THE MASTERS

A NOVEL BY

John Creasey

OF BOW STREET

Simon and Schuster
New York

To the British Police Force—
WITH ADMIRATION AND GRATITUDE

BOOK I
1739–1746

CHAPTER 1

The Hatred and the Hanging

THERE WAS the man who had killed his father; the man he hated as only a child who had been robbed of the man he had worshipped could hate.

Now, they were about to hang the murderer, and he, James Marshall, had come to see the hanging.

He was among the strident thousands, most of whom had come to gape for the pleasure of hearing the condemned man's peroration, for this newly made "hero" would surely die with words of defiance on his lips, would die in the midst of his turbulent, pulsating, vibrant life; a man in whom there had once been the seeds of greatness.

And the seeds of evil.

The boy, who was ten years old on this fifteenth of September 1739, did not know but sensed these things; could not explain the thoughts in his mind or the thumping of his heart or the mist which sometimes covered his eyes.

James, son of Richard and of Ruth Marshall, had come not in vengeance but to see vengeance done. He had followed the carts containing the manacled prisoners from Newgate Prison, each sitting on his own coffin in the groaning, creaking tumbrel, and had watched when, with the others who were to be hanged, his father's murderer had been half carried, half led into the alehouse to have his last free drink and make his last macabre joke.

Today there were two carts carrying seventeen condemned men headed for Tyburn. Most, by some strange miracle, behaved as if they were going not to their executions but to their weddings, although one youth, who could be no more than sixteen or seventeen, sat staring straight ahead of him. Most were dressed in their best or else in borrowed finery, but Frederick Jackson was by far the most resplendent. He wore a bright-green velvet coat with elaborate brown trimming, a nosegay of fresh flowers surely made by someone out of love for him, and breeches of bright-yellow velvet, the knees tied with multicoloured ribbons. In his two-coloured hat he had a huge white cockade, a silent declaration of his innocence.

In the cart with him, two were dressed already in their shrouds. Also in the cart was the Ordinary of Newgate, a prison chaplain concerned more in extorting confessions from each man so that he could publish and sell them tomorrow and in the weeks to follow. In between his pleading for confessions were mechanical words of comfort, but wine was a greater comforter than any God this priest could conjure up.

As they had left the alehouse, the Bow Tavern in St. Giles, one of London's foulest rookeries and a city of vice within the metropolis, Frederick Jackson had shouted to the mob: "Harken to me, fellow citizens! I am in the mood for singing. Who knows 'As clever Tom Clinch . . .'?"

A roar of approval had cut across his words, and like a bandmaster he had used his hand as an imaginary baton and had led the singing:

> " 'As clever Tom Clinch, while the rabble was bawling,
> Rode stately through Holborn to die in his calling,
> He stopped at The George for a bottle of sack,
> And promised to pay for it on his way back!' "

There, on the steps of the alehouse, the landlord had roared the words as loud as any. Even the hangman had chanted, and was smiling broadly now as he slipped the ropes over the condemned men's heads.

On that mellow autumn day in 1739 the boy stood on the fringe of the milling crowd at Tyburn Fields on a rise in the stony earth from which were visible the carts and the gallows, the black-draped preacher and the victims. But the boy saw only Jackson, his dark head held back, sharp chin thrust upward and outward, the noose not yet tight about his neck. Between the boy and the murderer were the thousands of sightseers, yet he saw no one; not man or woman or suckling babe or skirt-clinging child. No seller of ballads or pamphlets telling of the dying speeches of rogues who had died this way before; no seller of oranges or chestnuts, of gin or beer, of coarse bread dipped in beef drippings or mutton fat; no seller of pasties or of tarts, black puddings or favours; none of the gentry and their ladies seated in the windows of nearby houses or on especially constructed stands near the place of execution. All were agog to hear what Frederick Jackson, whom many thought a bolder villain than Jonathan Wild, would say in the minutes left to him before the horses were thwacked and made to bolt, so that the cart was jerked from beneath his feet and he and the others were left dangling and kicking.

The boy did not really see the other condemned men. He saw no whores, no pickpockets, no stealthy probing hands; James Marshall, son of a murdered man, son of a thief-taker, son of a God, was vividly aware only of Jackson's black head and, perhaps in wish-demanded fancy, Jackson's flashing dark eyes, the bright clothes and the brave medals stolen from some dead hero.

He heard no single voice, but all the voices. The chants of the tiny religious groups that had come to sing and pray for Jackson's soul, the shouts of the hawkers, the raucous voices of men whose hands were slapped from some pretty girl's breasts or buttocks or, if the press were tight enough, from the warmth between her thighs. He did not hear the preachers calling on Jackson to repent or the dozens of men and women crying out: "Dying confessions, as written by the Ordinary of Newgate—one penny." These were true enough, although the confessions were not of today's victims but those of the last mass execution, two weeks ago.

Suddenly, James saw the lips of the man he hated part, and, as if some magic had been cast, the noise ceased and silence fell, broken by one man's voice, which made the silence seem even deeper.

"Hear me all who have come here to watch me die, to see my legs kicking and my body tossing, hear me. Never in the history of Tyburn was such a monstrous crime committed, never a more innocent man condemned. . . ."

Four people besides the boy listened with intensity which matched his although none knew the others—except that the boy's mother was one of them. Each was present with a special purpose; each had come early and found a point of vantage. Each had waited with enforced patience, knowing that the hanging could not be over too soon or the people would scream their rage in disappointment and nothing was uglier or more difficult to control than a riot at a hanging on Tyburn Hill.

There were some people here who hated, many who feared, and one who loved the man who was about to die.

She was Eve Milharvey—the condemned man's mistress; in all but name, his wife, as beautiful as the years could leave a woman in her thirties who had been ravaged by the brothels and the stink and the torment of London; a woman who, had she been carefully nurtured and protected and married to a man who respected even if he did not love her, would have been the mother of a family now and mistress not of a murderer, thief, cheat and fraud, but of a household.

But she had been born in a cottage behind a row of brothels in Westminster and her world had been one of filth and lust and brutality, of stealing from a man who had her willing mother pressed against a wall. At twelve she had known men and what they wanted and what they did. At thirteen she had found herself, alone, in a dark alley on the edge of her world, surrounded by leering drunken men who all wanted their way with her and from whom she could not run because they hemmed her in while they peered at the black spots on thrown dice to decide who should take her first.

There was hardly a crime Frederick Jackson had not committed, hardly a savagery or brutality he had not exulted in, except one.

He had never taken a woman against her will.

He had succoured her.

His voice now was not loud, but was as clear as it had been on the night he had come upon her and the seven men tormenting her. She had not seen or heard him, heard only the triumph and the roar of the man who had "won" her first, who pushed the others away from him and sent them, muttering and grumbling, to wait; a great hulk of a man whose weight would crush her. Already, he had one hand beneath her petticoats and another easing himself free of his breeches to take her.

A man had spoken in a quiet but carrying voice: "Release her, Matty." And when the man in front of her had taken no notice, had

12

just fumbled and had nearly fallen on her, the stranger had called: "If you want to lie with a woman again, Matty, let her go." And she had seen his face above the hulk's shoulder and his hand on the big man's arm. Suddenly, she had seen the winner stagger, had heard him swear, had seen him turn to strike the man who had dared to interfere.

"Gawd!" he breathed. "Jacker!"

On the instant all lust seemed to vanish from him; he turned and ran at a shambling gait toward the end of the alley. And all the others had gone. She was alone with one man who now stood looking at her from the height of at least six feet, as if studying every feature closely in the light of a fading torch. He put out his right hand and cupped her chin in the crutch between thumb and forefinger, slowly turning her face from left to right. At last, when she was facing him, he let her go.

"Are you a whore?" he asked.

"Yes," she answered in a voice he could hardly hear.

"Speak up, girl!" His tone hardened as if her timidity angered him. She drew a deep breath and answered more clearly, "Yes, sir."

"An honest whore," he said, and laughed. "Do you work for Moll Sasson or anyone else?"

"No—no, sir."

"Speak up, girl!"

"No!" she almost shouted, not from courage or boldness, but out of fear. Moll Sasson controlled this area; nearly every prostitute paid her for both introducing customers and for protection against certain kinds of perverts.

"Then whom do you work for?"

"I—I work for myself," she answered.

"A chit of a girl like you? Don't lie to me."

"I am not, sir. I swear it, I work for myself."

"No bully? No twang?"

"I'm nobody's moll," she insisted, and her voice grew stronger, drawing some courage from the man. "I'll take a man standing or I'll take a man lying down but I won't take his pouch and I won't have a bully to take it *or* to protect me."

"Upon my soul, I'm inclined to believe you," he said, and laughed again. "Don't you know what Moll Sasson would do to you if you were caught working on her territory?"

"I—I wasn't working here, sir. They set on me. They know I'm always alone."

"I can believe that too," he said, and took her arm, turning her toward the nearer end of the lane. "You take my advice. Never work on Moll's territory. She'll do a lot worse to you than those drunken oafs would have done; a breastless woman's no pleasure to them. Where do you live?" he added abruptly.

"Where do you live?" The meaningless question echoed inside her head.

In the gutters, in the alleys, in the taprooms and the brothels, in the fields, in a barge upon the river, in a warehouse, in a coal house; anywhere she could lay her head. Bent and crooked over the troughs or tubs outside in the bitter-cold courtyard, in the sewers with the rats.

The man stared down at her and she dared to look up at him.

"Who are your customers?" he asked.

"Whoever comes by," she said.

"Faugh!" he barked. "You stink. When did you last have a bath?" he asked her. "When did you wash all over?"

"In May," she told him with near-eagerness. "In the river by the meadows at Chelsea."

"In May! Three months ago!" He looked at her as if with new disgust, and she did not know what had displeased him. Suddenly he demanded: "Whom do you belong to?"

And she replied; she could hear her voice now, even fancied there was a ring of pride, *pride* in those days of such squalor.

"Myself," she said. "I told you, sir."

"Speak up, girl. Whom do you belong to?"

"I belong to *myself*, sir."

"M'God!" he said in a voice which was half filled with laughter and at least touched with respect. "I believe you do." After a while he went on: "Will you come with me?"

"Yes—yes, sir," she replied meekly. "If I please you."

Cobbled lanes and cobbled streets, like the cobbles she stood on now, bare feet slipping, sore toes hurting, while he walked as if he were a king and it did not occur to him that she could not keep up such pace. Past dim-lit inns and dark closed houses, past decrepit old watchmen leaning on the poles they could scarcely carry, past a carriage and two horses close to Moll's, past a flaming torch outside a bank, along a narrow lane to a flickering oil lantern over a doorway. She knew the place and now she knew him and could understand why her molesters had disappeared so quickly and without protest at his approach; why the man he had called Matty had released her so swiftly.

Up the narrow wooden stairs into a room twice as large as any she had ever been in, along a passage with other rooms leading off. A woman, an old woman, saying: "Yes, Jacker, yes, Jacker, yes," obeying him literally, taking Eve into a small room which struck warm from a huge fire over which two caldrons of water shimmered and steamed, ordering her in a high-pitched voice to do just what he had already ordered.

"Fill the bath . . . take off those filthy clothes . . . throw them on the fire. . . . Throw them on the fire, you brat, or I'll throw you onto it!"

Her only clothes. She dragged the heavy hip bath from a corner; she placed her hands at her skirt, which was loose at her tiny waist, while the heat stung. "Off with your clothes!" Suddenly the old woman was on her, acting with much more strength than she seemed capable of, skirt off, petticoat, shift. She was being whirled about, hardly able to keep her balance, and in despair saw the hag throw her clothes into the fire where they blazed with blinding light.

How she had cried!

Copper pans full of hot water, cold water, mixed and bearable on her fair skin, heat from the fire, pain from a scrubbing, everywhere, everywhere; and suddenly, quiet and stillness, a chill blast from the door as it opened and Frederick Jackson came into the room.

She stared at him, covering her woman's breasts with her child's hands and half crouched so that the old woman scolded: "Stand straight, you ingrate! Don't pretend a man's never set eyes on you before."

"Leave her be," Jacker said, and the firelight made his face look half saint's, half devil's; filled her with hope and chilled her with fear. "Give her a cloak," he ordered. "Give her some food, and bring her to me."

She had known so many men but had never before known gentleness, or the softness of a feather bed, or the lingering of kisses on her lips and places of such rare intimacy. And afterward, back in the room where she had been bathed, a meal with beef sirloin that he cut from a huge piece on a turning spit, bread, cheese, cabbage, ale, and a cake with whipped sweet cream. A fantasy.

The whole of London, perhaps the whole of England, knew her now; the girl who had enticed so many rich men into her embraces and into Jackson's ruthless clutch; the girl who had made them so easy to blackmail. The woman who had grown more cunning and skillful in all the ways of her sex had never married and yet was forever Frederick Jackson's woman. The woman who had grown in stature as

15

he had grown in wealth and notoriety, laughing at her fears and scoffing at the threats of those who hated him.

"Hang Jacker? Never fear, my love, they'll never hang me."

Perhaps—perhaps they would not have brought him here and placed the noose about his neck and listened in awed silence as a legend prepared both to die and to grow stronger; perhaps it would never have come to pass—but for John Furnival.

John Furnival, also, was surely here today.

She did not know for certain because she had not set eyes on the big, honey-blond man with the near-yellow eyes and the massive strength, and yet she felt quite positive. He would not miss this day of triumph, after twenty years of conflict between him and Jacker, a conflict already fierce when Jacker had plucked her from the cobbled lane and taken her to Loxley Yard, near Gray's Inn and the fields, and claimed her for himself.

Most of the other condemned men were quiet now. One was calling on his nearby friends and relatives to rescue him; one, dressed in rich brown velvet and green shoes and hat, was tossing halfpence among the crowd, where the old and the young scrambled for them. Throughout Jackson went on talking in that carrying voice; it was as if he believed that for as long as he could talk, so he would defy the noose and the hangman and the men who had sent him here.

". . . among you here today are many thief-takers, justices, constables, each and every one of them more corrupt than I. Guilty of more crimes. Pariahs living off the people, living off you, the good, honest English people . . ."

A man near the platform shouted: "He's right!" Another, from the midst of the crowd, roared: "Hang them all!" Roars of approval came from a dozen places; close to the platform a surge of people was carried forward, threatening, and from all parts of the crowd came cries of:

"Cut him down!"

"Free him!"

"Save Jacker!"

"Hang the thief-takers!"

From close by John Furnival, who stood with only three of his own paid officers, there came other cries, deeper and more menacing:

"Hang Furnival."

"Kill Furnival."

"Kill the devil."

"Hang him—kill him—cut his throat—cut off his head."

Now the cry "Hang Furnival" became a chant, taken up not in two or three, not in a dozen, but in a hundred places. Men and women turned to see him as he towered above their heads, the timid began to move to a safer distance, the bold ones cursed and screamed at him, while Frederick Jackson's ruffians forced their way through the crowd toward him, ugly and menacing, harsh-voiced with hatred. The crowd divided to let them through. From the fringes many ran so that they could watch with greater safety while the cutthroats and the highwaymen, the thieves and the murderers, who got their living from Frederick Jackson or else were protected by him, pressed mercilessly on toward Furnival.

A small company of soldiers stood by the gallows, with the sheriff in charge of the executions, splendid in their bright-green uniforms and cockaded three-cornered hats, muskets grounded, sun glistening on long, narrow bayonets.

John Furnival saw the ruffians coming from all directions, saw the people near him scatter, knew how deeply they were afraid, knew that his aides would stay by his side even if they were cut to pieces trying to defend him. He had anticipated some such attack and had made arrangements with the sheriff. If it were possible, he desired to win this confrontation unaided; such a victory would be of great value in the future. Unless the sheriff ordered in the troops, few if any of the citizens of London would dare to help; most would prefer to see him hacked to death so as to be able to tell their children and their children's children of the hideous sight they had seen on the day Frederick Jackson and John Furnival had died.

He stood tall and aloof, as if impervious to any danger, and with great deliberation took out his golden snuffbox and placed a pinch of snuff on the back of his left hand. In his ears the chant was ringing: "Hang, hang, hang Furnival."

Slowly, he raised his left hand to his nose and sniffed delicately, an almost feminine gesture in so big a man. As the snuff went up his right nostril a single shot rang out, so sharp and clear that it echoed high above all other sounds, even the chanting which drowned the words spilling from Frederick Jackson's lips.

Furnival's movement had been his signal to the sheriff and the shot had frightened off those who would have attacked him.

Jackson was still haranguing the crowd.

". . . these are the guilty men, who batten on the poor, who drag the harmless whores into their courts and charge them for plying their trade, who . . ."

Suddenly, he stopped, for relatives and friends climbed into the carts to bid the condemned farewell, while the executioner and his assistants finished fastening ropes around the necks of those about to be hanged, then thrust them toward another huge cart over which the gibbet hung. Weeping and wailing now took over, drowning the voice of the Prison Ordinary, now chanting psalms, but nothing stopped the sellers or the performers among the crowd.

When the executioner covered the eyes and the faces of the condemned with black caps, Jackson kept trying to speak again but failed. The chaplains and the visitors were driven off, and then the executioner thwacked the horses fastened to the cart and they dashed away. There, kicking on the empty air, were seventeen human beings, soon to die. On the instant, some relatives pulled at the hanging bodies to hasten death, one belabouring a swinging man's breast with a heavy stone to stop the heart from beating.

Jackson hardly moved; no doubt the executioner had been well paid to make sure his neck was broken.

The crowd's attention switched now from the gangs forcing their way through to Furnival toward the victims, and there came a deep sigh, as if each person present drew in a breath at the same moment.

Eve Milharvey uttered a gasp and buried her face in her hands. James Marshall stared at the swinging man as if mesmerised by the sight. Ruth Marshall, for whose husband's death this man had died, watched with swollen eyes in a face drained of colour, then slowly lowered her head and locked her fingers in silent prayer.

The soldiers looked on impassively. The Reverend Sebastian Smith, a small, plump and mild-looking man, invoked his God in tones which only those close by could hear for all whose souls had departed this earth.

"Oh, Lord, have mercy on this man, Thy creature, spare him the fires of hell, take him to Thy bosom. . . ."

His voice and all other sounds were drowned in the fresh chanting, in the noise of movement, as Frederick Jackson's men fought to get at Furnival.

"Hang, hang, hang Furnival."

Furnival had not moved.

He raised his left hand again and sniffed the biting snuff into his left nostril, and almost on the instant there was a bark of command.

"Quick—*march*."

And from the direction of Hyde Park, from main roads and narrow side streets, came large numbers of dragoons, marching with their muskets at the ready. Furnival, as Chief Magistrate of Bow Street, had arranged their presence, rare at Tyburn, because he had been alive to the possibility of riot after Jackson's death, or even before. The tramp, tramp, tramp of feet now echoed to the chanting, while from the crowd more of Furnival's hired men moved with military precision and formed a ring around the magistrate.

Furnival looked toward the groups of men who had come to kill him. A stone struck his left shoulder but he did not appear to notice.

"Go home, all of you," he called. "Go home and hold your wake ınd you'll have nothing to fear this day. Stay and make more trouble ınd I'll have every one of you in Newgate within the hour."

Another stone glanced off his arm.

A man growled: "We'll kill you one day."

"But not today," said Furnival, and he turned his back. "Go home."

Not a single man approached him further; and as the men who had come to kill dispersed among the crowd so did Furnival's men, watching for the more blatant pickpockets; and as the minutes passed, the festive air, which had been everywhere before the hanging, began to return; laughter came in spontaneous gusts; the sellers of food, of gin and of ale, those who offered all the fun of the fair, began to do a roaring trade; men and women and some children sprang up as if from the ground carrying sheaves of single printed sheets. These were the forged or fictional stories, some based on things Jackson had said in prison, but few cared to wait for the official one the Ordinary would produce tomorrow morning.

"Last speech and dying testament of Frederick Jackson, his very words, from first to last, only twopence. Read all the things you couldn't hear because of the din. Jacker's own words, words you'll never forget."

And others hawked more newssheets and bills, whilst a few, with furtive air, began to offer pieces of the rope taken from Jackson's neck; if genuine, each piece would fetch several pounds.

"Death speech of Jonathan Wild, not a word missing, printed on special paper, only one penny."

"Who'll buy *The Daily Courant?* Read all about the 'orrible things that 'appen in the Fleet . . ."

And so they went on, raucous and never-ending.

At one spot, eating hot pies and drinking lemonade, one family group was busy reading aloud pieces from the confessions while another was arguing amiably.

"Tyburn's the best place, I tell you," one man declared.

"I like Newgate better; you don't have so far to walk," the woman argued.

"What's the matter with Putney, then, or Kennington? You can take a coach to the gallows and watch everything without moving out of your seat."

Others of the party began to join in, some preferring the hangings in the Old Kent Road and Wapping, some showing a liking for those outside a shop where a thief had been caught and summarily tried.

"There's a book I read," the first man said, "calls London the City of the Gallows. The author says you can't come into London by road or by the river without passing some."

A child, running, fell and began to cry and all thought switched from hanging to the scratches on his knee.

John Furnival, with his three close attendants, walked through the thinning crowd toward Tyburn Pike, where his carriage was waiting. As he neared a little mound which commanded a good view of the hanging, a lad dressed neatly in tweed breeches, a jacket which reached halfway down his thighs and a shirt with ruffles at cuffs and neck ran forward. His slouch cap, of hogskin, was pulled over his left eye. He wore heavy boots, patched at the toes, with thick nails already wearing thin. Before Furnival realised what was happening, the lad took his hand and pressed it to his lips. For a moment the magistrate stood still, aware of the cool lips and the upturned face and the dark curls and touched to emotion because of the lad's fervour; something stirred in his memory, too, but before the vision grew clear, the boy turned and ran, choking back tears. Furnival strode on, pointed out by hundreds, until suddenly he saw a woman in a dark-gray cloak and black bonnet standing in his path and staring at him.

Again he stopped abruptly. The three men also stopped and put their hands to their pistols and looked about but no one who threatened danger stood nearby, unless the woman hid some weapon beneath the cloak she wore as a disguise.

Furnival said, "If you need help, Eve Milharvey, come to me."

"I'd sooner ask help of the devil," she said. "I hope you die in agony, John Furnival."

She turned and walked away at a good pace, head held high, eyes still blazing with the hatred she had for the man who had hounded down her lover.

No one followed her or recognised her. She was near the creaking cart on which they were now taking Jackson's body away, drawn by two heavily built farm horses, when she saw a boy. Had she seen him only full face she might not have been so startled or so sure who he was. His profile allowed no doubt at all; the high forehead and the dark curly hair; the hooked nose; the deep-set eyes which might have been carved from marble; the full lips, seen even from where she stood as bow-shaped and beautiful, lips more rightfully a woman's than a man's. And the square, thrusting chin, too large in comparison with his other features, making him jaw-heavy, as his father had been. She had seen him once before and recognised him as James Marshall.

His father had worked as a court officer for John Furnival, and had been one of three who had gone to arrest Frederick Jackson for a robbery he had planned and helped to carry out. Jackson might have escaped from that charge of robbery, although some of the stolen silver and coin was still in his home, the home in Loxley Yard to which he had taken her nearly twenty years ago.

But he could not escape the charge of murder. And he had shot Richard Marshall through the heart, not knowing two other of Furnival's men had been outside the door, waiting to pounce on him when he came hurrying out.

And now here was James Marshall, watching the body of the man who had killed his father as it shook and shifted in the death cart.

And she, Eve Milharvey, felt no deep stirrings of compassion for him, even though she saw no hatred in his eyes but only tears.

He turned blindly, passed her, and ran toward Hyde Park and the turnpike there. Soon he was swallowed up in the crowd and she hurried and caught up with the people following the body, some walking alongside the cart as if they would be pallbearers. Some she knew; among them were the most vicious and cruel of the scoundrels who had looked up to Frederick as their leader.

A question which had often been in her head seemed now to burst inside her. Why had he led them? Why had a man of such caliber placed himself at the head of an army of brutes? What had driven him to the cruelties she knew he had committed when with her he had always been gentle and kind?

The horses' hooves and the iron wheels clattered over the gravel, the ungreased hubs groaned in a journey to the burial place she had bought for him, just as she had bought the body and the clothes from the hangman, whose property they became. Most bodies were purchased by friends or relatives who could afford them; a few by the Surgeons' Hall. Once there the surgeons would seize upon them in their greedy thirst for the knowledge which only fresh dead bodies could give. At least she could save Jacker that indignity. No one recognised Eve as she walked with her head bowed, the frills of her black bonnet drawn low over her forehead. Gradually, thoughts blurred and almost died away, but one remained: that more and more of the men who owed Jacker their lives and their livelihoods dropped out of the procession, a cortege fit for a caricature by Hogarth. Some stopped at a grogshop for a pennorth of gin; some saw a face or a pair of eyes or a low-cut revealing dress and followed it.

Outside the tavern in St. Giles the hangman himself was auctioning pieces of rope, and even young girls were buying pieces and fondling them, putting them to their cheeks or down their bosoms. From inside, the sound of drunken revelry was at its height and the words of the song which Jacker himself had sung came clearly into the street, making Eve catch her breath.

> " 'He stopped at *The George* for a bottle of sack,
> And promised to pay for it on his way back!' "

Once, near the open space of Lincoln's Inn, where lawyers lived and worked, she saw a boy and thought mistakenly for a moment that it was young Marshall. And once she saw a man with hair the colour of John Furnival's, but a smaller man, large enough to remind her of her hatred of the magistrate but not, in her grief, to make it blaze to life.

CHAPTER 2

Two Furnivals and Word of Others

JOHN FURNIVAL sat well back in his carriage and took the jolting with inward protest but outward calm as the two well-groomed horses and the four iron-banded wheels ran over the cobbles toward the Strand and the narrow streets beyond. He preferred this route when not in a hurry or anxious to travel secretly, for fear of giving notice to his forthcoming victims that he was on his way. The coachman, knowing his whims, took him into the great piazza of Covent Garden, where stood the big houses built by the Duke of Bedford, who had spared no expense to make this the heart of fashionable London.

But this whole area had lost much of its quality. Between here and Bow Street sleazy brothels and thieves' dens, gaming houses and wooden lean-tos and sheds had been built in once-spacious roads, making hiding places for thieves, assassins and criminals of every kind. Even the Ordinary of Newgate had complained of the danger of the area.

There were good spots, nevertheless, still guarded by private retainers, a kind of militia which could in emergency work together. John Furnival was able to have a stronger force than most, needed if he were to carry out his work as magistrate efficiently, because he was wealthy in his own right and chose this way of spending much of his money, helping to clear London of crime.

At last the carriage turned into Long Acre, where now buildings were making inroads into the fields. Mostly these big barnlike sheds housed wheelwrights and carriage makers of all kinds, but there were long stretches of small houses, near-hovels, some open land, a cemetery in front of the Church of St. Anselm, and many small shops. At the far end this wide thoroughfare narrowed and the carriage crossed Bow Yard into Bow Street. The horses began to slow down from habit. For here was Furnival's new home, above the offices adjacent to the building which he used as a courtroom, temporary prison, and sleeping quarters for his staff. As the carriage stopped, the footman leaped lightly down onto the raised pavement outside the buildings and opened the door wide. With slow deliberation, Furnival climbed out, so big a man that it was a marvel how he had squeezed himself into the carriage, a greater marvel that he should not get stuck in the door.

Bow Street itself was wide and a number of substantial houses stood back from either side of the road. Almost directly opposite Number Three, which Furnival now leased, was an inn. The government leased the house adjoining Furnival's, where the official quarters stood. This was considered the center of London's criminal courts, and suspects were brought here from as far as Hounslow Heath and Hammersmith as well as many villages in between.

Near these two houses was a row of shops as well as an alehouse, the Bunch of Grapes, frequented by many villainous-looking porters from Covent Garden Market as well as by Furnival's men. Farther along the street on the same side as Furnival's house was another, bigger carriage, with gilt borders and a coat of arms on the door panels. Furnival gave it only one glance, then spoke to an elderly man who came out of the offices, down the stone steps and past the stout oaken doors and polished brass torch holders.

"How long has my brother been here, Moffat?" Furnival demanded.

"Not ten minutes since," the man answered. "I came to give you an advance intimation, sir."

"Is he in a bad humour?"

"I think perhaps he has come to remonstrate with you, Mr. John."

"As you would like to," Furnival said dryly, and the older man did not trouble to deny the charge. "Will he burst if I keep him waiting for ten minutes d'you think?"

"I believe he would be most put out, sir."

"And so do I," said John Furnival. "And so do I. He may be so put out that he will leave me in peace. Take him word that I shall be with him as soon as I can," he added, and strode into the offices, with Moffat following, anxious and troubled. His skin had the look of delicate porcelain: a porcelain saint.

"Mr. John—"

"He won't bite you, man!"

"Mr. John, he knows you have another guest."

"Damme, he does. And who is the guest, pray?"

They were in the paneled hall of the old building now, where a log fire burned high in a deep fireplace, its cheerful flames reflected on pewter and silver, on glass and on books behind the glass. The ceiling was beamed and so low that the top of John Furnival's head missed the lowest part of the middle beam by a bare inch, perhaps less, and sometimes it actually brushed his silky hair. A broad staircase of dark oak, with a banister on one side and panels on the other, led straight from the front door. A passage ran alongside the stairs on one side; beyond this was the court and behind it the cells; one room to the right of the stairs at the back was his own private "resting room." This room could be most easily approached from Bell Lane, a narrow street behind Bow Street. And there his personal guests always waited for him.

"Mrs. Braidley is here, sir."

"To be sure, Mrs. Braidley. I'd forgotten her! But don't inform her of that, Silas. Tell her—damme, I'll tell her myself!" Furnival strode along the passage.

"Sir," Moffat pleaded, "remember your brother is waiting."

At first Furnival went straight on and his hand was on the resting-room door when suddenly he turned and looked back at Moffat, who seemed to shrink. For a few moments there was utter silence, and then Furnival threw back his head and roared with laughter.

"Does my brother think I could be in and out in ten minutes? No time for dalliance, no time for—" He almost choked with another gust of laughter and then managed to say, "Tell him to hold his patience for ten minutes and I'll be with him." Then he thrust open the door and entered the room to see a smiling Mrs. Braidley.

She was perhaps forty, so ten years and more younger than Furnival, and she was very handsome, with fine brown eyes and full lips, as ready to kiss as to smile. She had laid her colourful hat on a chair and her low-cut dress more than hinted at the milky-coloured fullness of her bosom. She had dark hair, slightly streaked with gray, and was dressed in the fashion of the Court; few women had a better dress-maker than Hewson's in the Strand, although his prices were reasonable since he did not have to pay the high rents of the west side of the city. One of the best-known women in London, she had given to the word "whore" a quality of refinement, and in truth she was a courtesan who possessed unusual qualities of character and intellect. Everyone who was anybody knew the truth about Mrs. Braidley; knew that although men fought for her favours as if she were a virgin, yet they invited her to the theater and to concerts, to the salons and often to social gatherings at their homes, but she seldom left her own house in Arlington Street to receive her patrons; John Furnival was one of the few for whom she made an exception.

"Why, Lisa," he said, going forward and taking her hands and drawing her close. "What a restful sight you are, to be sure."

"Do you think your brother William would agree?"

"He'd agree although he might not say so," declared Furnival. "What a house this is for secrets! You know he's here, he knows you're here, Moffat knows you are both here and is frightened in case I dally with you before seeing William! Lisa, favour and spoil me. Pour me a glass of brandy and whatever you would like for yourself, and then help me get these damned boots off. I swear the gravel at Tyburn is the stoniest anywhere in London!" He dropped into a huge armchair which faced a fire that glowed but gave out little heat, for he liked his rooms cool. Stretching out his long legs, he watched Lisa's graceful movements, then closed his eyes. He heard the glass being placed on a table by his side, heard her breathing and the rustle of her dress. Next, he felt the boot on his left leg being pulled, and he braced himself as she tugged until it came free. Then she pulled off the other boot and placed both, together, at the side of the fireplace.

"Bless you, my dear," he said. "Bless your good heart."

She did not ask "Are you tired, John?" She stood with a glass of dry sack in her hand as he picked up his; she sipped, he drank deeply, legs still stretched out, body limp in the great armchair, shadows beneath his eyes.

"Must you see William?" she inquired.

"Yes," he answered. "Much though I'd rather stay with you."

26

"I wonder which of us would exhaust you more," she remarked, and her eyes danced.

"The most exhausting thing in the world is boredom, madam, and I shall never be bored with you." Her eyes kindled now and she sipped again. "Can you come back?"

"No," she said.

" 'Tis a heavy loss, Lisa."

"It's no loss at all," she declared. "I cannot go and come back but I can rest until you are back from the bosom of your family."

He stared at her for what seemed a long time. Then he tossed down what was left of his brandy and sprang up, so swiftly and suddenly that he startled her. Before she could move away he put his arms around her and kissed her, holding the kiss until her breasts began to heave. At last he let her go.

"He may be in one of his stubborn moods and stay a long time," he warned her.

"I'll outstay him, never fear."

"There is no man or woman in London I would worry about less," his voice boomed. He kissed her again but this time lightly and went to a cupboard, opened it and hooked slippers out with his toes. "I can manage," he said as she came to help, and he used his forefinger as a shoehorn; but he was breathing heavily as he straightened up. She looked concerned, but she did not question him, however, as he nodded and walked toward the door, then she heard him walking up the stairs slowly and, for him, heavily.

She waited until she heard a door close, heard voices, the closing of another door, followed by silence above. Then she pulled at a bell cord which hung by the fireplace, and soon Silas Moffat came in, a small man compared with his master, and fragile.

"I'll be here for a while," she said. "I shall dine with Mr. John."

"I'm very glad to hear that, ma'am."

"I wonder," she said, but did not push the doubt although she looked at the man's face with great intensity. Moffat was neither embarrassed nor perturbed; nor, it was obvious, was he at all surprised by the question she then asked.

"How often is he short of breath, Moffat?"

Moffat said quietly, "Too often, ma'am."

"Don't prevaricate, man. How often?"

"It is a long time since I first noticed it. Once a week at least," reported Moffat, "and sometimes two or three times a day."

27

"Do you know what causes this shortness of breath?"

"That I do not."

"No man in the world resents an interfering woman more than your master," stated Lisa Braidley, "and no man could be worse served than by a servant who allows him to ignore the state of his health. Find out the cause, Silas. If needs be, make him see a doctor. Bring one here on some pretext. Do you understand me?"

Silas Moffat looked at her, his lips curving gently in a smile, but anxiety in his eyes, as he rejoined, "No man in London scents a pretext more quickly than he, ma'am. But I will find a way."

She touched his hand, nodded, and turned from him. He left the room and walked to the foot of the stairs. In the courtroom a man was shouting; outside, a carriage was approaching at a furious pace, and Moffat paused, head held high in expectation lest it should stop. But it passed, and with obvious relief he went up the stairs. From the landing he could hear the high-pitched voice of William Furnival, but he did not hover by the door to find out what one of his master's younger brothers had to say.

William Furnival was not much shorter than John, but a lean man who had the hard, weather-beaten appearance of one who spent much of his time out of doors, in energetic pursuits. Whereas his brother looked less than his fifty-three years, he looked more than his thirty-nine. He was dressed in the height of fashion, with a wide-skirted coat of wine red and dark-green trousers caught by garters of rich gold; the tops of his shoes were of pale-brown leather and his shirt frills at neck and sleeves gave him the look of a dandy. His three-cornered hat of green velvet was on a chair. He wore no wig and no make-up and was as immaculate and authoritative as a man could be who had driven across London's dusty streets. When John entered he was by the window looking out on the vegetable market of Covent Garden, where a few stall holders lingered although customers were few, for the freshest fruit and vegetables were always gone in the early morning. A group of men were gathered, some standing, some kneeling on the cobbles, praying. Two drunkards sat outside the alehouse, one man's breeches unfastened.

The room in which William waited was above the hallway and much the same size, with a fire glowing, comfortable chairs set about the brick fireplace, two walls lined from floor to ceiling with books which had a well-read look; most were lawbooks. The broad, uneven floor boards were strewn with Indian and Persian rugs of rich colours. Set in one corner was a huge couch which seemed to have been squeezed under the plaster ceiling and now helped to support it.

William Furnival turned slowly and deliberately as his brother entered and closed the door. John's breathing was normal now, and he was smiling very differently from the way he had smiled at Mrs. Braidley.

"Good afternoon, Will," he said.

"John," said William without preamble, "you must stop this lunacy. You've seen Jackson hanged as you always said you would. Now you must stop it."

"So I must," John said, his lips arching. "And is this just your opinion, brother, or that of all my brothers and cousins combined?"

"I speak for all," William declared.

"Then you speak for a host," replied John dryly. They eyed each other, men so different that it would be easy to believe they came from different parents, William sharp featured and dark and with a slight cast in one eye. "Sit down, Will."

"There is no alternative but for you to give up this dangerous work," William insisted. "No alternative at all." He moved nearer the fireplace but did not sit down although John raised the skirt of his coat and lowered himself into the chair farthest from the fire. "We are all of the same mind. At Tyburn today I have it on the most reliable information that you were within an ace of being killed."

"You should change your informers or go to watch events for yourself."

"Go and see that—that rabble? That mob of thieves and cutthroats who make sport out of seeing men swinging? Faugh! The very thought makes me want to vomit!"

"Nevertheless, you should go, some time," declared John. "Among the rabble you may see grief and sadness and good men striving. You might also find a little humility—"

"I'll never go to Tyburn to see a hanging and you know it," interrupted William. "John, I tell you the time has come to resign your appointments, except any you hold directly under the King, and come back to the House."

"Ah, the House of Furnival," echoed John. "The precious guild, the beloved bank, the venturesome ship-owners, the goldsmiths and the silversmiths. The makers of fortunes." He placed his big hands on the

29

arms of his chair and looked up at his brother. "I do not believe it is the life for me, Will. I prefer to be the Chief Magistrate of Westminster."

"You even lie to yourself," William rasped. "There is no Chief Magistrate of Westminster."

"You are not quite right. Chief Magistrate may be a courtesy title but surely well earned. After all, I am a justice of the peace for the City of Westminster, the counties of Essex, Surrey and Hertfordshire, and by your leave I have been even"—his voice was laughing but his eyes were serious—"the justice of the peace for the Commission of the Tower of London. And as there are other justices at some of these places—"

"Justices? Profligates and thieves, the scum of the earth who will condemn an innocent man to death for their share of the State's forty-pound reward. Do you know what they called the man who preceded you here? Do you—"

"Permit me a word, William," interrupted John Furnival. "If his desires had been more temperate—if he had not needed so much money to live on, that is—he would probably have lacked sufficient motives to carry through the—" Furnival paused and looked at the ceiling before adding abruptly, "Ah, I remember! Through *a* multiplicity of business so important to society." He paused again and then asked, "Have I recalled the phraseology, William?"

"Have you remembered that his business was condemning men to death or transportation to the Americas for life?"

"Bad men, William. Wicked men. In one of his petitions to the government he boasted of having sentenced to death or transportation nearly two thousand men, and asked for some financial reward."

"Thought of him makes me sick."

"It should not. He was a clever and courageous man and he fought crime as best he could. So do I. So shall I. I tell you the future you offer with commerce and banking is not the life for me."

"You speak as if it were offensive to you."

"No, Will."

"The very expression in your eyes and the tone of your voice are derogatory and disparaging."

"Whereas your tone and expression about my chosen occupation are full of reverence and praise," John retorted. "Will, you and the family do well enough, far better than most. What did I read in *The Daily Courant* only yesterday? That Furnival and Sons is now the third most powerful private banking house in London, second only to the Mattazinis and the Gallos. And one day last week the Goldsmiths' Guild gave high praise, the Lord Mayor said you are the richest and most powerful, while of all the magnificent imports brought from the Orient more than one-tenth is carried in Furnival ships and stored in Furnival warehouses. The spices and the unguents, the silks and the carpets and the jewels. And you have a finger in most large building firms. Why, before the century is halfway through you will own every other fine square in London! You don't need me."

"You've no right to sneer," William objected.

"I don't sneer, Will. I marvel and respect. But I don't envy you."

"It is not fitting that a member of our family should spend his life dealing with thieves and thief-takers, with people who stink of corruption. The stench of every other magistrate is on you. You must see what discredit this brings upon us." When his brother made no immediate answer, William Furnival took a step nearer, held out a hand as if in supplication and actually bent one knee. "John, give all this up. Corruption will only corrupt you. You have lost two wives of broken hearts already, good women who could not live to share your folly. Come and rejoin the family circle, marry a woman who can give you the sons the family needs. There are not enough males of the younger generation with us. Must I remind you that you are past fifty, John? Fifty, and with no issue."

He broke off.

He saw the expression in John's tawny eyes and on the face that could be so mild. He saw the thin line of lips which could be so well shaped and full of laughter. He stopped, straightened up and drew back. A log, part glowing red and part white ash, fell heavily in the iron dogs of the fire. He remembered such an expression only once before when he and other men of the family had said many of the same things and so set off the most explosive quarrel ever known among them.

Slowly, very slowly, John Furnival's tension relaxed and he even began to smile again.

"I told you before, you should change your informers," he said. "Efficient ones would tell you that I have fathered more sons than the rest of the family put together, even if each is a bastard! I know, Will; or I know about most of them, for I see that neither they nor their mothers starve. Nor do I interfere if the mothers marry and give the brats good homes. As for marriage, I want no more vapid women

31

swooning over me and screaming at the sound of a pistol being cocked, and I want no puling infants." He placed his hands on the arms of his chair again and stood up very slowly, appearing, because of his size, to tower over his brother. "I'll tell you other things I don't want. I don't want to sit around a big table with my brothers and the rest of the family discussing how to take more money out of London.

"You can afford to protect yourselves properly while the protection of the ordinary and decent people is left to the corrupt and the decrepit. As you and your kind have made London grow until the system of parish councils and watchmen has broken down, you have also created a race that appears more animal than human, people who live like rats in holes, and who, when they gather together in any one place, become the mob. If we don't find a way to create better conditions for them, one day they will turn upon us and devour us. All the government does, all the King does, is create new capital offenses, and those like you think this will be sufficient deterrent. Our present King has approved more than thirty new capital crimes. Such monstrous crimes as stealing a shilling from a man's pocket or five shillings from his shop, for taking clothes from a bleaching ground, for entering grounds with intent to kill game or rabbits, even for being on the highway with a blackened face and a shotgun to drive off footpads.

"That is the London you are creating, William—you and your colleagues protected by your hired guards. I had no desire to tell you what I think about you and your kind and some of the things you do, but you leave me no choice. Many of the results of your activities are as evil as those of any in London, and worse than most because you use a cloak of piety and respectability to cover your deeds." John Furnival drew a deep breath. "Do you understand me, Will?" he roared. "Go back and tell the others no, no, a thousand times no! I'd rather swing at Tyburn than go your way to hell!"

Lisa Braidley heard his raised voice. So did Moffat. Two thief-takers, men who had come to see the justice, were stepping out of the courtroom precincts, impatient at long waiting. One of them cocked a thumb toward the door and Moffat saw them go into Bow Street only a few seconds ahead of William Furnival, who came quickly down the stairs, his face pale with anger. A third man waiting to see John Furnival saw but did not appear to be noticed by William, who stalked out before Moffat could reach the door into Bow Street and open it for him.

"I'll come back in the morning," the third man said to Moffat in a low-pitched voice.

"How urgent is the matter you came about?" asked Moffat.

"I've had a report that Dick Miller is close to Tyburn Turnpike," the other man said. "If he is then we could set up a catch for him. It's not a certainty, howsoever—"

"You wait here for another ten minutes," decided Moffat. "If the magistrate is not down by then I'll send a message to you later."

"Later could be too late," the other man grumbled.

Neither of them had heard John Furnival come through the upstairs door which his brother had left open or saw him at the head of the stairs, but they heard his mild-sounding voice which confirmed what Moffat already knew: that the justice had never lost his composure, that the bull-like roar had been as considered as was everything he did, uttered only to infuriate his brother and send him off in a rage. Moffat was quite right: John Furnival wanted William to convince the other members of the family that it would be a waste of time to try to woo the eldest brother from his chosen occupation.

"What did you say about Dick Miller, Harris?" he asked.

The man with Moffat turned his head slowly, thick neck bulging over his tight shirt. He had more the look of the yokel or farm labourer, for his clothes had a homespun appearance and he wore leather gaiters over tough leather boots marked at heel and instep by stirrups. He was indeed of farming stock, for his family owned fifty acres near Highgate; he was also one of the very few of Furnival's men whom the justice trusted implicitly. He had been a close friend of Richard Marshall's, and a principal witness that Jackson had murdered Marshall.

" 'Tis said he's close by Tyburn Turnpike," he replied, "lurking there to pounce on any wealthy merchant who was at the fair. He's one of a dozen highwaymen waiting there, but the only one I know of any consequence."

"What would you have me do?" asked Furnival as he came down the stairs. "Speak up, man, I haven't all the time in the world!"

"I would send out a decoy," replied Tom Harris, "a young dandy and a lady for my preference. Miller can never resist a pretty face. And I would have enough men close by to take Dick the moment he attacks."

"Or else take a bullet or a hail of shot from a blunderbuss," Furnival retorted. "And the decoy take a chance that Dick will carry off his

33

lady or rape her in front of his eyes. Do we have any heroes and heroines willing to take the chance?"

"I think so, sir."

"Who?" demanded Furnival suspiciously.

"Red Foster and his wife," Harris answered. "Things have been bad for them since Red came out of Newgate and he doesn't want to go back. For ten pounds he and his wife would act as decoys, and a share of the blood money if we catch Miller."

"If I remember her, she's a pretty enough wench," mused Furnival reminiscently. "Silas, give Harris ten pounds from my personal box for the Fosters, and spare the lady a prayer. And you be careful, Tom. I don't want to lose you."

"You won't lose me if I can prevent it," Harris replied dryly.

Furnival chuckled. "I'll wager that's the truth!" He nodded and turned toward the room at the end of the passage, where Lisa was waiting. Halfway there he turned back and called in his clear, quiet, but carrying voice, "Have you seen Marshall's widow of late?"

"Yes, sir. I see her two or three times a week."

"How is she and how are things with her?"

"She took her husband's murder hard, sir, but she lacks nothing in courage. She works as a seamstress when she can get work, and her son earns by carrying messages and delivering goods for a merchant in Long Acre."

Furnival looked at the other for what seemed a long time, then nodded and turned away. The front door opened on to near-darkness, the flickering yellow-red of the torch flares of a coach-and-four, the clatter of hooves on the cobbles. The door beyond the stairs opened to Lisa Braidley, now dressed in a robe, bending over the fire with a log held in a pair of iron tongs. Nearby, a table was set for two, with a three-holder silver candlestick casting a pale glow. Beyond the table a back hallway had been converted by Furnival into a sleeping alcove with a double bed, a dressing table and a wide mirror on another wall.

"Come, my dear," John Furnival said, and took her shoulders and delved to her breast beneath the robe. Soon, when his clothes were draped over a carved oak chair and they were lying together, he said huskily, "We'll be quiet for a while." And soon, he said, "Would there were milk in your fine breasts, Lisa. I'd suckle and draw strength from you."

He caressed, playing, teasing, was gradually soothed, and soon was stirred explosively in his loins.

CHAPTER 3

Ruth Marshall

JAMES MARSHALL walked from Tyburn to Newgate
Prison, in the face of the thousands making their way toward the turnpikes and the small country villages beyond. Walking time was much
less than an hour, although the execution procession took twice that
long. He had often made the walk, sometimes with his father, and had
occasionally ridden behind his father on Dare, a horse he had known
since he could remember; twice he had ridden proudly alongside his
father on a borrowed hack or pony. As he drew nearer Newgate all
was quiet, but farther along Holborn and approaching Newgate Prison
itself the crowds grew thicker. Many entered the gin palaces; others
stood and watched the bearbaiting, hearing the snarling fury of the
goaded animals and the sharp ring of the goading sticks against the iron
cage; small, tight groups of men watched two gamecocks, laying their
bets as the birds tore at each other's eyes and bodies with steel-tipped
claws. Lights flickered over the entrances to alehouses; prostitutes
stood bare-breasted at the open doors of the brothels, some actually
on the main highway; men and women coupled in nearby passages,
and small children with silken-touch hands stole wallets for their way-
ward mothers, or the women themselves, pretending warm embrace,

35

lifted wallet or watch, purse or snuffbox, while their victims strained and grunted, gurgled and gasped.

The boy was oblivious of these things, for on the nights of the Tyburn hangings they were as normal as breathing. He passed Tyburn Tree, long since replaced as the gallows; indeed, the weight of a man on many of the branches would bring the branch down, the tree was so old. He passed along Oxford Road, with its small shops and taverns, down Holborn Hill and at last reached Newgate, not long ago part of the wall of London.

He had always been fascinated by the story of the prison, rebuilt on the greater part of Sir Richard Whittington's fortune, which he left for good works after he died in 1423.

James liked to imagine that Dick Whittington had desired a prison which was clean, and where there would be justice above all. But Dick Whittington's prison had soon become a place of infamy and terror. It stood until burned down by the Great Fire of London in 1666.

So this was the fourth prison of the name.

There it stood, tall and black-gray, with its arched gateway and narrow windows, the three statues just above the great arch. Atop the castellated roof a windmill turned sluggishly in a light wind, drawing some of the foul air out of the prison and dispersing it into the skies, driving a slender draft of cleaner air down into the cells and even to the dungeons. There debtor and murderer, highwayman and coiner, man and woman, boy and girl, lived in the stinking filth, fed, if they were lucky, by friends or relatives, or by turnkeys who took their money and charged extortionate prices for food which was almost impossible to eat.

When James had been here before, he had known that his father had come to question the prisoners in the murderers' and not in the debtors' side. He knew also that his father had taken food that he had seen his mother prepare to men he had arrested or helped to arrest and who would one day be hanged; meat pies and fruit turnovers, with slices of savoury-stuffed veal or rich fat pork, cheese wrapped in its muslin cloth and a small wooden dish of butter.

He had never been able to understand what moved his parents to pity, but some such emotion had stirred in him when he had seen the cart jolt away and Frederick Jackson swinging.

Was it pity?

Was it what his mother and father had felt?

36

He heard the clatter of iron hooves on the cobbles, moved hurriedly to one side and saw a well-known thief-taker and an assistant hustle a captive inside. He watched the jailers as the carriage door opened and three men climbed out and hurried toward the lodge, where the jailers seized the prisoner and took him into a small stone building attached to it. Clearly they had been warned of his coming, for manacles were clapped onto his wrists before a word was spoken and he was hustled away.

A smaller carriage arrived and the coachman called out: "I've one for the Master Debtors' quarters. Who'll come for him?"

A man dressed in the height of fashion climbed down, looked disdainfully about him and walked, unescorted, to the lodge. Only a single jailer came to him, a big-bellied man who touched his forehead and said, "Mr. Eustace, sir?"

"Yes. That is my name."

"All ready for you, sir," the jailer said in a hoarse voice. "Everything's as comfortable as it can be. If you want anything just let me know." It was difficult to judge whether his ugly brown teeth were bared in a smile or a snarl.

James Marshall turned away, disgusted. A "master debtor," thanks to his friends, could afford to pay for the best, as if this were a hotel. And while he had money, even the senior jailer would toady to him.

James knew the prison was comprised of the Master Debtors' Side, the Master Felons' Side, the Common Side for Debtors and the Common Side for Felons, as well as the Press Yard, the Castle and the Gate. Both the Common Side for Debtors and the Common Side for Felons were supposed to be for women only, but he knew from his father that the whole prison was a jungle. The terms "Master Side" and "Common Side" referred to the lodgments of those who paid and those who did not pay the keeper of the jail for their accommodation.

James's legs began to feel achy and tired but it did not occur to him to stop. He was two miles from the rooms he shared with his mother and two sisters, chosen because of their proximity to Bow Street and his father's work. The only change was that his thinking was blurred now, and he did not look at the sights he passed, did not feel the raw chill of the autumn night, did not hear the laughter of drunken men or the wailing of women or the sounds of evening traffic.

It was nearly ten o'clock when he turned off Long Acre into a side street, then into a yard, or small square, close to Bow Yard, and slipped into a narrow alley lit by two flares sheltered inside glass frames. Here was Cobbold Yard, where tradespeople lived, prosperous enough to keep servants, to pay for "protection" in the form of two men even now dozing in the doors, staffs aslant, placed so as to give them a sharp crack across head or shoulder if they slipped because the men slept.

One woke enough to ask in a sharp but frightened voice: "Who is it now? Who passes?"

"It's all right, William," the boy said. " 'Tis only I, James Marshall."

"I don't know what the young are coming to, coming home in the middle of the night. And your poor mother, scared half to death she is because you didn't get home on time."

"Good night." James Marshall strode briskly to the door leading to the back stairs which led to their two rooms. He started up them quickly but confidently enough, but slowed down as he drew near the door which his mother might open at any moment. He did not know why he was afraid, for his mother would at most remonstrate with him. Had his father been alive he could have expected a beating for being out so late; he had often been frightened of returning late without a good excuse.

Yet he felt differently now—worse.

He did not know, although later the years told him, that on this day when Jackson's execution could not fail to awaken painful memories of the shooting, already six months past because Jackson had used every device to postpone his trial and to buy false witnesses, he should have been with his mother. He simply knew that there was disquiet within him; new sensations which were not simply fear.

Ruth Marshall heard her son's voice in the yard, and the querulous tone of the guard, but she did not get out of her chair. A glow of red embers which filled the fireplace and cookstove provided the only warmth in these two rooms. The younger children were already in the smaller room, asleep, one at each end of a bed built from the wall; her bed was beneath it, much wider: her bed and Richard's. With Richard and the quilts there had been no cold nights, but now she was often cold. An iron pot was warm on the black iron stove, filled with meat soup which James liked; bread stood on the table with some cold vegetables and a piece of dried-looking cheese.

It was such a supper as she had often shared with both Richard and

James on nights when they had been home in time to eat and talk before going to bed. In a strange way she missed their discussions more than any other single thing except her loving with Richard.

How father and son had talked!

How proud Richard had been of the boy! Even though he had never said so in James's presence, for fear of making him swelled-headed. For from a very early age—earlier than that of Beth today, with her childish prattle and her giggles and her easy tears—James had used words as if taught their significance in the womb. A prodigy, Richard had called him.

"We've brought forth a scholar, Ruth," he would say. "A boy with a man's mind already."

Richard had had access to many books through his friend the Reverend Sebastian Smith. He borrowed and read them, then allowed his son to read them before discussing with the boy the author's meaning, the significance of the phrases and the philosophies. The more complex facts he would explain with extreme care, and his son always remembered. As the boy grew older, his interest in the rest of the world, in trade, in the figures quoted in the Annual Register, developed. There were two coffee houses in which he was permitted to sit for hours over a single mug of coffee, reading newspapers, absorbing the events of London especially, reading about crime and criminals, about his father's work and about that of John Furnival and Bow Street. Afterward he would talk over what he had read with his father, forever seeking explanations and information.

Sitting and listening, Ruth had absorbed a great deal of knowledge, just as, at James's age, she had from her own father. But she could not expound, as Richard had; and today as always she found it difficult to talk with her son except on homely matters.

She knew that he still read a great deal.

She could only guess how much he missed the talks with his father.

She heard her son hesitate outside the door, but still she did not move.

Slowly the door opened and he came in.

There was nothing furtive about the way James entered; there had never been anything furtive about him. She did not understand his expression but was aware of something different about him; perhaps it was due to the candlelight, but whatever the cause, he seemed older, older and very tired. He closed the door as cold night air swept up the narrow staircase and stood looking at her for a while, as if he were seeing something different in her, too. Quite without warning he crossed to her and went down on his knees, leaning against them and looking up into her face. She opened her mouth but no words came. Her right hand moved and touched and then soothed his forehead. He could feel the roughness at the end of her forefinger where she pushed the head of the needle; too often she sewed without a thimble.

It was like looking down on her husband, but this mood of nostalgia did not hurt. "What made you so late?" she inquired at last.

"I could not rest."

"You feel warm although 'tis cold outside. Have you been walking far?"

"Very far," he replied. "But that is not new to me."

"No," she said, echoing his words, "that is not new to you. Where have you been?"

He did not reply immediately.

He was ten years old, yet in some ways a man. He was ten years old yet felt a great burden of responsibility for his mother and his sisters, and he felt shame because he had left them alone all day, one of the few days when he was free because the merchant for whom he worked knew that it was useless to open his shop on a Tyburn hanging day. It was the poor people's holiday, and no one worked except those who must.

"James," she said, "you must tell me where you have been."

It was still some time before he answered, but there was no defiance in him, so she let him be, not trying to hurry him. Suddenly he buried his face in his hands and sobbed, so hard that she could feel the shaking throughout her body. Now both of her hands covered his head with a light touch which she hoped, prayed, was reassuring. He did not cry loudly and there was no fear that he would wake the others.

When at last he quieted and drew back, she asked, "Have you eaten this day, my son?"

He shook his head, his voice too hoarse for words.

"Go and wash," she told him, "and then come to the table."

He moved away, watching her, but she did not linger. She was young to be his mother, not yet twenty-seven; her body had natural sprightliness and she moved without effort. He went to a corner where there was a wooden slab with a bowl standing in a hole cut into it, a tall jug, and some soap so coarse it scraped the skin. He used very little of the precious water, emptied the waste into a pail, and rinsed in only an inch or two in the bottom of the bowl. He dried himself on a patched linen towel and, feeling refreshed, went to the table.

Two pewter bowls of soup steamed at either end. He sat down and his mother sat opposite, head bowed and palms placed together in prayer. Half a minute passed before she said, "Thank God from whom all blessings flow, all food and sustenance comes, all health and all courage."

"Amen," breathed James Marshall and, when he was sure that she had finished saying grace, he began to eat; only when he started did he realise how ravenous he was. But his mother did not offer him more soup; that was for tomorrow. He had a crust of bread and some cheese from a wooden trencher, for all their china had been sold, and washed these down with water; then he pushed the roughhewn wooden chair back, feeling much better.

"Can you tell me now?" his mother asked.

"I can and will but I do not know if it will please you."

She looked at him for a long time and, unbidden, what little he knew of her history passed through his mind. She was the daughter of a dissenting minister who, somewhere in Berkshire, had gathered supporters and had built a small chapel until, persecuted by more orthodox Christians, he had become a wandering preacher, visiting inns and, on the fringe of London, alehouses and even brothels to carry his message. Richard Marshall had once saved him from a gang of ruffians in an alehouse and had taken him home. That was when she and Richard had first met.

James realised, as what he knew of these things drifted through his mind, that his mother was about to speak so he did not try to find the words he needed. Slowly she went to where a basket stood on a narrow side table. She fumbled in the bottom of the basket and brought out a folded paper with black printing.

He caught his breath as she unfolded it and held it out for him to see.

"Is this where you have been?" she asked.

The face of Frederick Jackson, drawn true to life, stared out of the page, and across the top were the words:

Confessions and Last Utterances
on This Earth of the Famous
Frederick Jackson—Hero

James stopped reading halfway down the page of the injustice done to Frederick Jackson by his persecutor, John Furnival. There was so much more in the same malicious vein, no insult not heaped on the head of the man who had provided the evidence at the trial of a man he had been trying to bring down for twenty years.

The boy said, "They are lies—all lies!"

"The only truth is that Mr. Furnival sent him to his death and he was hanged this afternoon."

"He was a murderer, a thief, a devil in human form."

"This is what Mr. Furnival is to some people," his mother replied.

"*You* don't believe that!"

"No, I don't believe it," Ruth assured him. "I believe him to be as good a man as your father, except in one way, and most of these statements are lies. But many will believe them, my son." Almost in the same breath she asked, "Why did you go to Tyburn today?"

"It was not possible for me to keep away."

"Had you planned to go?"

"Yes, Mother. I was set on it."

"Why?" she asked, puzzled and frowning. "*Why?*"

"If there is an answer it is that the ghost of my father drew me there," he said huskily. "I wanted to see for myself what he had often told me happened. And it did. Mother, did you know that he came near to worshipping Mr. Furnival?"

She nodded mutely.

"And that was because he believed in all that Mr. Furnival believed in, and hated what Mr. Furnival hates. The evil system of thief-takers, who live by catching men, often innocent men, and having them hanged—like the seventeen I saw today!" His voice grew louder, fiercer. "Except for the men Mr. Furnival pays, and a few paid by others who abominate the system, there is no honest thief-taker, scarce an honest magistrate, for each wants his share of the government's blood money. Mr. Furnival believes the laws aid the criminals. They leave the safety of the wards and the parishes in the hands of these grasping justices. They allow two or three sheriffs to represent the King—and to make a profit out of crimes as best they can, by charging prisoners for favours, and by selling the body and the clothing of the men they have just hanged. And that is not all," tumbled on James, so fiercely that his mother gave up trying to interrupt him. He finally broke off as if hearing something of significance, and then cried: "Hark!"

In the stillness that followed, a frail voice sounded: "Eleven o'clock and all's well. Eleven o'clock and all's well!"

"*There* is our sole protection against criminals, save for any we pay for ourselves. The Charlies!" He sneered the word. "Men of the watch

42

hired by the wards to patrol the streets to keep them safe. Those useless hour bawlers who will croak 'all's well' if a house is on fire or a girl is being raped or a man robbed in front of their eyes! They are nothing but bumbling old fools who doze in their boxes or in the watchhouses and keep themselves out of trouble. *That* is how the peace of London is kept. *That* is why crime is always increasing and justice has no meaning. And that is what my father pledged himself to fight—and what Mr. Furnival is fighting with all his strength."

At last, exhausted, he stopped.

Looking up at his mother, it came to his mind that he had not seen her smile or heard her laugh since his father's death. He realised also that except for the younger children these rooms had been rooms of mourning for half a year, yet before then they had been filled with laughter and song. He had never come home to find his mother crying or vexed and he had known so few other families—then—that he had not realised what a remarkable thing that happiness was. He had never come home to an empty table, to curses, to punishment unless it was merited. In this past half year his mother had become a different person, and so had he.

But his answer was not the full explanation of why he had gone to see his father's murderer hang. He had not even known that morning, had not known for certain until he had climbed these stairs and hesitated—not for fear of having hurt her, but for fear that hope would not be realised. For he had gone to Tyburn to see the end of the man who had brought such heaviness upon him and his mother and he had thought that with the murderer dead the weight would be eased.

But there was no easing of his heart or, he knew, of hers. He drew a deep breath and spoke so quickly that it was difficult for her to follow the words.

"I thought it would exorcise the devil of hate from us, that's why I went. I thought when life departed from him—"

"No," she choked, "no, my son, don't tell me that."

"If 'tis not the devil, then who is it?" he cried. "Why is this like a house of death?"

As he saw the tears well up in her eyes, he knew how he had hurt her but became aware of something else, of a secret to share with her: he knew deep within him that she had suffered the same fears; that since his father had gone it had been as if they were possessed of the devil.

But why, why, why? What wrong, what evil had they done?

"James, my son," she said in husky whisper, "it is very late and you must be at the merchant's by six o'clock. You will be hard to wake. In the morning you will have forgotten all such talk of the devil. Why, you should be ashamed and so should I! Your father laughed at all mention of the devil and declared that God would not allow him to exist."

She laughed. Then for the first time in so many months they both laughed; together.

But when he was on the straw mattress in a corner of this room and his mother had gone to her bed, he saw those thrashing legs and he heard the voice of the Reverend Sebastian Smith asking God's mercy for the man who had killed his father.

Then he remembered his father, *alive*.

He bit into the coarse sheet which covered him and forced back the stinging tears. He must not cry, he would not cry, a *man* never cried.

About the time that James Marshall reached his home, Red Foster and his pretty wife passed the pike at Tyburn, his horse prancing between the shafts of a fancy gig hired for this night's work. It was very cold, and dark except for the clear light of the stars and lights at houses and taverns on either side of the highway and on other carriages. In the distance, lights showed at the windows of great houses and from farmhouses or from barns where cows were calving and in need of help. Now and again they passed little groups of people, tipsy-drunk, walking back to their country homes after the day at Tyburn Fair. Outbursts of laughter, oaths, shrieks of protest, came from the road which was usually deathly quiet except on the nights of death.

Foster was in his late twenties, a man from a good family which had disowned him for his gambling; but he took that ostracism easily, for he had won his Lilian at the gaming table and she was worth all the money he had ever lost. She held his arm as they went toward the Owl, an alehouse two miles from Tyburn Pike, where it was known that the notorious Dick Miller spent much of his time.

"Red," Lilian said, "I think I'm very frightened."

"Fie! With me to protect you? And Harris and his men close by?"

"But I haven't seen them," she protested. "I haven't caught a glimpse of them, and—and you know what Miller is like."

"Exaggeration, ma'am. Old wives' tales which should never be believed by young wives. I—"

"Red!" she gasped. "Look!"

And there, not far ahead and directly in their path, was a man on horseback, coming toward them. He had chosen his spot well, for a ditch with banks too steep for horse and gig was on one side, while on the other side was a high stack of hay. From both hay and ditch there came a stench which made all who passed this way wish to hurry.

Red, perforce, slowed down.

Ahead, the solitary figure on horseback came on, and from behind there was a movement and a noise loud enough to make Lilian look over her shoulder in alarm. Silhouetted against the light of a big house was another horseman.

"It's one of Tom Harris' men," Red muttered. "I swear it."

There was no way of being sure.

There was only the darkness, so full of menace, and the riders both in front and behind, the snort of a horse, the creak of leather and the chink of bridles, for the wheels of this gig ran smoothly and made little sound. Red Foster's wife was beginning to take in long breaths as deeper fear possessed her; knowing the risk of what they were doing, knowing Miller's reputation, made the sense of danger far greater than if she had not known that she, at least as much as her husband, was a decoy.

Suddenly the rider in front spurred his mount and called: "Stand there! Stand and deliver." He came straight on into the path of the carriage and Red pulled at the reins and the horse slowed down. The man who had called out waited only for the carriage to stop before he moved to the side.

"Get down, the pair of you," he ordered. He looked huge and menacing in the light from the carriage lamps. His pistol was leveled at Red Foster but his gaze was on Red's wife, who was little more than a girl. Foster draped the reins over the rail and climbed down.

"Take all I have," he begged, "but do not alarm my wife more, I beg of you."

"And how much have you got?" demanded Miller, and he roared with laughter. "Precious little if I know anything about young gallants who bring their wives out of London without an escort. Or are you lying? Is she your wife?"

"I swear it! I—" Foster cast a desperate glance behind him. The man who had followed the carriage was dismounting and Foster now needed no telling that he was Miller's man; there was no sign of Tom Harris or any who worked with him. He handed Lilian down and Miller rode close, covering them with his pistol and still looking at her. "I'll give you everything I have! I was lucky at the tables tonight, I've ten gold pieces and—"

"Deliver to my friend all you have," Miller ordered, and as he spoke the other came up, a slimmer man who looked as if a boy's face might be hidden by the mask he wore. "Stand over him," Miller ordered his assistant, and slid from his horse, making a mock bow and a sweeping motion with his right arm. "Ma'am, it is my earnest desire to make your closer acquaintance," he declared. "It is a long time since I have seen a prettier wench." He made a swift movement and plucked her off the ground and into his arms. She cried out and kicked and beat at his face and shoulders but he did no more than laugh at her.

"I beg you, do not take my wife!" Foster flung himself down on his knees.

Miller placed his right foot against Foster's chest and pushed him backwards, and at that moment one of Lilian's nails scratched his cheek beneath the right eye. She could smell his gin-soaked breath, the odour of his clothes and body, and terror possessed her.

"So you want it rough, my pretty," he growled. "Then rough you shall have it, with your fine husband looking on!"

He tossed her at the foot of the great stack of hay and, while Foster grappled desperately to free himself from the viselike grip of Miller's assistant, unbuckled his belt and let down his breeches. Lilian, staring up at the menacing figure, knowing that in a moment she would feel his hands, would have her clothes torn apart, would be another victim of Dick Miller, was so terrified that thought of Tom Harris went out of her mind.

Miller came down on one knee by her side and she felt his hand at the neck of her dress.

"No!" she screamed. "God help me! God help me!"

"As much use to call to Him as to your husband," Miller growled.

"Perhaps someone else heard her, Dick," a man called from the top of the stack of hay.

Suddenly the place was alive with men who sprang down behind Miller and on either side. It was as if they had come out of the night air.

"Leave your breeches down,'" Tom Harris ordered, rough laughter in his voice. "The lady's husband may like five minutes to lambaste you before I take you in."

Red Foster was already running. He ignored Miller and flung himself down by his wife's side, while Miller stood helpless and his assistant was seized and manacled. When a man pulled his mask from his face he showed for what he was: a lad of seventeen or eighteen. The girl was sobbing, Foster trying to reassure her. Miller began to hoist his breeches after Harris and another of the thief-takers had taken his pair of pistols and his dagger.

"Let me go," begged Miller. "Let me go and I'll put a name on a dozen thieves, each worth as much as I. Five hundred pounds' worth, well nigh. Take what I have and let me go!"

Tom Harris clapped the heavy manacles on him, and rejoined: "The only place you're going is Bow Street, and after Mr. Furnival has questioned you, to Newgate to wait trial. Do you know what I would do with the likes of you, Miller? I'd hang you from the nearest tree and swing on your genitals until you died. Get on your horse!" He gave a sardonic laugh. "Get on *my* horse, Miller; it's mine in forfeit now."

Soon, all of them were riding back to London, the carriage last except for one of Furnival's men who had come with Tom Harris. Lilian was quiet now, her head resting on her husband's shoulder, while Red Foster talked with an undertone of excitement in his voice.

"There'll be forty pounds each for the prisoners, m'dear, and the horses will be worth half as much again. We won't know how much money Miller has on him but Furnival is an honest man; whatever there is we'll get our share and I can be out of debt." For a moment he was silent, and then he went on: "I've been in terror of going back to Newgate, Lil. God bless you for keeping me free."

She did not answer. She was crying.

John Furnival was sitting in the back room downstairs when Moffat came in a little before midnight. Lisa Braidley had been gone for nearly two hours, and Furnival had been reading, his legs up on a stool with a feather cushion on it, a blanket wrapped around him and a voluminous jacket over his shoulders. The embers glowed both red and gold on the half-full glass of French brandy by his side, and a book was open and supported by another pillow on his thighs. When the mood took him he would go to the bed in the alcove, perhaps to sleep at once, perhaps to ponder.

He heard Moffat but did not look around.

"I have news you would like to know, sir," announced Moffat.

"Then why keep me waiting?"

"Dick Miller was taken tonight, with a youth believed to be his son. Both are lodged in the cells here, the better to be questioned tomorrow."

"So the trick worked," Furnival said with satisfaction. "How many witnesses do we have?"

"Five, sir."

"Not even the most besotted jury could argue with that," declared Furnival. "One rogue the fewer to haunt the highways." He picked up his glass and added testily, "Come where I can see you, man!" When Moffat appeared by his side, so gray, so tired, Furnival looked at him intently for a moment and then said, "I would want to talk to you but sleep will be better for us both. Tell me one thing, Silas."

"If I can, sir, I most surely will."

"Oh, you can, for I want only your opinion. Does it seem to you that for every rogue we hang at Tyburn or at Newgate or at any gallows, two grow in his place?"

Moffat spread his hands toward the fire, not only for warmth but for time to think. His master did not urge him, just sat up bundled in his warmth and comfort while Moffat looked as if his flesh were too thin to hold any warmth at all.

At last he answered, "Yes, sir, it does. But it also seems to me that if the one wasn't hanged there would be three instead of two."

"You're a great comfort, Silas," Furnival said. "King Solomon could have been no wiser. Now off to bed with you."

Soon after his man had gone, John Furnival stirred himself and went to the necessary room behind the alcove. In one corner a brazier glowed, and there was an overpowering perfume of flowers, which always reminded Furnival of the flowers the judges carried to overpower the stench which came from prisoners "fresh" from Newgate or one of the other stinking holes.

It was a good night for John Furnival, sleeping with the window open, for he could afford the window tax and preferred both light and air.

Out beyond Soho the city ranged, and already streets were appearing between there and Tottenham Court and Marylebone, beyond Clerkenwell and Hoxton to the north and Bethnal Green and Mile End to the east. Old houses might collapse, like thunder, even new ones fall, but the growth in numbers continued. The fields and the farms were beginning to yield to the great houses, while to the west, Hyde Park's fences were under siege to builders voracious in their hunger for land, egged on by great landowners who served both King and Parliament and ignored the laws which had been passed to try to prevent London from growing too large and so beyond control. Even Knightsbridge, even the south bank of the Thames was being developed far beyond the Borough of Southwark. And there was much talk of more bridges, one at Westminster and one at Charing Cross, to speed the stagecoaches and the riders.

Nothing, it seemed, could stop London from extending its boundaries beyond the limits set by King and government. These laws were circumvented in two ways: by the wealthy who, believing in the future of London as the heart of Britain, bought great tracts of land, bribing officials for permits to build; and by small merchants and houseowners who, too frightened to break the law, built onto existing houses.

The jealousies and animosities between the City of London itself and Westminster grew worse, not better. Within the City walls was the greatest concentration of families and businessmen, including the guilds of all crafts and most professions. Beyond the walls and the seven gates was the two-mile highway which led to Westminster. Once nothing but a road between open farmland running down to the Thames on the south, this was now built up to the north with inns, alehouses and brothels, and the great terror of the Strand was the highwaymen who lurked there after dark, making the journey deadly dangerous unless one traveled with a group or a strong escort.

Within the City, divided into wards and parishes, there was some pretext of law and safety, but most responsible citizens were too careful to trust the watchmen patrols and so paid for their own peace officers. The profession of thief-taker, so abominated by John Furnival, arose because anyone could charge a man with a crime punishable by death, and anyone could bear false witness, often to his advantage, since he received a reward for his service to the community. And he could be even better rewarded, for if he arrested a man and had him committed, then he received a certificate which exempted him from any otherwise compulsory service in his parish, from jury duty and many such tasks. "A thief-taker is a thief-maker," Charles Hitchins had said more than twenty years earlier, and that was as true as ever.

Rich landowners built the nuclei of small towns in and beyond the villages, where there were no restrictive laws. As these spread they drew closer to the permitted limits of London and so the day came when the gaps closed and they were virtually part of the city. These building projects slowly changed the face of London, and while some took over green fields by which the city breathed, others tore down rat-infested slums and did much good.

From the forbidding walls of the City of London, at that time a free port for the goods of all nations of the earth, the Strand led to the City of Westminster, which was without walls and proud of its position.

Both places crawled with beggars; with the destitute, the sick, the frightened; and with criminals who lurked by night and sometimes were bold enough to strike for a rich prize by day.

The Strand became more infested with highwaymen every week.

The Thames, the other great means of communication between the two cities, was infested with thieves and footpads and "mudlarks" and was crowded with shipping from across the world as well as from the coasts of Britain and of Europe. Thirty watermen plied their little wherries for hire, and the calls of "Eastward Ho!" and "Westward Ho!" were forever hovering on the river.

No law denied a man the right to build on the side of his property, or atop it, or beneath it, and so those who feared the law added rooms and shops, encroaching onto streets already narrow; and attics were built with narrow wooden stairways and sometimes only ladders, making such firetraps as London had not seen even before the Great Fire, which some old people could remember.

London's burning, London's burning.

Bringing different dangers were the cellars, dug into the gravel beneath the city, where damp rose and struck at the bones and joints of young and old, rats and other vermin thrived, and the seeds of the great plague festered until some special set of circumstances caused them to erupt into epidemics so fearful that the death carts could come again to the narrow streets. These ghettos, or rookeries, had narrow passages and connecting doors used to harbour thieves on the run from the law.

So London spread both up and down and at the seams until she swelled like a human being whose lungs were bursting.

The young novelist Henry Fielding, already stirred by a deep social conscience, said bitterly of the Charlies, who kept their slothful watch:

> They were chosen out of those poor old decrepit people who are from their want of bodily strength rendered incapable of getting a living by work. These men, armed only with a pole, which some are

50

scarcely able to lift, are to secure the persons and houses of His Majesty's subjects from the attacks of young, bold, stout, desperate and well-armed villains....

In the cellars or the attics of grogshops the drunks lay in their stupor on bales of stinking straw; soon they would wake and stagger to the taproom and buy their pennorth of gin so as to drink themselves back into oblivion. Much of the gin was bad, for all of it was illegal under the hated Act of 1736. Despite the public whipping ordered for all caught drinking gin, few tried seriously to enforce this, and none succeeded. In open defiance of the law, seven thousand quarters of wheat out of London's yearly importation of twelve thousand quarters was used for alcohol, not one per cent of which was licensed.

The sober workmen slept.

The night watchmen, who were old and scarcely capable, dozed in their watchhouses.

The thieves slept as morning drew near. The whores and the good women slept with the same peace.

Lisa Braidley and Eve Milharvey slept, and so did the Reverend Sebastian Smith, next to his buxom wife and in a room apart from their five children, with whom the Marshall children sometimes played.

Even Dick Miller slept; and, exhausted by both tears and fright, so did Lilian Foster, by her husband's side.

Only one of the Furnival family did not sleep well that night. She was Sarah McCampbell, sister of John and William and crippled Francis, Anne and Cleo. Recently widowed, she and her three children, two girls and a boy, were staying with Cleo while an apartment was being made ready for them. That night she lay awake, tossing and turning in the great four-poster bed, thinking of her husband; thinking, also, of her children, and in particular of her son Timothy, already a favourite with his aunts and uncles.

All of this family except John lived in various houses and in flats in Great Furnival Square, built not far from Tyburn Lane and Hyde Park; then it had been two miles outside the limits of the metropolis but now most of the space was built up with fine squares and streets with easy access to Piccadilly and to Westminster: When the Square and the arches and the colonnades had first been built, there were many who had called it Great Furnival's Folly. On the south side was the great house, taking up the whole of that side of the Square and facing a garden planned by Giacomo Leoni, the famous Italian who had laid out the gardens for the palaces of kings and noblemen. In this verdant garden grew trees and shrubs and flowers, roses such as never appeared on London streets; and there were gravel paths for the nursemaids to push their charges and for all who had authority to walk.

By night and by day there were six middle-aged watchmen in the garden and the surrounding streets, armed with staves and with pistols and muskets close at hand. There were also six younger watchmen inside the great house, almost a museum, where the grandfather and the father of John and his brothers and sisters had lived. To the east and west were individual houses for members of the family. In one, William and his wife and seven children lived—five girls and two boys. In another lived Francis and Deborah and their two pale and puny children. Anne, oldest of the sisters, lived in another house with her husband, Jason Gilroy, whose banking and trading business had merged with the Furnivals' on marriage. Gilroy traveled extensively in India and farther east, and Anne lived the life of a widow with her two children, boy and girl twins now aged fourteen. Next door to Anne was Cleo, long married to Robert Yeoman, Member of Parliament for one of the City constituencies. Two of their daughters were already married to young men who, if they chose, could each play a leading part in the growth of the great enterprises which had come to be known as the House of Furnival. Cleo also had a daughter aged seven and two sons, one slightly older and the other younger than Sarah's son Timothy.

The Furnival family had first come to prominence in Queen Elizabeth's day, with William, a banker. His oldest son, John, a man of great strength of will and unbounded ambition, had brought the business enterprises to great power, had built Furnival Tower House, so near the Tower of London, had even built some docks across the river and, of course, had created Great Furnival Square. Largely because of substantial loans he made to the Court he had been knighted. *His* oldest son, John the Second, had extended all the enterprises, and of his male children—John the Third, William and Francis—had expected most of John the Third.

At first these expectations promised well. John the Third traveled the world, came to know the vast Furnival empire, and made a report of great detail and value to his father and brothers. Then he had simply stated his intention of withdrawing from business, taking his inherited money with him, and becoming a justice of the peace for Westminster.

Nothing had dissuaded him.

There had never been a justice like him, for he could afford to keep peace officers and far more court officials, had great personal courage, and was incorruptible. He had become the scourge of London's criminals; with a dozen like him, he might have cleansed the City and Westminster of crime. Certainly he tried without ceasing. When he had left the business he had also left his house in Great Furnival Square. By inheritance his, it was now occupied by poorer relatives; he did not keep even one room for his own use.

Here in Furnival Square and in nearby streets hundreds lived, but none who was not a Furnival, a relation of the family, or working for one or the other of the businesses.

It would have been difficult to find a square better kept or more attractive to the eye.

Three miles away, in the heart of the City of London, close to the Tower and with its warehouses fronting the river and St. Catherine's Docks, were the Furnival offices, substantial and comparable with the biggest business houses, designed by Colin Campbell, whereas Furnival Square had been designed by the first John Furnival, working with a builder who had been one of those who had helped to build the Covent Garden piazza. Here were the head offices of all the Furnival businesses, from banking to shipping, importing and exporting; there were few branches of commerce with which Furnival and Sons was not associated, either directly or indirectly. Here, in Furnival Tower House, there was a private force of guards, or peace officers; and in the hundred years of its existence, none had ever succeeded in breaking in, although at least a dozen had been caught in the attempt. They had been taken to the mayor and to aldermen, to justices at the Guildhall and the Mansion House, from where they had been committed to the Sessions in Newgate or Bailey Street.

No matter what the trade, or from whence it came, the Furnivals were involved. At first they had been discreet, often buying small companies, such as shipping merchants, small coastal shipping lines, small banks, and wholesale distributors who brought in the food from all of England as well as from distant lands. They owned farms in Scotland and Wales as well as in Lincolnshire and Leicestershire, from where cattle and sheep were driven to London's markets. There were

53

Furnival-owned dairy and pig farms in Norfolk, herds of which crowded the rutted, muddy roads; they had farms in East Anglia, coal mines at all the strategic points for shipment to London by sea. They owned drays and carts in and near London, and had gradually extended their trade until, in the previous generation, it had been impossible to hide the enormous size of their trading empire. In the same year, 1705, they had founded the third of the great fire insurance companies; a year later, the land on which Great Furnival Square was built had been bought—then virtually worthless farmland.

No one knew how much their businesses were worth; but now they could compete openly with the great ducal landowners, with families that had been wealthy for centuries.

This, then, was the Furnival empire, controlled wholly by the family, with John the one "rogue elephant" who would not conform to traditions created by his forefathers. And in all of the houses in Great Furnival Square people slept safe in their beds.

Soon London stirred.

Long before dawn the journeymen were on their way to work, leaving narrow doorways and lanes, stepping over piles of yesterday's filth, stepping over some old sot who, not knowing it, had drunk himself to death on the day of Tyburn's frolic.

And they stepped over foundling babes, some stark naked and blue with cold or even stiff with death before the light of day shone upon them, some bundled up in rags or blankets, perhaps sleeping, perhaps crying, all left by girls often no more than twelve or thirteen; the warm ones left by their mothers in the despairing hope that *one* child at least would be picked up and fondled and perhaps wet-nursed by a mother in desperate need of the relief of milk from her breasts, suckled, and cared for and even—loved.

The great Foundling Hospital, with a royal charter, was in preparation because of the unyielding persistence of Captain Coram. Dukes and earls were to be on its board of Governors; some even said the Prince of Wales, the Minister of State and the Archbishops would be, also. But so far, it was only an empty patch of wasteland near Holborn Garden.

CHAPTER *4*

The Proposition

JAMES MARSHALL began his day at six o'clock, arriving only minutes later than Morgan, his employer, a good enough man as men went and a member of the Reverend Sebastian Smith's congregation at St. Hilary's, a small church soon, it was said, to be pulled down. Morgan was a true believer, who had taken James on because he had promised well and his mother needed help. For sixpence a day James laboured from six in the morning until eight or nine o'clock at night, delivering groceries as well as vegetables and fruit to the big houses nearby, to inns, dining rooms, coffee houses, brothels, and wherever food was needed.

Morgan professed to have great hopes of the boy. He might one day rise to a position behind the counter of this shop so redolent of spices, coffee and tea.

It was James himself who had thought of making a yoke, like an ox's, and stringing larger bundles to it so that they equaled, as well as balancing baskets on his head and pushing the two-wheeled cart, so heavily laden when he set out that it was all his young muscles could do to shift the wheels.

But shift them he did—even on that morning.

It was gray and overcast, with a spit of rain in the air, enough to make one's clothes damp, one's hair wet and the cobbles slippery, so that it was difficult to guide the cart. Alone, seen by hundreds and noticed by none, he started the cart moving and was soon at the Bell Hotel, where a porter was waiting to unload; next he made several calls in Covent Garden piazza, going to back entrances and seeing none of the fading splendour.

By nine o'clock this round was done, and he pushed the empty cart through heavy rain, finding it almost as difficult to control as when it had been full. He was given a cup of thin vegetable soup and was then loaded and sent off again, this time toward Holborn. Horses and carriages splashed mud over him and the canvas sheet covering the packages in the cart and the yoke and baskets, making progress much slower and more difficult. Most of the people at the roadside were bowed against the rain; many brought their capes from their shoulders and covered their heads. The wooden posts driven along the road to separate horse-drawn vehicles and horses from those who walked were bent and broken because of so many accidents. Close to Newgate Street a solitary rider, going much too fast, swung into the path of a coach-and-four coming from Holborn. The driver tried to swing his horses away but the near-side front wheel crunched into one of the posts and a horse squealed as it banged a knee against another post. The rider went on, ignoring the shouts of the driver and passers-by. A crowd soon gathered. At the fringe a boy, perhaps seven or eight years old, with a skeletal face and huge, hungry-looking eyes, darted forward and snatched at the packages beneath James's canvas, but a man saw him and cuffed him away.

"Thank you, sir," James said gratefully.

"They're thieves before they can walk," the man growled. "You be careful with your master's goods, boy."

"Be sure I shall use my best endeavours, sir."

Wherever he went during the next two hours he was haunted by that skeletal face, the hungry eyes, and the venom in the voice of the man who had prevented him from being robbed. Passing a grocer's shop in Holborn there was a roar of "Stop thief!" and the boy, the same one, came racing out of the shop, the owner or his man rushing after him, but stopping as the rain struck him like a wall of cold water. The little thief got away, hugging a loaf.

The big man shook his fist and roared: "If I catch him he'll hang as sure as my name's Jack Roberts!"

And the child *could* no doubt be hanged; or might at least be transported.

James Marshall went on and delivered his goods and walked back a different way from the road he had come. Whenever he could use a different route, or enter a lane or a yard he had never seen before, he would do so even if it meant running part way back to make up for lost time. He had four journeys to make, and whatever time it was when they were done, he could go home.

Tonight, it was half-past eight. There was still enough strength in his wiry legs to enable him to run through the rain toward his home, and as he was about to turn into the narrow lane, he stopped, despite the rain, and splashed into a puddle where the cobbles had worn thin. For along the street was a rare sight here: a coachman sitting in his cape and cockaded hat on the high seat of a coach-and-pair. The man stared at him blankly, and James turned into the lane, wondering who had come to see Mr. Leonard, the owner of the house. Once inside, he could hear the rain pelting on the wooden roof and sides, and a stream of water was coming from the landing where a window was broken.

He opened the door of the larger of the two rooms, and again he stopped, utterly still, more astonished this time than he had been at the sight of the coach-and-pair. For he heard the unmistakable voice of John Furnival.

His astonishment was such that James missed some of the words even though he recognised the voice instantly, but gradually the words themselves became distinguishable and even their import, although for a while he was not really sure that he understood.

"Think about it, Ruth. I'll not try to rush you. But you'll be a foolish woman if you refuse. You need more than you can earn honestly to bring up three children well, and if you see them going hungry you won't mind how you get the food to feed them with, never mind send them to school. If you marry again, your man might be good to them but—" Furnival broke off and then growled as if to himself, "I'll not try to persuade you, either."

James heard his mother say, "No one could have been more kind, sir."

The boy moved swiftly away from the door as footsteps sounded, heavier than any he had heard in the room before, and he reached a dark corner where the rain splashed on him as the door opened and John Furnival appeared. Had he looked at the corner or even at the window he could not have failed to see James; instead, he turned his back so that he could gaze into the room, and there was a gentler tone in his voice as he went on: "And you owe yourself some comfort. Never forget yourself, Ruth. It is a rule of life."

He turned to the stairs, his back still toward the boy, and went down slowly but lightly.

The door did not close.

James's mother appeared, looking toward the man who had been to visit her, not moving even when he had disappeared. Immediately the rattle of the carriage wheels sounded, and Ruth Marshall turned on her heel and ran swiftly back inside the room. When, five minutes or so afterward, the boy ventured in, she was standing at the tiny window and staring out.

Diffidently James said, "Mother, all my clothes are wet."

She pirouetted from the window, obviously taken by surprise, then rushed to him, beginning to scold him for getting so sodden before heeding his protest that he could not cease his deliveries just because it was raining. She stood him in front of the low fire and stripped and rubbed him vigorously with a rough towel, saying as she finished, "Now wrap a blanket from my bed about you and get your supper. Don't wake the others, they can't have been asleep for long."

She did not mention John Furnival's visit.

He did not tell her what he had heard and seen.

"What did he propose?" Tom Harris asked Ruth late that night.

The rain had stopped and the stars were shining. The room struck cold. Harris had called on the way to Bow Street to make a report on his day's mission, as he often did, to find out if there was anything she needed. She had never been more glad to see him. They talked in undertones in front of what was left of the fire because James was asleep in his corner and there was no other space for them to sit. She had poured out the story of Furnival's visit, both fearful and excited, and now here was Tom, the most stolid and the most unexcitable man she knew, asking in his flat voice: "What did he propose?"

"He offered me the position of general provider of food for him, at the court and in his home," replied Ruth. "He declared I would live with James and the girls in a cottage he owns at the back of the building and his offices." Had the candlelight been stronger or had this taken place in daylight the red flush staining her cheeks would have shown scarlet, but she went on without hesitation and scarcely a tremor in her voice. "And he promised to send James to school until he is fourteen—a school for boys close to Saint Paul's. I have heard of the school, Tom. 'Tis a highly respected one."

"None finer," agreed Tom Harris equably. "And then he will pay you enough to keep your children at home?"

"He will provide all food and fuel and also pay me one guinea a week."

"He was never mean with money! Did he tell you what else he would expect from you besides taking care of his food?" asked Harris bluntly.

The flush had subsided and, in spite of the implication in the words, did not return. She eyed him steadily; all she could see was the outline of Harris' solid body and head, and a glow on his eyes from the dying embers. He could see no more of her. They sat silent for so long that it was as if they were dozing, but at last Ruth answered.

"Yes, Tom. I needed no telling but he told me frankly he would require me to warm his bed at times. I mean it when I say I needed no telling; Richard often told me about Mr. Furnival's ways but said no wife of one of Mr. Furnival's officers would be at risk with him."

Harris did not make the obvious retort: "Only their widows." He stirred, coughed, and unexpectedly put out a hand and touched hers where they were folded in her lap.

"Think well before you decide, Ruth," he advised. "Long and well if you must. Be sure of one thing."

"What is that?" she asked, aware of the rough skin of his palm and fingers.

"What he promises, John Furnival will do. When he makes a bargain he will keep it, but"—the already deep voice deepened still further and the pressure of his hand grew firmer—"he'll expect the partner to the bargain to keep it, too. You'll not be the only woman to warm him, Ruth, and if there is any jealousy in you, refuse him. He killed two wives because of his ways."

"*Killed*, Tom?" She sounded shocked.

"They were jealous of the other women and he paid their protests no heed. I'll grant you, 'killed' is too strong a word, but they were no match for him. He's a great bull of a man." He took his hand away and shifted his chair back, indicating that he was about to take his leave.

"Tom," Ruth stayed him, "what would you think if I accepted the proposition? Tell me truly."

"I'd think you might rue the day," answered Tom Harris, "and I would hope you would have strength enough to leave him, if ever you did. I would not disapprove, if that is what you are really asking me. I've seen the same situation work well with others, and John Furnival would not flaunt you. Everyone who knows him well would be aware of the relationship but no one else would learn of it from him."

He rose slowly to his feet.

"Tom," Ruth said, putting out a hand to delay him again, "will you do one thing for me?"

"If I can, Ruth, you know that. What is it you want?"

"I would like to know what the Reverend Smith would think. I have worshipped in his church for many years and our children have played together often. I would not like to have no blessing from him."

A change came upon Tom Harris, one which was evident even though she could see so little. He stood very erect and she could hear him breathing through his nostrils, as if his lips were set tightly, as they were likely to be when he disapproved or was angry. What had she said that could make him angry?

The boy in the corner stirred in his sleep and turned over.

"Ruth," said Tom Harris, "you don't have to please me and you don't have to please the Reverend Smith. You have to make a decision for yourself and for your children. If Smith is half the man I believe, he will acknowledge one thing: whatever you decide he will think it was because you thought it best. This is what Richard would have asked of you, also." He stopped, and now his breathing came through his mouth, harsher and more laboured, as if mention of his friend and her husband had broken the tight hold he had kept on his emotions. "Do what you think best, woman. I've told you that all the world need know is that you are housekeeper at John Furnival's."

"But the Reverend Smith knows Mr. Furnival well," Ruth said in a meek voice. "He is a frequent visitor, interceding for his parishioners."

"I cannot make your decisions for you, Ruth, and you don't really wish me to. Think on it hard. And it's late now, I must bid you good night." He took her hands and, in a rare gesture for him, kissed her on the cheeks. Without another word he turned from the room and went heavily down the creaking stairs. She crossed to the window and watched as she had watched Furnival. One torch flickered in a tall bracket but there was light also at an open carriage, unattended, and light in a room opposite. That told her that the child of neighbours,

60

across the yard, was so very sick that the doctor had been brought out to see him late as it was.

The ailing son was the only child of two people in their forties; their all. They would make any sacrifice for him.

She would make any sacrifice for her children.

Tom Harris' footsteps sounded on the hard stones and she could see him as he walked toward the narrow arched passageway, the only means of entering or leaving the yard. When he had gone and all was quiet, the sound of the horse champing on his bit seemed loud. She considered whether she should go to see if she could help her troubled neighbours, but the doctor came out, top-hatted and cloaked, with a man whom she recognised as a brother of the neighbour's wife: so they were not without help. At last she snuffed out the candle and went in darkness to the other, tiny room. She undressed, pulled a heavy woolen nightdress over her head, oblivious to its scratchiness on her fair skin, and climbed into bed.

She did not go to sleep for a long time, yet she was up before James woke, to get him some hot mash of oatmeal and water and some cold loin of mutton and send him on his way. He looked so tired in the first light of dawn. But soon the other children were calling, one laughing, one crying, and by seven o'clock she must be done with everything needed for them and leave for the dressmaker's shop in the Strand, where she would perhaps work for a few hours or, if the day was good, bring the cottons and linens and even silks back here to work on. The pale silks, the rich brocades, the poplins, the velvets—all of the best materials were sewed on the premises; Mr. and Mrs. Hewson, who owned the shop, had some of the finest clients in London, men and women of fashion, even some who were at King George II's Court. Not a stitch, not a ribbon of the dresses for such honoured customers left the premises. All the cutting was done by Mr. Hewson himself, much of the designing by his wife, and on the two top floors of the premises the women and girls worked for as long as there was light.

Ruth was out by seven, the children clattering after her—Beth, aged six, and Henrietta, aged four. She admonished them to stay in the yard to play, checked that the three fire buckets which had to be outside each front door were filled with water, and swept her own patch of courtyard before doing a small corner patch for old Mrs. Blackett, who had a room in a building close to the passageway. She would keep the children from going out—when she was up, that was, and if she did not go nodding off to sleep. But soon other children would come and the yard would echo to their laughing and their shrieking, and to the women sweeping and filling buckets.

Ruth went across the yard, picking her way over puddles and dung, and up to the rooms where the sick child was. The man whom she had seen the previous night came out of the main room, a finger at his lips.

"I came only to inquire after Leslie," she whispered.

"Glory be to God, the child's still sleeping, and his mother and father, too," the brother-in-law answered. "The doctor who bled him prophesied the crisis would come during the night, and it both came and went." The man himself, veined and bulbous-eyed, looked tired out. "I will tell them you inquired, Mrs. Marshall; they will be very appreciative, that I'm sure."

"Is there anything I can do?"

"Nothing, ma'am, nothing at all. The good Lord has sent them all they need and spared the life of their beloved son."

She went off, aware of dislike of the man and chiding herself for the feeling. He had been at hand in time of the family's great need. What more could one ask? She went down the creaking stairs and picked her way to the alley and the street.

Until Richard's death she had stayed at home, or else had taken the children with her to the market or had helped to keep an eye on the children of the less fortunate mothers who had to go out to work.

The night's wind had dried the streets. Only here and there were patches of wet mud, and most of the dirt had already turned to dust, which was sent in clouds by horses and wheels. Here and there the big holes were still filled with rain water. A boy no older than Beth stood with his dung cart on the corner of Drury Lane and the Strand, and when horses spilled their droppings he would dart forward and gather as much as he could on a wooden shovel, toss it into the cart and rush back for more, desperate to get there before more carriages came and made the harvest more difficult. Ruth saw him dart in front of a coach-and-four and scrape as if his life depended on it, then dart out of the way of the heavy hooves and merciless wheels only just in time. Sedan chairs passed him within inches but these he ignored.

The Strand was wider than most thoroughfares and, even so early, full of traffic, while many shops on the north side were open. The great houses on the south side built by Inigo Jones, such as Essex House and York and the Savoy palaces, were beginning to lose much of their magnificence, although terraces and artificial streams still ran from their higher gardens to the river and the small piers or landing stages. It was rumoured that some would soon be pulled down to allow more shops on the south side of the street, and smaller houses between the Strand and the river. Many of the owners had already moved west, never likely to return to these vast houses.

Muddy water splashed as carriages and wagons went too fast through deep ruts; the walkers moved as far away from them as they could but few could avoid being spattered. Ruth was within ten yards of the lane where she would turn when a carriage-and-two went dashing by and mud splashed her from foot to waist. Two prostitutes standing against the open door of Charlie Wylie's brothel, dresses tight at neck and obviously going shopping, roared with laughter.

Ruth turned into the lane, then into the open door of Hewson's, as a woman of much elegance was assisted into a bright-red sedan chair; the chairboys nearly scraped the chair against Ruth as she pressed against the wall. Mrs. Hewson, tall and high-cheeked, looked down her nose as Ruth bobbed.

"Good morning, ma'am."

"Don't you know better than to come in here with that filth on your clothes?"

"I'm sorry, ma'am, but I was splashed just before I came in."

"Do you think I'm blind?" Mrs. Hewson demanded. "I hope Madame Tover did not know you were coming here or she would be shocked. You can't be allowed in the sewing room like that. Go to Mrs. Hay, and if there is any work to take home, she will give it to you."

There was only a little, some petticoats for the children of a merchant, but she would earn enough at least to keep the family for two days.

Ruth took the bundle wrapped in coarse cloth and hoisted it beneath her arm, grateful for what she had but stirred nearly to anger by Mrs. Hewson's manner. She went this time toward White-hall because if she walked along St. Martin's Lane she might find some scraps of beef and some bones. Hennessy's, the butcher's, had been raided by robbers two years ago and the old man and the two sons who owned the business had been badly injured and robbed of three hundred pounds. Within a few days Richard had caught the thieves; within three weeks both had been hanged. For a few months Richard had arrived home on Fridays with a joint of beef or a leg of mutton, a gift from the grateful Hennessys. Now at least they would save scraps for her and, she believed, sometimes "scraps" they made up for her. It was her turn to be grateful whether she liked to beg or not.

As she waited at a corner for traffic to slacken she saw a woman inside a brougham with a handsome man at her side. The woman glanced sideways but did not appear to notice her. Richard had pointed her out to Ruth one Sunday two years ago. It had been near here when they had been walking through St. Martin's Fields and admiring the magnificence of the new church.

"There she is, my love, the famous or the notorious Mrs. Braidley, take your choice. They say she is the highest paid whore in London."

"Richard! You should not say such things!"

"You speak more true than you realise," Richard had replied, still laughing. "If the great John Furnival were to hear me he'd throw me out of his service, and then where would we be?"

"You mean *he* goes to *her*?"

"No, m'dear. He is one of the favoured few; they do say there are only three left. She goes to *him*."

"Have you actually seen her, close to?"

"I've even held the lady's cloak and been bewitched by her dazzling smile," Richard had boasted, eyes laughing at Ruth. "Haven't you noticed the time when I've come home walking on air?" A few minutes later, very soberly, he had gone on to say, "Mr. Furnival and Mrs. Braidley are good friends, Ruth. She doesn't go to him simply a-whoring. I've heard him laugh with her more than with any woman —or any man, for that matter. She's good for him, and a man who works as hard as he does needs to relax."

"And how hard do you work, sir?"

"I do my relaxing at home with my wife!"

They had laughed together and had soon forgotten.

Now, she remembered. She asked herself what Richard would have her do, and unexpectedly smiled; the notion was so absurd. For a few moments she caught some of the lightheartedness she had so often known with Richard and it did not go immediately when she went into Hennessy's tiny shop and saw the two brothers whispering, one small and one big, each in blue-and-white apron with cross stripes, the white stained with blood. The larger of the two greeted her heartily while the small one vanished into the storeroom.

"Well, what a sight for my poor eyes!" the Irishman boomed. "And

64

'tis the truth I'm telling ye when I say ye look a prettier woman than I've ever seen before in all me natural. How are ye keeping, Mrs. Marshall? And that bonny broth of a boy, a strapping boy if ever I saw one. How is he?" There was a momentary pause before he asked, "What can I be doing for ye this morning, Mrs. Marshall, sweetheart?"

"If you have two pennyworth of scrag and bones I would like them."

Almost at once the door behind him opened and the small brother came through with a package wrapped in thin mutton cloth, stained pink from the meat inside. He handed it across the wooden bench, which was roughened with marks of choppers, and gave her a timorous smile.

"Take these with our blessing and may the Holy Mother look after ye and yours," the big brother said, but his words and the accompanying smile were forced and he lowered his tone as he went on. "The word is out that we're not to serve ye, Mrs. Marshall. Friends of Fred Jackson came to us yesterday and warned us, that they did. The next time must be the last time, they said, as true as I'm standing here. From the bottom of me heart I'm sorry, ma'am, but I've me own safety and the safety of me family to consider."

"And mine, remember," the little man said. "And mine, Michael."

"And me brother's, too," boomed Michael Hennessy.

Ruth wanted to throw the package into his face, and gripped it so tightly that the blood oozed through the wrapping and onto her fingers. She stared at the big man, who looked thoroughly ashamed, and made herself speak.

"Have you sent for the peace officers, Mr. Hennessy?"

"Now, ma'am, what good would a peace officer be to me if he came and found me with me throat cut? Not even John Furnival himself could guard the shop and me home all the time."

"Or mine, Michael, or mine!" came the echo.

"All day and all night they would need protecting, and how could a poor tradesman like me afford watchmen on his own? The streets are so full of villains, why, I heard that Mr. Walpole was attacked in Piccadilly only last week! 'Tis sorry I am, Mrs. Marshall, but 'tis the truth I'm telling ye."

She continued to look at him until both he and his brother grew uneasy under the scrutiny of this young and comely woman, with her chestnut-brown hair showing beneath her small bonnet with its lace fringe, and the clear blue eyes and the full mouth and skin almost without a blemish. They could not be expected to understand that she was no longer thinking of them but only of what they had told her and what it meant to her.

If the friends of Frederick Jackson had put the finger of fear upon those prepared to help her, whom could she count as friends? If she had no friends, how could she live?

"Mrs. Marshall, 'tis nothing personal I'd have ye understand, 'tis—"

"Fear of Jackson striking you from his grave," she interrupted. "I know, Mr. Hennessy. And how do you think people will ever become free from fear if men like you cringe at a threat and will do nothing in defiance?"

Before either man could answer, she turned away; and she was a hundred yards along Long Acre before she realised that the package was dripping onto the coarse wrapping cloth of the work for Mrs. Hewson. She stood still for a moment, outside a saddler's shop, then gingerly placed the package into her basket and walked on. Deliberately, she went out of her way to Covent Garden piazza and the still-magnificent though dilapidated houses and walked along the path toward the south side so that in a few moments she could pass Mr. Morgan's shop and perhaps catch a glimpse of James opposite the establishments with their small windows set in weathered boards stained with pitch and topped by big fascia boards on which the names of the merchants were beautifully and elaborately inscribed. A new market building was going up and dozens of labourers were moving piles of red bricks and stacks of wooden scaffolding, others carrying iron-cast guttering and pipes, others digging a huge ditch to carry away the waste; already an offensive stink rose from the ditch. Hammering, banging and shouting combined to make a deafening noise and she almost wished she hadn't come.

There was James! She had never seen him so loaded. From each arm of the yoke hung three baskets at different levels so that as they swung to his walk they would not bang into one another. Three round baskets were balanced on his head, and he pushed the laden cart out of the shop.

"Hurry, James,'" Mr. Morgan called. "I want you back by noon and not a minute later."

"Yes, sir,'" James replied and he turned hurriedly in the opposite direction from his mother.

As he worked seven days a week it had been a long time since she had seen him in morning light, and this was a bright crisp morning when it should have been good to be alive. He looked tired out already, yet he began to move forward at a slow jog, watched by Morgan from the door. A black-haired man, Morgan wore a clean white apron from neck to knees, and his fat calves were covered in black stockings rucked up over highly polished black shoes. Heavy-bearded except at the chin, itself clean-shaven, he glanced in her direction as he went back into the shop but did not recognise her, and she did not make herself known.

That was the moment when she made up her mind to accept John Furnival's proposal.

That was the moment, also, when Eve Milharvey woke for the second morning of her "widowhood" in the apartment to which Frederick Jackson had first brought her, so long ago. There was heaviness in her breast, a sense of loss and of grief, and she lay alone and looked at a bright patch of sky. She heard the old woman whom she had met on that first day moving about in another room and scolding a chambermaid for dallying at the window. Easing herself up on her pillows, she pushed back the bedclothes, but as she swung herself over the side of the bed she felt the onslaught of nausea. When she stood up she could only keep steady by gripping one of the fluted oak posts of the bed. She lowered herself again and belched, but hardly eased the nausea. She placed her well-shaped, well-kept hands on her belly, feeling the softness of the silk Fred had liked her to wear; it was the nearest cloth to feel like the smoothness of her skin.

"I can't be," she said aloud. "It isn't possible!"

But of course it *was* possible. She had been to see him in Newgate, where he had the use of a private room; not once, not twice, but a dozen times she had helped him to forget his danger.

And if she had a child it could only be Fred's.

Ruth Marshall heard the footsteps on the stairs and moved toward the door. She was quite calm, and indeed had been much calmer since reaching her decision than she had expected to be. She opened the door to find Furnival at the head of the stairs. He took off his hat but still had to stoop to get through the doorway. It was daylight and yet gloomy in this room, and the sound of the children shrieking in the yard traveled clearly. So did the stomping of a horse's hooves. She realised he had come on horseback, consequently alone; and that in its way was a great compliment to her. She closed the door as he tossed his cloak back over his shoulders; she noticed that he was breathing hard, as if the ride had been furious or the climb up to this room had been exhausting. He took a folded paper from his pocket and she recognised the note she had sent him yesterday, the day following her decision. James had delivered this to the offices in Bow Street only last night. She had written:

If it still pleases you I would be proud to enter your service in the manner of our discussion.

She studied the strong face and the massive body of this "great bull of a man" and was aware of the appraisal in his tawny eyes. His lips were unexpectedly shapely when he began to smile as he asked, "Who taught you to write, Ruth Marshall?"

"My father, sir."

"And what was your father, pray? A teacher? A parson?"

"He was a preacher, sir, and in his spare time a carpenter and wagonmaker."

"And could read and write well enough to teach his children. You were fortunate in your father."

"I have long been aware of it, sir."

"No doubt he had a ready tongue, also," said Furnival dryly. "What made you make up your mind so quickly?"

"A variety of reasons, sir," she answered, "and the most telling was that I did not want my children to go hungry or my son to miss the chance of going to school."

He nodded slowly and then added in a quieter voice, "By your leave I will sit down.'"

She was angry with herself for not offering him a chair and pushed forward the armchair in which Tom Harris had sat two nights ago. The arms were carved, and polished with age, and he rubbed them with each hand as he went on.

"What other reasons, Ruth? I want to know them all."

She stood in front of him and words like "out of respect" and even "out of affection" came to her mind but she could not utter them. He waited, watching. She remembered Richard telling her, "He can smell when a witness is lying or telling half the truth. I've seen him on the bench make a man confess to a horrid crime simply by staring at him and saying: 'I want the truth, only the truth.'"

And she could understand that as John Furnival stared at her now until she was driven to say, "It would be false to pretend deep affection for you, sir."

He started. "Affection? For me? You may have to wait months before you can even tolerate me!" He actually laughed, and she had never liked him more. "But there was another reason for such haste. Speak frankly, Ruth, and fairly."

"There was," she admitted.

"What was it, pray?"

She told him, faltering at first, about her visit to the Hennessy brothers' shop and what had transpired there, and his laughter and the softness of his expression faded. He was silent when she finished, as if he expected more from her. So she said in a husky voice, "Life would be difficult enough on my own without Frederick Jackson's friends conspiring against me. There are so many harmful things they could do. They might—they might try to turn James against me, sir, or lure him to drink or to crime. They might—"

"That is enough," he interrupted. "I know all they might do and fully understand why you reached so quick a decision."

"And you are not angered, sir?"

"Angered? By a woman who uses her head as well as her heart? No, Ruth, that way you'll never anger me. Many things do. I need—" He broke off abruptly. "Do you need time to consider afresh?"

"No, sir. I am firmly decided."

"Then the cottage will be ready for you on Monday," he promised. "As for James, he should give his master fair notice, a week or perhaps two, and then he can find out whether the school near Saint Paul's can teach him as much as his grandfather taught you." He palmed the carved heads on the arms of the chair and asked, "Is this his carving?"

"Yes, sir, it is."

"Whatever else you wish to bring to the cottage with this, tell my man Moffat, who will come to fetch you on Monday morning with a cart large enough to carry all you have." He stood up, placed his hands on her shoulders and pressed, and then smiled at her again. "Ruth," he said, "I think we shall become good friends. But we never will if I frighten you. Do I? Or does my reputation?"

69

"No, sir," she replied thoughtfully. "I am apprehensive but not frightened—not even by your reputation!"

She sensed that he was trying to make sure that she was telling the truth, and indeed she was. Suddenly he laughed and took his hands away, swept her a mock bow, and turned toward the door.

She was more lighthearted than she had been for at least six months, and she felt positive that she had reached the right decision. She was so preoccupied with his manner and her new lightness of heart that she did not move until she heard his horse on the cobbles, and by the time she reached the window, he was through the alley and gone.

CHAPTER *5*

"Robbery" in Fleet Street

"Is it the truth?" demanded Eve Milharvey, a week after the morning when she had fought the nausea and been frightened by its significance. She was walking in the warm sunlight in the piazza of Covent Garden with Peter Nicholson, one of Fred's oldest friends, who had been present at the hanging. The grass in the squares divided by post and rails had been freshly scythed and boys were sweeping the cuttings into great piles; the scent of the new-cut grass was as overpowering as a French perfume. A few people, mostly couples of middle class, judging from their clothes, strolled on the gravel paths, and from the windows of the rows of fine houses on either side, old people and young were basking in the sunlight. A street seller of oranges was singing, voice touched with melody.

"Sweet China oranges to sell, sweet China oranges."

"Aye, 'tis the solemn truth," Peter assured Eve. "She has moved into the cottage, and the whole family is with her."

"And she spends much time in Furnival's offices?"

"She is the food provider for him and the court officials and mistress of his offices and rooms," replied Peter, with a lopsided smile. He was a tall, silky-haired man in his late thirties, foppish after a

71

fashion, wearing a pale-blue cloak over a striped green-and-dark-blue shirt and breeches with pale-blue bands beneath the knees. His boots were of pale hogskin which looked as pliable as silk. He inclined his head toward Eve as if to make sure that no one else could hear and there was an undercurrent of excitement in his voice.

"Mistress of his bed, more like!"

"With him, she'll be that too."

"I wonder what Lisa Braidley will say to this new competition?" Eve asked, obviously wanting no answer. "The woman is young and comely, you say?"

"Yes, Eve, in all fairness that must be said."

"And she goes to Sebastian Smith's church, Saint Hilary's?"

"Yes," answered Peter Nicholson. "Her husband would never go but she always does."

"Peter," Eve said, touching him on the arm with her gloves, "make sure that Lisa Braidley is made aware of this new situation soon, and make sure the Reverend Smith is also acquainted. Neither of them will be fooled by what kind of mistress she is called."

"It shall be done, Eve, and quickly."

"And carefully, remember, as a piece of gossip, not as by the common informer!"

"As a delightful morsel of gossip," he assured her. "And the Reverend Smith, with his nose for prudery, will be in a right mood to admonish her!"

They walked on for a few moments in silence, reached a yard leading to Long Acre, and turned and began to walk back. The singer's voice seemed to have died away and there was very little traffic in the roads which ran about the great square.

Suddenly Eve Milharvey said, "The boy. What is the boy doing?"

"The boy James?"

"Who else would I mean?" she demanded impatiently.

"He is still with grocer Morgan, who sells coffee and tea and spices."

"He won't be for long, if I know John Furnival," she said, and her voice became momentarily strident. Another silence followed and lasted until they were close to the south entrance, when she took Peter's arm again and said with quiet venom, "Listen to me, and make sure everything is carried out as I say. Have a boy of Marshall's age dressed as he dresses and carrying parcels and pushing a cart as he does. Have this boy go into a shop ahead of Marshall and leave by the back way. Do you understand me?"

"I do declare I even understand what you are planning," her companion said, his eyes glowing.

"As young Marshall passes the shop have the shopkeeper raise a cry of 'Stop thief!' And be sure," went on Eve Milharvey, "there is a thief-taker at hand to stop the Marshall boy and search his baskets." She looked levelly into her companion's eyes and went on slowly. "It will not be difficult to find the stolen money in one of those baskets. Make sure the shopkeeper will swear to it and make sure some independent witnesses are stopped who will swear they saw the boy go in and come out again. If there is no one who can be proved an honest citizen, Furnival will get the boy out. We shall need them all in court when he comes up for hearing, and at the Sessions their evidence should be enough to have him hanged. Take all the time you need in which to prepare."

"Eve," Peter Nicholson said, "you are magnificent!"

"I trust you will be competent," Eve said coldly.

"I know the very shopkeeper to do just what he is told," Nicholson assured her. "A silversmith off Fleet Street close by the Cheshire Cheese, and there is a magistrate close by. I will pay five pounds each to two thief-takers who will whip the boy off to Newgate before Furnival or anyone else knows what has happened." He gave an excited laugh. "Truly, m'dear, it is worthy of the great Fred himself!"

Early on a Friday, a few days later, James Marshall set out for Morgan's. It was a damp morning with a hint of rain but in places a promise of sunshine. He had two hundred yards fewer to walk to work from Bell Lane, and this was his fourth morning of leaving home from the cottage behind Bow Street. He had been surprised by the news, a little dubious about going to school, but a room to himself on the second floor of the tiny terraced cottage was ample compensation, far beyond anything he had dreamed of possessing. He could shut himself away from Beth and Henrietta when the weather was bad and they could not go out and he could pore over the books of London and English history which so fascinated him, back to the days of Roman occupation and even earlier. He had an oil lamp of his own, and a desk once used by one of John Furnival's clerks now stood beneath the window so that it caught all the daylight there was. His sisters slept in a room at the back while his mother slept downstairs

73

in the front room. Wet or fine, she could cross Bell Lane in a few seconds to attend to her duties in the Bow Street premises.

It was good to have her so much happier, and to be lighter hearted himself. It was good always to be warm, for there was no shortage of wood or coal and the fires were banked with slack on autumn's cold nights. So much was good that apprehension over school was easy to forget.

The morning grew warm, and his jacket, a little too tight, made him feel hot; the thickness of the woolen stockings inside his ankle boots made his feet itch even before he reached Morgan's. For the first time since he had been coming here he felt a sharp distaste for it all; for Morgan's persistence in loading him with more and more, for the gloomy interior of the shop, for the horseplay of the assistants who would stay here or run shorter errands during the day. But soon the sun brightened and as his burden began to lighten after a few deliveries, his heart lightened, too.

His next call was at the Cheshire Cheese Inn, in a court off Fleet Street. Long before he reached it he could smell the aroma of the steak-and-kidney puddings; he had known times in a high wind when that aroma had tormented him even as far as the Royal Exchange.

Fleet Street had other fascinations for him, for two morning newspapers were published from offices situated there: *The Morning Cry* which, whenever he could read it, appealed to him much more than *The London Courant*. Already the street was bustling with the traffic it carried from the northern and northeastern provinces, and he had to watch the swinging of his baskets, for there was little room between the thoroughfare where the fast traffic moved and the doorways of the shops. Every fifty yards or so was an alleyway which led into a courtyard like the one leading to the Cheshire Cheese. He saw the hanging sign outside this alley, with a huge yellow cheese made into the face of a grinning man; it never failed to attract him. On days when he was here later in the morning he would linger in the hope of seeing some of the celebrities who came and gathered here to drink and talk. He had seen Benjamin Franklin and Alexander Pope, as well as Henry Fielding and Dr. Johnson and many lesser figures.

Suddenly he heard a cry: "Stop thief!" from behind him, and turned his head cautiously for fear of swinging his burdens too fast. A woman brushed past him. A short fat man in dark clothes except for an apron like the one Morgan wore came rushing from a silversmith's shop, the cry shrill on his lips: "Stop thief!" As James turned, the man pointed. "There he is! *Stop thief!*" From farther along the street a big and burly man came running, from the sidewalk on the other side came a second, adding to the din. "Stop thief!" People were slowing down and the shop doorways were filling up.

"That boy!" cried the shopkeeper, flapping his apron. "He came and struck me across the head and emptied my money box!"

One of the big men clapped a hand on James's shoulder while the other lifted the yoke and turned it upside down so that the precious packages fell out, fruit and cheese, spices and butter, everything which had been so carefully packed and loaded spilled and the wrappings burst.

"There's the little varmint!" the shopkeeper screeched. "He ought to be hanged outside my shop! He ought to be—"

"That's enough loose talk," one of the big men said, and upturned a basket. "I'm a thief-taker by profession, but fair's fair—"

Coins began to roll in all directions as the goods fell, making the self-styled thief-taker stop abruptly.

"There's your proof!" cried the shopkeeper.

Until that moment James had been stunned by the swift sequence of events; even when the big man had gripped his shoulder he could not believe that anyone really suspected him. When the packages showered their contents over the ground he was so shocked that for a few seconds he could not even think, only stare in horror. As the money struck the pavement and coins from a half crown to a penny and some halfpence and even farthings fell between the cobbles, a shiver ran through him.

He looked up into the face of the man who held him and protested, "But I didn't go into the shop! I didn't take—" He saw only cruelty and hardness in the face and eyes, enough to make him falter.

"I saw him go in," a little old man called.

"So did I," a woman asserted. "Bold as brass he did."

"But I swear—" James began.

The man struck him savagely across the face and sent him reeling. The other big man came up and gripped his hands, pulling them behind him. Cold iron bands clasped James's wrists as the shopkeeper cried again, "He ought to be hanged outside my shop, as an example to all the young thieves who pass this way. That's what I say!"

"That's right," called the woman so eager to assert that she had seen James enter the silversmith's. "Let's have a hanging. Why should Tyburn have all the fun?"

"A hanging, a hanging, a hanging!" seemed to pour from the throats of the crowd that gathered, stretching halfway across the road, forcing carriages and coaches to slow down. "Hang the thief!" men cried. "Hang him, hang him!"

"He'll be hanged, never fear," said the man who had clapped the manacles onto James. "But only after committal and a fair trial." He looked at the other thief-taker and said so that only James and those near could hear, "Get him through the Cheshire Cheese and out the other way or they'll stretch his neck as sure as I stand here."

"But I did not steal—" James began.

The man buffeted him so hard that his head rang and for seconds he seemed to have lost his senses. He felt himself pushed, then half dragged through Wine Office Court toward the Cheshire Cheese alley, past the closed doors of the inn. No one followed because other men hired by Peter Nicholson filled the entrance to the alley, and gradually the crowd thinned.

Beyond the passages and the huddle of wooden outhouses was another lane, and James was hustled along this. At the far end a small coach was standing, and before he realised what was happening the door was opened and the man who had manacled him lifted him by the scruff of his neck and the seat of his trousers and pitched him inside, then climbed in and slammed the door. Almost before the door had closed the coach began to move.

Struggling to a sitting position, forced to perch on the edge of his seat, James looked into the harsh face of his captor and said pleadingly, "I am innocent, sir, I swear to you. Some mistake was made—"

"The mistake you made was robbing the shopkeeper," the thief-taker said roughly. "You take advice from me, boy. When we get to Newgate you admit you stole the money. Things might go easier with you then."

"Newgate!" cried James in a sudden onslaught of dread. "You can't take me to Newgate! I must go before a justice; I must be taken to Mr. Furn—"

"You've been before a justice and have been committed. Don't gab so much." The man leaned across and struck him in the mouth and blood began trickling down his chin. It was shock as well as pain which made James silent. Newgate, most dreaded of prisons, which had horrified his father and was a living hell, a stinking blot on the face of London. The man had no right to take him first to Newgate; only a justice could commit him there.

The carriage stopped close to the spot where he had stood on the night of Frederick Jackson's hanging, and a jailer came out of the gatehouse as the thief-taker pushed James out. He slipped and, unable to help himself, fell heavily. Over his body the thief-taker and the jailer spoke briefly.

"Is this the young rapscallion?"

"Take him and put him in the Stone Hold, 'twill be good for his soul," the thief-taker said, and roared with laughter.

The jailer bent down, yanked the boy to his feet and pushed him toward the lodge and beyond.

In the saddle on a gray horse opposite the main gates Peter Nicholson waited until jailer and boy had disappeared and the thief-taker was back in the coach. The man winked at Nicholson through the window and Nicholson winked back, then slapped his horse and made for Eve Milharvey's house in Loxley Yard. He tied his horse to a wooden post and went lightly up the stairs. The old creature who had served Frederick Jackson for much longer than Nicholson had known the criminal was coming out of Eve's bedchamber. She was bent half double.

"She's still abed," she croaked. "And she won't want any but good news this morning."

"I've all the good news she can ask for," Nicholson replied, and rapped on the door, calling out, " 'Tis I, Peter. May I come in?"

After a moment she called, "Come in and keep your voice low. My head is splitting."

He opened the door and saw her sitting up in bed with a tray in front of her. Her hair was well brushed and she wore a frilled jacket, high at the neck. He walked toward her, clapping his hands together yet making little noise.

Her eyes were glistening.

"So you got him, then?"

"Tight as a drum!" boasted Nicholson. "He's in Newgate at this moment, and he won't come out of there except to talk at his trial and then onto the hangman's cart. We've three witnesses who *saw* him go into the shop and a magistrate who committed him to await trial. The trick worked perfectly. I told you before, Eve, you're magnificent."

She stared at him, her eyes no longer shining.

"I want to know how Furnival responds to this, and also the boy's mother. Do you understand me?"

77

"None better," he assured her. "No one will be better informed." He blew her a kiss and gave a little bow before going out.

"Eve Milharvey," he whispered, "the day will come when you won't talk to me as if I were a lackey. You'll beg me for help."

His smile was hard and set as he went downstairs.

Eve lay back on the pillows, not smiling, looking up at the heavy tapestry canopy over the bed and feeling the weight of the tray on her stomach. She now had no doubt that she was suffering from morning sickness, and sometimes this elated her and at others enraged her.

Did it explain, at this moment, why she felt that she hated Peter Nicholson?

In a much larger and lovelier room, of pale blues and greens and golds, with French furniture shipped from Rouen especially for her, Lisa Braidley also lay on her pillows with a breakfast tray beside her. The bed was huge and billowy soft, and on one of the four pillows were some short, dark hairs from the man who had spent much of the night here. He, at thirty, had been full of tremendous vitality and she was tired. That was not unusual, for her lovers were seldom placid or content first to lie with her and then by her side; and there was no reason why they should, for to get into this room cost a fortune: to less than a hundred guineas she turned a cold face.

But she was tired.

And the young man who had been with her, Lord Fothergill, had exasperated her with his prattle and, she admitted to herself, stung her with one piece of gossip.

"They do say that John Furnival has taken a new wench to his bed, and installed her as mistress of his household. 'Tis age taking its toll, Lisa, the man wants his slippers warmed as well as his bed."

She remembered John's need of comfort when she had last gone to him and wondered whether the "new wench" would lead to any relationship with John. If there were a man in London she would like to marry it was John Furnival, but the very thought was folly; so was the sting of jealousy. She knew he had a hundred mistresses, would even take witnesses into that little apartment to "question them" in private—oh, he was a sexual profligate, it was his sole weakness. She had never been in any doubt about that, so why should the fact that he had installed a new wench under some fancy name sting her?

She did not know; she only knew that she was badly stung.

In the corner of the tiny entrance to the cottage in Bell Lane was a grandfather clock that fascinated the younger children with its pictures of the moon and the sun and stars which changed each day, and with the deep-tone *whirrrrr* which preceded the striking of each hour as well as the *boom-oom-oom* of the notes themselves. It had a dark oak case already shining with years of polishing. Ruth did not at that time know its history and at first it troubled her; it was in fact the only thing about her new home which caused her any anxiety. She was afraid the whirring and the booming by night would disturb both her and the children, but the children had not appeared to be troubled even on the first night, and although she woke for a night or two to the striking of each hour, she was soon so accustomed to it that she slept right through.

On the fifth night, Friday, she heard the *whirrrrr* begin and she knew that it was eleven o'clock, very late for James. Fridays were long days for him; he was often not home until half-past nine, but eleven was rare. The clock began to strike in a deep and melodious tone and she counted; conceivably she had been wrong at the last striking and it was now only ten. Her hands clenched and her whole body was tense as she counted.

". . . eight . . . nine . . . ten . . . eleven."

So it had been no error and she simply could not understand the lateness.

Because visitors often came late at Bow Street and someone was on duty there all night, Bell Lane was much better lit than Cobbold Yard had been, with two flares on either side of the back entrance, and there were other flares placed at John Furnival's orders because he wanted to make sure that the guard he employed to keep Bow Street and Bell Lane secure could see anyone who turned into the lane from either end. As Ruth went up the narrow stairs she saw some of this light shine through the open door of the boy's room and spread a glow into the larger chamber where the two girls slept.

Ruth went into this chamber. Beth, fair-haired and chubby, with curling eyelashes and already coquettish, lay on one side of a bed larger than Ruth and Richard had ever known, a bare arm bent over her head, the other snug. Ruth moved the cold arm gently and Beth opened her eyes, stared blankly, and closed them again at once. Henrietta, the younger, had jet-black hair, and only the top of this showed above the linen sheet. Ruth moved the sheet so that the child should not breathe her own used air and crept out and down the stairs. The hall, though narrow, had a recess near the kitchen where hats and cloaks could be kept, and she took her heavy woolen cloak from the peg, pulled the hood over her head, then went into Bell Lane.

She looked in each direction along the row of cottages but there was no sign of James.

She moved toward Drury Lane and a guard carrying his lantern on a pole in his left hand and a cudgel in his right was quick to see her. He called in a low-pitched but carrying voice: "Stop there!"

Instead, she moved slowly toward him. For all the man knew she might be a whore looking for business, or even a visitor to John Furnival, although it was some time since the chief magistrate had brought a girl in off the streets; for one thing, he had become much too fastidious. But not all who worked at Bow Street were, and one or two even of Furnival's trusted private retainers were not above a little dalliance while on duty with a witness who needed a favour or a supplicant who needed help for a husband.

Ruth stopped in front of the man and he said in surprise, "Mistress Marshall, bless my soul! What are you doing out so late as this?"

"I'm worried about my son James," she replied. "I hoped you or one of the other watchmen had seen him."

"Not this night," the guard answered. "But I'm to meet Joe Kidder at the front of the court building. Come with me and we'll find out if he's seen anyone."

She was glad of his company although the streets were deserted; tomorrow, Saturday, would be the night for noise and crowds and drunken brawling.

The other watchman was shorter and stockier, reminding her of Tom Harris.

"No, I've not set eyes on him and I know him well," he replied. "Have you inquired of the merchant where he works?"

"No. I must go and ask—" she began.

"Mistress Marshall, this is no time for you to go anywhere alone," the first watchman interrupted. "Tiny, do you know if Tom Harris is still here? . . . He is? . . . Then we'll tell him what is worrying Mistress Marshall." He smiled down at Ruth and informed her, "After every hour one of us has to make a report to the chief officer on duty, and it's my turn. I can see Tom at the same time. Will you come in and wait?"

"No," she said quickly. "If it pleases you I will stay here."

She waited with the shorter guard for no more than five minutes before Tom Harris came out, buttoning his cloak at the neck; she thought from the look of him that he had been sleeping, but there was nothing sleepy in his manner as he took her arm and began to walk toward Long Acre.

"There'll be nothing to worry about," he reassured her. "That old skinflint Morgan is making James work late to avoid paying another boy, that'll be the truth of it."

She felt no certainty but was easier in her mind until they approached the shop.

It was in darkness; so were the windows above, where some of the assistants as well as the Morgans lived. Nor was there anything to suggest that the premises had only just been closed. A smell of rotting fruit hung heavy in the air. All of Ruth's fears came crowding back.

"He could have gone home by a different way; the boy has the biggest nose for odd corners I ever knew." Tom still tried to be reassuring. "But we'll see if Morgan can give us any information."

A few days ago Ruth would have been horrified at the thought of disturbing James's employer but now she could think only of one thing: finding out what had happened to her son.

She stared up at the dark windows as Tom bellowed: "Mr. Morgan, sir, wake up. Mr. Morgan, sir!"

A watchman swinging his lantern came hurrying toward them, an old man who looked scared but who summoned enough courage to demand, "Who are you to disturb the peace?" He peered shortsightedly at Tom, then suddenly recognised him and exclaimed " 'Tis Mr. Harris, I'll be bound. I can tell 'ee this, Mr. Harris, Morgan and his wife sleep in that room. I'll bang on the window with my pole and you call out again."

Slowly he pushed the pole up against the window and then began to tap, taking so long that it was all Ruth could do not to snatch the pole from his frail hands. But with this banging and Tom's shouting they woke Morgan at last. The merchant pushed up the window and leaned out, woolen bedcap falling over his shoulder on one side, a blanket clutched about him.

"Sorry to wake you, Mr. Morgan," called Tom. "But Mrs. Marshall's boy James has not reached home yet. Do you know what time he left here?"

"I can tell you . . ." began Morgan.

Ruth's heart began to beat sickeningly as she heard the querulous voice relaying that James had not returned from his first round; that he, Morgan, had been compelled to send a man out to check on his

81

deliveries, fearful of an accident; that James had delivered to three
addresses in Fleet Street and then had disappeared; a peace officer had
found his yoke, his cart and his baskets in Wine Office Court, with no
more than half of the goods left in them. He had not even delivered
his goods to the Cheshire Cheese! There was some talk of a robbery
and of James's running away.

"And you knew all this but didn't tell Mistress Marshall?" growled
Tom.

" 'Tis her responsibility to look after her offspring," replied Morgan tartly. "It would be different if the boy were to become an ap-
prentice but he is leaving this Sunday, did you know that? To go to
school." The man's sniff could be heard from the window before he
went on. "It won't surprise me to find that he doesn't want to go to
school and has run away to sea."

"Where is the man you sent after him?" demanded Harris.

"Where he should be, I trust—in bed asleep and getting ready for
tomorrow's work."

"I want to know where to find him," Tom interrupted. "Will you
tell me now or must I come up and make you talk?"

"He's in one of the sheds at the back," replied Morgan complain-
ingly. "By name, Tip Hill. Don't wake the others with him; we need
everyone up early on a Saturday morning." He withdrew his head
and slammed the window.

No other window in the street had opened; no one had dared to
show his curiosity, for there was no telling where it would lead if he
interfered with any fracas by night. Tom Harris turned to Ruth in
the narrow, silent street, sharing the anxiety which showed so clearly
on her face.

"D'you want to come with me and find out what this man Hill has
to say?"

"Yes," she replied tensely. "Oh, Tom—what do you think has happened?"

"I mean to find out," rasped Tom.

Alongside Morgan's premises was an archway for delivery carts to
turn and this led to a yard where there were four sheds, each in darkness. The all-pervasive odour of rotting fruit and hay was worsened
here by the stench from a nearby privy. The watchman pushed open
two doors, where no one slept, then when he opened a third the
light shone on the faces of three men, lying close together for warmth
on some bundles of hay.

"If I didn't know better I would say this was a ginshop," muttered

Tom Harris, while the watchman poked at the men until they stirred and he found out that Tip Hill was the one who slept in the middle. He sat up, blinking in the pale glow, a thin-faced, fair-haired youth of sixteen or seventeen with something girlish about his appearance. The others were older men.

"I want to know exactly what you learned about James Marshall," Harris said in a tone which brooked no delay. "Be quick about it, Hill."

One of the other men opened his eyes and listened; the third appeared to remain fast asleep. Hill edged himself to a more upright position, and only then did it become obvious that he was wholly naked, which no doubt accounted for the fact that he was sandwiched between the others.

"I—I told Mr. Morgan—" he began.

"You told Mr. Morgan what you were told to tell him," interrupted Harris in a flat, accusing tone. "It was only half a story even though he did pretend to believe it. Now I demand the truth, and if you don't want to appear in court on a charge of sodomy you'll tell me the whole of it."

The fair-haired Hill said fearfully, "I can't tell you much more, Mr. Harris. I swear I can't, but there was a thief-taker near Cheshire Court who told me what had happened."

"Describe him to me," Harris ordered.

"He was a big man, taller than you, sir, and he had a scar beneath his right eye, from a knife I would say. He—he went into a shop in Wine Office Court when I'd gone away; I saw him from the other side of the road."

"What shop was it?" demanded Harris.

"A silversmith and cutlery shop, where knives and scissors are also repaired, and some silver articles are hand made, Mr. Harris. I didn't see the name. I swear—"

Harris said in that same flat voice which carried so much menace, "If you've lied to me, you'll rue the day." He took Ruth's arm and led her out, making her walk fast once they were in the comparatively fresh air of Long Acre.

Neither of them spoke until they were in sight of the lights of Bow Street. Ruth found it difficult to breathe freely, so deep were her fears. The speed at which Tom made her walk added to the breathlessness, so that even as the thoughts went scalding through her mind she could not find breath enough to speak.

At last, Tom broke the silence between them.

"Ruth, I don't like the sound or the smell of what I've heard," he declared, "and the quicker I begin inquiries the better for us all. By noon tomorrow I want to be able to tell John Furnival all there is to know, if I haven't found young James. It will be hard on you, but you'll have to work and wait."

She looked at him intently and in a choking voice asked, "Tom, what do you think has happened?"

"I don't deal in guesswork," Tom Harris replied gruffly. "I want the facts and I'll get them, Ruth. I'll tell you as soon as I know them all."

"Tom," she persisted, "do you think this is part of revenge for Frederick Jackson's hanging?"

Tom replied, "If it is, then I'll know where to start looking." He slowed down as they neared the front door of her cottage, and opened it for her but did not go inside. She had never seen him so forbidding; and in herself, she had never felt such fear. "And if I haven't found out where he is by morning, I say, I'll tell John Furnival. If I know him, he'll put every available man on to finding out what happened."

CHAPTER *6*

John Furnival Goes Visiting

FOR JOHN FURNIVAL, Saturday morning was likely to be a light period in court, a good day for clearing up his records, making brief and factual notes in his diary, and reviewing pending cases. John Furnival saw a great deal, most of it through the eyes of a man steeped in the morass of London's crime. He felt, on such days as this, very lonely: perhaps more truly on his own. There were two other justices, one each for the County of Middlesex and the City of Westminster, and though fair men, Furnival doubted whether it had occurred to either of them to try to change some of the iniquitous laws: those, for instance, which made hanging the penalty for a child of seven or eight caught stealing bread because of his hunger. He had long since given up arguing with them or, in fact, with anyone whose understanding could not help him to reach his goal: a substantial police force to patrol the whole metropolitan area of London and keep down the murderers and robbers, the highwaymen and cheats, paid for by the citizens or by the State and paid sufficient to make most of the peace officers incorruptible.

He had no illusions. The difficulties were enormous, for there was not one city but three, although the distinctions were growing more difficult to see. First there was the original walled City of London with its many gates, the rookeries and slums built close to the stone walls, many of these with tunnels beneath so that criminals could come and go at will.

One great route out of the City of London was the Strand, the highway to Westminster, the seat of Parliament, the home of royalty. With a hundred and fifty thousand people in ten parishes, it had its great houses and its unbelievably foul slums. The other and even more important highway was the crowded Thames, crammed with ferries, small boats plying between the two cities, and small vessels which could pass beneath London Bridge. They had a strong but unorganised force against thieves.

All three groups, the two cities and the Thames workers, as well as the County of Middlesex, made a solid front against any attempt to create a force which could both prevent crime and catch criminals. And not one, of all these parishes, was properly protected. Each was becoming more and more vulnerable to thieves and footpads, highwaymen and murderers.

Londoners, then, indeed the English generally, regarded the concept of a national police force with genuine horror. They pointed to France and to other Continental nations and said in tones of dread: "A national police force can only lead to a police state, and no Englishman will stand for it."

So, instead, there were the private forces, such as that organised by the Furnival family and by most of the great banking and commercial corporations and all who could afford to pay for loyalty, which also meant for honesty. But it was loyalty to their employers, not to the nation, and many of these men outside their own strict duties would break the law with any man who could get away with it.

Justice could be bought and sold. Perjury was heard in every court at least as often as the truth. Honest witnesses were either bribed to lie or else were terrified into lying. Hardened rogues would cheerfully give evidence against a man they had never seen, even though it meant sending him to the gallows, for a share of the reward. Furnival never allowed himself to forget that most justices and peace officers were as corruptible as any, for they had to make their money out of payments made by the government for catching a man or from victims whose goods they "found" for a handsome reward, shared with the thieves. With more than a hundred crimes now punishable by hanging and more being added yearly to the statute book in the false belief that vicious punishment would reduce the amount of crime, there was a lively and thriving trade in every kind of malpractice.

He did not yet know about James Marshall but such affairs were an everyday occurrence, and Furnival believed this would remain and perhaps become worse until there was a professional force to replace the thief-takers, the watchmen and the parish constables.

This morning he came in his diary file upon a petition which he himself had placed before the Minister of State, Sir Robert Walpole, exactly a year ago. Without the help of his family, he had begged that the nation take on the responsibility of the payment of such a force, and had offered to continue to maintain his organisation centered on Bow Street.

A secretary had acknowledged the petition, and Furnival did not know whether it was still in existence or whether it had been destroyed. But here was a copy in Silas Moffat's beautiful copperplate hand. Every petition, every recommendation that he made was carefully copied and recorded; at times Moffat employed two clerks who did no more than stand at their sloping desks making copy after copy of some long plan which would be sent not only to the Minister of State but to other Cabinet ministers, and to many of the lords and commoners outside London who might take some interest.

Very few did.

He read this particular petition slowly and shook his head, but he did not feel the anger which usually assailed him on such an occasion. He was in a calmer mood than he had been for some time but had not yet attempted to stand back from himself to try to discover why. Sooner or later, he would do this.

He replaced the petition in a pigeonhole marked *September 1739* and as he did so he heard voices outside the room. Moffat's voice was unmistakable. The other man's—ah—it was Tom Harris. Neither would disturb him unless convinced that the matter was of utmost importance. He waited for Moffat's tap at the door and called, "Come in."

They entered, Harris close on Moffat's heels, both looking so concerned that Furnival said jestingly, "What bad news do you bring me?" He paused, then added, "Has Fred Jackson come back from the dead?"

"You might almost say that is what's happened," growled Harris, and there was no doubt of the seriousness of his words. He hesitated, giving Moffat an opportunity to take up the story, but the older man stayed silent, while Furnival stared at them both with those compelling eyes that could "see" a lie. " 'Tis Eve Milharvey's work, if I know owt, sir," Harris continued at last.

"It would help me if I were to know what work," remarked the justice.

"Sir, it is not the easiest of stories to tell. I beg you to excuse me if I make heavy going of it. Last night the Marshall lad did not return to the cottage in Bell Lane, and his mother confided in me." Both men saw the tightening at Furnival's lips but he did not speak and Harris went on. "So I pursued inquiries, sir, and without going into detail, which I can, however, provide, having written it all down in black and white, the upshot is that he was charged with theft from a silver-smith in Fleet Street. The charge was heard in his absence before a trading justice in a nearby shop and he was committed to Newgate to await trial. It is four weeks to the next Sessions, and in four weeks the lad can be turned into a lecher or can be so used by the men that he—"

"Have you been to Newgate?" Furnival interrupted.

"I've come straight from there, sir. For a fee of ten shillings the head jailer allowed me to see the entry and the charge. He would not tell me where the lad has gone, sir."

Furnival stared from one man to the other and finally back to Harris.

"How well do you know the boy?"

"I was at his baptism, and know him almost as well as I knew his father."

"Is there any chance that he is guilty?"

"Absolutely none, sir. I swear my own future on it. I can find no one else who has reason to hate the boy or the family, but—there's more, sir."

"Go on."

"Peter Nicholson was seen at the gate when the boy was taken into Newgate and must have ridden straight off to Eve Milharvey, for he was seen there half an hour later. I've checked closely, sir."

"Ah. What more?"

"The justice who committed the boy is Lionel Martin of—"

"I know where that drunken rascal lives. More?"

"The silversmith is a friend of Justice Martin's, sir, and the two thief-takers who took the boy were very conveniently at hand at the time of the alleged robbery."

Furnival ran his thumb and forefinger over his chin and after a few seconds remarked in a hard tone, "What are the worst aspects of the situation?"

"There are at least three eyewitnesses who swear they saw the boy go into the shop and come out again. One I would trust; the others would lie away a life for a few pounds. James stated that he did not go into the silversmith's, having no reason to, and I believe him."

"Then how can you believe—" began Furnival, only to break off before adding the words "young James?" It seemed a long time before he went on. "You think there were two boys?"

"That is my considered opinion, sir."

"And a very carefully laid plot."

"To discomfort you, sir," Harris declared.

"And well it could be," conceded Furnival. After another pause he asked bitterly, "How does one handle such sniveling cowards who will strike at a boy and a woman to avenge themselves on a man?" Obviously he did not expect an answer and Harris attempted none. Furnival closed his eyes and in those few moments looked very tired; his voice lacked its usual strength when he went on, his eyes still closed. "How long will it be before we get rid of the corruption and the treachery, I wonder? How long must one suffer the trading justices who will sell a man's life for a few pounds?" He opened his eyes and they seemed to be on fire. "Go on, Thomas Harris, give me an answer!"

Harris answered quietly, "Too long, sir."

"Hah! With a dozen men as wise and as experienced as you what couldn't I do with this cesspit they call London!" He turned to Moffat, who might have sunk into the floor for all the notice taken of him or the disturbance he made. "Silas, hie you to Justice Martin and ask him to have the courtesy and grace to meet me in the lodge at Newgate in one hour's time. Tom, hie you to the two thief-takers who say they caught the boy in the act and find out whether they'll retract best if we frighten them or if we cross their palms with silver. On your way tell Forbes to have my horse saddled and bridled in fifteen minutes. Bring me word at Newgate." Now he was speaking at a great rate and all signs of tiredness had gone. "Hurry, hurry, I can't bear a man who stands still when there's much to do."

But when they had gone, he stood motionless by his chair in front of the fire until he pulled at the pigeonhole and took out the petition again. He read it, slowly and deliberately, then put it away and pulled a rope at the side of the fireplace, ringing a bell in the kitchen which would bring a maid hurrying. In a few moments he heard light footsteps outside and a creaking board at the door before there came a tap.

"Bring me an undershirt and stockings," he called, "and have my riding boots brought up as soon as I've had time to dress." The footsteps sounded again and he doused his face in cold water, which was standing in a porcelain basin near the necessary room, then sat on the side of the bed and pulled off his shirt, showing fullness at chest and stomach. He pulled off the undervest and sat in his breeches, staring at the tiny window until once again footsteps sounded and there was another tap at the door. "Bring them in!" he ordered, without turning, and the door opened and he could hear the swish of a girl's dress. "Put them by me," he went on, still staring at the window, "and tell Mistress Marshall I wish to see her in five minutes. Not four, not six, but five."

"I will return in five minutes, sir," Ruth replied.

Furnival looked around, startled. He felt a rare thing for him: self-consciousness about his half nakedness. She was sober of mien and he could see the dark shadows beneath her eyes, an indication that she had slept badly, if at all.

Abruptly he said, "As you're here, put that undershirt over my head; the way they shrink when washed 'tis like squeezing a quart into a pint pot."

She picked up a vest and unfastened the buttons and stretched it, then placed it over his head and pulled one sleeve as she so often did for the girls and had done, not long ago, for James.

"Those boots," he added.

"They are at the door, sir."

"Get them," he ordered.

When she turned around with the shining boots in her hand he had shrugged himself into the undershirt and was drawing on a ruffled shirt, cream in color. As he drew this down she picked up the woolen stockings and stretched them, then held them so that he could push his feet into them.

"Do you think I'm helpless?" he grumbled.

"I think you are very—very kind, sir, to try to help my son."

"Help anyone who suffers an injustice," growled Furnival. "Your son or—" He broke off, looking at her as she knelt in front of him with the other stocking ready. "Don't worry, Ruth," he said in a different tone. "But for me he wouldn't be in trouble, and I'll soon have him out."

"That is not—" she began, but broke off. Furnival fastened the breeches below his knees, then pushed his feet into the black boots which she held ready.

Soon, he was outside on the cobbles of Bow Street, mounting his horse from a high platform placed there officially to make it easier for all comers to get in and out of carriages and on and off their horses. Forbes, his broad, short groom and man of all work, held the bridle. He rode off at a fair clip through thick traffic and the inevitable cacophony of clattering hooves, but did not plan to go straight to Newgate Prison, which was barely a mile away. He need not be there for half an hour and he did not intend to wait on the magistrate Martin; rather the other should wait on him. He passed the jail and the Old Bailey beyond, riding faster to the Tower, and as he rode, cloak loose about him, fair head bared to the morning sun, people stopped and pointed him out. A man hurled an apple at him, missing by two feet or more, but on the whole the people were more well disposed than ill, and he sensed this. A great many had been against his hanging of Fred Jackson, the highwayman, who had won many friends, but it was over now, and there was respect for that rare creature: an honest justice of the peace, a man who could not be bought.

Furnival was not thinking of any of these things, but of the face of Ruth Marshall and the way her son had been trapped—and the reason why.

He turned into Thames Street and there at the foot was Furnival Tower House, with its five stories towering over most of the others. A guard at the doorway recognised him and came hurrying, staff held like a lance, wearing a breastplate, three-cornered hat pulled low over his forehead, the ribbon of the Furnivals in a bow at one side, rosettes at each lapel of his jerkin and tied, like garters, beneath each knee.

"Why, Mr. John. 'Tis a long time since you honoured us with a visit."

"If honour is the word," Furnival retorted dryly. "Is Mr. William here?"

"Why yes, sir. And Mr. Francis." The constable handed Furnival down and took the reins.

Furnival strode up the steps and into the building, and thought as he had thought a dozen times before that it was like a palace, with its magnificent paintings, its mosaics on the floor, the dome which spread light everywhere, the great staircase. A dozen managers and clerks were moving about, all hurrying except two middle-aged men who held papers near the foot of the staircase. One was tall and elegant in a suit of smooth pale-gray wool; the other was more roughly dressed in homespun tweed, a sailor, probably the captain of a Furnival ship which had just come into the Port of London. The elegant man glanced up at Furnival and seemed to freeze.

"Very good to see you, Mr. John."

"Tappen," Furnival acknowledged, and went up the stairs, hurrying at first but slowing down when he was halfway up, for he did not want to be breathless when he met his brothers.

The offices of all the members of the family were built around the staircase so that the light from the dome fell upon each of the tall, honey-coloured polished doors. The colour of the doors and of the balustrade and of all the woodwork was no accident; John Furnival's grandfather had himself gone to Florence to be sure of the quality of Italian marble and to Venice for the superb craftsmen who had created the many-coloured mosaic around the inside of the dome, where the theme was discovery, exploration and trade. The design depicted great sailing ships on pale-blue oceans and an outline of the once-unknown continents of America, Africa and much of Oriental Asia.

The middle of the seven doors led into the board room; on either side were lodged the senior members of the board, now William and Francis; in the rooms adjacent to these were William's two sons, not yet fully experienced and never likely to be as bright as their forebears, Robert Yeoman, and, when in England, Jason Gilroy.

The smaller offices were used as a training ground for the younger staff members, apprentices and clerks who handled the shipping and the exporting sides of the business and kept close track of the way Members of Parliament voted, checking on those who it was believed would allow a fat bribe to sway their vote.

The women seldom visited Furnival Tower House, a male stronghold where most of even the most menial work was carried out by men or youths. At the head of the stairs and on the landing were messengers and guards, and John Furnival was well aware that word had been carried to his brothers the moment he had entered the building; perhaps before he had dismounted. So it did not surprise him when the middle door opened and Francis appeared.

Francis had the face of an angel, the misshapen body of a cripple, and the mind of a Machiavelli. His long dark hair, over which he seldom wore a wig or a peruke, was a frame for a face of such exquisite beauty that Leonardo da Vinci or Michelangelo or, more likely, Titian might first have painted and then breathed life into it, for there was a sheen of red in the dark hair, a tinge of honey in the complexion. Here on the windowless landing the light from the chandeliers enhanced the Titian-like red, the golden skin.

"Why, John!" Francis came forward, dragging his left leg so badly that it was hurtful to see, and dropping low on his left side with each step, although he gave no impression of effort or of pain. "This is an unexpected and welcome pleasure." He offered his hand, small, beautifully shaped; only his arms and hands and face had escaped the deformity with which he had been born. His grip was firm, and lingered, while John responded with equal warmth.

"I hope it remains a pleasure," John replied. "I've but a few minutes, Francis; I've urgent work to do at Newgate."

Francis smiled deprecatingly. Appearing behind him, William, at first surprised, drew his lips and brows together in a frown. He, too, came forward and shook hands, then drew John into the great room. It was forty-five-feet long and thirty wide, paneled in honey-coloured Spanish cedar and hung with portraits of the family. A long table, shaped like a wide horseshoe, was centered in the room, with ample space for thirteen carved chairs. Six were on either side of a chair on a raised platform that faced the door. According to one's mood this could be seen as a throne or as a judge's seat. Even were the chair occupied, no head and shoulders would have been large enough to hide the magnificent view of the River Thames through the long, high windows. Several doors at that end of the room opened onto a terrace overlooking the river. The tops of oak and beech trees showed immediately beyond the terrace, and beyond these, gardens as beautifully laid out as those in the great squares at the King's palaces. Farther on was the crowded river, caught now by the sun, mirror-smooth save where rowboats, wherries and ferries plied up and down; and great sailing ships rode at anchor or at the quays, their cargoes being unloaded into flat-bottomed barges or onto the stone quaysides. Beyond were more docks and squat warehouses, church spires rising sharp and clear above the huddle of buildings.

John Furnival took in all of this at a single glance as, with a brother on either side, he moved toward the windows.

"Will you sit down, John, and join us in a glass of port?"

"I would if I had the time," the justice replied, "but when I said I had urgent business I was not joking." He looked from one to the other. "In truth I come as a messenger from myself, anxious to make you understand that I mean what I say."

"Was there a time when you did not?" asked Francis.

93

"I pray not and pray that there never will be. Perhaps I should have said I want to convince you!" He gave that remark time to sink in and then went on with great deliberation. "In spite of what I said to William when we last met, I am in a mood to make an arrangement with you all."

Even Francis caught his breath.

"You mean, retire from the bench at Bow Street?" William demanded incredulously.

"On certain conditions," replied John Furnival, "and I would wish to discuss them with all the family at the same time, not speak to appointed delegates." His eyes danced as he looked at William. "When is the first opportunity?"

"Why, we can make one at any time to suit you," Francis declared. "Is that not so, William?"

"Provided it also suits us," William replied. "Whom do you mean by all the family, John? The menfolk? Or the women also?"

"I've a strong preference to have both sexes hear what I'm going to propose," Furnival replied, "but I'd not make it a condition."

"I don't know what is in your mind," Francis said, "but a good time would be two weeks next Sunday, October thirteenth, when we are all to dine together at Furnival Square. Siddle and Montmorency will also be present, with some of our associates from the City here, bankers and merchants with whom we may shortly expect some family ties. Either before dinner or after would be suitable."

"Then before," answered John promptly, "and there will be less danger of anyone present—even our tame Members of Parliament—becoming comatose."

"Talk at one-thirty, then," said Francis, "after everyone is back from church and we have had some refreshment. Will you be at Great Furnival Square at twelve noon?"

"I shall be there," promised John.

"Will you give us no clue as to what you intend to ask of us?" asked William.

"No, William," John replied. "Not a single one you haven't had already." He pulled his gold watch from his fob pocket and raised his eyebrows. "I must be on my way or I shall be late for an appointment with a fellow magistrate and the Keeper of Newgate. But first, I would like to step onto the terrace."

"I will open a door." Francis limped with surprising speed to one side, turned a key in the lock and pushed the door open, then stood aside for his brother, who dwarfed him.

Only out here did one realise the magnificence of the site which the old John Furnival had chosen for the offices and for this room. Not only was the whole south bank of the Thames visible; also one could see London Bridge spanning the river, crammed with foot and wheeled and horse traffic. An extra L-shaped platform had been added at the eastern end of the terrace, the foot of the L the great towers, and the white stone walls of the Tower of London seemed so close that it appeared possible to jump down to the parapets and join the scarlet Beefeaters. One could even see the ironwork of Traitors' Gate, the cannons mounted on the parapet pointing along the river. Looking at the broad surface of the river, alive with flat-bottomed craft, was like looking at a colony of giant ants.

John Furnival raised his eyes and looked above him to the tall, majestic monument with its crown of gilded flames towering above the spires of the churches as a constant reminder of the fire which had destroyed much of London less than eighty years ago. Beyond was the magnificent dome of St. Paul's, looking bright in the strong sun. He looked at this for a few moments and then his gaze shifted to Newgate.

He turned away.

"With such a view of London I marvel that you don't want to see it the best and cleanest and most trouble-free city in the world," he remarked. And with a sardonic smile he asked, "Did it ever occur to you that since the City marshals will pay as much as three thousand pounds for their posts, which carry no salary, they must have some way of making money? Such as corruption, perhaps?" As neither of his brothers answered he shrugged, smiled more freely, and asked, "How often do you come onto the terrace?"

Still neither man answered.

"It is as I feared," went on John Furnival. "You have lost your souls. You have until two weeks on Sunday to find them!"

He turned away, but quick as he was, Francis reached the terrace and the landing doors ahead of him, opened them and shook his hand.

"Good-bye, William," John called, and William replied, "Goodbye, brother."

He waited in the room until Francis came back from the head of the stairs, and as the door closed he asked, "What do you think it is he wants? Something very big or he would not humble himself to come here."

"We have certainly never been more of a mind than about that," opined Francis. "He is to try to strike a bargain which he wants very much indeed. As for what it is—we shall have to wait to find out. I will admit one thing about brother John," he went on. "He inspires absolute loyalty in his servants, from Moffat down to a groom. We'll never get a squeak of what he wants until he tells us."

"We can put two and two together," growled William.

Not Tom Harris but another of the Bow Street retainers, Sam Fairweather, was outside the gateway at Newgate Prison when John Furnival arrived some time later. Three men were being bundled out of a cart and pushed and kicked toward the lodge, all manacled together; each looked innocuous compared with the savage thief-takers who were committing them. Furnival did not comment; at times part of his mind was closed to the iniquity of London. Fairweather, a little wizened-looking man with the most powerful hands and forearms of any man Furnival knew, gave him a hand down from the saddle.

"Tom's inside, sir," he said, "with the two thief-takers and Lionel Martin."

"Good," Furnival grunted. "How would you describe them, Sam?"

Lines leaped into the corners of Fairweather's face as he screwed up his eyes with merriment.

"Apprehensive, sir," he answered. "It has not been my pleasure to see more apprehensive gents for a long time."

"Better still," said Furnival. "Has Silas Moffat been here?"

"And gone, sir. The Keeper is expecting you."

Furnival nodded and turned toward the archway, and immediately a small inoffensive-looking man came from the gatehouse lodge, bringing through the open door a whiff of the prison stench. He touched his cap and said, "If you will please follow me, sir," and led the way to the chamber where all who were committed to Newgate were taken. About the walls were iron rings for restraining violent prisoners; and there were heavy leg irons, balls and chains, as well as manacles.

No more than a dozen men and women were sitting on the stone floor and there was no sign of James Marshall.

The man led the way to another door which was opened at once and more potent stench wafted through; everywhere was the pervasive Newgate stink which nothing could ever really overcome, try though one might with scents and flowers or the Frenchies' garlic. In a front room with Tom Harris, all standing, were the three who had been instrumental in manufacturing the charge against James Marshall. The magistrate, a ship's chandler who was a well-known spare-time

96

justice, was short and plump and flaccid-faced. He doffed his three-cornered hat as he said, "My pleasure, Mr. Furnival, truly my pleasure."

"I hope it will remain that way," replied Furnival grimly. "You can take your choice, all three of you. Retract the evidence and the committal, in which case I'll say no more about it, or be charged with conspiracy to defraud and to bearing false witness and accepting payment in consideration thereof. Which is it to be?"

The magistrate gulped. "But there were independent witnesses to the theft!"

"You can take your choice but not your time," retorted Furnival. "It won't take long to find plenty of witnesses to say there were two boys, and that the wrong one was caught."

This was the only explanation he could envisage, and the reaction on the faces of the men convinced him he was right. Their hypocrisy was nauseating enough to turn Furnival's stomach but this was no time to say what he thought of them. He had one purpose: to find and release James Marshall even if it were only release on bail. But if these two thief-takers retracted, the boy would have complete freedom.

"It *could* be a case of mistaken identity," muttered the magistrate.

"D'you swear to that?" Furnival demanded. "In front of these witnesses?"

"Readily," the first thief-taker declared. "No one would want to see an innocent lad convicted of theft. Why, he could be hanged for it!"

"One day you'll make a mistake too many and you'll be hanged," Furnival said coldly. He looked demandingly at the other thief-taker. "Do you swear to a mistaken identity, Godden?"

"Why, surely, sir, I do!"

"If you ever cross my path again and I find you've given false evidence, I'll see you hanged, the pair of you. Now get out." He frowned as they scurried away, then turned to Martin. "It will take too long to withdraw the charge at the lodge and half the jailers are probably in the plot, anyhow. We'll see the Keeper and you'll tell him the two men who arrested James Marshall have retracted and you have canceled your notice of committal. Just that and no more. D'you understand?"

The man who dealt in justice for profit looked at him with unexpected defiance and replied, "Yes. But one day, John Furnival, you'll go too far. If the hangman doesn't get you, the thief-takers will."

"I can remember Frederick Jackson saying that very same thing,"

Furnival replied derisively. He turned to the inoffensive little man with thin features. "Have you orders to take us to the Keeper?"

"Yes, Mr. Furnival, sir, I am one of his turnkeys. I have already sent for the boy to be found and brought to the Keeper's office. What a terrible miscarriage of justice nearly took place, sir." He took two strides for every one of Furnival's, and the ship's chandler's length of stride came somewhere in between. "But the Keeper himself is in the country, sir, and his assistant will be seeing you, a Mr. Heywood."

He talked on ceaselessly as he led them through the dark, forbidding corridors of gray stone, the walls high on either side, every window, large or small, barred to make escape impossible. Yet without the bars and the darkened windows, the building could have been a palace rather than a prison, so nobly was it proportioned and so fine was the decorative work on the ceilings.

The Keeper, Furnival felt sure, was somewhere in the living quarters of the prison, anxious not to meet him face to face, so that he could deny any part in or knowledge of what had happened. His assistant, a one-eyed man, was fulsome in his greeting, offered wine, assured them there would be no difficulty, heard the ship's chandler's cancellation and the statements of retracted evidence, jumped when a tap came on the door, sharp and clear, and called "Come in." At once a huge man entered, keys clanking from the thick leather belt at his waist. He was handsome in a bold and rugged fashion, with glossy black hair, clean-shaven at the lips and chin but heavily hirsute on the cheeks. There was an air of the brigand about him, a swagger emphasised by the belted jacket and full-cut breeches and leather boots and gaiters. Everything about him was the more impressive because of his size.

Furnival had expected to see James Marshall with him but the jailer was alone.

"Well, Bolson, where is he? Where is the boy?" demanded the Keeper's assistant.

"He can't be found, sir, nowhere," declared the huge man. He looked not at the Keeper's assistant but at Furnival; it was difficult to judge whether there was more defiance than triumph in his eyes. Very deliberately he went on: "You know what can happen if the prisoners take a fancy to a boy."

Furnival stood absolutely still when Bolson declared that the boy could not be found.

Tom Harris exclaimed: "In God's name, *no*."

Heywood put a hand to his one eye as if to hide from the expression in Furnival's and said stridently, "It could not have happened!"

"I've known them dead before the men have half finished with them," the head jailer said. "I've known them live, too." He touched his forehead with a meaningful gesture. "They ain't never been the same, though."

"Mr. Heywood," said Furnival in a cold voice, "I desire to make a thorough search of every ward in the prison, male and female, debtors' and felons', until the boy is found. Tom," he barked at Harris, "go you to Tilt Yard at once, riding any horse if you have none of your own here, and tell the colonel in charge, be it Colonel Treese or Colonel Hammond, that a company of dragoons must be available to quiet an expected riot in Newgate Prison. Go then to Bow Street and send every available man to act as messengers. Is that clearly understood?"

"Perfect, sir, perfect!" Tom turned to go.

"Mr. Heywood," went on Furnival in the same cold voice, "if anything happens to or delays Constable Harris on this errand, I shall hold you personally responsible and charge you with conspiring to cause a miscarriage of justice." He turned his head slightly. "Head jailer—"

"You're wasting your time. I've already searched, I tell you." Bolson was aggressively sure of himself.

"You are in charge of the inmates of this noisome place and if any harm has befallen the boy Marshall you also will be charged with conspiracy, and you had best pray that he is not dead or grievously hurt. Mr. Heywood, will you escort me in person, if you please?"

"I— I—" began Heywood, and he looked as if he would burst into tears. "If the Keeper were here—"

"Either come with me or send for the Keeper, wherever he is hiding." Again Furnival turned to the head jailer, who still smiled faintly, as if he were enjoying this fuss and feared no harm. "Your name is Bolson, I understand."

"Yes, sir. Jake Bolson."

"We will go to the Stone Hold first."

Bolson looked astounded, but much of his expression seemed put on.

"The *Stone* Hold, sir? Why, it wouldn't be safe for a gentleman like you."

"We shall find out if it is safe for a scoundrel like you. Lead the way —at once."

Bolson hesitated, looked at Heywood, and obviously realised that there was no help coming from him. He shrugged and turned to the door. Over his shoulder he slung a single sentence. "No blame to me if they cut your throat." He turned into a stone-flagged passage and then down a narrow stone staircase; the stench which rose was enough to make Furnival choke. Jailers were at iron gates leading to other wards, or holds, astounded at the sight of Furnival.

Bolson and Furnival were halfway down the second flight of steps, lit only by rush flares in iron wall brackets, when the Keeper's assistant called, "I am coming, wait for me. I am coming!"

Bolson growled, "More fool you, you—"

Furnival stretched out a hand and held him loosely about the throat. The hard voice was cut off. Bolson looked over his shoulder as if for the first time he knew a moment of fear.

"Head jailer," Furnival said, "if we have to fight, I shall kill you, and if I have to kill you, it will be a happy day for thousands of poor wretches fated to come here. Lead the way." He released the man, who turned and moved on, saying no word; cowed.

The stench was now so thick and nauseating that Heywood began to cough and Furnival had to fight to prevent himself from being sick. They came upon a sight so awful that Furnival, who had heard of this place and who had been to other parts of the prison he had thought so bad that nothing could be worse, was appalled. Inside one huge stone-floored dungeon, with only dim light from a barred window built high in the wall and two casements, there must have been three hundred people. A dozen, mostly men, were banging on the gate and rattling it so noisily that it seemed that it must break; others were quick to join them. The stench of human body odours, excreta and gin came in a revolting wave. At one side, clearly visible, a man and a woman were copulating. Lying on their backs or on their stomachs or bent double as if in pain were men and women with gin flagons by their sides, so that apart from the rattling and the shouted threats there was snoring from dozens of throats. Against one wall another couple sat; within hand's reach of them was a girl with an infant at her full, milky-white breast. She looked dazed and oblivious of her surroundings as she suckled the child. In one corner, sitting in a circle, were six—or was it eight?—women all dressed in dark clothes which spread beneath them, all with their heads bowed as if in prayer. Each wore a white collar and had white cuffs. An old man was leaning against one wall, vomiting. Three children, two boys and a girl, were racing about the room, threading their way among the occupants, squealing with delight. A middle-aged woman stood in the midst of a small group, reciting the Ten Commandments in a high-pitched voice. Sitting or squatting, many men and women were in attitudes of dejection and despair.

The men by the gate stopped rattling it for at least ten seconds and then one of them screeched, "It's the bastard Furnival!"

"The hanging justice!"

"Let me get at him!"

"Send him in here, Bolly boy. We'll tear him to pieces!" screamed a man who was much the same build as Tom Harris.

Bolson drew back, a huge key in his hand attached to a bunch secured at his waist; and in the poor light his sneer showed and it sounded clearly in his voice.

"*Now* do you want to go in?"

"Open the door at once," ordered Furnival.

"No, sir, I beg you—" Heywood began.

"I myself wouldn't go inside that hellhole with them in that condition," Bolson declared.

"I can well believe you," said Furnival icily. "Are you going to open the door or must I open it for you?"

He moved forward as if to pull the key from the other's hand and Bolson screeched, "They'll kill you!"

"Every man in this hellhole knows that if I were to be murdered here he would be hanged next hanging day," said Furnival in a clear, carrying voice. "And you among them, for putting them up to this idiot behaviour."

"I—I—That's a lie," gasped Bolson. "I never did!"

Furnival wrenched the key from the man's grasp, thrusting him close to the bars so that he, Furnival, had room to insert and turn the key. He needed both hands and on the instant that he took one hand from the small of Bolson's back he was at the man's mercy. He felt Bolson thrust weight backward, then heard Heywood cry: "Enough!" Out of the corner of his eye he saw the Keeper's assistant's pistol thrust against the jailer's neck, and for the first time since he had sent Tom Harris off he felt that he was not alone. The key groaned in the lock as it turned. There remained the risk that one of the prisoners would attack him; and if one started, the others might follow.

"Kill the devil!" one man rasped.

"Choke him to death!"

"One more threat and one single act of violence and you will all be

101

placed under sentence of death for attacking a magistrate," Furnival said in that clear, carrying voice. "Who among you wishes to be hanged so that Bolson can line his pockets?" He paused long enough for the significance of his words to sink in, then added, "Let me pass."

There was still a chance that some of the men would rush at him, but instead they drew back, as if the cold gaze from his eyes and the thin line of his lips intimidated them. He trod on slime; the floor was running with a filthy ooze. He looked at every man and woman and especially at every child, but he did not see James Marshall.

As he neared the middle of the hold, he heard singing.

At first it was so soft that it seemed far away, but it was the voices of women raised in harmony, and he looked toward the group of dark-clad women in the corner, who seemed as out of place here as a virgin in a brothel. He went slowly toward them, noticing that those of the prisoners who were sober looked at them and listened, while even some who had been in the depths of misery glanced up, as if for a moment the awfulness of their plight was eased.

Gradually the words of their hymn became clear and pure in sound:

> " 'He that on the throne doth reign,
> Them the lamb will always feed.
> With the tree of life sustain.
> To the living fountains lead.
> He shall all their sorrows chase,
> All their wants at once remove,
> Wipe the tears from every face,
> Fill up every soul with love.' "

And as they sang they rose to their feet and from amongst them came James Marshall, whom they had kept hidden from the savage beastliness of the men in this awful den. The boy's eyes were feverishly bright and his face had a sickly pallor but his gaze was as direct as Furnival's.

Furnival's heart leaped as it might have had this been his own son.

There was growling and grumbling from the men who had threatened Furnival, but no move toward him or the boy. Furnival, turning, saw two of his Bow Street reliables by the open gate, pistols cocked.

The head jailer was at one side, and the Keeper's assistant was demanding, "Who are those women? Why have they been committed here?"

"I don't know. I swear I don't know!" Bolson's voice was unsteady.

"Then go and find out, you dolt." The courage that had poured into the little one-eyed man was sterner than had seemed possible, and he pushed the hulking Bolson toward the steps as he ordered the other jailers, "Bring those women out and take them at once to the Press Yard. See also that they have good food and drink, whether they can pay for it or not." He looked up at Furnival, his one eye blazing. "Thank God you were in time, sir."

"Thank God indeed," said Furnival dryly. "Boy, go with the ladies to the Press Yard, where the air is clean and no one will assault you. I trust you know well how to say thank you to those ladies."

"I shall be forever in their debt, sir," James Marshall declared in a quivering voice. "And in yours, sir."

"Remember the debt you owe them because you will never be able to repay it," replied Furnival.

He stood aside as the women, seven in all, walked out of the Stone Hold with their heads held high; all but one were in their twenties and thirties, each comely, the eyes of each lighting up at the sight of the rescued boy and of Furnival. They filed up the stairs, one jailer ahead and one bringing up the rear, while Furnival locked the gate as his own constables watched.

"Stay here until the jailers return," said Furnival. "Then one of you report to the colonel in charge at Tilt Yard that the emergency is past at Newgate Prison, thanks"—he looked into that one blazing eye—"to prompt action on the part of the Keeper's assistant. Can you spare me a few minutes, Mr. Heywood?"

"Gladly, sir, gladly." Heywood sounded as humble as he had earlier sounded afraid.

They went up past the middle holds of the prison, from which came the same stench, and alongside the Press Yard, from where it was but a short distance to the assistant's office.

"If you will partake of a little refreshment with me, Mr. Furnival, I shall be delighted. Port, perhaps, or coffee—"

"Good of you," said Furnival, "but I must be on my way. I trust you will report the incident in the greatest detail to the Keeper."

"The greatest detail, sir, I do assure you."

"And I will take it kindly if you will inform him that in my opinion Bolson was bribed by someone outside the prison to persuade the men to make that show of violence against me, and that I might well be dead but for your action."

"You are past grateful, sir. I declare I did no more than my duty. A duty in which I might have failed but for your example. If I may suggest—a letter, the shortest of letters, to the same effect to the Keeper. If it would not be too great a bother."

"It shall be done. And will you tell him, or be yourself assured, that I will pay for the privileges which are accorded the ladies, however long they are here. But they must be permitted the Press Yard and the best treatment and accommodation."

"Be assured of it, sir."

Furnival nodded and turned, saying, "I would like to go for the boy."

"And I will come with you." The Keeper's assistant could not get to the door fast enough to open it for the justice of the peace for the City of Westminster and the County of Middlesex, and they walked side by side, followed now by the two Bow Street constables. Behind, the Stone Hold was secured and guarded by jailers again.

Heywood led them along narrow passages which were pleasantly lighted by large windows, then through a doorway which opened onto the Press Yard. And almost the first thing Furnival saw was young James, gaping about him with a wonder surely as great as the terror he had felt when he had been in the dungeon.

James was as wide-eyed as a young monkey while he looked about him in this place they called the Press Yard, for it was almost impossible to believe this was part of the same prison. The air was clear and pleasantly warm and there was no unpleasant odour. Apart from the heavy barred doors and the barred windows it was like being in a small London square, and the men and women here—nine men to every woman at least, save for the seven who had just come in with him—were dressed in expensive clothes, some with diamond pins in their cravats, all showing or at least pretending an elegance which seemed part of a different world. A group of four was playing cards, and he recognised Sir Roger Pilaff, a Member of Parliament accused of treason. He remembered his father telling him that at Newgate—as in all the prisons—men and women of wealth could "buy" their own apartment, their own wine and food, and could live in luxury, having wives or mistresses whenever they wished, and having their own servants. For these prisoners the jailers would run errands for a price which varied vastly according to the means of the patron.

Much that James's father had told him he had only half absorbed, but from the moment he had been committed here until his release, he had been terrified, for he had experienced all there was to know about the helplessness of the poor prisoners, the near-certainty of conviction, and hanging or transportation for the humblest of thefts.

To him there were now two Newgates: this bright and airy part, where so many well-to-do lived and idled their hours away, and the nightmare beastliness of the stinkhole, where, he knew, he might have been killed by the more brutal inmates or from which he could have been raised into the death cart to be jogged and shaken on the way to Tyburn.

He could "see" Frederick Jackson's legs; and how soon they had gone still in death.

To James Marshall, moreover, there were two kinds of men: those whom he knew from Bow Street, with John Furnival leading them like a knight in shining armour, and men like the thief-takers and the head jailer. It seemed to him that all of life as well as all humankind must be divided in this way, and that bitter conflict was waged increasingly between the good and the bad.

He had been in the Press Yard for less than an hour when John Furnival came to fetch him. Before he left he went hesitatingly to the group of women who had succoured him, but when he reached them, all sitting cross-legged in a half circle and listening to the oldest of them, he could not find words; whenever he tried, his lips quivered but the words would not come. The oldest woman rose to her feet with ease and approached him, holding out her hands for him to grasp. He could see the deep lines etched at the corners of her eyes and mouth.

"Go with God, James," she said gently. "And remember, we shall always thank God that we were able to help you. If you wish to thank us—" She paused long enough for him to nod vigourously and to cry out "Oh, I do!" Then she went on in the same gentle but authoritative voice. "Then thank us by remembering that the greatest heights to which a man or a woman can rise are the heights of serving others." She paused again and, as he nodded, mute, went on: "Simply remember that, James, and pray for us."

She did not draw him to her.

He was aware only of her, although all were watching.

He did not know that a strange and rare silence had fallen upon the whole Press Yard. Every man and the few women present had stopped talking, stopped doing whatever they were at, and watched. Even Sir Roger Pilaff sat silent, cards fanned out in his hand.

Completely oblivious, James slowly went down on one knee and pressed the woman's fingers to his lips, held them tightly, then sprang up and ran toward the door leading to the main passage and to the lodge, with John Furnival striding after him.

It was a long time before movement in the Press Yard began afresh and low-pitched voices broke the silence; but even as the talking grew louder and behaviour returned to normal, many a curious glance was cast toward the dark-clad women, whether they knelt in silent prayer or listened to their leader or walked in twos about the yard quietly rejoicing in their comparative freedom.

CHAPTER 7

The Daring and the Danger

JOHN FURNIVAL returned to Bow Street straight from Newgate to find three accused footpads waiting for a hearing, and two debtors, one an elegantly dressed man attended by a servant and by a lawyer. None of the accused realised how reluctant he was to send anyone to Newgate or to the Fleet, which was at least as bad as the larger prison. Yet the evidence against the footpads was so great that he had no choice but to commit them for trial at the Sessions which would be held in Bailey Street in ten days' time.

The lawyer for the accused debtor said, "If it please you, your worship, I wish to enter a plea for a denial of the debt claimed. My distinguished client—"

"Why doesn't he plead for himself?" demanded Furnival.

"Indeed he will, sir, on your insistence, but if I may prevail upon you to hear me . . ."

He claimed that his client was being sued for debts he had not incurred; for clothes which a tailor had not delivered, for perukes which a wigmaker had made ill-fitting and of poor quality, for a horse, saddle and equipage which had been unsatisfactory. On any other day

Furnival might have questioned him closely, but he was in no mood to listen to the lies or half-truths of a fop.

"I shall commit the accused to Newgate but suspend the committal," he declared. "He may remain at liberty until called upon by a court official if he deposits one hundred pounds as security. See the court usher."

He nodded and banged his gavel. The lawyer, obviously shrewder than he appeared, quickly ushered his client away from the bench. There were no other cases, and Furnival went out by the side door and into his offices and then into his ground-floor apartment. A fire was burning brightly enough to show that fresh coals had been placed on it not long before. Slippers were by the side of his huge armchair and two churchwarden pipes lay by a jar of sweet-scented tobacco. Resting against the jar was a folded paper, which he took up and opened. He read:

> *May God thank you, sir. I shall never have the grace to give thanks enough.*
>
> *Ruth Marshall*

The writing was clear and bold, and not a word was wasted although the note said so much. Furnival sat down and read it again and then folded it and tucked it into his fob pocket. He leaned back and closed his eyes and must have dozed, for he became aware of sound and a presence. He opened his eyes to see Silas Moffat backing toward the door.

"What is it? What is it?" Furnival demanded.

"It is not important, sir—"

"It's important enough for you to creep in and find out whether I was asleep," growled Furnival. "What is it?"

"Tom Harris was here, sir. He has gone off to see into a robbery at the home of Sir Roger Cass; some French and Dutch paintings of consequence are said to have been stolen. Before he left, sir, he told me there is no doubt that the case against James Marshall was instigated by Peter Nicholson, but that he would not be likely to think of and carry that through without someone else's instigation, sir."

"Eve Milharvey," said Furnival flatly.

"There is a rumour about her," declared Moffat.

"Are you going to pass it on or must I go and find it for myself?"

"The rumour is that she is with child," Moffat told him expressionlessly. "She frequently visited Fred Jackson in the Master Felons' Side at Newgate."

Furnival sat absolutely still, looking at the beautiful complexion of his old servant, with the silvery hair like a frame on three sides, the high ruffles and cravat of pale blue making the bottom of the frame. Furnival was still for so long that the stirring of the coals in the fireplace was plainly audible. Slowly he gripped the arms of his chair, as if he were going to get up. But before moving he said bluntly, "Have not other rumours told us that Eve Milharvey was faithful to Jackson?"

"Any man known to touch her would have been castrated," Moffat replied simply. "She was absolutely faithful."

"Do you know what I've made you?" demanded Furnival, his grip on the arms of the chair tightening. "A cynic, Silas Moffat. D'you mean that love alone would not have kept her faithful?" He gave a bellow of laughter and sprang to his feet.

On that instant, he caught his breath. He would have fallen back had he not gripped the side of the chair for support. The colour drained from his face and he took in a dozen shallow breaths, until slowly the colour returned and, obviously, the pain receded.

"Sir," Moffat began, "I beg you to see Doctor Anson. He—"

"Tell Godden I want my horse," Furnival growled.

Silas Moffat did not move, but stood in front of him, hands held out in a kind of supplication and with deep pleading in his eyes.

Neither man spoke for some time, and then it was Furnival, who said roughly, "Oh, please yourself, please yourself. A carriage or a chair or a horse, I don't care which."

"I will arrange for your carriage," Moffat promised, and withdrew.

Furnival lowered himself back into the chair slowly. He no longer felt pain but was absurdly breathless, as if he had run a long way. He heard whispering outside and imagined that one voice was a woman's. If Ruth came fussing over him he would send her packing; he had no desire to be fussed over, wanted no surgeons bleeding him; they had some practices little advanced from barbarism and quacks. He waited for the door to open but it remained closed until Moffat came back, and by then he was feeling much more himself. He rose to his feet slowly, half fearful of what would follow, but the pain did not return and by the time he reached Bow Street he was taking his usual long strides. Godden was at the seat of an open carriage; a constable sprang to the door and opened it. He was Fairweather, a bronzed man with

close-curled white hair; something of his country upbringing remained in his appearance, something of the Lincolnshire vowels lingered in his voice.

"Is there anything you want?" asked Furnival, climbing into the
carriage. He pulled himself up by the top of the metal-banded wheel,
which was cold on his palm, and sat down with slow deliberation.

"Nothing of urgency," Fairweather replied.

"What is it, man?"

"I've a message from the Reverend Sebastian Smith," Fairweather
replied. "He would regard it as an honour if he could wait on you this
evening."

"Do you know what he wants?"

"He did not confide in me, sir."

"If it's money he's after I may find a little. If he wants to save my
soul tell him it's a waste of time. If it doesn't interrupt his prayers,
eight o'clock tonight."

"I am sure he will be here, sir," Fairweather answered. "He was
most anxious."

Furnival nodded, and Godden, taking his cue, made the reins ripple
along the horse's back, so that it started off gently. As they approached a street which led down to the Strand, Godden spoke without turning his head.

"Have you decided where to go, sir?"

"Does Eve Milharvey still live in Jackson's place?"

"Yes, sir. In Loxley Yard, close by Gray's Inn."

"Then that's where we'll go, by the Strand and Fleet Street to make
sure we are not followed."

Godden started to speak but checked himself and turned left at a
narrow lane and left again before he responded, and then he seemed to
be reluctant, perhaps even fearful. The clatter of a wagon full of
sheeps' hides drowned his words, the long, low-slung cart drawn by
six horses and going too fast for safety. Behind it, perhaps explaining
the driver's impatience, was a herd of cows, holding up all traffic
despite the desperate efforts of a drover and a boy.

"What do you want to say?" demanded Furnival. "Speak up, man!"

Now, two open carriages and a coach rumbled and clattered by,
two sedan chairs passed, the iron tips on the boots of their liveried
carriers making sharp sounds on the cobbles. Ahead of them lay St.
Paul's. The great dome was like a monstrous canopy. Godden turned
left before reaching the cathedral. No one had followed.

"All is not as it was at the house in Loxley Yard," Godden reported.

"How has it changed in a few days?"

"There are always men loitering—they say they are protecting the woman."

"And who threatens Eve?" demanded Furnival.

"Fact I can't give you, sir. Rumour I can."

"I'll not pass judgment on your accuracy, man!"

"It is said that Peter Nicholson wishes to marry her and she is reluctant. Since the boy James's kidnapping, Nicholson has been much bolder. He surrounds the place with men he says are enemies of Fred Jackson who want only to avenge themselves on her."

After a few moments, Furnival asked, "Is this Peter Nicholson as evil as he sounds?"

"Worse, sir. Before, the evil was overshadowed by Jackson, who dominated the man."

"And now that Jackson is dead he has become his tyrannical self," Furnival mused.

"Do you still wish to go there alone, sir?"

"No. I desire you with me."

Godden's massive shoulders shook as if in silent laughter. He turned the carriage along several narrow lanes and across a cesspit so rank that one could imagine the noxious gases that rose from it were visible to the eye. Close by were dead dogs and cats and rats, skeleton thin, but just beyond was a break in the houses which showed a square, almost as magnificent as the Covent Garden piazza at its best, where children played and lovers and old people walked. At another pit, fed by the foul sewers which led toward the Fleet River, a pale-faced, gaunt-looking woman stood with a child clutched in her arms. The child did not move and the woman stared yet seemed to be aware of nothing.

Two more turns and the carriage was in Loxley Yard, and at Jackson's house.

Five or six men, with perhaps more lurking, watched from corners and open doorways. Most of the brickwork was concealed by wooden huts or lean-tos, offering plenty of scope for hiding.

Furnival ignored them as Godden helped him down from the carriage but said in a clear, carrying voice, "You left word where we were coming, didn't you?"

"Everyone at Bow Street knows, sir," Godden answered, as clearly.

"Good." Furnival turned and strode into the doorway leading to Jackson's old apartment. Two men were at the foot of the staircase, each as villainous-looking as Bolson, the head jailer; the reek of one man's foul breath was like the stench from a drain. But as he went up the stairs Furnival became aware of cleanliness and fresh air and the odour of wood polish as well as of a log fire.

A girl in her middle teens appeared and asked clearly, but with obvious nervousness, "Is there something you require, sir?"

"Yes. To see your mistress," Furnival said.

"She is resting, sir."

"Tell her that if she doesn't make herself at home to John Furnival she may find herself resting in the women's side at Newgate."

"John Furnival!" The girl gasped and backed away as if she had seen an apparition; then she turned and fled into the room from which the wood smoke was coming. A door slammed but Furnival could hear the excited voice although not that of Jackson's mistress. He looked down the stairs and saw only one of the men there. Traffic noises filtered in but as if from a long way off. Then the door creaked open and the girl reappeared.

"Will you—will you please come this way, your honour?"

He was taken into a large room where a fire burned and a spit with a leg of lamb turned, the fat dripping into a pewter pan beneath it. At one side, the flames reflecting on her bony face and scraggy arms, on her old dress and her sparse gray hair, sat an old crone. She did not look up and gave no sign that she knew he had come into the room. From a door set in the other side of the fireplace wall came Eve Milharvey, her dark hair freshly brushed, cheeks pinched to give them colour, lips pale as his. She gave a mock curtsy and motioned to a chair.

"Will you be seated, your honour?" And when he sat down in a chair that he guessed had been built for Jackson by the finest carpenter and upholsterer, she went on in the same tone of mocking: "And to what do I owe the honour of this visit?"

Furnival stared at her for so long that her smile became set, but she did not look away. Suddenly he spoke with an emphasis the greater because his voice was quiet.

"I don't want to have to send you to Newgate or to Tyburn. But if I have to I will."

"A very gallant gentleman," she sneered.

"A very softhearted woman who would rob another of her son and have the harmless boy flung into jail and hanged. Let's not play with words, Eve Milharvey. Don't attempt to harm that boy again. Don't attempt to harm his mother or her other children. If you do either, I shall provide sufficient evidence to condemn you." He gave her time to retort, but she did not; in fact, for the first time since he had arrived she seemed truly frightened. "And even though you're carrying Jackson's child, it won't keep you out of Newgate and will only postpone the hanging."

She drew in a sharp breath, as if suddenly hurt.

"You know *that*."

"I know that," confirmed Furnival. "And I understand that Nicholson has been showing his claws since the devil's work with Marshall, and you don't know how to fend him off. Is this true?"

He looked at her as he had once looked at Ruth, as he often eyed criminals in the dock.

More sensitive because of her child, perhaps, or else because Nicholson had truly frightened her, she answered, "Yes, it's true enough. He thinks he can blackmail me into taking him to my bed."

"And you don't want him?"

"I would as soon have a pig!"

"Then I will tell you a way to deal with him," Furnival promised.

She had leaned back in her chair, shoulders touching the high back, and the firelight shone on her hair and her eyes, putting lights in them; there was fear in her and in that moment, perhaps, hope had been born.

"What possible way is there?" she demanded.

"Threaten Nicholson that you will tell me of his past crimes if he doesn't leave you alone," Furnival said. "Tell him you've lodged a list of these crimes at a bank, to be opened at your death. I could have taken him now, but if I judge the man aright, he has many criminal friends and will lead me to them if he's watched. If what I advise fails, I'll have him charged. I've evidence enough. But you will be in no danger from me if you attempt no harm to the Marshall family."

Eve looked at him as if she could not really believe what he was saying, and in an unsteady voice she asked, "What if *he* endeavours to harm them?"

"Why should he, except to win you?" demanded Furnival.

She did not answer.

He stood up slowly, using the arm of the chair as support, then bowed and moved to the door. He could not be absolutely sure that no man stood outside in the passage in menace, for there might be another way in, but he was certain that Godden would have found a way to warn him if more had come into the yard and were ganging up with the others to attack him.

Still inside the room he turned and went on: "You can tell Nicholson you gave me the sealed letter and I am to place it in a bank—not necessarily my own family's."

She did not answer.

The old crone stared into the glowing fire.

Fat splashed and the leg of lamb gave off a sudden spitting and hissing.

As Furnival stepped outside he saw four men, two at the head of the stairs, two at the far end of this passage. They were too far off to have heard what he had said but there was no doubting their menace, for two held pistols, one a long knife, and the fourth a flail with enough spikes on its head to cut a man's face to pieces with a few blows.

He thought with a flash of fear: They must have overpowered Godden or they wouldn't be here.

At the prison Furnival had been acutely aware of the danger but as sure as he could be that he could overcome it by his presence and his authority as a justice of the peace. But he had no such sense of certainty here. No words would stop these men from attacking him, and with such weapons as they carried they were not likely to leave him alive.

At least none of them moved, but one called out: "Close the door on him, Eve."

If she obeyed, then he would have no chance at all.

He heard a rustle of movement behind him, and at the same moment the two men with pistols drew nearer.

The rustling drew nearer.

He said in a casual voice, "How much will each of you get from Peter Nicholson for your part in this?"

The man at the head of the stairs took another step forward, pistol leveled at Furnival's breast. If he had a ghost of a chance it was to spring backward into the room and slam the door, for it had not closed behind him yet.

"Because I'll see that each of my constables who takes part in capturing you will get double."

Eve Milharvey, so close behind him that he could hear her breathing, moved swiftly past, pushing him to one side, and although the man fired and the shot roared, the bullet went high. Furnival entered the room on the half-turn and footsteps thundered. Eve's voice sounded strident and angry and she pulled at the door, slamming it behind her. As the reverberations sounded and died away, her voice came clearly.

"There will be no murder in this house!"

"Let us pass, Eve."

"Go away, I tell you!"

"What does he mean to you, you bitch!" one of the other men rasped. "Why should you defend him?"

"Stand aside, Eve," a man growled.

Furnival looked about him for a weapon. And there, over by the fire, were fire irons, including a massive poker. He crossed and picked it up; it was hot enough on one side to sting.

He went back to the door as Eve Milharvey said in her high-pitched voice, "Isn't there a man among you with any sense? If the leading justice is murdered here, every man at Bow Street and a thousand paid guards from the House of Furnival will join in the search for his killers. He's not going to be murdered in my house. Go away!" she cried. "Go away before his men come for him."

A man whose voice Furnival had not heard before said, "Perhaps she's right."

"We ought to go," said another uneasily.

"We must wait for Peter," declared a third, and after this, silence followed until footsteps began to sound noisily on the uneven boards and soon down the stairs.

At last, these stopped; and only when there was silence did Eve Milharvey open the door. She started at the sight of Furnival with the poker, and was baffled when he went past her and opened a door on the other side of the passage. There he saw a small window with diamond-shaped leaded panes which overlooked Loxley Yard. The room was an office or library, with richly coloured rugs on the floor, some oil paintings hanging on the panels, books stretching from floor to ceiling on two walls. He took all this in as he crossed to the window and peered out. Godden was there, standing by the horse!

And as Furnival watched, two other Bow Street men, one being Sam Fairweather, clattered into the yard on horseback. Godden had contrived to send a messenger to Bow Street for help! Furnival was smiling as he turned around, and almost bumped into Eve, who had come silently across the rug-covered floor.

"What are you looking for?"

"The man who was with me," said Furnival. "He's sent for others. Your friends will respect your wishes in future!" He moved aside so that she could see the two new arrivals, and when she turned she raised her hands to the height of her breast. For the first time he saw her free from tension and bewilderment.

"Fred always said you had eyes that could see through a man's skull and ears, that you could hear a penny drop when muskets were roaring. Can you also command your men by talking to them across a mile of London town?"

Furnival laughed, well pleased.

"I can rely on them to do the sensible things," he said, and as they both sobered, he became aware of her now simply as a desirable woman, and he knew that a few weeks ago he might have relaxed, dallying, and perhaps doing much to rid her of remembered hatred. The temptation to exert the magnetism he undoubtedly possessed over women was very strong. He thought of her being with child but there was little fullness at her belly. He thought of the hatred she bore him and the love she had had for Jackson, and he subdued the stirring of desire.

Quietly he went on: "I hope I can rely on you to do the sensible thing also, ma'am. I will send you a receipt from the bank for your confidential letter."

He bowed stiffly and went out.

At the foot of the stairs he saw two of the men who had been ready to attack him and noticed, for the first time, that what looked like part of the dark oak paneling on one side was a narrow doorway, now ajar; that was how the other two men had arrived without arousing Godden's suspicions. He ignored them as he walked to the carriage and returned the greeting of his men.

"Godden, I am going to take some coffee at Galloway's," Furnival said. "I shall write a note in there for you to take to a Mr. Tappen at Furnival Tower House. He will give you a receipt for it and you will bring it straight back to me." He climbed into the carriage as he went on to the others: "I doubt I shall need you now, but watch in case we are followed to Galloway's."

Galloway's Coffee House was in Fleet Street not far from the bridge over the Fleet River, an old building partly built of red brick, which was beginning to powder and flake, and partly of wooden boards. It was within reach of the new crop of newspapers which had come upon London, some replacing the daily sheets and the worst relying on a daily sale of at least a thousand copies. So this place was a center for newspapermen, gossips eager to pass on news, and men who were anxious to pick up information about overseas ships and conditions in foreign places; early news of a war or a ship's loss could be turned to good account in the stock exchanges as well as in other coffee houses frequented by bankers and leading investors and men from the big commercial enterprises. The better coffee houses kept *The Gentleman's Magazine*, *The London Magazine* and *The Spectator* as well as the daily or twice weekly newspapers. By far the most popular was *The Craftsman*, dedicated to the downfall of Robert Walpole.

Furnival opened the door of Galloway's to a heavy smell of tobacco smoke, which made a pale blue-gray mist, softening the sight of thirty or forty men sitting in groups at the little wooden tables, drinking coffee from tall mugs or smoking coarse tobacco. Three men sneezed, one after the other, with such violence that one feared for the safety of the snuffboxes in their hands, for one fallen box of snuff could cause more coughing, spluttering and sneezing than a canister of ground white pepper. Some of the customers wore long wigs, so old-fashioned was their dress, but many had the shorter perukes which fashion was now demanding, and one man actually wore full-length trousers fastened by straps under his boots, far ahead of fashion. Among the host of three-cornered hats were some with round brims and even some with high crowns.

At Furnival's entry there was a stir of interest and a lull in the conversation, making one man's voice sound very loud about the quiet.

"I tell 'ee, Will, the Jews were behind the South Sea Bubble, twenty years ago or not. Whenever there's money trouble look for the Jews. I'm against them having civil rights; if we're not careful they'll be operating all of London's business and—"

The speaker, one of the bewigged men, broke off when he realised that quiet had fallen upon the house. He, too, saw Furnival and his mouth stayed open. Tobias Clay, who was said to be the anonymous editor of *The Fleet*, was just in front of Furnival, together with the editors of *The London Journal* and *The Craftsman*. Two younger men, writers for *The Daily Advertiser*, were in a far corner.

"Are you against the Jews having citizens' rights, John Furnival?" Clay asked.

"I am in favour of all citizens having their rights," Furnival answered, "including safety in bed from robbers and safety on the highway from highwaymen and safety in the streets from footpads.

Aye, and safety in London from plague and safety in magistrates courts from jail fever." When he paused there was a general laugh, a few calls of agreement. He sat down and added, "I'd rather be a clever Jew than a foolish Gentile, and I'd rather be a dull-witted Jew than a Jew hater."

The man still bitter about the South Sea Bubble flushed beneath his side whiskers but did not take up the issue. A waiter came to Furnival with a pot of coffee and a clay pipe, marked with his name, and he looked through *The Daily Courant* and *The Spectator*.

Now and again Clay asked a question but Furnival did not look up until the man said, "Now that Jackson's dead, do you think crime will become less of a problem, Mr. Furnival?"

"No, I do not."

"So you think he was only one of many leaders of gangs?"

"Tobias Clay," Furnival said, laying aside *The Courant* and ejecting little puffs of smoke as he spoke, "if you, a renowned scribe attached to the press, whose ear is said to be closer to the ground than any other ear in Fleet Street, can doubt such a fact, then call your rag anything you like but not a newspaper."

"Forty or more words where one would suffice," retorted Clay smilingly, obviously taking no umbrage.

"I'll answer with one word when one will serve."

"Then answer this: What does the brightest luminary on the magisterial benches of London, Westminster and the counties of Middlesex, Surrey and Essex think will reduce crime?"

Furnival took the pipe from his pursed lips; no smoke came between them. He was aware that everyone was listening, that many were standing at the walls simply to see him. They leaned against the advertisements for soap, cure-all pills and physics, snuff, combs, pomades and other commodities in great variety. One man sniffed snuff wheezily, sneezed loudly once and smothered another.

"I will give you two answers," Furnival said slowly. "In the long term you need social justice to replace the iniquity of many of our present laws, the corruption in Parliament and among justices of the peace as well as all constables and their substitutes. Only a nincompoop would expect enough changes in less than fifty or sixty years although we shall move toward them. Our method of dealing with crime is the very breeding ground of crime and so of criminals. In the short term, in order to reduce the consequences of crimes which are born out of society, we need a strong force of trained men in

London, controlling the two cities and the Thames and the land between. And after that we want the same kind of force of peace officers in every city, large and small, working together. *Then* we would have less crime. But to make a good beginning on either would take at least ten years."

When he stopped, the silence seemed strange and disturbing. It was broken by the bewigged man who had been damning the Jews.

"Utterly unthinkable. Madness. We are a free people. We will provide our own security, but a professional force—it nauseates me. Positively nauseates me." He glared defiantly at Furnival, who had known exactly what to expect.

Another man called out, "You'd have us like the damned Frenchies, would you? A police army, that's what you'd have."

"Monstrous," another man declared. "Utterly monstrous."

"What empty-headed asses you are," declared a young man from a corner; though big and florid of face, positive of voice, he was blind. "Furnival's right. We'll never begin to be free of crime while we leave crime detection and keeping the peace to corrupt bumblers."

"Damme, Gentian," the anti-Jew cried, "you're as bad as he is! We want no police army in Britain, I tell you. The present system works. A few years ago I had two hundred gold pieces and as much in value in gold plate stolen. Within a month most was returned."

"And how much did you have to pay Frederick Jackson to get it back?" asked Furnival coldly.

"No matter! If he hadn't interceded, I'd have had none of it."

"For as long as the majority think like you do," the blind Gentian declared, "there will be no efficient way of fighting crime, and so more crime in London exists than there is stink in the River Fleet."

Furnival moved his chair back, stood up and crossed to the sitting man, and as he did so the door opened and Godden came in. Furnival signaled to him and went on to Gentian's table.

The blind man, editor of a small newspaper, raised his head and said, "Mr. Furnival. Very gracious of you."

"Very discerning of you," Furnival replied.

"My friends went so rigid, only one man in this room could affect them so. Yes, sir, I do believe completely in what you said, but damme if I can find enough others to agree with me to make up the fingers on one hand. You've one ally, though. Henry Fielding, the playwright, now at the bar."

"May we all three meet and discuss the matter?" suggested Furnival.

119

"My pleasure, sir. I am yours to command. But not, alas, for a few weeks," Gentian said in his curiously attractive voice. "Henry Fielding has to go to Paris to plead a case for an Englishman in some difficulty. I have no doubt that he will encounter a variety of Parisian crime."

"There'll be as much as in London, in spite of those damned police soldiers," a man sitting at the next table put in.

"Half the crime and a quarter of the hanging," Furnival replied. "I have seen recent figures from Paris."

"And far more manners, my dear sir," Gentian replied. "*Far* more manners. Mr. Furnival, sir, to our next meeting."

Furnival went out, to find the street more crowded although it was not yet five o'clock, very early for the heaviest traffic to begin. The only satisfaction, apart from relaxation, had come from the man Gentian and the information that Henry Fielding, playwright turning barrister, agreed with him.

It was six o'clock when he reached Bow Street.

Two of his retainers were on duty outside, talking to an old watchman, but no carriages and no horses waited, from which fact he drew hope that no one was waiting or demanding a quick hearing. The court and the offices were quieter than usual, and he was at the door of the downstairs apartment when Moffat appeared from it, bowed and remarked, "I am glad no harm came of your visit, sir."

"Who knows—some good may, in the passage of time," Furnival said. "Make me some tea, and then let me be undisturbed until a quarter to eight."

"But dinner, sir—"

"I will dine after the Reverend Sebastian Smith has been to see me," Furnival said and strode into his room.

Ruth Marshall was in front of the fireplace, toasting muffins. On a nearby table was a crock of butter, and there were few things he liked to eat more than muffins from which the butter oozed. A kettle sang and steam whispered from it as it hung from an iron hook by the side of the fire, and a teapot was warming with dark tea already inside.

Ruth looked up at him and made to rise but he said gruffly, "Stay there, stay there." He saw her cheeks flushed by the fire and her eyes glowing, and for the first time since she had come here she wore a dress cut so low that he could see the rich swell of her bosom.

He went into his alcove bedroom.

The bed was turned down as if it were night, his nightgown was

120

draped over one side, soft slippers of knitted wool stood by the bed. He drew the curtain and went into the necessary room with its strong, almost overpowering perfume of roses, needed less here because some years ago he had had a plumber drill a hole and fit a leaden pipe which was sluiced down with at least three buckets of water a day. He put on the nightgown and a dressing gown and made a great noise pushing back the curtain.

Ruth was pouring the boiling water onto the tea, holding the teapot close and tipping the kettle up with a small piece of angle iron. She allowed the kettle to straighten slowly, stood up as easily as a child and placed the teapot on the table.

"I think that is all you need, sir," she said.

"I don't know," he replied, looking at her. "I don't know, Ruth. Pull up a chair and get yourself a cup and just sit by me. I don't wish to talk and I don't wish to be alone."

She did as she was bidden and sat on the far side of the fireplace, sometimes looking into it, sometimes at him, toasting more muffins, smiling when he spread even more butter over any empty little holes. He noticed how delicate and small her wrists and hands and ankles were.

He did not know how long they sat there.

He did not know the moment when he stood up and stretched his arms out toward her, and how she came to him, neither shy nor bold; how for a moment his touch upon her seemed to create stillness and coldness in her body but soon these faded.

He was very gentle with her. At first he sensed that she was a little afraid, but after a moment he felt her respond, and before long their lips met, their teeth touched, their bodies were joined together.

He knew how different women were in their responses, how some lay almost frigid beneath a man and others pretended a passion which lacked the rhythm a couple should have. He knew well the practised ease of a woman such as Lisa Braidley, with whom it was impossible to be sure whether passion was real or simulated; and he had lain with women he had never known before with whom there had been no question but of passion and, after a while, some strange, all-possessing fire which blazed in both and exploded at the same fierce moments of climax. He had wondered, idly, how it would be with Ruth, aware that possession of any woman for the sake of lust, uncaring whether he saw her again, was no longer sufficient.

Now he knew near-perfection.

Afterward, *afterward*, he remembered how he had said to Lisa

Braidley that he wished her breasts held milk so that he could draw sustenance; and soon he found his lips gently about Ruth's nipples, drawing no sustenance yet drawing peace. The moment came when he fell asleep, his cheek against her breast.

When she felt it would not disturb him she eased herself away from him with great care, thankful that the huge bed did not creak. She stood for a few moments, naked, looking down at him and smiling. Soon she shrugged herself into her robe, drew it up and tied it at the neck, left the tea things on the table lest she should make enough noise to wake him, and went out. In the flickering light of candles in iron wall sockets Silas Moffat was reading a manuscript through the tiny lenses of gold-rimmed spectacles. He stood up immediately as she crossed to him, saying in a low-pitched voice, "I do believe that he will sleep."

"I hope it has not overtired him; I am troubled about his health. But pleasure followed by sleep can only be good for him," he added more happily. "I will go and see the Reverend Smith and try to find more of what he wants, and make an appointment for tomorrow, if it seems necessary." Ruth nodded and moved aside as he asked, an anxious note in his voice, "Must you go to your cottage?"

"Is Meg Fairweather there?"

"And will stay all night if needs be."

"Then I can stay here for as long as I am needed," Ruth said. "I will sit in a chair so that he will see me the moment he wakes and I can get anything he needs."

"Ruth," Moffat said, touching her hand with his gnarled and veined fingers, "I have served John Furnival for thirty years, and I do declare this is the first time I ever thought him lucky."

"Away with you!" she whispered, and kissed him lightly on the cheek before tiptoeing back to Furnival's room and across to see him. He had not moved, and his sleep was of deep exhaustion. She turned away, glanced at his huge chair, decided that it would not be wise to risk his waking and finding her in it, then found another that was comfortable. She placed coals with great care on the fire, then sat with the light from three slow-dripping candles shining on the tapestry which she had started long before Richard had died.

She felt completely at rest.

Furnival woke in near-darkness, to see her asleep in her chair, a silhouette against a faint glow from the fire; all the candles had burned themselves out. He looked at the watch standing now by the bedside. It was half-past three; he must have slept for eight hours or more! He went across the room and looked down at her, thinking: She is but a child. But she was not a child, and he had full proof! He eased his arms beneath her and raised her gently. She stirred. Carrying her across the room, he placed her on the bed, hesitated, and then undid the tapes at her gown. By God, she was not a girl! He moved her over as far as he could and then got in beside her, not expecting to sleep again, expecting, rather, to be teased by the desire for her.

Yet he fell asleep, and daylight showed at the tiny window when he woke again.

She was still beside him.

She woke at his touch, and stirred, and soon he knew that the fire he had kindled in her only yesterevening was one which would not easily be quenched.

CHAPTER *8*

"A Man of God"

THE REVEREND SEBASTIAN SMITH had a curious way of walking on the balls of his feet, so that he appeared almost to hop. Although a small man, the top of his head not reaching Furnival's chin, he was well proportioned, and reports came in from time to time that in defense of himself and his parishioners he had put many a ruffian to flight. He was fair-haired and his gray-blue eyes changed according to the light. He had a youthful look although he was a man of at least fifty and had been a curate at St. Hilary's for ten years before eventually becoming the vicar. He wore a black gown cut out at the neck to show that he was a cleric, with plain braid and buttons, and slit at each side of the shirt, which gave him freedom of movement.

The last time Furnival had seen him had been at Tyburn on the hanging day when Frederick Jackson had died. It was difficult to realise that this small, mild-looking man had such lungs and a voice which could boom above the noise of the mob.

He had a stubborn courage which made him take the Word anywhere he thought it would do good. He did not care whom he assailed with his tongue, the riffraff of the mob or the exquisite dandies who, deep-streaked with sadism, walked among the ruffians and the brutish poor. He might choose the Mall, most fashionable of promenades, where the aristocrats still promenaded. He might choose St. Bartholomew's Fair, crammed with side shows of actors or puppets, or one might find the Reverend Smith preaching earnestly at Ranelagh Gardens or Vauxhall Gardens, both of which seemed out of place in London with their Chinese and Greek, their Moorish or Indian pavilions. Whenever a new tea garden was opened, be it at Marylebone, Pimlico, Pentonville or Hampstead Wells, there sooner or later he would be seen.

Some who knew said that it was less the spirit of the Lord than the spirit of the flesh, titivated and tantalised by all he saw. Whatever the cause he was forever at work, either among his parishioners at St. Hilary's or in those places "spawned by the devil."

It was four o'clock in the bright but chilly late afternoon of the day following Furnival's visit to Eve Milharvey. By rare chance few cases had come up for hearing and no one of importance was waiting for his turn in court.

Moffat had brought Smith upstairs to the big study-cum-library and sun filtered through a corner of one window onto the leather spines of books, turning them from brown to russet colour. A newly fed fire blazed; a decanter of sack stood on a table between two chairs.

"Mr. Furnival, it is very gracious of you to see me," Smith said, both looking and sounding nervous. This was unusual, for whenever he gave evidence as to the character of one of his poorer parishioners in court, and whenever he interceded with one of the parish constables to increase a sum being given to a destitute family, he was quiet but confident. What, then, would make this man whose faith in his God gave him such confidence in himself act almost as if he were afraid?

"I should see you twice for being asleep when you were due here last night!" said Furnival. He looked and sounded as fresh as he had been for a long time. "How can I help you, Reverend?"

Quite unexpectedly Smith said, "You can help to get the release of the Methodist women from Newgate. And also—" But he could not go on and sat back in his chair, looking deeply troubled.

"The Methodist—You mean the women who saved young James were followers of John Wesley?" Furnival was quite taken aback. "What are they doing in London and above all what are they doing in Newgate? I've heard of Wesley's preaching in the provinces, but I did not know he had come to London."

"Nor has he, yet," rejoined Smith, gaining some confidence. "The ladies and their husbands came to prepare the way for him, and they fell foul of the law. It is a ridiculous story and I'm not sure we yet know what is really behind it," he went on. "They went to the market in Covent Garden and were told to help themselves and pay when a tally was made. Before they had finished they were charged with theft and were thrown into Newgate. And the devil of it is, sir, looked at one way it might have been theft, for they cannot identify the two men who told them to help themselves. They could be lying." He looked more boldly into Furnival's eyes and asked, "Could you spare enough men to find out, Mr. Furnival?"

Unhesitatingly Furnival said, "Yes. I will send an officer with you to Newgate to get a full description of the men and do whatever I can."

"I have their descriptions writ down, with notes on the clothes they were wearing and the sound of their voices. One man came from Lancashire, one from Norfolk, that is why the women trusted them. They are good but simple folk and familiar-sounding voices disarmed them."

"I hope the day will come when they will meet and recognise some honest Londoners," Furnival said, with a smile in his eyes. He leaned forward and pulled a cord at the side of the fireplace. Almost immediately footsteps sounded in the passage, then up the stairs, and a young clerk came in.

"Thomas, which men are standing by?"

"Tom Harris, sir, and Ebenezer Noble. And two of the others are at the Cock Tavern, within call."

"Send Tom up to me," ordered Furnival, "and send Ebenezer to get the two men from the Cock to replace him and Tom."

"That I will, sir." The boy hurried off, unaware of the clatter he made, while the Reverend Smith stood up from his chair and spread his hands in front of the settling fire.

"Mr. Furnival," he said, "you are not only a good man but the most efficient man I know. I doubt London and Westminster or indeed the whole metropolis know how much they owe you."

"I doubt it, too," said Furnival gruffly, "and I doubt they'd believe if you were to preach a sermon on it from your pulpit! Will you have a glass of sack?"

"No, thank you, sir."

Furnival drew his brows together in a frown and then gave a deep laugh.

"But I haven't the best memory of any man you know, have I? I'd forgotten that you don't drink alcoholic liquor. Is there a reason for that?"

"When there is no drunkenness, when there are no ginshops, then I will drink wine to warm my stomach," Smith replied. "But don't let me prevent you—"

"I'll be better off without it," Furnival declared, and looked toward the door as Tom Harris appeared. Though twice the weight of the young clerk, he made not a tenth of the noise. "Come in, Tom," Furnival said, but did not ask the constable to sit down. "The Reverend Smith . . ." He repeated Smith's story almost verbatim, while the clergyman gave him three sheets of paper on which the writing was black and bold. "Take Ebenezer and find out what you can," Furnival ordered.

"We'll go at once," said Tom Harris. "But I shouldn't be too sanguine, Reverend. Men from all the midland and northern counties as well as the east come with their wagons and unload and are off again before you can say 'wink.'"

"I shouldn't be too pessimistic, either," Furnival retorted for Smith. "If you can't find these men you can find the one who charged the women with theft. I'll talk to him here," he added in a tone of great finality. "At any time."

Tom Harris nodded.

"And on your way out, Tom, have someone bring coffee—or would you prefer tea, Mr. Smith?"

"Coffee would be most welcome, sir."

Tom went off and Furnival leaned back in his chair, watching the parson. He himself felt calm, even contented, and the long night's sleep had done him more good than a dozen bottles of physic. But his alertness was not dulled, and he felt sure that he had not yet discovered what was really worrying Smith.

Casually he asked, "When will John Wesley be here, Mr. Smith?"

"He is due in ten days," Smith answered, "but whether he should be persuaded to postpone his visit I am not sure. He was persuaded by the Reverend Whitefield to preach with him in Bristol, out in the open air since few churches would admit him. Mr. Wesley was reluctant, I am told, but soon found it acceptable and a way of reaching multitudes.

"Now he is due to come here. In truth, sir, I am persuaded that the man has in him the spirit of God, and he carries it not only to the rich and to the middling men but to the poor. We are in sore need of such a man in London, where the Church has lost its fire if not its faith. It has certainly lost its tolerance," Smith went on wryly. "I heard Wesley preach in Birmingham a month ago and came back hotfoot to open the pulpits to him, but few welcome him, few if any want him. And I have been ordered by the bishop not to give him the hospitality of my own pulpit. To me this is a wicked wrong, depriving a man of God of his right to minister and denying thousands their right to ministry." He looked away from the fire and straight into Furnival's eyes. "You are not a churchman, Mr. Furnival, but you must see the iniquity of this attitude."

"The Church being as smug as it is, I'm not surprised," Furnival said. "I think you might have a bigger task stimulating the Church of England to action than I would in persuading the government that we need a professional force of peace-keepers!" He pondered for a moment and then asked, "What kind of voice has John Wesley?"

"A fine and powerful voice," declared Smith.

"Then you should certainly find him a pulpit in the fields here also," said Furnival without hesitation. "In Spitalfields or Smithfield, even at Tyburn when there's no hanging. He'd have every right, provided he preached neither treason nor popery. You'd find out whether the citizens of London would flock to hear a new prophet as they flock to see men swing."

Smith had gone absolutely still. A new light, near-radiance, filled his eyes, and he looked as if he were too full for words. That was how Ruth saw him when she came in bearing a tray with coffee and hot milk, sugar and some open jam tarts, and she was so startled by the parson's appearance that she in turn stood still.

"John Furnival," said Sebastian Smith, his voice taking on the familiar booming note, "you'll never persuade me that you're not a man of God." He caught his breath. "That's what I'll do. I shall announce open-air meetings in the fields, as they have in other cities. More people will be able to hear John Wesley than if he preached thrice from every pulpit in London and Westminster!"

He spoke like a man inspired. He was hardly aware of Ruth as she set the table, and certainly he did not see Furnival close his fingers about her wrist for a moment and then release her. She slipped copies of The Daily Courant and The Craftsman into a slot at the side of his chair, then, without waiting to be told, poured coffee, placed the dish of tarts within hand's reach of each man, and went out.

When Sebastian Smith had gone—he had made no mention of Ruth —Furnival drew one of the newspapers from the slot and began to look through the inside news columns. Later he would look through the advertisements with a special eye on those of some of the bolder thief-takers, offering their services to look for stolen property, and those of more victims of robberies advertising for the recovery of their losses.

This was *The Craftsman*, a newspaper which so hated Walpole and his government that, like Henry Fielding with his plays, it might one day go too far. Two words seemed to rise out of the column and strike Furnival: "police force." He read closely, knowing how this had come about as soon as he read the first lines.

CHIEF MAGISTRATE DESIRES TO ESTABLISH GENDARMERIE KIND OF POLICE FORCE FOR LONDON

Mr. John Furnival, renowned magistrate at Bow Street, recently responsible for the capture and hanging of the notorious highwayman Frederick Jackson, gave forth at Galloway's Coffee House at the corner of Fleet Street and Chancery Lane yesterday on London's crime. The chief magistrate would have a professional police force to guard our liberties. However, what liberties would there be left to guard if the existence of such a force were—by its very existence— to take them away.

This newspaper is seldom in agreement with Sir Robert Walpole and the scurrilous crew he has gathered about him at Westminster. We understand that to Mr. Furnival's constant plea the administration returns a firm no. Liberty, it is obvious, makes strange bedfellows.

Furnival thrust his chin forward as he tossed the paper away and picked up *The Daily Courant*, which gave a shorter paragraph without comment. Those who did not actively oppose him would make no comment and might, he thought bitterly, just as well be hostile. Remembering an article he wished to read in *The Craftsman* he bent down for it and, in bending, wedged himself in an awkward, crouching position. He felt the blood go to his head and pressure grow in his chest and pain beneath his jaw.

He heard Ruth Marshall approaching and struggled to get up, but she was in the room before he could do so, and she, without a word, crossed and helped him.

"No," he said, though she was still silent, "I will not see a docto But I will have some tea."

129

CHAPTER *9*

Family Conclave

ON THE morning of Sunday, the thirteenth of October, 1739, John Furnival was driven in an open carriage toward Great Furnival Square. He was due to arrive to meet the family between eleven-thirty and twelve noon, and if he were to arrive early he would go to Cleo's home, or Anne's, for each would have been to church at St. Mary's and would be at home to anyone who called. "Anyone" would be members of the family, for no doubt it had been widely spread about that only family would be present. The sun was warmer than he had expected, and the Strand was almost empty, only an occasional coach or chair moving along and a few drunkards sleeping outside the grogshops or the brothels; the Sabbath had certainly quieted this part of London.

Seeing a throng of gaily dressed people come out of St. Martin's in the Fields, he wondered how Smith was getting on at St. Hilary's. Then he noticed a line of people dressed in dark clothes and wearing round hats with shallow tops walking by, carrying posters and calling out: "Go to the fields today to hear the word of God from the lips of His prophet, John Wesley." After a pause they repeated the same words, and Furnival saw that the times of the meetings were written on the placards. After the third refrain a man with a voice as powerful as Smith's boomed out: "John Wesley will preach at Tyburn Fields at twelve noon. At Spitalfields at three o'clock of the afternoon. At Smithfield at half-past five in the evening."

Furnival leaned forward and called up to his coachman, "Go up and down Whitehall and then to Tyburn Fields."

"Aye, aye, sir!"

It was a fine, clear day, and Furnival settled back to enjoy the sunshine. The roadways and the walks, already paved, were now crammed with people, and carriages and coaches were being drawn leisurely, some to go only as far as Westminster Abbey and the Parliament building, some to go along the embankment toward London Bridge, where they could cross for a Sunday at the gardens.

In these open thoroughfares on this beautiful autumn morning, the London of crime and treachery, of brothels and ginshops, of stinking sewers and rotting animal corpses, was easily forgotten. One could breathe clean air, could see contentment on many faces, could enjoy the sight of the couples arm in arm, some shepherding three or four children, the colourful fruit barrows, the cries of the street callers no longer strident. At the Abbey, where more throngs were leaving, the coachman turned his pair. They repassed St. Martin's and Furnival wondered why Smith had not arranged a meeting for Wesley in the surrounding fields. Soon they were moving at a good clip across fields where sheep grazed and a few cattle roamed and dogs barked. The sun became almost too warm, but the hood of the coach would go no farther back and there was a light breeze.

The coachman, whom Furnival did not know well but who was a protégé of Sam Fairweather's, recently released from the Navy, touched the flanks of the horses so that they quickened their pace along Piccadilly, and Furnival looked across the open fields toward Buckingham House which, some said, was soon to be pulled down. Traffic was very thick as they approached the turnpike at Hyde Park, and suddenly Furnival was aware of a hand waving and someone trying discreetly to attract attention. It was Lisa Braidley, magnificently arrayed, by her side the young Duke of Gilhampton. Furnival touched his forehead to her and smiled.

Beyond the turnpike was Tyburn Lane, with its farms and inns and tall haystacks, and people were streaming along, mostly dark-clad; he could hardly have imagined a more different sight from a hanging day. Furnival heard one pretty girl call: "Sheets of John Wesley's hymns, one penny!"

Groups were gathered in small circles, singing the hymns. Furnival recognised one of the women whom he had seen at Newgate, though she did not notice him. She had been out of prison for more than a week, for Harris and Noble had found the two provincials, porters, who had encouraged the women to take the goods so that they themselves could steal more and blame the women. Furnival had spent ten minutes with a tight-lipped merchant who seemed to have had no ulterior motive in charging the women but simply believed the porters' story, and also that anyone who stole should at least be transported for life.

The widening fields revealed several thousands of men and women; and in their midst others were hammering as if preparing a scaffold, but they were in fact making a rostrum strong enough to bear Wesley, and barriers to keep back the press of the crowd.

Sebastian Smith was amongst them, leading a group in singing, while the hymn sheets were being offered by eager-faced young people in vivid contrast to the harridans who had sold copies of Jonathan Wild's and Frederick Jackson's fabled last speeches from the gallows.

Thinner crowds were coming from the countryside and from the village of St. Marylebone, even some from Cavendish Square, as the coachman turned his pair along narrow, rutted side streets, with children playing in the open sewers.

Only five minutes away was Great Furnival Square, as remote from squalor as any place could be; called by many the most clean-smelling group of buildings in London, with a sewer system which carried wastes to distant fields, even with the newfangled water closets at ground floor and second floor level. Furnival thought of this as his coach drew up outside Number 17, Cleo's home. Before long he was going to be told that his family were in advance of any other in creating good, healthy living conditions for their workers, in taking care of them in times of adversity. He was going to be told that the patriarchal system developed by the Furnivals and many others served not only London but England best, for it kept all Englishmen free.

With short, dark, aquiline-featured Cleo on one side, in a gown of rich green, and tall, fair Sarah on the other, regal in a gown of ice-blue, which was drawn off her beautiful shoulders, John Furnival reached the head of the grand staircase and, arms linked, all three looked down on a scene almost as glittering as a ball by night. Outside, the day was full of sunlight, but there were no windows in this great circular hall, only doors leading to elegant rooms. All of these held tall windows but each door was now closed.

The huge glass chandeliers were glittering; the thousand candles, despite their flickering, gave a soft light which flattered both men and women, young and old. Although there must have been at least fifty people on the marble floor, with its signs of the zodiac inlaid with semiprecious stones, the hall seemed sparsely filled. Liveried servants stood at damask-covered tables with French wines, port and Spanish sherry, and even coffee and tea for those who preferred them. There were sweetmeats on one table, savouries on another, specialties like Cornish pasties, and *pâté de foie gras*, tiny sausages, ham rolled about asparagus tips; and game and hog pies for those who felt they needed heavier fare before dinner, which would be served by four o'clock in the main dining room behind the staircase.

Descending slowly, John Furnival picked out many of his relatives and family associates, some of whom he had not seen for years. It was strange, perhaps, that Francis, so exquisite of face and misshapen of figure, should be the most outstanding. Deborah, his wife, was with him, a thick-set mannish-looking woman. With them was Robert Yeoman, recently re-elected Member of Parliament for one of the seats of the City of London. An erect, hook-nosed man who could be taken in passing for the Duke of Gilhampton and was vain enough to want to be, he was a shrewd and calculating politician, Tory or Whig when it best suited him, who did not hesitate to speak up and vote against a government measure if it appeared to be against the Furnival interest. Cleo, his wife, took little outward interest in politics but carried out her social duties with ease.

With Yeoman was Martin Montmorency, one of the Members for the City of Westminster, and his elegant, laughing, beautiful French wife, in rich blue; when he had married her, Montmorency had taken one of the few risks in his career: of losing favour because he was married to a woman from a country for which few Englishmen had much respect.

There also was portly Jeremy Siddle, Member for St. Albans and a Furnival spokesman in the House, who was so red in the face he looked likely to collapse with apoplexy any moment. His wife was an Englishwoman of elegance but little other distinction. William Furnival, more elegant in pale green and a longer peruke than most, was talking earnestly with a group of men, all distant relatives by blood or by marriage and all with a share and an activity in the Furnival enterprise. Aldermen of the City of London and bankers, including a director of the Bank of England, great merchants, shipowners, men from Lloyds and other insurance houses, all were present with their ladies. Furnival realised at the first sweeping glance that his brothers had kept their promise in spirit as well as letter; here were the senior members of the family, with hardly a youth or a girl among them. He was to be taken seriously, and this was a measure of how much they wanted him back among them.

It was ten years since he had left all the boards, retaining only a few shares, for his own wealth had seemed fully sufficient for his need. Most years he visited here for Christmas, but seldom more often.

Cleo looked up at him as they neared the foot of the stairs and said, "You appear to be very stern, John. Do you know that even those who pretend to be indifferent are looking at you?"

"At you and Sarah, my dear," Furnival riposted. "The men in envy and half the women in malice, I'll be bound."

"How terrible it must be to be so often right." Sarah sighed and squeezed his arm. "John—"

"John—" began Cleo.

"What advice are my sisters going to give me?" asked Furnival.

"John," repeated Cleo, "you will speak with reason, won't you? You won't damn them all without giving them a hearing?"

"I shall speak with reason," Furnival assured her. "Who knows, I may wish to come back into the fold so much that I will even plead with them!"

He was aware of both women staring at him as if hoping that he meant what he said, then of William and Francis and their wives gathered near the foot of the stairs to welcome him, and his sister Anne, alone, telling him that Jason Gilroy was on one of his interminable journeys overseas. On that instant he was gripped by hand and arm and shoulder, his cheeks were brushed with warm, soft lips, and he was drawn to a dozen ample bosoms and as many that looked deprived despite their dressmakers. He was assailed by delicate perfumes and powders, the powerful odour of snuff freshly taken, of cigar smoke heavy on the breath of many men and of rum and port on the breath of others. He felt as he had never expected to feel here: like a prodigal son returning. Mellowed, he was told this piece of news and that piece of gossip and yet another of scandal. He was showered with invitations to dine, to attend home *soirées* and recitals. Even Handel, still in London and about to give a series of concerts, was offered as bait. The wives of the Members of Parliament, peers and men from the City of London were, according to their nature, insistent or effusive. No man during the first half hour spoke more than a courteous sentence or two. John Furnival went to the buffet with Francis' wife, Deborah, and with Anne, a delicate-looking woman with fine blue eyes in a heart-shaped face.

"Don't eat too much before you talk," advised Deborah, "or you will hiccup and that will spoil the effect of what you are to say."

"So I am to lecture, not simply talk to you one by one?"

"John," Anne said, "they all want you back. They still miss you, and every man concerned with Furnival's knows that you are the natural leader. Your presence will give the name even greater stature and—"

"They want me off the bench at Bow Street, where the stature of the name shrinks!"

"Fie, cynic!" scoffed Deborah.

"They would do a great many things to get you away from Bow Street," Anne agreed soberly. "But they know that they must listen to what you have to say and create the best circumstances for you to say it. Everyone present is a shareholder in one Furnival company or another, or in a company closely allied to us, and everyone will—"

"One or two of the women may decide it is not for them to listen or discuss, but to follow their husbands blindly," Deborah interrupted.

"True indeed," said Anne. Furnival was acutely aware of her fine eyes as she went on, and in his mind she rose greatly in stature while Deborah seemed to fade. "But most will come if only out of curiosity, some even"—her eyes glinted—"just to look on Handsome John! They will be with you in the library," she went on. "Enough chairs and couches have been placed there."

"My request could not have been taken more seriously," Furnival agreed.

"I tell you, John, there is not one among us who does not want you back," declared Anne. She took his hands and spoke as earnestly as anyone could. "Please, *please* come." She rose on her toes and kissed his cheek, then rested her fingers on the back of his hand.

"Francis is coming for you," she said. "John, what *is* it you want? If they can possibly give it to you, they will."

John Furnival looked down on her and smiled, gravely but with unmistakable affection. He was aware of Francis, approaching slowly, and knew that he had only a moment left. His smile broadened and he made a rare gesture, bending down and brushing her forehead with his lips.

"What I want is a change of heart," he said. "If they can give me that the rest will follow."

She gripped his hands so tightly that her rings hurt his fingers and he judged from her expression that she did not believe that he would be able to get that change of heart. Next moment Francis was by their side; a waiter came up and was waved away.

Anne and Deborah turned to mix with the others, and Francis said, "You and I will go into the library by the secondary door, John. If you wish you can wash in the closet before you go in."

John Furnival had first entered the library about thirty years ago by this same door when his grandfather, the first John Furnival, had sat at the huge carved oak desk, soon after the house had been formally opened and the families in Great Furnival Square had taken up residence. He, the young John, had been fascinated by the masses of books which rose from floor to ceiling and by the beautifully carved twisting oaken staircase to the gallery, from which one reached one section of the shelves. There had been few changes. Two walls were solid with leather-bound books and there were more on either side of the great fireplace.

Those who entered the library by the secondary door found themselves on a platform raised some eighteen inches above the wooden-block floor, from which one could see and be seen while speaking.

John Furnival stood on this platform now.

Every chair, every stool, every couch, was occupied; the fifty or so people who had seemed so sparse in the hall now crammed the room so that there could hardly be space for another half dozen. Husbands and wives sat apart, men on one side, women on the other, and the Members of Parliament and the men from the City of London were grouped together as if they felt they would be in need of protection.

A babble of talk had stopped as Francis entered and held the door open for his brother. They made a strange contrast, one so frail, the other so massive, but the disparity faded as Francis smiled and raised his hands as a priest might in a blessing.

"I don't really know whether we're going to hear a sermon or a political speech," he began, and was forced to stop as laughter, starting slowly, drowned his words. He allowed it to die away naturally, then looked around and up at his brother and added: "Or a boxing match."

Once again came a roar of laughter, and John Furnival found it easy to join in, glad that Francis was relaxed and amusing; this was the best side of his brother.

The others soon settled and Francis went on, still in a light tone but with obvious seriousness.

"No one could be more pleased to see him here than I—"

There was a chorus of agreement but John Furnival noticed little came from the solid phalanx of politicians and financiers and merchants. Could they have come to oppose for the sake of opposing?

"And I'm very glad that I am the host and he is not—"

A woman cried, "He means he's glad we're not at Bow Street!"

The phalanx of men relaxed into smiles this time, and John looked appreciatively at his brother, who was creating the most receptive atmosphere possible. Francis smiled back at him.

"I have no idea what he has to talk about; I only know that there has at last been a crack in that granite-hard mind of his, and he thinks there is a way by which he could rejoin us in our multifarious activities. I cannot imagine any prospect more to be desired."

Francis sat down on a monk's stool obviously placed in position for him, and John Furnival moved to the center of the platform. He knew exactly what he wanted to say and was adept in varying the way he spoke to fit the mood of a meeting. There was some applause, mostly from the women, as he looked about him.

"Why on earth you should want me when you have Francis—" he began, and immediately was drowned by a burst of applause. In a way this was a political meeting, and feelings were aroused much more than he would have thought possible. But the City group, though smiling, was still wary; and it was they, with his brothers and their sons, who would make the decisions. As the noise died down he went on more gravely. "I doubt that many of you present really understand why I left the—ah—bosom of my family and went to Bow Street, although the reason was simple and may be clearly apparent. I believe in the law, not a law merely for those who can afford it, not a law which a man can break with impunity if he has enough money to buy his freedom from prison or the hangman's rope, but a law free from corruption and indeed incorruptible, as rigid for the rich as for the poor, a protection for the poor who cannot buy protection for themselves. I went to Bow Street as chief magistrate and later became a justice of the peace for Westminster and the County of Middlesex in the faith that I could create—or at the very least help to create—such a law not only in London but throughout the land. I could do what few others could: pay for reliable men to serve Bow Street and the law. I could and did afford to pay each man enough money so that he did not need, for his stomach's sake, to accept bribes or depend on a share of the blood money. So they were able to be thief-takers, not thief-makers."

For the first time, he paused. There was not a sound in the room and not an eye was turned away from him; it was as if all those present had stopped breathing. He looked from one side to the other without focusing his gaze on anyone before going on.

"I was able, also, to pay constables in some parishes, or those hired by constables to do their work, money enough to keep them—or most of them—from temptation."

"There is no such thing as an incorruptible man," a member of the City group rasped. "Men are wholly trustworthy only when they are watched." The speaker, a lantern-jawed man with a heavy mustache and mutton-chop whiskers, was Cornelius Hooper, the husband of a sister of Sarah's husband and one of the wealthiest merchants in the City, with shares in most great banks and companies. Wherever the Furnivals married, they made sure of strengthening their position and gaining support for their policies.

Furnival heard him out and for the first time felt a stirring of anger, but he suppressed it and actually smiled as he said acidly, "I have at least twenty retainers whom I would trust with my life and my possessions, Mr. Hooper. I am sorry that your philosophy has made you less fortunate. Now if I may proceed?" No one interrupted and he went on: "Thank you. Taking as a guide a count over six months at all the magistrates' courts in the two cities and the counties, however, for every reliable constable employed by the parishes there are at least fifty men who call themselves thief-takers. These men will falsify evidence, perhaps themselves accept bribes, falsely accuse the innocent, all for the sake of their share of the government reward paid to every thief-taker for a conviction. If this were not bad enough, for every magistrate with a court and court officials, such as at Bow Street, there are twenty trading justices. These hold court in taverns and alehouses, yes, and even in brothels, and commit men to Newgate and other abominable jails on evidence they know to be false simply for their share of the reward." He paused as several of the women drew in their breath, and then went on with great deliberation. "It is not justice, it is a prostitution of justice. When you see a Hogarth picture of the people of London you see many as they really are, not—"

"I must protest!" Hooper interrupted. "Hogarth seeks out the drunken lechers and the gin-sodden who present nothing but the filth in which they live. Nine citizens of London out of ten, aye, ninety-nine citizens out of a hundred are decent and respectable. You'll do no good making the situation out to be worse than it is."

"If there is to remain a London it cannot become any worse than it is," Furnival retorted. "Because you keep the crime at a distance from you by employing a strong and well-paid force of private peace officers, you will not be able to hold it back forever, any more than by having water closets and sewers here at Great Furnival Square and at Furnival Tower House you can keep the stench of open sewers and open cesspits away when the wind carries it from outside your walls. You may carry the waste to fields and keep it from the Thames and the Tyburn, but others don't, and they befoul the air you have to breathe. So the crime in the rest of London befouls the House of Furnival and all those like it. It is useless to be farsighted if all you can see is a brick wall."

He stopped, glaring at Hooper. Robert Yeoman put a restraining hand on Hooper's arm, and, without getting up, Francis spoke in his bell-like voice, "Brother John, if you could continue uninterrupted for—for a while—not too long," he added, smiling, "would you answer any questions afterward?"

"Yes," barked Furnival.

"Then I shall be absorbed in what you have to say—and fascinated to find out what you want us to do."

"So shall I," growled Hooper.

Furnival was aware of Anne watching him intently, and her expression suggested that she was pleading with him to keep the peace, to avoid an open quarrel. That was right, of course, and what he had to do, but it was far from easy.

"Telling you what I want is simple, but only useful if you see the need to support me," he said. "We have in this huge city and its close environs three quarters of a million people, more, perhaps, than are gathered in any other area in the world except possibly the capital cities of China and Japan. Among these in the metropolis of London we have an estimated one hundred and fifteen thousand people who live on the proceeds of crime. We have a small, exclusive number of very rich people who live better than they could anywhere in the world since London has long since been the greatest port for the importation of exotic foods and spices in the Western Hemisphere. We have—and you will see how little we have changed since Defoe's figure of 1720—about one hundred and fifty thousand people of middling income, who, if they work hard, can eat and clothe themselves and their families well; and we have more than five hundred and fifty thousand who can barely earn a living, who are hungry most of the time. This is the breeding ground of our drunkards and our criminals. It exists. And we have to clean it up just as we have to clean up our streets and our sewers and our rivers. The Act of 1737 demanded half as many watch boxes as there were watchmen, so that each parish area should have one watchman patrolling and one at a box. But there are neither the required number of boxes nor the required number of watchmen. Only the old and frail and useless will do such work—or pretend to—for five shillings a week. This is a mockery of protection as the trading justices are a mockery of justice."

He drew a deep breath, and expected another interruption, but no one spoke and he sensed a tension which now touched them all. He was quite sure that to many of the women the figures he quoted came as a shock, which was why he had wanted them here.

At last he went on with great deliberation.

"There is only one way: a strong peace force, as I would call it, paid not by individuals who can afford to protect themselves and devil take the others, nor by parishes, which avoid paying every penny they can, but by the government." He went a step closer to the edge of the little platform and raised his hands waist high, the first gesture he had made. "If the House of Furnival, with all its influence in Parliament, with the King and with wealthy merchants and the guilds, will commit itself to fighting for such a professional force, I will resign from Bow Street and devote myself to all the affairs of the Furnival enterprises.

"I ask for no money, no charitable foundations, no work for other good causes, but simply for this.

"For if we prosper out of the sickness and the poverty, the hunger and the desperation of the mass of the people, the time will come when there will be a terrible reckoning."

When Furnival stopped, the silence was even more profound; none among the City group stirred; everyone was watching him as if expecting more. Yet without repeating himself there was nothing more to say. His mouth was dry and he was sweating at the forehead and the neck although he did not know whether anyone else was aware of that. He expected Hooper or one of his group to speak but it was Robert Yeoman, sitting behind them but not one of them, who rose to his feet, and standing against a well of books, he looked more elegant than among the crowd. He placed a pinch of snuff on the back of his hand, sniffed up each nostril in turn, and then said, "Most eloquent, John; never heard such eloquence. You belong at Westminster or in the Bishop's Palace. Such sentiments do you credit, great credit. At the beginning you told me that you are what you are because you believe in people. 'Tis not for me to argue with you about how many people are in the mob or whether they could improve themselves by hard work or endeavour. That can be a matter of opinion and no doubt always will be. But it is for me to tell you, John, that anyone who tried to persuade Walpole to create such a peace force would be wasting his time. Walpole will have none of it, nor will the King. Cromwell tried it and left scars enough. A peace force is an army used against the people, John; these people you say you wish to help and protect. An army, I say, in England, to be used against the people day in and day out, not simply at times of riot and disturbance or to keep order on hanging days. You forget one thing, John. You forget that before their possessions, before the sanctity of their homes, aye, and even before their families, Englishmen love freedom. The worst of them, the lowest of them, the murderers and thieves who will hang at Tyburn or Tower Hill, would call for freedom with his dying breath. And you would have their streets patrolled by armed men. You would ravage the sanctity of their homes by sending soldiers to search and pry. Who could believe that a man's wife and daughters would ever be safe if troops patrolled—"

"May I inquire," interrupted Furnival coldly, "whether you are speaking for the King, for Walpole, for the people, or for yourself?"

"As God is my witness, for all four!"

"May I say a few words?" Plump-faced Martin Montmorency stood up, and Yeoman immediately gave way to him, as no doubt he would on a day when the House of Commons was behaving courteously.

Furnival felt quite sure what had been planned: that each man should speak in turn, opposing whatever they felt he would propose, if they were of a mind, showing the rest of the family that opposition was not from one but from several men with different interests and different causes for loyalty to the House of Furnival. It was as if witness after witness were standing up to give evidence on behalf of a rogue they knew to be guilty, hoping to impress by weight of numbers even if they could not do so by fact.

Montmorency had a plummy voice, a countryman's voice upon which a London or Westminster accent had been imposed, but he spoke to the point. "I have to agree with John about the shameful conditions among some classes and parts of London. I have to agree with him that much needs doing. But I strongly oppose the concept of a peace force as un-English—un-*British*, I will say. I concede that it might be practicable for those of us who employ private guards— I can only say *might*; it is a situation which should be explored—to find a way to work together so that in wards and parishes we might spread our canopy of security over the less fortunate. I will myself recommend such an investigation. But a peace force paid by the government—no, sir, never. Over my dead body—"

"And well it might be," Furnival said roughly.

"You exaggerate, John, and I am sure I may use a colourful figure of speech!"

"If I may interpose—" This time it was Jeremy Siddle who stood up, several places away. Gracefully, Montmorency lowered himself snugly into a chair, and had Furnival needed confirmation of the "opposition plot" he had it now. "There are aspects of the situation in our fair city which you overlook, John. There is much that is good here, if also much that needs doing. One thing, as my colleague Robert Yeoman said, is to teach the people the benefits of honest toil. Another is to improve living conditions. You talk of the sewers, of the living conditions of the House of Furnival, as if they were bad because they do not improve the condition of others as fast as you would like them to. But they are an example to others and an example to the government. Here is a way in which we could, and I truly believe should, try to improve our beloved London. We can work ceaselessly in Parliament and in the City of London until great public works, not only of new sewers—we are not *rats*, John—but of new highways and improved roads, and a water supply purified and brought closer to the houses of the people so that they do not need to carry it so far, are undertaken.

"And we need not one but two, even three, new bridges across the Thames. It is a disastrous situation when London is the only bridge on which to cross, crowding the river dangerously with small row-

142

boats and with ferryboats, a great danger to shipping. There is more, much more. London has become the greatest port in the world, as well as in all Britain: more than three-quarters of our trade with the Empire and with nations overseas goes through the Port of London, but it is now so crowded that there is too little space to load and unload in a reasonable time. We need twice as much dock space as we have.

"No, John Furnival. We do not want to restrict the rights of the people.

"The House of Furnival has more vital work to do: to use its influence in Parliament to get great projects into being and to help to finance such undertakings as will give more employment while making our magnificent city the greatest in the world."

Siddle bowed in all directions and sat down to a loud and prolonged burst of applause which was certainly spontaneous. Furnival, who had taken in everything Siddle had said, and even admired its cleverness and the indisputable truth of much of it, was at first angry, then quite calm. There was no hope at all for support for his proposals and it would be useless to try to find it; wise only to accept defeat without worsening the situation between himself and the rest of the family. Was Anne pleading again? Was Cleo deliberately avoiding his eyes and Sarah only pretending that her nose tickled?

He did not know what made him glance up but for the first time he saw four or five of the younger members, nieces and nephews, sitting in the gallery above the doorway. He smiled at them as he rose to an uneasy silence and his smile seemed to ease the tension.

"Not in my lifetime, not in the lifetime of all these unimaginative old fogies down here—I mean really old people, like your uncles, Timothy!" This brought a chuckle from many and delighted the youths and made Sarah, mother of Timothy, stop worrying her nose with a tiny lace handkerchief. "But in your time, the life of all of you in the gallery, there will be a peace force here in the metropolis of London. It will not be an army, it may not even be armed, but"— John looked down from the gallery and to the assembly, now happy because obviously there was going to be no storm of temper, no bitter recriminations—"between now and the day when it comes, much unnecessary harm will have befallen London and the whole of England because we have no organised peace-keeping force to see that the law is carried out."

He paused, then gave a great bellow of a laugh before going on:

"Nothing is going to force me into the House of Furnival, either, but if you don't do all those fine things Jerry Siddle has promised in your names, I'll haunt you with ghosts of the thousands who will die and the tens of thousands who will be driven to crime because of your failure."

And he sat down. He did not know what caused them but the pressures at his chest and beneath his jaw came upon him suddenly, and for a few minutes he could only sit there unmoving. Mercifully, no one approached until the pain began to ease.

"We would still like you back," William said when the men were alone in the dining room after dinner, the great room a blue-gray haze of tobacco smoke, as port, sack and cognac were being passed around. "We really want the same thing, John."

"There can be no doubt of that," said Francis. "Come back, John."

"No," replied Furnival quietly. "We should forever be in conflict over priorities and I would be forever convinced that I should be working for one thing and one thing only. Profit. I can't get help from you, but there must be others who think as I do."

"I can tell you one such." Robert Yeoman, close enough to overhear, joined them.

"And who is he?" asked Furnival, surprised.

"Henry Fielding," answered Yeoman. "Yes, the playwright who lost his Little Theatre in the Haymarket for his lampooning of our distinguished Minister of State and members of his Cabinet. There is little doubt that the closing down of all theaters except those licensed by the Lord Chamberlain was really to crush him."

"Surely with success," remarked Furnival, remembering what Gentian had said in the coffee house. "Didn't Fielding dismiss his company and give up without a fight?"

"He's no coward," Yeoman declared, "but you can't defeat King and Parliament. He has studied for the bar. He may make a good lawyer, and he certainly has no time for trading justices—"

"I saw his *Debauchees* and his *Justice Squeezum*," Furnival interrupted. "I will keep an eye open for him."

"You may find him at your court, John! As for your present notion, I doubt if any Member of Parliament will support you. But as London grows larger and the problem of population grows greater, then one day something may have to be done about it. You're ahead of your time, that's the truth of it."

144

Furnival gave a throaty laugh.

"And I'm two hundred years behind the need," he retorted. "At all events, thank you for the information about Fielding. I'll be grateful for any other names of people who may take a sympathetic view."

"That we can prepare," William promised. "And we will."

Rising from the table, they went out into the garden and relieved themselves in a long covered shed which had a porcelain barrier to prevent them from splashing their shoes and stockings with a mixture of mud and urine; the waste was washed into the sewer from here by men tossing buckets of water at one end. They strolled about the grounds for a while afterwards to drive the smell of smoke out of their clothes and hair, and were sprayed by footmen with eau de cologne so that when they went back to the salon to join the ladies there was hardly a whiff of tobacco and little of the male sweat some men always carried. Furnival was anxious to leave, now; but to have gone before dinner would have been churlish, and both William and Yeoman had shown that at least he had moved them to gestures if nothing more. The need he saw was so glaringly obvious that he could not believe that intelligent men would hold out indefinitely. They must eventually realise that unless the city was safe for all, the time would come when it would not be safe for them without a strong guard.

Three of the children were playing a Bach concerto on a harpsichord and violins, a piece which was the rage since it had come to England from Leipzig only a year before. They were much more proficient than Furnival would have expected. He heard this out and joined in the clapping, then sought out his sisters and sisters-in-law to bid his adieus. He could not find Anne, and was sorry, feeling that she understood what drove him more than any of the others. William went with him to the front door.

"Will, tell me this," he said slowly. "Were the defenders prepared so well because they knew in advance that I was going to ask for their help in creating a peace force?"

"They knew it would be something to do with law officers or Bow Street, and Siddle has Walpole's ear. Walpole told him you had petitioned for peace officers to be employed by Bow Street and paid by the court, and the newspapers talked of your endeavour recently. So adding two and two together wasn't difficult."

"No," agreed Furnival, in a voice edged with bitterness. "I was defeated before I began to speak."

"John," William said as they stood on the porch and looked into the square, which was bathed in a pink-and-mauve afterglow of quite rare beauty, "if we had agreed to help we would have got nowhere, and we would have damaged what influence we have. We have a lot, you know. If we put money into a bridge or new docks or a new water supply from the country, not out of the Thames, other money soon flows. On at least three occasions we have led the way and the directors of the Bank of England have followed. If we espouse the wrong cause we can do much harm to other causes which are equally worthy."

"I suppose so, I suppose so," Furnival said, a touch of despondency in his voice. "What no one seems to understand is that it won't serve London if a bridge is put over the Thames at Westminster and thieves can escape more easily with their loot. It won't help trade if you build more new docks and the dock workers and the dock owners vie with each other to cheat and steal. It won't—but no matter, Will. I meant what I said to young Timothy!"

He shook his brother's hand and strode down to his coach, already waiting, with a footman at the door and the young coachman in his seat, the two bays tossing their heads. As he put a foot on the step and gripped one side to haul himself in, he was aware of a woman sitting in a corner, and she uttered a low-pitched "Husssh." So he did not cry out or back down, and as he sat, his heart lifted as he recognised Anne.

"Forgive me," Anne said, "but I wanted to talk to you without the others and there was no way at the house."

Furnival sat by her side and took her gloved hand.

"You make me feel like an eloping lover," he declared. "And damme if I don't wish I were!" He kissed her cheek, and there was enough light for him to see her flush of pleasure. "Do you want us to start?" At her affirmative nod, he pressed the horn for the coachman to hear and immediately the horses began to move. "What is so secret, Anne?"

"The others don't want you to know this because they think it might excite you and make you talk about it. They don't realise that not all Furnivals are fools!" She covered his hand with hers, and he could see and was touched by the brightness of her eyes. "John, you have more sympathisers than you think. Walpole is adamant but he won't always be First Minister, and the King, who doesn't dislike the idea of an army of peace officers in the way Walpole does, might have more power over his next! I know it will take time and you are desperately impatient, but there are things you can do to quicken the pace. I shall prepare, with Will, a list of influential people to whom you should write, inviting their interest, and, if it suits you, you could send your missive together with a printed copy of your speech today, and what followed."

"There is no such copy!" Furnival objected.

"There will be if you will be so good as to read it and make the corrections you wish," Anne told him. "Behind you in the gallery was a Mr. Letchworth, who has developed a new form of quick writing in which he puts down the essential words of a sentence and links them with strange symbols I do not understand. He will prepare a complete rendering, he promises me, in three days." Before Furnival could interrupt and while the radiance was still on his face, she went on: "You made a wonderful case, and if you insert some more facts and figures it will be brilliantly convincing. The presentations of what the others said will show exactly what kind of opposition you are facing. Tell me this is a great help, John."

"I declare it to be more help than I have ever received from another human being," John Furnival said huskily. "And I include those who have died trying to do what I have told them and they believed to be right."

He held her tightly, then sat back, gripping her hand. He could not really believe it but tears squeezed themselves beneath his eyelids; he could not remember the time when he had last cried.

"Will you come in, Anne?" asked Furnival as the carriage turned into Bow Street.

"No, John, I must be back before I am missed. Come and see me, soon. *Please.*"

"Anne, I would be greatly honoured if you would bring me this exposition in person," said Furnival. "And if it is good I would like to meet this Mr. Letchworth. He might be of great service in proving how often a man perjures himself in contradiction in my court." He backed out as the door was opened by Godden, kissed Anne's hand and stood to watch her go.

147

CHAPTER *10*

New Life

IT WAS A woman, Ruth told herself, I know it was a woman. Then aloud and angrily: "And why not, pray? Do you expect him to change his whole way of living for an innocent like me? He can have as many women and as many mistresses as he wishes, from Lisa Braidley down to—"

She could not bring herself to say "me."

She was in the big room upstairs where she had been stoking the fire in case he chose to sit there rather than in the room below, and had heard the carriage out of the window. All she had seen was the way he had bent low over a hand—and whose hand would it be but a woman's?

She heard the men downstairs speak, heard his voice. Three prisoners were awaiting a hearing, Sunday or no Sunday, two of them for robbery with violence, the third charged with assaulting a curate who had been handing out hymn sheets at John Wesley's meeting at Spitalfields. She had wished he could avoid the court but knew that he could not. She heard him walk along to the back room downstairs, which in a strange way had become their room, although she had shared his bed only on that one night. Since then, however, she had sensed a deeper affection, had felt that he wanted her and had been content. She had thought of Lisa Braidley and of his many "loves" and had persuaded herself that these were a part of him different from the part which had become hers. She had known about them long enough, goodness knew! Why, she and Richard had laughed about them when he had described their appearance and their imagined charms.

Now, Richard was so far away in her mind, in some ways almost as if he had never been.

But he had been, and but for him she would not be living here in this great comfort, with James at the School for Young Men and her two daughters fed and clothed better than they had ever been, and looked after much of the time by Meg Fairweather, who was virtually a grandmother to them. The Fairweathers shared a cottage next door with Joe Godden, who was long since a widower. Everything in her present life stemmed from Richard's love for John Furnival and Furnival's affection for him. She could even remember the time when she had been jealous of John Furnival, for Richard had hero-worshipped him and had spent so much time working, hunting criminals down, and so little time even at night with her.

Now she was jealous of a hand she had glimpsed.

"It cannot be so," she said clearly. And then with great determination: "It must not be."

She sensed rather than reasoned that if she allowed herself to be jealous she might ruin the comfort she had, might rob herself of the daily grace of helping him, might make him reject her. It was madness. If she felt any twinges of jealousy she must overcome them within herself as well as never show the slightest sign of them to John.

John.

His voice sounded and she caught the words: "Where is Ruth?"

Godden answered, "She is in the library, sir, no doubt tidying."

"Room doesn't want tidying," Furnival growled. "I want tea in the back room before I go and hear those accused."

Ruth came hurrying down, not smiling but relaxed and comforted. She said, "The kettle is boiling, sir," and slipped past the two men and along to the back room. Furnival glanced at her but did not speak as he went to the bedroom, washed, and kicked off his shoes. By the time he was back the tea was made and she was holding a muffin in front of a warm toasting fire. He sat in his big chair and she rested the fork on an iron fender and held his slippers out for him, kneeling in front of him, and to her great relief her heart was light.

"I'll not need much to eat tonight," he said. "I'm not sure I should eat those muffins, but no doubt I will. Some cheese and perhaps a piece of cold lamb and some coffee at eight o'clock, say. If you want a heartier meal, Ruth, will you eat between now and eight o'clock?" And she nodded, eyes glowing, as he went on: "And will you ask Meg to keep an ear open for your girls tonight?"

Now her heart leaped, for he wanted her here.

"Of course," she said, with a catch in her voice.

He leaned forward and cupped her dark head with one hand, then leaned farther forward and cupped her right breast with the other. They sat like that for several minutes until he smiled and withdrew his hands and she picked up the toasting fork again. Soon they were both spreading more butter onto the muffins.

Ruth, prepared for him to be hungrier than he expected, had a small caldron of pea soup simmering over the fire when he came in, a little after eight o'clock, as well as a wedge of cheese from Wensleydale, a Yorkshire specialty to which he was very partial. She also had homemade bread, and butter which she bought from a stall in Covent Garden, knowing the dairy produce came from a nearby Hampstead farm and the butter, salted as he liked it, was churned fresh daily, while even on the hottest summer day the milk kept fresh in the red earthenware jars in which she stood the metal containers. Afterward there were fruit tarts with whipped cream and, something he had never tasted before, small tarts made of short pastry which melted in the mouth, filled with a deep yellow confection.

He tried one cautiously and his face lit up.

"What have you been doing, keeping this from me?" he demanded. "What is it, lass?"

"Lemon curd," she answered. "My mother's recipe, and one I have not used for a long time."

"In future, at least once a week," he urged, taking another and then another. "With this I could even make my sisters envious!" He had never before mentioned his family to her, and had said not a word about what had happened that day. He drank more coffee and then patted his heavy stomach. "Now I've eaten too much," he declared. "You'll have to discipline me, Ruth."

"Is there any man or woman who could?" she asked meekly.

He laughed. "I know one who could discipline you!" She was reaching out to collect the crockery, but he stayed her with a hand at her waist. "Leave all this and come and sit on a stool by me."

She obeyed, and after pulling the table farther from the fire, she shifted the stool and he the chair so that she could sit against him and he could slip his hand beneath her bodice, more for comfort than for play.

After a while he asked, "Forgive me if this is a difficult question, Ruth, but I would like to know. Did Richard talk to you much about his work, and about Bow Street?"

"There were times when I doubt he talked about anything else," she replied.

"Did it weary you?"

She turned her head so that she could see him, and he could see her face, foreshortened, slightly flushed by the glow from the fire.

"Only when it made him forget that I was a woman. And I confess—" She broke off and looked away, doubtful whether she could go on with what she had started to say.

"Confess," he ordered.

"If I must, sir. I confess I blamed you more than him."

"For forgetting you were a woman?" Furnival teased.

"All he was aware of on such nights was Justice of the Peace John Furnival and the crusade for the law." She placed a hand on his, hers outside the bodice. "Does that affront you?"

"It amazes me that any man of any age could ever forget that you are a woman," he declared, and laughed; and she flushed with the pleasure of it and yet felt an edge of shame because they were talking of Richard in a way which many would feel was one of disrespect. "Ruth," Furnival went on, "I've sent all three men charged to Newgate, to await trial, and they will be in that noisome place for at least six weeks before they are tried. Two men are common thieves, and if anyone deserves such a fate, they do. The other is a religious bigot, enraged by John Wesley's preaching at Spitalfields. There should be a different place to send such men who are awaiting trial. There should be . . ."

He began to talk, discursively at first, but gradually a pattern took shape and she could understand what drove this man, what powerful force of human passion was in his head and what cold contempt there was in his mind for those who opposed what he believed to be right.

He told her what had happened that day.

He told her what Anne had promised, so that she learned whose hand he had kissed.

He told her what he had said to Timothy and the other youths who had been present.

After a long while he stopped talking and she thought he had fallen asleep, so she freed herself with great care and slowly and cautiously moved the table toward the door and into the passage, then went back and sat in a chair opposite him, studying the strength of his jaw, the shapeliness of his lips, the breadth of his forehead. A "bull of a man" Tom Harris had called him but he was much more than that: a giant of a man. He did not look as tired as he had but he must be tired to drop off to sleep so quickly. Some coals fell in the grate and she got up to move them so there would be no risk of their falling on wooden floor or carpet, and as she turned around he opened his great arms and trapped her, pushed her bodice down with his chin and kissed her bosom, then lifted her as he rose from the chair and without a word carried her across to the sleeping alcove. He placed her gently on the bed, looked down on her, and then began to untie the tapes of her dress.

There was ecstasy and frenzy, there was warm comfort and contentment. It was as if this had always been and would remain forever. Her one anxiety was that he breathed so hard, afterward—but he did not speak of it. The peace was soon shattered, for there was a knocking at the door which she heard first; a knocking which did not stop. She eased herself to the foot of the bed and over the foot panel and wrapped a cloak around her as she went to the door. "Who is there?" she called, and immediately fears for the children surged over her.

" 'Tis Tom Harris," was the reply. "And no matter how deep his sleep I must see the justice."

She opened the door to see Tom's big shoulders against the yellow light from the oil lamps and candles.

"Come in, Tom, and I'll call him," she said. "What is it that's so important?"

"I've something for his ears alone," Harris said.

When she reached the sleeping alcove Furnival was sitting up, and she brought a candle guttering in its stick and told him what Tom had said. His hair was ruffled and he had nothing on but the sheet up to his waist, so she helped him on with his nightshirt, in no way harassed by his urging her to hurry. Before she had finished pulling it down to his buttocks, he called, "Come in, man, come in! What are you behaving like a virgin for?"

"I've news you'll thank me for waking you to hear," said Harris, and excitement made his voice quiver. "You'll never believe it, sir. Mr. Martin Montmorency was waylaid by a highwayman on his way home from Great Furnival Square tonight, on the outskirts of Westminster, and was robbed of his purse, containing thirty guineas, and his gold-topped cane. And his wife was stripped of her jewelry, valued at over a thousand pounds."

Harris paused. Furnival stared up at him with a strange expression on his face and his lips pursed, as if he were fighting to keep words back.

"And that is not all," Harris went on, his voice still quivering, and it seemed to Ruth that he was trying to keep back laughter. Why should such a thing amuse him? "The house of Mr. Cornelius Hooper was broken into while he was out this afternoon, his guards were attacked, and all his gold and silver plate was stolen."

Furnival exploded with laughter. Harris, reassured, slapped his great hands on his stomach and rolled as if this were the best joke he had heard in many years. For a while their laughter was the only sound in the room, as Ruth moved slowly, placing small coals on the embers of the fire; they might catch without the need for kindling.

At last John Furnival said, "And I'll wager you'd had a report on what went on this afternoon."

"Aye, sir—from one of the footmen."

"The man should be dismissed for gossiping, so whatever you do, Tom, don't remember his name." Furnival gave another snort of a laugh but when he went on he was wholly earnest. "Now we've had our fun. Send out every man we have here and find out the name of the highwayman; I want him in irons by morning. If you have to pay to loosen some rascal's tongue, pay what you must but make sure you get the truth. When we've caught him, and only then, see what you can find out about Hooper's silver and gold plate. It's probably on its way out of London by now; no one would steal such unwieldy valuables unless he had a ready market. If you can't get word on it soon, let me know. Hooper will be hearing from a thief-taker soon and he'll do a deal for the recovery of the plate rather than let it be known publicly that he was robbed." Furnival gave a great spurt of laughter again. "But we could tell *The Daily Courant* of the unfortunate episode, couldn't we?"

"Aye, we could spring a leak," Harris said, and he too was shaking with laughter when he went out.

"Ruth," Furnival said, "I think I'm too wide awake to sleep. You get to bed and I'll read for a while." He chuckled. "My, my! I would have given a fortune to have seen their faces and to have asked them whether they'd like a peace force now." He slid out of the deep feather bed, and as he stood up his mood changed and he looked down on her, frowning. "Highwaymen at the gates of the city. The two miles between here and Westminster are infested with them. It's no laughing matter, Ruth, no laughing matter at all."

For some reason that she didn't understand, she began to laugh at him.

Tom Harris and a young constable named Brown were back in triumph within two hours, with the highwayman who had robbed the Montmorencys manacled between them. They had found him in the Old Cock Tavern, next door to Charlie Wylie's brothel in the Strand, gambling his loot away on a cockfight. They had two witnesses ready to swear his life away.

From the bench, wearing a long cloak over his nightgown, John Furnival said, "You must be made a lesson and a warning that our highways must be kept free for honest travelers, and I shall send you for trial at the next Session. Before your trial you shall be lodged in Fleet Prison."

The highwayman, a fair-haired youth in his early twenties, actually shivered before he was taken away. For the Fleet, in many ways, was worse than Newgate.

In the middle of Thursday morning, a cold and blustery day with leaden skies reminiscent of winter's snow, Anne Gilroy came.

Her first message was a greeting from his brothers and congratulations on the capture of the highwayman; her second to pass on a report that Hooper, whose gold and silver plate was still missing, was at his surliest with his business associates.

"He will be a hard man to convert," Furnival said. "Those who believe in man's inevitable evil and greed always are. Now! Do you have the renderings?"

"Mr. Letchworth calls them extensions," she said. She handed him a sheaf of papers containing all that had been spoken in public on the previous Sunday, with some additions which, an explanatory note in exquisite penmanship said, had been gleaned from the private conversations which had taken place afterward. The general tenor of these was that no matter how bad the crime situation might be, an organised professional peace force paid by the State would cause more crime, rioting and anger and would have serious repercussions.

"Will you have some tea while I read this?" Furnival asked. They were upstairs in the study.

"I would rather go downstairs and see Silas Moffat and some of your men whom I know," Anne replied. "I will come back as soon as you call for me." She went out without giving him time to protest.

Furnival heard Moffat speak, and then lost himself in what he read. He was surprised by the conviction in his own words, surprised by the convincing remarks of some of the others, particularly Montmorency. He began to itch to pick up a quill and alter and add to those facts and figures, and when he was through he felt quite sure that this was a most powerful statement of the case both for and against his dream.

He had started reading again when Anne came back.

"I'm sorry," he said quickly. "I had almost forgotten—"

"That I was here!" Anne's blue eyes were at their happiest; even as a child she had been both the most serious and yet the most light-hearted of the family. "Do you think it good?"

"I think it can be improved but basically, yes, very good. There is one thing: It will need at least four pages of print unless the print is to be uncommon small and tedious to read."

"My!" she mocked. "It will be as large as an edition of *The Daily Courant* or the *Dying Confessions of Jonathan Wild!* John, will you work on it, and when you are ready, send it to me for the printing and—"

"I can arrange for the printing," John interrupted.

"Indeed you can. There is nothing the great John Furnival cannot do better than all others except possibly take a little help when it is proffered. John, I would like to bear the expense of this, and Will has told me that he will arrange for its distribution, without comment, to all the family and shareholders of the House of Furnival and associated houses, as well as shareholders of other banks and many merchants in the City. Yeoman will see that it reaches Walpole, as well as some of our more radical Members of Parliament and peers. We cannot yet give you all you want, but this we can do."

"Anne," said Furnival in a helpless way, "Anne, I have never been good at saying 'thank you'—not even to you. But—"

"Good gracious no, don't thank me with words!" she interrupted, her eyes dancing. "Thank me with deeds. Take Silas Moffat and this pleasant Ruth to the country for a few weeks. Silas is nearly seventy-five and he needs a rest even if you don't bother. And you really *do*, you know. I noticed after you spoke to the family that you were exhausted. Take Ruth and her brood to St. Giles Farm, 'tis empty but for the servants, and get them out of this contaminated city before it poisons them!"

"Anne—"

"You have not taken one weekend away from London except on business for ten years," Anne insisted, "and you need a rest."

"Anne," he insisted, "why do you say 'take Ruth'?"

"Because she is good for you," declared Anne. "Why, everyone expected you to have apoplexy last Sunday—we even had Doctor Anson in attendance. But you were so calm it was not natural. So I asked Moffat to explain why, and he explained enough." She paused and then asked in a sharper voice, more intent than before, "Did you know that Timothy was at the School for Young Men near Saint Paul's?"

" 'Pon my soul, I had no idea!"

"Well, your Ruth's son and Sarah's are school companions," Anne said, "and I'm not sure Sarah will approve but I do, John. I would even have James at Great Furnival Square when you were away if you would only go to St. Giles."

"I wish I could," John said regretfully.

"What is there to stop you?" she demanded.

"A task unfinished," he replied.

"Oh, John," she said. "Oh, brother, John, will you kill yourself for your cause?"

"No doubt. As my father and his father killed themselves by over-work and overdrinking for theirs."

"I don't understand—oh! You mean, they killed themselves because they could not rest from making money." She pouted momentarily, and then laughter crept back into her eyes and she went on: "I am not sure whose motive is the better, but I do know my big brother John will kill himself if he doesn't rest more often, and if he kills himself who will fight for his cause?"

"That is what I have to be sure of before I go on to the next world," he said soberly.

"Goodness! You make yourself sound almost serious!"

"Never more so," John Furnival declared. He smiled at her gravely and the mischievousness died away from her eyes as he went on: "Anne, is Silas a sick man?"

"He is an old man, and tired," she said.

"Then I shall send him to St. Giles for a few weeks."

"He would be happier and so would I if you would go with him," Anne declared. "But I won't press you, John." The laughter came again. "I must work on Ruth!"

Furnival found himself chuckling.

He went to Bow Street to see Anne off in her carriage, and as she turned the corner and disappeared, a coach swept around, not only too crowded and too far on one side of the road but also going too fast. Furnival looked with cold anger at the face of the driver of the team of six horses, angry because the man could so nearly have caused an accident to his sister. To his surprise the coach began to slow down, and he went inside, not wishing at that moment to tell the driver what he thought of him. He went to the back room, which was empty, left the door open and so heard the man who came from the coach call out: "I want Judge John Furnival. I have an urgent message for him."

Moffat's voice came quietly in reply, "I can take the message."

"I was told to see him myself," the man grumbled. "If you don't tell him, let it be on your own head. He's to send no more prisoners to Newgate until the Keeper raises the ban. There's a bad epidemic of jail fever, and worse, there are two proven cases of cholera. I'm taking new prisoners from Newgate to the Fleet, and I stopped on the way. You tell him, now."

"I will tell him," promised Moffat. But as he turned toward the back room he saw Furnival and knew there was no need to pass on the news.

It was a year since there had been a serious outbreak of cholera in London and the realisation brought fear, for so many were stricken and there was so little to be done. Next to smallpox, which was always with them, it was the worst disease after the black plague.

"There isn't much we can do, Silas," John Furnival said, "but we will heed the warning, of course, and I will commit as few prisoners as I can to any prison." He knew that cholera seemed to carry itself from prison to prison, plague spot to plague spot, and that it ran like fire through the already overcrowded hospitals.

The keeper would have warned the City authorities, of course, and they would have told the Middlesex and Westminster authorities; probably for a few days there would be a ban on travel between any of the places until the full extent of the outbreak had been discovered. If this epidemic proved comparatively small, only a few thousand would die of the evil disease.

CHAPTER *11*

The Sickness

THE FIRST that John Furnival knew of Moffat's sickness was on the third day after the old man's collapse. He, Furnival, had spent nearly a week conferring with other magistrates about general matters. He was particularly concerned by the continuing addition of laws passed at Westminster, now extending the death penalty to more than two hundred crimes, from stealing bread to murder. The government appeared to believe that by increasing the severity of the punishment they would discourage the crime.

It was true that many of the death sentences were now being transmuted to transportation for life, or, in some cases, only ten or twelve years; judges at the Sessions applied the capital sentence with much care. But it was said that half of those who set out on the transportation vessels died long before reaching port, either from disease or malnutrition, since the ship's captain had an allowance to buy food and could be just as generous, or more often mean, with it as he chose.

Coming home in low spirits, for so many of the other magistrates appeared to side with the government, as if they actually enjoyed sending men through to the Sessions where the harsh penalties were passed, Furnival expected to see Moffat, but no one was in either the

159

downstairs or upstairs apartments. The fires were alight in both, and kettles were singing and tables were laid against the time when he reached home. He felt exasperation. Why wasn't Moffat here? Why wasn't Ruth? He wanted the comforts he was coming to expect from her and when he glimpsed her coming from her cottage he did not notice her distress.

She came into the back room and he said gruffly, "Where is everyone this night? Go and see if Silas is—"

He broke off because of her expression and waited for whatever news she had to tell him. One of her children sick of the cholera, perhaps? Or one of them dead? He did not know what to say to help her.

She said in an unsteady voice, "Silas is in the hospital at Saint Bartholomew's, sir. I have just come from there."

"You've just come from a hospital where cholera is rife? Are you mad, woman?"

"I had to see Silas," she protested, "and I have been to my cottage and bathed in salt water they gave me at the apothecary's and put on fresh clothes before coming here, sir. My girls are with Meg. All the boys at the school have been kept inside the walls because of the outbreak, and no case has yet been reported there." She stood in the doorway, helpless and entreating. "I had to go to Silas, sir. He—he was asking for you."

Furnival exclaimed, "My God! And I blamed you." He raised his voice as she had never heard it raised before. *"Godden, my horse at once!"* He turned to her and took her hands. "Where shall I find him, Ruth?"

"But, sir, if you go—"

"Where shall I find him?"

"He is on the second floor, sir, the third bed to the left from the door. But let me come with you, I beg you."

"When I get back I'll need to wash all over with that salt water and to change my clothes," he said gruffly. "And I shall be hungry. You get things ready for me, and if you can wait that long have your meal with me."

"I will do as you say," she promised and turned away.

But before she had taken a step he gripped her by the shoulders and turned her around, looked into her misted eyes and spoke in a grumbling voice, "Don't you get cholera! Do you understand? Don't you get cholera!" He made to thrust her away but instead drew her to him and held her so tightly that she could hardly breathe. A moment later he turned and strode into the hall as Godden appeared; his horse was saddled and waiting.

Never had John Furnival seen such sights.

In Long Acre and Holborn there were few people and most of those, he suspected, were thieves or looters looking for easy pickings at the houses of the dead or sick. But as he drew near Smithfield and St. Bartholomew's, the streets were crowded with young and old, men, women and children; and as the dogs clawed among the stinking piles of rubbish for food and so stirred up the noxious gases and smells which carried sickness, as if the cholera was not bad enough, the human beings struggled toward the hospital, and none could doubt that all were sick and many were dying, and that the only hope they saw was in the hospital wards.

At the approaches to the hospital was a line of dragoons, their muskets sloped, staring over the heads of the crowds, and in the entrance itself was a barricade manned by a dozen soldiers, with space for only one person or one horseman to pass at a time. In the pale afterglow and flickering lights of torches the soldiers stood gay and bright. As Furnival slowed down at the barrier a young officer who looked little older than Timothy approached from the other end of the barricade.

"John Furnival, justice at Bow Street," Furnival stated. "I have official business."

The youth peered up as if doubting his claim and a sergeant, close by, saluted Furnival and said, "It's Mr. Furnival, sir. Same gent as fined me a shilling for being drunk and belligerent, when some would have sent me to the Fleet to cool my heels."

"Take Mr. Furnival to the main door, sergeant."

"Right, sir!"

Furnival looked into the unshaven face of a man he could not remember having seen before and nodded his thanks. He dismounted and the sergeant tied his horse to a post and then led him to the closed door, guarded by four soldiers. They opened the door and as Furnival stepped inside it was like going into a place of death, some awful charnel house. For along the passages and along the stairs there were people, dead or dying; and there was a moaning sound which was like a chant of the damned. Here and there a woman or a man knelt by the side of a patient, and at the first floor was a desk at which sat an elderly woman giving instructions to messengers and answering questions of demented-sounding people who wanted news of husband, wife, son or daughter. Stretcher-bearers were taking some cloth-covered bodies away.

Furnival reached the second floor and went past a similar desk and scene into a great ward where the floor seemed to crawl with people. Only here and there was an oasis of stillness and of quiet, and one of these was at the third bed to the left of the door. At first glimpse Furnival thought that Moffat was already dead, he was so pale and lay so still. It was hard to believe a man could become so emaciated, so hideously thin, in such a short time; but for the unmistakable profile Furnival would not have recognised him, he was so wasted away.

As Furnival reached his bed some kind of awareness must have stirred in him, and he turned almost closed eyes toward his master and pleaded in a voice that was barely audible, "Send for Mr. Furnival. Please send for Mr. Furnival."

Furnival took the bony hand gently and said very firmly, "I am here, Silas. You can go to sleep now."

"Mr. Furnival," Moffat spoke in a louder voice, and he tried to open his eyes wide. For a moment there was some kind of responding pressure in his hand but that ceased and his arms and whole body sagged as the wraith of life departed.

In the weeks which followed Moffat's death, Ruth saw a side to John Furnival that she had never suspected. The high spirits and laughter had gone and were replaced by the constant sternness he showed to nearly everybody with whom he was in daily contact. He worked with an application and single-mindedness which affected everyone, and frightened many. Only with her and on occasional visits from Anne did he relax at all, but it was not the complete relaxation of those few, now precious, occasions when he had forgotten everything but Ruth. In court, Tom Harris and others told her, he took statements and made decisions more quickly than ever, giving lying witnesses little latitude, but giving more scope to accused men who he believed might be victims of conspiracy. He sent fewer men and women to Newgate and the Fleet, especially when a charge involved the death penalty.

And whenever a new death-penalty edict reached him from Westminster, he sent a formal letter of protest in which the form was almost unvarying: protesting the imposition of such a savage penalty for so minor a crime and beseeching repeal of the decision.

For his pains he inevitably received a courteous acknowledgment from the Private Secretary and occasionally from Walpole himself; and eventually, note of an additional crime for which the death penalty had to be ordered.

Occasionally, late of an evening, he would talk of this to Ruth, with an edge of bitterness but with a greater sense of sorrow.

All this time, with unrelenting persistence, he wrote to Members of Parliament, the leaders of the guilds, everyone with influence at high and middling levels, urging formation of the peace force. Few even acknowledged, fewer still sent a considered reply, although he did get a letter from Henry Fielding saying that he was "vastly interested" and hoped before long to create an opportunity to discuss the whole matter. Most of Furnival's missives were delivered by hand, although those in the farther areas of London went with street postal carriers by the new penny post. None was sent by the House of Furnival, although each week a messenger came with a few additions for the list of those who might support him.

He did not replace Moffat and came more and more to rely on Ruth for personal things, although insuring that she obtained ample and sufficient help in the kitchen and with the housework. As each week passed she came to love the polished dark oak, the brass and the ironwork, the warmth and the comfort of the rooms upstairs, where now she had a room for her exclusive use. While she looked after Furnival's wardrobe in his spacious bedroom overlooking Bell Lane, she had never slept on the huge four-poster bed. It was the back room below and the small alcove which woke his strongest desire for her, and his greatest affection; and she grew into an abiding love for it, also.

Two things had changed: he did not now use the room for quick peccadilloes with female witnesses and he did not bring Lisa Braidley here. He went to see her in Arlington Street, Ruth knew, and there might be others of whom she was unaware, but this caused her no distress. The longer she lived here with the men she had known so long and with others whom she had only come to meet recently, the more she learned about the way of life between so many couples. She had not realised how sheltered she had been with Richard, how little she had really known. If a man could not afford a mistress he could always afford a prostitute for sixpence, sometimes even for a single drink of gin. If a woman of quality, even of the middle class, did not think she was taken to her bed by her husband as often as she should be then there were many houses of assignation she could frequent. And whether a house be elegant and the patrons able to pay their guineas, or a stinking brothel or a ginshop where favours were exchanged for pennies, these places were the breeding grounds for crime. Information about stolen goods would pass freely; stolen goods would be offered at very low prices; the thief-takers who knew where to "buy" stolen goods and have them sold back to their owners often met the victims here, for their own safety from the few rigidly incorruptible constables.

All these things became part of Ruth's understanding and acceptance of life.

She was in one way grateful and in another troubled by one thing: James's future. For soon after the cholera epidemic, when the pupils had been kept in long dormitories, the School for Young Men had decided that since there was so much dirt and squalor, foul air and filth, and that those living among these were most vulnerable to the worst diseases bred, it should become a school for boarders. When Furnival had asked if she would agree to this, she had been living in the shadow of Moffat's death, and some cholera victims were still dying, while there had been two outbreaks of smallpox. Once smallpox really took a hold nothing could control it; only those who were naturally immune were safe. So she had said yes, eagerly, and in deep relief. But now she saw James so little, although he came to the cottage each Sunday—or on those Sundays when the risk of infection seemed at its lowest. He was growing fast and was more like Richard than she had realised; he was a little too formal with her and extremely formal with John on the few occasions when they met. But once launched on a recital of events he became his old self, and she could see the colour in his cheeks and the brightness of his eyes, and understood that his lean figure was due to exercise, not to lack of food. Among those things he most liked were tours, under strict supervision so that little contact was made with passers-by, to such places as the Tower of London, the Mint, the great palaces, even to theaters where performances were given for pupils from a restricted group of schools.

She had no doubt at all that he was happy; little doubt, either, that he was growing away from her, although occasionally when he romped in a wild rough-and-tumble with his sisters at the cottage, it was as if the distance between them did not exist.

It was in December of that year, on a brisk, bright day, that Ruth saw a carriage draw up at the back entrance to the house in Bell Lane and watched from the window of the cottage as a footman climbed down and, a moment later, opened the door to a lady of such elegance and so adorned with furs that at first she thought she must be one of John's sisters. But if so, then why should she come so furtively? Ruth did not know whether John was in court, and she unfastened her apron and hurried across to find the young clerk in a state of obvious embarrassment staring up into Lisa Braidley's face.

"I—I dare not disturb him, ma'am, m'lady, he is in the middle of a c-case. If you w-will wait—"

"Upstairs in Mr. Furnival's study, perhaps?" Ruth stepped forward and smiled, but her heart was thumping. She did not want to take Lisa Braidley into "their" room, although it was possibly the only room the other woman was familiar with.

Lisa Braidley said quite easily, "You must be Ruth Marshall."

"Yes, ma'am. That is my name."

"If you will take me to the study I shall be grateful," Mrs. Braidley said. If she had the faintest idea why Ruth had headed her off from the back room she did not show it. She followed Ruth upstairs, her clothes rustling, and stood for a moment in the doorway, the light from a huge fire flickering over her. "Such a beautiful room, I had almost forgotten," she said. "Have you time to bring some tea and drink it with me?"

"I will gladly bring you tea, but—"

"I simply must talk to someone," declared Lisa, and she had never looked more beautiful even though her age was showing clearly; Ruth had the impression that she had made no real effort to conceal it. "I have such exciting news, and I cannot wait for Mr. Furnival to know." She leaned forward and her eyes danced in such a way that Ruth believed she could really like the woman. "I am to marry the Duke of Gilhampton, my dear."

John arrived half an hour later, and Ruth made fresh tea and brought a fresh supply of the lemon curd tarts, now part of the daily teatime meal. John looked tired but took Lisa's hands and drew her close, gave her a hug and a kiss—and over her head gave Ruth a broad wink. Ruth went out, her heart as light as could be. She heard them laughing and talking, and deliberately went back to the cottage so that he should not think for one moment that she had been spying. Within half an hour the coach took Lisa off and for a moment John was outlined against the open door as he waved her good-bye. Then Ruth saw her name framed on his lips as he turned inside. He was in the back room when she returned, shutting the door against the cold.

She affected to be surprised when she saw him, but something in his expression touched her with shame, and she said laughingly, "I saw you in the doorway."

"So you saw the future Duchess of Gilhampton driven off," observed John, looking at her with his head on one side. "I expected she would marry an old man who would soon die, but Gilhampton's healthy enough in body even if he isn't the brightest intellectual star in the firmament. Ruth, my love, you are the most discreet person I know or have known. Who taught you the value of silence?"

"My father," she replied simply.

"That remarkable parson and craftsman in wood! Tell me, how much do you know about my past?"

Her eyes danced.

"All I wish to know, sir!"

He laughed in turn, deep down inside him, and she had not heard him laughing since Silas Moffat's death. His body was still quivering when he put an arm around her and kissed her cheek.

"I'll be bound you do! And I'd pay you for that rejoinder if there weren't seventeen miscreants waiting to find out what bad news I have for them!" He hugged her and then stalked off without a backward glance.

From that time on he began to mellow, was more often his old hearty self, laughter came more often and more freely. The periods of silence which had followed the gathering at Great Furnival Square and Silas Moffat's death all but ceased, and never once did he voice any bitterness toward those of the family who were so determined not to help. For much of the winter Anne visited him regularly and then in early March of 1740 she came with a mingling of excitement and regret. Jason Gilroy had decided to stay in Calcutta and to maintain offices in conjunction with the East India Company there, and for the bad seasons of the year they would go to nearby hills, where it was much cooler, if Anne would bring the children there to join him.

"Go?" John roared. "Of course you must go; it's past time you had some pleasure out of that man of yours!"

166

He took Ruth to the St. Catherine's Docks, not far from the Tower, to see her off, but would not join the mass of the Furnival family crammed onto the terrace outside the director's room at Furnival Tower House. She sailed with a dozen others going to help establish the new headquarters, on a day early in April 1740 when the sun struck hot enough for June, when the daffodils were out in the window boxes, one of those days when it was so easy to forget the ugly side of London. The ship, a four-masted bark of the Furnival Line, was taking supplies to Bombay and Karachi, and also enormous bales of cotton cloth from the north-country mills for the Indian natives. A band of the Royal Navy played on deck and every man on the quay and on other boats, great and small, roared his farewell.

"It is surprisingly easy to be glad for someone else and sorry for oneself," John said when they were back at Bow Street. "Well, Ruth! Now you've seen Furnival Tower House from the grounds of the Tower of London. Did you wish you were on the terrace with the rest of the family?"

"When I am with you it does not enter my mind to wish I were somewhere else," Ruth said, and was astounded when he responded with obvious delight.

The sadness of Anne's going did not weigh upon him too heavily, and he now seemed fully recovered from the loss of Silas Moffat. With the men and the officials in court, Ruth was told, he was less brusque and gruff and would listen with more patience. His manner with his fellow magistrates, who visited occasionally for coffee or port, or even some of Ruth's lemon curd tarts, which had become famous, was much easier. There was less noticeable change in his manner with her; he was affectionate all the time, very seldom abrupt or impatient, occasionally he would tumble her with the abandon of a youth, and always, afterward, he was gentleness itself.

She did not know the actual occasion, although inevitably she could place it within a period of three weeks, when she conceived. It was six months after she went to live at Bell Lane and Bow Street. The possibility had been in her mind for a long time and had worried her, partly because she did not want to add to John's problems and the decisions he had to make. She used a sponge whenever she felt sure they would make love but his desire would sometimes come at the most unexpected moment. She did not want to believe the truth at first, but when she was three weeks late with her flow, and each morning she felt nausea, not yet severe but quite unmistakable, she was certain. For the first time since she had recovered from Silas Moffat's death, she longed for the old man: it would have been easier to break the news to John with him at hand. The only other person who might have helped was Anne.

On the day when she decided to tell John, there was a great stir in Bow Street, for a man who had become almost as notorious as Frederick Jackson had been caught by two Westminster constables and Tom Harris, working together. He was Peter Nicholson, who had waylaid a wealthy Member of Parliament with a friend just outside the City walls; the friend had tried to run and had been shot dead. On such days the tension spread to all parts of the court, the cells and offices as well as the private quarters. Ruth caught a glimpse of the manacled man who had helped to plot the case against her son; a tall, handsome, bearded creature. He wore a long peruke and the most fashionable of clothes, a red coat and bright-green breeches with red hose and green shoes. Although so helpless, there was courage in his mien and he tried to sweep her a bow as he was hustled into the courtroom.

Would this, after all, be the day to tell John Furnival?

She had found an excuse to put it off twice already, she reminded herself, and each passing day would make it more difficult. She wished only that she had some idea of how he would receive the tidings: whether he would want her to stay here.

CHAPTER *12*

John Furnival's Son

FURNIVAL CAME to the back room late in the afternoon, looking very tired. Word had come to Ruth through Tom, Sam Fairweather and Ebenezer Noble that a dozen witnesses had been brought into court to swear that Nicholson had been with them at a cockfight at the time of the holdup and the problem was how to cast doubt on these statements. The landlord of the inn, his wife and two taproom men had sworn in Nicholson's favour; the Member of Parliament as well as one of the Westminster constables swore on oath he had been the highwayman. When Ruth had last heard, John had not made his decision; she wondered whether he was still undecided. At first she thought that the case had cast him back into a mood of silence and bitterness, but as she brought tea to the table and placed it by the side of a dish of muffins, he laid his hand gently on her shoulder.

"I do not know what I would do without you, Ruth."

"I do not know why you should think you might have to," she countered. "I think it would be—"

"Go on," he urged. "What would it be?"

"I do not think I should say what was in my mind," Ruth replied, and she went very pale. "It was not fair, Mr. Furnival." She handed him two muffins on a silver dish as he looked at her, half frowning.

Unexpectedly he asked, "Has the day made you reflect on the past, too?"

"The past a little, the future much," she replied.

"You know, except for my sister Anne, you are the only woman I have ever met who has a way of putting significance into every word she utters," remarked Furnival, and he ate a muffin and dabbed his chin before going on. "I have just sent Nicholson to Newgate to await trial at the next Sessions. At one time I thought he had corrupted too many witnesses to make that possible, but one of them had spent the night with a girl from a nearby farm, and once his testimony was broken, that of the others collapsed. Can you imagine who was in court?"

"No," she answered.

"Eve Milharvey, Jackson's onetime mistress," Furnival replied. "Now a Mrs. Nash."

"But I thought she had borne Jackson's child and lived in the country, at Saint Albans!"

"She was in London visiting friends," Furnival told her. "When she heard of this trouble she came to see Nicholson and offered him whatever money he needed to buy his creature comforts in Newgate. Had he not been manacled I declare he would have slapped her across the face!" Furnival spread butter on a muffin with almost sensual pleasure, and then held it out for her to take a bite. "I spoke with her after Nicholson had been taken away. Her child is growing fast, and she dotes on it."

"Is it a boy or a girl?" asked Ruth.

"A boy, Frederick by name—Frederick Jackson, to boot! More, she is married to an elderly farmer and is happy enough—and again with child," Furnival went on. "She is one of the few who have thanked me for intervening in their lives. Did you know that I suggested she should leave London?"

"Yes," Ruth answered. "Silas told me."

"Ah," breathed Furnival. "There was a man of great faith and loyalty." He leaned back in the chair, resting his hands on the arms, stared into the fire for a while and then turned to smile at her. "Enough of my meandering, Ruth, What ails *you*?"

She caught her breath, but was quick to reply, "Fear of you, sir!"

She tried to make that sound lighthearted, tried to put laughter in her eyes, but her anxiety showed clearly; his expression convinced her of that. She was seated in a small chair opposite him and he held out both hands. Slowly she placed hers in them and he held her firmly.

"Never be frightened of me, Ruth. Never be frightened of those who love you."

Her heart, already beating fast, gave a wild leap at the word "love," which he had never uttered to her before. Yet she was no more certain how he would receive her news than she had been, and the only word to describe her emotion *was* "fear."

"What is it?" he asked patiently.

"I am with child," she said in a voice pitched high above the thumping of her heart. "Your child, sir, lest you should think that I have known another man."

He sat utterly still. His grip tightened until his fingers hurt hers, but she made no attempt to draw free. He scrutinised her face as if it were the face of a stranger. His breathing seemed to stop, and the period of silence seemed agelong. Footsteps sounded in the passage, hoofbeats and carriages outside, and still he did not speak. Now her heart was beating in long, slow, painful thumps, for she could see that this was a shock to him but could only guess what was passing through his mind.

Slowly his grip on her eased; slowly the muscles of his face relaxed and she became aware of the delicate shape of his lips.

"Ruth," he said, "I would not like our child to be a bastard. You know me as well as any woman ever can. Do you think that you can do me the honour of becoming my wife?"

They were married at St. Hilary's by the Reverend Sebastian Smith at the end of the month of May in 1740. William and Sarah, with Francis and Cleo, were present, as well as those at Bow Street who could be spared from their work. It was a quiet wedding, and immediately after the ceremony they set out by carriage and pair for the farm at St. Giles, which was some forty odd miles from the Hyde Park Turnpike. The turnpike road led northwest and had many turns, one to Oxford, another to Aylesbury, and theirs which would take them to Dunstable, thence several miles beyond to the village of St. Giles. St. Giles Farm lay only a few hundred yards east of the road. The spring day was damp and misty, the rutted road was slippery, and now and again they passed single horsemen and others riding in pairs, any of whom might be highwaymen, but not only did the daylight discourage an attack: two guards from Great Furnival Square armed with

171

muskets rode just behind the carriage. Of them William had said jestingly, "Let them act as an escort for you. It would not do if John Furnival were held up on his honeymoon and his pretty bride carried off. Dick the Raper has been very busy in these parts."

"I'll be glad of the guards as a privilege," John said, "and today I won't even declare I want it most for the protection of every man's birthright."

"You did *not* say that very effectively," Francis retorted.

Now Ruth was reflecting that every Furnival she had met had been possessed of some quality which made them extremely likable. Whatever the rights and wrongs of their attitudes, their policies and their actions, as humans beings they were good.

What would John's child be like?

And would she bear a boy or a girl?

Although he had not breathed a word she was sure that John wanted a son. She glanced at him as they went along at a steady pace, the carriage itself swaying. He was staring across newly ploughed fields and meadows where sheep and cattle grazed together, his profile clear-cut and handsome, his lips relaxed. When he turned in response to her appraisal, his mouth puckered in a smile and he slid an arm about her waist.

The sun had broken through and it was warm when they arrived at the farmhouse, of which Ruth had heard so much, but nothing to prepare her for its size or its distinctiveness. Built of rich red brick and with the tall chimneys of the Tudor period, it stood against a rising stretch of woodland, oak, beech and birch, thick and beautiful. A stream from the hillside ran past the house and meandered toward St. Giles village, which looked about a mile away to the north. Some cricketers were playing on a green between here and the village, a pleasant sight. Close to the house the stream had been dammed with a brick wall and a pond had been created, on which ducks and geese and three snow-white swans were swimming. The path from the pond to the wrought-iron gateway of the drive was paved in irregular fashion with broken paving stones, and the driveway was also paved to prevent ruts caused by cart and coach wheels. Two footmen, who, Ruth later learned, served also as groom and coachman, and three maids were at the front doorway to meet the newlyweds, and the huge oaken door with heavy iron studs stood ajar. It opened onto a red-tiled main hall from which led other rooms with narrow-strip oaken floors.

Upstairs, that night, in a bedroom overlooking the stream and the pond and the lights at distant houses, Ruth said, "I can hardly believe this is real, John."

"The longer you stay here the more real you will find it," he promised her.

Two days later he asked if she would like to stay there all the time, with the children, while he came for weekends. The suggestion brought to the forefront of her mind an anxiety which had been hovering for many months, and now she was torn in two directions. To leave the children with others for so much of the time was against all her instincts, but she was sure that John needed her companionship and help. However he might refuse to admit it, he was not well, and she hated the thought of being away from him for long periods. She alone could help him relax; on his own he would work like the giant he was, to the point of disaster.

But no matter how much she wanted to be with him, and how great his need, how could she deny her daughters the magnificent air of the countryside, all the fresh garden products and the freedom from the squalor and disease of the city?

It was a long time before she made up her mind, though with much misgiving. Meg and Sam Fairweather, already deeply attached to the children, would soon need a place to live in retirement, for Sam was getting too old for Bow Street. She could trust them absolutely with the girls, and there was no one with whom she could leave John.

She decided to leave her daughters here with Meg and Sam, while she stayed at Bow Street, coming here frequently for as long as she could wisely travel by coach. That would be until the seventh month of her pregnancy, she anticipated.

When the time came, for some reason she did not understand, leaving the children at St. Giles Farm worried her less than leaving James at the school had done, but as the weeks passed, her preoccupation with her fourth child, John's obvious delight in the prospect and the level of high contentment in her life with him made her misgivings recede. But they were never far away.

Apart from this, her life seemed too good to be true.

Life for John continued in a domestic contentment he had never known before, despite increasing frustrations at Bow Street and an increasing sense of failure over efforts to win support for a peace force. Crimes increased beyond even his worst dreams, and more and more were decreed suitable for the death penalty. The thief-takers reveled in rewards for their evidence, true or false, with which to convict a man. The filth of London grew until the stench could be carried for miles on the wind and nowhere was there freedom from the effluence, and the water from the Thames became noisome and stank as it was drawn from the street stack pipes. But the parks became more beautiful than ever, the great houses more prosperous; as criminals multiplied so did those who made a good living at every craft under the sun. New docks, new warehouses, new shops, drew more and more trade from ships which not only brought rats to swell the rodent population of the city but also rich silks and tapestries, spices, and tea and coffee.

Not only did trade from abroad increase bewilderingly and so bring more people in from the provinces to do the work, but trade from the provinces kept doubling and trebling itself. Since the first Turnpike Act in 1663, giving parishes on the Great North Road the right to take tithes from all who used it, the money going to road maintenance, a dozen new turnpikes had been added and all had become furiously busy. Whether from Derby or Manchester, Gloucester or Hereford, Oxford or Birmingham, Bath or Bristol, Chester or Coventry, Hawick or Dover, Portsmouth or Chichester, each bore thousands of tons of heavy-goods traffic to and from London.

Rutted or rock-strewn, muddy or waterlogged, well surfaced or bad, each turnpike was part of the forward-surging economy of the country, which was still based on London.

Distant from all this, on the fifteenth of December, 1740, a son was born to John and Ruth Furnival, attended by Dr. Anson, who had come from Great Furnival Square, and by Meg Fairweather as midwife.

Both mother and son throve.

On the fourth Sunday after his birth the child was baptised and christened in the parish church of St. Giles, the Reverend Sebastian Smith assitsing the vicar. Smith held the baby in his arms, sprinkled his wrinkled forehead and thin black hair liberally with holy water without waking him, and preached in a subdued boom until finally he said, "In the name of the Father, the Son and the Holy Ghost I hereby give to this child the names of John William Francis and I pray that he will add to the great name of Furnival still greater lustre and distinction. Amen."

On the lips of the hundred people present there came the prayer: "Amen."

The child gave his parents no anxiety. He appeared to have inherited the strength of his father with the equable temper of his mother and an intelligence which might have come from either or both. Soon after his ninth month he was taken to live part time at Bow Street, for Ruth would leave neither young John at St. Giles for long at a time nor her husband too long alone at Bow Street. They went seldom to Great Furnival Square, Ruth because she did not feel at home or happy there, John Furnival because the gap between his purposes and those of the family had widened yet further.

In the early years of the marriage, troubles of a different kind fell about their ears. Already Walpole's yielding to powerful demands for war with Spain brought war with France to a dangerous crescendo. At last Walpole was defeated. The whole of Europe seemed to go up in flames; no nation of real consequence seemed at peace; or if there was peace, it was short-lived. George II led the British and allied armies against the French and won a victory and an uproarious burst of popularity, but rumours in newspapers and from government sources were right—the French prepared to invade across the Channel. All this time, new and more burdensome tasks were thrust upon Furnival. The repeal of the Gin Act in 1743 had eased the flow of charges for illegal sale and manufacture, but greatly increased the number of crimes which arose out of drunkenness.

Westminster became a victim of a different kind of plague: fear of spies. Furnival was charged with seeking them out and searching for arms dumps cached for a Jacobite uprising in or near the metropolis. For not only was France threatening but the Scottish were said to be rallying around Prince Charles, who might soon become strong enough to march south with an invading army and take London and the throne. In his new position as Chief of the Secret Service, Furnival had to report daily to Thomas Pelham, Duke of Newcastle.

As the threat of an invading army increased, so did the temptation to send Ruth to join the girls at St. Giles Farm, but if the invasion did break through, rebel forces might travel very swiftly, and he might not be able to get them away from the Bedfordshire village in time. So he kept Ruth and the child at Bow Street.

In the strange mixture of war and peace in which all Europe seemed involved, hundreds of French footmen were imported to London, putting as many English counterparts out of work. A group of English footmen called a meeting to discuss action and, rumour of this leaking out, Furnival was ordered by the government to prevent it. His first step was simple: to deny them use of the room where they wanted to assemble.

Almost without warning, hundreds of Englishmen marched on Bow

Street. Some bribed or fooled a servant to admit them and found Furnival alone in his downstairs office.

"You allow us into the meeting room," one man said, "or you'll die where you sit."

Ruth, puzzled by the crowd outside, had gone down to see what was the matter, and went into the office. As the men swung around, fearful of an attack, Furnival snatched up two pistols and pushed past them to the door.

"You go upstairs with the baby," he ordered Ruth. "Send Harris or any man you can find to summon troops and our men—but let our men not attack the mob by themselves. They are to protect the rear." He did not utter a word to the invaders, who, taken aback at the sight of the pistols, retreated to the hallway. Ruth safely out of sight, Furnival stood at the foot of the stairs, pistols in hand. The front door crashed in and dozens more of the footmen rushed into the hallway— but stopped at sight of his guns. Upstairs, the baby was crying; everything on the ground floor was wrecked, windows and furniture were smashed and documents were burned. John Furnival moved neither forward nor backward, but if any man drew near he leveled his guns.

Two and a half hours later, when he was at the point of exhaustion, troops arrived in Bow Street, and Furnival's men, who had been keeping hundreds at bay, rushed to his support. Once the crisis was past, he felt once again pressures at his jaws and chest, and, breathing heavily, he groped for a chair, Ruth helping him.

He sat heaving for a while, and gradually recovered, saying when he could speak, "I confess I have never been more frightened. Has my hair turned white?"

"Nothing but a distinguished gray," she assured him; and he blessed her for her cool head. "But mine will if you do not see a doctor."

For once he conceded, "I will think of it."

He was allowed little rest, even after that invasion of Bow Street.

Orders came to round up Roman Catholic priests who might be working for the Jacobites, and the rate of crime steadily increased. It was little consolation that the government accepted responsibility for the damage at Bow Street after the footmen's riot and offered a hundred pounds in gold over and above all other rewards for the arrest and conviction of any street robber until May of 1745.

There could have been no greater incentive to the thief-taker; to those giving false evidence; to those prepared to condemn the innocent.

Pressed by Ruth, John at last saw a doctor, who advised him to take more rest and to eat less and gave him a medicine to take twice each day. From then on his attacks lessened in severity until he all but ignored them.

On little John's fourth birthday in the blustery December of 1744, when a party was to be held to celebrate in the upstairs apartment at Bow Street and John was in court, a visitor came, different from any they had known before: a King's Messenger, carrying a sealed message which he would hand only to John in person. The young clerk who had copied so many of Moffat's appeals, and was now a married and family man, took a message into the court and John came out into his offices and then up the stairs. Ruth judged from his expression that he had been filled suddenly with hope that at last one of his pleas had been answered favourably, else why should a special envoy be sent? He broke the seal of the heavy envelope and straightened out a piece of parchmentlike paper with two folds. He began to read, and Ruth had never seen such hope or tension in him. The messenger watched with supercilious interest, until he was shocked—like Ruth—by the sudden laugh which burst from John Furnival's lips, a laugh which went on and on and shook the walls, reminding Ruth vividly of the night when John had come back from Great Furnival Square and learned of the highwayman's attack on Montmorency and the theft of Hooper's gold and silver plate.

The envoy looked outraged, but before he could speak Furnival moved toward Ruth and held the missive so that she could read it.

Before she even began, Furnival gasped, "The King is rewarding me for my services to justice—he is making me a knight! *Sir* John Furnival, m'dear, how does that sound? Will the death sentence sound more pleasant from the mouth of *Sir* John, will the—"

"Your pardon," the envoy interrupted coldly. "His Majesty is to hold a ceremony tomorrow at Westminster Palace which he has graciously invited you to attend to be dubbed Sir John. May I report to His Majesty that you will accept? Or shall I tell him you were so vastly amused that you could not make the decision easily?"

"Oh, both," answered John Furnival. "Both, by all means! That I was vastly amused by the unexpected nature of the missive and humbly beg to accept. I will present myself tomorrow at Westminster Palace, if you will be good enough to tell me what time I should be there."

"At three o'clock, sir."

"And may I, as is the custom, have the company and support of my wife?"

"As it please you," the envoy replied, supercilious again. He bowed stiffly and turned and went onto the landing where the young clerk was waiting to escort him.

The young clerk was at the Bow Street door when the carriage returned from Westminster, and as he handed Ruth down he said in a clear voice, "Good afternoon, my lady."

Ruth was so surprised that she slipped and would have fallen had the youth not supported her and if Tom Harris, standing by, hadn't come to lend his weight. Upright again and looking quite beautiful, she breathed heavily, for the welcome had been a shock. They had not discussed it and until the moment when she had been called "my lady" it had never really dawned on her that she would be known by the title. She caught a glimpse of John, smiling down at her, and felt sure he had deliberately not talked of it before the knighting to make sure that she would get the full effect of "my lady" the first time it was used.

There was a boisterous party in the apartment, the other magistrates, clerks and officials coming to pay their respects, most of them wanting a word afterward with John Furnival the Fourth, who had been "banished" to the cottage for the great occasion. At last, however, the visitors ceased coming and little John was brought back and put to bed, while soon afterward Ruth and John Furnival ate a simple meal, cooked exclusively for them, in "their" room.

"And now I am going to prove to you that Lady Furnival gets no more respect from Sir John than Mrs. Furnival used to get from plain John Furnival, Esquire," declared Furnival.

Had Ruth had any doubts before, she knew now that he was deeply pleased with the knighthood, although within a few days he would no doubt be sending off his protests again, and trying to find out whether the "Sir" prefix would procure him a better hearing.

In August of 1745 the dreaded invasion of the Young Pretender began. Landing in Scotland to a rapturous reception he began his march of triumph south and was proclaimed King of Scotland in

178

Edinburgh. As he took Derby there was panic in London; tens of thousands left the city; thousands besieged the Bank of England; even the King was advised to flee to Hanover. All this time Furnival maintained his work as magistrate and secret service leader, keeping Ruth and the baby in London.

"The Prince will never get here," he would insist. "He'll be turned back. The north will not support him."

And the north, where the Prince's great hopes had lain, watched as he passed by with his Highlanders and did not lift a finger to help; at the same time, in the Scottish Lowlands, loyalty had swung back to the Hanovers.

John Furnival had taken a night off duty so that he could give Ruth a rare treat, an evening at Drury Lane. Rebuilt only a few years after the fire which destroyed it, a light and lively play, written, produced and acted by David Garrick, was being staged, and the evening was made the greater for Ruth because the King was in the Royal Box. Few saw the equerry who went to speak to him, but all saw the incredible sight of the portly sovereign climbing onto the stage, gesticulating wildly and shouting phrases in guttural English which no one could understand, then bursting out into German.

As his excitement increased and the audience and players began to wonder whether he had gone mad, an equerry joined him and announced clearly, "His Majesty has been advised of the complete and bloody defeat of the Jacobites at Culloden. He—"

His next words were lost in a roar of cheering, shouting and stamping, while only here and there appeared a pale, shocked face.

"One danger over," Furnival said in the carriage as he and Ruth were driven home.

"You mean you expect a bad winter of crime?"

"You are a discerning woman," he declared.

Because of the preoccupation with the Jacobite rebellion, concentration on the criminals in London had been impossible for Furnival or anyone else, and crime during the winter of 1745 to 1746 had been the worst ever known.

But in some ways there was change for the better, as a number of the people to whom he had written over the years were persuaded by the worsening crime figures that an organised peace-keeping force in London would have made it much easier to search out the Jacobites.

179

A slow, steady stream of support was developing, and almost two years to the day since the King's accolade, Sir John Furnival, as active as ever at Bow Street, arranged for missives to be sent out to thirty gentlemen, including three peers and five Members of Parliament, to attend a meeting at the Printers' Hall in the City to discuss ways and means of bringing more pressure on the government and the King. For the first time Ruth left her fourth child at the farm so that she could give her undivided attention to her husband. In one way she was puzzled, for now that the great opportunity was at hand and there seemed a prospect of receiving the support he needed, he was more on edge than he had ever been.

"I know, Ruth, I know," he said when she remarked on it and asked if she could help. "So near and yet so far—is that the reason, I wonder? I have been working for this day for so many weary years that like you I can hardly believe it is real." A smile broke through his frown and he held her by the arms. "Now the boot is on the other foot! Ruth, will you remember, I wonder, the day I set out to bargain with my family? I had such high hopes then. I did not really see how in all reason they would refuse and yet I was so frightened that they would. When the actual Sunday came I was nearly as much on edge as I am now. Am I a fool, do you think? Or have I been fooling myself?"

"No man was ever less of a fool," she replied. "What you lack is faith in those you are going to meet." She stood over him as he sat back in his chair and went on gently: "You should rest tonight—with no exertion. No exertions of any kind, sir!" Her eyes teased him. "I will go and get some lemon curd tarts; they are in the oven, warming."

She went out of their apartment and was away for perhaps ten minutes. Everyone except the court officials and two retainers whom she did not know well had left to attend a fight between two famous pugilists at a big new amphitheater near Tottenham Court Road. She preferred things as they were, for she felt an overwhelming desire to be alone with John that night, having a sense that he had great need of her.

When she returned, his head had lolled forward, chin on chest, as if he had fallen asleep, and she placed everything in position before going closer to him. If he were in too deep a sleep she would not wake him.

She caught her breath, for he looked so strange.

His lips and nose and part of his cheeks were blue in colour, his mouth drooped open, his eyes were neither open nor closed but a little of each. Ruth felt in that awful moment that he was dead, but she steeled herself to feel for his pulse and detected a rhythm; she could hear breathing deep in his chest, too. She straightened up and ran out of the room, calling "Tom, Tom!" but it was another constable who came hurrying to her. "Get a doctor!" she cried. "Doctor Anson if possible, but please hurry for a doctor!"

A youthful doctor, partner to elderly Anson, came within fifteen minutes, by which time the servants were in the room where John Furnival now lay on two chairs, more comfortable, while Ruth stood over him, bathing his forehead.

Soon the young doctor said with assurance, "I have no doubt, Lady Furnival, that your husband has suffered a major seizure of the heart. I would recommend constant care with the best possible trained assistance. The Royal Physician will come, I am sure, and I can recommend excellent women to care for him until such time as we can be sure he will recover. But I am hopeful, ma'am, most hopeful."

"Lady Furnival," the King's physician said, two weeks later, "with care and constant attention your husband will live for many years, provided he can accept what is now, I fear, inevitable. His left side is paralysed, and he will not be able to walk. His will be a life of enforced retirement from public affairs and I would strongly recommend that the whole household move to St. Giles Farm. It will be a terrible blow to him, ma'am, and a great burden upon you, but I see no alternative."

Quietly Ruth said, "It will be no burden, sir. If he can use his mind, I can be his arms and legs and can do whatever he wants of me. Is he able to understand what is going on about him now?"

"Vaguely, I fear—but vaguely."

"Then we should have him taken to St. Giles before he recovers well enough to protest," she said, "and I will be grateful if you and Doctor Anson will make what medical arrangements are needed. I will call upon his brothers and get their permission to move permanently to St. Giles."

She did not add that she would implore one of them, at least, to take up where John had been forced to stop.

"Ruth," said Francis, standing beside his desk, "none of us can continue with the work he was doing because we do not believe in it sufficiently. But two things we can promise you. We shall never stand in the way of any man who follows him. And we shall forever regard you as one of ourselves because you are so much part of John."

BOOK II
1751–1783

CHAPTER *13*

The Invitation

"HAVE NO DOUBT," Timothy McCampbell, Sarah's son, said to James Marshall, "I believe you should come, James, and persuade your mother to come also. It will be a very great occasion, and properly used it could mend a breach which I think should have been mended long ago. If it were practicable for your father to be moved I would urge that he come as well."

They were walking across the new Westminster Bridge. The setting sun of that autumn day of 1751 threw the spires of nearby churches into sharp relief against the sky and reflected on the roof and the two towers of Westminster Abbey, solid and impressive. The great buildings of Mayfair and Piccadilly, and, closer, the Royal Stables at Charing Cross, gleamed whitely, and they had but to turn their heads to see the clear outline of the dome of St. Paul's. Below were the flags of gaily bedecked ships with their masses of passengers, many coming to see this year-old bridge for the first time. The watermen of the Thames, who had fought so bitterly against the proposal to build a bridge there, fearing loss of trade, now made a fortune taking Londoners and hosts of visitors from the provinces through one of the

185

great arches as far as the open countryside between Westminster and Chelsea.

A stiff breeze filled the sails of big ships and small, and ruffled the muddy-looking surface of the river; and it stirred James Marshall's jet-black hair, which he wore exposed to both sun and wind, seldom wearing a peruke or any covering save a soft leather cap. The sun caught his high forehead, and his hooked nose, deep-set eyes and thrusting chin drew the gaze of many a girl and matron who passed. He was of a height with Timothy McCampbell, but a more striking contrast it would have been hard to imagine, for Timothy favoured his mother, with her blond hair and pleasantly rounded features. Timothy, who gave no outward sign that he could match James's strength of will and character, was a follower rather than a leader, and he laughed easily, his cornflower-blue eyes crinkling readily at the corners. •

Both young men were passed by hundreds of workers, hastening home mostly from shops and small manufacturers near Westminster, and the road was thronged with carriages, sedan chairs and groaning carts.

When James did not respond at once, Timothy asked, "Do you have no answer?"

"I have two," James replied. "My mother will not come without John Furnival and I am reluctant to come without her."

"For what possible reason?" demanded Timothy impatiently.

James shot him a sideways glance and his lips curved in a smile as he answered, "None whatsoever, except custom and prejudice."

"Which are not worthy of you! Here, I tell you, is a great occasion, the opening of the new Furnival Docks, opposite Furnival Tower House, the finest and most modern in London—in all the world, more like. There will be a great procession on the river, an escorted visit to the new docks, and a ceremony as the first ship enters, all this followed by a show of fireworks the like of which you have never seen. Doesn't the prospect entice you?"

"You forgot to remark upon the delectable food," observed James.

"There are times when you are exasperatingly impossible!"

"I am aware of it," conceded James Marshall. "I marvel at your patience but would be a sad man if you lost it. I am inclined—"

He broke off as an enclosed one-horse cart came smartly toward them. On a high board above the head of the driver, as well as on the sides, was printed:

EBENEZER MORGAN & SONS
ALWAYS THE HIGHEST CLASS IN GROCERIES

Finest Fresh Dairy Produce ... Tea, Coffee, Cocoa
and Spices all of the Finest Quality
Long Acre and Establishments elsewhere
in London

Timothy looked at his companion thoughtfully. "Do you live much in yesterday, James?"

"I like to remind myself how much I owe John Furnival," James said. "Sometimes I wonder where I would be and what I would be doing had I stayed with Morgan."

"Driving that old cart, most likely!"

"Or one like it, yes. I hear that Morgan actually has nine other shops in different parts of London now instead of just the one in which I worked. Timothy, I have decided what to do. If John Furnival has no objection to my visiting you, then I will come, even if alone. But not if it is against his will."

" 'Tis fair enough," responded Timothy in a tone which implied that he did not really think so. "Will you go to St. Giles this Saturday and Sunday?"

"Yes."

"Then you will have your answer by Monday," Timothy remarked with restrained satisfaction. "I hope you will convince my uncle that everybody desires his presence."

"I have never fully understood what happened in the family," James said, "but I do not think there was ever an open quarrel."

They walked from the northern end of the bridge into Whitehall, past the palace, past the stables, where crowds gathered to watch the Royal horses and their brilliantly clad grooms, down the wearing stone steps toward the crowded Embankment. The two friends walked on past the statue of King Charles, then turned right at the Strand into such a commotion of traffic that it was hard to comprehend. Four or five sailors, mostly middle-aged, were being thrust out of Charlie Wylie's notorious brothel, while in the doorway stood several middle-aged prostitutes, shaking their fists and screaming at the sailors. Two men carrying staves, from Henry Fielding, chief magistrate at Bow Street, were in the middle of the road, endeavouring to make a passage for one vehicle at a time in each direction, but with little success. The traffic was piled up in a great mass as impatient

187

riders and drivers pressed on from behind, not knowing the cause of the holdup. Three small boys and a girl no more than six, all barefooted and in rags, were darting about among the crowd, dipping into fob pockets and purses and dashing off with their loot.

Suddenly a cry was raised: "Stop thief! Stop thief!"

James's breath hissed through his teeth and Timothy was startled at his set face.

There was a raucous bellow of laughter as a woman at a second-floor window emptied a chamber pot over one of the sailors.

One of his companions was roaring, "We'll have you for this, you bitches! We'll have the lot of you!"

James and Timothy crossed the road and turned toward St. Martin's in the Fields, nearing the pillory, where two men stood with their heads and hands through the holes, a small boy hurling tomatoes at them. At last the crowd began to thin and the traffic moved more freely.

"Does the cry of 'Stop thief!' still affect you?" asked Timothy.

"No matter how I try to prevent it, yes."

"Time will make you forget the hurt. Have no fear, James. Have you decided yet what to do with your life?"

"Not fully," James replied thoughtfully.

"There is ample scope for you at Furnival Tower House, you must know that."

"And I am not unmindful, Timothy."

"Is there anything I can do to help you come to a decision?"

Very slowly James shook his head. They walked on in silence for a few moments, then turned into Mee's Coffee House, which was within sight of Whitehall and of Leicester Fields. The one large room was half empty, and they went to a corner opposite the foot of a narrow staircase. As they sat down a girl giggled, and a moment later a slim young woman with a frilly dress caught high at the neck and at the hips came toward them, tray in hand.

"I declare this is the first coffee shop where I have been served by a wench," Timothy remarked.

"I hope it won't be your last, sir!" The girl, merry-eyed but pale-cheeked, bobbed a curtsy and took their order of coffee and seed-cake, then disappeared into a room beneath the staircase, where, out of sight, she giggled again. A few minutes later she brought their order, and said, "I hope you are aware that you can get all the comforts of home here, young gentlemen!" She pranced off.

"What on earth does she mean?" asked James, baffled.

Timothy laughed. "James, you are truly the innocent of innocents or a better actor than any who appears at Covent Garden or Drury Lane! She meant, if you wish to know, that this establishment has not been making enough money selling coffee, tea and cigars, so it has hired a female staff that will take you upstairs to bed for a modest sixpence or a shilling! James, don't take me so literally! And I declare I've seen less attractive bed companions than our young woman. If it weren't for fear of the French disease I might be tempted. That is one thing which I have learned, where to go to disport myself. There are some young ladies whose freedom from the disease can be positively guaranteed." Timothy picked up his coffee, sipped, and shook his head sadly. "Abominable stuff! I well understand why they had to stoop to such tricks to keep this shop open!"

"Did you know what manner of place it was when we came in?" asked James.

"Do you think I would willingly bring you so close to the gates of hell, Jamey?"

"I confess I don't know what I think you would do," declared James. He was smiling, and out of the corner of his eye he caught sight of another girl coming down the stairs. Still looking at her he remarked, "No, Tim, I don't think you can help me make my decision."

"One thing I warrant: you'll never be a justice or a judge!"

"What makes you say that?" flashed James.

"You take too long to make up your mind," replied Timothy. "My! You are a sensitive creature on some spots; even I can light on them without intent." He drank more coffee, made a face, and went on: "Well, my future was decided from the day I was born. Given the death of two uncles and a variety of relatives I shall one day be chairman of Furnival's! Meanwhile, please God, Uncle Jason will decide he needs extra help in Bombay or Calcutta, in working with the East India Company, or else I shall be dispatched to the American colonies, where they say there is much danger from Indians and outlaws but much money to be made. To this end I have been sent to the great seat of learning at Oxford and covered myself with degrees and glory. Whereas you covered yourself with more degrees in Leipzig and this past year at Oxford. There can be few with more. What *will* you do with your doctorate of law, Jamey? Or your doctorate of literature? Old John will want an answer from you soon."

James laughed, but there was a somber note in his voice as he replied. "I doubt if he will much like the desire which takes me most."

"Then you have a desire! You old fox—you have been pretending uncertainty all this time but in fact your mind is made up!"

"No," James said. "Not quite."

"You'll wait and let him make it up for you, will you?"

"No," replied James, taking the suggestion seriously, "but I'll know for certain when I see him on Saturday."

"Am I to be given no inkling?"

"I prefer not to be laughed at in a public place."

"No place could be better than here, it is all giggles!" But despite his words there was earnestness in Timothy's expression. "What is in your mind, James? You can't say so much without telling me all."

James looked his friend very straight in the eye. "I would like to go to Bow Street and work with Henry Fielding. I greatly admire much that he is doing to reduce crime. I doubt I am old or experienced enough, but there are some things in my favour."

Timothy looked worriedly at his companion. "You mean that, don't you?" he asked thoughtfully.

"With all my heart."

"But *why*, man? Why waste all that learning on the scum you will have to deal with? Why risk losing your head in a fight with cowards and killers, why—" Timothy broke off, and with a rare gesture touched the back of James's hand. "I am sorry, Jamey. I've no right to talk so wildly."

"Everyone else will," remarked James with a wry smile. "Loudest of all, I imagine, my mother. Such a prodigal waste of education, of opportunity, of—" He too broke off. "You will have no difficulty filling in the gaps."

"No difficulty at all," agreed Timothy. "Is this because—" He paused and looked away, as if momentarily touched by shame. "No matter! Will you have more coffee?"

"No, thank you. Were you going to ask if I had this desire because my father was in the employ of Sir John Furnival at the time of his death? And whether I have a hatred of crime because my father was murdered by a highwayman?"

"Truly I was, but it is none of my business," Timothy replied uneasily.

"But I would like to answer. This is a difficult decision and it will help to talk to someone who can be detached, as I believe you can be.

190

It is not because my father worked at Bow Street against criminals. It is because I believe in what John Furnival has been trying to do these many years. I think, as he does, that we need a much stronger civilian control over crime than we have. The second day I came back to London, my first visit for three years, I went a-walking to all the old familiar places, and—"

"Sentimentality," Timothy interrupted. "Mawkish sentimentality, nothing more."

"Stench," countered James.

"What did you say?"

"I said 'stench.' The same stench. The same filth in the streets. And as much crime. *More* crime than is usual in summer, in fact, and it is always worse in winter. Why, when John Furnival was at Bow Street the highwaymen kept outside the city walls, and even footpads seldom ventured into the wide thoroughfares. Today, *today*, as soon as darkness falls, they are everywhere; in the Strand, in St. James's Square, no one is safe without an armed guard, so no one who cannot afford an armed guard dares venture afield. They—"

James broke off as two middle-aged men came past the table, glancing curiously at his tense, white face and glittering eyes. When they had gone he continued, his voice throbbing with emotion.

"Yesterday I saw a man being taken out of the stocks, his head and shoulders smeared with refuse, I saw gin-soaked men and women in the middle of the afternoon at Grog Lane, I saw some of the streets and alleys as bad as the wards in Newgate, and I saw thieves going among the drunkards, stealing what little money they had and snatching rings off the fingers of the women." He spread trembling hands across the table. "Oh, yes, I know what you will tell me: that I have walked across a fine new bridge and seen some fine new buildings and much prosperity. But I haven't seen a street safe to walk in after dark —or a single yard or alley lit as the law demands. And why not? Simply because criminals terrify the householders into dousing them. *This* is why I want to work at Bow Street. The laws *must* be enforced; criminals *must* be brought to book; people *must* be protected."

Timothy had listened with surprise and alarm, turning, finally, into obvious distress. He was silent for an appreciable time after James had finished, and then asked quietly, "Was this not in your mind before you came down from Oxford?"

"No, Tim. I swear it."

"What had you in mind at that time?"

"Oh, the law. Then I read Henry Fielding's *Enquiry into the Causes of the Late Increase of Robbers, with some proposals for remedying this growing Evil.*" James gave a sardonic laugh. "He asked for fresh legislation against receivers of stolen goods and fresh control of the sale of gin. And he also claimed that some thief-takers were most honourable men."

"No doubt he meant those who work for him," Timothy said dryly. "What was the result of this *Enquiry*?"

"In some ways, good. Hogarth, long a friend of Henry Fielding's, executed his famous engraving *Gin Lane*, and that helped to bring about the new Act compelling all who sell gin to do so through alehouses, under license. But the law has to be strictly enforced and Fielding needs helpers without being able to pay for them."

"James," Timothy said after a pause, "you know, don't you, that thief-takers are held very low in public esteem, despite Fielding's defense of some."

"Yes," James answered, "I do."

Neither of the young men spoke until Timothy asked abruptly, "Will you come with me tonight?"

"Where to?" asked James in surprise.

"For some feminine company and frolics. You need to free your mind of the horrors you have seen and the weighty problems you are considering. This place to which I would take you is not a brothel or a grogshop, it is a house, well run and—"

"I would prefer to go and see some of my old friends," James replied, not letting Timothy finish. "You go to your ladies, Tim. Call me a prude if you like but certainly I am not in the mood for frolics."

"That I can see." Smiling, Tim asked in the gentlest of voices, "Have you ever slept with a woman, James?"

James flushed a dusky red. "No," he replied shortly.

"I will tell you this," said Tim earnestly, "before I would be happy at your marrying a sister of mine I would want proof that you had taken lessons in how to treat a lady!" Laughter as well as seriousness showed in his eyes as he went on. "But I must admit there is evidence to suggest that some men are born celibate. Are you ready to leave?"

"Yes, at once."

"I will walk with you as far as Long Acre," Timothy said as he placed a coin on the table and then led the way out. "And I will show you this haunt of vice where I shall pleasure myself. Why"—he glanced around him—"it is nearly dark. Are you not afraid of footpads, Jamey?"

"I must confess thought of them causes me some uneasiness," James Marshall admitted. "But nothing to the uneasiness I should feel were I to accompany you this evening."

"Are you sure you won't come with me?" Timothy asked again.

"I am going to see the Reverend Sebastian Smith," replied James. "Are you sure you won't come with *me*?"

James walked alone along Long Acre and past the site where St. Hilary's had once been. Already the walls of another building, not a church, were going up and great piles of bricks and wooden scaffolding were piled where the pulpit had stood. Buildings on the other side of the street had been demolished and there were great gaps which showed the now starlit sky. Every so often a horse whinnied but there was little traffic, all was in darkness. Shadows at corners and in doorways seemed to move and sounds that he thought were muffled footsteps were not far behind him. At some doorways flares gave a meager light but most of the time the only break in the darkness was from lighted windows. He approached the spot where he had once worked and stood stock-still—astounded.

The old building was not there!

In its place was a taller one, four stories high at least, with six shops on either side of a high arched passage. Over this archway, protected by an iron grille, was the largest flare James had seen that night, its flames illuminating an announcement on the huge board fastened to the wall above it similar to that one he had already seen on the horse cart:

EBENEZER MORGAN & SONS
ALWAYS THE HIGHEST CLASS IN GROCERIES

and on the bottom line that almost unbelievable statement:

103/109 Long Acre, and 9 Establishments
Elsewhere in London

James listened, and there was now no doubt at all that he heard footsteps approaching stealthily on the other side of the road. When he judged the moment right, he quieted his thumping heart and spun around, calling out sharply, "Who is that? Who follows me?"

To his relief he saw only one person, dark against the shadows, who stopped the instant he turned and called. On the same instant, footsteps sounded from the archway and a guard came running, tall pole in hand. The man behind turned and ran for his life, while the watchman slackened his pace and approached James.

"What manner of fool are you to walk alone at night?" he demanded in a gruff voice.

He was nearly as broad as he was tall, massive enough to fill the archway, and James knew at once that he was Tom Harris. Tom, one of the finest constables John Furnival had ever had, working as a night guard for Morgan!

"Well, speak up, or how shall I know you haven't come to steal?" Harris growled.

"And if I do speak up, Tom, how will you judge whether I am telling the truth?" James asked.

"You know me better than I know you," Harris said suspiciously.

"I doubt that, Thomas Harris," James replied, much warmth in his voice. "You will know me well once you have looked back to the days when I was a young boy always at your side."

"James Marshall!" Tom Harris cried in sudden recognition. "By all the gold in the Bank of England, 'tis Jamey!"

They met in the middle of the road and clasped each other firmly before Harris backed away and looked searchingly at the younger man. Then questions poured from his lips. How was James's mother? How were Beth and Henrietta? How was the old justice himself? As his excitement quieted Tom showed how much he had aged, how lines were carved in the broad face, how far the hair had receded from his forehead.

At last he said with great reluctance, "I must go on my rounds, Jamey, and that will take an hour at least, but I can come back here for a while afterward. Will you have time to wait?"

"I would rather use the time by seeing the Reverend Smith."

"You'll find him in the same house; he is allowed to live there until the place is knocked down as the church has been," Tom answered flatly. "Will you try to come back in an hour, say?"

"I will come back," James promised.

As he walked along the road he was puzzled. First, why was Tom doing this and not working for the Fieldings? Second, why had his tone been so flat and troubled at talk of the Reverend Smith? And third, why hadn't he inquired after John Furnival the Fourth, now ten years old? It must have been an oversight; what else could it have been?

The rectory of St. Hilary's was at the back of the church site, in a

narrow lane which had once had fields all about it but now was surrounded by houses. Outside the front gate a torch flickered unsteadily. James opened the gate, having to push hard and making it squeak
on the gravel of the path before he could get through. Another dim
light showed on the stained-glass fanlight above the doorway. He
rang the pull-type bell and heard it clang but no one came. He pulled
again, surprised at the chill which had crept into the night air.

Suddenly he heard Sebastian Smith's voice booming in the hallway.
"That will be another of them. Can we get no rest?" His footsteps
sounded and he opened the door abruptly, speaking before he could
see who was on the doorstep. "I can't help you, I wish I could, but
I've nothing in the church poor box, and the constable keeps the
parish box. You'll find him at Bow Street."

There was a note of exasperation, perhaps of helplessness, in the
clergyman's voice, and he kept a tight hold on the door, as if ready to
slam it in the caller's face at the slightest provocation. Shadows moved
in his study behind him. It was not Sebastian's wife there, as James's
mother had written in a letter that she had died of smallpox two
years ago.

James was aware of the intense gaze from the little man when suddenly Smith cried out in a very different tone, " 'Tis James Marshall,
in the name of goodness. Jamey! Come in, lad, come in! You've grown
so much I didn't recognise you. Come in, come in!" He clasped
James's arm, drew him inside and slammed the door. " 'Tis not often
I have a welcome visitor by night, 'tis always the poor come to beg,
and how their ranks grow thicker. We poor clergymen are always
their target. We are supposed to be able to make manna fall from
heaven, and if we fail them we get cursed for trying!" He ushered
James into the old, familiar room, with its Queen Anne desk, religious
samplers on the walls, the row of churchwardens, the huge jar of
tobacco. "Mary, who do you think has come to see us? Jamey Marshall of all the people on earth and in heaven!"

A young woman rose from a chair. She held a needle and thread in
her right hand and in her other hand was one of her father's surplices.
High on the wall above, two candles burned to give her the light she
needed for mending, and at the same time showed her face vividly; it
had changed from that of the awkward girl he remembered, full of
life but with nothing extraordinary to commend her. Now, she was
beautiful; and for a measurable time all he could do was stand and
stare at her.

CHAPTER *14*

Mary

IT SEEMED to James Marshall that, as their gaze crossed, some message passed between them, or some spark of understanding, perhaps a sense of shock. As he was amazed at the change the years had wrought in her, so might she be at the change in him. The moments could only have been few. Sebastian Smith hardly seemed to have stopped moving and talking; perhaps he had not, perhaps James had been blinded to all else but Mary.

"Get some coffee, Mary—you'll partake of coffee, Jamey? And sit down, my boy. My! You've turned into a man in a few short years —hasn't he, Mary? And the very image of his father, the spitting image! Mary! Some coffee, my dear!"

"Hullo, Mary," James said, and his voice sounded strange in his own ears.

"Good evening, James."

"I'm very glad to see you again."

"It is a pleasure to see you."

"Coffee, Mary!" Smith almost spluttered in eager insistence. "Do you want our guest to stand up all the time he's here? Will you sup with us, Jamey?"

"No thank you. But coffee will be very welcome."

"Then bring him one of your pasties, daughter. Show him that some Londoners can cook; not all the good food stays in the country where 'tis grown. Sit down, lad, sit down!"

Mary looked straight ahead as she went out, as if not wanting to see him as she passed. She was tall now for a woman, and the top of her head must come at least up to his eyes. Her father cleared a leather slung-seated chair of a mass of papers, turned his own chair from the crowded desk, and stretched up for a churchwarden which was hanging nearby. He groped about at the bottom of the huge tobacco jar and began to fill the blackened bowl; and he talked all the time, asking questions but giving James no chance to answer.

The only other sound was the clatter of a horseman, riding fast, and Sebastian Smith said, "That will be one of Fielding's men, be sure of that, going to head some villain off. There is a short cut through to Covent Garden piazza from here now that the old houses are down, did you know that? How long is it since you were here, Jamey? Don't tell me, don't tell me! It must be all of four years! How old are ye now, lad? Don't tell me, don't tell me!"

He paused and consulted the heavy beams of the ceiling, as if he were praying. But the answer came not from him but from Mary as she entered the room carrying a tray.

"He is twenty-two, Father. And it is three years since he was here, but four since I have seen him."

"Be sure if she says so, she is right," declared Smith. "I never knew such a girl for remembering. In fact, she is my memory these days; my own is failing fast."

He put the unlit pipe down while James watched Mary place the tray on a table within reach of all three of them; steam rose from the coffee and from a pitcher of milk, and there were three pasties as golden-brown and appetizing as any his mother had ever cooked.

As he drank and ate, he answered all their questions about his family, his life in Germany and at Oxford, but was vague as to his hopes. He had wanted to ask things of them both, but was now reluctant to do so, for clearly there had been changes in this household. At least two fine pieces of furniture had disappeared since his last visit. Was the nearly empty tobacco jar also symptomatic of a change in Smith's fortunes? And the clothes he was wearing were patched, whilst Mary was mending a garment which had the faint brown shade which years so often gave to black cloth. She sat in the corner sewing while the two men finished coffee.

197

Out of the blue, her father said, "You aren't a blind man, James; you must see that all is not as well with us as it should be. Don't say you'd noticed nothing; there's no need to study my feelings, lad. Since I threw in my lot with John Wesley much has gone wrong for me. The Bishop frowned upon my association from the beginning, and the more successful Wesley became the more bitter the opposition from within the Church. St. Hilary's was full of beetle and dry rot, 'tis true, but any other church would have been saved. Instead, they built a new one a mile away. And most of my people lived in the houses here which are now pulled down, and many are old and cannot come back to me."

"But surely the living—" began James.

" 'Twas always a very poor living here, James, supplemented by one or two steadfast believers, of whom one was Ebenezer Morgan. Ebenezer has endowed the new church on one condition: that a new parson is given the living. I'll have none then."

"But what will you do?" James found it hard to utter the question.

"I shall become one of Wesley's preachers. Blessed be to God their number is increasing. And I can have all London as my parish. I shall live with friends while I am in a particular part of London helping to establish a congregation, and I shall no doubt be comfortable. It will be strange but my heart dictates this course."

James thought in alarm: Then what of Mary? He glanced toward her, but her eyes were cast down at her sewing.

Sebastian Smith was saying, "The truth is that absolutely everything has changed and there are times when I am very bitter. Have you ever known me to turn away the poor? These days I have to, and I put a hard face on it until I grow hard of heart. I never knew your stepfather refuse to help, lad, but Henry Fielding, good though his heart is, hasn't the money." He paused a moment, while James looked at him in silence, then banged a clenched fist on the table. "What happens, James? The law leaves its handling to parish officers and vestrymen who hoard as much as they can to stuff themselves and their cronies with a great feast at Christmas and at Easter. Why, 'tis wickedness itself. In John Furnival's day 'twas not so noticeable about here but it was terrible in other parts of London and the nearer towns. How is he, d'you say? Is there any hope of his coming back?"

James had a swift mental picture of the huge figure in his special chair that he could propel for short distances himself by means of cogwheels, but always he had to be helped in and out of the chair for the closet or the bedroom.

James shook his head slowly.

Footsteps sounded in the alley and as Sebastian Smith rose resignedly, as if knowing that they would be those of yet more destitute people coming for help, James rose with him.

"Stay, lad, 'tis none of your affair," Smith said.

"At least let me give you this to help them." James had two half guineas and some pennies in his purse and he shook them onto the palm of his hand.

With great care Smith took all but two of the pennies but did not touch the gold pieces. As he left the room James moved closer to Mary and he raised his voice a little over a banging door to ask, "Mary, what are you going to do?"

"I propose to secure for myself a post as housekeeper," Mary replied promptly.

"Is it all settled?" he demanded.

"Yes, I think so. My father has yet to give his final approval but there is little choice. The family is a respectable one and there are five young children. No doubt the work will be hard, but"—she smiled—"I am used to hard work."

Voices sounded from along the hall; then the door closed and Sebastian Smith's footsteps drew near again. He called, "I'll be back very soon. Don't run away, Jamey!" There was a hint of the old spirit in his voice as he hurried toward the rear of the house.

"Do I know the family you are to serve?" James asked.

"I think it most unlikely," Mary replied. "They are by name Weygalls, Paul and Mathilda Weygalls. Mr. Weygalls is a merchant in Covent Garden. At one time he worked for Ebenezer Morgan but he was affluent enough to begin a business of his own. He is not only a grocer but an apothecary, and he also supplies surgical instruments to doctors." She stretched out her left hand, and when James gripped it she said, "Don't look so forlorn, Jamey. I shall be well cared for and content."

"I feel as if I've found a jewel only to lose it," James told her. He felt deeply distressed.

"You are very gallant, sir!"

"I feel as gallant as a clodhopper! Mary, can you delay a while?"

"Not more than a day or two," she replied, "and although my father makes a great fuss of giving or withholding his approval, he must, in fact, give it. One week from today this house will be demolished—yes, as soon as that! Father can live with his friends although it will be hard for him not to have a home of his own. I cannot inflict myself on others, there being none on whom I would even wish to! And such posts as the Weygalls offer are few and far between. I might go half a year without finding another, and"—her eyes glowed with merriment—"you would not have me resort to the streets, would you?"

James remembered playing with her and her brothers and sisters as a child. Now Mary looked at and accepted the world as it was, had weighed up all the alternatives and made her choice. Why did she not marry? It was on the tip of his tongue to ask but a door banged: Sebastian Smith was coming back.

James moved farther away from her and then said urgently, "Delay the decision, Mary. I beg you to."

"Should you not talk to my father, sir?"

"You can twist your father around your finger, and well you know it!"

"But I cannot twist James Marshall, I perceive! If it pleases you I will delay until Monday but not later than noon on that day. I will not ask why you wish the delay because I trust you not to play with my future!"

"I need time to think," James said huskily. "I need to—"

He broke off, unable to say more because his heart was thumping so hard. He knew what had happened to him since he had stepped into this room yet could hardly believe it, and for a few moments his head whirled and a jumble of thoughts raced unbidden through his mind. He saw a different expression in Mary's eyes, as if she caught a glimpse of the truth, and they were regarding each other in silence when Sebastian Smith came in and began to boom. How grateful the couple at the door had been, how glad he was to see Jamey again, he hoped they would meet again soon, if not in this house then in some other. He looked very tired, James thought, as he took his leave.

He was halfway along the lane leading to Long Acre, the picture of Mary's face still vividly in his mind, when he became aware of the murmur of muted voices. Would anyone lying in wait for a victim talk so audibly? James wondered. But perhaps they had not heard him approach. He was walking on soft earth and made little sound.

He heard a man say clearly, "Here she comes!"

Now he could make out the shapes of four or five youths lurking in the shadow of a tall building. Across the road was light from an alley and down the alley came a girl. Reaching Long Acre, she paused, looked up and down, saw no one, and began to hurry, half running, in the direction of Morgan's new building. On the instant, the youths leaped from their hiding place and raced after her, whooping with glee. Two of them passed her and stood in front so that she could not go in any direction.

"No," she gasped in terror. "No!"

"Don't worry, little one, we won't hurt you!" cried one.

"Just have a little fun," another called.

Two of them swooped again and, obviously with long practice, one seized the girl by the waist and whirled her upside down, so that her skirt dropped over her head. Two shoes shone in the reflected light as she kicked and struggled. But the other youths moved forward, and while one seized her right leg and one her left, another slipped his hand under her petticoats, ignoring her now muffled cries.

All this had happened so quickly that James Marshall was at first astonished, then shocked, and then furious. He moved forward to cry out, but there was a movement behind him, a hand closed over his mouth, and a viselike arm encircled his neck. Aware of what was happening to the girl, he could now do nothing to help her until he had dealt with his captor.

Very slowly, James shifted his position.

In Germany he had met a student from whom he had learned an ancient Japanese art known as jujitsu. He knew where to grip a man's wrist or arm, shoulder or leg, to cause great pain and also a numbness which robbed the other momentarily of his strength. James moved until he had the right grip on his assailant's wrist, then twisted. The other gasped. Exerting little strength, James heaved him over his shoulder. The man went flying and struck a partly built wall, the thud making the youths look around.

James stooped down, picked up two bricks and hurled them at the pack, then seized the fallen man's staff. As he rushed forward, the youths fled along Long Acre, one of them limping where a brick had caught him on the knee. The girl was in a huddled heap, her skirt and petticoats still tumbled over her head. He could hear her sobbing as he pulled her clothes about her more tidily until her tear-stained face appeared. She could be no more than fourteen or fifteen, and in spite of the tears she was pretty, her fair hair in long ringlets.

"Thank you, oh, thank you!" she managed to say, obviously wanting to get up. "Thank you a hundred times, sir. I—I beg you to say nothing of this to anyone. If it were known that I had been attacked by the New Mohocks I would live in shame; no one would believe I was not raped." She began to pull herself free of his hand as the words spilled out. "I shall be safe now. I have only to go a short distance along the street. I do beg of you, say nothing."

She turned from him and ran.

James stood watching, baffled, because for all she knew the gang that had attacked her could be waiting in some doorway or alley, but when she reached the archway between the Morgan shops she turned down it and disappeared. Did she lodge nearby? he wondered.

He was sweating freely and had no heart for another encounter but he thought of the man who had attacked him and whom he had thrown so heavily. Was he still on the ground or had he also taken flight?

The fellow was standing by the wall and he moved as James began to cross the street, but he limped badly. James judged that he was a much bigger man than the striplings who had tormented the girl. Holding the man's pole firmly in his hand, he went toward him.

"If I had my way—" he began, and was going on to add that he would strip the watchman of his job when, with savage certainty, he realised that this was Tom Harris. *Tom* had tried to prevent him from rushing to the girl's assistance; *Tom* had lurked in wait for him, would have allowed the young brutes to have their way with the child. James could hardly get the words out when he said, "Tom, if I didn't know it was you I would never have believed this, but I cannot doubt the evidence of my eyes."

"No," Tom muttered, "no one would expect you to."

Questions rushed one after the other into James's mind but he did not voice them; at heart he was afraid of hearing the answers. Just as he had felt exhilarated only a few minutes ago, with Mary's face thrusting everything else from his mind's eye, now he felt a heavy weight of near misery.

Tom said gruffly, "I wanted to prevent you from interfering, Jamey. I was afraid of what they would do to you if you attacked them. At least two carry knives, and I did not want you hurt."

"Obviously it did not matter what happened to the girl," James replied bitterly.

"Oh, it mattered. Such things have scored my heart a dozen times, but the situation in London has become worse and worse. These New Mohocks are as bad as the first of their breed. After dark no woman or girl is free from the risk of being molested."

"I've known the time when you would have cracked their skulls."

"Aye," Harris agreed, "and no doubt I should have, but I know two of them are sons of Ebenezer Morgan, and I work for Morgan. Without the pittance he pays me I would be one of the poor wretches who go begging to the Reverend Smith and often come away empty-handed, since how can a man who has nothing give anything?" When James did not respond Harris went on: "I did not save much money when I worked at Bow Street; I was never much for blood money. When Henry Fielding told me I could not stay with him, I had less than enough in my stocking to live for a year. I tried to get work, but no one would employ one of John Furnival's men except as a Charlie. That's the truth, Jamey. I am ashamed of what happened tonight and of what I have become but"—he drew a deep, hoarse breath—" 'tis better than living the life of a pauper, in and out of the work-houses."

James said huskily, "I am more sorry than I can say, Tom."

"Yes, you would be."

"But," James's voice rose in protest at believing all that he had heard, "couldn't Fielding keep you at Bow Street? Or one of the other courts? It is a crime to throw away a man of your experience!"

"Oh, I don't know," Tom dissented. "I am too old for the work that has to be done, and both Fieldings are doing the best they can on very little money. I've a friend at Bow Street; do you remember David Winfrith?" James had a quick mental image of an overeager young man who had acted as a messenger between the court and the private quarters at the Bow Street house. "He is still there and he tells me what goes on. There are times when David is so like Silas Moffat that I swear Silas must have sired a son no one dreamed about, unless John Furnival knew and gave him the post as clerk. If you want to know what is happening, talk to him. You'll find him in the Chapter Coffee House in Paternoster Row each morning after court. He gives the newspapers tidbits of information about cases important enough to warrant their having a man at a hearing."

"You mean Fielding admits the *press*?" James exclaimed.

"Not officially—but the newspapers have their paid men present very often," Harris said. At last he stirred, putting his leg on the ground gingerly, then taking a few paces.

James went with him, troubled and confused, and as they reached Long Acre he asked, "These New Mohocks, Tom. Is no one safe?"

"No one fool enough to venture out alone after dark. They're not the same breed as footpads and highwaymen; they do what they do for excitement and enjoyment."

"Would Mary Smith be safe?"

"No one is safe, Jamey. Mary would not risk venturing out alone, mind you."

But Mary would soon be working for the merchant Weygalls, thought James, and living in this same area where the young Morgans and their cronies conducted a reign of terror over the local women. And in the meantime, what would happen in an emergency, for instance, if Mary had to fetch a doctor for her father?

James shivered.

Suddenly Tom said, "Hush!"

Soon James became aware of voices and footsteps and marveled at the sharpness of the older man's ears. Presumably the group that had attacked the girl had entered Long Acre from a nearby alley, and at the same moment a stench as from an open sewer assaulted James's nostrils, carried on the wind. Would the New Mohocks have opened a cesspit or a closed sewer? Or could they—

Tom Harris made a funny little noise and James realised that he was stifling a laugh. Then he saw two of the youths go ahead of the others into the Morgan archway; the flickering light showed that their clothes were matted close to their bodies. The other three kept well to the windward of them as they all disappeared, and now Harris laughed aloud, howbeit keeping the sound low.

"The builders dug into a cesspit this afternoon and did not cover it; those two must have fallen in. Please God each was a Morgan and may the stink stay with them all their lives!" he said bitterly.

One of the youths who had fallen into the open pit was Gabriel Morgan, the other the son of the owner of one of the big houses in Covent Garden, by name Jacob Rackham. They first washed the dirt off with a hose in the stables and then stood naked while the other youths poured buckets of water over them until the odour was all but gone. Their clothes were ruined but they were old, worn only on nights when the group went out for their "fun."

Gabriel Morgan shivered as he wrapped a cloak about him, and he said in a flat, deadly sounding voice, "If I ever find out who that man was tonight, I will cut his throat."

Rackham growled, "I'd draw him first to enjoy his screaming, then hang and quarter him. And I'd expect everyone here to help." He glared around at the others and demanded of them one by one:

"Do you swear, Saul?"

"I swear."

"Do you swear, David?"

"Upon my soul, I swear!"

"And you, Charles?" the youth demanded. "And you, Gabriel?"

Solemnly each man swore that if they ever learned the name of the man who had robbed them of their entertainment and who had sent them running wildly to safety and the cesspit, he would help first to draw him while he was alive, than hang and quarter him.

Leaving the near-deserted streets behind him, James Marshall turned out of Bow Yard and came soon to the northern end of Bow Street. Here, at least, there had been no major changes since his last visit. One man stood outside the courthouse doorway, and two horses were tethered to wooden posts, while several sedan chairs were placed nearby. At any other time James would have gone inside but he was virtually certain that except for Winfrith he would know none of the men who now served Henry Fielding.

Suddenly his thoughts switched back to the gang, copying tricks their predecessors had been infamous for thirty and more years before. James could picture the girl, running, trapped, upturned. He could see her vividly when he had straightened her clothes, and on the instant he pictured not her pretty tear-stained face, but Mary's.

Such a thing must never happen to Mary—and yet *no one* was safe, Tom had said. *No one.*

When he reached the top of the Strand a roaring sound penetrated the clouds of dread and confusion and anger in his mind and heart. For the second time that day the traffic in this great thoroughfare was piled up, and parish constables were calling out: "Go by Long Acre or Holborn, there is no path this way."

The one or two small carriages and a few horsemen who tried to go on were swamped by the mass of people on foot pressing toward the scene of the trouble. Suddenly James saw flames leaping out of the higher floors of a building. As he stared, aghast, two women jumped down onto the milling crowd below, mouths open in screams he could not hear.

People were shouting. A riderless horse was screaming, rearing up on its hind legs and thrashing at the crush of people thronging around it. As the flames leaped higher and the roof caught fire in a fierce and sudden blaze, James was knocked against a heavy sign which read:

His mother had once worked here. The sign was so heavy that he hauled himself up by the wrought ironwork which fastened it to the wall. In a few moments he was astride the top of the sign and had a perfect view of the astounding spectacle ahead. One glance was enough to show him that a dozen sailors stood in a half-circle about the burning brothel known as Charlie Wylie's while screaming women came rushing out of the brothel carrying chairs and feather beds and cooking pots. The flames now blew across the street, and clearly there was a danger of a conflagration starting there. James saw a line of men carrying leather buckets already beginning to toss water onto the walls of the tavern next door, but no one seemed concerned with the brothel itself. There was no sign of fire carts, either, which, with their hand pumps, could have worked much more quickly than men with water-filled buckets.

A hanging sign came crashing down while the crowd turned into a seething, screaming mob.

Gradually, above the din was heard the tramp of marching feet and a bugle sounded. James waited for a moment until the space beneath him was clear, then lowered himself and dropped to the cobbles. Sliping into a narrow lane, he soon reached the river, a splendid spectacle with the reflections of flares and lamps in the water. At the corners and at all gateways, guards and watchmen were posted; this part of London at least was kept comparatively free from crime, for it was well lighted and well guarded.

In a narrow street which led to Charing Cross, behind the Royal Stables, were three- and four-story buildings, many of which were let to young men on their own in London. Timothy had such a flat, whose windows overlooked the river to the tree-clad south bank and beyond to St. Paul's and the City. James was sharing this flat with Timothy until he made up his mind what to do, but the flat was now empty. He unlocked the door and was careful to lock it again from the inside before lowering himself into a chair by the window. Stretching his legs straight in front of him, he loosened his collar, Mary Smith, Tom Harris, the tear-stained face of the girl vividly in his mind.

He was dozing when Timothy came in, tired but excited. Had James seen the fire in the Strand and did he know what had happened? Five sailors from a four-master tied up at Greenwich had visited the brothel and had been robbed while disporting themselves. They had demanded the return of all their goods and had threatened to pull the place down unless everything was given back. Charlie Wylie, used to the braggadocio of drunken sailors, had sent them off empty-handed, not dreaming they would return with dozens of their mates, hell-set to wreck·the brothel.

"And they tell me Saunders Welch persuaded the officer on duty at Tilt Yard to send troops in time to help save the whole district from being burned to the ground. What do you know of this Saunders Welch, Jamey?"

"That he is a friend of the Fieldings and a man of like caliber."

"So fully approved by James Marshall!" Timothy stifled a yawn. "Did you do all you wanted to?"

"Not quite," James said. "But I hope to finish tomorrow and go to St. Giles the following day."

Once in bed, he tossed and turned, unable to get to sleep, haunted by his experiences of the evening and troubled, also, by the behaviour of the crowd. There would have been a vast area of destruction but for the troops. But why hadn't one of the Fieldings sent for them and not left the responsibility to a high constable?

As a result of his restlessness, he slept late, and when he woke, Timothy had gone. James went out, depressed and worried, had a breakfast of sausages, chops and coffee at a coffee house in the Strand and read in a late edition of *The London Advertiser* that the Fieldings had been out of town the previous night.

Outside, he saw crowds gathering, and they looked in an ugly mood. Two men whom he passed were talking.

"Any time they use the troops against the citizenry, I'm against it," said one.

"There's talk that those sailors will be back tonight, in hundreds," said the other.

As James drew nearer Bow Street, the crowds were even thicker, and to his astonishment they were outside the Bow Street court, yelling, brandishing clubs and iron bars. Some were chanting words which gradually became distinguishable.

"Release them!"

"Let the prisoners free!"

"Release the prisoners!"

"If they won't, we'll break down the doors and get them," a man near James growled.

Suddenly James heard the thud of marching feet; obviously this time Henry Fielding had called out the troops. As the crowd began to divide for twenty or more soldiers, some of Fielding's men appeared at the door of the house, a prisoner manacled to each man. The crowd began to hurl bricks and stones, but the troops impassively formed an impenetrable guard as the manacled men were marched off.

"Fielding's committed them to Newgate," a man said angrily. "There'll be trouble after this, you may be sure."

The next moment James heard a volley of shots, and one of Fielding's men on horseback came tearing around the corner and cried, "There are four thousand sailors on the march from Tower Hill. They say they'll set fire to all of London if their men aren't released."

"And there are a thousand men on the way to stop them. We had word of the gathering at Tower Hill," another added.

James would not have been surprised to hear the tumult of battle, but now all the streets were lined at intervals with troops, and very slowly the crowd began to break up in an uneasy peace. The disturbances of the morning made it impossible for him to see David Winfrith, for everything at the court was badly delayed. He walked back toward the end of the Strand and realised for the first time that Wylie's brothel and the Cock Tavern were rased to the ground.

"Wylie will have to find somewhere else for his girls to take their men tonight, and the old Cock won't be serving ale for many a month, if ever," Timothy remarked late that evening, when they were getting ready for bed. "What time will you leave for St. Giles?" he added.

"Any time before noon will be early enough," replied James. "I am told there is a coach leaving Hyde Park at every hour on the stroke, heading for Birmingham as well as Oxford and other places in the middle provinces and the north, and each will stop at St. Giles village." After a moment he asked lightly, "Did you do all you hoped to do?"

"That's a sly one," declared Timothy, laughing. "Will it be answer enough if I tell you that I am exhausted?"

James joined in the laughter but his was edged with anxiety. In one way he would have liked to talk to Timothy but he did not think the slightest good would come of telling him how he felt about Mary, so he said nothing, and it wasn't long before each was in his own small room, undressed and ready for bed. Again it was some time before James went to sleep, and for at least an hour he struggled with his thoughts and fears and listened to Timothy's rhythmic snoring.

The longer James lay awake the more vivid Mary's face became.

CHAPTER *15*

The House at St. Giles

WHEN JAMES left the rooms next morning, he carried his bag by sedan chair to the coach departure place at Hyde Park, had the baggage roll well marked with his name and destination, then set out for the Chapter Coffee House. The morning promised a fine day, and so he walked a northerly route until he reached St. James's Park. Some families were already in the park, children playing on the lake with small boats as their mothers watched. From St. James's he took another sedan chair, one of whose bearers was a Negro who ran between the frontshafts. James paid the Negro sixpence before stepping toward the narrow oak door of the Chapter Coffee House.

This, he knew, was a meeting place of at least three worlds. Men of letters, were they humble journalists or writers of renown such as Dr. Johnson, went there to talk with friends who shared their love of literature, of writing, and of the sound of their own voices. Book publishers and printers also attended, together with bankers and merchants from the area north of St. Paul's and a sprinkling of clerics from the cathedral or from churches within easy reach.

James was momentarily afraid that the coffee house would not be open, for it lacked five minutes of ten o'clock, but the door yielded to his hand and he stepped into a room so brightly lit from panels of glass in the ceiling that there was no need of lamps. On the walls were some front pages of various newspapers as well as some Hogarth sketches and caricatures of prominent men of letters, politicians and members of the Royal household. Racks of churchwardens, all marked with tiny labels, hung around the walls beneath the pictures, and some were suspended by leather thongs from the wooden beams across the ceiling.

That morning no more than a dozen men were present and James did not see Winfrith. He was hovering between waiting hopefully and giving up when Winfrith, emerging from a door marked CLOSET in a corner, approached a nearby table and sat with a thin-faced man with close-trimmed jet-black hair and beard. Winfrith glanced at James and then suddenly spun around to stare at him. In that moment the likeness between this man in his early thirties and James's memory of Silas Moffat was startling, the clear, pale, blue-gray eyes, with their innocent expression, the most similar of all.

"It *is* James Marshall!" Winfrith exclaimed, and sprang to his feet, both arms extended. In spite of his angular thinness the grip of his hand was firm. "Jamey, I can't tell you how glad I am to see you! Did you come by chance or to seek me out?"

"To seek you out," James replied. "I tried yesterday but you were busy. Two nights ago I encountered Tom Harris, who assured me you would be the one to tell me what is happening at Bow Street."

"Better even than Henry Fielding," declared the close-bearded man at the table. "Are you John Furnival's stepson?"

"Yes."

"I never met John Furnival but everyone who knew him tells me that is a great loss," the other replied. "I am—"

"James, I would like you to meet one of Bow Street's most worthy friends," Winfrith interrupted. "A man who serves us and what we are trying to do better than any other—Mr. Benedict Sly, of *The Daily Clarion*. What I forget, he can tell you. That is, if you have no objection to his presence."

"If the discussion is confidential I will at once excuse myself," declared Benedict Sly. There was a glint of humour in his eyes. "Although I confess I would prefer to be present."

"For my part, sir, you are very welcome," James assured him as he settled down to coffee. Some brandy snaps were placed before him on a porcelain dish which was marked MORGAN'S TEAS AND COFFEES— THE BEST IN THE WORLD.

Nine other establishments in London.

Two sons who were leaders of the New Mohocks.

A pretty, sobbing, outraged girl.

And Mary.

Neither man questioned him despite the tautening of his expression, and gradually all other pictures faded except that which now unfolded of the London these men knew so well, and of what was happening in Bow Street and other magistrates' courts. All James's fears as to the worsening state of London's crime were confirmed by what Winfrith and Sly told him, and he very soon had no doubts that the system was failing, and that the parish constables, sheriffs' officers and the private forces employed to maintain the safety and the security of the wealthy were unable to cope with the increasing boldness of criminals. No one was safe. A dignitary might take with him an armed guard of six or eight men and the guard might be vanquished by a gang as fiercely armed and twice as strong in numbers. Where householders did place lights they were swiftly doused, either from devilment or at the behest of the gangs, which preferred to commit their depredations under cover of darkness.

Neck and neck with the growth of crime, and part of the cause of it, they told him, was London's development as a commercial and industrial city. It was now not only the largest of England's ports but did twice as much trade as the rest of the ports put together, and migration from the provinces, as well as from Ireland and the Empire, swelled the population. With this came greater prosperity for some, but terrible poverty for others, leading to yet more lawbreaking.

Yet Pelham's Ministry appeared to have become moribund concerning the extent and the gravity of crime in London.

All of this poured out of Winfrith as if he had been longing for an audience.

When he had done and sat back to drink some coffee, the newspaperman Sly said dryly, "You must understand more clearly why the government does not concern itself with the condition of Londoners. It has its work cut out to keep a flow of trade and to protect British investments overseas. Our masters cannot find the time or the money to give us pure water, to bury the sewers deep, to help the starving. These urgent needs are left more and more to the private good will of individuals. And in the sacred names of freedom and liberty we have no organisation against criminals!"

Hardly had he stopped than Winfrith leaned forward and said

vehemently, "There is still worse!" He began to talk as passionately as before.

The government made laws that were bound to be broken, demanding licenses for music in an alehouse, making vagrants out of decent citizens who could not find work, condemning Henry Fielding for giving light sentences to those who, in desperation, stole food or clothing; and if a constable failed to see that laws like washing the street outside one's house or keeping a light burning were kept, then he could actually be fined. If he failed to make others carry out Sunday observance, if he permitted the sale of obscene prints . . .

"Madness!" Winfrith went on hotly. "It forces worthy men to evade the duty of constable and leads to bribery and corruption!"

The time passed with almost frightening speed; even so, they would have talked on much longer had not a man in his late twenties, carrying a constable's stave, come into the coffee house, now so crowded there was hardly a vacant seat at any table. The man bore down on Winfrith, who espied him and sprang to his feet.

" 'Tis not one o'clock already!"

"It is ten minutes past," the other declared, "and if you want to see Mr. John angry, keep him waiting just ten more minutes."

"After one!" gasped James. "I had intended . . ."

For several minutes there was a confusion of good-byes, promises to meet again, courtesies which seemed interminable, before Winfrith was gone and James looked with dismay at the clock on the wall.

"They make the most delicious pork pies and apple pasties here," Benedict Sly announced. "Join me in a meal, James, and allow me the pleasure of taking you to catch the next stage. There is one on every hour, you say? I have my trap close by."

The pies were as delicious as he had promised, the better for being washed down with fresh hot coffee, and as soon as they had finished eating, Benedict proved that he knew his way about London with any man, keeping his pony at a brisk trot along little-used roads and lanes so that when they reached the coach, due to depart at two o'clock, it had scarce begun to take on packages and passengers. Benedict did not linger and James watched him turn toward Kensington, the sprightly pony still trotting at a fair pace.

James felt more preoccupied than ever. Now he had reliable facts and figures from Winfrith and a dispassionate assessment of the situation. Benedict Sly, too, gave the impression of being a man who weighed his words before uttering them, and at least six times he had produced cuttings to illustrate the accuracy of what he had said.

One had been a reproduction of the pamphlet written by Henry Fielding headed:

Enquiry into the Causes
of the Late Increase of Robbers

I make no doubt, but that the streets of this town and the roads leading to it, will soon be impassable without the greatest hazard. There are eleven major causes.

Each had been listed, and at the end had come Fielding's final charge to the grand jury when he had been elected chairman of the Sessions.

James glanced through the morning's *Clarion,* which Benedict Sly had thrust at him, as he sat on top waiting for the coach to fill up, the driver and an assistant hurling cases and rolls onto the hold at the top. On the back page was a cartoon depicting a familiar-looking man down on his knees before a crowd of people, and beneath this was a brief statement:

Gin shop and brothel destroyed by angry sailors. Owner's plea of no avail. Firemen and troops arrive late.

Almost directly beneath this, in heavier type, was the headline:

JUSTICE FIELDING SUMMONS TROOPS
TO COMBAT SAILORS ON RAMPAGE.
COURT AT BOW STREET BESIEGED
BY ANGRY MOB

Beneath, in smaller type, was continued the telling of the events of the day before, concluding:

Why Englishmen are so opposed to law enforcement, whether by a military or a civilian force—the latter advocated by Sir John Furnival and it is believed supported by Mr. Fielding and his brother John and also the High Constable Saunders Welch—we cannot presume to guess. We only know that Mr. Fielding has aroused much resent- ment against himself for calling on the troops. The Londoners' hatred of such a course appears to make them risk another Fire of London.

His lips set in a curiously wry smile, James then scanned the newspaper for other news to do with crime. There were two reports of thieves committed to Newgate Prison by the magistrates at Bow Street, another of a Mr. David Hooper who had recovered all the property stolen from him two months ago, thanks to the good offices of a well-known thief-taker named Hardy.

On the same page he came across a small paragraph headed:

THE PLEASURES AND COMFORTS OF NEWGATE PRISON

We hear that a new scheme is on foot for enlarging the prison of Newgate by knocking down bakehouses near the Sessions House yard. It is intended to erect piazzas so that the prisoners may have room to walk about in the open air, as well as facilities for receiving prostitutes.

This will be a great comfort to all prisoners who are wealthy.

James lowered the newspaper as the elderly driver started the team of six horses. Soon the coach began to move at a fair pace, passing Tyburn Fields, where some youths were playing cricket. Gradually these sporting events gave way to green and cultivated fields, and soon every neck was craned to see a strange machine cutting the stalks of late corn, while men walked behind to gather it in sheaves, and women and children followed to pick up the gleanings that were left by tradition for the farm labourers and their families.

"That is a rotary reaper," declared the driver. "It was invented by Jethro Tull. The harvest can be reaped in half the time it takes with scythes."

"And a quarter of the men," a gray-haired passenger complained. "These machines are of the devil."

It being broad daylight and the sun warm, a large number of riders and carriages was on the road, especially when they clattered through straggling villages, past churches, farmhouses far back from the road, and here and there an inn, each with its thatched roof and narrow doors.

In the villages the road surface was tolerable, but on the open road there were great ruts, and sometimes stones and flints jutted up from the surface high enough to lame a horse or to overturn a coach. The driver showed uncanny skill in avoiding the worst places without slowing down. Only two huge flocks of sheep, their thick wool filthy with the mud of a hundred miles of being driven, forced him to a standstill, as did one big herd of cattle.

Two and a quarter hours after he had left Hyde Park, James saw blue smoke rising from the tall chimneys of St. Giles against the wooded hillside. On one side of the highway a small group of people waited, some to catch the coach, some to welcome alighting passengers. As he drew nearer he could discern the shape of the building clearly, and the rich, warm red of the bricks where they caught the sun. The walled garden with its bushy fruit trees was ablaze with color and for a breath-catching moment he recaptured the sight of the burning brothel in the Strand. Next moment he recognised Beth and Henrietta running down from the house toward the highway, whilst far behind them, hurrying, a youth pushed a wheelcart, doubtless to carry his luggage.

The driver began to pull at the leaders' reins, the brakes were applied gently and the coach drew up. Even before his bag had been handed down James was being hugged by Beth and Henrietta, both so excited that for a moment it was as if they were still children. Then, as both girls drew back, he became aware of the fact that—like Mary Smith—Beth had grown from girl to woman since he had last seen her, golden hair now piled high on her head, whereas Henrietta still had no more shape than a boy, her hair dark and glossy as a raven's wing, hanging sleekly to her shoulders. Together, they walked to the house, whilst the youth trundled the cart behind them. Beth chattered on without ceasing, Henrietta making no attempt to speak but seldom looking away from her brother.

"And such news I have to tell you," Beth declared, gripping his arm. "I am soon to be married! And to such an elegant gentleman, the son of Sir Mortimer Tench, who lives in St. Giles parish. Sir Mortimer is the justice of the peace and a great landowner. Everything is arranged between the families! Is that not wonderful news?"

"Magnificent, Beth! I wish you every happiness."

Yet he could not understand why a curious sense of depression weighed on him. She was of an age to be married and obviously eager and agog. It could not be that he would miss her for he had seen her so little. It was a feeling for his mother, he decided, whom he saw walking from the main gates. He broke free from his sisters and ran toward her. As he drew near and as the light blazed on her face he realised how beautiful she was, and his heart smote him, that she should be shut up in this place, virtually a prisoner, taking care of John Furnival. His own feelings toward his stepfather had always been, at best, ambivalent. He did not know the man, only the love and devotion he inspired, and it occurred to him now that his mother's love and devotion were costing her too dear.

On that instant he drew close enough to see her clearly; she was not only lovely of feature but serenity and happiness glowed in her, and the brief thought that caring for John Furnival was costing her much faded in his pleasure at being with her again. Talking and laughing, they entered the drive, with its grassy banks, tall elm and oak and beech on either side. Soon it widened into a carriageway large enough for a coach-and-four to swing around and stop at the great front doors; and there, framed in the open doorway, sat Sir John Furnival.

He was in his same wheelchair, although it was immediately apparent that changes had been made at the sides of the chair. Slowly John Furnival moved his arms and hands and by turning a wooden wheel on either side propelled the chair forward with surprising speed. So he had regained a little use of his left arm and hand!

As James moved ahead of his mother and sisters he saw that Furnival, though still heavy at shoulders and belly, had a hardier appearance than when he had been here those three years ago. His hand grip was firmer, too, and with great deliberation he said, "It—is—good—to—see—you—James."

Only the right side of his mouth moved; the left side of his face looked lifeless except for the brightness of his eyes. But it was a triumph that he could utter any words clearly, for over the years only Ruth had been able to understand him clearly, interpreting what he had said to others; she was not only his eyes and ears but she was his voice and she shared his spirit.

James had heard by letter that his half-brother, John the Fourth, had been sent to a small but highly respectable school in Kent, where he would have boys of his own age for company and where he would be trained to overcome a slight speech defect. He himself had written short missives to young John, who was known in the family as Johnny, but had received none in return, and he had not written for at least two months. So he asked his mother, shortly before dinner, how the younger boy was.

"The reports from school are satisfying and apparently the lisp with which he was troubled has been overcome," she replied. "It does not matter how I scold him, though, he will not write to me beyond the few lines demanded by the school."

"When will he be home?" James asked.

"At the end of the month," his mother answered. "Indeed I hope that you will be able to go and fetch him from Rochester in Kent. It is a long journey for either of your sisters and I do not like to send a servant."

"Unless I am bound hand and foot, I will go!" James promised extravagantly.

While the others were getting ready for dinner he went for a walk through the walled garden and across the nearer side of the hill, recalling with pleasure all the nooks and crannies he had rediscovered soon after Johnny had started walking and running. He wondered how the child of seven, already very like his father in appearance, with the same determination and a streak of wilfulness, which Sir John had no doubt possessed in his early childhood, had matured in the past three years.

Hearing the gong sound for dinner, he hurried back to the house, preoccupation about Johnny forgotten. His stepfather would not be there, for he was sensitive about his difficulty with eating, but his mother would be, and both of his sisters.

"Is he strong enough to talk about serious things?" asked James of his mother. It was after dinner and they were together in the bedroom which had been his since the move to St. Giles.

"The day when he cannot talk about serious things will be the day he dies," Ruth replied. She sat on the side of a small four-poster bed, looking at James as he stood against the window. "He has made great efforts to talk but comparatively few sentences exhaust him. However, he will listen to you all night if you have news of London; and he will understand and consider and give his opinions, which are as valuable and as well weighed as ever. Have you much to discuss with him, James?"

"With him and with you."

"Then start when we are all three together. He has a remarkable sense of perception, which his illness has increased rather than diminished, and if I am given prior knowledge of any subject, he will know."

"Then I will wait. Mother—are you happy about Beth's wedding?"

"I shall be content when she has settled down," Ruth answered a little hesitantly. She considered her next words with great care. "She has been a flighty one, and sometimes I think she is too pretty for her own good. For a while I feared she would find herself with child before she was married, fathered by a farmer named Nathaniel Cook, from the other side of St. Giles, but all now seems well."

James made no comment except to ask, "But will you not miss her?"

"In one way, yes, but in another I shall be glad," answered Ruth. "When the time comes for Henrietta to leave home that will be very different. But here am I, gossiping! We must go downstairs and talk to Mr. John!"

So she still thought of her husband as "Mister," James noticed.

Furnival was now in a huge chair in front of a fireplace where only a few embers glowed, for the room was warm. Sitting with his legs bent at the knees, it was difficult to believe that he was so disabled. A maid came in bearing tea and coffee and a dish of lemon curd tarts, which James loved but could hardly find room for after the huge dinner of roast beef and chicken, pasties, strawberries and cream, and delicious-tasting cheese.

"Now—tell—me—what—you—know—of—London," John Furnival asked, and he gave a one-sided smile.

James began to talk readily enough.

First he spoke of his own vivid impressions, skating over the molesting of the girl but talking of the New Mohocks, saying what he thought about the change in Tom Harris and Sebastian Smith. Through all of this John Furnival sat, stern-faced, while Ruth knitted, making only the faintest of clicking noises with her cream-coloured whalebone needles. Soon James talked of his discussion with Winfrith and Benedict Sly, recalling most of the salient things each had said.

"If I am told aright," he finished at last, "then the Fieldings are as frustrated as ever you were, sir, but they have a grave disadvantage."

Furnival raised his right hand and articulated very slowly, "No—money?"

"That is so, sir."

"Mr. Furnival makes some donations, paying for the wages of one clerk, and he also donates to the poor box at the court and to the foundling homes," Ruth interjected.

"My—money—spreads—thin—these—days," Furnival declared.

James needed no telling that he could not ask his family for money to spend on Bow Street, wealthy though they were. He also knew that Furnival, expecting to die soon, was anxious to leave the largest possible competence for his wife.

The older man was trying to find control of his voice, and at last words came.

"Do—you—feel—strongly—about—conditions?"

"Bitterly angry to think so much work has been wasted."

"Mr. John does not think the time or the effort has been wasted, James," Ruth interrupted. "He has come to believe that the conflict between society and its criminals is an agelong war in which only the first battles have been fought. I can tell you this: he is anxious, as I am, to know what is in your mind."

James said hoarsely, "I would like to join Henry Fielding."

"As one of his men, you mean? A thief-taker?"

"Yes. What else? Both the Fieldings must be in desperate need of men. I know they can afford to pay little, but I would manage somehow, and would put all blood money in the poor box—and like Mr. Fielding himself I would if necessary adopt an additional occupation."

"I read in *The Daily Clarion* that he has just finished a new book called *Amelia*," his mother remarked.

It was not until John Furnival looked toward his mother that James realised how the news that he wanted to join Fielding might affect her, and he turned quickly, expecting to see her troubled. She was not outwardly affected, however, and he had a feeling that she was neither shocked nor surprised.

"I think Mr. John is asking the question which is uppermost in my mind," she said. "With your law studies behind you and your degrees assured, could you not use your knowledge to better effect, perhaps as a barrister who will one day become a magistrate or a judge, or as spokesman for the poor who cannot properly speak for themselves in court? Have you thought of that, James?"

She turned toward him, her expression empty of emotion, trying simply to help make sure he had considered all aspects of his situation.

John Furnival raised his hand and both of the others watched and waited until he said, "Yes. Also—politics."

"Not politics!" exclaimed James. "Politicians are more corrupt than merchants, in their way as bad as the worst thief-takers!"

Furnival raised his hand again and this time the waiting became almost interminable until he said with great effort, "And—always—will—be—while—" For the first time he stammered, and something of the frustration and bitterness James knew he must feel showed in his expression until he said, "While—g-g-good—people—stand—a-a-aside."

"Of course you are right, sir," James replied more quietly. "But I cannot imagine myself as a politician. I can imagine myself assisting the Fieldings out of my knowledge of London and of crime, and also out of my knowledge of the law, which truly would not be wasted. And it is too early for me to be considered for the magistracy or the Sessions. Unless you have strong objections I shall go to see Henry or John Fielding one day next week."

To his surprise he saw Furnival relax and smile, while his mother said with a glint of humour in her eyes, "And if either of us has strong objections you will still go to see the magistrates, no doubt. James, it is your life and neither of us would try to live it for you. I ask only that you do not take wilful risks."

She paused as if to make sure that he understood that she meant exactly what she said, and Furnival's nod of approval was quite vigourous. Then she turned the conversation to the Reverend Sebastian Smith and revealed that both she and Furnival were well informed about what was happening, for several of Furnival's old Bow Street men were watchmen, like Harris, and some came to visit and report. At St. Giles they also kept abreast of affairs through *The Craftsman* and *The Daily Clarion*.

It followed naturally that Ruth should ask after Timothy, and Furnival immediately showed keen interest. So James told them of the invitation to attend the opening of the new docks opposite Furnival Tower House. It was difficult to judge from Furnival's expression how he reacted, but again he seemed to pass on the words he wished to utter to Ruth, who said, "I believe Mr. John would like to think on this, and perhaps discuss it further in the morning."

Furnival nodded his agreement. He looked exhausted, and Ruth stood up and began to push his wheelchair nearer to him. James watched the way he maneuvered himself into this with the help of his powerful right arm, and he had never before felt greater admiration for his stepfather. He walked with them, Ruth pushing the chair to the ground-floor room which had been converted from drawing room to bedroom, and bade them good night.

He was mentally very alert and did not wish to go to bed yet, so he went out by a side door which would be left unlocked until midnight. Strolling in the pleasant night air in the walled garden, he suddenly heard a breathless kind of giggle which reminded him vividly of the girl in the coffee house in St. Martin's Lane. He was too close to the sound to turn back without increasing the risk of being seen, so he went on more slowly, his footsteps making hardly a sound on the springy turf.

Next, he heard a girl say, "Oh, I love it so, Nat. I love it so."

The voice was Beth's, and Nathaniel, James remembered, was the name of the farmer with whom she had dallied, not the name of the man to whom she was affianced.

Silence followed save for murmuring and rustling which grew louder as he passed close by and died away as he neared the wooden gate at the far end of the garden. James opened it and went out, closing the gate again with great care. Out of a sense of unbelief came a feeling first of shock, then of revulsion, so that he walked faster and farther than he intended, reaching the top of the hill where a giant oak grew in a hollow which, it was said, had been scooped out by Britons in the days of Roman occupation.

When at last he reached the house again he was still trying to rationalise Beth's behaviour. It was the nature of some women as of some men to be promiscuous and to enjoy the act of mating for its own sake, he told himself. He was so absorbed in his thoughts that he jumped wildly when a figure appeared from a doorway leading off the passage near the head of the stairs, a silhouette against soft candlelight.

It was Henrietta, still fully clad.

"James, did you see Beth?" she asked.

"I both saw and heard her," James answered in a tone which betrayed his feelings clearly. "I can just understand her having lovers before becoming affianced, but at such a time as this it is beyond my understanding."

"It should not be," Henrietta replied as they turned into his room. "For as long as she lives Beth will have lovers, but don't allow this to affect your love for her, Jamey. She is the gayest soul alive and she will give herself to her husband with the same abandon as to any lover. It may well be that as she begins to have children circumstances will persuade her to be more faithful, but the desire will always be in her."

Henrietta, little past her sixteenth year, spoke with the wisdom of maturity, and at the same time was anxious to make sure he did not show hostility or disapproval toward Beth. Who else knew? he wondered. Had his mother had this at the back of her mind when she had talked so freely about Beth and, later, said that he must live his own life, no one could live it for him? Was that how she felt about Beth?

At last he said, "I shall be here only tomorrow; it should not be difficult for me to feign ignorance. But what of you, Henrietta? Do you yet feel the same desires?"

"I have still to be awakened," she replied simply, "and I pray that it

221

will be by the man I love and whom I marry and that I shall want none other than he." She touched his hand and put her cheek up to be kissed. "Good night, Jamey. Don't stay away for so long again."

It was late the following morning before James saw John Furnival. He was reading *The Daily Clarion* which James had brought with him but set this aside at once. Ruth appeared a few moments afterward, adjusted a cushion at the small of Furnival's back, then drew up a wooden stool for herself. She wore a dark-blue dress of a patterned Irish linen and a bonnet of the same colour.

"Mr. John would like to go to the opening of the new docks," she announced to James's pleased surprise, "and he would like also to visit the house in Bow Street, if that can be arranged. Doctor Leonardi will be here after church and will advise us what we must do to make the journey the least exhausting."

"I could not be more delighted," James declared, and the brightness in his eyes was matched by that in Furnival's.

Dr. Leonardi was a young, dark-haired man whom many took to be Italian but who had been born and bred in St. Giles and had followed his father as the only doctor, except for old Dr. Marsh, for many miles around. He spoke little until left alone with James for a few minutes.

Then he said, "I am in favour of allowing Sir John to do whatever he wishes, for the strain on his heart due to emotional distress might be as great as the physical strain imposed by making the journey. However, I must warn you, James, that he may have another attack at any time, brought on by the flimsiest of reasons; and he is as like as not to drop dead without more warning than a rattle in the throat. I have warned your mother and it is as well that you be warned, too."

"Then is it wise for him to travel?"

"Wait six more months and it might be impossible," Dr. Leonardi replied. "He himself knows the risk and it is one he readily takes. My advice to you is to allow him to enjoy this visit as much as he possibly can. The one service you can render him is to ask his brothers and close relatives to avoid causing conflict, for unless they travel to St. Giles it is not likely that they will see him after this occasion."

Deeply concerned, particularly in view of his newfound feeling for his stepfather, James faced up to the need for telling the other Furnivals of this. He would ask Francis and William to grant him an interview as soon as he was back in London. He had another decision to make at the same time and one which pressed heavily on him. He was reluctant to discuss it with his mother but needed to talk to someone who might see the situation more dispassionately than he.

That afternoon a tall, fair-skinned young man wearing a big old-fashioned peruke, the son of Sir Mortimer Tench, called for Beth to take her to his home for dinner. He was a fop, thought James, personable enough but of little stature, and a man whom Beth would probably find easy to deceive.

Furnival rested in the afternoon and Ruth stayed with him, leaving James alone with Henrietta. While strolling on the banks of the stream he told her, simply, about Mary; he had already told her and Beth of his decision to apply to Bow Street to become one of Henry Fielding's men. It was hard to believe that Henrietta was so young, he thought suddenly; she seemed to have a wisdom far in advance of her years.

Gravely, but without hesitation, she said, "If you work for the Fieldings, Jamey, you will have no time for family life, and your wife will be lonely and much of the time afraid. I think you will have to make up your mind which is the more important to you—Mary, whom you know very little, or this task to which you declare you are dedicated. You surely cannot honestly have both at this early stage."

He was forced, with the greatest reluctance, to agree.

He was up at six o'clock the following morning and, taking a fine bay horse from the stables, rode to London, where at eleven o'clock he called on Mary. In one way he dreaded the meeting, realising that he must have led her to expect that he would have some practical proposals to make; but in that event she made it very easy for him, affecting to have expected nothing but his charitable thoughts.

"One thing is very pleasing, Jamey! If all goes well with the Fieldings you will be near at hand!"

He left her at half-past eleven with no idea that, as she watched him from the window, tears were streaming down her cheeks.

Preoccupied now with his next task, he rode to Bow Street, finding that although no one was on the bench, debtors and felons, thief-takers and sheriffs' officers, constables and witnesses, even wives and relatives, crowded the court. Winfrith was there and was delighted to see him in a small anteroom.

"I know both brothers will be able to see you at three o'clock this afternoon," he promised. "Will you be back then?"

"I shall not delay a moment," James promised.

He took the horse to a livery stable and walked along Bow Street into a sprinkling of rain out of what had seemed a clear blue sky. It was colder than when he had arrived, too, which meant that there was a sudden change in the weather which would make it difficult to get about. As he neared Thames Street a gust of wind brought the unmistakable stink of fish from Billingsgate Market, and he saw a group of fishwives, none with less than four full baskets on their heads, gathered about an alehouse near the Monument. Their language was so coarse that he could understand only part of it and was astonished by the obscenities which flowed from their mouths. Walking quickly past, he turned into a narrow alley and came to Thames Street and the great building which the years had mellowed very little. Close by was another edifice in the same style, reached by a covered way from the main building. That was a measure of the growth of the House of Furnival.

Two guards questioned him before he was allowed in; another, carrying both night stick and pole, questioned him when he was inside. It was like entering a closely guarded palace. A youth in honey-brown uniform with violet sash and stockings carried a message up the great circular staircase and within two minutes was hurrying down again, saying, "Mr. Francis will see him!"

Slowly James mounted the stairs. Dwarfed by the magnitude of the building, trying desperately not to be overimpressed, he was nonetheless on edge when a door on the right opened. Next moment all sense of intimidation disappeared, for Timothy came hurrying out, both arms extended.

"You are as welcome as a man can be," he declared. "Come in, come in."

Except that his thick hair was nearly white, Francis Furnival looked little different from glimpses that James had caught of him several years earlier, and still retained the honey complexion he had had in his youth. He dragged himself around the big desk, shook hands, said that Timothy had been talking about their hopes and plans; no one could have been more friendly.

When they were all sitting down he smiled and said, "While I could hope that you have come to see if there is an opportunity for you to work at Furnival House I am not persuaded that this is likely —at least not yet! How can I be of service, James?"

"I am really here with a message from my stepfather," James began, and saw the other's face light up. "He would very much like to come to the opening of the new Furnival Docks."

Soon, Francis was saying warmly, "I hope you will tell him that this will be one of our greatest pleasures. Three Furnival ships from Bombay and Kiamari will be docking that night, to baptise the new docks, as it were. One of them carries mail and there should be some from our sister Anne. John could not have chosen a more fortunate time. And you may be assured that we shall exert ourselves in every way to make his visit easy. You yourself must tell us where to put ramps for that ingenious chair of his!"

There was no doubt of the warmth and sincerity this man felt toward his brother, yet James knew there was a deep chasm between them which had never really been bridged.

As he replied, something of the puzzlement he felt showed in his face, and Francis asked, "Is there some doubt about bringing the chair, James? D'you think he will be self-conscious and embarrassed?"

"In no way, sir, or he would not have agreed to come," James said. After a moment's hesitation he went on in a gruff voice, his cheeks turning red. "It puzzles me that you should make both me and Sir John so welcome and show such obvious pleasure yet at the same time be so often in conflict."

"Ah," Francis breathed. "I can understand your bewilderment because we have never been able to sink our differences. If they were matters of policy we would have no problem, but the clash is one of principle. The rest of us do not believe in a national or even a city peacemaking force; we are convinced it would infringe too deeply on the freedom of the individual. John would sacrifice a measure of this freedom to combat crime in a way which might not succeed even if it were tried." Francis leaned back in his chair. Few lines betrayed his forty-six years, although his eyes crinkled at the corners as he asked, "Have you committed yourself to one view or the other, James?"

"Yes, sir," James answered. And when both Francis and Timothy waited for him to go on, he added quietly, "There was a big fire in the Strand a few nights ago, when some enraged sailors broke up a brothel. Had troops not arrived there would no doubt have been a

225

greater fire. But for firm action next day, when Mr. Henry Fielding called out many more troops, four thousand sailors together with rough elements from the mob might have caused a most serious riot. Had two or three Bow Street men been present at the outset they could not only have prevented the fire altogether, but could have averted the following day's trouble. I believe that the property of all people should be protected by the government, sir—so I am with the Fieldings."

"A brothel keeper and a dozen prostitutes and no doubt some pimps and bullies—are their rights to be protected, too?"

"In this case, as I have said, much damage and a serious riot threatened. But in *any* case I believe that the rights of all should be protected, sir. Where is the line to stop, sir, if there is not to be one law for all? Who is to be judge of who must obey a law and who may defy it?"

James fell silent, acutely aware of the scrutiny in Francis' eyes and of Timothy staring at him with uncommon intensity. The slow relaxation of the older man's expression convinced him there was no disapproval.

At last Francis said quietly, "Your reasoning and the manner of presentation does you much credit. If you change your views about the need of a professional peace-keeping force there will always be a position of distinction for you here."

"Thank you, sir, you are very kind."

"I perceive that if you do not waste your efforts or your talents you have a bright future. Now! Timothy, why don't you take James to see the terrace and, indeed, show him all over Furnival Tower House? The tour may impress him with the great scope offered here."

He stood up and leaned across the desk; his parting grip was very firm.

"You know, Jamey, you have almost made me a convert," Timothy declared as they stood on the terrace and looked out over the seemingly unending panorama of London. James was amazed at the scene of the thriving activity on the river and at the docks, the mass of buildings spreading now in all directions. "If I didn't know that more than half—nay, three-quarters—of the people of London were well fed and happy and unaffected by crime or criminal tendencies, I would be with you," Timothy finished.

"If you could convince me that there were a thousand families wholly free from the influences of crime I might agree with Francis," James said. "But that day will be a long time coming."

He left Furnival House with barely time to arrive at Bow Street by three o'clock, and to make sure that he was not late he hailed a hackney carriage from a stand just outside the Furnival building. He was at Bow Street a little before three o'clock and Winfrith took him immediately to Henry Fielding, who was in a small private room near the one James's mother had once shared with John Furnival.

James was surprised to see how ill and weak the magistrate appeared, but there was no weakness in his voice when he said, "James Marshall, the day will come when my brother or I will call upon your services, but at this time we feel the need for men with extensive knowledge of the slums and criminal haunts of London. To take on a single new officer without such knowledge could be disastrous. So I beg of you, do what you can in court for any accused whom David Winfrith deems worthy of your help, and be prepared for the day when I can welcome you as I would dearly love to now. And meanwhile, pray say nothing in public about the Bow Street men." The lined face twisted in a wry smile as he added, "Officially, they do not exist."

James hardly knew how he excused himself and withdrew. It had not occurred to him that he would be rejected, especially in such a way; that what had become a great dream would be smashed so swiftly.

He was empty of hope when he left the court and walked the streets of London for so long that he grew footsore. By the time he reached Timothy's rooms he was damning himself for what he had said to Mary and hating himself because in his hurt he had not told Henry Fielding that John Furnival would like to visit Bow Street. He forced himself to go back and, by chance, met John Fielding, who moved with such freedom and assurance that it was difficult to realise he was blind. James told him about Furnival, praying that John Fielding meant what he said about the wholeheartedness with which Henry would welcome his predecessor.

When eventually James saw Timothy, the other's delight about the visit to the pageant was so great that for the first time the raw hurt of disappointment began to ease.

227

CHAPTER *16*

The River Pageant

"MY DEAR SIR JOHN," Henry Fielding said, taking Furnival's hand, "I cannot recall a greater pleasure. This gives me hope that you might once more take your seat on the bench."

"And none with greater right," John Fielding declared.

Blind though he was, he found his way about with great expertise and he too shook Furnival's hand. Warned in advance that Furnival would not be able to converse and would like only to be wheeled about the court and the downstairs rooms now occupied by the Fieldings, they extended not only great courtesy but obvious respect to the man who had once been chief magistrate. Furnival sat through the hearing of two cases, one against a man charged with the rape of a young girl, one against a youth charged with causing the death of another by unlawfully hurling stones at him while he had been helpless in the stocks. When the first part of the visit was over, the Fieldings entertained their guests in the room at the back of the offices, "their" room to Ruth for so long. For the occasion a long table had been placed the full length of the chamber, and this was covered, if sparsely, with hot and cold meat pies, oyster stew, baked potatoes and baked carrots, and bread as good as any ever tasted at St. Giles.

If James ate sparingly it was because he did not want to eat too much of this food, provided with such sacrifice. In any case, at Furnival Tower House a great banquet would be prepared for a vastly greater number, and he could eat there without the guilty sense that he was robbing someone else. He was fully aware that John Furnival was deeply affected and could imagine how he longed to be able to express his thanks. His own regard for the Fieldings rose enormously; no one could have shown more concern and affection than they for old John.

At last the eating and drinking of wine and beer were at an end, and by four-thirty a carriage came to take James and John and Ruth Furnival to Furnival Tower House. Leaving the big table, James saw his mother glance at the door leading to Bell Lane, and he followed her to find, with common astonishment, a crowd of at least a hundred people, men and women, mostly in rags, lined up outside.

It was Winfrith who, coming to join them, said quietly, "After you have gone these people will come in and finish the food. It will be of interest for you to know that every one of the Bow Street men as well as all the magistrates contributed to the expense incurred. That is how well Sir John is remembered."

"I will tell my father," James replied, "and I know I can express his very sincere gratitude for all that has been done."

He saw his mother glance at him sharply, saw Winfrith's eyes widen as if in surprise, but gave neither any thought as Henry Fielding came to escort his mother to Bow Street. For a second time James was astonished, for a much larger crowd had gathered here, obviously good-natured, and containing nearly as many women as men. All were watching with fascination as John Furnival, sitting in his chair, was being raised on boards by two chairmen. Once the chair's wheels were level with the door of the carriage, the chair was turned slowly so that he was pushed inside. Only a carriage with an especially wide door would have allowed this, and compared with the great strain and effort of getting him into and out of the carriage before, this was ease and comfort itself.

Once he was inside there was a burst of cheering and shouting.

With Ruth and James opposite him, the carriage set off, and James had never ridden in one which jarred the passengers so little over the uneven roads. Nothing which could be done to make the ride easier for his father—

He stopped in the middle of his thinking: astounded. *That* was

229

what had surprised his mother and Winfrith: he had for the first time in his life called John Furnival his father; and it could only be because he had thought of him as such!

The older man was leaning back against a cushion. In the darkness of the coach he looked pale and tired but the one good side of his mouth was curved in what might have been a smile of contentment. Still pondering his "discovery" and not sure how he felt about it, James glanced through the carriage window and received a second, very different kind of shock.

Amongst a crowd waiting at the corner of the Strand until such time as the horse and carriage traffic should slacken so that they could cross was Mary Smith. She looked very stern as she peered ahead, and in more ways than one reminded him of his mother. He had no idea whether she had glimpsed him; if she had, she was making sure that he did not know.

Two of the House of Furnival guards took advantage of a lull in the traffic to halt a number of sedan chairs so that their carriage could turn into the Strand. Mary was lost to sight on the turn. James sat back, aware of the interested gaze of his mother but in no mood to talk.

If only he had spoken differently to Mary at their last meeting. Now it was too late.

Mary Smith knew who was in the carriage because she had been among the crowd in Bow Street to watch the party come out. Her father had business at a Wesley congregation on the south side of the city and so had not been able to accept an invitation to attend the dinner; she suspected that he had arranged the business deliberately so that he could avoid mixing with old friends at a time when his clothes were patched and the heaviness in his heart showed so markedly in his expression.

But she was not thinking of her father then, only of James Marshall. She could not remember the time, even when they had both been children, when she had not loved him. But when, four years before, she had last seen him, he had been so unbelievably tall and handsome, while she had still been so plain, that she had tried to put him out of her mind. And until he had come on that fateful night, she had almost forgotten him, or at least had been able to think of him without longing.

230

On the night of his first visit, hope had flared within her because his concern had been so evident, and although she had warned herself that nothing would come of this interest, that her deep love for him would never find response, she had lived in the clouds of fancy until after his last brief call.

Now, she was installed as the housekeeper of the Weygalls. He knew only that they lived above their general merchandise shop near Long Acre. And now he was driving off in a magnificent carriage to a world Mary would neither know nor share. She did not believe he had seen her. Now she had shopping to do, mostly for fabrics to make dresses for the three daughters of the Weygalls, and it was to Hewson's in the Strand that she was heading, while fighting back her tears.

Among others who had watched the celebration at Bow Street was Gabriel Morgan, the oldest of the Morgan brothers and one of the gang that had attacked the young girl. At that time he had no thought that James Marshall was the man who had put him and his friends to flight, ending in the ignominy of the cesspit. He was going to one of his regular meetings with others of the group soon, and among those present would be Jacob Rackham, who had become their leader.

"Jamey, a number of us are going up the river to see the sights," Timothy McCampbell announced. "Will you come with us? Your stepfather will be well cared for and your mother is already surrounded by a positive horde of aunts and cousins. If you don't come with us you will miss one of the greatest spectacles on earth."

"Then I would be a fool to stay behind," James said.

It was now after six o'clock, and the excitement of arrival was gone, yet a glow of elation remained. For a while he had been in a whirl, meeting Furnivals of all ages, as well as elderly men like Sir Cornelius Hooper, who had for two years been Lord Mayor of London, and was said to be the only one in thirty years who had proved incorruptible. He had also met a succession of beautifully dressed young women and was aware that several had eyed him with speculative interest. At least two of the young ladies were Timothy's sisters and one, fair-haired Penelope, had caught his eye more than once.

He followed Timothy through a maze of passages and staircases until they approached a small inlet from the Thames by a flight of stone steps leading to a gaily decorated barge in which at least a dozen youths were already crowded and four watermen sat ready at the oars. A fifth helped Timothy and James into the barge, making it sway slightly, then cast off.

James saw gates opening slowly between the inlet and a much wider section, not the river itself but so close to it that, as the barge swung through, a great expanse of the river showed.

He caught his breath.

From this level, only two or three feet above the surface, the panorama of London's river was revealed in a way it could seldom be. The great sailing barges, the clippers, even three men-of-war with their great figureheads, towered high above the host of smaller ships, and each one seemed to be in full sail; whilst moving in and out of this armada of sailing ships were hundreds of small craft: some, tiny cockleshell dinghies with only one man at the oars; some, brightly painted barges. It seemed like water bedlam, a mass of uncontrolled movement with a cacophony of sound, from loud voices to squeaking winches, firecrackers to bells and wooden rattles used by the watchmen to raise alarm by night. Among the small craft, however, were many in which stood liveried watermen employed by the great shipping lines as well as by the port and river authorities to make order out of chaos, moving ships from one position to another, arranging anchorage, working with colleagues on the quaysides to tie the larger ships to stanchions.

But still more than all this magnificence, making the spectacle absolutely breathtaking, were the flags and pennants of every imaginable size and colour. Every tiny ship, even the smallest dinghy, had its flag bravely flying, and it seemed as if there was no room for other craft to move.

As the barge drew farther into the river James saw that more watermen were keeping a space clear. It was yet three hours to full tide but already the river level was high and most if not all of the mud flats were covered with water. From the banks naked boys dived and swam, going up to ships riding at anchor and holding out their hands in supplication. Most of these were water thieves by night, the mudlarks who swam close to the ships to secure and swim away with stolen articles of all kinds tossed overboard by crew members or by rat-catchers or other workers from the city.

There were masses of people.

On ships and on quaysides, on terraces and on roofs, there were people. On the castellated walls of the Tower of London there were people, for the Tower Gardens had been thrown open. On the cannon and on the walls, people sat and watched and waited, while street sellers moved among them, never still, never silent.

"Look!" cried a youth next to Timothy, and he pointed with joy toward a church steeple. On the top two lads were clinging, getting the finest view of all London and the pageant. If only they did not fall and break their necks, thought James grimly.

Slowly the barge turned the curve in the river between Temple and Charing Cross, and gradually Westminster Bridge came into view. Sated though they were with spectacle, not one among the company failed to gasp in astonishment, for here there were more ships, banked tight at the sides, three more men-of-war and thousands of small craft.

At the steps by one of the arches, elaborately adorned with flags and pennants and with carved crests and shields painted in bright hues, was the Royal Barge. There were enough men aboard, all bustling fore and aft, to make sure that it was shortly to be used.

"Is the King coming to Furnival's?" a young man called out in awe.

"It is unlikely," answered Timothy. "But those of you who wish may doubtless be presented to the Prince of Wales." He waited for the chorus of exclamations to die down, then went on: "His Majesty was gracious enough to send a message of congratulations and good will, and the assurance that he will be represented, and I have it from the Lord Chamberlain himself that the Prince of Wales will join us. Now perhaps the time has come to explain what has been planned. For the first time in history a pageant has been organised by a private company, with the cooperation of all the guilds concerned as well as that of other great houses, shipping companies and dock owners. The new docks opposite Furnival Tower House will be known as Furnival Docks, where there are sufficient berths to house ten ships at one time—not little coastal vessels but ocean-going merchantmen with a weight of a thousand tons."

Timothy paused, for the barge went beneath one of the arches, and instinctively everyone on board became silent, although there was ample room for two of the oarsmen to keep the barge in motion, and the quiet was uncanny as they passed. On the far side the scene was very different, sylvan and meadowed in long stretches on either side, with only small craft on the river, for no ship with a mast much higher than fifteen feet could pass with safety. As the oarsmen swung the barge round for the return voyage, Timothy resumed his peroration of the coming events of the night, as if there had been no interruption, but he soon had to raise his voice because of the increasing noise from the crowds.

He broke off again as a dinghy with one small boy in it, naked to the waist, came across their bows, both arms outstretched. His ribs stuck out against his skin; it was a miracle that he had the strength to row. Several of the guests tossed pennies, and his cries of gratitude wafted after them as the barge plowed on through the water and Timothy resumed speaking.

"After the formal approach of the craft and the receiving of the masters by the directors of the House of Furnival, there will be a reception in the main hall and on the terrace, with more than seven hundred guests, including officers from the ships, the Prince of Wales and his entourage, the Lord Mayor of London, the Governor of the Tower of London, at least three bishops, no less than seventeen Members of Parliament . . ."

Through gaps in the buildings and in between the sails, James caught fleeting glimpses of the gallows at Tower Hill, and thought again of Tyburn and the day Frederick Jackson had been hanged. He had no doubt that pickpockets and cutpurses were active among this crowd, that every kind of theft was being perpetrated, and that some would be caught and sentenced to death or to transportation for life. Yet, by whatever standards he judged, this was a great day.

All of the group which called itself the New Mohocks were downriver from the new docks, at the beflagged windows of a tall warehouse. But the flags did not hide the sign which was fastened to the wall:

EBENEZER MORGAN & SONS

Nine Other Establishments in London
Fine Teas   Coffees   Spices   Rare Fruits   Nuts
Finest Produce from all Corners of the World
All Goods of Highest Class

Jacob Rackham put a naval telescope to his eye and studied the gallows at Tower Hill across the river. When he lowered the glass, he spoke through a tight-lipped smile.

"We shall catch our man one day, Gabriel, and he will know what it is to suffer."

But Gabriel Morgan was too full of the pageantry and colour of the day to think about revenge. He was far more concerned lest it should rain.

Among the crowds on the riverbank and the quays were thousands of people who would join the revels at every hanging day at Tyburn. The same sellers of fruit and pies, newssheets and notices, the same thieves, the same singing groups, the same beggars. And most of the men who by night donned masks and became highwaymen or footpads were here also, jostling with others, enjoying every moment of this great occasion.

Frederick Jackson, now over eleven years of age, was with some other youths, a handsome but sober-faced lad who had begged his mother's permission to come to the pageant. Most people who had known his father might be aware of the likeness, perhaps puzzled by it until they heard the lad's name—he had been given Jackson's name at birth at Eve Milharvey's insistence.

Already on board one of the great barges at Westminster was Lisa, Duchess of Gilhampton, and also on board was not only her husband but at least five men who, in the past, had received her favours; yet few ladies received more respect than she. The Hewsons were on another barge owned by a customer whom they had "dressed" for two generations. Tom Harris, whose duties left him free until dark, was also present; a subdued Harris, whose knee had not yet recovered from the sprain received when James had thrown him over his shoulder.

One other person known to James Marshall was among the crowd, one of five boys who had broken out of their school in Rochester and had persuaded a wagon master to bring them as far as the southern end of the new bridge. From there they had walked to the Tower, and the ringleader of the escape was astride one of the guns, ignoring two Beefeaters who stood near. In the Tower, companies of dragoons were being dispatched to vantage points throughout the City and Westminster as well as the connecting highway. If trouble threatened after the pageant, as well it might, for much drink was already being tossed down hardened throats, the troops would be at hand to keep order.

The boy astride the gun would have been even more readily recognised as his father's son than Frederick Jackson as his, for this was

Johnny Furnival, looking at least four years older than his ten years and startlingly like John Furnival had been in his youth, with the same honey-blond hair and honey-brown eyes which missed little. He was not only big but very strong for his age, and dexterous, too. Every now and then he espied a carelessly open pocket or a loosely held purse, and he would leap from the gun, snatch what he could find from the pocket and take away the purse, then return by a circuitous route to the cannon, where his friends kept a place for him.

Had anyone told Johnny Furnival, son of Sir John and Lady Furnival, that for a single one of the offences he committed he could be hanged or transported, he would have laughed and scoffed, for whatever else was bad about him, he had high courage and great daring.

Soon after the barge returned to the steps at the side of Furnival Tower House, the Prince of Wales arrived, and the roaring of the crowd, which had a strong affection for the fledgling prince, grew deafening. Then the first of the merchantmen came into sight around the bend of the river at Wapping, and yet another wave of cheering began. Bands played on the decks of some of the larger ships, the men-of-wars' bands struck up, and pipers who had been brought down from the Furnival offices in Glasgow and Edinburgh stirred everybody's emotions with their swirling dirgelike tunes.

The cheering was now so wild it had become a kind of hysteria. As the last merchantman was tied alongside, three guns boomed in salute, and as the echoes died away, every band struck up the national anthem. Suddenly the voices of the multitude were raised in singing "God Save the King" as if this were the most popular king England had ever known, not just a thirteen-year-old princeling.

When the singing died away there were wet eyes everywhere until the bands swung into tunes known to be favourites with the Prince of Wales as well as with the crowds.

Darkness came early because of the overcast skies, but so far no rain had fallen. Flares began to dance on the sides of the ships as well as on the buildings, none brighter than those on the terrace at Furnival Tower House as first the Prince and then his companions stepped from the Royal Barge. Only when they had been received did the ships' masters arrive from their proud vessels.

James could see all this perfectly, and he also saw John Furnival and Ruth, placed so that they were part of everything that went on.

The reflected light from the flares turned John's pallor into the flattering colour of his middle manhood. The music had stopped and the crowds were now silent.

The first of the sailors, a small man with a straggly black beard, carrying a leather box, reached the welcoming group, bowed low to the Prince of Wales, but somehow created an impression of impatience during the courtesies and said to William Furnival in a clear and penetrating voice, "It is my honour to place in your hands missives from members of your family and of your staff in India. It is my deep regret—"

The man behind called out, "Not now, Henry, not now!"

Already there was bewilderment and embarrassment that the master should speak while the formal welcome to the Prince was not yet finished.

William covered the awkwardness with a loud-pitched: "Captain Gamble, we shall be happy to see you for private discussions at the earliest moment. Captain Mortenson—"

He presented two more sailors and there was some formal exchange of compliments before a military band once again played "God Save the King," and then William and Francis escorted the Prince down to the great hall below. Here, a huge circular table was piled high with dishes of every description, dozens of footmen, chefs and wine stewards standing discreetly by. Music from two string quartets was now being played, and while two of the Furnivals' most attractive young women were presented to the Prince, James Marshall—at the balcony on the second floor—saw Francis and William leave the hall and go up the staircase to a room which led onto the terrace. Timothy's hand was on James's shoulder.

"I know a short cut to the terrace," he declared. "I want to hear what that idiot Gamble has to say."

One of the few guests remaining on the terrace, where it was much cooler than in the hall, was John Furnival, in his chair, with James's mother and an elderly great-aunt sitting beside him. As the two young men came within earshot, Francis spoke in a sharper voice than James had yet heard from him.

"Captain Gamble, what news is of such significance that you choose a formal occasion to relay it?"

"I am sorry, sir." Despite his words there was nothing in Gamble's voice to suggest that he felt distress, only a sense of injured pride. "I was charged both by our own representatives and by the East India

Company on leaving Bombay with relaying this news at the earliest possible opportunity, and to have delayed would have been doing less than my duty."

William answered in an unexpectedly conciliatory fashion. "Be sure we are aware of your attention to duty, Captain. Will you now be good enough to present us with the news?"

"With no pleasure, sir, no pleasure at all and only with the deepest regret. Shortly before we set sail from Bombay we received a fully accredited messenger from the office in Calcutta. I have the message in the box, sir. It appears that Mr. Jason Gilroy was ill advised enough to travel by road with his wife and their son and daughter between Delhi and Calcutta. At dusk one evening, when they were approaching a village only a day's journey from Calcutta, they were attacked by Pindari bandits, their guards were killed, they themselves were robbed and slaughtered."

Captain Gamble paused as if to make sure that the full significance of the news was understood, and then went on.

"My instructions were to advise you to notify His Majesty's Government at the first opportunity and to request that they make urgent representation to the Maharajah of Gwada to heed the East India Company's request for the immediate apprehension and punishment of the murderers. The outrage was committed in the Maharajah's province."

For a moment there was complete silence, until Timothy said in a broken whisper, "Aunt Anne!"

Then William spoke in a strange, taut voice. "Is there no doubt at all about this, Captain Gamble? No possibility of error or mistaken identity?"

"None whatsoever, sir. The envoy was in fact Mr. Gilroy's most trusted Indian servant and guide, who escaped during the attack and went back to the scene of the crime after the bandits had gone. He saw that each member of the family had been slain in the most despicable fashion. Moreover, sir, two smaller and faster vessels out of Karachi passed my ship and signaled the news to me."

No one spoke until Francis said, "Anne, dear Anne."

Someone out of sight exclaimed, "What a day for such news to come!"

"I cannot be blamed for the circumstances, gentlemen," Captain Gamble said aggressively.

"No one is attempting to blame you," Francis assured him, "but this is grievous news to pass on at such an occasion. If there were time to stop the fireworks—"

Almost on the instant a great crack of sound came from across the river and a rocket burst high above the crowds, spreading white, blue and pink stars against the dark sky. In a moment there came another, then another, and suddenly the terrace was crowded as the guests from below came to see the display. Finally, there was a tremendous explosion and, high above the roofs of the new warehouses, one word and one word only burned as bright as day:

FURNIVAL

Whilst on the terrace, head lolling, body slack, Sir John Furnival lay back in his wheelchair: dead.

CHAPTER *17*

Johnny

JOHN FURNIVAL was buried in the churchyard at St. Giles only two days later, attended by his brothers, surviving sisters, and some other close relatives and friends. Among those not of the family who came to the simple funeral ceremony was John Fielding, who brought condolences and deep regret from his brother. Tom Harris came, too, and old Sam Fairweather, so crippled with arthritis that each step caused pain. Benedict Sly was also present, and the Reverend Sebastian Smith, who had journeyed with friends across London and had then taken the stagecoach from the Hyde Park Turnpike.

When it was over, the members of John Furnival's family departed from St. Giles except for Francis and his wife, Deborah, who were to stay the night. Beth and Henrietta stayed with the Tenches, and only Francis and Deborah, Ruth and James, were together at the farmhouse dinner of roast beef and batter pudding.

"Ruth, this may not be the night to talk about the future, but I would like you to be sure of two things," Francis said. "For as long as you wish to stay at St. Giles, it is yours, and if there is ever anything you need that we at the House of Furnival can provide, that is yours also."

Ruth had said very little since her husband's death, the only indications of her grief being pallor and a redness at her eyes. Now she looked at Francis with thoughtful intentness.

"You are very kind," she replied. "I believe I know what I must do."

"You see, Francis," Deborah said, "I told you so."

It was seldom that Deborah spoke when in the company of those not part of her immediate family, so her intervention made James and Ruth look at her in surprise, but no greater surprise than that of Francis. Deborah was a short, broad woman, with not particularly attractive features; at moments, when on horseback or out walking, she could be taken for a man. There were those who wondered whether her masculinity had appealed to Francis because of the contrast between them: his delicacy, her solidness; his almost feminine good looks, her plainness; his beautifully shaped fingers, her broad, flat-tipped ones. She wore few adornments and this evening looked even more somber than usual in her unrelieved black dress. Only her eyes, pale gray, gave her any brightness.

"What did you tell Francis?" Ruth inquired mildly.

"That you would know what you desired to do, and would be as stubborn as—" Deborah broke off, perhaps because of the expression on Francis' face.

"As my husband," Ruth finished for her.

"Deborah did not mean—" began Francis.

"Francis, perhaps Deborah would always speak more freely if you did not talk for her," Ruth interrupted, and James was astonished that she should speak in tones of rebuke. But Francis laughed, and his laughter brought a smile of relaxation from Ruth.

"Indeed you may be right," Francis agreed pleasantly.

"Well, he *was* as stubborn as a mule," declared Deborah.

"As an ox would perhaps be better," countered Francis.

"As a man who had great faith in what he was trying to do," Ruth put in equably. "Yes, he was stubborn, thank God! And he began changes in the thinking of men and women that will one day come to fruition. Francis, you have always been kind and affectionate toward John, and I would not reward you if I were to tell half-truths or pretend what I do not feel. I am grateful for your reassurance and it would not be surprising if one day I came to you for help. You know that John took all his inheritance and sold his shares in the House

241

of Furnival so that he could spend freely on his chosen task. Yet he left me a goodly competence. Notwithstanding that, I cannot live here or for that matter anywhere else and do nothing. My life was full in every minute with John, and while I could serve him I was content. Now James is more than old enough to fend for himself, Beth is soon to be married, and Henrietta is an independent young woman who will decide her own future. I shall return to London and seek a post in one of the foundling hospitals for which I shall need no salary. I shall be dealing with those too young to have become incurably contaminated by the evils of the world." She paused a few moments, then asked, "Does that shock you?"

"It doesn't *surprise* me," declared Deborah.

"I am not shocked but I am surprised," Francis replied. "I believed you loved this place."

"John came to love it."

"And you loved it only because of that? Ruth," Francis went on, getting up and drawing close to his sister-in-law, "you are a most unusual woman, but reasonable also. Will you ponder your decision at least long enough for us to sleep on it?"

"You'll never bribe *her* to change her mind," Deborah declared. "That's a thing you've never learned, Francis—the good are the most stubborn people on earth. Did you ever hear of a martyr in a bad cause?"

Quite suddenly James began to laugh, and his mother followed; soon all of them were laughing.

James spent a few minutes in his mother's room before going to his own, staying long enough to assure her that whatever decision she made he would support her. In fact, the only anxiety he felt was about Henrietta, but even that did not weigh enough to prevent the best night's sleep he had had for some days. Yet the next morning he was up before the others, striding through the grounds—until suddenly he realised with a shock that he had forgotten Johnny.

But his mother could not have forgotten her youngest child. Had some arrangements been made for Johnny's future? Or did she expect to be able to keep him by her when she laboured? Utterly confused, James stood by the little stream watching the early-morning mist rising almost invisibly before he hurried back to the house. Soon, they were all at breakfast in a pleasant room overlooking the hillside. Dust was already rising as the first stagecoach of the day from London approached at what seemed even from there a wild speed. That was a sight which, a few years before, Johnny had loved to see. He would rush down toward the stagecoach, pointing a wooden gun and crying in his unmistakable voice, "Stand and deliver! Stand and deliver or I shoot!"

"No, Jamey," his mother said, "I had not forgotten Johnny." There was a strange expression on her face.

"Then what is to happen to him?"

"His father and I did not attempt to deceive ourselves," Ruth Furnival replied. "We knew that our time together would be limited, and we discussed my need to serve. We agreed that Johnny should be cared for by one of his uncles or aunts. Because John had left the House of Furnival there is no reason to deprive Johnny of its benefits. That is one reason why he was sent so early to school. Had there been more time to talk, my son, you would have been told of this."

"It is not important whether I knew," James replied, and yet he had a sense of hurt. His mother could have written to him while he had been away; he had a right to know what was happening to members of his family, especially to Johnny of whom he was inordinately fond. It was on the tip of his tongue to make some comment when he reminded himself that his mother had suffered too great a loss to be harassed because of his stung pride. Lightly he substituted, "But it would be interesting to know what else my absence has kept from me."

To his surprise his mother looked away, and he saw Francis draw his brows together as if at some distasteful prospect. Had his remark been so sharp as to earn their disapproval? Only Deborah, who was slicing a large steak on her platter, appeared oblivious of any undercurrents.

"There is one other thing which has been kept from you," Ruth admitted slowly.

"About Johnny?"

"Yes, about Johnny."

"I should be very glad to hear it."

"You may be very sorry to hear it," replied his mother, "but you would have been told and indeed consulted had you not been away. As it was, I believe I was glad you were not here." She paused, and when James said nothing, she went on: "You brother has always been self-willed and intractable. You well know that at one time only you were able to make him behave; you were the one person among us all whom he would heed. When you went away to your studies, this wilfulness became much more pronounced. He began to run wild,

243

tormented his sisters, defied us, and spent much of his time with lads in the village, always the ringleader in escapades that were dangerous and caused much distress and trouble. Because of who he was and because countryfolk often have more tolerance of the waywardness of the young, he escaped severe punishment. When many a lad would have been taken before the justice, Sir Mortimer Tench, Johnny was brought home for correction. But on one occasion when he had, with some others, trapped a fox and let it loose in a farmyard with the gates closed so that there resulted a great slaughter of fowl, he *was* taken before the justice. Indeed, that is how Beth met her betrothed, who was given the task of bringing him back here. For a while after this Johnny was more subdued, but before long he was at his tricks again."

"You make him out a little monster!" protested James, horrified.

"He *is* a little monster," Deborah declared.

"Aunt Deborah—" James began hotly, only to be stopped when his mother stretched out a hand and touched his arm.

"There were additional and even stronger reasons for sending Johnny to the Gordon School, where there are many others of his own age, activities which will absorb his high spirits, and a strict code of discipline. Had you been here I am sure you would have agreed that this was the best course."

"I must say I wish I had been told," James said. "I might have come back and brought influence to bear on him."

"At sacrifice of your own good and your own opportunities," his mother replied.

"A man has a right and a duty to help a member of his family!"

"A mother has a right and a duty to do what she believes best for her children," Francis interpolated. "This your mother did, James, both for Johnny *and* for you. She consulted Johnny's father to the full. This matter was discussed at much length, and I for one have no doubt of the wisdom of the course that was taken. Johnny *is* a headstrong child who is maturing at remarkable pace."

"He is a little *monster*," declared Deborah once again.

"I am sorry but I cannot sit here and listen to such words about my brother," James declared, rising to his feet. "I will ask you to excuse me."

Deborah leaned back in her chair.

"You won't get anywhere if you don't face facts, Jamey," she declared.

"But if I am not satisfied that they *are* facts, ma'am?"

"James, your Aunt Deborah and I must return to London later in the day and afterward I have no doubt that you will have much to discuss with your mother," Francis put in. "I urge you to endeavour to see this situation without heat. And I hope you will not leave us at this juncture for I would like to talk to your mother about her own plans and it would be helpful if you were present."

Reluctant to create a more difficult situation, James drew his chair back to the table. A hundred questions burned through his mind, but all his training told him that Francis was right and he should take time in which to consider the news dispassionately. By now, moreover, he was able to accept the justice of the implication that he had been away in his own interests and could hardly expect family decisions to have been postponed until his return.

"So you have slept on my plans," Ruth remarked, turning to Francis.

"Yes, sister Ruth, I have slept on them. May I ask you some—a very few—questions?"

"Indeed you may."

"Do you love St. Giles?" asked Francis.

"Greatly, yes."

"Is your reason for desiring to leave due to the pain of its association with John?"

"In no way," Ruth Furnival replied without hesitation.

"Have you a great love for London?"

"Affection perhaps but no great love. Brother Francis, may I explain that to serve one must go where the need exists, and there is great need in London for work of charity among the newborn. Many are left to die, as many are born out of wedlock to young women who are then never likely to find any life outside a brothel. It is a known truth, sir, that mothers kill their babes because they cannot suckle or feed them, and the parish authorities do nothing to prevent this, not wishing to spend funds on keeping them alive in misery."

"Oh, I don't dispute what you say for one moment," Francis declared. "In fact, I can tell you that in the year 1750 there were more than three thousand foundlings left in the streets and alleys. It is said that most of those who do find homes of any kind are taught to steal as soon as they can walk. The situation is a grievous and shameful one, and the foundling hospitals are already overcrowded. Nor are they properly staffed, and they are situated in parts of London where smallpox and cholera are most likely to originate."

"One must accept the situation which exists and try to help as best one can," Ruth rejoined.

"I do not think that is the proper philosophy for the wife of John Furnival," said Francis, but the tenderness in his expression eased the words of any sting. "He would insist on changing the situation."

"While nevertheless overworking to alleviate conditions within that situation!"

James had never seen his mother more animated.

"True enough," agreed Francis, placing some honey on a crust of bread. "I believe there is a way in which you can do both." He popped the morsel into his mouth, thus leaving time for Ruth or one of the others to comment, but no one did.

Something in Francis' manner suggested that he was wholly confident that what he had to propose would appeal to his sister-in-law but it was difficult to imagine what it was, and clearly Ruth was as baffled as James. Deborah, who had finished her steak, was now eating bread and honey with intense application, as if nothing that had been said affected or interested her; perhaps it did not.

"I shall be most happy to hear of such a solution," Ruth Furnival said at last.

"Very well, I will submit it for your consideration! Instead of going to London to alleviate the sufferings of a trifling number of foundlings brought to places we know are already overcrowded, why do you not help to create a foundling home here at St. Giles? *In this house*. The conditions are well-nigh perfect, and additional buildings could be erected at little cost. You would find foster mothers and nurses eager—aye, anxious!—to work here, far away from London. You would be able to have a resident doctor and yet be so close to London that more experienced doctors and surgeons would always be available. You would have—"

"Francis," interrupted Ruth very quietly and deliberately, "are you saying that the House of Furnival would finance such a home?" She was pale, and a hand which rested on the table trembled slightly.

"I believe that it would, yes. If there were some legal impediment or other objection, I would myself finance—"

"*We* would invest the necessary money." Deborah cut across her husband's words. "What Francis could not afford, I could." She stared belligerently at Ruth as if defying her to refuse.

James, astounded, looked from Deborah to Francis and back to his mother and saw what he had not seen in his life before: tears spilling from her eyes.

Beth and Henrietta were back and stood at the gates with James and their mother as Francis and Deborah drove off with their own pair, brisk in a sultry morning's air in which rain threatened; rain had been falling on and off for several days and there were reports of huge thunderstorms in the West Country and in the Midlands. A streak of lightning showed vivid in the sky to the north but the thunder which followed was distant and overhead the sky was blue. Beth was full of excitement at plans for the wedding, now only two months away, and James left his sisters together while he went up to his room and stood looking at the wooded hillside where a hawk hovered and swooped downward.

The pleasure and excitement he shared with his mother about the future of this house was subdued by the burden of other problems.

When he had come here he had been concerned with only himself. Now there was the problem of Johnny. Surely the boy could not have changed as much as had been suggested. And even if he had, should he, James, acquiesce in the others' plans for him? He was worried, too, about Henrietta's future—it was almost as if his mother was planning a life in which her children had no part. At any other time he would have talked to her frankly, but the sight of her tears at the breakfast table had told him clearly what Aunt Deborah had confirmed when they had been left alone for a few moments.

"Your mother has been living in a state of high tension which is bound to cause a collapse or an outburst of some kind. Be kind to her, Jamey."

Yet outwardly, once the paroxysm had ended, Ruth had been almost her old self again and obviously pleased at the prospect of making a home for foundlings in the house she had learned to love.

There was a great deal James did not understand but he had no doubt of the basic goodness of Francis and the kindliness of Deborah.

He was contemplating this when he heard footsteps outside his door, and then heard Henrietta say, "You are so excited I declare I do not know how you can wait two months!"

"Everything is so wonderful," Beth said. And then in a voice pitched in a lower key, "If only Johnny does not spoil it."

James stood motionless for a moment as if struck with an axe, and then strode toward the door, but as he opened it that of another room closed and both girls were lost to sight. He fought the temptation to go to them and turned to a spiral staircase which led down to the back of the house and to a door into the walled garden. He strode through this, then set off at a furious pace across the fields.

247

How *could* Johnny spoil Beth's marriage?

He was fulminating over this and at the same time warning himself that he must be dispassionate, must review the situation as an intellectual, not an emotional, problem, when he saw a horseman leave the highway and turn in the direction of the house. He was a man in his middle thirties, James hazarded, wearing no hat, and with fair hair blown wild in the wind; judging from the lathered sides of his horse he had ridden a long way.

James hurried back to the house to meet the stranger, but when he arrived he found the man already waiting by the open front door and a maid's voice sounding clearly:

"I will tell Lady Furnival that you are here."

Ruth arrived at the door as James approached from the side. The stranger bowed to her and spoke almost at once.

"Lady Furnival, I am grieved to bring you harassing news. I am a master at the Gordon School and have my credentials in my pouch. My task is to inform you and the parents of four other students that your son and theirs ran away from school two days before the river pageant and have not been traced beyond London. It is my hope that your son has come here."

Ruth closed her eyes and seemed glad of James's steadying arm as he stepped to her side; the rider drew the back of his hand across his sweaty forehead and waited for her answer.

"This is most disturbing news," she said at last. "No, he is not here, sir. But you will have ridden a long way and need rest and food. Will you not come in and recover from the journey? And if you will, tell us what makes you think my son went to London."

"The evidence was conclusive," James said to Francis when he reached Furnival Tower House late that afternoon. "Johnny was leader of the truants and they made it clear to their fellows that they were going to visit the river pageant. The messenger talked with an innkeeper at the Kent Road Turnpike and identified the five chiefly by describing Johnny. It's a thousand pities the boy looks so much older than he is—although the innkeeper swears he would not serve them with beer, simply gave them bread and cheese and sent them on their way. This was in the early afternoon of the day of the pageant."

"How can we search for him in London?" Francis asked in a harsh voice. "Who can possibly find them if they do not want to be found?"

"If I may suggest it, Uncle," said James, "Mr. Henry Fielding's men are the best trained in London and I have no doubt he would immediately organise a search for Johnny. He would, however, require funds to use as bribes and persuasion to loosen the tongues of watchmen, turnpikemen and their like."

"He may name his own sum," said Francis briskly, "and not a moment should be lost."

"It is an opportunity to prove our worth such as we have seldom had," Henry Fielding declared as soon as he heard the request. "I will ask my brother John to take from you a description of your brother and have him send this description, printed in a pamphlet, to all parish constables, watchmen, trading justices, alehouses—yes, and bawdy-houses, too. I shall be disappointed and surprised if the boy is not found, with his friends, in forty-eight hours."

Only an hour later, the blind brother of the magistrate raised his head and declared, "This description might well be of a younger John Furnival—the father, not the son."

"There could be no better way of describing him," James declared.

"Then we shall have no difficulty at all in finding him and I do not think there need be the expense or publicity of a printed notice. We can spread this by word of mouth. With the proper use of fifty pounds, by tonight a hundred men and by tomorrow night a thousand will be on the lookout for the boys. Will you see that the House of Furnival is made aware of this?"

"I will tell Mr. Francis myself," promised James.

He told Timothy that night, and Francis the following morning at Furnival Tower House, where there was great commotion because of a report of the loss of one of the Furnival Line ships in a hurricane in the Bay of Biscay.

But while he waited for a word with Francis before leaving to take part in the search, a messenger came posthaste from Bow Street with a missive for him, written in Winfrith's small, easy-to-read hand. James tore it open and read:

All five boys have been found unharmed except for the fact that they are drunk on gin. Your brother appears likely to become conscious sooner than the others.

Yours obediently,
David Winfrith

The five had been discovered in a cellar next to an alehouse, and it was believed they had paid for the gin, so no known crime lay at their door. Word was dispatched to St. Giles and to Gordon School, where all five would be returned under escort from the House of Furnival. The discernment of the doctor who had examined them proved excellent: Johnny came to full consciousness some hours before any of the others, and James went to see him in a room at one of the cottages in Bell Lane. The boy still wore the knee breeches, green stockings and plaid shirt of Gordon School, but had lost his shoes. He had bathed before James's arrival, and his face had an innocent expression which momentarily deceived James.

"Jamey!" the lad exclaimed. "What a sight to see! I imagined at best a Furnival underling or even a lout from Gordon School. How are you, Jamey?"

"Why did you run away?" demanded James, not to be distracted.

"To see the sights of London's river! I asked permission to come and was rudely refused so I took what I believe is called French leave. Were you at the pageant? Wasn't it a truly glorious spectacle?"

James hardened himself against his brother's glowing eyes.

"Yes, Johnny. Why did you defy your masters?"

"To obey them all the time would make life unbearably dull. I am too old for school. I wish—"

"You are not yet eleven years old," James interrupted.

"Compared with some of the young gentlemen"—Johnny sneered the last two words—"I am a full-grown man. And I am too old and too intelligent to have to take orders from masters who are my mental inferiors, get up at four-thirty each morning, go to chapel for a service of worship I do not believe in, have three hours of lessons which are not worth learning before breakfast—"

"I am well aware of school routine; it is similar at most," James interrupted. "If you consider yourself superior, why not prove it by industry and example?"

"Jamey, you sound like a scolding woman! I've known some sent to the stocks for less!" Laughter seemed to bubble in the lad's eyes, bloodshot though they were. "I have had my glimpse of freedom and will now go back to jail and take my punishment. Leave me happy memories of you."

"Johnny, you can't reject all discipline—"

"I'll not talk about it," the younger brother interrupted, suddenly cold-faced and sharp-voiced. "What I do I do, and that is all there is to it."

"Johnny," James said, "your father died on the evening of the pageant."

"I am aware of it. I read both the notice and the obituary in *The Daily Post*. What does it matter? He was dead while he was still alive. Am I to grieve for a corpse?"

Slowly, out of sudden pain, James said, "You could grieve for your mother, and for yourself."

"When the day comes, I may grieve for myself," Johnny retorted. His expression softened as he stretched out a hand and touched his brother's. "There is only one other person in the world for whom I could grieve, Jamey, and that is you. My mother gave me nothing; her love and care were all for that wreck of a man. If there is one good thing to be said of my father, he lived his own life and damned the rest of the world. In such a way I shall live. Can you not live that way also?"

"You make one mistake," replied James, speaking very quietly. "He lived his own life but he damned no one except lawbreakers and the wicked."

Across the other's face passed an expression which was difficult to understand unless it was one of cunning or deception. The moment it was gone Johnny gripped both of James's hands in his, held them tightly and declared, "I will think on what you say, Jamey, have no fear."

James sensed two things in that moment. First, despite the warmth of assurance, the boy's words had a hollow ring of insincerity, more hurtful than anything else which had transpired. Second, although Johnny was so many years the younger, he seemed, in that moment, to be the elder and the more dominant of the two.

Before either brother could speak again there was a flurry of movement outside the cottage and the sound of approaching footsteps, and in the next moment Francis limped in, accompanied by one of the senior members of the guard of the House of Furnival.

On the instant, Johnny's expression changed yet again and became soft and cherubic, his eyes touched with humility, as he said, "Uncle Francis, how can I tell you how sorry I am to have caused so much commotion? I do declare it was simply born out of my eagerness to see the river pageant, a tribute to the House of Furnival which my masters denied me. But I know now that I should not have behaved so, and that immediately afterward I should have come to ask your forgiveness."

No one could have sounded more contrite, and it was hard to believe that this was the arrogant boy who had spoken with such truculence only minutes ago.

"The important thing is that you seek and obtain the forgiveness of Mr. Gordon," Francis said, "and that you realise how much distress such escapades cause your mother. We are ready to start the coach for the journey back to Rochester. Your unfortunate companions are already in it." There was no sternness in his tone, and it was obvious that Johnny had fooled him with his show of contrition.

James, however, felt with acute distress that he was now seeing his half brother as he really was.

After the coach in which Johnny departed turned the corner, Francis swung round and said to James, "I don't know what magic you used, Jamey, but you made a remarkable impression on your brother! Your mother has told me that when he was younger you were the only one of the family to whom he would listen and for whom he showed any affection." Francis placed a hand lightly on James's shoulder, and, looking at his uncle, James was suddenly acutely aware of the hidden strength in this man who had mastered so completely the handicaps of his infirmity. "But then," went on Francis, "they would be strange human beings who would not have affection for you."

James flushed scarlet as he stammered, "Y-you are too generous, sir!"

"Not many, if any, would agree." Francis gripped James's shoulder for an instant, then released his hold and began to limp toward his carriage. "I must go back; seldom has so much happened in one day. The name of Johnny has not been blessed at Furnival Tower House! But before we part I have a message for your mother which I hope you will give by word of mouth. It is the firm opinion of my brother and sisters that the foundation of Saint Giles should be a matter for us all as individuals, and we pledge the sum of five thousand pounds each, a total of twenty thousand pounds, together with such an annual sum as may be necessary. We shall consider it a memorial to our brother. Now, James! I must be on my way."

Dazed by news of such munificence, James watched as Francis was handed into the coach and was driven off. He glanced at the turnip-shaped silver watch in his fob pocket: it wanted fifteen minutes of five. He must ride back to St. Giles at speed, but before he fetched his horse he must have a word with Winfrith and perhaps one or both of the magistrates. Turning, he found Winfrith and Benedict Sly coming toward him.

"I cannot thank you or the justices enough—" began James.

"Do not try," interrupted Winfrith. "Your uncle has already done so magnificently. He rewarded the boys' actual finder with twenty-five pounds, all our officers with ten pounds each, and deposited a further fifty pounds in the poor-law box."

"Handsome is as handsome does," remarked Benedict. "And I swear that a kinder family I have never met." He threw back his head, laughed, and then went on in a challenging voice, "Jamey, are you prepared to spare me an hour of your time?"

"An hour? You know well that I plan to start back immediately for St. Giles!"

"If you can delay for this hour I believe you will find it worth-while," Winfrith assured him earnestly.

"There is ample time for you to come with me and still reach Saint Giles this evening," Benedict urged earnestly.

"Do we need horses?" James asked.

"It will be quicker to walk," Benedict replied, and James fell into step beside him.

Soon they had plunged into a rabbit warren of lanes and yards lined with dilapidated buildings where there was an unrelenting stink, the worse to James because he had become unfamiliar with the noxious-ness of open sewers. Then, suddenly they were in open fields, close by Lincoln's Inn. Here and there small houses had been built, new and clean-looking, even though the all-pervasive odour was still discern-ible.

One such building proved to be a small church, with a house adjacent.

James had never seen so small a church, but its size was explained when he saw the noticeboard outside, reading:

UNITARIAN CHURCH
THE FIELDS

Minister: The Reverend Thomas Rattray

A sign in the small garden of the house said simply MANSE and James was more and more puzzled at being brought here, until a youth of fourteen or fifteen appeared from the side of the vicarage, and James knew on the instant what Benedict wanted him to see.

This youth was remarkably like Johnny: so alike that they might be brothers.

253

CHAPTER *18*

The Half Brother

THE YOUTH, carrying a milking pail and a three-legged stool, drew nearer, and as he did so, what differences there were between him and Johnny became more apparent. He had a placid expression, and his eyes were a darker brown than Johnny's, although his hair and the rest of his colouring was much the same. He had a scar about an inch long above the right cheekbone from a wound which must have come perilously close to blinding him. He was broader and more solid-looking than Johnny but about as tall, perhaps because Johnny was far above average build for his age.

"May I help you, gentlemen?" he asked in a well-modulated voice.

"I was passing and wanted to find out details of the Reverend Rattray's sermon times this Sunday," Benedict Sly answered.

"He preaches thrice, at nine o'clock in the morning and six o'clock in the evening from the pulpit, sir, and once at three o'clock in the Lincoln Fields."

"Are you his son?" asked Sly.

"That is my privilege, sir. I am Simon, the eldest of his six children."

"You are very kind to give us the information so freely," Benedict said. "Let us not delay you further."

The lad inclined his head and moved out into the field, where two cows grazed among dozens of busily pecking fowl.

When Benedict and James were back among the huddle of buildings, Benedict glanced sideways at his companion and asked, "What occurs to you, Jamey?"

"Was Simon Rattray discovered in the search for Johnny?"

"Yes."

"Can there be serious doubt who his true father was?"

"I would say very little."

"What more do you know?" asked James.

"No more than you about the family, except perhaps that Thomas Rattray has an excellent reputation and his sermons are more thoughtful than is usual."

"His—wife?"

"Her name is Dorothy and she is, I am told, known for her charity to the sick and the poor among the congregation. It would not be difficult for me to find out more."

James frowned. "Without stirring up trouble for the Rattrays?" he asked.

"That is the last thing I would wish to do," Benedict assured him. "I would cause no trouble for his church, either." He broke off and suddenly changed the subject. "Is it still in your mind to become one of those who serve at Bow Street?"

"More than ever," James assured him, "and only one thing would stop me now: the continued refusal of Mr. Fielding to accept me."

"Oh, he'll accept you sooner or later," Benedict Sly declared with confidence. "Once he is convinced that you know the dangers and are ready to face them. David asked me to give you some advice." The black-bearded face broke into a contagiously attractive smile. "It appears that Mr. Henry and his brother are having some difficulty with the government, who require Bow Street to put down crime in the metropolis but do not wish to pay for the service."

"That is hardly a new situation," James pointed out.

"However," went on Benedict, "the Fielding brothers have lately come upon three cases in which trading justices have held their courts in alehouses and have accepted gifts of money from witnesses and thief-takers. So angered are the Fieldings that they are placing the facts before the Minister of State and asking that the iniquitous system of trading justices be investigated."

"Have they any hope of success?" asked James eagerly.

"In my opinion—and David's also—none whatsoever. There has been less crime of late, due entirely to the Bow Street men and the Gin Act, but this may be only a temporary lull. It could be almost suppressed if the government would pay for only twelve parish constables," said Benedict bitterly. "Instead, Fielding's eight have to rely on what they earn as thief-takers."

"And yet I would gladly join for no reward!"

"They consider you too young and inexperienced."

They were now at the stables close to the Bow Street offices, and seeing James, a stableboy went to get his horse.

"So you advise me that there is little use in my approaching Mr. Henry?" James asked.

"David advises you that a more appropriate time will come."

"Then I will be guided by him, if reluctantly."

"And one of us will tell you as soon as the right moment approaches," promised Benedict.

The horse was brought out, saddled and bridled, and James placed a piece of hard bread saturated with dried honey on the palm of his hand and allowed the horse to lick it from him, slipped two pennies into the stableboy's hand, then checked the stirrups. He sprang into the saddle effortlessly, unaware of the imposing figure he cut, and equally unaware of the fact that Mr. Henry Fielding was peering at him through a small window in the Bow Street house.

"Do *you* have any advice for me?" James asked Benedict Sly.

"Since you ask, I dare offer it! Yes, Jamey. Come and live in London, near Bow Street. Offer your services as a man of the law to poor defendants and others who need legal help but can afford only a little for it. Develop some other business if you must, as Henry with his writing and John with his Universal Register Office. But first and foremost, prove to the court that you are truly familiar with the extent of crime in London and are aware of the need that many have for protection from both crime and the law. You will probably not make a fortune but you will prepare the way for becoming a very rare bird."

"Rare in what way?" demanded James.

"A well-liked, well-respected thief-taker once the Fieldings called on you!"

Both men laughed but James's smile faded as he started out, then picked up the main highway to the northwest and St. Giles. Rain was falling steadily now and the road was greasy, while mud was beginning to collect in the treacherous ditches at the sides of the road.

Most of the traffic was agricultural or commercial. Two herds of cattle caused hopeless tangles as their drovers tried to keep the animals on the road and out of the ditches and unprotected fields. A carriage-and-pair which had been caught in a large flock of sheep got clear and the young driver, obviously furious at the delay, whipped his horses to greater speed, making the carriage tear past James and everyone on the road. One of its wheels caught in a mud-and-rain-filled rut and the carriage went crashing to one side, pulling the horses with it and flinging the driver twenty feet away. As the horses screamed and struggled, they became entangled more and more in the harness.

The driver lay still; he was dead of a broken neck.

It was dark before James reached home, but a reddish glow from a flare at the gate guided him. Soon he had changed into dry clothes and was sitting in front of a huge log fire, telling his mother and Henrietta what had happened. Beth was with the Tenches again for some family celebration.

Neither his mother nor sister was surprised at Johnny's escapade, although both were troubled.

At the same time they were overwhelmed by the news about the promised finance and annual support for the home, and it was a good time for James to ask, "What will you do, Henrietta?"

"I shall stay here and work with Mamma," answered Henrietta promptly. "I would have gone to work with her in London, had that been necessary. What will *you* do, Jamey?"

He answered without a moment's hesitation. "I shall take rooms in London, close to Bow Street, where I can both live and have a law office. I shall set up as a poor man's legal adviser together with whatever other business finally attracts me. Also, I shall be available for Mr. Henry or Mr. John Fielding as a Bow Street man at any time."

It was after dinner, while they were still at the table, that he asked, "What could Johnny do to upset Beth's plans to marry Randolph Tench? If there is a real danger of that, I do believe that I should know."

"Sir Mortimer has always made it clear that if Johnny should get into any more trouble with the law it would compel him to withdraw his approval of the marriage," answered Henrietta. "And there have been times when I have believed that Johnny would do some unlawful thing simply out of spite, for he hates Sir Mortimer Tench."

"I truly believe that Beth fears he will commit some outrageous deed at the wedding," Ruth Furnival remarked in the lull which followed. "If he does, Beth will never forgive him, and I shall find forgiveness difficult."

In the event, the wedding passed without disturbance. Beth was at her loveliest in her bridal gown; not only was the small church of St. Giles full but hundreds gathered outside in the sunshine and a huge table groaned with food and drink on the lawns of St. Giles Farm, where every villager was a welcome guest. Sir Mortimer Tench, an older and more mild-seeming man than James had expected, was very conscious of his duty to those who lived on his estate. Beth was radiant and her tall, somewhat too-elegant groom was obviously delighted with himself and his bride.

It was as if the wedding closed a door firmly on the past and opened another to a bright future.

In the odorous, dirty, overcrowded court, pleading for accused who were victims of circumstances or corruption, James Marshall learned more than he could have hoped to learn in any other way, with the help of David Winfrith and Benedict Sly. *The Daily Clarion* was the property of three young men, of whom Sly was one, dedicated to social reform. Much of its material was based on the Fieldings' reports and opinions, so that the newspaper became an unofficial second means of attack. Moreover, its columns often printed advertisements at very low cost, asking victims of robberies to report their loss to Bow Street immediately.

With increasing admiration James began to understand how the Fieldings worked and saw that progress *was* being made with the recovery of stolen property and the arrest and committal of thieves.

"But until there is official support, progress will be slow," Winfrith declared.

There seemed no doubt that he was right.

By September 1753, two years almost to the day since he had returned to London, Beth had had her first child and seemed thoroughly happy; the work of converting St. Giles farmhouse was long since finished, and the first foundlings had already been taken there; and since his outbreak at the time of the river pageant, Johnny had behaved in exemplary fashion.

Moreover, James's own affairs prospered. His presentation of case after case was so skilful that news spread of it throughout London, and people who had grievances or believed they had been wrongly accused came to him frequently, able and ready to pay a reasonable fee for his help. These fees he gave to the poor or to help with Bow Street expenses. While the legal side of his business expanded considerably faster than he had anticipated, another venture also prospered. He did not really know how it had started, except that Benedict Sly had convinced him that he should be able to turn his exhaustive knowledge of London and her environs to account.

"You should place an advertisement in *The Daily Clarion*, Jamey. Now let me think. How would it be if you were to declare yourself an expert on all matters pertaining to London?"

"Expert is much too strong," James had protested.

"Very well, then. How about this: 'Whatever you require in London Town "Mr. Londoner" knows where to find it.'?"

After pondering, James had replied, "But who would want to pay me for such a service?"

"Let us strike a bargain," Benedict had suggested. "I will insert the advertisement in our columns without charge daily for two weeks, and you will pay only if it brings you results."

On the day following the first advertisement a man had come by to find out if "Mr. Londoner" knew where to obtain a certain kind of French pomade, two women had requested his assistance in buying Spanish mantillas, and an elderly man from the North American colonies had wanted to know if the place of his birth still existed.

"I dare not traipse about London looking for the place where I was born," the man deplored. "It frightens me even to look at the rush and tear on the roads. The name of the place I can remember—Skelton Yard, near Saint Paul's Cathedral."

"There are but a few houses left there," James was able to tell him. "Take a sedan chair . . ."

He knew, also, of a shop in Covent Garden where Spanish and Portuguese as well as some Indian bric-a-brac was sold, and recommended a French hairdresser in the growing suburb of Knightsbridge as one likely to know where the pomade could be found. He made no charge for the information, asking only for a fair fee should his guidance bring results. Within two hours the man from the North

259

American colonies was back, overjoyed; he had found the cottage and a cousin and now requested help to find other relatives.

"I don't care what it costs," he said grandly, placing two guinea pieces on the table where James sat. "There are plenty more where those came from, Mr. Londoner!"

More and more inquiries came, some from the advertisements, mostly from recommendations by word of mouth. At the doorway leading to his rooms, one of Benedict's printers did a nameboard with the words "Mr. Londoner" written across wash drawings of St. Paul's and the Monument. James was seldom unable to answer questions.

His own knowledge of the City and of Westminster grew even more extensive and he was so busy that he had little time to brood about what could be improved and what could be different. Now and again he saw Mary Smith, who had settled into the Weygalls' household and, although looking thinner, was comfortably dressed and outwardly at least content. Sight of her never failed to stir him but he still had a sense of needing time before committing himself in marriage. All this time he waited for a summons from John Fielding. He had learned much about the way his men worked and of their unswerving loyalty, and he was grieved that despite their efforts the early part of that winter of 1753 showed crime had risen to fantastic heights. A few highwaymen began to work regularly close to the turnpikes, and some holdups were actually staged within the City of London. Reports claimed that these were mostly the work of one bold gang of ruthless thieves known as the Twelves, one of them having boasted that if he were taken, eleven men would come rushing to his rescue.

Everyone who knew Henry Fielding realised that the burden of his work, his long hours in court and his constant fight for official assistance were making him ill. He suffered, among other sicknesses, from dropsy, and his brother and friends, including Saunders Welch, persuaded him to go to Bath to take the waters. He was about to leave when an urgent message reached him from the Secretary of State, the Duke of Newcastle. At last the government had been stirred to anxiety and demanded of Henry Fielding a detailed plan to fight crime in the coming winter.

Fielding canceled his visit to Bath and spent four days working on a plan which he submitted to the Duke. In his report, Fielding revealed the existence of his volunteers and pleaded for six hundred pounds to buy horses so that the men could move faster and for funds with which to pay messengers and buy information. Now the government knew exactly what Henry was doing.

The waiting began again until finally George II said in a speech from the throne: "It is with utmost regret that I observe that the horrid crimes of murder and robbery are increased . . . I urge that everybody should contribute their best endeavours against the criminals."

The following day *The Daily Clarion* and other newspapers quoted the speech.

James, going into the smelly, crowded court a few days later, saw Winfrith beckoning him.

As soon as he drew within earshot, Winfrith whispered, "There is to be an official allowance of two hundred pounds a year, Jamey."

James gasped. "Two *hundred*! Not two thousand?"

"It is a start," Winfrith said with a sigh. "It is a start."

CHAPTER *19*

The Battle

OUT OF the blue one morning at the end of November a summons came for James to wait upon John Fielding at Bow Street. This was the first time for several years that he had been in the private office, behind the court: a room once used for very unofficial purposes.

"Mr. Marshall, I am keenly aware of your eagerness to assist us at Bow Street in our pursuits," the magistrate said. "But your father was killed in such service and your stepfather made great sacrifices also. I have been reluctant to subject you to the dangers involved. However, one grievous problem preoccupies us—in which your special knowledge of London and of this particular district might be of help."

"I am wholly at your service, sir."

"Thank you. You will have heard of the activities of a gang known as the Twelves. We have received some intelligence that members of this gang live in the Covent Garden area, venturing out at night and riding their horses to attack our respectable citizens with the utmost violence. No one is safe."

"If I can help put an end to it I will be greatly rewarded," James declared.

"I am aware of it. My proposal is that you use your knowledge of the topography of the area to discover exactly where these blackguards live and where they hide or dispose of their ill-gotten gains. You will be alone in your early endeavours unless you can think of one other who, not being an associate at Bow Street, would have the courage to accompany you. Should good fortune attend you, then every available man will be used to crush the Twelves."

"I will exert myself in every way," James promised, fighting down his increasing excitement. "It might be of assistance, sir, if I could study the record of the depredations of the Twelves to ascertain where they have struck, whom they have attacked, what valuables they have stolen, and on what nights they have been active."

"Such a record has been prepared. Mr. Winfrith will put it into your hands."

"You are very kind," James said.

He left the house in Bow Street, still eager and yet becoming slightly apprehensive. He carried a leather case containing the information Winfrith had given him and went straight to his rooms and studied the documents for three hours. Dizzy with the concentrated effort of reading he walked to an alley in Fleet Street in which there was an eating house where the food was good, plentiful and cheap. He had been there for only ten minutes when Benedict came in, still wearing an apron smeared with printer's ink. In the latter part of the day he set up in type the stories he had garnered during the earlier hours. His eyes had the bright glitter of a man who was tired.

"I was told you were here and came to take a glass of ale with you—I must not stay long or there will be no *Clarion* tomorrow!"

"I have been taken by an idea," James said suddenly. "Although it wasn't in my head a minute ago, I offer it to you eagerly. Will you join me in risking life and limb in an endeavour"—he lowered his voice and leaned across the scrubbed wooden table—"to catch the Twelves and put them in jail? This *is* a secret matter, mind you."

"Fleet Street is the right place to bring secrets," Benedict said dryly. "Are you serious about this, Jamey?"

"Never more so. When I have your word on secrecy I will tell you the whole story."

Three-quarters of an hour later Benedict said earnestly, "I am your man. And I can help in a way the court cannot. *The Daily Clarion* holds a record of incidents in the whole of the Covent Garden area, where we sell many of our newspapers, but many are told to me and my partners, for payment if used. I'll warrant there was no mention of the New Mohocks in the secret record."

Startled, James said, "There was one—they left a girl all but dead in an alley. Even then it was said only that they were suspected."

"We have a list of most of their little escapades as well as hundreds of others not attributable to them."

"I am very glad, but why should you keep such a list?"

"Jamey, everything is grist to the mill of a newspaper," explained Benedict. "One can never be sure when a piece of gossip or a trifle of information may not lead to a story of great public interest. If you will finish eating that treacle pudding I will take you to the office and get the diary."

The office and printing house were only fifty yards away and the steady beat of a machine sounded clearly as they crossed the cobbled yard. The print shop itself was heavy with the odour of printing ink and hazy with smoke from pipes and oil lamps as the men stood at the machines and the boys rushed about with loads of newsprint. The office, in one corner, was little better, and James could only just make out, through the haze, two men sitting at a long desk.

There was good-humoured banter between Benedict and the two men before the diary was taken down from a shelf. James was astonished by the detail, the minutiae of information about that quarter of London which contained both Bow Street and Covent Garden. It was kept on a day-to-day basis, most entries being set in the hours between sunset and midnight.

As James turned its pages, one entry kept occurring: a single line reading "New Mohocks." Occasionally there was the name of a victim of their outrages or an address of a house where they had created a disturbance, but for the most part there was just "New Mohocks"— identifiable because of their method of attack on women, which had sometimes developed into rape by four or five men in succession.

"Bring that back intact or 'Mr. Londoner' will cease to exist!" one of Benedict's partners threatened.

"I'll bring it back, purified!" James laughed.

By the time he reached his rooms it was already nine o'clock but he studied the entries for another two hours, by which time the candle was burning low and his eyes were so heavy that he found it hard to keep them open. The following day, when not at court or attending to callers, he studied both the Bow Street report on the Twelves and the dairy, and read and pondered late into the night. Up at six the next morning, he breakfasted on cold beef and pancakes with heavy black treacle, and had barely finished his ale when a thought stabbed into his head. Pushing back his chair, he sprang to the table where the diary lay. He began to look through it furiously, placing in the diary a tiny dot on those days when the Twelves had been active anywhere in London.

On no single night of the Twelves' depredations had the New Mohocks been active. Not one single night.

"You think they might be the Twelves one night and the New Mohocks another?" Benedict sounded incredulous and David Winfrith showed a kind of resignation.

They were in James's bedroom, large enough to be a living room also, and at night an office. On one side of the hearth were bookshelves holding mostly law and English and European history.

"I think it probable," James replied. "Even five years ago the New Mohocks were old for such youthful gangs and today some of them must be in the middle twenties and none younger than twenty-one or -two. Would raping women and arousing the fear of neighbours satisfy young men of that age? Could the attacks on women not be a cover for more serious activities?"

"I like your reasoning," Benedict replied.

"And I," agreed Winfrith.

"There is an easy way to find out," declared James. "Have each of the New Mohocks watched and followed to their homes after their next attack and then at dusk each night for a week, say, have them watched and followed wherever they go."

"Practicable but I doubt easy," said Winfrith. "The watchers would be denying themselves any of the customary rewards of thief-taking and protecting private houses. They would need some retainer, a shilling a night at least."

"I will pay whatever is needed," offered James.

"I will pay half," Benedict added. "Get skilful men, David, accustomed to following suspects without being seen."

Winfrith replied, "I am quite sure that Mr. Fielding will agree to this and will be grateful for your generous offer."

The surveillance began that night with constables from adjoining parishes taking positions of vantage, sometimes in doorways, sometimes in rooms of houses owned by friends, in the alehouses and near the brothels. For two nights there was nothing to report, but on the third, several men suspected of being New Mohocks left their homes and forgathered at the Angel Inn, near a corner of Covent Garden piazza. An hour later they left the Angel and split into two groups, one concentrating near a big house in Leicester Square, the other in Long Acre. Each group was watched and followed secretly.

The first group ran amok through the great square, terrifying people in the houses and in the streets, cutting horses loose, kicking down protective fences about the flower beds and disappearing after ten minutes of bedlam.

Disappearing, that is, as far as they knew. In fact they were followed, one by one, to a big warehouse belonging to Ebenezer Morgan & Sons.

The second group lay in wait for a girl and set upon her, but before they could harm her, two riders thundered by, Bow Street men, who gave the girl a chance to escape but did not reveal their identity.

The next night nothing happened.

On the fifth night of the vigil the New Mohocks met again at the Angel Inn but this time they did not stay so long. In twos and threes they left in the direction of Hyde Park Turnpike and went on to the Pack Inn, a mile beyond the turnpike. Within a quarter of an hour they left by the ill-lit back door, took horses from the stables, and approached the highway; each one was masked. Since they were mounted and Fielding's men were on foot, no chase was possible, but the Bow Street men were near enough to identify the riders as they held up two carriages and one coach. Frightened men and women were made to dismount and were robbed of all their valuables, and two young women were so roughly handled that there seemed some danger of rape, but a small company of dragoons, dispatched at Fielding's request, came at a gallop before great harm could be done and the highwaymen scattered.

Each one returned to the Morgan warehouse through the archway in Long Acre.

By the time James and Benedict were summoned and reached the spot, all Fielding's men were at the approaches to the warehouse. John Charleston, one of the oldest and most reputable of the men from Bow Street, advanced into the middle of the yard in front of the warehouse, while others crept to the doorways, where a pale light glimmered through the cracks.

Suddenly there was a cry from the roof.

"On guard there. On guard!"

On that instant the doors were thrust open and the men who had been followed rushed out, knives and pistols in their hands.

Charleston, face to face with a man who raised a pistol, called out clearly, "Drop your weapons! We are officers of the law. You are under arrest."

The man in front of him fired on that instant, and a bullet caught Charleston between the eyes; several more shots sounded as, heedless of danger, more Bow Street men rushed forward. Benedict saw one of the highwaymen creeping close to the wall and leaped at him, while James, no more than three yards behind but hidden by shadows, watched the man who had shot and surely killed Charleston slipping along the archway toward Long Acre.

If James called for help, the other would hear and shoot him in his tracks.

If he followed the man alone, he would be in nearly as much danger.

No lights were on except the one at the archway and every step made it more difficult to make out the other's shape; all at once he turned into an alley, and James stopped moving. Nearby was a doorway which would give him shelter. The noise of the battle continued; there was no more shooting but much bellowing and scuffling.

Soon he heard the chinking of bridle and stirrups: Charleston's killer was mounting a horse. James crept into the empty street. Sharp and clear, the horse's shod feet sounded on the cobbles, and as James drew nearer still, the murderer nosed his mount into Long Acre. James's one hope of stopping him was to let him pass and then spring at him.

The masked rider peered in each direction but did not see James. Slowly he inched his mount forward, giving James time to draw level with the horse's hindquarters. He keyed himself to leap, confident that once he could grip the rider's arm he could throw him with one twist of the wrist, bringing him off the horse, but just as he was on the point of jumping he caught his foot on some piece of metal in the road and it clanged with an alarming noise.

The man turned swift as sound in his saddle.

There was just enough light from the flickering flares to show the pistol thrust forward. James flung himself to one side as a shot roared and flashed. He felt a thud in his left shoulder and crashed onto the cobbles so heavily that consciousness died.

The highwayman put his horse to the gallop as men began to stream out of Morgan's archway in time to find James with his badly injured shoulder but too late to catch the man who had killed John Charleston.

All the other members of the Twelves were captured; all were taken to a special session at Bow Street, where John Fielding committed them to Newgate to await trial. One of them was Gabriel, son of Ebenezer Morgan.

James was aware of pain in his shoulder and a throbbing ache in his head. He could smell something sharp and astringent which reminded him of a hospital. Light came into the small room from a window placed high in a wall. All was quiet. Very gradually he recalled what had happened and suddenly he realised the simple, overwhelmingly significant truth: he was alive! Cautiously, fearful of making the ache worse, he turned his head and saw that the ceiling sloped down to a door in a corner opposite the fireplace. He did not understand where he was, but at least he *was* alive.

Had the others caught the highwayman?

Was Charleston dead?

These thoughts drifted slowly through his mind, while his head seemed to become heavy even on the pillow and his eyes closed. He did not know how long he alternately slept and dozed but the next time he woke he felt an alertness of mind which told him that all drowsing was done.

He tried to sit up but the effort brought such blinding pain to both shoulder and head that he desisted, lowering himself gently back on the pillow. Hardly had the pain eased than he heard footsteps on stairs which creaked loudly, followed by more footsteps groaning on the boards of a passage. A few moments later the groaning stopped, the latch lifted quietly and the door opened.

Mary Smith came into the room.

In that first moment it was like a dream; she could not be real, must be a figment of his imagination! But as she crossed toward him and, seeing his eyes open, smiled with pleasure, he had no doubt that she was there in the flesh. He raised his right hand to her and she took it between hers, pressed gently, then drew back and sat on a slung chair. What light there was shone on her face, and he had a swift thought that in the little bonnet and dark dress with white ruffs at neck and wrists she was very like his mother. She had the same colouring, the same shaped eyes and forehead.

"How long have I been here?" he asked in a voice husky through lack of use.

"Since last night," she answered, leaning forward and taking a small mug of water from a table at the side of the bed, putting her other hand at his head and raising it a few inches. He moistened his lips and then drank a little, surprised at the great effort this cost him. She lowered his head onto the pillows again. "You had a bad fall, and we were anxious for a while, but the doctor took the bullet out of your shoulder and assures us that although you may have cracked your skull it is not broken. You are to rest and sleep as much as you can, eat a little food and drink some soup. If you are obedient to your nurse he expects you to be as good as new before long." Her eyes smiled as she went on: "And you are not to be worried or anxious, and I am to answer all your questions as far as I can."

James looked at her searchingly and asked slowly, "Where am I and how is it you are here?"

"You are in an old cottage attached to Mr. Weygalls' house, and he commands me to give your needs my prime attention."

"But his family—"

"Jamey," she interrupted, "last night a miracle happened in this part of London. The New Mohocks were broken up and are never likely to re-form. Mr. Sly made it clear that you were largely responsible, and except possibly for Ebenezer Morgan, who dares say no word since one of his sons was involved and one of his warehouses was used to store stolen goods, every person in the neighbourhood knows how great a debt they owe to you."

"Nonsense! The Fieldings—"

"To the Fieldings, too, but they are remote from us. Jamey, I think you have talked enough. I will come whenever you call for me, and you have only to pull this rope behind your bed."

She drew the end of a rope forward so that he could reach it without strain, but before she could move away he rested a hand on hers.

"Mary, why is this room like a hospital?"

"You had best not allow Mr. Weygalls to hear you say that. He considers hospitals to be stinking places, where patients die even more quickly than they would outside, but with perhaps a little more comfort. This is a sickroom for his family. You were within a stone's throw of this place, and Benedict Sly brought you here. Now you must rest."

"One more question," James pleaded. "How many of the New Mohocks were caught?"

"By the strangest coincidence eleven New Mohocks and eleven members of the Twelves! Only one, the man whom you tried to stop, escaped."

"Is it known who he is?"

"You will have to ask others that, later."

Mary stood up and squeezed a sponge in a bowl of water on the table, wiped his head, face, hands and wrists, and emptied the bowl into an earthenware pitcher which she took out with her.

He thought he would stay awake, she was so vivid in his mind, but in fact he fell asleep quickly and slept soundly and without stirring for some hours. He woke only to doze off again, and when he opened his eyes next it was daylight. He did not want to harass Mary but doubted whether he could get out of bed safely by himself, so he pulled the rope and heard a faint ringing some distance off. In a surprisingly short time her footsteps sounded.

Mary helped him out of bed and to the commode, which was a tiny closet outside the door, and he was surprised to see one of the Harrington flush systems installed, while there was virtually no odour. It made a noisy clatter and the roar of water was like a waterfall, so he was laughing when he went back into the bedroom. Mary had made the bed and had propped pillows up against a wooden rest covered with sailcloth, and this greatly eased his shoulder. After tucking the blankets around him, she said she would get his breakfast. Ten minutes later she reappeared with a tray on which were scrambled eggs, fresh bread and butter, and a pitcher of hot milk and another of hot coffee.

"Ring for me when you have finished," she said.

"Can you not stay and talk?" James pleaded.

"There are children clamouring for their breakfast in the kitchen!"

"Oh, I'm sorry," he said. "I had forgotten you had others to care for."

"I only wish—" she began, but broke off without finishing.

Using his right arm James was able to handle the food without difficulty; it was not until he began to eat that he realised how hungry he was, and how good the food was. He was sipping coffee when he heard voices downstairs, one of them Benedict Sly's.

Approaching the door, Benedict called, "How is the people's hero this morning?" Pushing the door open, he strode in, his usually calm face filled with excitement. Suddenly his eyes blazed and he burst out, "The hero is being pampered, which is as it should be. Jamey—you,

Bow Street and the capture of the Twelves are the talk of the town! Every newspaper carried the story in great detail and never have more newspaper reporters crowded into Bow Street. Jamey, you should see the store of ill-gotten wealth that was unearthed, close on fifty thousand pounds' worth! Have no doubt the thieves will hang—and have no doubt you and all concerned will be much the richer when it is all over."

"Richer? How?"

From the inside of his jacket Benedict drew copies of *The Daily Clarion* and *The Public Advertiser* and spread them out in front of James, who saw the bold announcement in the middle of both pages, identical except that they were in different type, stating that all jewels stolen by the New Mohocks were recovered intact and that the owners reclaiming them upon producing identification were to reward James and his men—

James put the papers aside and said, "It was wrong to single me out for praise, Ben."

"I don't agree with you," Benedict Sly said. "Had John Charleston been alive he would have been named with you. Full credit was done to him in yesterday's newspapers. It is a triumph for Bow Street and for you. Revel in it while you can!"

In a room on the first rickety floor of an alehouse in Kensington a man lay in bed with a pretty, blue-eyed girl beside him, looking at his strikingly handsome face with adoration. He was reading the announcement which James Marshall had just read, and he was scowling. Suddenly he flung the paper aside.

"I know what I would do with the likes of them," he growled. "I'd draw out their vitals and then hang them high and while they had life left in them I'd quarter them, too." He broke off as the girl's eyes widened, only to go on: "Never mind what I say, Nell."

His strong hand covered her breast and made a number of firm, bold strokes down to the pit of her stomach, until her whole body began to quiver.

Afterward, when he lay half asleep, she whispered, "Will you take me to see, Jake?"

"Take you where?" demanded Jacob Rackham.

"To see the man drawn and quartered. I have seen dozens hanged at Tyburn and Tower Hill, but never a drawing and quartering."

271

He drowned her words with a roar of laughter, but when that had stilled and they lay quiet, looking at the green fields beyond the window, he thought of what she had asked and of what he had said, and of the man James Marshall, who had come near to preventing his escape. Only once before had he felt such vicious anger toward a man, and that had been when he and the New Mohocks, early in their existence, had been amusing themselves with a girl and a stranger had come thrashing about them with a staff, scattering them until two had fallen into an open sewer. They had carried the stench for weeks; he, the memory for much longer.

Jacob Rackham made the same promise to himself now that he had made then.

Later that same morning, the door of James's room opened and, to his delight, his mother appeared, with Henrietta close behind. They were full of concern, eager in admiration, agog with their own tidings. Another building at the foundling home at St. Giles was almost ready. Even better news—a second such home was to be started near Staines, beyond Hounslow, by a friend of Sir Mortimer Tench's who had observed what they were doing at St. Giles and planned to emulate them.

It was hard to believe there was still better news.

"A report from Gordon's says that Johnny has made great advances in studies and has caused no more problems," Ruth said happily. "And there is a suggestion that before he goes for further study, he should visit all the Furnival offices throughout the world." She stood up from the side of the bed and took his hands, and once again he was reminded of her resemblance to Mary. "Jamey, it is no exaggeration to say that I am inordinately proud of you but also a little apprehensive —both feelings I had so often for your father." She leaned over and kissed his forehead, her voice unsteady as she went on. "Both he and John Furnival would have been so proud of you, my son."

Tears stung his eyes when she and Henrietta had gone.

Soon, however, he was shaken out of such a mood, for Timothy arrived, closely followed by David Winfrith with greetings and a note from the Fieldings.

Sitting down on the side of the bed, David said in a quivering voice, "Victims of the highwaymen are coming to inspect the recovered goods in droves, Jamey! And each—when he has satisfied one of the

Mr. Fieldings and has answered his questions about that particular robbery, for the more evidence against the Twelves the better—goes off with his once lost property, leaving a handsome reward. Already the total is more than one hundred guineas. It would not surprise me if it grows to more than a thousand. If it is agreeable to you, ten per cent will be set aside as yours and the rest distributed—"

For the first time since he had been here James was taken by surprise by the opening of the door, and Mary came in, smiling and yet scolding.

"Do you want him to die before he can use his share of the reward, David? You will have to stop talking, for he must rest."

"I confess I had not realised how fatigued I was," James admitted. "But, David, I do not require a greater share than others."

"Ten per cent also will go to the widow and family of John Charleston," David told him. "I had forgotten that."

He went out, ignoring James's protest at his leaving, and threw a teasing kiss at Mary as he went.

"There are two things I would like," James told Mary that evening, never having felt more contented. "To have you stay for a while, not bustling about, and afterward to meet Mr. Weygalls."

"The first you can have if it pleases you," Mary replied, to his delighted surprise. "A kitchen maid will fetch the tray from the head of the stairs and will wash the dishes, the children are abed, and Mrs. Weygalls will sit downstairs with them. Mr. Weygalls has gone to a meeting of surgeons at Barbers' Hall and will not be back until after you have gone to sleep." She took the tray out and when she came back she was without her apron, and looking as pretty as he had yet seen her. "Now that I am here what would you have me do?" she asked, a gay note in her voice.

"As the mood takes you I would like you to talk about yourself," James said.

He was asleep, about an hour later, when she left.

For five consecutive nights she sat with him and they talked or she read extracts from *The Public Advertiser* or *The Daily Clarion*, mostly about the stream of callers who came to seek their belongings. It proved that except for some gold plate stolen from a peer's dining room and a few jewels, the Twelves had stored most of the valuables. They had, however, spent all of the money. On the seventh day, when James was out of bed and beginning to feel fractious, wanting to go out of doors, Benedict and David arrived together. The reward money, so they told him, now totaled more than fourteen hundred guineas, and there might yet be more! They went off leaving another phrase ringing in his ears.

"Since Friday night there have to our knowledge been many fewer attacks by highwaymen. Neither the watchmen nor the Bow Street men have had a less strenuous time in winter."

Surely this was proof of the effectiveness of the methods Bow Street had adopted; surely more official approval and bigger payment would soon be forthcoming and London would be given a peace-keeping force competent to subdue all major crime!

Paul Weygalls proved to be a short, plump, rather fussy-mannered man, quite different from the mind picture which James had conceived. He would not hear of payment or recompense for what he had done, telling James that the atmosphere of Covent Garden and around was unbelievably improved. People now dared venture abroad at night with much less fear. And indeed the effect on all London was most remarkable, *most* remarkable.

"If there is a single thing I can do for you, Mr. Marshall, you have but to name it."

"There *is* one thing, sir," James said quietly.

"Then as I say: name it."

Heart beating fast, James replied, "I would like permission to visit Mary Smith from time to time, sir."

"I suspect that if I were to refuse I might no longer have a housekeeper!" Weygalls smiled broadly and turned toward the door. "In the meantime, Mr. Marshall, I shall send her to see you straightaway."

Two days later, after James had been there for nine days, he went back to his rooms in the Strand. He was surprised to find three persons on the stairs, and in the office where he interviewed his callers, six more, four gentlemen and two ladies. Behind the desk were Benedict Sly and a youth whom James had never seen before. He proved to be Benedict's younger brother Nicholas.

The Slys had maintained the business which, because of the publicity, had increased tenfold.

There was soon a much greater volume of work than "Mr. Londoner" could handle, so he employed Nicholas Sly to maintain the office throughout the day, at the same time renting a small shop alongside it. He soon discovered that the lad's love and knowledge of London rivaled his own, and it became Nicholas' greatest pleasure to visit out-of-the-way parts of London and buy any small curiosities which took his fancy, cleaning and polishing them before putting them in the shop. There was always a ready market among visitors from abroad and from the provinces. As the weeks passed, Mary found herself free to visit James during the day, when the Weygalls' children were at school. And when not engaged in work for Bow Street, James spent part of each evening visiting Mary, occasionally taking her to St. James's Park to see the ducks on the lake or to stroll among the perambulating crowds along the Mall. After the excitement of the triumph over the Twelves, life took on an even tenor in most spheres.

CHAPTER 20

James and Mary

As THE pressure of court work declined in the spring, a noticeable change for the worse befell Henry Fielding. As well as dropsy, he suffered asthma and jaundice. At last, and under great pressure from his brother John, he agreed to go with his wife to a warmer climate, where the warmth and sun alone might help him. He left his work at the court for the last time in April, and many believed that his death was near. But he hung on to life and even wrote a little, revised some of his earlier novels, and lived through a May during the whole of which, it was said, the sun shone on London only three times. In June, a vessel was found to take him and his wife and family to Portugal, but because of bad weather there were considerable delays, and it was more than two months later, early in August 1754, before they arrived.

Within two months Henry Fielding was dead; and his brother and his friends mourned.

In London, during this time, John was appointed to the magistracy at Bow Street and prevailed on the government to continue paying for the execution of Henry's plan. At the age of thirty-three, totally blind for fourteen years, he showed tremendous energy, courage and determination.

Saunders Welch was also made a magistrate, working sometimes at Bow Street with John Fielding, sometimes at his home in Long Acre.

The first years at the St. Giles Foundling Home were a complete success. A rigid standard of cleanliness was kept, and of the first fifty near-starving children taken in, only three died. St. Giles became a show place and an example.

In June of 1755, Beth had her second child, a daughter.

"And we shall call her Ruth Elizabeth Anne," Beth declared in a note. "She is absolutely *precious*, with blue eyes and golden hair which Mamma says she will lose but I cannot believe. . . ."

James was reading this, and smiling, when he heard footsteps on the stairs. Putting the letter aside, he was rising when David Winfrith burst in, pale and wild-eyed with anger.

"The treacherous sons of Westminster bitches, pimps to their own mothers! How dare they show their ugly faces in the House! How dare they behave like woolly-haired bullies, the dirty, lousy crows! They are not worth John Fielding's little finger! The Blind Beak can see farther than their stinking noses! There isn't a highwayman in London who would not put them to shame!"

He paused for breath and James was tempted to remark, "I perceive you are out of temper!" or some such, but stopped himself in time. Instead, he asked carefully, "What has distressed you so, David?"

"Distressed? I am livid with rage! If I had the necks of any one of the stinking sons of harlots here, I'd squeeze the breath out of them! Do you know what those demagogues at the Palace of Westminster have done? They've told John Fielding they are not likely to continue their support. There have been many complaints, especially from the City merchants, about what we are doing at Bow Street. Here, for a few paltry pounds, we are giving the whole of the metropolitan area within the tollgates freedom from criminals, for the first time we have armed men who will give chase the moment crimes are reported, for the first time citizens realise it is worth reporting all robbers and suspicious events quickly. And the government heeds a few City merchants who say we are driving criminals into the City! It is monstrous!"

He stopped short as Mary entered the room, then told her what had happened, this time speaking with more reserve.

"Possibly the government's mood will pass. Certainly *The Clarion* will come out strongly against the Lord Mayor's proposals."

"Perhaps among *The Clarion*'s readers there will be some to help," Mary suggested. "I must confess there are times when I almost wish Henry Fielding had spent more time writing novels than coping with crime. I declare I have never been more entertained than by *Tom Jones*."

"Then it is time Jamey found a better way to entertain you," David declared, his expression clearing. "Perhaps he could take you with him while he pelts the Duke of Newcastle with rotten oranges."

Despite having had ample opportunity, it was a fact that James had never had a love affair of any kind. Although occasionally he was stirred to interest by a young woman, he had felt no sense of urgent physical need, and although he had often been sexually aware of Mary, he felt a deep obligation not to take advantage of her friendship in any way. Yet the more he saw of her, the more he enjoyed her company.

Since the shooting affray he had become aware of a sense of loneliness. And he now had financial independence. The business, widely known as "Mr. Londoner," was making a substantial profit, and James suddenly realised that not only could he afford far greater comfort than he now permitted himself, he could also afford a wife and children.

Suddenly it came to him that Mary might have no desire to marry— or to marry him. Conceited fool, he told himself, what makes *you* so desirable?

From that moment on he could not wait to ask for her hand.

On the next occasion that Mary visited him, he was so nervous that at first she was puzzled. It was a cold night, a wind was howling, and her cheeks were rosy and her eyes bright as she spread her hands toward the fire. He did not believe she had ever been more attractive, and he knew that he had never been more tongue-tied. He went down on one knee to take off the big overshoes she wore, and quite suddenly he was on both knees, holding her hands tightly and peering up into her face. Still his jaws seemed locked.

Very slowly she bent down until their eyes were level, and she smiled and said gently, "How can you expect words to come when you are looking up at someone far less worthy than yourself?"

"Less worthy!" he exclaimed. "Are you mad, Mary? Why, you are worth—you are worth—"

Words stuck in his throat again, but he could see that her eyes were glowing, and he knew what her answer would be before he asked the question.

Huskily he said, "Mary, I love you."

"I love you, sir," she replied.

But he hardly heard her as he blurted out, "I—I beg you to marry me."

"I shall not find it difficult to do so," she declared.

"Now!" he cried, suddenly understanding and wild with delight. "Soon!"

"As soon as you wish and can," she replied gently, "and if you are sure you really desire me for a wife, or indeed really desire a wife at all. Or—"

He kissed her to silence.

He kissed her until he was almost dazed with joy.

He was more aware of her than he had ever been, and that no doubt was why, later in the evening, when it was nearly time for her to leave and after they had eaten fine mutton chops and mint jelly and fried suet pudding, he said, "Mary, I—I confess to some embarrassment."

"With *me*, Mr. Marshall?"

"With you, Miss Smith!" He touched her hands, and then with a boldness he had not known before, he stepped behind her and placed his hands on her bosom and drew her to him, so that they were close together. "I can say this best without looking you in the eye. I shall probably be disastrously inadequate on our wedding night."

"*Inadequate*, sir?"

"I can think of no better word. I—" He swallowed but made himself go on. "It has never been—I have never— Oh, damnation, where is my courage? I have never *known* a woman, Mary!"

She stood very still and he felt for a few moments that he had disappointed or troubled her, but slowly she gently pressed his hands and said in a voice soft at first but gradually gaining strength, "And I have never known a man, Jamey. So there will be two of us in the same—"

"Bed!" he cried.

"Bed!" she echoed. Then she drew away from him and said in a trembling voice, "If I stay longer, I shall not be able to say on our wedding night what I have just said."

279

"Provided we do not have to wait too long—"

"Jamey," she said, "I would like ours to be a very simple ceremony, performed by my father and with only close friends as witnesses. Will that hurt you? If my father had a church of his own it would be different, but I do not think he will ever have one again and"—mischief forced its way through her brief sadness—"that would mean too long a wait."

"As soon and as quiet as you wish," he replied.

Because Timothy was in the north of England, visiting relatives at Newcastle, only the Weygalls, David Winfrith and Benedict and Nicholas Sly were at the wedding. James had sent a brief letter to his mother and Henrietta and another to Francis Furnival, saying that when they received the missive he would have taken a wife and asking that all three come to visit them as soon as could be arranged.

After the ceremony they paid a brief visit to the home of Paul and Mathilda Weygalls, then went directly to the rooms over the shop in the Strand. Already James had moved up another flight of stairs, to a huge bedroom with a four-poster bed large enough for a dozen people.

"Jamey," Mary said, "I think we shall find that we know most of what we need to know already."

"Absorbed as we have lived?" he asked, with forced lightness.

"Absorbed into our mind as we have lived! For instance, I can assume from what your hero Henry Fielding has made clear in his novels that a bold bride would come to the bed undraped." Soon she said, "Whether 'tis fair that the woman should always lie beneath the man I do not know." Still there was laughter in her.

"Somewhere in my readings I have absorbed the notion that it is not always so." Happiness and eagerness and apprehension affected James. "Even as I lie here, doing nothing, I have a stirring in my loins."

"What a strange euphemism!"

"It has Biblical precedent, ma'am." His breathing was shorter now, and he kissed her, then drew back, and in the movement was closer to and even more aware of her. "But for tonight I'm happy enough to accept your judgment," he said, and gently began to stroke her breasts until suddenly, incredibly, she said in a voice he could hardly hear, "Arise, Sir James."

"What did you say?" he began—until he was aware of the gentleness of her hand on him and of so overwhelming a desire for her that all else was forgotten.

They did not go out of London for the week which followed their marriage and James took Mary to the City, where—to his astonishment—she had never been. The contrasts appalled yet fascinated her: the magnificence of St. Paul's and the Tower of London side by side with dilapidated alleys and buildings; the once great houses now grown over with grass and lichen, next to broken-down brothels with young girls old before their time anxiously waiting at the shabby doors and windows.

"I confess I am glad we shall not live in the City," Mary said at the end of their visit. "But this is a week I shall never forget, my love. A happy, happy week."

Their first child was born on the eighth day of October, 1756. He was named James, and they called him Jimmy.

The child put the seal on their marriage, which drew them very close yet kept neither from individual activities, and James spent as much time at Bow Street as ever.

There was no end to John Fielding's energy or determination, and as James watched him in court, he realised the absolute importance of this one man: but for Fielding and his handful of loyal workers, criminals might well have taken over the whole of the metropolis.

More and more James understood the vital need for a larger, fully professional peacemaking force.

To his deep satisfaction, no one agreed with him as much as Mary.

CHAPTER *21*

No Reward?

"IT IS a remarkable thing," David Winfrith pronounced, sitting on a carved oak chair in the Marshalls' living room, "They will not give John Fielding enough money, they will not give him men, they will not give him moral support for whatever that is worth, but they *will* give him a knighthood."

James Marshall, on one knee beside young Jimmy, now five years old, who was struggling with a set of building bricks, looked up sharply.

"No man deserves the accolade better," James declared.

"No man knows better what he deserves," said Winfrith. "The letter to the Duke of Newcastle in which Fielding suggested that giving him this knighthood would increase public respect for him was a stroke of genius."

"You mean he *asked* for the honour?" Mary, coming in from the kitchen, with a baby in her arms, was so surprised that she missed a step.

"That he did," replied Winfrith. "And if I know John Fielding, he will shortly write to say that a man who has been knighted by His

Majesty must keep up appearances and nowhere could money be better spent than on Bow Street Court and the Bow Street Runners."

"Runners?" Mary echoed.

She sat down beside James, the child in her arms suckling contentedly. From the kitchen beyond came a shrill cry from their middle child, three-year-old Charles. The Weygalls' eleven-year-old girl was playing with him, but Charles was not the easiest child to amuse.

"Runners they are and Runners I should like them to be called, though they're still known as Mr. Fielding's men," said Winfrith. "But men or Runners, today we have two less than we did seven years ago."

"And fewer highway robberies and footpads," James remarked.

"That is the bitter irony of what is happening," Winfrith said tensely. "Mr. John—*Sir* John!—works miracles with the six men he has. Imagine, six men to keep the peace of the whole of London at a cost of less than four hundred pounds a year! And because the incidence of crime is kept low, the government insists that the system is a great success."

"And so it is," a man said in a deep voice from outside the door.

"Ben!" exclaimed Mary. "I did not know that you were back."

"Truth to tell I hardly knew myself." Benedict Sly laughed. He peered at the child and patted Mary's shoulder affectionately. "So there is young Dorothy. Bless my soul, how time flies. It seems only a few days since it was Master James you were nursing and—let me see—it must be all of five years."

The past five years had been eventful and dangerous ones for Britain, with savage defeats abroad.

Of the three men, Benedict Sly had aged the least in appearance, despite a bushier black beard, which now gave him a fearsome appearance. He had put on no weight, and despite a long coach journey, his eyes were alert and his expression was bright. He had been to the Americas to see at first hand what had happened there since the French had been defeated in Canada and the northern colonies. His friends had known that he would soon be back but had not realised it would be so quickly.

David Winfrith had aged in appearance not five but nearer fifteen years. His face was deeply lined and his hair, once fair, was now almost white. Anxiety and anger, the loss of two of his three children in a smallpox epidemic, and the effect of this on his wife, whom the shock had turned simple-minded, had contributed much toward this aging. The rank air of the Bow Street courtroom, long hours of work on meager pay, insufficient food, and recurrent attacks of jail fever caught from prisoners had been responsible for the rest. Although his suit was shabby and his plain waistcoat and cravat were badly spotted, the piercing blue-gray eyes were unchanged. But there was a sharp edge to his voice as well as to his temper.

James Marshall was little changed. At thirty-two he was fuller at the jaw and middle, but still lean and upright. Years had made his chiseled face more, not less, handsome. He had not known a moment's regret at marrying Mary and indeed had little cause for sadness except for David's ill fortune. He had tried, and so had Mary, to help with money, but David's spirit of independence had grown fiercer along with age and the difficulties of his condition.

"If I take charity from a friend," he would say, "I lose a friend."

It was useless to argue with him.

The bitterness he had shown a few minutes earlier faded in pleasure and excitement at seeing Benedict Sly, who was taking off his coat in the warm room. Mary took the children into the kitchen, leaving the men on their own.

" 'Tis an excuse for wine," James declared; he kept wine for his friends but was himself adamantly teetotal. He poured the amber-coloured liquid into deep goblets and his two visitors were drinking when Mary came in with a platterful of biscuits and rock cakes. She had really brought these for David, James reflected, watching Winfrith hold back until Benedict had taken one.

Benedict finished his wine before speaking in a graver tone than he had used thus far. "I will do an editorial on America now I am back. But my first article will be to congratulate Sir John Fielding on his knighthood."

"And if you are still interested in reform I shall tell you what your second should be," said Winfrith.

"When I lose my enthusiasm for reform I shall be in my grave," Benedict replied. "What is the second editorial to be, David?"

"It should be a detailed story of the proposals which appear to have earned Sir John his knighthood but little money to help run the Bow Street men, still less set up an efficient peace-keeping force in London."

"He actually sent such proposals to the Duke of Newcastle?"

"Yes. And to Bute, who is Secretary of State today. Yet the truth of it is that they vary little from those Henry Fielding sent in the year

284

before he died, or for that matter those that John Furnival submitted more than thirty years ago."

Benedict said, "Have you a copy of these proposals?"

"I have, sir—held against your return."

"I will use it at the earliest opportunity," Benedict promised.

"Pause a moment," James demurred, drawing the gaze of both men. "Are they confidential, David?"

"Yes."

"Then if they appear in *The Daily Clarion* will it not be obvious that you supplied them to the newspaper? Would not Sir John feel that he had been betrayed?"

"I know not, nor do I care." Winfrith glared at James, fire smouldering in his eyes. "The time has come when some greater effort must be made to secure public support. If I sacrifice my livelihood trying to ensure that, is it any great matter?"

"You are a very great matter to us," James replied soothingly.

"Ben, will you publish or will you not?" demanded Winfrith.

"David, I will publish if I believe it good," Benedict Sly promised.

"Then I will go to court and get the copy now," Winfrith declared. He abruptly strode out of the room, his movements jerky and ill-controlled.

Meeting him in the passage, Mary spoke to him but he scarcely replied, and as his footsteps sounded on the wooden stairs she came into the living room. She had brushed her hair and had changed into a full-skirted dress of peacock-blue taffeta. James caught his breath at sight of her, for this was one of the moments when she looked her loveliest.

"What troubles David?" she asked, looking accusingly at Benedict. "You did not anger him, did you?"

"If anyone angered him it was I, but without the slightest intent," James assured her, explaining what had happened. "I do believe that, whatever he says, if he were to leave Bow Street he would break his heart."

"And I declare that if he doesn't, that court will kill him," Mary replied soberly. "How Sir John can sit in such an odoriferous place day in and day out I shall never know. It should be pulled down and another built, or at worst closed for a week and fumigated."

"Have you such an intimate acquaintance with the court?" inquired Benedict.

"I will have no impudence from you, sir! On occasions I have to go in. Should I allow some innocent child to be sent to Newgate for want of a witness to her character? And if I did not, then the stink of James's clothes when he spends a day there would tell me all I need to know."

James, smiling, said, "I am made to change all my clothes when I come from court."

"It would be a savage hurt for David should he leave the court and have nothing more to do with his life's work, but I believe he could do admirable service for *The Daily Clarion* as well as for Bow Street men if he would join our staff," Benedict said. "For *The Daily Clarion* is growing," he added, unable to keep the pride out of his voice. "During the six months I have been away our daily circulation has risen by nearly a thousand, so that it is now over three thousand copies a day."

"Remarkable!" James exclaimed. "Why, that must be more than either *The Daily Courant* or *The Public Advertiser*—more even than *The London Advertiser*."

"It is not far short of the total sale of them all put together," gloated Benedict. "And we anticipate higher sales yet. We are to move to larger premises in Fleet Street itself, James." He took a few moments to indulge his evident satisfaction, then went on in a more somber tone. "But nothing could bribe David away. He must be dismissed or else leave of his own accord before he would even consider taking work with *The Daily Clarion*."

"Even then he would regard it as charity," Mary said.

"Couldn't you influence him, Mary?" asked Benedict.

"Most certainly I could try," Mary replied.

David Winfrith's health and general condition had worried James for some time, for David had few comforts, if any, returning home after his burdensome day's work to a wife who was no help to him. Instead of having a meal prepared, she might well be sitting in a corner staring blankly at a cold fireplace.

"I have some coffee already in the making," Mary said, reading his thoughts, "and I have pasties and tarts heating."

She stood up and the others needed no telling that she had heard David returning on the stairs; he would be more likely to eat well before he left if the others also ate. As he drew closer to the rooms he was taken by a lengthy fit of coughing.

"We *must* get him away from Bow Street," Benedict Sly remarked quietly.

"Did you ever try to separate a mother from her babe?" asked James resignedly.

When David came in he was obviously weak from the coughing bout, and for a while he was content to sit in a large hide-covered armchair while Benedict read aloud through the "simple and yet so exceptional a plan" presented by John Fielding to the government.

There was utter silence when at last Benedict stopped, his voice hoarse. Without speaking, James poured him some beer in a pewter tankard.

Unexpectedly it was Mary who broke the silence, saying, "This must prove to be the best story you have ever written or *The Daily Clarion* has ever published, Ben."

"I shall earnestly try to make it fit for the best set of proposals ever made for the safety of London." Benedict drank, put down his tankard, and looked hard into David's eyes. "Unless David would be prepared to write it for me."

"I, man?" David gasped. "Where do you think I would find the time?"

"I only know that no one could present this better."

For a few moments all four were very still, until slowly a glow lit up David's face, encompassing every feature. But, as slowly as it had come, the glow faded.

"It is not possible," he declared. "There is no time. And Sir John would recognise my style on the instant. I do not wish for an open breach with him. He may suspect that I released this to you, but he would be sure if I were to write it. In any case, you undervalue your own ability, Ben. You are the journalist, not I!" As if to ease any awkwardness he asked, "Is there more coffee, Mary?"

Mary handed him another cup at once, hot from the hob, and talk became more general.

When at last David and Benedict rose to leave it was nearly ten o'clock, an hour when James and Mary were usually abed, for both would be up before five o'clock, Mary to make a good start with her household work before preparing breakfast, James to go through correspondence and other matters he would have attended to tonight but for their guests. Neither he nor Mary had as much help as they needed, but this was not because of the expense, for in his ten years in London he had greatly prospered, but because each enjoyed working, although Mary now had kitchen maids as well as help with the children during the evenings.

287

For increasingly long periods during the day she would be out, working for this charity or that, and she spent three mornings a week organising charity appeals at the lying-in hospital, where constantly increasing numbers of working-class mothers were delivered with no charge. Although this and other hospitals had been built by great philanthropists and had substantial foundations, the poor crowded so thickly into the wards that the costs were far higher than anyone had dreamed.

When Mary saw the silent, dirty crowds waiting for admission, she wondered how they lived. At least two in ten of London's people were so poor that they were likely to die at the onset of any illness, having little resistance to disease. At least a hundred thousand did not know what a satisfying meal was like. Was there any wonder, Mary often asked herself, that crimes seemed to multiply as fast as the mould in the rotting piles of vegetables, fruit and manure, the open sewers and cesspits?

Each man in his own way rebelled against these things. But whereas both Benedict and David discussed their feelings freely, James schooled himself not to show his emotions to others, controlling them so well that even Mary was sometimes taken by surprise when he exploded with anger over some injustice. She remembered a few weeks back when he had returned from Bow Street after giving evidence as to the character of a youth accused of robbery which he was sure the lad had not committed.

She could still picture the scene as he had described it, at great length and in passionate words. The youth of seventeen in the dock; Charley Green, son of one of the porters at Covent Garden market. He had gone to The Three Turks, an alehouse in a narrow street off the Strand, to have a draught of ale at the end of his day's work. A thief-taker had slipped a sleeping potion into his tankard, then murdered a Mr. Hepburn for his gold, placing two gold pieces on Charley's person, to be found there when the lad awoke. Charley, who had no recollection of what had happened, protested his innocence in vain. And thus the thief-taker had both the gold he had stolen *and* his reward for apprehending Hepburn's supposed assailant.

"God damn their misbegotten stinking souls!" James had railed. "When are the politicians going to realise that until a peace-keeper is paid enough to make sure he isn't open to corruption we shall have dozens—hundreds—of innocent lads like Charley Green convicted of murder and theft?"

He had tossed and turned in bed all that night and had for several days been moody and depressed, trying desperately to find a way of saving Charley Green. The magistrate had committed the boy for trial at the Sessions at the Old Bailey, and there was just a chance that some defense evidence would be forthcoming, but none had come up so far. All Green said was that he could remember going into the alehouse where he repaired every Friday and Saturday night to spend the tips he had received on his day's portering.

He had also remembered seeing a young girl sleeping at the door of the alehouse, Jane Wiseman, and James had searched for and found her, but she could not recall where she had been on the night of Hepburn's murder. Most nights she went onto the streets and had a man or two, then went and spent the sixpence they gave her on food and drink.

She was thirteen.

She had run away from a Lincolnshire farm to come to the golden streets of London Town.

On the day when Charley Green was hanged at Tyburn, with seven others condemned for theft, one for stealing bread and another for taking coal from a barge on the Thames when the river had been frozen over, James Marshall had been among the crowd.

He often mingled with the onlookers on hanging days, as Mary knew well.

At first she had been worried as well as puzzled by the macabre pilgrimage, believing that it brought back vivid memories of the day when as a boy he had watched Frederick Jackson hang. It was almost as if he went to gloat over the man struck down by vengeance, but that was completely foreign to everything else she knew about him. She had never ventured to ask him why, for on those occasions he was strange and different.

The hanging of Charley Green made a deep mark on him and she knew that he regarded it as a personal failure. Since then he had been more often at Bow Street and had worked with unflagging energy for any accused about whose guilt there seemed the faintest doubt, driving himself sometimes to a point of exhaustion in the effort to discover one of the suspected conspirators who had committed perjury. Once such perjury was proved, the magistrate would dismiss the charge, and twice in the past month he had saved the life of accused persons, one a boy of sixteen.

One day, Mary was sure, James would talk freely to her.

Meanwhile, she went about her own work and left word where she would be so as to be at hand whenever he needed her. They had been continent for so long now that occasionally it crossed her mind that he might have a mistress, perhaps even a serious love affair, but nothing in his manner ever suggested illicit happiness. He appeared bowed down by burdens within himself.

"Mary, I shall accompany Benedict to his rooms," James said on the night when David Winfrith had burst out with such outraged feeling. "I may walk back alone, but be sure I shall use only well-lighted thoroughfares and do not be troubled if I am late. You go to bed, wife."

She smiled at him, outwardly untroubled.

"Indeed I will, Mr. Marshall!"

"Such obedience!" declared Benedict. "You must tell me how you contrive to keep your wife in such subjection."

"The obedience is born in the wife, sir, not imposed by the husband," retorted Mary, and when she saw James laugh she felt a lift of her heart; obviously Benedict's return had cheered him up.

She watched them from the window walking along the Strand, thrust her anxiety for his return aside and went into the kitchen.

The scullery maid was upstairs in her tiny room, otherwise this apartment was empty but for Mary and the children. James had recently taken a second adjoining shop, together with three floors above it, for the activities of "Mr. Londoner," and doors had been knocked in the walls to make more living and sleeping accommodation. Moreover, there was a narrow staircase at the back leading to a yard and a rabbit warren of alleys beyond, so that the children could come and go by day without disturbing James.

She heard a movement on the back stairs.

Her heart jumped and she stared across the kitchen at the door, left ajar the better to hear the children should they cry. It would be a boy coming or going from the maid, she reassured herself. The girl was well on the way to losing a respectable job and becoming a prostitute. Nothing Mary had said, so far, had affected her.

The noise was repeated, just outside the door.

Thanks to John Fielding's persistence and thoroughness one or two reliable constables were always in the Strand, where their very presence could avert trouble.

"Who is there?" she called, her heart thumping.

No one spoke but the door opened wider and David Winfrith came slowly forward. There was a wild expression in his eyes as he slammed the door so hard that Mary feared the children might wake. But no cry was made and no alarm was raised.

"David," she said. "What is it? Is everything all right at home?"

He said, breathing very hard, "I can't go home."

"But David—"

"I tell you I can't go home," he went on fiercely. "I can't go back to a wife who is a living death, to a house which is a den of accumulated filth and to a fire that is always cold and dead, no fit place for me or the child. Mary, I tell you I can't go back!"

She did not speak, realising that no attempted persuasion would help him, but she went forward, holding her arms out. As he came to her, stumbling, she felt his thin body quivering and felt him racked with sobs. For a while they stood without moving, she not knowing what best to do, until she began to stroke the back of his head and his short hair. She behaved as she might with a troubled child, soothing him in his distress and seeking a way to help. He felt so thin and light against her that she longed to lift and put him to bed, knowing how much he needed sleep. But if she did so, his dignity would be sorely hurt, and this was not a time when he should be hurt more.

Slowly, slowly, she became aware of him as a man.

He was pressed tight against her bosom and she had not realised that as he had wept or as she had moved to ease her position, the top button of her dress had come undone; and she had changed hurriedly tonight and had not put on a petticoat. Suddenly, he began to kiss her between the breasts, as if he were in overwhelming need of her. He found words which at first she did not hear but which gradually took on clarity and substance.

"It is a year since Sarah and I have lain together, a year of torment! . . . Mary, Mary, you don't know, you cannot know, how I have come to love you. . . . Mary, darling Mary, don't turn me away, I beg you. Don't turn me away, I need you so much."

There was not only desire but there was unsuspected strength in him.

And there was weakness in her, and more loneliness in the nights than she had dreamed there could be, sleeping by James.

There was the strength of passion in him.

"Mary, Mary!"

291

His lips sought hers and crushed them, and suddenly they lay upon the couch, and she felt herself responding to him, unaware of shame or anything but a fierce surge of passion and, on an instant, utter stillness.

He lay upon her, and he was crying.

She did not remember what they had said or how long it had taken them to dress, or even how he had looked when he had reached the door and turned momentarily toward her.

But when she was in the great four-poster bed she was still aware of him, and she was saying over and over to herself in a shocked way: "Why should I want him? Why should I want him?"

And she, too, began to cry.

CHAPTER 22

The Decision

"JAMEY," BENEDICT SLY said as they reached the narrowing of the Strand, "you are very quiet tonight. In fact I would say that the only one of us who was truly himself was Mary."

"Mary is always herself," James replied.

They stood on a corner waiting for a lull in the succession of carriages and sedan chairs coming from the two great theaters. The Strand was alive with people, the alehouses were lit with more flares than one could count, and the clatter of iron wheels, iron-tipped boots and horseshoes was turned into a cacophony by a group of drunken sailors coming from Charlie Wylie's new coffee house.

A Bow Street man, carrying a pistol, rode fast along one side, recognized by only a few. His maneuvers caused a temporary halt in the flow and James and Benedict were carried over the road with a flood of people who had been waiting to cross.

"If no way is found to control the traffic, it will become as great a problem as crime," Benedict observed. "This is five or six times greater in volume than it is in New York." They reached the comparative quiet of Fleet Street and he changed the subject smoothly. "What is on your mind, Jamey?"

"David," James replied. "Also Sir John Fielding and Bow Street. And these accursed politicians. One day—"

"If it isn't Benedict Sly back from the colonies!" a man called from the doorway of a coffee house, dimly lit both inside and out. James knew him as the editor of a new daily newspaper which had appeared in London during the past months.

"Ben, you're back at the right time," the man called out again. "You must have a nose for news; you're a sly one!"

The pun on Benedict's name brought forth a gust of laughter and now half-a-dozen journalists spilled out of the coffee houses at this end of Fleet Street. It was late enough for most of the morning newspapers to have been "put to bed" and so the men might have been expected to be inside; many of them spent the night talking and dozing, and breakfasted here before going to their rooms. Clearly there was some cause for this exodus.

"What is this news you're talking about?" demanded Benedict. "Have we won a war or has the new king died?"

"You don't *know*?"

The man who had accosted Benedict seemed astonished; so did the others who had gathered in a circle.

"I hope I shall soon," Benedict replied. "Could the Cabinet have fallen?"

"That's nearer the subject," a man declared. "The Member for Minshall was killed in a collision between his carriage and a post office coach today. Died of a broken neck as clean as if the Shadows had attacked him." The Shadows was a name given to a newly organised gang of criminals. "You know what that means, Ben. Old Jerry Topham was for Pitt right or wrong, and no one could manipulate the House so well as he. Now Bute will have an even greater edge over Pitt, no matter who's returned for Minshall at the by-election."

"If the Tories can keep Pitt down, the King will have more influence, and he's already seeking too much," another put in. "We shall have peace abroad but at heavy cost."

Politically, this was news of rare importance, James knew.

James, little concerned with foreign policy, his sense of national pride battered by conditions in London and the obstinacy of both government and opposition to a national peacemaking force, was concerned only with the impact of these tidings on this particular situation. Minshall was one of the new boroughs close to London

294

which had a large population of houseowners. It could not be bought and sold or dealt with as patronage, like many of the rotten boroughs. Voting had always been close between Whig and Tory, and there was no way of telling who would win a by-election. His one hope was that the new member might be a champion of Sir John Fielding.

Bidding Benedict good night, he slipped quietly away. He did not quite know why he delayed returning to Mary; it was as if he were drawn by some unknown compulsion. First he walked at good speed to Ludgate, for a view of St. Paul's. Then he turned left, into the shadowy lanes, the old haunts, which, despite new laws demanding more lights for all hours of darkness, had little light save a crack here and there from a window or doorway. The darkness, the distant noises, the furtive movements of men, did not worry him. Here he was at home. Soon he passed the archway leading to Ebenezer Morgan's warehouses; there was the spot where he, James, had been shot down by the only one of the Twelves to escape; the narrow lane along which he had walked on the night of his meeting with Mary; the corner where he had flung Tom Harris against the wall.

Tom had since been a victim of the swift upsurges of cholera. And not a single man who had served John Furnival at Bow Street in a peace-keeping capacity was still there. Most were dead.

Just as the Twelves had at one time struck fear into the hearts of many, so now a new robber gang, the Shadows, made London an unsafe place to walk. Gradually a picture of the gang had evolved from tidbits of information from John Fielding's men and from turn-pike keepers as well as from victims of their attacks. The highwaymen struck swiftly and savagely out of the darkness. They used silent weapons: knives to drive between the ribs or into the bowels; cord of hemp with which to strangle; staves weighted heavily enough to crack a skull at a single blow. Increasingly reports came of attacks by footpads who wore cloth over their boots to silence all sound, stepped swiftly behind their victim, flung an arm about his neck, choking him to silence, then yanked his head back with such force that the neck snapped.

Hepburn, the man whom Charley Green was supposed to have killed, had died in such a way. The prosecution had made much of this because Charley's arms had developed such powerful muscles as he shifted boxes and sacks of vegetables and fruit at the market.

James wondered tensely about the government's reception of Sir John Fielding's plan, all-encompassing, yet at the same time within reach. The authorities must stop the dreadful folly of widening the crimes for which the penalty was death. It was now one hundred and sixty! And for such crimes! Stealing more than one loaf of bread, entering an enclosed garden, cutting down a bush or a tree!

Surely Bute *must* listen to the magistrate; all London must listen! He, James, must make the whole of the metropolis take heed; he must find a way to compel the government to act.

But how?

Out of the blue the answer came, glaringly obvious to James now that he could see it. As suddenly and as urgently he wanted to see Mary. His strides lengthened and quickened as he swung into the Strand from St. Martin's Lane. The crowd had thinned and many of the coffee houses were now closed, but he had no thought for anyone or anything but his wife.

He unlocked the side door of the premises and ran up the heavy oak staircase, calling, "Mary, Mary!"

Mary, lying awake with her strange, tormenting thoughts, said to herself: "I cannot talk to him tonight. I must pretend to be asleep."

James heard one of the children cough as he reached the landing and lowered his voice as he called again: "Mary, my love. Mary!"

There was no whispered response when he reached their bedroom, the light from flares flickering about the room, reflecting from the mirror and the high gloss of the pitcher and bowl on the marble surface of the washstand. He tiptoed in, more eager than he had been for a long, long time.

"Mary!" he whispered urgently.

She lay with her back toward him, facing the window. He could see enough of her face to feel sure that she was asleep. When he stopped by the side of the bed, he could see the regular movement of her bosom and her lips. He had rarely seen her more exhausted.

"Mary," he said brokenly, "never have I needed you so."

I cannot talk to him, she thought desperately. *I cannot because of what could follow. I cannot lie with him tonight.*

She heard the hopelessness in his voice when he said again, "Mary."

Silence followed, and was broken only by rustling movements as he turned away and began slowly to undress. He had come burning with the desire to talk, to tell her what had happened, and yet, if she was so exhausted, how could he wake her?

He did not try again.

He moved to the bed and began to shift the bedclothes carefully, so as not to disturb her, when suddenly one of the children screamed, and on the instant, Mary opened her eyes and stared beyond her husband to the door. James turned and hurried out as the child screamed again, and in a moment he saw Charles sitting up in bed, eyes wide with terror.

By the time he reached the bed, Mary was at the other side, hands on the child, saying in a soothing voice, "It is all right, Charles beloved. You were having a bad dream. It is all right . . . it is all right."

The child clutched his mother, but after a few minutes his eyes closed and Mary allowed him to sink gently back onto the pillows. She appeared to concentrate only on the child but she was thinking with unexpected calmness: It is the voice of God making me listen to Jamey.

Soon she smiled up at James, saying, "He will sleep now, I think. He dreams so much."

They moved toward the foot of the little bed, and James put his arm about her and she rested her head on his shoulder. In that position they moved to the other bed and the cot and Mary adjusted the bedclothes of both Jimmy and Dorothy before turning back to the door. As they got into bed, as she felt her husband's body against hers and the pressure of his arm, she gave a little shudder.

"Are you so cold?" James asked.

"I think I was a little frightened."

"You were waked out of a dead sleep. No wonder you were frightened!" He kissed her cheeks and held her more closely, going on in a voice of great contrition. "Mary, I know I have been difficult to live with during these past few weeks. I am sorry."

"Your trouble is your conscience," she said with forced lightness. "I suspect that you have tried yourself more than you have me."

"Bless you!"

He kissed her again, but as yet there was no passion and she sensed his deep preoccupation and what he was going to say. She even thought that his preoccupation might be so great that he would talk until he fell asleep.

"Mary," he said, "I have decided what I must do."

"And what must that be?" she asked. But before he could answer she went on: "If Sir John Fielding, with his position and his authority, his reputation and his friends, cannot succeed, dare you have even hope?"

"More," he said. "I am sure I can do it."

She looked into his face, and as she absorbed the warmth of his body, she felt the memory of what had happened with David receding. This night, if she could do it, she must be utterly his.

She made herself ask, without scoffing, "And how will you go about it, Jamey?"

"I shall stand for Parliament as the Member for Minshall." James explained what he had heard from the newspapermen, and went on with great confidence. "I am known well enough by the electors of Minshall to win the seat there, and I shall be the voice in Parliament and the country for all those things which must be done. I believe that once a voice *is* raised in Parliament, then both Members and the people will listen. And I have sufficient money, Mary, you need not fear. The business will flourish more when it is owned by Mr. Londoner, Member for Minshall!" There was fierce excitement in him. "Tell me! Is that not the answer? Don't you agree?"

She thought: Those he fights will marshal all their resources against him. What chance has he to win? But there was no mistaking the eagerness within him, and this was not the moment to pour cold water on his dreams.

"Jamey," she said, "it is the only answer."

"What a wife you are!" he cried. "I tell you I have not felt so much a human being for weeks. The hanging of young Green has haunted me, but this way I can avenge him and countless others. This way all the reforms so desperately needed can be brought into being.

"When they pulled down so many of the houses in Long Acre and in Cheapside most of the people moved to Minshall, and I myself protected their rights, made sure those who owned their property were properly recompensed. It is like the finger of God pointing the way."

The finger of God, she thought, in the death of a man on London's streets.

The voice of God in the scream of a child.

How long, *how long*, were human beings going to blame God for the way they lived and the things they did?

"Mary," James said in a husky voice, "I feel as if I have been away from you for a long time and am now back."

"I know how you feel," she answered him.

She felt his hands upon her, the desire in him, and she closed her eyes and tried to ease the tightness of her body.

"Mary," he said, "I love you. How I love you. There can never be anyone for me but you." He was kissing her. "Mary, I love you . . ."

When, not long afterward, he was asleep by her side and she lay between sleeping and waking, she was aware of shame and she was aware of David and of what had happened earlier that night. She recalled to her amazement that for several moments with James she had actually forgotten David. I am no better than a whore, she thought. And, more sharply, she wondered what would happen if James found out what had taken place between her and David. She answered herself: He can never find out. Only David knows, and he will feel as great a shame as I.

She did not expect to sleep, but when she awoke the following day it was almost as if that passionate interlude with David had been a dream, and she was soon plunged into a whirl of morning activity which prevented her from dwelling on what had happened.

James, still excited at the prospect he had conjured up for himself, spent an hour with Nicholas in the shop, where every imaginable kind of oddment, old and new, was now for sale; the one condition that it had been made or long existed in London.

James did not know when Benedict Sly would be at his office but thought it likely that he had been up late the night before and might not arrive until the afternoon. Headlines announcing the death of the member from Minshall were everywhere, but whilst several newspapers carried long stories about the accident they said little about its political consequences. James glanced at these, then opened *The Daily Clarion*.

Benedict had not ignored the political significance of the M.P.'s death, which he described in detail in his leading article, and which James read with the closest attention. He became aware of Nicholas Sly at the doorway; so rapt had he been that he had no idea how long the younger man had been present. Nicholas, now in his early twenties, was sharp-featured, with expressive brown eyes and full, well-shaped lips; it would be hard to imagine anyone less like Benedict. This morning he looked troubled, which was unusual.

"Are there any problems with which I can help?" asked James.

"No, sir, but most certainly there are problems," Nicholas replied heavily. "Have you seen the risks which Benedict has taken in his article, speaking out against the King? I fear serious repercussions."

"I doubt whether the King or anyone would force such an issue yet," James said. "But I am going to see Benedict forthwith and I will find out what he and other newspapermen think."

He fought back the temptation to tell Nicholas what was in his own mind, and went to Wine Court. The dining space there had been turned into a coffee house used almost exclusively by journalists, and James saw that Benedict was present and was surrounded in the smoke-filled room by at least a dozen other men of the press. James could feel the undercurrent of tension.

One man, the editor of *The Record*, which usually opposed everything *The Daily Clarion* stood for, was saying in a clipped, angry voice, "I'll support you to the hilt, Benedict. You must refuse to go."

"It is an outrageous command," another growled.

Benedict, outwardly the calmest of those present, looked toward the door and espied James. Immediately he smiled and waved, and the crowd about him made a passage.

"Come in, Jamey, come in!" Benedict cried. "You are in time to see a unique moment, aye, a historic moment in history." Despite his smile and the hint of amusement in his deep voice James knew that he was serious. "The first moment on record when every London newspaper is in full agreement!" There was a rumble of "Aye, aye" and "That we are!" followed with a thumping of fists on the table and feet on the floor. "It has pleased His Grace the Marquis of Bute to send a summons for me to appear before him and the Privy Council to answer a charge of sedition. To quote: 'Your comments are false, scandalous and seditious libel,' and I am accordingly summoned to show cause why I should not be tried for treason and why *The Daily Clarion* should not be banned from publication."

"My God, they lost no time!" one of the newcomers called out.

"You will refuse to go," said another.

"I *have* to go," replied Benedict. "And I have it on good authority that they plan to commit me to jail on a warrant sworn by the Secretary of State. Are you not glad you are not a journalist, Jamey?"

"I feel almost ashamed to be an Englishman," James replied in stunned, cold anger.

"What will you do if they take you under arrest?" called a man standing on a bench.

"Be guided by my lawyer," Benedict replied. "What would you have me do, Jamey?"

James said in a quiet voice which sounded everywhere because of the silence which fell, "I need a little time to think."

"Don't take too much," urged the editor of *The Record*. "It will not be long before they send mounted constables from Westminster. Now that they have started this iniquitous persecution they can only serve their purpose by acting fast."

"We shall have some warning," a bearded man pointed out. "We have paid street sweepers at various vantage points on the several routes along which a troop of mounted men would come, and these will signal to each other until one on the roof of the nearest building to us in Fleet will wave a notice of close approach."

"You sound almost as if you had been forewarned," said James.

"Only a dullard would have failed to see the imminence of an attempt to muzzle the press completely," the editor of *The Record* declared. He was short and stocky, boasting an iron-gray beard and a shock of iron-gray hair. "Parliament is once again becoming a tool of the King and the aristocracy, with the great bankers supporting them." His voice trembled with rage and he shook a clenched fist as he went on. "If there is no voice of the people and Westminster takes no heed, then there must be a voice in Fleet Street!"

His outburst drew another, louder roar of applause, so full of emotion that James believed this must surely be a unique moment. Slowly silence fell, and James spoke.

"There must be a voice of the people in the House."

"Jamey," Benedict said, "there are many voices but they are muted."

"There must be another in the new Member for Minshall," James declared. The smile was wiped off Benedict's face, and every eye was suddenly turned toward James. "I propose to submit myself to the electors as worthy of representing them. I hope you will all be able to support me." While gasps of surprise were still echoing he continued in a voice of absolute conviction: "You should allow them to take you, Ben, and then have every man here ride after you, demanding your release. I will go to John Fielding, and unless the Secretary of State accuses you of treason immediately, which I doubt, Fielding will soon have you out. This attempt to intimidate the press will fail, but its failure—and its purpose—will be ten times more apparent to the public if you are thrown into jail and then brought out."

"My God, Ben, you have a clever lawyer!" a man called.

"That will remain to be seen," James replied. "There should quickly be a special edition of every newspaper, if only a single sheet, condemning the move and demanding absolute freedom for free comment. Copies should be distributed everywhere in London and nearby. And a slogan is needed, a rallying cry—"

A man called: "Free Sly, free the Press and free the People!"

"Aye! Aye!" came in a great roar which shook the doors and the shutters on the windows and the mugs and platters on the tables. There was such a din that at first no one saw the door open and the small boy come in, with a mat of coarse hair, wearing a filthy, stinking, torn shirt and ragged knickerbockers, barelegged and with feet so dirt-stained they looked more like those of an Indian. But his eyes were bright and bespoke a quick intelligence.

He was breathless from running when he cried, "I'm the captain of the sweepers. I've to see Mr. Garnett!"

"I am Sam Garnett!" called the bearded man who had promised some warning. "Are the horsemen coming?"

"Indeed yes, sir—two parties of them, one by the Strand and one by Long Acre. 'Tis true, sir, my boys have warned me. There are six in each party, sir!"

Suddenly a man let out a cry much greater than before.

"The riders are coming!" he roared. "They're coming fast!"

"To your horses," James cried as Garnett tossed a small bag of coins to the self-styled captain of the crossing sweepers. As the boy pulled the string of the bag and gazed inside, dazzled at such munificence, the men began to stream out, and only Benedict, James and Jabez Peterson, the editor of *The Record*, remained. Hoofbeats clattered in the yard a few minutes afterward and footsteps sounded noisily on the cobbles until the door was thrust open and two men, both carrying pistols, strode in.

"I come for Mr. Benedict Sly," the first man stated, waving a document which crackled like parchment. "I have a warrant for his arrest signed by the Secretary of State."

"The Secretary of State has no such authority," James declared. "A warrant must be signed by a justice of the peace."

"The warrant is good enough for me," the man replied harshly. "Are you going to defy me?"

"I am going to fight you, but not with a sword," replied James, and looked at Benedict, who had not yet said a word. "You had better go, Ben."

"I would like first to go to my office and explain—" began Benedict.

"You are to come with me immediately. Others may explain for you."

James went into the yard, Peterson stumping behind, and watched as Benedict mounted a saddled horse brought for him. But barely had he and his military escort started on their way than a stream of carriages and horsemen appeared from the Ludgate Hill direction, others joining them from narrow streets. Hampering the soldiers in every way they could, the men of Fleet Street went not only ahead but on both sides, while behind there were at least another fifty; and as the strange assembly reached the church of St. Clement, the protesters began to chant:

"Free Sly . . . Free the Press . . . Free the People!"

Crowds on the sidewalk heard the words and began to cheer. Boy crossing sweepers joined in, high-pitched voices sounding above the rest. The cheering was carried swiftly along the Strand, people rushing from shops and houses to see what was going on, and all taking up the cry:

"Free Sly . . . Free the Press . . . Free the People!"

"Mr. Benedict Sly," said the Solicitor General, "since you refuse to withdraw these remarks I feel that I have no alternative but to have you committed to the prison of Newgate, where you will remain until your trial."

"But if you will disavow your scurrilous remarks this remand will be withdrawn," the Marquis of Bute declared.

"Not one word," replied Benedict Sly. "The press and the people have a right to say what they think, even about the King, sir."

"With the greatest regret I must ask the justice present—Mr. Lawler, please—to commit you on a charge of inciting to riot. A graver charge may follow."

303

"The one way to ensure a riot is to accuse me of treason on these ludicrous grounds," Benedict Sly said. "It is not I but you who have to think again, gentlemen."

As Benedict Sly was brought to the gates of the prison, two bodies still swung on the gallows from the morning's hanging. Children playing at the gallows foot ran to and fro beneath the corpses, leaping high to try to touch the limp feet. The jailer, seeing Benedict's clothes and cleanliness, greeted him with respect.

"For a few paltry pounds a week, sir, you may have your own room and the services of a warder, and if you wish it, a nightly visit from a respectable woman whose cleanliness I can promise you. She will ask nothing but your favour, sir."

"I will go where the felons without money go," Benedict said.

The jailer's face dropped.

"But that's no place for the likes of you, sir!"

"Nevertheless, that is where I will go," Benedict told him.

CHAPTER 23

"Free Sly... Free the Press...
Free the People"

"OUTRAGEOUS," MUTTERED Sir John Fielding when James had finished making his report. "This magistrate Lawler will do anything for money. I know of no precedent or justification at all. Do you, David?"

Fielding sat on a chair in the well of the court, James standing on one side of him, David Winfrith on the other. Apart from the three men, the court was empty. David looked as if he had not slept all night. He had talked little, and that brusquely, when James had first arrived.

"No, Sir John, none whatsoever."

"Then I shall sign the writ for Sly's release," Fielding declared, "and shall send two constables to the prison to serve it. If there is any dispute with the keeper of the prison, I will consider what steps to take." He turned to James as David started to prepare the writ. "What is this I hear about you contesting Minshall, Jamey? Is it true, boy?"

"How in heaven's name did you learn that so quickly?" gasped James.

"Oh, we have ears in many surprising places. Is it true?"

"Yes, Sir John."

"What little influence and experience I have will be in your support," promised Fielding, continuing before James could begin to utter thanks. "I will have the constables and their deputies in all the Minshall parishes examined, and where we can find an honest man we must set him to work. The parties can spend a fortune in bribery, and they can also terrify any who would support a candidate against their interests. One of the duties of a *real* peacemaking force, James, would be to supervise elections and make sure people can vote freely and without fear of any consequences. Ah, David! You are done, then? Good, good! I'll sign the writ. If there is any trouble, any trouble at all, I am to be told at once, whether the court is sitting or not."

"It is a wilful defiance," the Duke stormed. "I will not allow a blind man who is a magistrate by our favour to defy us. Is it not enough that he is always begging more money for his court? Did he not beg a knighthood and did I not give it to him? He shall not be heeded."

"I hope you will be gracious enough to consider other aspects of the situation," the Solicitor General murmured sleekly. "Sir John Fielding is highly regarded by many who give us their support and he's highly popular among the people."

"Damn the people!"

"It would be indiscreet to do so openly in the House," declared the Solicitor General. "I have been making inquiries. Had our action yesterday persuaded Sly to withdraw his remarks, little would have been said, but since he refused—Well, I confess I misjudged the response of many of our supporters."

"You really *mean* we must release the newspaperman Sly?"

"For the time being at least. Once that is done there will be less danger from the press of further vitriolic attacks on you or the King."

"We must find a way to keep these damned pests of Grub Street quiet," growled the Duke. "Find a way."

"I shall lose not a moment. And, meanwhile, I have your authority to order Benedict Sly to be freed?"

"Damn it, that's what you're forcing me to give you, isn't it? Yes, release him. And I hope he falls out of his carriage and breaks his neck!"

"We can hardly expect such good fortune twice in one week," murmured the Solicitor General.

"What? Good fortune? What—*oh*." The Duke began to laugh, the first sign of good humour since this interview had begun. "Topham, y'mean. Twice!"

He was roaring with laughter when the Solicitor General went out.

It was as if all London had erupted!

Masses of people packed the streets leading to Newgate, but unlike those gathered together in times of riot or on hanging days, these were well dressed and prosperous-looking. In thousands of hands a pamphlet fluttered, whilst pinned to every hat and jacket was the slogan printed at the foot of the pamphlet:

FREE SLY!   FREE THE PRESS!   FREE THE PEOPLE!

Never in London's history had there been such an uprising of the middle classes. Only on the fringes did the mob appear, some light-fingered, some joining in for the excitement, for the battle that looked inevitable.

From an open carriage hemmed in at Newgate, James Marshall, Nicholas Sly and Jabez Peterson watched with awed fascination. Outside the jail entrance they could see a ring of dragoons, sent hastily from both Tilt Yard and the Tower at the urgent request of justices in Westminster and the City.

"One act of violence and the whole crowd will riot," muttered James.

Tension was on the faces of all three men, when suddenly there came a cry from the direction of Holborn.

"Fielding! . . . Make way for John Fielding! . . . Make way for Sir John."

"God be praised they are not out of control," Peterson murmured.

Over the heads of the crowd they could just see the top of a sedan chair, two Bow Street officers in front and two behind. One of the leading officers, his stentorian voice worthy of a town crier, was roaring, "Make way for Sir John! Make way for the Blind Beak!"

As the cry was taken up, men pressed back to allow the chair to pass. Fielding was framed in the open doorway, the pale evening light showing the ruddiness of his face in a strange glow, the black ribbon over his eyes in sharp contrast. He wore his robes, chain of office, and big three-cornered hat with upswept brim. Every now and again he raised his right hand to acknowledge the roaring acclamation, the throng closing in behind his chair as it moved on.

At last he reached the clearing between the crowd and the dragoons, while the roar split the evening skies.

"Fielding, Fielding, Fielding!"

A youthful lieutenant came forward as the chair was placed on the forecourt and Fielding got out with surprising ease of movement despite his clumsy-looking body. He handed a rolled missive to the lieutenant, who unfurled it, read, saluted, then immediately turned on his heel and went toward the prison gates. Fielding moved, alone, toward the now empty gallows and walked up the wooden steps, as sure-footed and as nimble as if he were a man with full vision. Reaching the spot over which dying men so often dangled—men he himself had committed—he held up his hand for silence. For three or four minutes he tried in vain to make himself heard, and at last two of his Bow Street men went up to the platform, and David Winfrith joined them. Before they reached his side, however, the prison gates opened again and the lieutenant of dragoons appeared with Benedict Sly at his side.

At last quiet fell, while Benedict joined the chief magistrate and waited until the older man spoke in a voice pitched high enough to reach many standing out of his sight in the side streets.

"I came to ask you to disperse, since I hold the Solicitor General's authority to hear the charges against Benedict Sly in Bow Street, there having been some error when Mr. Sly was committed yesterday. I—"

He was forced to stop by the tumult, and it was several minutes before he could go on.

"I myself have examined the charge and will call on witnesses, and upon the evidence decide. . . ."

There was no difficulty in clearing a path for him and for Benedict Sly, no longer manacled, as they went to the waiting coach which would take them to Bow Street for the second hearing. Nor was there much doubt in James's mind, as he and Nicholas Sly and Jabez Peterson followed, that the Solicitor General's charge on which the committal had been made would be dismissed by Fielding.

At last, after the evidence and the witnesses were again brought forth, Fielding observed dryly, "I will admit that the incident has come near to inciting a riot, but I am satisfied that the cause was not the words written by the accused and published in a newspaper owned by him. I therefore dismiss the charge."

"And because the press of this great city kept the people informed of what was happening at Westminster," Benedict declared, "justice has been done. This is a great day for the newspapers, a day when they first spoke with one voice for freedom—"

But the crowd would not let him finish. The cheering went on and on, until it seemed that they would stay at the place of their triumph forever.

Suddenly James saw a party of twenty men or so holding a banner, two of whom carried a pole to which one end of the banner was secured. Painted in red on a pale cloth which looked like stiff linen was the now familiar slogan:

FREE SLY . . . FREE THE PRESS . . . FREE THE PEOPLE
IN THE NAME OF THE LORD

One of the pole carriers was a young and massive man whose appearance made James start, for at first he could have sworn that he was Johnny! Everything about the face and figure was uncannily like his half brother.

But this was Simon Rattray, officially the son of the minister of the church near Lincoln's Inn, but surely the natural son of John Furnival.

Benedict Sly, followed by James and Nicholas, climbed the stairs to James's rooms, long after dark, and dropped into a chair in the living room while Mary came hurrying from the kitchen. It had been two hours before the crowd had stopped calling on him to speak, two hours before first Fielding and then he had been able to get away.

Sly mopped his forehead and declared, "The rescue was a far greater ordeal than the arrest! Would you have believed such a rising, James?"

"I'd not given it a thought, but if I live to be a hundred I'll never know a greater day. Sir John was magnificent."

"Yes," Benedict agreed. "He was indeed. Why doesn't David come, I wonder? He would tell us how Sir John responded when the press had gone. I will wager—"

Mary hesitated, but none of the others had any reason to believe this was because she had heard that David was expected. But she recovered quickly, carried in coffee, and rejoiced with the men, masking her apprehension. Benedict did much of the talking, mostly about the horror of Newgate Prison, while James said enough to make it clear that conditions had not improved and that his own youthful experience still burned in him.

David did not arrive, that night or for many nights to come. It was as if he had dropped out of their lives.

CHAPTER 24

Traitor

AT THE coffee house in Wine Court next morning, James saw that *The Daily Clarion* and other newspapers all carried a straightforward if elated account of what had happened. Every newspaper but one, the Tory *St. James's Journal,* promised its help in electing Marshall. Until that morning James had not even begun to realise the impact he had made on either the newspapers or the public. For the first time Mary and others who had thought his candidacy hopeless began to believe that he might win.

The week following he received many letters of support from his mother, Henrietta, Timothy, Sir Mortimer Tench, Beth, and more friends than he realised he had.

A letter from Francis Furnival read:

My dear James,
I hasten to send you my best hopes for your success, in which William joins me. Indeed, I speak for all the senior members of the House of Furnival, the young, as always being a law unto themselves.

These past few years have been a most unsettling period in the House, and while it is always in the Furnival interest to maintain the highest possible volume of trade, it is increasingly evident that many social evils remain here at home, particularly in and near London. A strong voice drawing attention to these can only do good. No doubt you will campaign, among other things, for a peace-keeping force. I think if my brother John, your stepfather, were alive today he might find less rigid opposition. But opposition, nonetheless! I have a feeling that we may be moving into a new age. . . .

Another letter, from Johnny, was more disturbing:

Jamey, you are a fool. Don't do it.

The words, written in purple-coloured ink on a small sheet of parchmentlike paper, seemed to leap out and strike James. A sharper, more unexpected blow could not have been imagined. *Why?* he thought. *Why,* Johnny? He had seen very little of his half brother during the past few years, their meetings being mainly at family reunions at Great Furnival Square. Now and again Johnny had been to see his mother and his half sisters but he never stayed long. It was as if he were determined to cut himself as loose as possible from his mother's side of the family. He had grown into an extremely clever and shrewd young man and it was said that he always had a following of devoted admirers, and that he had conquered more feminine hearts than any man in London.

Moreover, the place held for him inside the business was very high. It was not simply that he was entitled to a high place by birth; his ability was beyond question, and many believed that in a few years he would be a powerful figure—perhaps one day the leading figure—in the great banking and merchant empire.

And there was no doubt that if ever he came to rule the House of Furnival, it would be with great—perhaps too much—strength.

None of these things was in James's mind at that moment, however. Two short sentences rang through his head.

"*Jamey, you are a fool. Don't do it.*"

James put the note aside and was thinking now of David Winfrith, of whom he had seen practically nothing for a month. David on the one side and Johnny on the other, both shunning him. It was the strangest and most painful experience. He felt guilty, blaming himself for failing to see what was responsible.

Slowly, he opened other letters, mostly of encouragement for the coming campaign, but none significant enough to draw his mind from gloomier reflections. The next envelope appeared to contain a stiff card, which fitted so tightly that he had difficulty in pulling it free.

As he did so he caught his breath for he looked down at an unmistakable caricature of himself hanging from a gallows. So vivid was the facial likeness that it was impossible to believe that whoever had drawn it did not know him well. He turned it over—and, unable to control himself, was taken by a fit of shivering. For on the back of the card was an identical picture of his face but here his body was cut into four as would be that of a man who had first been drawn, then hanged and quartered.

One word was printed in black across the foot of the card: TRAITOR.

"It could have been sent to frighten you, the work of some cartoonist with a twisted mind," suggested Benedict. "There is no doubt of strong opposition. What does surprise me is that the opposition should have remained so subdued. I would give this to David; he can show it to others at Bow Street who might recognise the work and be able to identify the artist."

It was on the tip of James's tongue to say that he had no desire to consult David; then he decided that this might be a good opportunity to break the barrier which had grown up between them. Rather than go to Bow Street he would invite David to dinner and discuss it with him afterward. When he suggested this to Mary he was surprised by her momentary reluctance, but she quickly infused warmth into her voice. The idea was stillborn, however; David sent a brief note that he was sorry but had no time as work at the court was getting heavier every day.

"If I did not believe it nonsense, I would say that David was deliberately avoiding me," James remarked to Mary. "Can you imagine any way in which I have upset him?" He hardly noticed that her "No" was very subdued as he went on: "This is the last straw. I shall go to see him and demand to know what it is all about."

"No!" Mary exclaimed. And then as if to explain her sudden vehemence, she went on hurriedly: "I believe he is very sick, Jamey. I do not think it will be good if you try to make him talk against his will."

"If he is as sick as that I should try to help him," replied James,

313

placing his hands gently on her shoulders and looking into her eyes.

For a moment she turned her head away as if frightened, but recovered her direct gaze almost at once as he went on.

"Do you know anything about David that you haven't told me? Have I been so busy with my own affairs that I have let you carry my anxiety, my burden?"

She gasped. "Oh, no. No, no, *no!*" Suddenly she was in tears and there was nothing he could do to calm her, but after a while she quieted and dried her eyes, forced a laugh and said huskily, "No, James, you are the last man in the world to neglect anything. I—I am tired and I think"—she caught her breath—"I think I am with child again."

"With child?" His eyes brightened. "Is that a cause for tears? Are we so poor or you so ailing that we cannot be happy at such a thought? But rest—yes, my love, rest you must. And there shall be more help in the household. I am not even sure we should not move into the country, where the air is so much fresher and—"

"No, James! I do not want to leave London. But—but when your mother was last here she was anxious to persuade me to take the children to St. Giles and spend some weeks with her. It would please her and if it would also please you—"

"Would it please *you?*"

"I think I would greatly enjoy it."

"Then it shall be arranged! And another thing, Mary—it has been in my mind for some time to suggest that with our next child you should go to St. Giles. You must talk to Mother about that."

She did not hear; she had heard him say "our next child" and her mind had boggled and gone hazy. *Their* next child. How could she be sure? What would happen if the child took after David Winfrith, or the man who many believed had sired David, Silas Moffat?

For once the courtroom was in darkness and the house at Bow Street was nearly empty for Sir John Fielding was away for a few days of sorely needed relaxation and all cases were being referred to other courts. At last James reached the door of David's home at one end of Bell Lane. This house was much larger than the row of cottages and there was a stable alongside it. Yellow light glowed at two windows and a flare flickered over the porchway, nearly dying when eventually David opened the door. He peered forward and suddenly James's name exploded from him.

"James! What are you doing here?"

"I need your help, David," James said, "and I could not find you at the court."

David hesitated, then stood aside. As they stepped farther into the house the smell of sewage and rotting vegetables assailed James's nose and in the candlelight he saw that it was in a state of almost unbelievable chaos. In the living room David's wife sat rocking herself to and fro while staring blankly into the fire. On the floor were a child's clothes, and James needed no telling that David himself had put their surviving child to bed. The conditions were so bad that James felt guilty at having come and the importance of the cartoons faded in his mind. He had to explain his visit, however, so he told David the story while showing him the card.

As he stared down in the light of two candles which stood in congealed wax in cracked earthenware dishes, David's expression changed and he said sharply, "I have seen such drawings before. Not depicting you, but by the same artist, I swear—and of men hanging. They have been found at the scene of holdups believed to have been the work of the Shadows. But why should *you* be a recipient?" He pursed his lips and then uttered the word "Traitor" with great deliberation. Then, more briskly, he went on: "I will take this to the court in the morning and find out if any of Sir John's men can throw a light on it." After a pause he demanded, "Are you frightened, James?"

"I suppose I am, a little."

"From now until the election at Minshall you should never travel abroad alone, and I shall hope to arrange for two good men to watch over you. This is either the work of a madman or one of the utmost viciousness and depravity. I am glad you came, Jamey."

In one way James was also glad. In another, he wished he had stayed far away from that terrible home. He knew there were thousands, perhaps tens of thousands, worse off; but—*David*.

James was greatly relieved that Mary was going to St. Giles, for he became more and more preoccupied with the coming by-election, knowing that to fight it effectively he must live for a while in Minshall itself. It was already known that both a Whig and a Tory would fight and there was a rumour that a man who called himself "All for Pitt" would also enter the fray. Three days after his talk with Mary, James went with her in a hired carriage to St. Giles, where, on his second evening at the farmhouse, he once again met the young doctor, Mario Leonardi, who was now resident doctor of the foundling home. James had been too concerned about his stepfather's health to form any opinion of the man at their earlier meeting. Now, talking with him at some length, he found that he took to him immediately. Obviously Henrietta was greatly attached to him, as obviously she was delighted that he had given James a good impression. Nothing was said, however; perhaps, thought James, the young man was too shy or too cautious to commit himself.

Walking in the grounds after the others had gone to bed, James was strangely ill at ease on this second night away. Yet Mary seemed content, and she, his mother and Henrietta always enjoyed one another's company. The night air was cold, and he walked more swiftly until soon he was among the trees on the hillside. In the distance some lights winked from the village, and a coach with four gleaming lanterns swung along the highway.

Suddenly a figure appeared between him and the village; someone very close.

"Who is there?" he demanded.

"You'll soon find out who's here," a man growled from one side, and as James spun around yet another hooked his legs from under him. Even as he fell, his arms were seized and he was forced face downward on the grass. Before he could think clearly, an evil-smelling cloth was slipped over his head and was drawn tight about his neck, and two men bound his wrists together behind his back.

Then a man said with a clarity which made him shiver, "Now you'll see what happens to traitors."

At the word James had a vivid picture of the cartoons, of his own face and the hanging man and the quartered body, with TRAITOR in bold black letters beneath. Shock of the recollection was as great as the shock of the attack. He was aware of the thud of heavy feet close by and, a moment later, of being picked up by the shoulders and ankles and swung between two men as if they were going to fling him into the air. Next he was dumped over a horse's withers and was held there while a man climbed into the saddle and began to ride. Every pace jolted his whole body, but a strong hand held him in position as they went uphill. Gradually he became aware of other riders, four or five or more, and realised they were threading their way through thick trees to the top of the hill behind St. Giles.

The constant jolting brought his teeth snapping, and his head, jerked to and fro, struck agonisingly against a branch. Now and again a blinding flash, as of lightning, shot through his mind, and every time it revealed the cartoons. Words seeped through cracks in his consciousness, always the same: "Now you'll see what happens to traitors."

The going became more steady; they were close to the top of the hill, where the trees were more sparse, but where, in a hollow which hid it from sight of all except those at very close quarters, there was a huge oak tree. Suddenly the truth slashed through him. They would hang him on the branches of that great oak!

His captor pulled at the reins and the horse stopped; others were dismounting. Muffled voices sounded, but his head was swimming and his ears were ringing and he was unable to distinguish what was said. He felt himself lifted by a man who must surely be a giant, slung over huge shoulders and carried no more than twenty yards. The sound of branches being pushed aside was all about him. Without warning he was lowered, feet first, to something flat beneath his feet. One man supported him and another pulled at the rope behind his back; he was being secured to the trunk of a tree.

Only then was the hood pulled roughly from his head. At first, he was aware of a flickering light and of chill, fresh night air. He breathed shallowly, then more deeply, and his vision began to clear. Not far off beyond the sweeping branches was a fire with half a dozen men about it; swinging from the branches were several lanterns, swayed by a soft wind. On a table in front of him gleamed the sharp blades of some knives. And the red-hot glow of a smaller fire lit up a butcher's chopper. The awful significance of these instruments struck with savage force. He was to be hanged; he was to be cut down and drawn while alive and his vitals burned; then he was to be quartered.

One man among the group moved toward him, grinning. He was strikingly handsome, the reflected firelight in his eyes giving him a fearsome expression. The fact that he did not trouble to wear a mask proved beyond hope that he meant to kill.

Others, including the giant who must have lifted James from the horse, came forward. It was this giant who drew close to him and, reaching up, took a noose from the branch above his head, lowered it, then placed it carefully around James's neck. The grinning man watched, without speaking, while the giant moved to one side and pulled the rope slowly until it was tight beneath James's chin. When it seemed that he was to be hoisted off his feet, the pressure eased. The man in front kicked at what proved to be an upended barrel on which he was standing. The barrel rocked and the noose pulled his head first this way and then that, but did not tighten enough to choke him.

The movement steadied.

"So Mr. Londoner is going to contest the Minshall constituency in the name of law and order," the grinning man said in an educated voice. "And Mr. Londoner is going to put an end to public hanging. And Mr. Londoner is going to clear London of all highwaymen and footpads, is he?" After a moment he swept his hand around and struck James on the side of the face. "Answer me, you traitorous pig. Answer me!"

The blow had been hard enough to make James's head ring, and a strange result followed. His head cleared of its buzzing and his mind cleared of dread. He now had no doubt of the inevitability of pain and death and perhaps because of that he ceased to fear them and was calm. He could see everything more clearly, too, and for the first time he noticed a coach drawn up, with a woman at the open door. A woman, here to watch him suffer!

"If you prevent me, others will do what I set out to do," he managed to say.

"Speak up! We want to hear you. Every condemned man has a right to speak!"

The man waved toward the giant and almost at once the pressure of the rope slackened, making speech easier. The ring of men stood still; one of the horses whinnied and pawed the ground, but there were no other sounds.

"If you prevent me from fighting to put an end to criminals like you, others will take my place. If you kill me, others will fight to bring a peace-keeping force to London and sweep you and those like you away."

"You're a bloody madman!" the man said roughly. "They've been trying for more than a hundred years; even Cromwell the Dictator couldn't control the country with his military. You've been wasting your time, James Marshall. All those like you have been wasting time. Well? Have you more to say?"

Still with that new-sent calm, James asked, "Why do you call me a traitor?"

"Because you insulted the King and conspired with every accursed newspaperman and busybody in London to insult him. Highwayman I might be, but no one is more loyal to the Throne."

"Or the system which lets you live on the blood of others."

"Enough of that!" the man roared. "And there are other reasons. It took me a long time to find out you were the fine hero who rescued a girl in distress and nigh broke my head doing it. And it also took me a long time to discover that you betrayed me and the Twelves to the Bow Street men. Yes, Mr. Londoner—*I* am the missing leader of the Twelves, now leader of the Shadows." He was almost hoarse when he finished and swung about, roaring at the others: "It is time we began. You have one more minute, Mr. Londoner, before you swing. And while you are swinging I'll play some little tricks with the knives to entertain the lady, before cutting you down and burning your guts! Hey, Nell! Here's what you begged of me." He backed away with one of the knives in his hand, his voice growing shrill.

He's mad, thought James. No doubt about it; the man is mad.

"One more question!" the highwayman roared. "Never let it be said that Jacob Rackham refused a dying man his last speech. *One more question.*"

"Who are you in truth?" James asked huskily.

The man threw up his arms and roared with laughter. Then he turned to face the others, shouting, "Hear him? He wants to know who the leader of the Shadows is. He is so innocent that he doesn't know the fame of Jacob Rackham, darkest of the Shadows!"

The angle at which James saw the man reminded him vividly of the moment when he had seen a rider easing his mount into Long Acre; the man who had shot at him as he had tried to leap. Every word he said was true.

Now he stood with arms upraised, as if he were invoking not the men watching but the devil, and he screamed, "Big Will, when I slash with my knife, pull!"

James felt a rush of fear, all calm gone in the tumult of terror, feeling the tightening noose and the rolling barrel even before that dreaded knife flashed. But while his heart thumped as if driven by some great unseen power, while the giant waited for the word of command, while the knife seemed to shiver as it was about to descend, a voice came out of the darkness, loud and clear.

"Cut him down, Jacob," the unseen man ordered. "Let go of the rope, Big Will, or I'll fill you so full of shot you will shake like a rattle." There was a moment of paralysis—of utter stillness—before the man said again, "Cut him down, I say!"

At that last word, James thought in stupefied disbelief: The voice is Johnny's. On that thought he fainted.

When James came around he was alone. He was on the ground close to the fire, which had faded to red embers; he felt a faint glow on his cheek and on his right hand. Soon he realised that he lay on the grass with a cloak thrown over him. His body ached, his head throbbed, and his neck was painful; above were the stars and about him the emptiness of the hillside, the only sound the stirring of night creatures. The past nightmare events were still vivid in his mind, the most vivid of all that swift thought: The voice is Johnny's.

Haunted by this thought, James began to move cautiously until he was on his feet and walking unsteadily downhill. There was enough light to see by, and soon he saw stars reflected in the stream; to reach the house he had only to follow the rippling water. Every movement was painful but at last he reached the side entrance and he knew which room was Dr. Leonardi's. A glow shone beneath the doctor's door. James almost fell against it, then banged on the panels until a moment later Leonardi appeared, eyes rounded in alarmed astonishment as James nearly fell into the room.

Half an hour later, rubbed from head to foot with a liniment which already soothed the pain, and with a draught of brandy from a supply Leonardi kept on his window sill, James was in bed.

"I don't want Mary or my mother and Henrietta alarmed on my behalf," he said, "so we will tell them I had a fall while walking. And I'll have a man drive me back to London tomorrow. There will be no more danger," he went on reassuringly. "I know the name of the leader and some of his men and the Bow Street men will have him and his gang before the week's out."

"If this is what you prefer, of course I am agreeable," Leonardi replied. "I am as anxious as you not to give the ladies cause for alarm, and—"

But James was already asleep; and after pulling the blankets up to his chin, Leonardi walked softly from the room.

James had been wrong about the speed with which Jacob Rackham and his ruffians would be caught. For a while there was a marked fall in the number of holdups and it appeared that Rackham had gone into hiding. Despite the names and descriptions James was able to give, the Bow Street men made no arrests.

"I'll tell you this, sir," said one of their older members. "Since you know the name and appearance of the leader, they may soon make another attempt to kill you. You need to be doubly careful."

James took this advice very seriously, not only for himself but for Mary, and even though it meant that he saw her only once every two or three weeks, it was not difficult to persuade her to stay at St. Giles until after the election. The country suited her, but he sensed she was troubled. Had Mario Leonardi let something of the story out? Whether or no, the election drew near, he was seldom alone, and after a few weeks he forgot the measure of the danger.

CHAPTER *25*

The New Member for Minshall

IN THE constituency of Minshall the candidates went from village to village, exhorting, pleading with, exciting the crowds. No by-election in the century had attracted more attention. The Tories had selected Lord Gellow as their candidate; the Whigs had as champion George Whitfield, a member of the Goldsmiths' Guild in Lombard Street, who had his home within the constituency and who was renowned for his good works; few men were better liked, and in his early fifties, he had the vigour and appearance of a much younger man.

Both men had wealth. Each man spent money without let or hindrance. All of a sudden, dilapidated cottages on the estates of supporters of each candidate were repaired; an army of carpenters, stonemasons, bricklayers, and plasterers descended on the constituency not only from nearby villages but from as far afield as London. At the same time, the landlords of the taverns were courted to display the blue favours of the Tory or the orange ones of the Whig, and free ale, free food, even free gin, poured from these places from morn until night. Farmers found new, high-paying markets for their crops; all they had to do was fly the colours of one candidate or the other. As election day drew nearer, newspapermen appeared from London and Oxford and other provincial cities; there was hardly a spare bed to be had anywhere in the constituency.

Gellow campaigned passionately for peace and absolute loyalty to the King.

Whitfield campaigned for Pitt and policies which would strengthen the economy by adding new territories to the Empire.

Throughout all this James fought quietly and steadily, with no great show of wealth, but with careful spending; no free beer or food or patronage but promises that if elected he would fight in the House for reforms. Whereas the other candidates were prodigal with pamphlets and campaign newspapers, he issued one pamphlet only, the front page carrying a picture of himself superimposed over a section of the "Mr. Londoner" shop and beneath it the slogan:

> FREE THE PEOPLE FROM CRIME . . .
> FREE THE PRESS FROM POLITICAL PRESSURES.

Most of the time he campaigned from a shop in the village of Minshall itself, lent to him by its owner, who, thanks to John Furnival's men twenty years before, had recovered the whole of his plate and money after a burglary. Streams of well-wishers came to take away supplies of pamphlets printed free of cost to James by *The Daily Clarion* and several other newspapers as well.

Two days before polling day a rider climbed from his horse outside the headquarters and approached James as he sat with Nicholas Sly, and for the second time James saw a man who at first sight might be his brother Johnny.

But this was not Johnny; it was Simon Rattray. Simon had become a larger man than Johnny and more solid, but the likeness of the features, especially of the eyes, was quite remarkable. Only one thing was missing: the glint of fire, of defiance. Yet these eyes were the same honey-brown, perhaps slightly darker, and when Simon spoke it seemed to James that Johnny's voice must come from those well-shaped lips. But this man's voice was deep and rougher in tone, though well controlled.

"Mr. Marshall, sir, I would be grateful for a little of your time."

"You will forgive me if it is indeed little," James said warily. Rattray did not look the fanatic that some reformers were, but there was no way of being sure whether a man was coming to offer solid help or advice or whether he wanted support for some crackbrained scheme or wild policy which was "*Certain to sweep you to victory, sir.*" He led the way to a small office at the back of the shop where he held confidential discussions. As he indicated a chair he went on: "It is Simon Rattray, is it not? We met once, some years ago, and I saw you in Bow Street at the trial of Benedict Sly."

"You have a good and gracious memory, sir!" Rattray could not be more than twenty-four or -five but he both looked and sounded much older. "I come with a warning and an offer of help, and will not waste your time. It has come to the ears of one of the congregation of my father's church that there is much concern among the supporters of your two opponents because of the progress you are making in your campaign."

"I would like to believe it," James replied.

"You can believe it, sir. I repeat that I have not come to waste your time, and I am sure of my facts. It is the intention of both opponents to employ a large number of men—men of the mob, sir, poor people, many of whom will cut a man's throat for a shilling. They are to descend upon the village and close off all the polling places and they will exert themselves to frighten away all who cannot be relied on to vote Whig or Tory."

Very softly James said, "I was warned by one of Mr. Fielding's men that some such persuasion might be attempted."

"It will be, sir. Have no doubt. The man who will arrange this is a fugitive from the Bow Street men and a notorious highwayman known as Jacob Rackham."

As he spoke, a change came over Simon Rattray—a glow, the light of fervour which put life into the eyes and passion into the voice— and now he was the image of Johnny, who had written: "*Jamey, you are a fool. Don't do it!*" And who, on that dark and terrifying night, had cried: "*Cut him down, Jacob. Cut him down, I say.*"

"He has already enlisted more than two hundred men, and the number will probably be doubled," Simon went on. "There is not one who would stop at murder. If they reach this constituency their very presence will keep all but your boldest supporters from the ballot."

Rattray's words struck cold apprehension into James. He had known of the strong current of support for him; he had also known what could happen if only a handful of drunken brutes was let loose on polling day to intimidate the voters.

"My information is wholly reliable, sir," Rattray continued. "The source is unimpeachable."

"It is grievous," James found himself saying. "And it will need the closest thought." Suddenly he remembered what else this man had said and asked, "What is the help you offer, Mr. Rattray?"

"Do you have a list of those who have promised you their vote?"

"Yes. And a list of those we expect to come over to me."

"But some of the voters are even now afraid to say what they would like to," said Rattray, and anger sounded in his voice again. "We cannot stop these men leaving London or reaching here, sir, but we can provide the protection of two guards for each of your known voters, and we can keep a watch on their homes after the voting. If you will accept that we will not expect much trouble."

"Nor would I," said James thoughtfully. "Would your men be prepared for violence?"

"Yes, sir."

"Then it remains for me to ask who they would be," James said.

He fully expected to be told that they would be members of the little church he had been looking at when he had first seen Simon with his milking pail and that strange air of maturity. But something in Rattray's manner warned him that it might not be so simple, and he squared his shoulders as he awaited the answer.

"It is necessary for you to know before you agree to have their help," Simon Rattray told him, "for there are those who say that mud sticks, and many would call these men mud. They are the workers, sir. Unskilled workers of many trades and professions who find it hard to earn a living wage and who desire to better their conditions. You could call them a Guild of Poor Men—but honest Englishmen, every one, each anxious to see you with a seat in Parliament. They seek political reform, sir, giving all workingmen as well as all property owners the vote, and thus making a true people's government for this country. They'll support any man of peace to the death if it will help them draw closer to their goal. But"—Rattray paused, then went on with deep deliberation—"you might regret allowing it to be said that the mob helped to elect you, sir. It would make you a people's candidate at a time when the people do not count for much in the minds of the upper and middle classes."

James sat quiet and still for what seemed a long time, the uncanny family resemblance of this man forgotten, everything forgotten except what Rattray's words implied. Slowly he stood up and moved to the window; as slowly he began to speak in measured words.

"Mr. Rattray, that is the first thing you have uttered to which I take exception. What makes you imagine that I would regret being known as the Member who has the support of the people, be they poor or not? Do you think I use the cry 'Free the People' simply as a catch phrase?"

That was the first time he had seen Simon Rattray smile.

Rattray's men came in farm carts and delivery wagons, in drays and on horseback, by battered coach and shaggy donkey; some even came by foot. Never had James seen a more motley collection of patched breeches and worn-down boots; but each shapeless hat bore a white favour with three words printed on it in black: *Vote for Marshall*. They brought staves and poles but no other weapons, pouring into Minshall from all directions and taking up positions in doorways, at street corners, and outside alehouses and inns. They were of all ages, all strong men with impassive faces. Each brought a cloth filled with food, and a leather flagon hung from each belt. None went inside a tavern or any place where beer was sold, and when on the morning of the day of the election the mass of Rackham's hired men arrived on horseback or by coach it was as if they had come upon a brick wall. Wherever they went they were followed, and few got near enough to the voters even to begin to harass or threaten.

"It was the quietest election day since elections began," said the mayor of Minshall as he prepared to read the result outside the town hall. "We people of Minshall may be proud of our respect for law and order." Despite the words he seemed uneasy. "I have the honour to announce in the name of the King," he added huskily, "that the following votes were cast for the candidates: Lord Gellow, one thousand and seventeen; George Whitfield, Esquire, one thousand one hundred and fifty-two; James Marshall, Esquire, two thousand and one. I duly declare James Marshall elected to . . ."

A roar went up from a thousand throats that split the evening heavens. No one who saw them that night would ever again call Rattray's men impassive.

A few weeks after the election, Mary's fourth child and third boy was born. Even from the earliest hours there was no doubt of his descent: he was the Reverend Sebastian Smith in miniature! From the beginning everyone dubbed him Little Seb, although they christened him Jonathan.

Sebastian Smith was much happier than he or Mary had dared to hope. The life of travel, of being an important figure in the growing Wesleyan movement, suited him. Moreover, the initial Wesleyan conflict with the Church of England lost its fire. To the discerning it was obvious that one day they would become two different establishments, but for the moment there was a state of suspended hostilities if not peace.

CHAPTER *26*

The House by the River

Two FACTORS persuaded James to seek a house which had some open land about it, and where the air was cleaner than in the heart of the City. Not only were the rooms in the Strand now too few to house the family comfortably, but the business of "Mr. Londoner" was expanding so fast under Nicholas Sly's handling that it would have to take over more space or move elsewhere. Having the two shops and the rooms above them for a rent of only sixty pounds a year, with nine years of a lease from the Duke of Bedford still to run, it was clearly advantageous to stay.

James considered Southwark and beyond. Of the places he liked, however, Chelsea stood out as the most suitable. It was only ten or fifteen minutes from Chelsea Steps to Westminster by waterman's barge, and it was possible to walk to the House when he had reasonable time. The broad expanse of the river, the meadows sweeping down on the other side broken by tiny villages, pleased both James and Mary, and at last they found a house only a hundred yards from the riverbank with an uninterrupted view over fields where cattle grazed, and where fresh milk, butter and eggs were freely available. Moreover, there was a dame school nearby, attended by children of the Chelsea pottery workers as well as other families that had moved from the crush of London itself. The house was of red brick, only twenty years old, and available on a long lease for forty pounds a year from the ducal estate.

Built on two floors, it had rare spaciousness, with one huge room stretching the width of the building, and mullioned windows which provided plenty of air and light. The main entrance was at one side, a wide carriageway in front, and brick columns supported a porch. The big room had three doors: one leading to the dining room and, beyond, the kitchen and outhouses; one, to the hall, with its fine oak staircase; and one to a suite of small rooms, one of which was to be James's study. On the floor above were eight main bedrooms and three wash-rooms, while a second, narrower staircase led to ample accommodation for servants.

The front and sides of the house, which was referred to as The House by the River, had lawns and some formal gardens, but at the back was open pasture and a fine walled orchard, with the stables be-yond. And beyond the stables were two small hothouses, one with a promising young vine.

Both Mary and James fell in love with The House by the River at first sight, early in September of the year 1762.

Mary's one doubt was whether James could afford it, but he assured her that even if it were reasonably staffed they would still be able to live within their means. The business of "Mr. Londoner" now flour-ished so much that considerable sales were made by post, and goods were shipped as far afield as the colonies of America, Hong Kong and India, where the growing British population cherished mementos from England. It would prove, James fervently hoped, their one and only home, large enough for great numbers of grandchildren.

With the birth of her fourth child Mary had recovered much of her old spirit and liveliness and, as always, she showed a shrewd interest in what was going on. Able to play in an orchard of apple, plum and pear trees, the children throve. Paul Weygalls' oldest daughter, Betsy, who now spent more time with the Marshalls than with her own parents, helped to look after the children, and Mary had four living-in servants. It was a comfortable household, and both James and Mary blessed the day they had first seen The House by the River.

Then, out of the blue, came a triumph for Sir John Fielding. The government at last replied to his recommendations, rejecting his pro-posal for detachments of troops near the turnpikes but authorising a civilian horse patrol of eight men, with an inspector, and allowing Fielding six hundred pounds for this patrol, just enough to pay each man four shillings a day for the six winter months. Never had James seen Fielding more jubilant. Within days the success of the plan seemed assured. Lurking highwaymen actually ran away at sight of the Bow Street Horse Patrol!

All who had supported Fielding were deeply pleased.

In his domestic life James was as content as a man could hope to be.

From time to time, however, a hideous memory would flash into his mind, of Jacob Rackham wielding his long knife, of the fire, of the pressure of the noose beneath his jaw. And occasionally a voice would come out of nowhere, sharp and incisive: *"Cut him down, Jacob."* *Could* it be possible that Johnny had been that speaker? Johnny now held a roving commission on the continent of Europe, crossing the English Channel frequently to visit customers and associates of the House of Furnival. There was no way that he, James, could be sure that he had been in England that night.

The darkness of this lurking shadow became less intense as the months passed, and from his seat in the House of Commons in the Palace of Westminster, a hall so small and crowded he could hardly believe that so much history had been fashioned there, he watched the many-coloured pageant of the future in the making.

Two more moves were made to follow the suggestions of Sir John Fielding, but no credit was given to the magistrate himself, whose proposals had been pigeonholed for so long. The first and simplest was a great improvement in street lighting, a responsibility which was now accepted by the government. The second was likely to be by far the most far-reaching.

Following the well-tried example in the City of London, five new "public offices," or magistrates' courts, were to be set up, one near Bow Street and the others widespread.

But James was acutely aware of the folly of the King and the oligarchy he placed at the head of the nation's affairs. All the time working to find supporters for the rest of Sir John Fielding's police plan, James nonetheless was drawn into the vortex of passionate debate on matters not directly concerned with his closest interests.

One factor loomed larger in James's mind all the time: the vast gap between information given to the House and the wild rumours which spread outside. No member of the press was able to attend parliamentary sittings, so no truthful reporting was possible, since Members

who were bribed for information either wilfully or unwittingly mis-
led the press.

All James and a dozen or so Members could do about the many in-
equities was to protest. Never had he so hated party politics, the
double-dealing, the secret pacts, the support given to the King by
those Members whose families received titles, honours or substantial
pensions in return. The power of the King was absolute although it
was exercised under the cloak of representation of the people. Only a
few honourable men stood out against the system.

It was the anniversary of the opening of Furnival Docks. Across
the room at Furnival Tower House, James saw Johnny.

Francis was present, looking old and parchment-faced. William had
a fine bold presence. Sarah retained much of her ebullience. Timothy,
at James's side, remained irrepressible and unstinting in his support for
James. Jeremy Siddle and Martin Montmorency had been dead for
some years, and now other, younger men were the unofficial representatives of the House of Furnival within the House of Commons.

When he had agreed to come James had wondered whether he
would meet his half brother. Now Johnny was watching him from
across the room. He had with him a young, elegant and beautiful
Italian woman, with whom he was known to have established a
permanent liaison; he had not yet married, but the capitals of Europe
were said to be littered with a trail of his neglected mistresses. This
woman had changed her religion to please Johnny, James knew, and
was now a member of the Church of England. Timothy, also still a
bachelor, was obviously glad to escort her to the buffet while Johnny
made his way toward James, who went forward to meet him, and as if
of one mind they moved toward the terrace. It was a fine October
evening, and still warm. The river was congested with boats of all
sizes and they could see the new outline of London Bridge, denuded
of its shops and houses since a barge had rammed one of the piles and
made so much weight unsafe for the old structure to carry. Otherwise
the scene had hardly changed.

"Well, half brother," Johnny said in a jeering tone, "I told you you
were a fool and would be wasting your time."

"No minute has been wasted," James retorted.

"Every minute, everything you do is a waste," Johnny declared.
"We will never have rule by the mob here, and the time will arrive

when the King's rule will be absolute. When that day comes be careful they do not have you executed for a damned rebel."

"Or hanged, drawn and quartered."

"Even that," agreed Johnny, but his eyes were aglow, as if touched by some demon's humour. "There is still time to become a King's man, half brother."

"I am an England's man."

"Fine sentiment from one who consorts with the mob that wants to bring the nation to its knees. I am warning you again. Remember the day." Johnny shrugged and looked over the river for a moment before changing his tone and asking, "How is Mary?"

"She is well."

"And our delightful mother?"

"Well and happy, but neglected by her youngest son."

"She wants none of me; I am not cut off the right block. Better I neglect her than cause her distress whenever I reveal how different I am from my father. You are much more in his mould though not of the same blood."

"You are the image of him in appearance," James said quietly.

"Aye, in appearance but in no other way. Have you heard it said that he left at least a dozen bastards when he died, farming them out on families that needed the money he would pay?" When James did not comment the younger brother went on: "That's another way I am not like him, half brother. I've never met the woman yet who could bear me a child. Isn't that a relief to you? When I die my like will die with me."

"Johnny, what has hardened you so?" asked James.

"Hardened?" Johnny replied, the jeering note still in his voice. "I'm the same as I always was, half brother. I was born with different qualities in me, and it is against my nature to conform. Every now and again I become sentimental, but I'm a hard nut, Jamey. Don't waste your time trying to reform me." He threw back his head and roared with laughter so that a few people who were sauntering back from the bigger rooms looked across at them in surprise. "The truth is that God and the devil merged in John Furnival's nature, and I'm from the devil's side."

"No side of your father was a fool," James retorted.

"*Touché*! Only a lunatic would behave as I sometimes do. All right, half brother! But rather a fool than a tool of the papists."

The switch in conversation was so sudden that James was taken completely off his balance and echoed, "Papists? Where do they concern us?"

"They concern everyone," declared Johnny, a harsh note springing to his voice. "The devils are everywhere, plotting against the Church and the State. Why do you think France and Spain hate us so? And even Ireland! We're victims of a papist plot, Jamey, and anyone who is not against them is for them. Just as"—gripping James's arm so tightly that the pressure hurt, he lowered his voice so that only James could catch the words—"anyone who is against the King is for the papists. Open your eyes, half brother! See what goes on about you instead of wearing your heart on your sleeve for the mob."

Turning on his heel, he strode off, rejoining the beautiful young Italian, now talking to a tall youth whom James recognised but could not immediately place. James was still puzzling over Johnny's words when Timothy caught his elbow.

"Cousin, if I didn't know you better I would say you were trying to avoid me," Timothy declared. "It isn't like you to go sneaking off with Johnny or anyone else on these occasions. How is Mary? And Little Seb?"

"They are both well," James assured him, still looking across the crowded room and the host of beautifully dressed people. "Who is that with Johnny? Do you know?"

"Shame on you! Are your thoughts turning from Mary at last? That is Isabella—"

"I mean the youth."

"Oh, how unromantic," protested Timothy. "I thought I had found your Achilles' heel at last. That is Lord George Gordon. Johnny has been seeing much of his family lately. But let us consider Johnny's plight. Could his companionship with that young fop explain his reported failure as a man? One hundred mistresses and not a single babe!" Then, seeing the shadow cast over James's face, his tone changed. "Oh, fie, Jamey! May I not joke?"

"I was feeling sorry for Johnny," James remarked, "and I did not expect ever to feel like that about him."

He walked away, still remembering the sudden cry that had saved him: *"Cut him down, Jacob. Cut him down, I say."* Even over the years there seemed no doubt whose voice it had been.

CHAPTER 27

The Papists

THREE WEEKS later James was faced with what he considered a crushing blow.

Just at the time when most people were beginning to feel that the metropolitan area *had* been cleared of the worst criminal elements, the government refused Fielding's request to make the patrols permanent. It agreed that they were successful and that the people did not object to the use of troops, but insisted that the cost was too great.

"A thousand pounds a year too much for the security of the whole metropolitan area!" James exclaimed angrily in the House of Commons. "This is the most senseless and penny-pinching decision I have ever heard!"

But despite a chorus of "Hear! Hear!" from both sides of the House, the government was adamant.

By now the condition of the watchmen in the parishes was so bad that many citizens joined together to employ other, stronger men, and at last the government agreed to a committee of inquiry, to which James was appointed. Fielding presented the case for more and younger watchmen who should be better paid. But one by one the main proposals were dropped by the nation's leaders.

Sir John put as many of them into practice as he could afford, one being the keeping of a register of all crimes reported to the office.

"It is a disgrace that the government will not pay for the register," James told Mary as he sat with her after a long day at Bow Street, "but it must be prepared. That register leads to more arrests than anyone would guess."

Partly because of the register's success, Fielding was now considering producing a journal giving news and descriptions of all known criminals, to be circulated to all in authority throughout Britain.

"But how long it will be before the government will finance it is a matter for conjecture," he said wryly at the end of a day's hearings.

"What will you call it, sir?" James asked.

"Perhaps your friend Benedict Sly will have some ideas!" Fielding smiled thoughtfully.

The journal was founded in the autumn of 1772, and after a number of variations the name was finally settled; the expression "hue and cry" now became the name of the official peace journal.

One of the first things reported was the robbing by a highwayman of the Prime Minister, Lord North, but even this would not persuade him to work for the return of the horse patrol.

"With the patrol and the journal together we could stamp out crime in all England," Benedict Sly growled. "Why is the government always so reluctant to pay a trifle to fight outrages which cost the people hundreds of thousands?"

"It is a kind of blindness," James said resignedly. "I never cease talking to fellow Members, never cease pointing out the obvious truth, but few listen. True," he added grimly, "they have cause for deep anxiety these days. There is talk that as a result of our tax policies there is much unrest in the American colonies and even sentiment for open rebellion. If that is true . . ."

In the year 1775 came war with the colonies.

A war that would be over in weeks, boasted Lord North.

And at last, in 1781, surrender.

Slowly the wounds of war began to heal, and for a while the madness was done.

During those years, James maintained his friendship with Benedict Sly and often visited the coffee houses patronised by editors and reporters. He made some friends among the more independent-minded men in the House of Commons, was constantly in touch with his constituents, and occasionally met Simon Rattray, who would sometimes ask him to raise some matter in the House or with the government—always a reasonable request. He saw little of the Furnival family except Timothy, who had helped when he had fought and won Minshall at the General Election, and he spent much less time in Bow Street, although he still interceded for poor clients whenever need arose. He was at "Mr. Londoner" at least one morning each week and came to look on Nicholas, now married and with three children, as a younger brother.

The one man he seldom saw, except in court, was David Winfrith. And David now looked so gaunt that his face was like a skull. He had withdrawn from his old haunts and friendships. Nobody could persuade him to visit or to receive callers, and conditions at his house became so bad that fewer and fewer tried. Sir John Fielding, as concerned as any, tried to ease his mind, but the death of his two children and its effect on his wife had made too deep a mark. Mary had been to see him, offering help with the remaining child, but he would not admit her to the house. Whenever the front or back door opened a great stench billowed out, and David himself smelled as bad as if he had come from the Fleet or Newgate.

No one knew for certain but it was rumoured that a Bow Street magistrate had told him that unless he cleaned himself there would be no position for him.

One morning early in 1777, David did not come to court, the first time he had missed since his children had died. Word came from Bow Street to "Mr. Londoner" on a morning when James was there, and he hurried out, called a sedan chair, and was carried at a sharp pace to Bell Lane. As he turned into it he saw people streaming toward the corner where David lived and an eddy of smoke sweeping down from the chimneys; the word "Fire!" was bellowed once and was immediately taken up in a great refrain. The parish fire engine was already at the scene and men were working the wooden pump and trying to make sure that the flames did not spread. The house itself was already a charred ruin, the roof burned through and only two walls standing.

"Was anyone inside?" James demanded.

"No one came out," a neighbour told him. "They perished in the flames, that's what they did. Tell you one thing, the 'ouse ain't no loss, like a stinking sewer that place was."

James had never seen Mary cry so bitterly as when he told her. It was several weeks before she seemed fully to recover.

Meanwhile, much had happened to change the face of London.

If he were called upon to name the change he most approved, James would say, "The covering over of the Fleet River!" Like many other once open sewers, it had been completely covered. Many of the old rookeries had been pulled down because of the danger of fire, whilst in the Strand the greatest palace in all London, Somerset House, was now near completion.

Much was stirring, also, in the fields of science and invention. James Watt was making a new kind of steam engine, which, it was said, would not fail, as earlier attempts had done, and some prophesied an enormous revolution in industry.

More traffic than ever crowded London's roads and thronged on the nation's highways, some no more than rutted tracks linking towns and villages, some—controlled by the Turnpike Boards—improving whenever they were close to the larger towns. Many towns were now growing beyond a population of fifty thousand as industry moved north. Lancashire proved to be far better than London for the treatment of cotton, with the greater use of Arkwright's spinning machine, Hargreaves' spinning jenny and Crompton's mule. Yorkshire was better for the treatment of wool, but silk weavers stayed a long time in Spitalfields. London became more sharply aware of competition from other ports as well as industrial towns, yet continued to grow at an almost frightening pace. More than three thousand miles of canal now eased traffic on highways and inside many great cities.

One day, after three men had been brought into Bow Street and charged with inciting to riot, Sir John Fielding dismissed the charges so summarily that those who knew him well were surprised. He had been ailing on and off for years, but never had he looked as ill as then.

He was helped from the bench and was taken home. Now and again in the next year he returned, but slowly it dawned on James and on Benedict Sly that this great and powerful man had little longer to live.

Other magistrates sat at Bow Street although no one was appointed to replace Sir John. James now found Bow Street and the nearby streets and yards strange and unfamiliar. He knew few people, for many new houses had been built and more families had moved in. Only when he went into the courtroom itself did he find the same grimy walls, the same stale odours, the same hapless prisoners; there everything was unchanged.

Caught up inextricably in parliamentary work, gradually accepted by many who had at one time cursed his name, he had become a familiar figure at Westminster, renowned for slowly delivered, well-informed speeches and for never missing an opportunity for calling for a London, if not a national, police force. He was gray at the temples now, and his face had acquired dignity as well as greater handsomeness; the hooked nose and deep-set eyes had begun to feature in cartoons, as had his bow-shaped lips and thrusting chin.

It was his custom to meet with any who wanted his help.

One day in late May of 1780, a day when the sun shone from behind the Abbey onto the far bank of the river and gave the whole scene a golden cloak of beauty, he glanced up from his table in Miller's Coffee House to see Simon Rattray and a stranger.

Rattray looked not only older but thinner, and gave the impression of a man who did not get enough to eat, but nothing of this reflected in his manner as he bowed before James and said, "Jack Bowyer, sir, a friend of mine."

"Mr. Bowyer." James half rose and indicated two empty chairs to Rattray and a small man with a leathery face and piercing blue eyes.

"My pleasure, sir," he said in an unexpectedly well-modulated voice, and they waited until a lad brought coffee. As James poured from an earthenware pitcher, Rattray spoke again.

"I brought Mr. Bowyer along because he is my chief informant, sir. He is a potboy at a coaching inn called the Coal Hole, at Blackfriars, and they do a big trade."

"Very big trade indeed, sir, and much bigger since the Blackfriars Bridge went up." Although it had now been there for ten years, it was still talked of in awe.

"And a lot of people meet to make plans there," Rattray put in. "For years it was a favourite haunt of highwaymen, and certain trading justices still hold court there."

"Four, that's a fact, exactly four," Bowyer declared.

"And they have private rooms where groups can meet and cellars for secret meetings," continued Rattray.

"Secret meetings, that be the truth," affirmed the potboy.

Knowing Rattray, James did not doubt that all this was going to lead up to a revelation of much significance, although nothing yet said gave a hint of what it was. Usually Rattray was quick to reach the point, but now he edged slowly toward it, as if anxious to build a strong foundation.

"There was one last week and two more this week," he went on, "attended by the same people and for the same purpose, sir. To plan an uprising in London against the papists."

"To do *what*?" James gasped.

"That's right, sir, and a terrible thing it's going to be," declared Bowyer. "They'll likely plan some terrible deeds. Lord George Gordon has been battling for the repeal of the Catholic Relief Act, but Parliament won't take it back, sir, will they?"

James thought back to the passing of the Act, which gave Catholics privileges they had not had for generations, and the accompanying protests and demonstrations.

"I doubt very much if they will," he replied. "There is a petition before the House for repeal but I expect it to be heavily defeated."

"If it is, sir, then the Gordon lot—begging your pardon, sir—are going to attack all papists they can lay hands on, *and* anyone who tries to stop them. A terrible thing it's going to be."

James thought: *Papists!* And had a swift mental picture of Johnny and the way he had spat the word out.

"Murder and pillage will be the result," went on Rattray in a low-pitched voice. "I'm no papist, heaven forbid, but whatever his religion a man has a right to practise it. It's already under way, sir, a very big uprising indeed. Mr. Bowyer informs me that paid rabble-rousers and rioters already have been sent to many points of vantage to whip up riots. They're bound to pillage and to burn, sir."

"Bound to, certain as can be," Bowyer echoed.

"Unless you can have them stopped in time," Rattray continued. "You've little enough time to work in, I'll admit, but no one needs telling who the leader is. The crowds will follow Lord George Gordon, sir. If you could have him put in some place to cool his heels it might all come to nought."

James thought: Johnny is involved in this. So great was his sense of shock that for a few moments he made no reply, thoughts of his half brother excluding all else from his mind. What had Johnny said? "But rather a fool than a tool of the papists. . . . The devils are everywhere, plotting against the Church and the State. . . . We're victims of a papist plot, Jamey, and anyone who is not against them is for them."

To emphasise the words he had gripped James's arm so that the pressure had hurt. In another strange mental flash James seemed to hear Johnny's voice from even farther back in time: "Cut him down, Jacob."

He saw Simon Rattray move forward and peer at him tensely.

"Did you hear me, sir?"

"I heard you," James assured him, forcing his mind to return to the present. "I heard very clearly. Mr. Rattray, can you or Mr. Bowyer give me any evidence, any proof, that paid rabble-rousers and rioters have been sent to points of vantage to whip up the riot?"

"No proof, sir. But certainty."

"I have to deal with people who will demand proof before they act," James said. "How many rabble-rousers? Can you say?"

"They'll be everywhere, everywhere," Bowyer declared. "How many, sir? How many I cannot say."

"Dozens? Hundreds?"

"Many hundreds, sir." Bowyer appeared to be making a great effort to concentrate on what he was saying; being an echo to Simon Rattray was one thing, speaking for himself was obviously another. "It is said that the Shadows will be present, sir. And every highwayman and footpad in London. They—" His concentration wavered and he dropped back in his chair. "Every highwayman and footpad in London will take advantage of the troubles," he muttered, his chin on his chest so that the words were barely audible. "Fact," he muttered. "Certain fact."

"He told me that supporters of Lord George Gordon are giving ten shillings to each man who will start a fight and twenty to each who will start a fire, sir," added Simon. "And I can tell you beyond all doubt that money has been offered to some of my friends—men known to be ready to march anywhere in protest against the workers' conditions. My friends won't take bribes, what they do they do out of principle, but some people are well known for creating public disorders, hence the offer." After a pause he went on: "Have we convinced *you* of the seriousness, sir?"

"Yes," replied James. "If only Sir John Fielding were at Bow Street."

"Is he not there, sir?" Rattray seemed shocked.

"He is very ill at his home," James answered. "And with Mr. Welch out of the country, the remaining magistrates are not likely to take swift action. I will try to help," he promised, finishing his now cold coffee, "but if I know the authorities they will not act until it is too late." His eyes met Rattray's and they seemed to be Johnny's eyes. "I know what is needed but I do not think it can be arranged, Mr. Rattray."

"It will be a grievous day for London if it is not," Rattray replied.

"You are absolutely convinced of what is to happen?"

"As I believe in God, sir."

"I know what is needed," James repeated. "Every parish constable and every deputy, every peace officer and every Charlie, should be put on the alert; the Bow Street officers should be mounted and ready to move to trouble centers at short notice. And the first men to cause violence or start fires should be taken before a magistrate at once and committed to Newgate, Fleet or Gatehouse. If the affair could be crushed before it really began, then the use of troops could be avoided."

He broke off, aware of the relief on the faces of the other two men, who saw in him the one possible means of averting grievous disaster. They could not see into his mind, however; they could not begin to understand the immensity of the task. With help from Sir John Fielding or Welch he might have a chance of success. Without it, what magistrate had the strength and courage to call out the troops and risk disaster?

"Do you know when this is to begin?" he asked.

"Very soon," replied Simon Rattray. "Messengers will take the word around and trouble will begin in a dozen places at the same time."

"So as to prevent a concentration of forces against the rioters," James reasoned. "Mr. Rattray, will you and Mr. Bowyer obtain as much information as possible about the timing of the raids and the places where trouble is to begin and leave it as a message for me at the offices of *The Daily Clarion?*" It did not occur to James to doubt that Benedict Sly would help. "I will acquaint the senior justices of the danger. I will also inform the Bow Street men, who, once they have authority from their acting chief magistrate, will be of much value, especially if the riot is quickly controlled."

"Be sure we will ferret out everything we can," Simon Rattray promised, rising to his feet. "I trust it will be possible to avoid calling on the military, sir. For when the Army is called to stop civil troubles many who are on the side of law and order are deeply resentful."

Silently James nodded.

Ten minutes later he was riding along Fleet Street, which had never seemed more crowded. As he tied the reins about a hitching post outside the new Fleet Street offices of *The Daily Clarion*, a thought flashed into James's mind.

It had not once occurred to him that Simon Rattray might be wrong. And it had not once occurred to him to go first to the Minister of State responsible, so sure was he that no action would be taken.

Benedict Sly, gray showing clearly in the darkness of his beard, took only a few seconds to answer.

"Yes, James. I shall put a reliable man at a desk to take messages and keep a close record of them. Whenever news of significance is brought in I will send a messenger to you. Will you be at the House of Commons?"

"As soon as I have seen the magistrates," James answered. "Ben, will you find out for me whether Johnny is in London at the moment, or abroad?"

"I will," Benedict promised.

The two men who shared the bench at Bow Street listened, one attentively, the other with impatience. The attentive one replied, "When there is clear cause for action we shall take it, Mr. Marshall."

"If the parish constables are not alerted—"

"Allow us, sir, to know how to handle our own affairs."

The three men who sat on the benches in the County of Middlesex listened with haughty patience.

"We are grateful for your information, Mr. Marshall. At this juncture we see no cause for alarm."

The two magistrates at Westminster said, as with one voice, "We have heard such rumours countless times, Mr. Marshall. Nothing would cause more harm than to organise our constables before need, for that would antagonise the greatest number of people, peace-loving citizens who respect freedom of religion."

The most helpful of James's fellow Members at the House of Commons were concerned but far from persuaded that danger was imminent. They had, they said, no doubt that if a wave of rioting did

342

begin, it would be taken care of quickly. The magistrates were well aware of what they were doing. All this could so easily prove a false alarm.

The Secretary of State for Home Affairs, Lord Stormont, could not or would not see him.

Word came from *The Daily Clarion* while James was at the House of Commons listening to a fruitless debate on keeping open all sea lanes to the various parts of the Empire:

> *The time is tonight, at eight o'clock.*

And with this was a note in Benedict Sly's own handwriting, saying:

> *Your half brother is in London. He spends little time at Furnival Tower House and even less at Great Furnival Square.*

On that sharp, sunny day in early June, Parliament rejected Lord George Gordon's petition with almost cynical indifference and James felt there was no hope at all of avoiding trouble.

Reports began to come in of isolated outbreaks of violence at brothels, theaters, alehouses and crowded thoroughfares. None of the incidents seemed connected, but each demanded the time and urgent attention of Bow Street men and local justices and constables. Details came in quickly one upon another, convincing James of the complete truth of Simon Rattray's story. The riots were beginning. And it seemed to him that the one remaining hope was to go again to the Secretary of State and implore that troops be stationed at vantage points about the whole area of the metropolis.

"Mr. Marshall, no one respects your integrity or your good will more than I," said Lord Stormont pompously. "And few disagree more vehemently with your beliefs and your support for Sir John Fielding. There is overwhelming evidence that the present method of keeping the peace and fighting crime is most effective. I see not the slightest cause for alarm and am horrified at the thought of summoning troops, whose presence invariably inflames the mood of both the middle classes and the mob. Good day to you, sir."

343

When James rode from Whitehall and the Palace of Westminster, crowds were gathering at the Charing Cross approach to the Strand, always a trouble spot. On a platform on a corner near Hennessy's, the butcher's, a man was standing and roaring so that his voice traveled with frightening clarity.

"We'll burn them out of their homes. . . . We'll drive them into the sea. . . . To the devil with the papists! What do we say?"

"No popery!" the crowd roared. "Let's get the papists on the run!"

There was a bellow of approval from dozens of men in the crowd, a waving of staves and muskets, a vivid lighting of flares, a terrifying sense of purpose—to pillage and to burn—as the cry reached the rooftops and the skies.

"No popery! No popery!" they roared. "No popery!"

A vast crowd of sixty or seventy thousand men, with Lord George Gordon at their head, set out to march from St. George's Fields, in Southwark, to the Houses of Parliament, and there was none to stop them. Soon they were a rabble pouring over Westminster Bridge, smashing carriages and setting on peers and Members of Parliament. Far too late Stormont sent for Army help.

Day after day the riots went on, the June weather nearly as cold as winter, constables and watchmen helpless, the magistrates impotent. Yet still the government vacillated.

If James had any comfort it was that Mary and the children were safe at Chelsea. He stayed between Westminster and "Mr. Londoner" whilst reports grew more and more alarming.

CHAPTER *28*

To Pillage and to Burn

IN LINCOLN'S INN FIELDS, close to the Unitarian church of Simon Rattray's father, a mob descended without warning on the Sardinian Embassy in which was a Roman Catholic church, smashing down doors and windows, pitching furniture into the street, using flares to start huge fires. As the mob danced and sang in gin-sodden revelry, the scream "No popery!" seemed to drown all other sound.

At the same time a vast crowd stormed and set fire to the Bavarian Embassy in St. James's, until the conflagration showed in the sky all over London, whilst in a dozen other places the homes of wealthy Catholics were sacked, their inmates escaping narrowly with their lives.

Uneasy quiet came with the night, when Simon Rattray arrived at the *Clarion* offices while the story was being set in type. He was wild-eyed, his face bruised, his hair scorched.

"I hoped I'd find you here," he said to James. "Tomorrow night there's to be a mass attack on the weavers of Moorfields, sir. They are mostly Romans who live there. If there could be a company of dragoons it might still prevent the situation from getting out of hand."

"Can we get the justices to act?" asked James.

"*I* can't, sir, and the Lord Mayor won't try. He's nought but a brothel keeper. And it's a waste of time relying on the parish constables; you only have to mix with the crowds to see how many wear the cockade of the Protestant Association. I sometimes come to hate that blue," Rattray said in a grating voice. "If ever troops in large numbers were needed this is the occasion, sir."

"Jamey, this has all the smell of revolution," Benedict Sly groaned when Rattray had gone. "Is there no hope of help from Parliament? Can you not see Stormont again?"

"I try each day," James said grimly.

And once again it was his first act when he reached Westminster the next morning. Being on foot, ignoring the thinning crowd, he was not molested, but his heart beat fast nevertheless. He did not have to wait long for word from Lord Stormont this time.

"I have sent for troops in strength," he said.

About that time, two Irish servant girls, cowering behind a staircase while rioters wrecked and burned a house in Leicester Square, were driven out of their hiding place by smoke and fire. As they appeared in the hall leading to the street a man leaped at them, dragged them into one of the rooms, stripped himself and them naked and raped first one and then the other. Done, he struck their heads together and dropped them, unconscious, into a corner where flames were already creeping. Still naked, but for one girl's dress over his shoulders, he strutted out among the mob, which roared its approval as he paraded himself in stolen finery.

Fire after fire was started, in shops, in houses, in churches. No one was safe as the cry raged everywhere: "No popery! No popery!"

When at last the mob seemed to tire of its own violence, men moved among the people, thrusting gin into their hands, spurring them on to further destruction, or went off to start still more trouble wherever the crowd was not yet sated.

All over London the rioting continued. One great mass of rioters assembled close to the House, another debouched into the side streets, the grogshops and the taverns. Great piles were made of the wreckage and the fields were dotted with fiercely growing fires.

James Marshall, denied entrance to the Palace of Westminster by the mob, stayed on the fringe of the crowd. His clothes were torn and blackened, his face was unshaven, and he looked as villainous as any of the rioters. Utterly helpless, all he could think of was how to prevent the riot spreading. If there were a way, it was to catch the ringleaders. Without the Bow Street men and with hardly a constable who might serve, the only source of help was Rattray's men.

Rattray might be at *The Daily Clarion's* office.

James pushed his way, on foot, toward Fleet Street, when he heard a cry: "Bow Street! On to Bow Street!" A great fear choked him as the cry was taken up and a man standing in a cart raised his huge voice: "Bow Street ahoy!" One moment James was ahead of the crowd; the next he was helpless in its midst. Men carrying lighted torches raced ahead, and what he had thought to be impossible happened. The hordes streamed into Bow Street, smashing the windows of the house he knew so well and tossing their torches through the broken glass.

James saw three or four Bow Street men beating out the flames inside the court. Could they save it? he wondered distractedly.

Suddenly another huge roar came from the man in the cart as it came crunching along the street.

"Newgate!" the man roared. "They've got some of our men in Newgate. Newgate ahoy!"

"It isn't possible," James breathed in a strange despair.

Now the rioters, maddened by success, surged in a solid mass toward Holborn until they came within sight of Newgate Prison. At their head was the man in the cart, and now his voice reached a volume it was hard to believe could come from human throat.

"Newgate! Open the gates and let the prisoners out. Break down the doors!"

As he roared the words, the Keeper appeared with six or seven of his men, all armed and ready for defiance; but suddenly a new sound came: the thud of running feet. Could this be the troops? James wondered. Then he saw a dozen men appear, not troops but constables and their deputies, lashing out with staves. At last all the justices had stirred.

"At them, men!" roared the man in the cart. "Cut them down!"

The rioters, armed with swords and knives, hammers and axes, pitchforks and iron bars, went forward like a solid phalanx. But James hardly noticed the horror that ensued.

He hardly noticed the way the constables were battered, their staves smashed and set alight; how the Keeper and his bodyguard were swept aside while the mob hacked at the bars of the huge prison, climbed the roof and beat great holes in it, set fire to the massive doors and finally broke in, met by a horde of prisoners bent only on escape.

He did not see the beginning of the fires which took hold of Newgate Prison and began its burning.

In his ears rang a single cry, uttered in the stentorian voice, yet with a cadence he could never forget.

"At them, men! Cut them down!"

"Cut them down!"

Cut—*him*—down!

The man in the cart was Johnny; his half brother Johnny, disguised with filthy wig and clothes that no one who knew him would recognise. But that one phrase had brought the truth home. James Marshall had no doubt at all.

The leader of the rioters was Johnny.

All over London fires raged. Everywhere, rioters surged and raped and pillaged. Prison after prison, great house after great house, were wrecked and set on fire. Two thousand more prisoners escaped from fetid jails and mixed with the mob, only a few trying to make their escape into the country. There was smallpox and cholera. There was jail fever. There was rioting and looting such as had not been seen in London since the Great Fire.

But at long last sufficient troops were summoned, it was said, by the King's command. Gradually they forced the rioters back and thinned their ranks; gradually the noise and fury abated.

While James, back in the House of Commons, was haunted day and night by one man's voice: the voice of his half brother.

"Ben, there is no doubt of it," James said on the morning of June 9, the first day after the back of the riots had been broken. "It *was* Johnny. And unless he is caught he will try to organise another revolt, another riot as bloody as this one."

"What do you want me to do?" Benedict Sly asked.

He had not slept except for odd hours during the whole seven days of the rioting. Now his eyes looked like glass, his cheeks were hollow, and his face had no colour at all. He had not washed and had hardly eaten. Nor had the men with him, setting type, running the machines, bundling up edition after edition as each came off the press.

348

"Print Johnny's likeness and name him as the ringleader," James replied.

"Must it be you who has to identify him?" Benedict asked heavily.

"I know of no one else who can," said James, "and no one else who should. I shall go to Furnival Tower House and tell them what I have done. And Ben—"

Benedict waited for him to go on.

"Ben," repeated James, "such a story should go to the other newspapers, too."

"On that we are agreed," Benedict acknowledged reluctantly. "No newspaper is keeping information of great significance to itself. It will be in all the papers, Jamey, with a likeness of Lord George Gordon alongside your brother's. And it will come in the same edition as Lord George Gordon's arrest and committal to the Tower on a charge of treason." He gripped James's shoulder. "I do not like your task, Jamey, but you have no choice."

"I am in full agreement," William Furnival said. "You have no choice, James."

"None whatsoever," Francis agreed.

"But you must give thought to one aspect of it," William went on very quietly. "It will cause your mother great hurt, even though she may agree on the need."

"Yes," James said slowly. "Yes, I know. And you are both very good."

"You are exhausted," Francis observed. "Will you not rest for a few hours, Jamey?"

"I wish I could," James replied, "and I am grateful. But I must take my seat in the House this afternoon. There is an early session. Then I must go to Chelsea. I have not been home since the first night of the riots. No, no, there is nothing to fear," he went on hastily. "The house has been well guarded and I have been able to send Mary a message every day."

"At least you will let us take you to Westminster by the river," insisted Francis.

Both the older men walked with James to the steps he had descended with Timothy on the night the new docks were opened. Both watched as he was rowed away, and he waited until they were out of sight before looking about him. On the river itself, crowded as ever, there was

349

no sign of the rioting, but along the north bank he could see great palls of smoke, while everywhere great smuts from the fires lay like black snow, as if the city had been sent into mourning.

The boat was to wait for him.

He walked to the Palace of Westminster and took his place among the other Members. Never had he seen the House so silent and so grim. Men who had never acknowledged him before spoke with courtesy, and some made their way toward him, saying, "Such a thing must not happen again, Marshall. Now we can see why you have fought so bitterly for a peace-keeping force."

But although at least a dozen said as much, a hundred growled their protest at the shooting of "innocent civilians" by the troops without a magistrate's order. They blamed the magistrates, the government, the high constables, the troops, but never once themselves for leaving the nation's capital open to such violence.

When James tried to say so, they shouted him down.

In the House of Lords at this same time, another man, Lord Shelburne, fought against the tide of popular opinion.

"The peace-keeping in Westminster is an imperfect, inadequate and wretched system," he declared. "It ought to be entirely new-modeled and this immediately. Recollect what the peace-keeping by the police of France is like. Examine its good but do not be blind to its evil."

The Lords turned on Shelburne.

"It is all evil. . . . There is no good in the French police. . . . Englishmen must be free. . . ."

While the bodies of seven hundred dead were collected from the streets and rain washed away the reek of blood, Sir John Fielding lay near death, mercifully unknowing that both Houses at Westminster were as bitterly opposed as ever to his great dream.

The river lapped against the jetty in sight of The House by the River, and the boatman handed him out and thanked him gravely for his shilling tip. Slowly James walked along the path toward his home, seeing two or three of the children in the orchard with one of the maids. At least six men stood in various places nearby: Simon Rattray's men, thought James, sent as protection against any marauding party from the rioters. Had Rattray's warning been heeded, the riots would never have got under way. As it was, and despite the initial reaction of the politicians, this might be the beginning of a new era, of a different attitude toward the problem of maintaining law and order.

James wondered idly why Rattray's men had not gone home; did they believe that danger remained?

He walked around to the side of the house and saw a single horse tied there but did not recognise it. Turning the key in the heavy side door, he pushed it open, exasperated because they had a visitor at a time when he had so wanted to be alone with Mary. Then alarm shot through him at the thought that this might be a messenger from St. Giles: such a messenger would only come with bad news. He heard Mary speaking, heard her finish.

"I tell you I have no idea when he will return. He has not been here for a week."

"Then he is not likely to be long," a man replied. "I shall wait, sister."

Only one man in the world would call Mary "sister" in that half-jeering way; and there was only one voice like that in the world.

Johnny's.

On the instant that he recognised Johnny's voice, James wondered: Are the men outside Simon's or Johnny's? There was no way of being sure, no way of knowing why Johnny was here. Closing the door, James glanced over his shoulder, sensing rather than hearing a presence, and felt a stab of fear as he saw a tall, heavily built man coming from the front room, head bent so that he could get under the lintel.

This was the giant who had been at his "hanging."

The man called out, "He's here, Mr. Furnival."

James heard Mary's sharp intake of breath, then a chair scraping on the boards, and a moment later Johnny called out in deep tones of satisfaction, "So he's arrived at last. Come in, half brother. Come in."

Heart thumping, James pushed open the door.

Johnny still sat in the chair but it was turned toward the door. He had never seemed so massive. He wore a flowered waistcoat worked in gold thread, a long jacket of dark-brown velvet, knee breeches and stockings to match; it was hard to believe this could have been the ragged, unkempt creature who had fanned the crowds to such violence. His face was wreathed in smiles but there was no humour in his eyes. Mary was standing by the tall fireplace, and there was fear in her.

351

"Don't drag your feet now. Come in, I tell you," Johnny said.

On the table by his elbow was a pistol, and beneath his outward relaxation was the strong suggestion of a lion about to pounce on its prey.

James walked on, the giant remaining in the doorway. He looked steadily at the younger man.

"This is the last place you should have come, Johnny."

"Others would say it was the first, half brother. Come in, Jamey, don't stand close to the door; Big Will might get you this time. I was just telling Mary of the occasion when you nearly got hanged, drawn and quartered. I should have let Rackham have his way with you. There's another thing, Jamey." Johnny placed his hands lightly on the arms of his chair and leaned his head back, cold light in his eyes negating the bright smile on his lips. "I was always fonder of you than any man or woman of my family. Why—I was going to bring my love to you and ask you and Mary to look after her while I was away, for I knew the metropolis would be too hot for me for a while. She is with child, Jamey! I am not a sterile creature after all. Isabella is to bear my child. And I wanted her with someone I could trust. In all innocence I was coming here when I was given a copy of *The Daily Clarion*. Have you seen a copy, half brother?"

"I know what is in it," James Marshall replied.

"Do you think that was a grateful thing to do?" Now Johnny stood up very slowly. He moved first to the table and picked up the pistol, then toward James. His lips were stretched taut across his teeth; no one could be deceived by his smile now. Taking a folded newspaper from his pocket, he spread it out so that James could see both picture and story. "Or would you call that *betrayal*, Jamey?"

"The only betrayal is yours," James returned heavily.

"What did I hear you say?"

"You have betrayed your father, your mother, your family, all—"

James broke off at the sudden change of expression on Johnny's face, at the hatred in his gaze, and on the instant Johnny flung newspaper and pistol aside and leaped at James with both arms outstretched. James clutched at Johnny's wrists but already iron fingers were tightening about his throat and the breath was being choked out of him.

There seemed no hope of life.

Then, through the mists of his mind, another voice sounded. Hands descended on Johnny Furnival, pulling him off. James, dimly seeing

Johnny swing around, suddenly realised that his half brother was face to face with Simon Rattray and that they were only a yard apart, whilst Big Will lay on the floor, blood running from a wound in his forehead.

Simon let Johnny go, and each drew farther from the other, but neither turned away, and neither uttered a word until Johnny said thinly, "Another of his bastards." Both men were breathing heavily, their lips and jaws set; it was as if each were looking at a reflection of himself in a mirror which stood between them.

Suddenly Johnny leaped.

He could have snatched at his gun. He could have seized a knife. Instead he flung himself bodily at Simon, who was ready to resist the onslaught and did no more than stand. For a few terrible moments there was a flailing of arms as Johnny groped for Simon's throat and Simon fended him off. Then, as suddenly as Johnny had leaped, Simon moved, thrusting both arms around the other in a mighty hug which brought a gasp from Johnny's lips and made his hands relax. With another swift movement Johnny tried to counter the pressure by driving his knee into Simon's groin but had no room in which to move. Simon did not ease the pressure but tightened it until Johnny began to gasp with pain and sweat gathered at his forehead and rolled down his cheeks.

Simon freed him, took one arm, then pulled him around so that instead of being face to face the one was behind the other. Johnny backheeled but there was no power in his kick, and the next moment Simon's right arm was across Johnny's neck, bending the head back— and farther back—and farther back still.

The crack of the breaking neck sounded throughout the room.

Mary uttered a groaning sound, went limp, and would have fallen but for James's support.

Slowly, slowly, Johnny's body crumpled, and Simon stood back and let him fall. Simon's chest was heaving, veins were swollen in his neck and forehead, and he stood without moving for what seemed a long time.

At last he turned to James, who had lowered Mary to a chair. There was a strange light in his eyes as he said hoarsely, "It was he or I. There was no other way." He moved toward the table and leaned on it with both hands, the colour gone from his face and the strength drawn from him as he looked up at James from beneath his brows and spoke with a great effort. "It is better—this way. The other way he would have gone—to some prison. He would have been tried and found guilty. He would have been hanged—perhaps worse than hanged. It is—much better this way."

James said, "I think that also."

"There is a—Furnival boat still at the landing stage. Shall he be sent to Furnival Tower House?"

"I know of no better place," James said. "No better place at all."

So many died in the riots that no one inquired into the manner of Johnny's death. He was buried in a City churchyard, and only James and his mother grieved.

Slowly the city recovered from the riots and the dead were buried; work had already started on rebuilding the houses and the prisons which had been burned down. Slowly the House of Commons returned to normal, its resistance to any creation of a peace force becoming, obtusely, even stronger. To James, the greatest tragedy of all was that Sir John Fielding was now too weak to take part in any new efforts to break down this resistance.

On that day in September when Sir John was buried with only a few to watch and mourn, James rode with Benedict Sly and Nicholas from the cemetery to the *Clarion* offices, where he read first the obituary, then a leading article in which Benedict had asked:

Who will be next to lead Bow Street?

Who will be next to work for the great ideals of this man who killed himself in the service of his fellow citizens and the city he loved? Let the government make the appointment of chief magistrate with great care, and let the people scrutinise Sir John Fielding's successor in the knowledge that their own future will be involved with it.

This great city will never be freed from the criminals who feed like vultures upon it until there is in being an incorruptible peacemaking force paid by the State and dedicated, as were the Fielding brothers and Sir John Furnival before them, to the war against crime.

James put the newspaper down and said slowly, "If Fielding could have read that he would have been a happy man."

Once again Benedict put a hand on his shoulder.

"There are other factors which would have made him happy, and should help to make you much happier, Jamey," he said quietly. "I have a report from a secret source at Westminster which says that the government is, after all, to use Bow Street as the first experiment in creating the force we need. They will pay for a foot patrol, and if it is successful in keeping law and order and reducing crime in the streets, they will extend it. There is opposition but little doubt that the plans will be approved. Do not be surprised if you are consulted, nor hurt if they neglect you. Politicians are notorious for their ingratitude."

"If they will do this, they can forget that I ever existed!" James cried.

CHAPTER 29

The Last Tyburn Hanging

"YOU UNDERSTAND that there will be strict limitations on what we are prepared to do," Lord North said to James the following week, "but the government feels that your knowledge of Bow Street and its—ah—unofficial methods in the past is so extensive that you can be of great assistance."

"You are most kind," James replied.

"The government is not unmindful of your endeavours even if at times it has regarded you as being—ahem—considerably ahead of your time. There is one other matter. It is the desire of the Sheriffs of London to put an end to public hanging and the subsequent rejoicing thereafter. Knowing of your deep convictions on the subject . . ."

This was a task James could work on with good heart.

Then he found in Sheridan, the playwright, an enthusiast for a new and coordinated force, heard him propose in the House of Commons that in the case of civil riot the Army should be available to intervene without the order of a civil magistrate.

"I am opposed to any alteration of our system of peace-keeping," the Solicitor General said in reply. "The Gordon Riots were a single instance of a defect in a civil power which in all probability will never occur again."

And the proposal was overwhelmingly defeated.

On the morning of July 1, 1783, more than two years later, James woke to sunshine streaming in at the window and to the noises of the children in the garden. Turning on his side, he saw Mary moving quietly across the room so as not to disturb him, and he called out. She came toward him, smiling, startlingly like the Mary he had seen that night when he had called on the Reverend Sebastian Smith.

She sat on the side of the bed, her hands in his, laughter lurking in her eyes as she said, "This is not a day for you to be late, Mr. Marshall."

"What is there to make me hurry?" he demanded.

"I do not believe that you have forgotten. This is the day of the last Tyburn Fair. Shame on you that you would dally on such a solemn occasion. I have been reading an article by our friend Benedict," she went on. "He is wryly amused by the great reform sponsored by the Sheriffs of London, Sir Barnard Turner and Thomas Skinner. What genius they have to put an end to the hangings in Tyburn and to have them instead outside the gates of Newgate Palace! And such solemn occasions hangings shall be, with the gallows to be draped in black and only a man of God to stand beside the condemned men and the hangman. Also, there is to be a drop, the floor giving way beneath them so that death is quick." She tightened her grip on James's hands and asked, "Do you think it will be an improvement, Jamey?"

After a pause he answered, "I think it will be a step forward, not a step back. I had not forgotten the day, my love."

"Did you desire to drown the memory in me, Mr. Marshall?"

"I think I wanted to be here with you when the accursed cart is moving," he said, "but—" He broke off, half frowning as he looked at her.

"Nay," she said. "For whenever we were together in bed we'd have the gallows for company. If you are not at Tyburn to watch the last hanging you will regret it, husband. You would be drawn there, whatever I say." She drew herself free and stood up, asking gently, "Would you have me with you, James?"

"No," he said most positively. "You are right and I should be there —but I should be alone."

357

He stood on the spot where he had come as a boy to watch Frederick Jackson hang.

He saw the hordes of people, many half drunk, the fashionable men and women in the stands, the price of which had doubled for this last great occasion. He saw those selling the "Last Words and Confessions" of many who could neither read nor write. He saw the orange and apple sellers, the sellers of pies and pasties, of sweetmeats and gin and lavender. He saw the cutpurses and the pickpockets; and he saw the six men hanged.

He did not see young Frederick Jackson, grandson of the first Frederick, who was present with his father.

He did not see Simon.

He did not see Timothy.

He watched the swinging bodies and the creaking carts carrying them to the new Butchers' Hall and to new hospitals where surgeons needed bodies on which to experiment and so learn to save lives. After he had turned away and walked for what seemed a very long time, he saw the house at Bow Street with strangers on duty both inside and out. The men of Bow Street no longer lived only on a share of blood money or of reward money; their livelihood now depended, at least in part, on their acceptance by the government.

In his mind's eye he saw the mob coming to tear the courthouse apart and burn it to the ground.

But there it still stood, the home of true justice, a house of hope for those who, if they were innocent, need fear no longer. A monument to miracles of achievement and an even greater monument to failure. It was utter madness that the growing metropolis, now spread far beyond the cities of London and Westminster, should be without a civil peace force. He must not cease to fight. He must harry whatever government at every opportunity, presenting the Ministers always with cold facts, the viciousness of corruption, the fact that justice could be bought and sold. . . .

A chill wind blew from Westminster, making him shiver.

BOOK III
1784–1829

CHAPTER *30*

A Promise of a Bill

"I REGRET the need for so constantly harassing you, sir," James Marshall said to William Pitt. "I have no doubt you will be weary of me. Yet I persist because the need is as great now—indeed, far greater—as it has ever been. With the press of population and the increasing number of soldiers back from Europe and America, many now without work, as well as increasing trade and prosperity, the present system of parish watch and constable is nigh on collapse. I dare remind you that at the time of the Gordon Riots four years ago—"

"Yes, I recall the subject," the Prime Minister interrupted with heavy sarcasm. "Nor am I unmindful of your persuasiveness or your pertinacity. I have discussed the matter further with Sir Archibald MacDonald, since it is within the province of the Solicitor General. He is to take advice from the magistrates at Bow Street and, of course, his own department, and on that advice prepare a bill which shall be submitted to the House of Commons as soon as practicable. I have no doubt that Sir Archibald will both need and welcome your guidance, and I trust the issue will be favourable. Good day to you, sir."

As if he had conveyed a message by some unseen means, a tap came at the door of Pitt's office in Westminster, and he rose from his padded chair, tall, strangely supercilious in manner. A secretary came hurrying in, wig askew, and James Marshall could do no more than bow and stammer his thanks.

"I—I am overwhelmed, sir. The—the—the nation will be grateful."

Pitt did not seem to hear him, and the moment James had finished the word "grateful" the secretary began to speak. James, escorted by a youthful flunky in uniform, went out of this part of the Palace to the lobbies with which he was more familiar and where a few Members stood about talking as they waited for interviews with Ministers or for committees.

At that moment James was in no condition to talk to anyone; all he could think of was getting into the open air, by himself, and repeating the incredible tidings . . . "prepare a bill which shall be submitted to the House of Commons as soon as practicable."

A bill—a peacemakers', or a police, *bill!*—prepared on the advice of the Bow Street magistrates! Drawn up by the Solicitor General! As the fullness of the truth burst upon him he wanted to shout *"A bill. There is to be a police bill!"* at the top of his voice. His excitement showed in his eyes and on his face, and several Members stopped to point at him, while one called out: "Hast come into a fortune, Jamey?" Once again it was on the tip of his tongue to cry "There is to be a police bill, glory be to God!" when a man appeared at his side, the disheveled secretary who had entered the Prime Minister's room as James was leaving. The man's wig was set even more on one side and his breathlessness was greater.

"Mr. Marshall, an urgent matter," he whispered hoarsely, close to James's ear.

James looked at him uncomprehendingly, beginning to realise that he must regain his composure.

"Mr. Marshall, I come to you with an urgent message," the secretary declared earnestly. "Mr. Pitt asks that you keep this matter in strict confidence until such time as the details have been decided and the form of the bill assured."

"In—*strict* confidence?"

"In absolute confidence, sir, lest its opponents be able to plan the bill's defeat even before it is presented."

"I understand," James assured him, relieved that the message had caught up with him in time.

"Have I your assurance, sir?"

"My absolute assurance," James replied, and suddenly he smothered a laugh, for this man, who had obviously been sent rushing after him because the Prime Minister had been too preoccupied to enjoin him to silence, would never dream that two minutes later he would have come upon James Marshall, M.P., doing a jig. As it was, James went out of the chamber and into Whitehall walking on air.

The huddle of buildings which crowded upon Westminster Palace had lost its dilapidated appearance, and even the alehouses close by the main entrance, where too many Members repaired not only for refreshment but to dally with wenches beneath the crooked upstairs ceilings, were places of beauty. He was tempted to go into Minus, his favourite coffee house in the area, but other Members were sure to be there, mostly in heated discussion, and seeing his preoccupation would begin to harry him with questions. For the first time he regretted the need for silence.

Instead, he went toward Westminster Bridge and stood close to the Royal Steps, looking for a chair. He must sit quietly for a few moments, giving himself a chance to calm his excitement before he reached the offices of *The Daily Clarion*. For there was one man on whom he could rely: Benedict Sly could be trusted even with State Secrets, and indeed, on occasions, he had been.

James *had* to talk to someone.

"I could not be more pleased and excited," Benedict declared, as they sat together in his Fleet Street office, which was both private and quiet. "I could not congratulate you more, Jamey. I hope they will consult you closely and not put too much faith in today's Bow Street magistrates, who are not remotely of the same caliber as the Fieldings. How I wish the Fieldings were alive to know of this!" He appeared to be overcome with satisfaction. "If there is any way at all that I can help be sure I will."

From Fleet Street James went by hackney to Chelsea. Many buildings had been recently erected in the Strand and much activity was going on about Somerset House. The contrast between the magnificence of this palace and the huddle of hovels opposite it, hemming in the ancient church of St. Mary-le-Strand, was as unbelievable as it was incongruous.

Out by the gates of Hyde Park he had his hackney stop at an apple stall, buying some apples to munch instead of going into the nearby

Hercules Pillars for a mug of ale and a pie. Here and there, beyond the park, many houses were being built, and the farms and farmland were severely reduced in area, but this was not James's day for bemoaning the inroads of the city on the countryside.

He reached his Chelsea house in soft rain falling from skies which seemed to become heavier every moment. To his relief, none of his children or grandchildren appeared, and he found Mary sitting in his big chair, reading the newspapers which had been delivered since he had left for Westminster. Startled at his early return, she turned to look at him with an obvious anxiety which instantly faded at sight of the elation in his eyes. When she took his hands, he held hers with great firmness.

Before he spoke, she said, "You have talked with Mr. Pitt and he has seen the light at last! Is that what has brought you?"

"He has not only seen the light, he has enjoined me to silence about it. Had he known how quickly my wife could read my mind he would have known that was a waste of time!"

"Oh, Jamey, Jamey, I am so glad for you," she cried, and as if without conscious effort added, "and for London, for everyone. Oh, Jamey, if only the Fieldings could know!"

He pulled her to her feet, held her close, and kissed her . . . and quite suddenly they were stripped of their years and they were together in the flesh and in the spirit as closely and as perfectly as they had ever been.

When, afterward, they lay together in the four-poster which had been so much trouble to move from the house in the Strand, James felt a deep contentment which her very stillness told him that she shared. Suddenly he heard cries from below; some of the grandchildren had arrived.

"Keep quiet and pretend you are not here," James urged Mary lazily.

"They would think the world had come to an end," she protested.

Watching her dress, James pondered what she had said.

"So their world would come to an end if you were not here to welcome your grandchildren?" he mused.

More cries followed his words, and, distinctly, the call "Grandmamma!" came from below.

"You take me too seriously, Mr. Marshall," Mary laughed.

"Not seriously enough," he replied. "If you weren't here *my* world would be at an end, Mary."

364

"Oh, tush!" she exclaimed, but there was pleasure in her eyes.

As the door opened the sound of voices calling "Grandmamma! Grandmamma!" billowed out more loudly; when she closed it behind her, her responding call came clearly.

And to think he had nearly lost her, James recalled with strange tension. He had gone that night to her father's house and had been so attracted that he had persuaded her to postpone taking the post of housekeeper to the Weygalls—and then he had turned away from her. It would have been so easy for her to have met and married someone else. He had nearly thrown his future away.

These musings still hovered in his mind when he heard a scream from below of such piercing shrillness that it set his heart pumping and made him spring to his feet. There was great commotion as he hurried to the stairs, servants rushing, womenfolk running, one mother whose voice he could not identify crying, "Stay absolutely still. Don't move, child. *Don't move!*"

What was it? Some unsuspected danger from a feared creature; a rat, perhaps? Then he came to a spot on the stairs where he could see a ring of women and children with one small boy standing in the middle, black from head to foot. Behind him was a trail of black footprints. His face was so smeared that his eyes seemed abnormally bright.

"How on earth did you do it?" cried his mother, Esther, frantic at the sight.

Mary was kneeling in front of the lad, far more reassuring than the excitable mother, while James called out, making everyone turn around like so many puppets on the same string.

"It is the price of progress," he declared. "There is some experimenting on tarred and macadamed roads nearby and—and—and"—*what was the child's name?*—ah!—"and Charles has obviously stumbled on one of the stretches where tar has been spread. Your sense of smell surely indicates that."

"But how are we going to get him *clean?*"

"Grandmamma will wash me," small Charles declared, and a general laugh followed. Mary, who had sent a maid for an apron, wrapped this around herself and picked the child up.

"What did you use to clean the boy?" asked James later in the evening.

"There is a new soap which lathers badly but cleans well," Mary replied. "Thank goodness I didn't have to rub him raw."

James, in high spirits, laughed with satisfaction at his wife's skill. It did not take much to make him laugh that day.

The rapture of the day was soon lost, however, in anxiety and uncertainty. James did not understand what went on about the proposed bill during the next months. Secrecy was one thing but to hide what was happening from him was surely carrying secrecy too far. He was not summoned to the meetings which, he learned, were taking place between MacDonald and the Bow Street justices, and on the several occasions when he attempted to see the Solicitor General at Westminster he was rebuffed.

Distressed by the situation but not prepared to make any formal request for information, he buried himself in his other House of Commons duties. Whenever a plea for assistance was made from one of the parishes, he was summoned to advise. Whenever a new charitable institution was formed, one which should be free from all obligations of tax, he was placed on the investigating committee. He became so busy that at times he wondered whether this was done deliberately to prevent him from taking a deeper interest in the police bill. The idea was less absurd when, one day nearly a year after Pitt had made his great concession, and as James was just about to leave for Westminster by the river, a carriage appeared at the side of the house and a servant came hurrying after him.

"It is a Mr. Sly, sir, who begs leave to see you."

Benedict? wondered James. Or Nicholas? Had there been some disaster at the premises of "Mr. Londoner" in the Strand? He turned back from the garden, where he had been walking on a rain-sodden path toward the mist-shrouded river, and saw that it was Benedict. Benedict's beard was as thick and close-cut as ever but instead of being jet-black it was now uniformly gray. They met in the red-tiled hall and James drew his old friend into the small room which he used as a study.

Benedict was seldom perturbed and as seldom showed his emotions but there was no doubt of his distress.

"James, I now have an explanation of why you have not been consulted over the police bill for London," he stated without preamble. "The bill proposes to put all authority for the police and the maintenance of law into the hands of the three justices of Bow Street. The other magistrates in London will be under them, and will lose money by receiving salaries instead of fees. Can you be surprised that the magistrates, except those who now lord it over Bow Street, are cold toward you, since no doubt they believe you have inspired this?"

James, standing by the side of a big chair, felt as if all the blood in his veins had been chilled. Most certainly he needed no more explanation. From the days when his stepfather had first conceived the idea of a police force paid for by the State, it had been assumed that the administration of the police, as of justice, should be in the hands of those who were most closely associated with the processes of the law and had the methods necessary to apprehend criminals and to discourage them. In the manner now suggested, the apprehension of criminals and the administration of justice would be under the same control, but there was not a justice outside Bow Street who would not fight such a bill bitterly. James had no words with which to answer Benedict, but he raised a hand in a helpless gesture, as if the news were too much for him to bear.

Mary appeared in the doorway. She did not speak, not even to welcome Benedict, but her expression showed that she had heard enough to be deeply concerned. James glanced at her and forced a smile.

At last he said, "So all but the Bow Street justices are to be reduced in authority?"

"Yes. And the most bitter opponent is Sir Douglas Rackham," answered Benedict. "It is said he will resign the magistracy of Westminster Courthouse and go to the House of Commons to fight what he calls these iniquities."

James did not know Rackham well. He was a distant relative of Jacob Rackham but that could hardly be held against him. His reputation was that of a decisive man without sentiment, who applied the law strictly to the letter and with little regard for circumstances. It was not surprising that he would fight against being passed over, for Sir Sampson Wright and Sir William Aldington, now at Bow Street, were not men of great stature, and Thomas Gilbert was even less impressive.

"The concept is that the other justices should administer justice, not control the police or any form of police, such as the parish constables or the Bow Street Runners; the police would be controlled, as I have said, by three salaried commissioners. The whole of the metropolitan area of London would be divided into nine divisions, each with its own chief constable, and"—Benedict paused and drew a deep breath, as if fully aware that he was about to deliver his next bombshell—"the

367

City would be one of these divisions. All its present powers would be withdrawn, its effective system of law enforcement would be destroyed, and the City itself would have no say in the administration of the force or of the numbers of constables employed or—"

"But this is madness!" exploded James. "The City will be up in arms the moment it learns of those last provisions. No one with any awareness of the opinions of City bankers and merchants would contemplate such a force. Why, the City must have as many constables and peace officers as the rest of the metropolis put together! To reduce such an organisation to the status of one-ninth, and that ninth without any real authority, is—I tell you there is but one word for it: madness!"

"I will go along with that," Benedict agreed. He began to pace the room, continuing to talk as he did so, speaking with great vehemence. "It is now abundantly clear why MacDonald gave you a wide berth. He knew you would try to prevent this, for you are known to be related by marriage to the Furnivals, suspected of having one foot in the City and the other in Westminster. You know what has really inspired this—this—"

"Wickedness," Mary put in very quietly. It was the first word she had uttered, but both tone and expression reflected her anger. "Wickedness, mixed with folly and ignorance. And largely born out of the hatred Westminster has for the City."

"You could not be more right!" Benedict spoke warmly, paused as he looked at her, and for the first time since he had arrived his expression softened. "Mary, how clearly you get to the heart of the matter! I am not sure we should not turn you loose on Mr. Pitt and his colleagues! How can a man of such wisdom in some affairs be so blind in others?"

"Because he does not give such matters as this sufficient thought," James answered, and he too was calmer although still deeply troubled. "How did you find these things out, Ben?"

"I have seen a copy of the bill," Benedict replied. "It is still a matter for shame how many Members of Parliament, indeed, Ministers of the Crown, will betray their oaths of secrecy for a sum of money. James, I wonder if you see the dangers which go even beyond what we have discussed."

"I think I do," replied James. "Once this bill is published the City will blame me for the hostile provisions in it. I shall have few friends in either camp." He gave a half laugh. "One thing is now clear. I must see Timothy and tell him of this before he hears it from some other source. And I shall tell the Prime Minister that I now feel released from my oath of silence—if oath it was. Ben"—James held both hands toward his friend—"I cannot tell you how grateful I am. Had my first intimation been at the reading of the bill in the House of Commons I could never have repaired the damage." He gripped Benedict's hands tightly.

And Mary said quietly, "God bless you, Ben."

"Enough sentiment!" Benedict tried to sound gruff but could not prevent his voice from cracking. "Are you coming to the City with me, Jamey?"

"Without losing a moment," James said.

Since William's death, Timothy McCampbell had taken his place as chairman of the companies of the House of Furnival, a slender, youthful-looking man for one who was now in his late fifties. His hair, although graying, had much of its original fair color and his complexion was fresh and pleasing.

Known now as Timothy McCampbell-Furnival, he advanced across the landing to welcome James, ushered the other into his office, motioned to a chair, and, as he himself sat down, remarked soberly, "I can see you come on heavy business, Jamey."

"Business I wish were nonexistent," James replied, "and business which is for the moment highly confidential. I came because I do not want you to believe that I have taken leave of my senses or have developed some bitter animosity toward the City."

"I am vastly intrigued," Timothy said. "Can you give me a hint of what the business is?"

"I shall give you much more than a hint. Timothy, has rumour reached you of the preparation at Westminster of a bill which, if passed, will establish a police force for the whole metropolis of London, including the City?"

"Rumour, yes—with your name attached."

"As I feared." James sighed. "That is what I am most anxious to make you understand. I am doubtless responsible—or partly responsible—for the principle of the forthcoming bill and that will hardly surprise you. Until today, however, I had no intimation of its provisions."

Timothy raised both hands in obvious amazement. "You mean that

Pitt and his Minister did not consult you in the drafting of the bill?" he asked, leaning forward and thumping his desk, his voice rising. "It is a monstrous insult, Jamey. I did not expect to lose my respect for Pitt but such an act as this could only be done by a poltroon! What on earth could have possessed him?"

Heartened by Timothy's anger, James began to tell his story. The effect on Timothy was much the same as that of Benedict's recital on James only two hours earlier, although Timothy continually interrupted with exclamations of disgust and indignation. Yet when the whole story was told he was bereft of words. After a while he rose from his chair and strode to a window, threw it open, and stared out over the panorama of the City. James, understanding what was in his mind, left him there for a minute or two and then joined him.

Timothy's whole body tensed and his voice was unsteady when he said, "You know I will have to fight this with all my power, don't you, James?"

"Yes."

"And the other bankers, merchants, aldermen, everyone who lives in the City, will fight it, if necessary with their lives."

"I don't think it need come to warfare," James said, and to his surprise and relief he actually laughed.

"It is not a laughing matter," Timothy rebuked. "This is why all my family and friends have opposed the very thought of such a force, why it is anathema to us. Not only would the politicians ride roughshod over the City's ancient rights and privileges, but they would weaken us so that we would never again be able to stand against them. You do not realise how much you owe to the City, James. You—"

"I know the City could not possibly permit this," James interrupted. "And if the bill were to be presented to the House in its present form I should have to vote against it." With a twisted smile which did not conceal the hurt he felt, he went on: "So I wish you good fortune in making sure that the bill is not debated!"

"I shall make the task my first, and that in spite of the fact that I scarce know which way to turn for work. You would be surprised how often I wish you had decided to come into Furnival's! We need men of stature on whom we can rely. It had never occurred to me that being in command of such an organisation would carry with it such responsibility."

When he left, James was calmer in his mind and much more reflective than he might have expected. Timothy's last cry had unquestionably risen from the heart.

For three weeks the bill came under remorseless pressure from the City, from the Middlesex and Surrey justices, and from every newspaper of substance in London. It was damned on all sides until finally Pitt, admitting a technical error in the originating and presentation of the bill, withdrew it before the House had opportunity to debate it.

"I don't know how deep the hurt will go," Benedict Sly said to Mary on the day the bill was withdrawn. "James knows, and many others must know, that had he been allowed to draw up the bill based on the detailed proposals of the Fieldings it might have had some success, certainly a debate strong enough to register deeply on the public mind. But this wipes out the very thought for a generation, perhaps for generations, to come."

"The hurt will go so deep that he will grow busier than ever to heal the wound quickly," Mary replied. "Ben, I can understand the folly, I can understand the long-standing jealousy between the City and Westminster, but I cannot understand men like Sir Douglas Rackham. Why should such men fight a measure which their intelligence and experience must tell them will be of great value?"

"It will be of much *less* value to them," James said, coming in quietly. "The most difficult task will be to overcome the few who profit out of things as they are. Wherever there are rich and powerful criminals, there will be those corrupt enough to be bought by them."

There was another man in London who had been savagely opposed to the bill, one Todhunter Mason, a young man who had become the leader of a powerful gang of thieves and cutthroats at least as deadly and dangerous as the Twelves of earlier years, and in some ways much more menacing to society. For whereas the earlier gang leaders and the most notorious thief-takers had been commonly known, many boasting of their achievements in the manner of Jonathan Wild, and had satisfied themselves with a small band of ruthless followers, Mason kept his own part secret, using members of his gang to organise thieves, receivers of stolen goods, coiners, prostitutes, everyone who was on the wrong side of the law. He saw the possibility of controlling most of the criminals of London by offering them help, hiding places when on the run, a ready market for whatever they stole, and organised attacks on the Bow Street Foot Patrols to make sure there was little danger for robbers when they broke into houses or held up carriages.

The son of a now prominent member of the City who did not know he existed and of a Lincolnshire girl long since dead, he had clung to life through the horrors of an orphan childhood, living by his wits, often within an ace of the gallows but never caught. He knew the conditions of London as few knew them. Although only twenty, he was familiar with all the thieves and their doxies, and he had a good, clear mind which was never bothered—and why should it be?—by a twinge of conscience. He did not know how he had come by the name Todhunter but his other name, Mason, had been given because for several years he had lived in a rat-infested shack in a stonemason's yard near the river.

He could not know that he and Sir Douglas Rackham made an identical resolve after the defeat of the police bill: to make sure that no others would be presented.

"There is one aspect of the bill I would like to think more upon," James told Benedict a few months later, when they were together in the Rialto Coffee House on the Adelphi terrace, overlooking the river on a blustery day when wind whipped the surface to anger. "And that is the provision which would separate the justices from the police. When I first heard of it I was appalled, but the more I consider it the greater its attraction."

"There isn't a justice in England who would agree with you," Benedict reminded him.

"I think the ferocity of their opposition gave me most cause to think," said James. "What have they to lose, Ben? Simply money? As justices administering the law they would get salaries and some allowances, as they do now, and in the course of time, no doubt more. They would lose some of the more arduous tasks and more irksome responsibilities, yes, but would such losses in themselves create such a furor?"

After a pause, Benedict picked up his mug, drank deeply, and said in a musing voice, "Could you imply that they might also lose their *power?*"

"What else but power, or authority? They should have sufficient with administering the law, but as things are they are responsible for the police, the constables, the keeping of law and order, the keeping of the King's peace. Should that really be under the control of those whose task it is chiefly to say whether the law has been broken, and if it has, what punishment shall be meted out?"

"I confess this aspect has never occurred to me," said Benedict.

"Nor to me until now. But— Well, I will consider the issue very deeply," James declared. "Because inherent in this may be the root cause of opposition to a police force. It may be that the truly honest opponents do not want to feel that the justices should be given power over a wide area. The success of Bow Street has always seemed to me proof of the value of such a force, but if it means accepting more widespread authority for certain justices, then can one be so surprised at the adamancy of the City? I tell you, I have come to believe that before a police force is established in London the cause of the opposition from the City must be found and removed. Timothy McCampbell-Furnival made it crystal clear that the City would actually mobilise its guards and constables if its self-government were threatened."

"I once quoted a City alderman as saying that 'no greater alarm would have been caused if a torch had been set to the Royal Exchange and the Mansion House,'" Benedict said slowly.

"So the rich reject a police force to maintain the law, whilst condemning charity to the poor and thus making crime inevitable," said James. "Ben, I recall wondering how we could win and I came to the conclusion that we must find a way of introducing the police so that the leaders of the City will *not* object. The rest of the opposition will probably melt away if once they agree."

"What you are really saying is that you desire to create a police force the City would support—or even, if it had the wit, wish to create." Benedict laughed. "To James Marshall *all* things are possible! Meanwhile, I came agog with other news before you took my breath away with this. The Dublin Parliament is said to be considering Pitt's bill for itself. Now there is irony, Jamey—more law and order in Ireland than in old England." When they had finished laughing at such improbability, Benedict went on: "James, there is to be a special banquet for newspapermen on the ninth of July."

"On the ninth of July, this year and every year, I am irrevocably engaged," replied James. "It is Mary's birthday, and we celebrate the day as if it were the birthday of everyone in the family. And the next is one of unusual importance because all the grandchildren are coming. *Grandchildren*, Benedict! Where have the years gone to? How quickly they have passed. But they've been happy years, and I have been truly blessed in having Mary for a wife. If I could only bring Pitt and his Ministers to their senses, I should be well satisfied."

When he reached The House by the River that night, about his usual time, he saw a lathered horse outside and sensed the urgency of the messenger who, judging from the warmth of the horse's neck, had come within the hour. He did not recognise the young man who came from the house, but from Mary's expression, just behind the man, he could tell the news was bad.

"I deeply regret it, sir," the young man said. "I am assistant to Doctor Leonardi at Saint Giles, and I come with grievous tidings."

Before the man uttered the next words, James felt sure that his mother was dead.

Ruth had seemed well and happy when he had last seen her, and the news struck James deeply.

One of the infants brought to St. Giles for succour had been suffering from smallpox. Ruth Marshall Furnival, who had first handled the child, insisted that only she could nurse it through the illness; and she herself had suffered the fever in its most virulent form. The messenger, away at the time of the tragedy, had been told at a distance what had happened and where to come with his tidings.

The infant was recovering, he reported. No one else had been infected, and both Henrietta and her husband, Dr. Leonardi, were distressed but well.

No one must visit the house for at least two weeks, and long before that time Ruth Furnival would have been devoured in flames kindled in a pit dug into the hillside beyond St. Giles.

Slowly the gap left by his mother's death began to lessen, partly due to Benedict Sly, who would hustle James out to see a cricket match at the new ground opened by a Yorkshireman named Lord or would send him two tickets for the Drury Lane Opera House or to Covent Garden Theatre with a note saying: "Edmund Kean is magnificent in this" or "You will never forget Sarah Siddons' performance, I promise you." So James would take Mary to the theater and afterward to supper. She sat enthralled at the performances; he really believed she enjoyed playgoing more than any other outing.

Occasionally, too, she relished a day at the races, for the sake of the picnic and the great crowds and the side shows which never ceased to make the children ecstatic. James viewed the colourful scene more realistically.

"One hundred thieves were there to every constable, watchman or peace officer," he remarked in disgust when they left a racecourse in July. "If the King had been here the story would have been very different."

Almost three months to a day after making this remark he was walking along Whitehall toward Parliament when he heard the trotting of horses and some sporadic outbursts of cheering, which told him the State Coach was approaching with the King inside. Then suddenly a roar came from thousands of throats as a group of men burst out of side streets and doorways, throwing bricks and trying to rock the coach and push it over.

"The guards managed to keep the crowd at bay; they say the King was purple in the face when he reached safety, offered a thousand pounds for the arrest of those involved, and harangued the magistrates to keep better control of riots," Benedict reported.

Would no one *ever* understand that a strong force of peace-keepers, of policemen trained to deal with crowds, was the only sure way to control such outbursts *and* the drunkenness? thought James bitterly.

Half the fires—perhaps more—were caused by drunken men knocking over lamps or striking flints carelessly.

"Let me show you why," said Benedict Sly one day, when James was taking him on a quick tour of the City and nearby. Here and there was a good brick building, but for the main part they were wooden buildings, dry as tinder. And in some streets every other house was licensed to sell alcohol.

"You know," James remarked as they turned a corner in High Street, Shadwell, "they *are* dreadful places. And yet, compared with the days when you and I were young, much *has* improved. There are fewer slums, less utter destitution—"

"Stop talking like a Tory," growled Benedict as the carriage pulled up and two boys rushed to take the horse, one of them filthy and in rags, one almost clean.

"Good morning, Mr. Marshall."

"Good morning, sir!"

James touched the dirty head as well as the clean one.

Inside the coffee house they entered were the usual advertising posters, more crude than those in the City and West End, but tables, chairs and floor were scrubbed and the newspapers were clean. A little pot-bellied man came forward, smiling a welcome.

"Good morning, Mr. Marshall. What is your pleasure?"

"Coffee, Dan, just coffee—eh, Ben?"

"I wouldn't object to a steak pie," Benedict said.

"And coffee and a steak pie for Mr. Sly."

The potbellied man went off and James turned back to Benedict.

"You have just seen Daniel Ross, one of the few trading justices in London who won't accept a share of reward or blood money, and I would as soon see him at one of the police offices as any magistrate I know."

Ross had obviously heard the remark as he passed on the order to a young waitress, and he came to the table and drew up a chair.

"Wouldn't have one of those jobs for a fortune," he declared. "Not for a fortune. Do you know what those magistrates have to do, gentlemen? Judge and jury in a hundred cases a week—it's only the serious ones like murder and high treason and fraud they send on to the Sessions. Why, they have to decide if a man's guilty and pack him off to jail—summary jurisdiction, they call it, don't they?"

He paused when three mugs of coffee and one hot pie in a pottery dish were placed on the table, then, as Benedict ate and James drank, he went on:

"And they've got to license public houses, issue search warrants, frame orders to parish officers, and decide such matters as parish removals, the billeting of soldiers, applications for admission to workhouses or for other assistance, and hundreds of other problems. And if that's not enough, they're the heads of the police in the district. No, sir, none of that's for me. I like to sleep at night."

"I have a belief that you do sleep," Benedict said.

"Fair to middling, sir, fair to middling, if I don't start worrying. Why, it couldn't snow on Saint Paul's Churchyard without flakes falling on one thief in every two."

"If you feel like this, why are you a trading justice?" asked Benedict.

"One simple reason—very simple. If I wasn't here there would be someone else a lot worse."

When the two men left the coffee house the two boys were waiting in a light drizzle, still watching the horse.

Benedict Sly said unbelievingly, "How do you find such characters, James?"

"I keep my eyes open," James replied. He gave each boy a penny, then, pausing before the filthy one, he asked, "Is your father still in Marshalsea Prison?"

"Yes, sir," the boy replied brightly. "He keeps going in and he keeps coming out, sir."

As this dialogue was taking place, the door of a shop next door opened with the loud clanging of a bell and a big, bearded man with a peg leg stood in the doorway, grinning. The small window was crammed with odds and ends from ship's breakers' yards, and as they drew nearer, Benedict saw that the shop itself was even more crowded; there was scarce room to move.

"Well, I'll be blowed down, sir, I'll be blowed down if it ain't the Prime Minister himself," Peg Leg said. "I bin hoping you'd come, sir, come upon a find I did." He lowered his great voice to a hoarse whisper. "Coins, m'lud, coins from an old ship sunk in the estuary. Come and see, Mr. Prime Minister." He winked behind thick curly eyebrows at Benedict Sly and went on: "Glad to know you sir. Glad to make the acquaintance of any of the Prime Minister's friends. And if he isn't the Prime Minister then he ought to be, sir, that's what I say."

The shop stank with mildew and wood rot, but here and there a polished brass rail or a clean hurricane lamp, a ship's wheel or a pair of lamp holders, showed brightly from fresh burnishing against light from candles at the back of the shop, which gave an eerie effect. Stepping over rusty metal, old ropes, rotting wood, rotting sailcloth and canvas, Peg Leg at last reached a corner where a cupboard was fastened with a huge padlock. He opened this with a rusty key, then took out a box of coins and held them up to a candle.

"There they be, Mr. Prime Minister. Old Roman coins if you ask me."

"They are no more Roman than they are ancient British, and you are well aware of it," replied James. He poked among the coins, picked out two or three, examined them through a glass he took from his pocket, and then said, "They are Dutch, I think, Polycarp—old Dutch, perhaps. I don't know their value. I'll give you two pounds for them all or take them away and put them in 'Mr. Londoner' and give you half what I get for them."

Polycarp was breathing hard as he listened, hesitated, and then said, "It's not that I don't need the money, Mr. Prime Minister, but I'll do better with half the price you get. If I run very short of cash, can I come and collect the two pounds?"

"Yes. At any time."

"Then it's a deal," affirmed Polycarp, and he began to scoop the coins into a canvas bag. "Things are bad, I don't mind admitting, and why you and them other Members of Parlyment is thinking of paying for them river police I'll never know. Look what it'll cost. Five thousand pounds for the river guard, over four thousand for the quay guard, and that's only the start of it. It's robbery."

"I shouldn't worry too much about it, Polycarp," soothed James. "The merchants would have to pay for all of this, and it keeps the river safe from thieves." He struck an attitude which startled Benedict and alarmed the other. "Do you pay *your* share for the protection? You use the Port of London, don't you?"

After a shocked silence Peg Leg managed to say, "A joke's a joke, Mr. Prime Minister, but you don't have to frighten the wits out of an honest man."

Driving back toward the Strand, Benedict Sly said after a long silence, "You are a difficult man to know, James. Have you others like that tucked away?"

"In every part of London, although they are two of the best," James said. "Ben, I never understand it but I am more at peace in this part of London than anywhere else except Chelsea. There is something about the docks which fascinates me."

As they drove through thick traffic near St. Paul's, Benedict said quietly, "He was wrong to call you Prime Minister, James. Mr. Londoner is the perfect name for you."

CHAPTER *31*

The Party

ONCE AGAIN it was Mary's birthday, and the party was at full swing.

James Marshall, sitting in the massive armchair which his grand-father had made nearly eighty years before and which on this occasion had been brought onto the terrace, watched the pageant of the river and the children playing in the orchard and heard the laughter in the house behind him. How many grandchildren had he, now? Sometimes he forgot! He began to recall them in a desultory way, less because he was keenly interested than because he was mildly exasperated with himself for not remembering.

Jimmy had four—no, five, children. Jimmy, his and Mary's first-born, whom he hardly remembered as a child and with whom he had spent such little time. Jimmy had been born in 1756; my goodness, he had a son of forty, who had married at seventeen, some of whose children were married and living in faraway places, one in Australia and one in America. One did not have to be a jailbird or felon to settle in the colonies any longer, and one did not have to be a rebel to prefer America to England.

James's thoughts began to wander. It had taken him years really to recover from the fiasco of the police bill, years in which street robberies inside the built-up area of the metropolis became so numerous that the Bow Street Foot Patrols were extended, five new patrols being used to patrol the London streets, as well as the eight which continued to work outside. But all these worked by night; the government ignored the rising crime by day.

Yet what a success to have the government accept responsibility for all thirteen patrols in—when was it?—1790, that was it, April 1790. His memory was not so bad after all! And two years later had come a further development which would have delighted the Fieldings and John Furnival. Another private Member and he, with support from Pitt, got the Middlesex Justices Act through the House of Commons. There were to be in all seven "public offices," each with three magistrates who would be paid for their services and not permitted to accept other fees. Moreover, each office was to have six officers, like the Bow Street Foot Patrols, who would be paid twelve shillings a week and also expenses. All of these men were still free to receive rewards for successful prosecutions, and many earned a substantial sum.

A great move forward, but with drawbacks, for there was no central control, each office worked autonomously; and the small fee led to corruption among some men. Sir Douglas Rackham had led the opposition to the bill, but the House was against him, despite his cold, detached case against paid justices and the fact of his own resignation from the bench in order, he declared, to concentrate on work in the House of Commons.

"If ever there were a rascal, that man is one," James said aloud. "But I will say one thing for the man: he never seems to grow a day older. I wish I could say the same about myself!"

Now, not far away, a young man was walking across the garden toward him. Reaching a brick wall, he sat on it, his legs dangling, his gaze on his grandfather. This young man, first son of Jimmy, had inherited his grandfather's hooked nose and thrusting chin, his high forehead and the well-defined lips which even James's heavy white mustache and mutton-chop side whiskers could not disguise.

Seeing him, James's thoughts returned to his children. Jimmy, then, now in full charge of "Mr. Londoner" and with five children of his own.

Next came Charles, handsome in a way which had caused much bother before his marriage to Muriel Weygalls, the youngest of the Weygalls family. Both of Charles's children were boys.

Aloud, James asked, "How many then, so far? Five, six, *seven* grandchildren."

The young man on the wall stopped swinging his legs and watched and listened intently.

"And next, Dorothy," James said, loud enough for his grandson to hear.

Dorothy, the only one of his children at all like dark-haired Henrietta, and whose two children had died in early infancy. Just how deeply Dorothy felt about this James did not know; outwardly she was always calm and composed.

And lastly, Jonathan, thought James.

He had wanted to name their fourth child David, after David Winfrith, who up to the time of the boy's birth had played such an important part in their lives, but for some reason that he never understood Mary had been adamantly opposed to this. They had compromised with Jonathan, who, as he grew older, became more and more like his grandfather Sebastian Smith. Like Sebastian he had gone into the Church, and now had a living on the south bank of the Thames almost directly across the river from where James sat; James could see the spire of his church standing straight as a needle stabbing the sky.

Seven and eight makes fifteen—*fifteen* grandchildren, mused James.

The wind off the river grew fresher, but he did not move. Between the houses he saw the small craft, the barges, some gaily bedecked coasters which reminded him of the great pageant of nearly fifty years ago. Well, forty-five! How strange it was to realise that one was nearly sixty-seven, so much older than most of one's friends when they died. Nicholas Sly had been gone for ten years, but Benedict was still alive, although crippled by some disease of the bones which made walking impossible and movement difficult. And Mary, thank God, his Mary was still alive on yet another "family" birthday, like an extension of himself, still spry, still able to smile readily and to tease more wickedly than most. None of the children or grandchildren really took after Mary, unless it was Richard, the eldest son of Jimmy and his wife. The boy was said to look like him, James, in face and body but there were undoubted qualities of Mary in him. Over the years James had watched him with his brothers and cousins, and if ever there was a peacemaker it was young Richard, even at a youthful age.

A stiffer wind caught James's hair and blew it straight up from his forehead; for the first time he felt conscious of chill following the warm day. He eased himself forward in the chair, which did not creak or squeak, but before he rose to his feet Richard's voice sounded from one side and his grandson appeared.

"Can I get you anything, Grandfather?"

James, recovering from a start at the unexpected sound, said, "New bones, my boy, new bones for old."

"If Uncle Charles is to be believed they may one day be able to do that," replied Richard.

"They? Who do you mean by 'they'? Be more precise, Richard, more explicit. More harm is done in this world by the failure of one human being to understand another than by any of the seven deadly sins. Do you know the seven deadly sins, my boy?"

"Most of them only by reputation, sir!" Richard's gray eyes creased at the corners.

James, well pleased, growled back, "You are an impudent young pup. I am too old for such flippancy."

"That I cannot believe, sir."

"Eh? You disagree with me?" James was startled into speaking in a normal tone. "Have you no respect for age?"

"A great deal, sir; most of it learned from study of you," Richard retorted, and, smiling, he moved in front of his grandfather. "That is not flattery. 'Tis honest truth. I never see you as an *old* man, though, and I refuse to believe you are too old for anything to which you set your mind."

James, taken even more aback, placed his hands on the arms of the chair and returned the other's gaze. He warmed to the youth, who could be little more than twenty-two, if that. He had a comfortable feeling with Richard, who obviously felt the same with him.

"Flattery," he insisted at last. "It will get you nowhere, Richard. D'you always mean what you say?"

"Nearly always, sir!"

"Do you really want to know if you can get me anything?"

"I would be very happy to fetch whatever you want."

"Then first I want to go inside, my boy, into a corner where small children won't fall over my feet, and next I want some tea, *fresh* tea, you understand, and after that I wish to give my regular birthday performance and then to go for a drive. Are you competent to drive a carriage?"

"Middling, sir, middling competent."

"True modesty is the milk of the humble, mock modesty is the vinegar of fools."

James allowed himself to be helped from the chair, and as the stiffness eased from his joints he walked to and fro, still looking at the river, then turned toward the house. At one side, away from the big main room, was a smaller one where he and Mary often sat when they were alone together, and he turned toward this. As he reached it he became aware of a strange silence which had fallen upon the children, but it did not last for long, and suddenly the chatter in the other room was broken by a roar of "Punch and Judy!" and loud cries of delight.

The noise did not worry him; indeed he found himself listening to the shrill, clear voice of Punch and the thwacking of Punch's wife. He could picture the puppets—old-fashioned ones made of wood if Mary had found the puppet master with his strange name of Swatchelcove. He had heard this show every year for at least fifteen years and could distinguish not only Punch's voice but Judy's, the clown's and the ghost's, the beadle's and the constable's and even the hangman's.

A clink of cups sounded outside the door and Mary came in, carrying one tray, with Richard behind her carrying another—with a silver-plated kettle, still steaming, and some cakes and biscuits. Mary wore a silk dress of dark blue, drawn in at the waist and off the shoulder. Her hair still had streaks of dark in it, and the lines at her eyes did nothing to lessen their brightness.

"Richard tells me you forgot to add that you also wanted him to bring me to join you," she said, placing her tray on a small, low table.

"After these many years why should I suddenly change?" asked James, and Richard chuckled. "Pour me out some tea, Mrs. Marshall, and have less to say for yourself."

"If I failed to speak for myself who would speak for me?" she said, smiling.

She poured out and James sat back on the cushions, as contented as he had been for a long time. In the past few years he had lost the sense of urgency which had driven and at the same time so troubled him most of his life. The outburst from the children stopped at last; the first calls for them to get ready to leave brought the inevitable cries of disappointment.

Mary, as relaxed as James, asked unexpectedly, "Why did you ask Richard if he were a good driver?"

"Because I would like him to take me for a drive," answered James.

"A drive to where?" asked Mary.

James hesitated and it was some time before he answered, "I was going to say wherever the fancy takes me, but I can be more precise than that. I want to go from here to Westminster Bridge and thence by Charing Cross and the Strand to Bow Street, and next . . ."

She heard him out, without interrupting, and when he had finished, said quietly, "You had best take the large carriage, Richard. And I must remember your grandfather's old bones and pack the seat with cushions. I'll do that before I see the children off." She stood up, smiling at James, and love glowed in her eyes. "You wish to remember, Mr. Marshall, and *I* wish you would remember, some of the everyday things. You have to go into the family room and place a wrapped gift into every child's hand, and you have to remember you do not name a single one, because—"

"Because even if I get it right I may disappoint the ones I forget!"

"I do declare there is hope for you yet!"

Mary leaned down and kissed his forehead, and James, watching her walk across the room with as much freedom as she had twenty and even thirty years ago, felt a deep contentment. And Richard's chuckle was an added pleasure. No, he thought, there was no doubt at all that between him and Richard existed a rapport which he had not known with any of his children or any of the other grandchildren.

When tea was over he got out of his chair more quickly than usual and walked proudly upright toward the family room, outside which stood a huge wicker basket now overladen with gifts, including sweets and confections in packets small enough for him to hold two at once, just the right size to fit the tiny hands of the smaller children. This was a time-honoured ceremony and not only the parents but most of the children were eagerly expecting him.

There they spread, some sitting on the floor or on chairs and couches pushed back to the sides of the room, some kneeling, each one expectant. As Richard carried in the basket, piled high with gifts, the cry was as great as that for the Punch and Judy show. But with a difference. Now he could see them all, the brightness of their faces, with here and there one downcast and tearful from some earlier disappointment. The whole brood, together with the servants' children and a number from neighbouring houses— Why there must be sixty young souls gathered there, he thought, from girls who were nearly women and young men dressed to ape their fathers and uncles to tots who could hardly walk. Here and there hair had been freshly brushed or plastered down with water, but mostly it was a disheveled motley, grubby and sticky-mouthed, but with excitement everywhere.

"Well, you young people—" James began.

"Be quiet!" Dorothy whispered to two of his grandchildren who were talking, and they went as still as frightened mice, so that there was hush everywhere.

"I've never known such a noisy bunch," went on James. "I can hardly hear myself speak."

One or two of the older ones laughed, as he had intended that they should.

"I've never known so many people to have a birthday on the same day, either. Grandmamma, can you explain that remarkable series of coincidences?"

There was more laughter in which some of the smaller children joined, either because they understood or because they sensed this was the time to follow their elders.

"I want to tell you that your grandmother and I love to have you all here. I can't understand why we should but—"

The laughter came freely now, few having to pretend.

"So there must be something nicer about you than I can see. Eh, Mrs. Marshall?" He peered about, as if trying to look over couches and beyond chairs, and shook his head. "Well, I suppose you *must* have some nice qualities or you would not have so many friends here to join you. I have, in this little basket"—he glanced at the basket, which now rose higher than his head, and won another delighted laugh—"a small gift. A birthday gift and yet rather more than that— a way of saying how glad we are to see—and *hear*—you enjoying yourselves. Some of you don't understand what I am saying, of course —will those who have understood every word indicate by shouting aye?"

A few called "Aye!" in a startled way.

"As few as that?" deplored James, looking about again and pursing his lips. "I *am* disappointed."

"Can we try again, sir?" a young man called.

"Hey? What's that? Try again?" James hesitated and then waved his hands. "Oh, very well. Will all of those—"

"*Aye!*" came a roar from three quarters of those present.

"That's much better," approved James, glancing at Mary, who enjoyed this charade at least as much as he. "However, if you haven't understood me, don't worry. There is always next year, and during that year you will have learned much—or *I* will have learned how to make myself understood better." They chuckled and laughed and one boy began to cough. "In any case, a large number of grown men and women don't understand me when I talk—eh, Mrs. Marshall?"

"Even *I* don't always understand you," Mary retorted.

Now this was as happy a group as could be. Soon they came forward one by one to collect their gifts, not only sweetmeats and gaily coloured dolls for the young, but handkerchiefs and porcelain figurines for the older ones, with almonds and chestnuts in a lace bag. When it was done and the young people had roared their thanks, with a little guidance from two of the mothers, James waved to them all and went back to the small room.

Quite suddenly he felt exhausted.

He lowered himself slowly into the old chair—brought in now from the garden—as the strength seemed to ooze out of his body. He was hardly aware of the others, Mary and Richard, but felt the glass in his fingers, and his hand raised by her, and the bouquet of cognac stealing into his nostrils. Gradually he lost his overwhelming sense of fatigue and looked about him, first at Mary, who was obviously anxious, then at Richard.

"You put too much effort into what you do," Mary scolded.

"Would you have me pay the children less respect than I do that mob of monkeys at Westminster?"

"I would have you conserve your strength," Mary retorted.

He smiled at Richard, sipped, and said, "Have you ever known such a woman?"

"No, sir, nor ever expect to," Richard replied.

"You are a perceptive young man," James approved. "Have you yet decided on your future?"

"No, sir. I am considering some alternatives while I am studying in my room at 'Mr. Londoner.' "

"I trust the alternatives are all pleasing," said James, "but I asked for a more selfish reason, Richard. I am too tired to go out this evening, much though I wish to. If tomorrow promises a fine day, I would like you to drive me to a number of places."

"And such good sense, not to go out tonight! I declare I hardly recognise you," Mary applauded, and slipped away.

Would Richard do what he, James, would so like him to? wondered James. He looked at the lean face, tanned as if the young man spent more time out of doors than in. No other member of his family except Jimmy had ever taken more than a passing interest in the establishment still known and even more famous as "Mr. Londoner."

James himself had gone into the offices at least once a week while he had still been an active Member of Parliament but he had not contested the last election: Parliament was for younger men. At first he had missed the House of Commons so much that there had been hours of anguish but now he was much more resigned.

"I shall present myself at ten o'clock and be at your service for as long as you wish," Richard said. "Is there more I can do now, sir?"

"No, Richard. I need nothing more."

Thoughtfully he watched the lad go off.

CHAPTER 32

Richard

THE NEXT morning James awoke feeling as fresh as he had felt for a long time. Richard arrived a little before ten o'clock and drove him through all those parts of London he knew and loved. Then, finding themselves outside Morgan's Coffee House, Richard suggested they go in.

"Do you know, my boy, I think you have the makings of a keen intelligence allied to common sense!" said James. "That is exactly what I would like to do."

Richard looked affectionately at his grandfather as he helped him from the carriage. From the earliest time he could remember he had loved and respected the older man, enjoying his company far more than that of his own father. When at school close by his home at Holborn, he had frequently walked the four miles to Chelsea, and could remember to this day his sense of disappointment on those occasions when his grandfather had not been there. When he had been told that "Your grandfather is in the House," he had been puzzled, for he was nowhere to be found, until he learned that "the House" meant the House of Commons, the seat of government at Westminster Palace.

So he had become interested in politics and the activities in "the House" at a much earlier age than most.

His curiosity had long been insatiable. He had raged when his grandfather had been opposed—often harshly and maliciously—in what he was trying to do, had hugged himself with delight when some great national figure, such as Jeremy Bentham, had applauded instead of damning him. He had a boy's sense of admiration, even hero worship, for highwaymen, who were often glamorised at their hanging and glorified after death, but the constant fight which the older man made for Bow Street officers caught his imagination. Soon he had taken to going to Bow Street and offering to do odd jobs such as holding horses or cleaning the brass or leather of harness or carriage. Not only had he come to know every officer by sight, from the youngest, de Beer, who had the courage of a lion and the skill of a veteran at seventeen, to the oldest, but had often been drawn into conversation with them.

Richard did not believe that he would ever forget the pride which had filled him when, on learning his identity, Todd, greatest of all the Bow Street men of that period, had told him the time-honoured story of the clash with the Twelves, alias the New Mohocks. His grandfather's part in this had become legendary, even to the account of his singlehanded attempt to capture the escaping horseman. Clearly there was not a man among those now at Bow Street who did not regard James Marshall as a hero.

When Richard had decided to study law and had become articled to a lawyer in Lincoln's Inn, his interest had been concentrated on criminal law, much in the way of his grandfather. He had applied his knowledge to real-life problems, often assisting in the interrogation of prisoners—or more often suspects—and was often consulted by the Runners on points of law which were obscure to them. All had a nodding acquaintance with most laws affecting arrest, detention and trial, but there were areas in which they were in doubt. Seldom wishing to consult any of the magistrates, who were kept under inexorable pressure of business in the court, the Runners would consult Richard.

Inevitably, the boy had come to know the seven other magistrates' courts. He was also familiar with the prisons, especially Bridewell and Tothill Fields, the Palace of Newgate, as the Runners called it sarcastically, the Fleet, Gatehouse and King's Bench in Westminster, Coldbath and Clerkenwell. As inevitably he came to know London and its labyrinthine maze of streets as few others knew them.

He constantly marveled at his fascination even with the worst parts of London, and while he had never talked of this to any of his family, he had often wanted to discuss his activities with his grandfather. But despite his fairly frequent visits to the House by the River, he very rarely saw James alone; and on this particular occasion he needed all his concentration on guiding the carriage.

That was why, on seeing the coffee house, he had suddenly decided that he could wait no longer to unburden himself and had suggested they go inside.

Morgan's Coffee House was a revelation in comfort and appearance. Its seats were high-backed, more like those of a chophouse, so that there was a degree of privacy if patrons wished, but at the same time each booth offered a view of much of the rest of the long, narrow room, especially that section in the middle where there were dozens of padded armchairs with copies of newspapers and journals fastened by long chains to a central table. Here, one paid, but not excessively, for comfort and quality. The floor boards were narrower than most and dull-polished, not being covered with sawdust, and the benches were ornately carved with the heads of great figures in literature and the arts. Each booth had a different likeness and the appropriate name carved on the wall panel at one end of the booth. James peered at these names intently.

Ben Jonson was there, of course, and Hogarth, with Defoe, Gray, Sheridan, Garrick and Gainsborough. Obviously James was on the lookout for a particular name and he stopped abruptly by an empty booth, peering as if he were not sure of the words. But no one could be of two minds about the likeness carved on the front panel.

Richard chuckled.

"I should have known, sir."

"Is that Henry Fielding?"

"And with it are some of his characters, Tom Jones and Amelia—"

"I am more concerned with Henry Fielding himself," declared James, and he eased into the booth on one side as Richard slid opposite him.

When the tray of coffee and biscuits was placed on the table Richard began to tell his grandfather the essence of what he had been doing and how much he had learned. The more he talked the more he found to tell; not only was he explaining to his grandfather, but he was also explaining to himself, and during the recital he began to feel more than ever sure of what he wanted to do with his life.

James sat back in his seat and listened closely. When at last the young man fell silent he leaned forward.

"Tell me, what would you do about the situation as you see it?" he asked.

"Engage it in battle, sir!"

"A praiseworthy purpose but how would you go about it?"

"I would follow a time-honoured and proven successful course, sir."

"There is no such thing."

"I believe there is, grandfather," Richard replied quietly. "The Fieldings did not really fail; they simply did not live long enough to see their plans come to fruition. I would follow them, sir—which means that I would follow in your steps to the best of my limited ability. I would watch for all abuse of the law, all injustice, and use every means in my power to bring about improvements. And I could want no better mentor than yourself."

When he stopped, the expression in his eyes was one of pleading, both for his grandfather's approval and for his guidance.

He means every word, James Marshall said to himself, in great exultation. I *must* be sure not to dampen his ardour, yet at the same time I cannot allow him to think this is an easy path. He saw the eagerness in the eyes so like his own, and in a moment of deep feeling he stretched out his hand and covered Richard's. He could feel its warmth and strength.

At last he said, "Nothing will make the task easy, Richard, but for you I believe the achievement is much nearer. Do you wish to become a Bow Street—ah—Runner, is it?"

"I am not sure what way is best, sir."

"I found that the legal help I was able to give the poor and the unjustly treated was of great value," remarked James, "and I am sure that much odium is going to be cast on the Runners—"

"But *why*, sir?" Anger sounded in Richard's voice.

"Because a substantial number of people for a great variety of reasons do not want them to become the foundation of a metropolitan police force and will therefore do all they can to discredit them. I think you would be wise to choose some other way."

"As a lawyer, do you mean?"

"I know of none better. Unless you decided to go early into politics! In a nation where a young man in his early twenties can be so powerful as was Pitt, you are not too young."

"I do not think I have the making of a politician," Richard demurred.

"Why not, Richard?"

"I become too angry at conniving and trickery."

"Yes, and so do I," James replied with feeling. "But it is the government which makes new laws and changes or improves old ones, and as the years pass I think you may look on politics differently. For the present, the law would earn you a living and give you the influence you need." When Richard did not answer, James went on with a dry smile. "But a poor living, I declare. Have you ever felt any desire to work with 'Mr. Londoner'? Your father would welcome you." He did not add that Jimmy, who was ailing, had never been a great enthusiast for the shop.

"*Is* there scope, sir?"

"God bless my soul!" exclaimed James. "There is always room for expansion in any business. And as I know well, both the work for 'Mr. Londoner' and for Bow Street can be carried out at one and the same time. It is possible to buy a great variety of *objets d'art*, curios, and even small antiques from the little shops in the byways of London. Your father does not enjoy buying, but you might. Give it deep thought, and if you decide that this is what you would like to do, tell me so at once." He smiled into the other's eyes and went on: "It will be a great comfort to me if you decide to accept the sobriquet of 'Mr. Londoner' after your father, and your grandmother will be as pleased as I."

"I can think of nothing more likely to persuade me," Richard said.

James nodded but made no further comment, and they were just about to leave when heavy footsteps sounded from the shop door and a newcomer drew the gaze of most of the men at the middle table. Many began to whisper to their companions.

The man appeared suddenly at the end of the booth, and Richard exclaimed, "Mr. Godley!"

"The very man I am seeking," said Henry Godley, perhaps the second most famous of the Bow Street Runners. He was massive and deliberate in movement and manner, black-haired and with a short black beard. He doffed his round hat to James and went on: "It is an honour to meet you, sir. I saw your carriage pass by a while since, hence I knew you were in London. I have a message of some urgency for you."

"For my grandfather?" Richard exclaimed.

"Indeed yes, sir. The message is relayed from your residence in Chelsea, where a messenger arrived in haste soon after you had left to ask if you would be gracious enough to visit the home of Mr. Simon Rattray. I have his address by me, sir. Mr. Rattray is ill and I understand he has expressed a wish to see you."

Even before the Bow Street man had finished, James was beginning to get to his feet.

"I will go and bring the carriage." Richard turned toward the door.

"I have a coach waiting outside," said Godley. "I did not know how far away your carriage would be stationed. Mr. Rattray lives near Lincoln's Inn, so the journey will not take you long."

For James, the years rolled back with painful vividness.

As the coach passed through streets where there had once been green fields and reached the tiny Unitarian Church he had first seen forty-odd years ago, he recalled the lad, so startlingly like his half brother Johnny, walking toward the gate with his empty pail. He had come from a cottage behind the church, he remembered. The church remained, dwarfed by houses nearby, but the cottage had been swept away and had been replaced by a row of houses at least three stories high, built of warm red brick with slate roofs.

As the coach drew up, the door of one of these houses opened and a woman appeared on the step who, James believed, was Simon Rattray's wife. She approached them quickly, her heavy wool dress falling like a sack about her, her pale face deep set with luminous eyes.

Godley, who had stayed with them, opened the door and climbed down, then put a strong arm up so that James could steady himself.

Richard heard the Runner say, "I'm very glad we found him, Mrs. Rattray."

"And I am eternally grateful for your coming, Mr. Marshall," the woman said. It was impossible to doubt that the words came from her heart. "And to you for your help, Mr. Godley." Despite the obvious gravity of the situation she looked at Richard, saying, "There can be no doubt that this is your grandson, sir. I am very glad to meet you."

"My pleasure, ma'am," Richard replied. Then he asked, "Have I your permission to walk in your garden while my grandfather visits Mr. Rattray?"

"You are most understanding," Mrs. Rattray said.

Richard watched the three go into the house, Godley bringing up the rear. He followed slowly in their wake but before he had gone far there was a movement behind him and, turning, he saw a young man of about his own age, but heavier and more thickset, with powerful shoulders and a short neck. The most arresting thing about the new-comer, however, was the colour of his hair and eyes; the colour of honey fresh from the comb.

He walked with beautifully controlled movements, inclined his head and said, "I am Simon, the son of Simon."

"I am Richard Marshall."

"No name will ever win greater respect in my family than that of Marshall," young Simon Rattray declared. "I believe my father has kept himself alive so as to see your grandfather one last time. He had what the doctor calls a seizure during the night."

"I could not be more sorry."

"It will be a greater loss than most men realise," replied young Rattray. "Will it interest you to see a collection of his speeches and the work he has done for the advancement of the poor? They are kept in his office at the back of the house."

"I would like that very much," Richard said gratefully.

Among the medley of thoughts that passed through the mind of James Marshall as he followed Simon Rattray's wife into the house was that he had never visited Simon Rattray here, and wished now that he had; and also that this house was at least twenty years old and had a solidness which he found pleasing. The passage beyond the front door was wide, a curved staircase rising at one side. Opposite the bottom stair a door stood open, and Mrs. Rattray led the way in.

"It is Mr. Marshall, Simon," she announced.

Obviously this room had been converted into a bedroom from its original use as a study. One tall, narrow window overlooked the garden, and light from this reflected on the glass of a large bookcase which rose from floor to ceiling. In a corner facing the window stood a double bed with a solid carved head panel, as solid a one at the foot. In this lay Simon Rattray, propped up on pillows, his eyes closed. He opened them slowly and turned his head toward James, who saw with shock and pain how thin he had become, sunken cheeks now more like dried parchment than leather; even his once bull-like shoulders seemed to have shrunk. His hair had turned snow white and looked as soft as down. Only his eyes remained as James remembered them, bright, yet mellow. He moved a brown and beveined hand slowly, and although his grip had no power, it was firm. James stood so that the other could see him without twisting around.

"It is good to see you," Rattray said in a tired-sounding voice.

"It was good that you sent for me," replied James.

"I have lain here for a long time and spent much of it looking back over the years," said Rattray, "and there are few things for which I have no regrets. But I have none at all over my acquaintance with you, Mr. Marshall."

"It has been a long and valuable friendship, little though we have met," James agreed.

"It has been friendship to you, also?" Rattray's expression kindled.

"Deep and abiding," James assured him.

"I have never felt more rewarded." Simon Rattray gave a wry smile. "I do not often consider the matter of reward, but I suppose no man can live without some share of them. The three most bountiful for me have been my wife, my son, and James Marshall." Rattray withdrew his hand slowly but made no attempt to hoist himself higher on his pillows. "We should have allowed our families to meet, not selfishly kept them apart." Before James could say that he had been thinking that very thing, Rattray went on: "May I have your attention on two counts, sir?"

"Readily."

"You are very kind. The first concerns a young man who came to help in the organisation of our work only two years ago and has since proved invaluable. I do not know whether his name will be familiar; it is Jackson, Frederick Jackson."

The name struck into James's mind like a knife cut, laying open the past so vividly that for a moment he was silent. Frederick Jackson, Jacker, the highwayman who had killed James's father and whom he had seen kicking from the gibbet in Tyburn Fields. Even the roar of the crowd came to his ears; the sound of marching soldiers, the way John Furnival had faced the hostile thousands. He could recall the facts he had learned about Eve Milharvey, Jackson's mistress, that she had borne a son by the highwayman after his death. Those things which he had learned at later periods were dimmed but these, includ-

395

ing a picture of Eve Milharvey herself, were very vivid. He could not recall ever discussing how his father had died but Rattray had many sources of information. He had not discussed Jackson's son with Simon Rattray either, but Simon would not wish to talk of this youth unless he was sure of their association.

As if he could read what was passing through James's mind, Rattray went on:

"You recall his grandfather, then?"

"So he is a grandson of the highwayman."

"Yes, and is aware of it," answered Rattray. "He is the son of Eve Milharvey's first child, to whom she gave the surname Jackson. This grandson of hers is one of eleven children born in the village of Saint Marylebone, as poor and needy a family as one could find. This has fired him with great zeal to reform, Mr. Marshall, and I commend him to you as a young man with much potential. He lives in a cottage with a widowed sister, the only other members of the family to rebel against their lot. The sister's husband was killed in a riot during a march by the workers and apprentices of the Steam Engine Company. Both are dedicated but I do not believe they are fanatics or that they have any sense of personal injustice. If you can help them you may make yet another great contribution to the greatness of London."

"I shall most certainly try," James promised.

He was tempted to urge the other to relax, for his speech had plainly tired him. It would not have surprised James had Rattray's wife now enjoined him to rest but she remained silent, and at last Rattray went on:

"The second matter concerns my son, Simon."

"If there is a way in which I can help him, it is as good as done."

"I will be forever at peace if I know he is to be told who his forebears were, and of his blood relationship to the Furnival family. I chose to ignore this and to make no attempt to win their interest, but a man has no right to make such a decision for his son. I have not told him, although the temptation has been great these past five or six years. He was a mature man at sixteen; today, at twenty-two, he is exceptional, both as an organiser and as a leader. I would like you to tell him, Mr. Marshall. I do not know what the effect of such realisation will be, but I am sure that he should know. He works with me and the men trust him, but I confess I do not believe his heart is with them, as mine has always been. I have been prepared for him to go his own way, and I suspect he has stayed with the work out of consideration for me, but that he will seek fresh fields when I am gone. This is another reason why he should know the truth about himself from someone who will make it clear he has no claim on the Furnivals but that he has their blood."

"I shall acquaint him with the truth," promised James.

"You are very kind, sir."

Simon Rattray's hand moved and rested for a moment on James Marshall's, and the parchmentlike face relaxed. He closed his eyes and it began to look as if he had finished, but when James attempted to withdraw his hand, Rattray pressed more firmly and uttered two words which were only just audible.

"Wait, please."

"For as long as you wish," James promised.

For some time it was difficult to be sure that Rattray was still breathing, he was so still, but his wife showed no particular concern, which was surely an indication that she was familiar with this stillness, as if Rattray were hovering between life and death. How long it was before the man's eyes opened it was difficult to say; at first they appeared dazed and reflected bewilderment, but soon they cleared and he spoke with unexpected firmness and precision.

"I am now able to do something for you, James Marshall."

"There is no need, none whatsoever."

"There is every need," insisted Simon Rattray, the dry, wry smile manifesting itself again. "You and I are both aware of the narrow gap between poverty and crime. Poverty can turn basically honest and good men into footpads, kind men into cruel, generous men into greedy brutes, but this you know."

James nodded.

"However, there are other causes of crime," continued Rattray. "Some men have evil born in them; greed and lust and a savage enjoyment of making others suffer. And many have a hunger for power, which I sometimes believe is the greatest crime of all. Such men have infiltrated into the ranks of the parishes and the constables, accepting for their own nefarious purposes the work as watchmen. I believe some are even members of Bow Street patrols, and I am fearful lest they create conditions which could lead to revolution as bad as that in France, riding to power over the bodies of men who fight truly for a just cause."

Again Rattray stopped.

There was no call for James to respond, and in truth there was little new in what Rattray said. James was virtually sure of what was coming when Rattray went on.

"I have warned many people of this danger, but they have not listened. There are few who do not have great regard for you and your judgment, however, and you are regarded as a man of the world, whereas I—partly because I oppose violence so bitterly—am regarded as an impractical idealist. Use all your influence to make the poor understand the truth, I beg you. Do not allow yourself or them to be deceived."

After a long time, when he was sure that the other man had finished, James Marshall answered.

"None shall be deceived if I can help it."

"You do not know what good you do me."

Rattray's voice was now so husky that the words were difficult to distinguish one from another, and when he finished his chin slumped on his chest and his eyes closed. His breathing was shallow but not laboured, and his face had the calmness of a man at peace.

The following day a messenger came from Mrs. Rattray to say that her husband was dead. Only *The Daily Clarion* gave him space for an obituary. But ten thousand mourners jammed the fields near Lincoln's Inn when he was buried in the tiny graveyard of the church where his stepfather had been minister.

CHAPTER *33*

The Young Simon

RICHARD, NOW that his mind was made up, plunged into the activities of "Mr. Londoner" with great vigour. At the same time he made himself available to plead for any victims of injustice sent to him by Bow Street. While he had no official association and, in fact, was not on personal terms with any of the magistrates, the members of the Bow Street patrols and patrols from other offices sent many needy men and women to him, some so old it was hard to understand how they could survive, some so young it was impossible to believe they had committed the crimes of which they were accused.

But, as the population increased, so did crime. And the consequent near breakdown of law and order brought yet further opprobrium on Bow Street.

Richard saw the causes only too clearly. The men were possessed of great courage, but their interest was not in the murderers and footpads who committed violence for a few pounds; there was little profit in blood money compared with that in finding stolen goods and receiving handsome rewards for the recovery. Catching the thieves was incidental. Very few men argued against their motivation; even Jeremy

Bentham declared that the only way to fight crime was to give the fighter a prospect of substantial reward.

Some of the great Bow Street officers, such as Godley and Todd, received handsome fees for guarding the Royal Family on special occasions, for attending the Bank of England when dividends were being paid, and for being on hand at many great events. The larger the reward, it was believed, the greater the endeavour to earn it. Some Runners were employed by foreign governments to protect their envoys and also to guard valuables being transported from one place to another. No great ball or banquet was without its Bow Street men, handsomely rewarded to make sure that nothing was stolen.

So the rich benefited; seldom the poor. All of these things James Marshall observed from the big chair in his room at Chelsea as the months passed, or heard from Richard, who lost some of his hero worship for the Runners, but little of his liking.

James had discovered one thing which had pleased him, if somewhat wryly. Young Frederick Jackson had applied for a post with the Bow Street patrols and had been accepted. His great ambition, it appeared, was to become a Bow Street Runner! James arranged for Richard to inquire after Jackson from time to time.

Every week, Richard came to Chelsea for an evening meal and sat and talked with his grandfather, giving him news and learning from him more of a past which in some mysterious way they seemed to share.

On one of these nights, toward the end of August 1796, Richard brought young Simon Rattray to The House by the River.

Throughout the meal James watched the young guest, who was so like his father and his father before him. The boy had the same deliberate way of speaking, giving the impression that he said nothing without considering it deeply. Yet he was not difficult to talk to, had a sound general knowledge of London and affairs, and a firm grip on political realities at Westminster. It was not possible to judge whether he knew why he had been brought there. Mary, who had developed the habit of retiring to bed soon after the evening meal, bade them all good night, and James noticed a little anxiously that she looked more tired than usual.

He poured port for both the young men and offered them tobacco, but neither smoked or took snuff.

Settled in the big chair, James placed both hands on its arms and asked, "Have you ever been curious about your family, Simon?"

"No, sir, I cannot say that I have been," Simon replied. "I was grateful for the mother and the father that I had, and for my grandfather. Did you know him, sir?"

"The Reverend Thomas Rattray?"

"Yes, he was my grandfather. He adopted my father."

"I met him occasionally and had great respect for him," James replied. He hesitated before he asked with some diffidence, "So you knew that he was not your grandfather by blood?"

The honey-coloured eyes did not change their expression.

"Yes, sir. I did." Simon raised his hands in a defensive or apologetic gesture. "I was not unaware that a great number of children were foundlings and of these only a few fortunate ones were adopted by good families. I did not inquire beyond what I knew because I did not wish to find out whether my antecedents were good or bad." When James did not respond, the young man asked in the same steady voice, "Are you about to inform me, sir?"

"Yes," James replied flatly.

"At my father's wish?"

"But for that it would not have occurred to me to interfere."

"What if I were to say that I did not wish to know, sir? Would you regard continued silence as betrayal of a promise to my father?"

James pursed his lips and rubbed them together in concentration before answering.

"No. I would regard it as a failure of my obligation to you."

"Despite the fact that I really may not wish to know?" insisted Simon.

"A greater failure," replied James, smiling very faintly. "I do not think it is characteristic of you to turn your face from the truth if it is possible for you to see it. If it is hidden from you, you have no guilt, but if it can be revealed—"

"I am sorry that I have been obstinate," Simon interrupted quietly. "If you have the truth I would most certainly desire to hear it."

"Then I will tell it as simply as I can," James promised. "The simplest way is to remind you that my mother married Sir John Furnival many, many years ago, and of that union there was one child, a son—not your father but so much like him that there could be no doubt of the relationship. Your father and my half brother stemmed from the same tree. A newspaper friend of mine went to some considerable trouble to make sure, and there was no doubt that your grandmother was at one time closely associated with Sir John Furnival. I can tell you that your father was aware of the relationship and that the Reverend Thomas Rattray was doubtless aware of it at or about the time of his marriage to your grandmother. And I have sufficient knowledge to convince me that it was a very happy marriage."

James's voice faded into silence. His body seemed to shrink farther into the chair and his hooked nose and thrusting chin dominated the deeply lined face. He did not look away from the youth, who showed no sign, immediately, of having heard.

Richard found young Simon's silence painful, and sensed that his grandfather did, also. He had never seen age written so clearly on the old man's face. But at last Simon Rattray stirred, and both to Richard's surprise and relief the strong face broke into the relaxed expression of a smile.

"You could not have told me more clearly, sir, or with more consideration, had you been my father. I am grateful. As for my forebears, I am most interested to hear, and I understand now why my father on occasions discoursed on the qualities of Sir John Furnival! If I am to believe what I have heard, it is likely that I have a great many uncles and aunts and a positive proliferation of cousins in London, few of whom know of my relationship. It is not my nature for such things to weigh heavily on me, I may say."

James replied, obviously with much relief, "You make a not unreasonable assumption."

"Are there any of my contemporaries known to you?" asked Simon. "Or your half brother, for instance. Is he one of the partners in the House of Furnival?"

"He died in 1780," James answered.

"Without issue?" Simon wanted to know.

"Leaving one son."

"Do you know the son, sir?"

"Very slightly," James answered. "He lives at Great Furnival Square with his mother, who was accepted by the family, although—" James broke off abruptly.

"Although there had been no marriage?" Simon asked.

"As you infer, there had been no marriage. But the family felt an obligation to her."

"But may not to me—a man. What does this son do?"

"He is active but too young to be a leader in the affairs of the House of Furnival. Since his mother is Italian he is bilingual and I understand that the business between Italy and this country, particularly with Milan and Rome, is thriving. I do not know the details but he is being trained to take charge of all or part of that side of the business."

"Does he also bear the unmistakable stamp of John Furnival?" demanded Simon, and for the first time there seemed a touch of bitterness in his voice.

"No," James answered. "He is very like his mother."

"Then I need have no fear that I shall at any time meet my double!" The bitterness, if it had ever been there, was gone completely. This young man, so like his father, had qualities which had never been apparent in the older man, humour and lightheartedness; he would not take life with the unadulterated earnestness which had characterized the first Simon Rattray. "May I think on this matter, sir?"

"How could it be otherwise?" James inquired, and his eyes twinkled.

Simon chuckled. "I mean think with a purpose! I do not know whether I would like to be received into the bosom of my grandfather's family, even if they were willing. Did you give my cousin a name, Mr. Marshall?"

"His name is Peter, in Italian Pietro, and he carries his mother's name of Levandi."

"I have a distinct sense that I would like to meet with my cousin Pietro, whatever else," young Simon said. "But I am presuming, sir. Would it be practicable for you to introduce me to the House of Furnival if such a thought grew in my mind?"

"Indeed yes," answered James, "but I would advise you not to delay too long, for Timothy McCampbell-Furnival is at least as old as I!"

"Your grandfather really is a most remarkable man," Simon Rattray declared when the young men were together. "It was a pleasure to meet him. As it is a pleasure to have met you, Richard."

"I do not know when I have had greater satisfaction from a short acquaintance," Richard said, more prosily than he meant. "I wonder how you will find the chairman of the House of Furnival?"

"Do you know him?" Simon asked.

"I saw him once at a distance when there was some occasion on the river and the family was taken to see the fireworks. My grandfather used to know him well. And liked him," Richard added with feeling. "They were very close friends."

Timothy McCampbell-Furnival was, in the opinion of those younger than he, likely to live forever. At sixty-seven, those who knew him declared that his grasp of affairs was better than it had ever been, and certainly there was no one in the House of Furnival who had anything like so exhaustive a knowledge of all aspects of the business.

Both of Francis' sons had died in their teens of the galloping disease which ate their lungs, and the same disease had taken Francis after he had been driven by continued periods of sickness to try the climate of Italy. For some years William had ruled as chairman, but he too had had periods of ill health, and Timothy, who had taken the family name, now reigned virtually supreme.

He had grown in stature out of all knowledge, yet remained the Timothy whom James Marshall had known and liked so well. There was still and probably would always remain a streak of conflict between them, for despite the fact that Timothy had once said that James had all but converted him to the need for a metropolitan police force, the House of Furnival remained adamantly opposed to this. Rather than meet in conflict, they now met seldom. Yet each retained a deep affection for the other and cherished happy memories of their old friendship.

On a morning in September 1796, Timothy McCampbell-Furnival, was standing on the terrace overlooking the docks. A Furnival ship had tied up alongside the previous night, and Timothy had letters from a dozen major company offices on his desk; they told the constant story of expansion and the need for more men to head the various branches, men capable of accepting weighty responsibility. He watched the small boys begging for money from the crew as they swam and trod water, frowned as he saw one of the sewers emit a rush of evil-smelling mud just downriver from the docks. Six or seven men with poles and rakes and nets were wading among the filth, searching for treasure-trove. Many a golden guinea, piece of jewelry, valuable snuffbox or watch was dredged up through the ooze which seeped through these men's fingers.

Timothy was not drawn to the terrace only by the ship, but because James Marshall was due to come to see him at twelve o'clock; he was to stay for luncheon. James's impending visit turned Timothy's thoughts nostalgically back over the past to the day of the great river pageant. He was sure that he would never see its like again.

He was interrupted by a clerk, who came from the room behind him.

"If you will excuse me, sir—"

"Yes, Abbott? What is it?"

"Mr. Marshall is in the front hall, sir. Will you receive him here?"

"No other place would serve so well."

"I will escort him myself, sir."

Soon Timothy heard footsteps and turned with his back to the railings to look at his old friend. While on the one hand he was surprised and even shocked by the ravages of time in that sharp-featured face, the directness of gaze remained and James was as upright as a man could be although he moved slowly and with the aid of a stick. The old friends stood and appraised each other for what seemed a long time before each approached more closely and they shook hands.

"I don't yet know what has brought you," Timothy declared, "but even if it is yet another effort on your part to enlist my support for your civil army, I am thankful for it."

"I am sure it is too late to open your eyes to the simpler truths," retorted James. He moved toward the railing and surveyed the dramatic everyday scene as he went on: "Do you ever think of Johnny?"

"Occasionally," replied Timothy, obviously surprised. "What brings him to your mind?"

"An unexpected encounter with a nephew of his," said James, still watching the scene.

"And which nephew may this be, Jamey?" asked Timothy. "Why does it please you to be mysterious?"

"I was not his only half brother, as you well know," said James. "He had many others, some of whom died, some of whom emigrated or were transported, some who are still in London of middling means. But there was one whom I believe only I knew, and who kept to himself because he had neither time nor love for those things that the House of Furnival stands for. Does the name Rattray mean anything to you?"

Timothy exclaimed, "Simon Rattray, the troublemaker?"

"Simon Rattray, the reformer."

"I read that he died quite recently."

"What you did not read was that he was John Furnival's son, and that he had a son much like himself and his father in appearance but, I suspect, very different from both in character and in attitudes. The son, also named Simon, learned of his real ancestry only last month, and that from me. I wanted to form some opinion of him before bringing him to you, and I had some Bow Street men inquire about him. He appears a highly reputable if sometimes forthright young man. He assisted his father in much of his work but since Simon Rattray's death has been seeking an occupation of a more commercial nature. Not unnaturally he is curious about you and would be pleased if you will see him. I have concluded that you will not be displeased."

"The son of Simon Rattray," Timothy said, as if he could not believe he was uttering the name. "And John Furnival's grandson! How old is he, James?"

"About the same age as my grandson Richard, I believe," James replied. "Twenty-two or -three. Richard has come to mean more to me than any of my children or other grandchildren, and I have learned to respect his judgment. He has formed a high opinion of this Simon."

"James," said Timothy, with a glimpse of his youthful heartiness, "I will gladly see him, and it may help if I were to see Richard, also. How soon can it be arranged?"

"If you wish, this very day," answered James. "I came with them and they are at this moment walking in the grounds of the Tower. If they have taken the route which I recommended they should soon be by the cannon on the ramparts overlooking the river."

Five minutes later, when the two young men appeared, walking slowly and taking in all there was to see, Timothy rang for Abbott and sent him hurrying to fetch them.

"What I require above all else is a young man to serve as my personal assistant and for the time being I have no more to offer but that. If you ask James Marshall here he will no doubt explain that I mean a lackey. The man for me should be a second pair of eyes and a second pair of ears, a second pair of hands and arms and a second pair of legs. He should consider my interests his own and remember that all interests are the interests of the House of Furnival. What knowledge he has of banking, shipping, the British Empire and, indeed, the rest of the world, of politics, of history—all of these things are unimportant save that he uses them to perform his single-minded task: to serve me. What he knows now is of less significance than what he will learn. Ignorance is no bar, but refusal, reluctance or inability to acquire knowledge would be the greatest barrier of all. Do you think you could fill such a position, Simon Rattray?"

"Yes, sir," answered Simon.

Richard saw the smile in his grandfather's eyes and felt a desire to laugh aloud, for that answer, uttered with such a ring of confidence, might have come with the same assurance—and with sound reason—from Johnny himself.

They had not touched upon this subject early during the meal, which was laid in a small annex to the terrace, in full view of the river and so of the shipping. Since Timothy had swung to the matter, however, none other had been discussed. First he had outlined his problems, his needs in general, and indeed his disappointment at the twists of nature which had left so few Furnivals taking an active part in the affairs of this mammoth concern. Then he had touched upon its widespread interests. No one could have drawn a clearer picture, and when it was done, Timothy had made it clear that he and only he was fully cognisant of the activities of the House of Furnival, and that while others had both knowledge and virtual control of specific areas, he must be consulted on all decisions of major significance.

"So I must be fully informed," he had finished. "My sources are many and my servants are loyal, but what I require above all else is a young man to serve as my personal assistant, an ever-present *aide-de-camp*. Do you think that you could fill such a position, Simon Rattray-Furnival?" he asked again.

"I do," said Simon.

"And will you, as I have done, add the name of Furnival to that already yours?"

"I would be proud to, sir."

"James," said Timothy in a strangely husky voice, "I do not know whether in this young man you have brought me my salvation or my damnation. But if he proves to be as valuable as I hope to God he will, the House of Furnival will find a way of making the politicians give you your police force!"

CHAPTER *34*

10,000 *Thieves*

EACH YEAR after that first meeting in 1796 Timothy McCampbell-Furnival invited James and Richard to dine with him and Simon Rattray-Furnival at the great business house by the Thames. From the beginning it was evident that Simon was likely to make a success of the position which had been thrust upon him with such little warning. Just as Richard was in rapport with his grandfather, so Simon was in rapport with his father's cousin. His mind was as quick and as sharp as Johnny's had been but he appeared to be completely free both from Johnny's sadistic streak and Johnny's bitter prejudices. Most people took to him. He did not presume upon his new position or his employer and very quickly gained the good graces of the other relatives and chiefs of departments. Given two rooms at Great Furnival Square in an apartment of the main house, he was always at hand should Timothy need him, yet had plenty of time to study the history of the group. Timothy made no formal attempt to train him, so he trained himself until, even after one year, he knew more about the intricacies of the House of Furnival than all but the most senior of its leading members and staff.

The first anniversary luncheon was, to James, a joy. He had never seen Timothy more free of troubles, or been so sure of a young man as he was of Simon. If he had any regret it was only that old Simon Rattray had not lived to see that day.

Richard, now a frequent visitor to the House by the River, came to collect his grandfather, driving the same open carriage, although Mary protested because it was spitting rain. Satisfying, or at least mollifying, her by taking an extra cloak, they started off, Richard, who had arrived earlier than expected, explaining that they were first to meet Simon at Morgan's Coffee House.

Arriving at Morgan's, James saw Simon already sitting at the booth which had the carving of the Fieldings. Simon was obviously delighted not only to see them but with himself, and Richard appeared to be in a very good mood. Was that because they had planned this encounter? James wondered.

He asked no questions but could not repress his own high spirits, until after ten minutes or so Richard said, "If I did not know you better, sir, I would think you had put brandy in your coffee!"

"My spirits always come from within," James retorted.

The younger men laughed, and Richard raised both hands from his coffee mug, saying, "Time to tell him, Simon, or he will be in so gay a mood he will not be able to understand."

"Tell me? Tell me what?" demanded James. "If you two have come to make a fool of me—"

"Neither of us would attempt the impossible, sir," Simon Rattray-Furnival responded gallantly. "On the contrary, I hope to be able to make a prophet out of you." He paused long enough to allow James to speak, but when the old man simply waited, he went on: "You once intimated to Mr. Benedict Sly that you needed to find a way to establish a police force which would not bring upon you the opposition of the City of London. Mr. Sly confided in Richard about this and Richard confided in me, on my promise to find out if there was a way of achieving such a purpose without being disloyal to the House of Furnival."

James felt his heart begin to thump painfully, for this young man would not treat the matter lightly, and most certainly Richard would not. He felt his throat very tight as he responded, "And what success have you, Simon?"

"Considerable, sir, I do believe."

Now James's blood began to drum in his ears and he thought that concern leaped into the eyes of the others as they faced him across the table. He made no attempt to speak. Simon's voice seemed to come from a long distance off, yet every syllable was precise and clear.

"It has been increasingly evident, not only to the House of Furnival but to every merchant who uses the River Thames, that every merchant vessel which comes from the estuary to London, every coaling vessel which comes from the northeast coast, and every passenger ship wherever it is from suffers from the depredations of the mudlarks. It is reliably estimated that at least ten thousand of these river thieves prey upon the river's traffic. Nothing is safe. Naked boys climb aboard in dead of night, thieves work among honest dock labourers, warehousemen are under constant threat from cutthroats. Of an estimated thousand watermen, one quarter is regarded as dishonest, living on the edge of poverty as they do. There is greater terror on the river than there ever was on the highway between the City and Westminster. And the City suffers most, sir, either in direct loss, by meeting insurance claims, or by having prices on the Exchange affected after a particularly daring robbery. I repeat, Mr. Marshall, the City suffers where it hurts most. In its pocket."

Now fully recovered, James murmured softly, "Yes. Yes, indeed." His voice gained strength and he leaned forward. "No doubt you have heard of Mr. Patrick Colquhoun, my boy, one of the Middlesex justices and a man for whom I have the greatest respect. Mr. Colquhoun went into great detail on this matter of a river police in his treatise published last year."

"The proposals have been closely studied and the prospects have been examined," Simon replied. "It is not possible to police the river with ordinary patrols, only with experts, and these would have to be well paid so as to avoid risk of corruption. I have little doubt that the merchants who most use the Port of London would contribute handsomely toward a Marine Police Force, as Mr. Colquhoun describes it, under one commander—under single control, that is. I do not believe a voice of substance would be raised against it. And since the bonded warehouses are within the region and the customs houses suffer great losses by smuggling, which such a force could restrict, I am of the opinion that the force would soon be taken over by the authorities. A *river* police force, sir—and one which could hardly fail to be successful since it would have everyone's support—would be a perfect example for the land areas to follow."

"Simon, you may well be right," said James quietly. "Have you discussed this with Timothy?"

"I have taken soundings, if I may use the phrase, and believe he would give full support to the forming of such a force. Moreover, Mr. Colquhoun's proposals set out an excellent plan which no doubt he would consider in even greater detail, knowing of the prospects of success. But I would like you to propose that Mr. Colquhoun be consulted. Mr. Timothy is mindful of his promise to you on the day when you first brought us together."

Into the brief silence that followed, Richard said almost apologetically, "This is why we wanted to see you before meeting Mr. Timothy for luncheon."

"That was most considerate of you," James replied, his heart beginning to thump again. He was looking into Simon's eyes—into Johnny's eyes—but did not know what he wanted to say to this young man. It was so much more than "Thank you." It was as if in some miraculous way Simon had wiped out the stains left behind by Johnny, as if he were the man everyone had prayed Johnny would become.

Perhaps because of the intensity of the older man's gaze, Simon looked away.

There was much to surprise the others in the sudden change which came over his expression. It was as if Simon had seen some vision which drove thought of everything else from his mind, even what he had just said with such controlled vehemence to James Marshall. Richard's glance followed Simon's—and immediately something like the same metamorphosis came upon him.

James became aware of several voices speaking a name at the same time, some lighthearted, some undoubtedly touched deeply by respect. "Miss Hermina." "Miss Hermina." "This way, Miss Hermina." "Such an honour to have you here, Miss Hermina." Other sounds followed, footsteps, shuffling, rustling. It was exasperating that this should have happened at such a juncture, although in one way it saved James from attempting to put his feelings into words. He wished to concentrate his thoughts on the burden of Simon's declaration, on the possibilities which dazzled him in much the same way that these young men were dazzled by the rare sight of a woman in a coffee house.

Being across the table from James on the side facing the door, they could see along the center aisle and he could not. But suddenly two women and a man appeared in his line of vision, backing away from— no doubt—this Miss Hermina. The name was familiar but James could not think why.

The man was the manager of the coffee house.

The two women, James believed, were his assistants.

Simon Rattray-Furnival, until that moment dumb struck, swallowed hard, then forced himself to look away from the new arrival. He smiled faintly and said, "Your pardon, sir. I interrupted you."

Richard, on the other hand, appeared transfixed; James had never seen or imagined that he could be so affected. It was as if he were hearing the voices of the Sirens. What a striking-looking young man he was! Slowly, he closed his mouth, and at the same moment the bowing and curtsying trio passed and "Miss Hermina" appeared.

James saw her glance toward the two young men opposite him.

He felt a quick response of the heart—yes, he, James Marshall, now in his sixty-eighth year! For this young woman was most vividly *alive.* Her vivacity, an enormous capacity for life, showed in her eyes, in the way her lips were set, in the flare of interest she showed in Simon and Richard. The next moment she was past, a vision in powder blue with a wide-brimmed bonnet, the simplicity of her clothes a tribute to her taste and her dressmaker. Her dark hair made the blueness of her eyes even more startling.

She was gone.

"I repeat, your pardon, sir," said Simon. "Such shameful behaviour. Eh, Richard?"

"Eh? Oh. Shameful indeed! I— Damme, *no,*" declared Richard, laughter sparking in his eyes. "There is nothing shameful about being mesmerised by beauty, is there, grandfather?"

"If I know your grandfather he will retort that our sudden distraction gave him time to think, and thus he will make a virtue of our ill manners. But in truth, she is a most beautiful woman." As Simon spoke a waitress passed and he put out a hand and touched her arm. "Tell me, pray, who is Miss Hermina?"

"Miss Hermina, sir? She is—well, she is Miss *Hermina.*"

"So I have come to understand." Simon smiled into the child's pretty face. "But Miss Hermina who?"

Before she could answer, James Marshall burst out, "Hermina *Morgan!*"

"That's right, sir! The daughter of Mr. Ebenezer Morgan, *the* Mr. Morgan."

James slumped against the back of the booth, overcome by a wealth of memories. Why, this must be old Ebenezer Morgan's granddaughter. Ebenezer Morgan & Sons . . . a small, hot, stuffy shop . . . a yoke across his shoulders, laden with parcels . . .

A voice penetrated his reverie. "Are you well, grandfather? Are you all right?" It was Richard, now holding his arm.

Across the table Simon, too, seemed full of concern. What contrasts came out of the mists fading in his mind. Richard's face, lean and narrow and sharp, an eagle's face, capped with hair black as a raven's wing and with gray eyes of compelling honesty; Simon's round and blunt, yet boldly handsome, a lion's face, with a lion's tawny hair and John Furnival's honey-coloured eyes.

"You see, I was more affected by the sight of such beauty than either of you," James found himself saying. "Upon my soul, I don't know what has come upon young men these days. To be so matter of fact!" The others relaxed and Richard took his hand away. "So, Simon, you believe that the City would support Mr. Colquhoun's scheme for the formation of a river police, in the beginning financed and controlled by the merchants in association instead of each merchant attempting to protect his own property with his own guards. And you conclude that the situation on the river is such that it would be only a matter of time before control, which means management, and finance, which means taxation, would fall into the hands of the government?"

"I have no doubt of it," Simon rejoined.

"Then indeed I *would* like to raise this matter with Timothy. If you can tear yourselves away from thoughts of Miss Hermina."

Hermina Morgan was talking to waiting friends and the bell-like clarity of her voice traveled clearly.

"I have been to see Mrs. Hewson. She has some beautiful evening gowns from Paris, but I was greatly taken by one from Vienna, in green velvet; if you can believe it, embroidered with gold thread . . ."

Timothy did not seem to be a day older than when James had seen him at the first of these meetings. He was bronzed, handsome and distinguished, and had no spare flesh. The lines in his face, though sharp and clear, made him look weathered but not aging. There was greater decisiveness in his manner, and he listened closely, giving his whole attention.

When James had finished, he said without hesitation, "Such a force on the river would have my support. What say you, Simon?"

"It was Simon who put it in my mind," James said quietly.

"No, I did not mean to take the credit—" For once Simon appeared to be almost embarrassed.

"Nor to have me know that you were in league with my old enemy," Timothy said dryly. He leaned back in his chair so that had he been a heavier man the back legs must surely have given way. "I

413

think we have a new Machiavelli among us, James. Simon, will you obtain a set of Mr. Colquhoun's proposals for my earliest consideration?"

"I will indeed, sir."

"And now I would like to discourse with Mr. Marshall," Timothy went on. "Perhaps you two young men could occupy yourselves usefully for an hour. Simon, you may like to take Richard onto the *Oriana* where there is a most fabulous collection of Chinese jade and ivory as well as Indian jewelry displayed for customs inspection."

He waved his hand as the younger men rose at once to leave. Once they were out of earshot he shook his head and spoke very slowly.

"I am nearly sure that Simon is the most remarkable man ever associated with the House of Furnival. In the year that he has been here he has lightened my work beyond all reason, and he anticipates my needs with uncanny accuracy. I will wager that he has a set of proposals for this river police already at hand, and after a decent interval he will produce them as if the need had not occurred to him until I asked. In nearly every way he has become like a son to me."

"I am very glad indeed," James said.

"And like a son he offers problems as well as much satisfaction," went on Timothy. "It is time he thought seriously of marriage but he shows no sign of that yet. The longer a man remains a bachelor the more likely he is to choose his own path and to become—I nearly said, a tyrant." As if he did not wish James to dwell on that word he went on hastily: "Is Richard affianced yet?"

"He appears to be as celibate as a monk."

"You have greater faith in monks than I! James, this river force of policemen could fill a great need. Did Simon tell you that sober estimates show that we have ten thousand thieves on the river, ranging from starving boys to modern-day pirates? I think there is little doubt that they can be overcome only by a strong body of men under a single control. With such a force we may well clear the Thames of crime."

"With such a force you could clear the whole of London of crime," James retorted. They both laughed, in the richness of friendship, before James went on: "I would like to talk to Mr. Colquhoun so that he is aware of your support."

"Then talk to him, by all means," Timothy agreed.

Soon they strolled out onto the terrace and watched the never-ending movement on the Thames. A soft rain fell, pitting the calm surface of the water, as an adept oarsman, knowing the tides, passed his small craft swiftly beneath the bows of a customs vessel, which could have missed the boat by only two or three feet.

"That is characteristic of Simon. He is utterly without fear," Timothy declared. "There are moments when I wonder whether he is utterly without feeling, also."

"I will tell you one thing," Simon said as he rowed so easily yet with such strength, "if the ships' crews were paid better, not so many of them would take bribes or help dump cargo overboard for mudlarks to pick up. If you care to take a slip of paper from inside my jacket" —he indicated where with a downward tilt of his chin—"you will see what I mean."

Richard took the paper, which listed the seamen's salaries from commander down to the lowest carpenter, and after reading it carefully he replaced it in Simon's jacket, but did not comment until they were within easy reach of the *Oriana*. Then he said, "That is one of our most difficult problems—to create conditions which will remove the temptation to be dishonest. Some men will always be lawbreakers, but such conditions *breed* criminals out of decent folk."

Soon he and Simon were clambering aboard the *Oriana*, a vessel of eight hundred tons which plied to and from the East Indies and the Far East, carrying a crew of more than one hundred. On the deck were a dozen men in Furnival livery, all with muskets, all ex-soldiers, well paid, and ready to risk their lives in defense of the treasures now being examined by a gray-haired inspector of customs and two assistants: ivory carvings of long-dead emperors and their consorts, jeweled swords and daggers, necklaces and rings. One necklace of diamonds and sapphires had surpassing beauty, and Simon stooped down and picked it up, holding it in front of Richard.

"Do you think that would sit well on Miss Hermina?"

"I cannot think of any jewel which would not."

"Which is a tribute to your gallantry but not to your sensitivity to ladies and the jewels they should wear," replied Simon. "This would be wasted on some women just as pearls would be wasted on Hermina. Richard, there is to be a ball at Great Furnival Square to celebrate Mr. Timothy's birthday. Will you come? I can safely promise you the widest selection of attractive young women in London, with comments, if you wish, on their delectability and the degree of persuasion they need for compliance in the bedchamber."

"If you have no objection," Richard replied, "I would rather find that last out for myself."

"But you will come?"

"I will come happily," Richard assured him, surveying his friend with amused interest. "I wonder what the odds are that you will have Hermina Morgan there, also."

"No man but a fool ever guessed what a woman might do," Simon rejoined. "But I shall reserve that necklace for her. What is it I once heard your grandfather say? Nothing beats trying but doing!"

On the morning following her visit to the coffee house, Hermina Morgan was looking at herself in her dressing-table mirror and applying a little of the face powder which Mr. Pitt, in his wisdom, had recently taxed when her maid came bursting in with a bunch of dark-red roses so huge that she had to hold her head on one side in order to see her mistress.

"Miss Hermina, you have a new admirer!" she declared.

"Indeed, Chloe, I did not think *you* had brought me roses as a gift," said Hermina. "And who is the gallant gentleman?"

"He gives no name and leaves no card."

"Does he not?" remarked Hermina. "Then put the roses in a corner where they will not hide those of less reticent admirers!"

On the next day, more red roses came, again without card or message, and on the third and the fourth day, also, and at the end of the week Hermina was sufficiently intrigued to begin to wonder who was sending them. Then came a single rose fastened by a narrow silk ribbon to an expensive parchmentlike envelope on the back of which was a crest and beneath it the words, "No Man Shall Be Afraid."

Slowly, and under the eagle eye of her maid, Hermina drew out the missive. It was a card bearing the same crest, and with a printed invitation.

Timothy McCampbell-Furnival hopes for
the pleasure of your company at
A BALL
to be held at Great Furnival Square in
Northwest London
On Friday, October 17, 1797
Your carriage will be welcome at
any time after 5 P.M.

"But he is an old man!" cried Chloe in anguished protest. "He must be very old. I am disappointed for you, Miss Hermina."

"An old man may have sons or grandsons," Hermina replied thoughtfully.

"You mean that you will attend?"

"I most certainly shall," replied Hermina Morgan. "And I shall go tomorrow to Mrs. Hewson . . ."

On the night of the ball the hall at Great Furnival Square was as magnificent as any palace. The huge chandelier spread a light, strengthened by a thousand candles in the wall fittings, which shimmered on colourful dresses and jewelry, much of which was beyond price, and it shone on the elegance of men whose colours were only a little less subdued and whose powdered wigs and faces gave them added romanticism. A string quartet played on each side of the gallery, whilst the library, where once old John had made his great speech, was given over to those men who wished to smoke or take a spell on their own. The passage to the dining room was lined with flowers and flunkeys guided the guests into the room where a dozen tables groaned under the weight of such food as was seldom seen. At several tables chefs wearing tall white hats carved turkeys, hams, beef and sucking-pigs, pies of a dozen varieties were served piping hot, and there was no delicacy imaginable which could not be found.

In another part of London, Todhunter Mason was sitting in the cellar of the Black Swan, an alehouse near London Bridge, putting the finishing touches to his plans for the next few hours. A man of slight build and narrow features, with pinched-in nostrils, he dressed in somber-coloured clothes made by a good tailor from Savile Row.

No one could doubt that a hundred times more jewelry would be exposed on feminine hands and heads and bosoms that night than on any ordinary night in any one place in London, and being at Great Furnival Square made the lure even more attractive, for Mason had heard of the House of Furnival's support for a river police and was determined to make its formation impossible. Now a man in his early thirties, wealthy as a result of his share of half the robberies in London, exquisitely tailored, he ruled with a tight rein. His organising ability was both thorough and brilliant, and his spies and informers were everywhere. Through a servant at Great Furnival Square, he

417

had been one of the first to know of the magnitude and splendour of this occasion, and he was fully prepared to raid when the ball was at its height.

He had drawn men from every part of London, armed them, and told them all to concentrate on Great Furnival Square. Promising to send up a flare bright enough to dazzle the coachmen, guards and Charlies waiting near the big house for the inevitable charity of food and ale, he estimated that within five minutes he and his men would have possession of the house and within fifteen minutes every woman would be stripped of her jewels. As he saw it, the greatest danger was that too many of his force would be excited by the beautiful women and there was likely to be wholesale rape, so he had to make sure the jewelry was collected by himself and other reliable and less impressionable men before the mob was let loose among the guests.

Sex did not greatly attract him.

Money and jewels fascinated him beyond all thought. They gave him a sense of power.

Seldom if ever could there have been such magnificence as there was that night. Seldom had a greater number of beautiful women gathered in one place. When the dances were at their height the ballroom looked like a glittering sea, each wave touched by a rainbow.

Just as the food and general arrangements were as nearly perfect as they could be, so were the comfort and pleasure of the guests. A dozen young Furnival men and women made sure that no one was alone for long, that introductions were made quickly and gracefully, that any embarrassing situations were avoided; and if a young man began to show himself the worse for drink someone was at hand to make sure he did not become offensive. Outside in the great square and in the streets leading to it were massed the coaches and carriages of the guests, and while the coachmen were eating and drinking in the places provided for them, Furnival guards, strengthened by older watchmen and four Bow Street Runners, took care that nothing was stolen.

Even for those who were used to such affairs, this was a triumph.

To Hermina Morgan, it was a breathless round of young and handsome men, any one of whom *might* be her mysterious admirer. She had been introduced to Simon and had recognised him, and she had also been introduced to Richard. Of the two, Simon was infinitely the finer dancer and conversationalist; for a while Richard had been almost incoherent. But she was used to young men being tongue-tied in her presence and coaxed him to talk until one of the young men acting as an escort came to them, a thickset, strong-faced man with graying hair at his side.

"Miss Morgan, may I have the pleasure of introducing Mr. Patrick Colquhoun?" he asked.

"My pleasure is much the greater," Colquhoun said in an attractive Scottish accent.

Colquhoun, Richard thought in surprise; he had not dreamed that the magistrate would be here. Later he saw him talking to Timothy and had little doubt that they were discussing the river police. He knew that his grandfather had spent several hours with the justice, no doubt offering some advice on those things which might lead to hostility within the City of London.

Quite suddenly, he wanted to leave this place. It had been exciting, fascinating, unforgettable—but he did not really belong. Simon did, but not he. Simon was now on his own on the staircase, surveying the multitude. Suddenly he moved and a few moments later Richard saw him with Hermina Morgan; if one had to say who was the most beautiful woman present, virtually all would have named her. Richard went out, past two footmen who were constantly opening the door, past the mass of carriages and men, who were laughing and talking in subdued tones. Soon he had left Great Furnival Square behind him. As he reached a corner a tiny figure darted out from beneath a carriage, hands outstretched in supplication.

"Please, sir, my stomach is empty. I need money for food. Please, kind sir."

Richard put a hand to his fob pocket and drew out his purse—and the urchin snatched it, gripped it tightly and ran off. Richard sprang after him, two words at his lips: "Stop thief!" But he bit them back. He heard the padding sound as the child's bare feet sounded on the pavement, and then he saw the tiny figure against a lamp on the corner of a house—and saw him recoil.

A larger figure appeared in silhouette and the boy screeched, "That's mine. That's mine!"

On that instant there was a vivid flash which lit up the roofs and the windows. As it faded, an even larger figure appeared, plucked the urchin from the ground and, to Richard's horror, flung him brutally to one side. Now other figures were moving and there was more light,

419

not only from the houses but from a host of flares; not two or three but dozens of men were approaching. The flash must have been some kind of signal, thought Richard, but who would be abroad at this hour and in this place?

He turned on his heel, stilling a desire to run, and began to retrace his steps. Soon he was approaching Great Furnival Square and could see the lines of carriages. No flares shone behind him now, but he felt sure men were still on the move. At last he dared quicken his pace to a run, but as he did so a man appeared out of the shadows, huge and terrifying.

"That's far enough," the stranger growled, and a powerful hand descended on Richard's shoulder. "Who are you and where are you off to?"

"Men are—coming," Richard gasped. "I think there are a lot of them, some with flares. They—"

He was interrupted by a shrill cry, the cry of a night owl; and this was taken up in several places, as if owls had suddenly swooped down from the rooftops. The man with his hand on Richard's shoulder turned and as he did so he released Richard and pushed him in the direction in which he had been going.

"If you want to keep your head on your shoulders, *run!*" he ordered.

Another man shouted, and almost at once more flares appeared in windows and doorways, spreading an eerie yellow glow and revealing dozens of men streaming out of the alleys and houses where they had been hiding. From not far off came the crack of a shot followed by a roar of voices.

Close by Richard was the wall of a garden. The chance of getting back to Great Furnival Square by the streets was negligible but he might be able to climb over the roofs.

He sprang toward the top of the wall, clawing to get a hold with his hands, missed once, tried again and caught the rough brick at the top. Gaining a firmer grip, he hauled himself up and edged his way along until he found himself on top of a house porch, able to see but not visible to any from street level. Dozens of men were clutched in hand-to-hand fighting, knives flashing, staves cracking against heads. Flares carried by some of the men were tossed toward waiting carriages and some caught fire. Horses began to rear and scream.

Richard realised exactly what was happening.

An enormous gang of thieves had come to raid Great Furnival

Square, doubtless planning to break into the main house and the ball-room. But the raid must have been expected, and the waiting coachmen had obviously included constables and peace officers ready for the fray. There was little shouting but he could hear the heavy breathing of men as they fought, the thud of blows, the occasional gasp or groan. He had no doubt that the defenders were winning at this spot, but was that true everywhere? Were there places where the attackers had the upper hand?

Richard looked up to the window above him and saw an overhanging ledge which would be within hand's reach if he stood on tip-toe. He stretched cautiously, grasped the ledge and began to haul himself upward. Two or three bricks were loose, giving him a fingerhold, and the idea of climbing up to the roof and clambering over other roofs until he reached a spot from where he could look down into the square became a practical possibility. Glancing downward, he saw that the fighting was still fierce. No one appeared to have the slightest idea that anyone was above. He stretched up to the next ledge and repeated what he had already done. It was easier than he had hoped, but by the time he stood on the second ledge he was gasping for breath.

No one noticed him. The shutters were fastened in the house, which seemed to be empty.

Richard stared up at the stars and saw two more overhanging ledges: the second would be the last! He began again. Dust from the bricks began to settle on his face, irritating his eyes, tickling his nose and making him want to cough, but he fought against it. The din from the street seemed to grow louder and three shots were fired in quick succession. A man cried out and there was a lull in the struggling until another screamed, "At them, boys! At them!"

Richard began to climb again.

It became easier to think, for now he could move more mechanically. There could be no doubt that the men near the square had been prepared for the raid; no one but he had been taken by surprise—he and that poor urchin who had been so roughly flung aside.

Richard shuddered at the recollection, tried to push it in the back of his mind, quickened his pace—and slipped. For a terrifying moment he thought he was going to fall. He grabbed at the last ledge but it was the one below, on which his foot caught, which saved him. For several minutes he stood spread-eagled against the wall, gasping, shivering at the nearness of disaster, but soon he felt better and started on his way up again, giving the task every ounce of effort and concentration.

At last his hands reached the guttering. He put his weight on this gingerly lest it should loosen, but it held until he was able to put one knee onto the roof. Now it did not matter what noise he made, and soon he was standing upright, still unobserved. Perhaps because he was higher than when he had looked down before, perhaps because he was more accustomed to the light, the scene in the street below was even more vivid. He could see knives flashing, small groups fighting with great ferocity, and here and there a couple locked in what looked like a death grip. The main body of the fighting was nearer the end of the street from which he had run; the defenders were pushing their attackers back.

Richard turned away and began to climb toward the chimneys. The sloping roof made it difficult; once again he nearly fell, and after this he dropped to his hands and knees, going up on all fours. Now he forgot the scene behind him and could think only of what he would see in Great Furnival Square.

He reached the chimneys and stood up in their cover but could see only a narrow segment of the square at the foot of the houses opposite. Sitting down, he edged himself forward, acutely aware of the danger of falling, until he could view the incredible scene below.

There must have been five hundred men in Great Furnival Square!

Two or three large groups were fighting and he saw Simon—*Simon* —leap into the fray with a sword. The double doors of the great house were wide open but the approach was empty, although a few stood, obviously on guard, close to the footpath. The fence about the garden in the middle had been crushed in a dozen places, flower beds and grass trampled into shambles. Bodies lay everywhere, while those who had been wounded were crawling toward open spaces as if looking desperately for ways of escape.

Men were hanging from the branches of three trees! At first Richard could not believe that this was so; then he saw three men grab another and hoist him high, saw four or five at the end of a rope heave as if this were a tug of war, saw the hoisted man swinging by the neck, kicking wildly but unable to save himself. The other end of the rope was then tied about a tree branch and the self-appointed executioners seized another victim.

Three men stood where that one had been plucked from, hands tied behind their backs, obviously in line for hanging. Richard wanted to scream *No!* but no sound came except that of heavy breathing. His chest was heaving, his whole body was clammy, and sweat dripped off his forehead into his eyes.

Through a blur, he saw a man sitting at a table brought from one of the houses and a group of manacled men on one side. One, standing in front of the table, was also manacled. The seated man clearly was acting as judge, the garden having been turned into a court for summary justice. From where he sat Richard saw his mouth open as he spoke, saw the victim drop onto his knees, saw him dragged away to stand with the others awaiting hanging.

The self-appointed judge was Sir Douglas Rackham; Richard was quite sure of that. Had there ever been clearer evidence of his lust for power?

The fighting was nearly done. More prisoners were taken to swell the size of the manacled group, and at least thirty men were now awaiting "trial" while ten or twelve were hanging and twice as many lay stretched out on the grass, some of them in the fine clothes of revelers at the ball.

Richard looked for Simon and saw him talking to another, bigger man. Who was it? Colquhoun, Patrick Colquhoun! Was such a man party to this travesty of justice, this horror piled on horror? Richard felt an icy coldness as Simon left the magistrate and went to the table, standing between Rackham and the latest manacled victim. What he said Richard could not hear but at once there was a roar of protest.

"No!"

"Hang them, hang them!"

So Simon was trying to stop this hangman's holiday.

Two of the bellowing men from a dozen or so who were acting as guards rushed forward, one with cudgel upraised, and Richard felt a rush of fear: if that descended on Simon's head it would most certainly kill him. Simon turned at the last minute, his sword flashed from its scabbard, and with astonishing ease he ran the man through. Others from the ball came running to his assistance, and the man who had been passing sentence of death with such swift pleasure rose from his seat and was hustled away.

All the fighting had stopped now, and Richard prayed that none of the Furnivals had been hurt. He was so far removed from the tumult below that he could hear distant sounds, then the striking of several clocks and, clear and shrill, a watchman who could not be unaware of the fighting calling out: "Eleven o'clock and all's well."

423

"All's well," Richard choked. "What use *are* the Charlies if they can call such nonsense?"

He began the hazardous climb down. Before doing anything else he must find that child.

Standing at the windows of the great house were the women guests and a number of older men. At one, by herself, was Hermina Morgan. She watched only Simon, and at the moment when he was about to be attacked she drew in her breath with a hiss that a sword might make being drawn swiftly from its scabbard. She saw Simon turn and run the man through and her eyes glistened with rare brightness.

CHAPTER *35*

Guardians of the River

RICHARD DROPPED from the lowest ledge, brushed himself down, hesitated, then turned his back on Great Furnival Square
and took the lane he had walked along earlier that evening. It was like
a battlefield, wounded men being attended by their friends, coaches
and carriages smashed and broken, sedan chairs in pieces, fifty or sixty
horses huddled together and kept calm by a youth who was talking to
them all the time in a monotonous Irish undertone. Richard reached
the corner where the lad had accosted him and walked more slowly.
There was no damage here but many people were standing about, and
others from nearby houses had come out and were offering them beer
and cider, some food as well.

He came upon a coat spread over the curb.

He hesitated, staring down, for from beneath the coat poked a boy's
foot. After a few moments he made himself go forward, bend down,
and draw the coat aside.

There lay the child: dead.

The face was unbruised, but the back of the head was crushed and
death must have come on the instant. As Richard knelt beside the

emaciated body he heard footsteps approaching. They stopped, and looking up, Richard saw a priest standing there.

"Do you know the child?" he asked.

"No, Father," answered Richard. "We—we met just once." He straightened up but still looked down. "Did you cover him?"

"Yes, my son, as I have covered too many on this sad night."

"Where will you take him?" Richard asked.

"Where else but the nearest poor hole?"

"To a grave of his own in a churchyard, the churchyard of Saint Anselm's if needs be. How much will it cost?" Richard asked, opening the front of his jacket, for in an inside pocket he kept more money than he ever carried in his purse. "Will two guineas suffice?"

"It is generous, my son, and will help to feed some who are hungry."

Richard said, "Bury the boy deep," and turned and walked on.

It was an hour and a half before he reached the Strand and his rooms at the top of the four-story building which now housed "Mr. Londoner." A candle fluttered at each landing of the narrow staircase, and he left them burning, for others who worked at the shop also slept here. Entering a raftered room with two gabled windows overlooking the roofs and smaller buildings at the back, he lit a candle, sat down in a William and Mary slung chair, which had a heavy leather back and was more comfortable than most of its kind, and put his feet up on an old milking stool. Everything in this room was old, and he had bought each piece himself, from the two Roman urns which stood in recesses on either side of the main window to the four-poster bed brought over by one of the immigrants fleeing from religious persecution in Holland before that country had established toleration.

The wooden floor was firmer than when he had moved in, for he had replaced many of the boards with more substantial ones from buildings which were being demolished; he got much pleasure from using tools and the wooden cleats fitted perfectly, while all the joints were level. The fireplace was part of the reredos from St. Hilary's Church; he had found it in a builder's yard, covered with chippings. On the floor were Persian carpets bought from sales at the old Somerset House before its demolition.

He loved the room, but just now he was too distraught by what had happened to take pleasure in it. Ten thousand thieves plague the river, Simon had said; many of them might have been drawn from the river that night.

Leaning back more comfortably in the chair, he closed his eyes. A clock at St. Mary-le-Strand Church began to strike: one, two. Two o'clock. He began to doze ...

It was daylight when he woke to heavy banging on the door. For a moment he stared at the door, too startled to move, and saw its stout oak timbers shaking and the big iron key quivering up and down until suddenly it fell out. Then, as he slid his feet off the stool, there came a cry.

"Richard! Are you there? *Richard!*"

That was Simon's voice!

He called out hoarsely, "Coming, coming!" Startled to full wakefulness he crossed to the door as a man said, "He answered." He could hear the breathing of several men outside, then Simon's voice, clear and authoritative.

"Wait until we see it is he. Then go about your business."

Richard opened the door.

Simon stood in the middle of a group of five men, two with staves, two carrying muskets. There was little light on the landing except that from the windows behind Richard, and this shone into Simon's face, showing his eyes, glassy and red-rimmed, his sweaty, blood-streaked cheeks, his torn jacket—it looked as if a sword or knife had slit it across the stomach; inches deeper and it would surely have disemboweled him.

Despite his obvious weariness, his smile was warm.

"I couldn't find you among the dead or injured," he said, "and I wanted to make sure you hadn't been carried off as a hostage. Three men were but we got them back. This was a well-organised affair and I don't yet know who was behind it, but I had sufficient warning to prepare a hot reception."

Richard stood aside, scarcely comprehending.

"Are you really all right, Simon? *I* am as well as I look."

"I need a wash, some breakfast and twelve hours' sleep," declared Simon. "When I wake I'll be as good as new. May I use your closet?"

"Of course." Richard opened the drawer of a chest and took out a clean towel, made sure there was soap in the basin, and left Simon to his ablutions. He himself went down two floors, where the maids who looked after his room were already up. He ordered breakfast for both Simon and himself and went back upstairs. Only now was he beginning to think clearly and the foremost thing on his mind was Simon's obvious anxiety for him. In this past few hours he had seen a different

427

Simon, much more mature and sophisticated. How could a man change so much in one short year?

But *had* he changed? Or was he only now showing his real self?

Richard heard him splashing and spluttering and peered into a square mirror with a rosewood frame which could swivel on brass hinges to any position he desired. He needed a shave and a wash but the shave could wait. Then Simon came out and Richard said, "Breakfast will be here soon."

Simon, still clutching the towel, remarked, "Did you see Rackham last night?"

"As well as you did."

"The man is a dangerous fool," Simon declared. "He argued, and will plead, that only by summary justice could he prevent a much worse slaughter and that the men, who were out of control, would have done the hanging anyway."

Simon had hardly finished when footsteps sounded outside: one of the maids with tea, which he, Richard, liked first thing in the morning. She put this on a table as Simon finished drying himself and while Richard went into the closet.

Almost at once he heard the girl exclaim, "Oh, sir, I beg you, no."

He stood very still and listened, wondering whether Simon was going to reveal another facet of himself, knowing that if he were then he, Richard, would have to intervene.

She was a buxom girl, not yet seventeen, wearing a square-necked dress, not as daring as most, yet showing the deep swell of her bosom. As she straightened from the table Simon stepped behind her and slipped an arm around her waist, hugging her close to him.

"Oh, sir," she gasped, "I beg you, no."

To her great relief, mingled with some strange awareness of regret, he released her.

"Why are you not pouring out some tea?" he asked, laughing.

In a gasping voice she said, "Mr. Richard likes to pour his own, sir."

"I like mine poured by a pretty wench," declared Simon, "and you'll pour it or I'll know the reason why."

She was giggling when at last she backed away, and when she was on the stairs she stopped and adjusted her bodice, placing her hand where his had been. Then the cook called her and she hurried down to fetch breakfast for Master Richard and this tawny-haired stranger who had so affected her.

Leaning back in the chair in which Richard had spent the night, Simon stretched out his long legs. He sipped tea slowly and had half a cup left when Richard came out of the closet, looking much fresher. Richard leaned against the foot of the bed and poured himself tea while Simon grinned up at him.

"So you were in the wars, too, were you?"

"I saw most of the fight from the top of a house," Richard answered. "I also saw—" He broke off, and then asked, "How long have you been an expert swordsman?"

"Since I was adopted by the House of Furnival," answered Simon. "Any man who spends much time on the river and in the City at night has to know how to defend himself. So you saw me employing my skills."

"I saw you stop that hanging, as I said."

"Ah. So I proved I am a law-abiding man. And so I am, so I am."

"You say you expected the attack last night?"

Simon nodded. "Yes. I have spies in many places, and several reports reached me—and in any case, only a fool would have been unprepared for trouble on such an occasion. I half expected the scoundrels to go to the river thinking that we would have taken most of our men away from there; had they done so they would have had as rude a shock there as they had at Great Furnival Square. Richard, if you've taught me anything it is that the only way to overcome criminals is by organisation. Only I'm afraid we have greatly postponed the day of a police force for London. The government will take heart, tell us what a magnificent job we have done, and command us to continue. But I have one good thing to tell you."

Outside there was the rattling of knives on a tray, of pottery clinking. Richard moved toward the door to open it, saying, "I'm glad of that, anyhow. What is it?"

"There will be a river police force within a month, and the government will sponsor it soon afterward. I talked to Patrick Colquhoun, who now has the ear of at least three Ministers. That man is a great worker! It was not until recently that I realised how much he does for charity as well as reform. Do they not call him the King of the Soup Kitchens for the Poor?"

Richard laughed as he opened the door and the maid came in, shooting one glance toward Simon, then hurrying with the laden tray and the wooden platters to a table beneath one of the windows. She set out steaks and sausages, eggs, butter, new bread, cheese and tankards of ale, then scurried out.

"She is terrified of you," Richard chided.

"Terrified? You are not used to the ways of wenches. There is nothing she would like more than a tumble with me, and she has you to blame for missing such a delight!" Simon hitched his chair forward and went on musingly: "You don't have to be a celibate in order to be a saint, Richard!" He laughed at Richard's expression and began to eat fastidiously, speaking from time to time. "I cannot imagine what you would think of me if we were to see more of each other. I suspect you would often be shocked! . . . I am told by Mr. Timothy that I have at least *some* of your grandfather's half brother, Johnny! . . . Come, man, that was not meant to hurt. If all I hear of Johnny is true, he would have been a great man but for one twist in his character, and in many ways he was the most lovable of individuals. Do you know his son, Peter? I thought not. He is a good and able young man without a touch of brilliance or a touch of badness, likely to be the most worthy of servants of the House of Furnival. Will you understand me, not think me disloyal, if I say that as a family the Furnivals have not done well in their bloodline? I suspect that at some time several of them married the wrong women and lost the fire in the blood." He drank deeply from his tankard, and for the first time paused to concentrate on what he was saying instead of flinging out remarks with indifference to their effect. Looking very straight into Richard's eyes, he asked, "Did you see Hermina Morgan last night?"

"What man could fail to?"

"No man worth calling a man! Now there is a woman with fire in the blood. I am determined to marry her, Richard."

Richard eyed him with the same directness and asked dryly, "Is she aware of her good fortune?"

Nothing in his voice or expression betrayed the contraction of his heart and the pain which Simon's announcement caused him. He had never known himself so affected by a woman as by Hermina. Had never dreamed of one, nor drawn her into his fantasies, as he did Hermina.

He had to make himself listen to his friend.

"It would not surprise me if she had not already determined to marry me," Simon replied with a gust of laughter. "She is a woman so used to getting her own way that if she has, then I shall have to show a proper reluctance." The words hovered in the air until suddenly he brought his fist crashing down on the table, making everything on it jump, and in a taut voice he went on: "To hell with reluctance! I'll not stoop to devious ways with her. But we'll marry. Have my word on it, we'll marry. And our children will put new blood into the line of the Furnivals. How is that for a grand jest, Richard?"

"Is it not how all great English families have remained strong?" asked Richard mildly. He was beginning to feel less acutely and realised that for a long time he had expected some such news as this.

Simon threw back his head and roared with laughter.

It was eight months before a Marine Police Force was set up for London's river, sponsored by the merchants, on the plan drawn up by Patrick Colquhoun. James Marshall read the details of the force in *The Daily Clarion* immediately after its formation. There were to be sixty full-time officers, all paid enough to make sure they worked with "utmost zeal, vigilance, prudence, discretion and sobriety." Within days a marked improvement became visible in the conditions on the river. Thieves and mudlarks no longer found it easy to raid ships and warehouses, pilferers found it more difficult to get away with their loot, prostitutes, with whom most of the thieves worked as bullies, found themselves hounded away from doorways and dark corners and kept away from ships. In months, the trade on London's river was nearly free from the depredations which had been costing, some authorities declared, at least fifty thousand pounds a month. In less than a year the government began to prepare a bill to take over the force, and by the year 1800 the Thames River Police became a public body through an Act of Parliament which won the overwhelming support of the House of Commons and of the Lords. A new Police Office was opened at Wapping Steps, with three magistrates: a police force was actually in operation in London!

Yet one evening in September of that same year, when Richard was at the Chelsea house, where a room was now set aside for his special use, James was more angry than he had been for many years, and his voice was vibrant as he said, "It must now be only a matter of time before disaster strikes unless we have the police force the whole of London needs, Richard. Not simply the river. *Everywhere*. Oh, I know, progress has been remarkable in the past decade, but it is not enough. The present situation is an invitation to disaster—"

He broke off, coughing.

"James," said Mary in a subdued voice, "you should not excite yourself."

"I am tired of not exciting myself," declared James crossly. "I cannot sit here and say and do nothing while I watch the situation deteriorate. I would like to go on the river now that it has been cleared of such a horde of criminals, and then I would like to go to those places in London where the paid criminals have repaired to. For the river police have not thrust them into the Thames and let them drown, I presume. They do still exist. They have to survive and they will feed off other sections of the populace. We need a police force for the City and the rest of the metropolis more desperately than ever. *Make the authorities understand that.* And I will try to make Timothy—"

He began to cough again, and Mary pushed her chair back and moved toward him, but James waved her back.

"I will try to make Timothy use his influence, while you, Richard, exert yours on Simon," he went on. "I am told that Simon is a remarkable man, a giant among today's Furnivals, more like my—my stepfather than anyone—anyone—anyone—"

Once again he began to cough, and this time he dropped back into his chair and began to breathe very heavily. Richard called one of the gardeners and together they carried him up to his room, where Mary and the housekeeper got him to bed, and a lad was sent to fetch a doctor.

"He has caught a chill and is grievously ill with congestion of the lungs," the doctor diagnosed. "Only with constant surveillance can there be any hope for him. I judge the crisis will come in the early hours of the morning. I will send a reliable and experienced woman to help, while you, Mrs. Marshall, must rest, or you will also become ill."

But Mary stayed up throughout the small hours while James fought for life. She was with him, and so was Richard, when he died as the first light of dawn spread from the other side of the river.

When it was certain that he was dead, Mary allowed herself to be led to another bedroom and took a spoonful of laudanum to help her rest. As the children and grandchildren came, too late to see James Marshall alive but hoping to console Mary, she slept, staying in the small bedroom overlooking the orchard for so long that when the doctor arrived to attend her the family was waiting anxiously for him.

Richard and the housekeeper went in with the doctor, who spent only a few minutes examining her, then straightened up and said, "She has been tired to a point of exhaustion for a long time. Now that her husband is dead she has no desire for life. It is doubtful even whether she will become conscious again."

Mary did not regain consciousness, and on the third day the two people who had loved each other so dearly were buried in the same grave in a tiny churchyard in Chelsea. Among those who stood by the graveside on that chilly autumn morning were Timothy McCampbell-Furnival and Simon; and there was Benedict Sly, the oldest of them all, who had printed almost everything that James had said, and who had conveyed some degree of his passion in an obituary which took up more than half a page of *The Daily Clarion*. It was the last action Benedict carried out as editor of the newspaper; a week later he was taken ill with jaundice and at the year's end he died also.

Within two weeks of Benedict Sly's death, Richard sensed a change in the character of *The Daily Clarion*. Gone was the forthrightness and the fearless challenge to authority; in its place was a loud beating of drums, as it were, in praise of the manner in which London was managed and governed; the City of London, its Lord Mayor and aldermen, its leading citizens, wealthy bankers and merchants, could do no wrong. Now and again the editorials urged the government to some action, but there was no breath of the old reforming zeal. Troubled by this, for Benedict Sly's newspaper had been of great value to all reform movements and an unceasing champion of the campaign for a police force, Richard went to the coffee house in Wine Court, where his grandfather and Benedict Sly had so often met and he himself had joined them, hoping to see Benedict's surviving partner. He was not there, but a bearded man whose breath whistled through his nostrils and rattled through his chest joined him at a table which needed washing. The heavy crockery was cracked and unappetizing; the place had obviously fallen on bad times.

"You don't recognize me," the bearded man said. "I am Neil, once of *The Times*, and a great admirer of your grandfather." The red-veined eyes held shrewdness. "Have you come hoping to find out what has happened to *The Daily Clarion?*"

"That, and Benedict's partner," Richard answered.

"He inherited *The Daily Clarion* and also its debts," declared the ex-*Times* reporter. "Benedict had been running the newspaper at a loss for ten years because there had been too much competition. His partner was compelled to get what he could, which was not much, Mr. Marshall. A syndicate of City men and Members of Parliament bought the good will and changed the policy of the paper overnight. It is now little more than a scandal and gossip sheet, but the syndicate uses it as a political front, too, relying on its past reputation to mislead its readers."

"Do you know any members of the syndicate?" asked Richard, more heavyhearted than ever.

"I know them all, especially the chairman—Sir Douglas Rackham," Neil answered. "Any man who can escape with only a reprimand from the Solicitor General for what he did at Great Furnival Square must surely have the devil on his side."

There was now no possible doubt; all support from *The Daily Clarion* had died with Benedict Sly, and the task of overcoming the opposition, both in Parliament and among the people, would become more difficult than ever.

And Simon was busy with the House of Furnival and his personal affairs.

CHAPTER *36*

The Attackers

HERMINA MORGAN watched Simon as he moved toward her. She felt her heart beating very fast, faster than it had ever beaten at the approach of a man. She was aware of the intensity of his gaze and knew that he felt raw, naked desire for her. She did not move.

She wondered, fleetingly and with only part of her mind, why she had allowed this meeting to come about. Why, with this man, she lost her inner composure. She had been taught and had come to believe that men were her servants and suitors, who always came a-begging for her favours, and so it had been throughout her years of maturing.

Now, as Simon came toward her, she felt for the first time in her life that she was not in control of her emotions.

They were in a cottage by the river at Putney, not far from the wooden bridge. A waterman sent by Simon had brought her to Westminster Steps on this warm autumn day in the first year of the new century, about a year after they had first dined together. Simon had behaved punctiliously but she had a sense of great power, even of danger, in him. On either side the old vineyards, now run wild, stretched down to grassy banks, the fields were dotted with tall beech and oak, hedges had sprung up since the Enclosure Act, and small farmhouses stood in a dozen places, each with its barns and outhouses, each with its cattle and free-running sheep, fowls and pigs, many with a path leading down to the river where dinghies and small boats were tied to rickety-looking jetties. A few people crossed the bridge, and children ran over it, making it swing and shake and causing nervous women to call out: "Don't run, don't run!"

But few heeded their pleas.

Simon had sent Hermina a dozen deep-red roses and inside the accompanying missive, a key; the note said that she would find a waterman waiting for her at Westminster Steps and that the man would wear the livery of the House of Furnival. She had told herself that she would not go, that nothing would make her.

The waterman had been waiting, ready to help her into the slender craft. At the jetty close to the cottage he had secured the boat and then had accompanied her part of the way. Was he accustomed to carrying out these preliminaries? she wondered. If this were so, he revealed it neither by word nor expression. He had left her when she reached a stile in a beech and hawthorn hedge, and she had walked in the seclusion of the garden to the weathered oak door, looking at the thatched roof and the leaded panes of glass and the pink and white ramblers till smothering the porch. The small lawn had been freshly scythed and the scent of flowers and newly cut grass went to her head like wine.

Before going inside she had fought a battle with herself. This *must* be the place where Simon Rattray-Furnival took his women, and by being here she was little better than a whore; she should not and need not stay.

She had felt hand and body quivering as she had opened the door.

She had waited for no more than five minutes in the front room, with its dark oak rafters and heavy beams. All was beautifully kept. The furniture had the luster of wood constantly polished over the long years, the brick floor had been newly painted, the brass of the fire irons in the inglenook fireplace gleamed brightly. A fire burned, low but welcome, for once out of the direct rays of the sun it was cool.

Now Simon approached. She had seen him rowing himself, not at speed but with calm assurance; he had moored alongside the other boat. For a few minutes he had been hidden from her by the hedge but now he was halfway up the flagged path leading to the front door. If he had any thought that she was at the window he gave not the slightest indication, and Hermina moved quickly back. Nothing she could do, however, could take the hot stinging flush out of her cheeks.

He opened the door and stepped inside, closed the door and deliberately shot the bolt. He turned and looked at her; it was as if he were stripping her naked with his eyes.

He smiled with swift, reckless gaiety and said, "You are the most beautiful creature I have ever seen."

"You are most gallant, sir," she managed to say.

He drew nearer, saying, "I have wanted you from the moment I first saw you."

"To add to your conquests?"

"No," he said. "To marry and bear my children."

She caught her breath as he stood in front of her. His eyes seemed to burn into hers and when he took her by the shoulders her flesh tingled beneath his fingers.

"Do you understand me?" he demanded.

"I—I understand full well."

"Since you are a woman of spirit I little doubt that you will make your own decision whom you will marry, and that you will have no difficulty obtaining your father's approval," Simon said. "You know that no matter how much wealth and how many possessions you have, I have more, so I cannot want you for your money." There was laughter in his voice but none in his eyes, and the pressure of his fingers became greater. "For your body and your childbearing—is that enough?"

She said, with sudden confidence, "I can promise you my body but I cannot promise you children."

"Have you reason for saying that?" he demanded sharply.

"None, except that some women *are* barren."

"Not you," declared Simon Rattray-Furnival with overwhelming confidence. "Not you, my sweet." His expression changed to a frown and he went on: "I'll have you know one thing. Once you are mine, you are mine, and I'd kill any other man who touched you. Do you understand *that*?"

"I've no wish to watch my husband die on the gallows," she retorted.

"You'll never see me die," he declared as if there could be no possibility of doubt. "But the choice is yours, Hermina Morgan. Marry me and I am the only man you will know for the rest of your life. Refuse to marry me and your life will be your own. How is it to be?"

He released her shoulders, lowering his hands to the small of her back, and pressed her close.

"Say no, and I'll go away," he told her. "The waterman will come and take you wherever you will. Say yes . . ." He paused. "Which is it to be, Hermina? Yes or no?"

She found her breath coming in shallow gasps.

She found thoughts flashing through her mind: that she could ask for time; that it was ludicrous that any man should propose in this aggressive way; that now his body set fire to hers; that if she delayed he might turn on his heel and stride out, and if he did, he might never come back. The pressure of his body grew more relentless, and now his eyes seemed to burn right through her.

"I'll ask you just once more," he said. "Which is it to be? Yes or no?"

She made herself say, "What if I cannot give you a child?"

"Yes—or—no?" he ground out between his teeth.

"Oh, dear God, save me," she cried, and suddenly her body went limp. "Yes, yes, yes, *yes!*"

Never had there been such triumph in a man's eyes as that which shone in his as he picked her up and carried her into the room beyond.

There was a moon when he rowed her back to Westminster Steps; a moon and brilliant stars, quiet lapping of the water, only a few other boats, the lights of London gaining in brightness, the flares at the foot of the steps. He left the boat with a Furnival waterman and they walked to the embankment where a coach waited and they were driven to her home, in Lancaster Square.

At the doors, Simon said with a droll kind of humour, "The quicker we arrange the marriage date, Hermina, no doubt the better."

"It cannot be too soon for me," she said.

"One month?"

"One month, and I can have all the clothes I need, every invitation out and answered."

She looked into his eyes. He did not stoop to kiss her and she did not show any outward sign of affection, but when she went to her bedroom she looked at herself in the mirror and pictured him beside her.

Every newspaper, every journal, every announcement, called this the most spectacular wedding of the decade. There were more peers of the realm, more Members of Parliament, more food, more finery, more magnificence than at any but a royal wedding.

Standing in close attendance, hiding both thoughts and feelings, was Richard Marshall. Even on this day Hermina's beauty could stab right through him.

A year almost to the day after the wedding, in October 1801, their first child was born. They named their daughter Grace.

Three years later, on October 28, their second child was born and to Simon's joy this was a boy. He was christened Marriott, and he took after his mother in both looks and colouring.

At the time of Marriott's birth London was undergoing one of the periods of panic which danger from the French and Spaniards could bring. For Napoleon, with much of Europe at his feet, was known to be mustering a huge army across the Channel, and a fleet of flat-bottomed boats to bring men and horses and cannon for the invasion which had been talked of for so long. Not only London but the whole of Britain was in the grip of fear, for if Napoleon once got a foothold on the Channel coast, what chance would there be of forcing the French Army back?

On the twenty-ninth of October of the following year, the Rattray-Furnivals' third child and second son was born, and not only to their own rejoicing. Out in London's streets and public places the people had gone wild. Church bells rang and rattles clattered, whistles blew and bands played, for Nelson's smaller fleet had smashed both the French and the Spaniards at Trafalgar, destroying any hope Napoleon might ever have of coming back to the Channel coast and launching his attack on England.

By the time the news came through of Nelson's death the gin and beer and joy of victory had carried the people beyond sadness. London and all Britain rejoiced, while Simon looked down at his second son, the shape of whose head and face made him quite unmistakably a Furnival in the grand tradition.

He was christened John.

Timothy McCampbell-Furnival felt tired but happy, relaxed and well fed. For a man of seventy-seven he was in remarkably fine fettle. As he stood on the terrace at Furnival Tower House and looked across at the lights and the bustle at Furnival Docks, heard the shouting and the squealing of winches and hoists, the lapping of the Thames in a stiff breeze, he felt not only contented but had a stirring of interest in having company in bed that night. It was only a passing thought and indicated fancy more than active desire. He did not feel seventy-seven; he had not felt sixty-seven ten years ago.

He had been present that afternoon at the baptism of Simon's third child—the second son, John, who was now nearly a year old.

In the years since Simon had married, he had also grown in stature. No one now seriously doubted his right to the leadership of the House of Furnival. Occasionally some of the other relatives conspired and played politics but he defeated them by sheer indifference, as if leadership was his by some kind of divine right. And his wife—what a magnificent woman she was!

It was not often that Timothy came to Furnival Tower House on a Sunday but two ships had berthed with precious cargoes from the Far East and he had wanted to be at hand to welcome the captains in the time-honoured Furnival fashion. Simon, of course, had been with him. Simon had wanted Timothy to leave with him, but one of the ship's masters was an old friend who would soon come across the river from the *Sea Lion* and together he and Timothy would repair to Great Furnival Square for the night. Timothy heard more lapping of water than usual but could see no sign of a ship's dinghy. He turned from the railing and looked at the windows and the lights of the docks reflected on the heavy glass.

He did not see the three men in the water close to the steps which led up to the terrace. Each had a bundle tied over his head; one had a knife between his teeth, one a heavy cudgel secured to his shoulders. They swam strongly but the noise they made was drowned by wind and tide.

It was strange, mused Timothy, that he thought of Simon as his son; not as his nephew, not as his grandson, but as his son. Consequently he saw Simon's three children as grandchildren and prayed that the two boys would inherit the qualities of their father.

Timothy often confused Simon with Johnny, of course. That was strange, because in so many ways his mind was as clear as ever. Simon —Johnny—Richard. He had not seen young Richard Marshall since

James had died. It seemed strange to Timothy that he should be so much older than everyone about him. His cronies were gone, even his enemies! Not that he had made many enemies and those few only because of their jealousy. Simon had the same trait of making friends.

Timothy did not see the men climbing up the wet stone steps, each clad in breeches cut short at the knees, each now carrying a weapon.

They had been sent by the man who held them and so many others in his thrall: Todhunter Mason.

In spite of the wind it was not cold on the terrace, which was protected from both sides, and the wind must be coming from the west. What a noise it made! What a night for a ship to set sail. And one *was* setting sail from farther up the river, a bark which Timothy thought came from Morgan's Wharf, a bonded tea and coffee warehouse belonging to the company which might soon be merging with Furnival's. He had discussed this with Simon who, in his decisive way, had said, "Yes, sir. But not yet, I beg you."

He had not explained why, but no doubt he would have a good reason.

Timothy watched the ship traveling faster than it should, as if the wind billowing its sails would soon take it out of the captain's hand.

The three men were now behind him.

Two were by the doors leading into the house; one was creeping up toward him, the cudgel, with its spiked head, in his hand. Not until the last moment did Timothy sense that anything was wrong. Some sound which did not merge with the wind and the water made him turn, and he saw the man, water glistening on naked shoulders, chest and arms, one arm descending with the cudgel gripped in it. Timothy made an involuntary movement but it was too late. A crushing blow fell on one side of his head. It did not render him unconscious but made him stagger. The man grabbed him by one arm, yanked him upright, and struck again.

A messenger came for Simon at half-past ten, when he was in bed with Hermina, teasing her about a fourth child; soon, he kept saying, soon: and we start *now*. When a servant knocked timidly on the door Simon could hardly believe anyone would dare cause such an interruption, but soon the knocking was repeated.

He pushed the bedclothes back and climbed out of bed as Hermina called, "It must be an emergency, Simon."

"I will teach them what an emergency is," Simon growled and opened the door.

The middle-aged man who looked after household affairs had not troubled to put a robe over his nightgown, had not even pulled his knitted sleeping cap off his bald head. He carried a candle in a tall brass stick and the flame quivered as he said, "It's Mr. Timothy, sir. Mr. Timothy. They say he is sick unto death!"

The master of the *Sea Lion* had found Timothy when, delayed by customs officials as well as by the drunkenness of his crew, he had been rowed to the steps and, not doubting that he would soon be met, had sent his boatman back. There was enough light to see the old man crumpled up on the terrace, even enough to see the blood on his head.

Now, facing Simon, who had dressed in a trice and had ridden to Furnival Tower House at wild speed on a horse kept close by against emergencies, the seaman looked haggard and old. Two doctors were there, members of the staff, and the guards who should have prevented this murder had they been alert. On a couch brought to the room from which the terrace led lay the lifeless body of Timothy McCampbell-Furnival. Out on the terrace were a dozen men carrying flares; the river between Furnival Tower House and the docks was alive with small boats showing all the lights they could so as to reveal anyone or anything unusual in the water. Godley, now the most experienced of the Bow Street Runners, was searching the terrace, while other Bow Street men were going through the building.

Every room within easy reach was wrecked. Paintings had been slashed, portraits of long-dead Furnivals had been ripped, furniture had been smashed and broken. All small ornaments, silver candlesticks, some plate, a collection of coins from various Furnival offices overseas and two superb ivory carvings from Tientsin had been stolen. Precious carpets small enough to roll and carry with ease were gone, too; larger ones had been ripped with sharp knives. In everything that had been done, naked hatred showed; and Simon, after staying close to Timothy's body for five minutes, turned and surveyed the scene, while nervous night watchmen stood at a distance and some of the office managers who slept nearby also watched.

442

There was no expression on his face, but his eyes glittered as if with great pain. When he moved, it was stiffly and slowly. There was no way of telling whether he actually took in what he saw or whether his gaze was piercing the curtains of the past. After a while, and when he had seen all the material damage, he turned toward the terrace. Godley was now at an open door, studying him. The Runner was tall and bony-looking, his hair cut short so that he looked gaunt, almost skeletal. He wore a loose-fitting tunic and boots which rose to his knees over tight-fitting breeches.

Simon beckoned him and sat at a Genoese silver table which had been badly dented with blows from a heavy object. He looked up at the man from Bow Street and then asked in a taut voice, "Your conclusions, Mr. Godley?"

"One or two men came first, swimming, and forced their way in. The water marks of feet are still on the terrace, but there are other footmarks of men wearing muddy boots. One of the swimmers surely killed Mr. Timothy for his blood is mingled with the marks of bare feet. Others followed, by boat. Marks on the stanchions show where a boat was tied, and already three men bear witness to seeing one moored alongside about the time this evil deed was committed."

"The destruction?"

"Hate, sir. Pure hate."

"The thefts?"

"By men who knew what they could sell, sir. This is an expert job if ever I saw one. Very experienced men."

"Would hate be an added motive?"

"Practised thieves can hate, sir. Many of them know Mr. Timothy favoured the marine police."

"What ideas do you have?"

"Ideas I like to keep to myself, sir. My trade is in facts."

"For the murderers of Mr. Timothy I will give a reward of ten thousand pounds," Simon declared. "For that I want facts, ideas, opinions—*answers* to any questions I ask. Do you want the commission?"

"Yes, sir, I do."

"What ideas do you have?"

"There's been a lot of talk for years, sir, among the criminal fraternity about getting back at the Furnivals for what Furnivals did at Great Furnival Square on the night of Mr. Timothy's ball. This could be one result, sir."

"After nine *years?*"

"Criminals have long memories, sir, as long as the law. Longer at times. And there's one in particular who remembers better than most, but we've never been able to prove anything against him. We get his men, but never him."

Simon leaned back farther in his chair and studied the gaunt man before him. Silence engulfed the room except for lapping water and an occasional movement on the terrace itself.

Where a lesser man would have started to justify himself Godley stood still, without shifting his gaze, and Simon stirred at last, asking, "Do you know this man's name?"

"Mason, sir. But I've no proof."

"Do I understand you have the Bow Street magistrates' consent to investigate this crime?"

"Yes, sir, Mr. Colquhoun's, who is there tonight, Sir Richard Ford being away. He told me to use my best endeavours and as many men as I required. Already I have asked for a descriptive list of the stolen property so that I can circulate it among pawnbrokers and others who might be asked to buy, but there is a good chance that this kind of *objet d'art* will be offered to private collectors or museums, sir. All inquiries possible will be made. I have asked for space in the major newspapers to advertise the list of missing articles and have offered a reward for reliable information."

"I will pay any rewards. I want the actual murderer quickly, Mr. Godley. Without losing a moment. We can deal afterward with the Mason man."

"With respect, sir—you couldn't want the murderer quicker than I do," Godley said. "If only—" He broke off.

"Well? Don't start a sentence and leave it unfinished."

"Your pardon, sir. I was going to say that if there were the same organisation in the City and everywhere else in London as there is on the river, we could have four thousand men working for us. As it is, we will be lucky to have two hundred. So progress may be slow, sir."

"The purpose of the ten thousand pounds is to overcome the obstacles," Simon said, his voice as taut as ever. "Have you questioned the watchmen who were said to be on duty here?"

"Yes, sir, but I have to see them again."

"If you suspect them to have connived with the thieves, then find the evidence necessary and I will charge them." Now Simon's voice rose. "Is it practicable for me to charge them with negligence while on duty?"

444

"Connivance there could be, sir, though I doubt it. Negligence there was not."

"Six men are on duty to guard these premises. They allow an army of thieves to come in and their master to be murdered—that is not negligence?" Simon now glared, and his right hand, on the table, began to clench and unclench. "I am becoming less sure that you are the right man for this investigation."

"If you would prefer one who will lie to you or tell you what he thinks you would like to hear, then I am not the right one, sir," Godley retorted instantly. He stopped and held silence, challenging Simon; indeed, defying him.

Somewhere, a man sneezed; it was like a shot from a gun. Some way off, downstairs, voices sounded; it was as if they came from a different world.

Simon said, "Why do you not consider them negligent?"

"They were instructed by Mr. Timothy to leave him alone, sir."

"Or are they lying so as to save their skins?"

"I know two of them well, sir. One was at Bow Street for two years before better conditions in private service took him away. He would not lie. It was the custom of Mr. Timothy to be alone on the terrace occasionally, as I understand it, and the guards say they thought nothing of it tonight. As for connivance, nothing of it shows on the surface, but I shall certainly probe deep to make sure."

"If there is the slightest evidence, they must be made to answer. If not—"

Simon did not finish, for now there was a disturbance at the main door; one of the guards on duty was keeping a newcomer at bay, and the newcomer's voice sounded in subdued protest.

"I wish Mr. Simon to know I am here."

The words traveled clearly and Simon looked away from Godley toward the door. There was a break in the hard surface of his expression; for a moment his face appeared to crumple, but in another moment he was in full control again.

"Day or night, I am to be informed," he said to Godley. "I will instruct all who work at Furnival Tower House to give you whatever assistance they can. Will the river police cooperate with you?"

"Fully, sir."

"Conceivably theirs is the negligence," Simon said with a flash of anger, but he stood up and moved toward the doorway, until he saw Richard just outside. The guard withdrew quickly.

Richard and Simon met, hands outstretched, and as they gripped, Richard said, "I could get here no sooner."

Simon did not speak. For the first time in their years of friendship, Richard saw tears shimmering in Simon's eyes, and the grip of his fingers was so tight that it crushed flesh against bone. At last Simon withdrew his hand and without a word turned toward the couch where Timothy lay. The face, even the forehead, was scarcely touched and the head had been expertly bandaged; the old man looked so young, so pleasant-featured, so peacefully asleep.

"Richard, I would beg a favour of you," Simon said in a voice which threatened to crack at any moment. "I would like to spend the rest of this hideous night in your rooms. And I would be grateful if you will tell Hermina what has happened and allow her to believe that I am busy about the investigation." He gripped Richard's arm fiercely and went on: "She does not believe that I have any of the human frailties. I would not wish her to see me distraught—and distraught I am."

"Would it not be better to send a messenger?" asked Richard. "I am reluctant to leave you on your own." In a strange way he, too, was reluctant to go to Hermina in such circumstances.

"Yet it is on my own or with some wench with a soft body to comfort me that I must be tonight," Simon replied. "Do you know of such a one, Richard? Or are you shocked to hear me talk so?"

"What you need tonight is whatever you feel you need," Richard answered.

They were taken by a youthful coachman to the premises in the Strand, which was dark except for a few flares. Only two taverns appeared to be open at this late hour, for it was after two o'clock. The coachman waited. Richard made sure that Simon had what he needed and left him, stony-eyed and weighed down by a grief which was only just beginning to tear at his mind and heart. Leaving the room door unlatched, he went quietly down one flight of narrow stairs and then along a narrow passage leading to the big room where the maids all slept. There were four, and Lucy, the one who had been present when Simon had come to seek him out after the battle of Great Furnival Square, was in the second bed. She had been twice married already, once to a man who had died of the pox, now to a seaman who had not been in London for more than a year.

One Sunday morning after Richard had been out late the previous night following a performance of a Beethoven symphony at the Covent Garden Opera House, he had slept late and had waked to find her in the room, looking down at him, smiling. No longer the timid child whom Simon had frightened, she had become more plump and cushiony, with a pleasing face and a merry smile which, at that moment, had a quality of seductiveness that Richard had not previously noticed. That morning her smile, the fullness of her bosom as she leaned forward, and her nearness, all combined to fill him with an urgent sense of desire. All of his past experiences with women had been largely unsatisfying because of a sense of restraint, even embarrassment, on his part, and a dislike of the boldness of his companion— always a casual acquaintance. Aware that most men of his age were vastly experienced in such matters, his own ignorance had added to self-consciousness.

There was one other deterrent factor, too.

On such occasions it was never possible to get the thought of Hermina out of his mind. She was ever present. Now that she was out of reach, since the wife or sister of a friend must by his own and most standards be inviolate, he was partly persuaded that he was naturally celibate, but on such a morning as that Sunday he had realised the folly of this notion.

Lucy had come to him with obvious pleasure, and there had been much mutual enjoyment while they had been together, without inhibitions or shyness. From that Sabbath on she had come to him early, and they had pleasured themselves for a while and then had rested until she had been duty bound to dress and go downstairs to begin her work for the day. He had expected that she would soon begin to make claims on him, to ask for some declaration of their relationship, even that he should set her up in an apartment of her own.

But she had shown no desire for any of this, and when one morning after their exertions he had talked of it, she had said, "Twice I've been tied to a man and had a man tied to me, sir. It does no good and turns pleasure bitter. I ask for nothing more but a continuance of your generous goodness."

Richard set aside a sum for her each week, and she made passing reference to it but did not make him feel that it was payment for their Sunday mornings. He had learned that there were at least two other men who received her favours, but that did not trouble him; in a way it reassured him that she was not dependent on him alone.

On this autumn morning she woke with a start and turned on her back to stare up at him for he had never come to her like this.

"Take no alarm," he urged, "but get up, Lucy, and make some tea and take it up to my room. Mr. Simon is here and in great distress. Say nothing of that, but if he needs your comfort, comfort him."

"*That* man needs comfort?" She gasped. "As likely comfort a raging bull!"

But there could be no doubt of her readiness, indeed, eagerness, to go to Simon, and little doubt that he would find in her the solace he needed.

A tired watchman with his lantern on the end of a cracked, squeaky pole sat on the porch at Simon's house. He held the lantern close to Richard's face and backed away, grumbling, but allowing him to pass. Inside the hall another watchman waited, with yet another at the first landing.

A young man whom Richard knew to be the senior footman came out of a room with a candle in his hand, recognised Richard and said, "I will have the maid find out if Mrs. Rattray-Furnival is awake, sir."

Richard waited for only a few minutes before the man reappeared from another room, part of the suite which Richard knew Simon and Hermina used when they were not entertaining.

"You may enter, sir."

Richard did not see the maid.

All the way there he had been fighting against a rising excitement which he told himself he must not allow Hermina to notice. Tonight of all nights it should not even be in his mind, he had such tragic news to convey. Yet in fact the shock at learning what had happened had not yet gone deep, for he had been concerned for Simon and was now, whether it was proper or not, concerned for himself. He tried to push awareness of Hermina to the back of his mind but could not do so. Now he saw the door of her room—her room and Simon's—standing ajar and tapped to make sure she was ready to receive him.

She called, "Come in, Richard," and her voice struck every nerve in his body.

He pushed the door wider open and stepped into the lofty room, beautiful in pale colours, with rich furnishings, and a huge bed without posts or canopy. He had expected her to be out of bed, but she was sitting up against the pillows, a froth of lace slipping from her shoulders. She smiled at him in obvious welcome, as if she did not care why he had come and was glad only that he had.

She was so beautiful that she made him catch his breath.

He missed a step and then stood still, his heart thumping against his ribs with heavy, choking beats.

He did not want to feel like this.

He did not want to feel the blood drumming in his ears, the dizziness in his head. He wanted to be calm and detached and friendly despite the mist which suddenly appeared before his eyes.

Slowly, it cleared.

Now she was smiling more broadly and her arms were outstretched. He felt as if he were choking.

She did not move or speak, but her smile and her arms invited him.

He did not allow himself to move, fought for self-control and for his voice. The first syllables came on a husky note, and he swallowed and tried again. This time the words were at least audible.

"I come with grievous news," he told her.

"But you have come."

"Simon sent me to—"

"I do not want to talk of Simon," she interrupted, and her voice took on a sharpness of tone he had not expected; nor had he heard it before.

"I have to tell you that Timothy McCampbell-Furnival is dead," he declared. "Most brutally murdered."

At last she listened, her arms dropped to her side, her mouth opened, her expression suddenly one of dismay. All this was as it should be and helped Richard to feel more normal, easing the tension which sight of her and her reception had created. He moved a step nearer and went on in a voice now under stern control.

"Simon has much to do, arranging the hunt for the murderer and the thieves. A fortune was stolen and much damage was done—they were vicious vandals also."

Hermina asked, "Did Timothy suffer?"

"The doctor said there could have been only an instant's pain before he died of a blow on the head. Hermina, Simon was concerned for you and anxious that you should not receive this news from a servant or from a stranger. I wish someone other than I could have been the bearer."

"I know of no one from whom I would rather have heard," Hermina said. She held out her arms again, and now he thought it was a gesture of distress, a need for comfort. Had he been mad to imagine the way she had moved and invited before had been any different from this? Had the tumult in him distorted the picture of what she looked like and his hearing of what she had said?

She was so beautiful.

449

She went on in a soft, enticing voice, "And I know of no one I would rather have by me now."

She was like fire in his veins.

"Where *is* Simon?" she asked, still softly.

"He—has many things to do," Richard repeated.

"So he will not be here for a long time," she said. "Richard—oh, Richard."

She leaned back on her pillows and with a gesture let the lace slip farther from her shoulders. They glowed in the soft light and seemed to call him. Farther still slipped the lace, and now her breasts were uncovered.

"Richard," she murmured, "come to me."

This was Hermina!

This was Simon's wife, the unattainable, the goddess! Richard's head filled with an unfamiliar roaring and his body was anguished by fierce longing. She was Simon's wife. But Simon was not here; he would never know what passed between them. He had only to move two steps, three steps, to be with her, to know a glory and a fury of possession. Three steps.

"Richard," she said, "you will never know how I have yearned for you."

For *him*. Simon's wife. It was as if false words forked her tongue, yet words that he wanted to hear above all others.

"Richard, come to me . . . I have yearned for you."

Her eyes were like magnets, drawing him. Her body began to quiver. Suddenly she flung back the bedclothes and with a twist of her hips she was kneeling, naked, on the bed, only a hand's reach away from him.

"Richard!" she hissed. "Come to me, come to me!"

She flung herself forward.

He opened his arms wide to save her from falling, and in that instant there flashed into his mind a single word: *No.*

As if she sensed his decision, her expression changed, rage turned her cheeks to flaming red, and she began to strike and claw at him.

Richard struggled desperately to restrain her, but she was like a madwoman, biting, scratching and kicking, and suddenly he knew exactly what he must do. Holding her off for a moment, he struck her smartly across one cheek with his open hand. On the instant her eyes rolled and she became a dead weight, body sagging, head drooping.

Looking up, he saw a pair of eyes and realised that they had been watched. His heart missed a beat, and then he looked away, shifted Hermina's position so that he could lift her and, lifting, called, "Come and help your mistress."

It was a woman, older than Hermina yet still young, wearing a loose-fitting robe of heavy wool and a bonnet. She came forward briskly, and as he laid Hermina on the bed, looking down at the flawless beauty of her body, she took a gown from a chair. After a moment of hesitation he raised Hermina to a sitting position so that the servant could slip the gown over her head and shoulders and place her arms in the sleeves. Then he raised her again while the other drew the gown beneath her, covering thighs and legs down to the slim ankles.

He stood back. He realised suddenly that he was breathing very hard, that he had seldom been so near exhaustion. Moving to a chair, he leaned against it as the woman drew the sheet over Hermina, who was still unconscious.

At last she was finished, and Richard made himself ask, "Does such behaviour happen often?"

In a measured voice, the answer came: "Too often."

"Does Mr. Simon know?"

"Too well," she said. "But I have never known her quite so bad."

"It must have been the shock of hearing of Mr. Timothy's death. I was too abrupt in telling her."

"It was the shock of having you refuse her," the woman said bluntly.

"That I can't believe."

"It is nothing but the truth. For many years she has longed for another man, for freedom from Mr. Simon's domination, and she has always felt much affection toward you. May I speak frankly?"

"So far nothing appears to have discouraged you from so doing," Richard said dryly.

"Had you succumbed, it might have proved her salvation."

"And mine? To betray a friend?"

"Mr. Richard," the woman said quietly, "there is much hypocrisy and ignorance over such matters. It is my opinion that if Miss Hermina could share her life with another, she would be less subject to such outbreaks of hysteria and Mr. Simon would lead a more peaceful life here at home. He is not enough for her."

Richard remembered much of what his grandfather had told him of Hermina's family, a story never related in one coherent whole but in bits and pieces which he had gradually woven into a picture which seemed part of his memory, the telling had always been so vivid.

Gabriel Morgan, a member of the New Mohocks and of the murdering, pillaging Twelves.

There was a bad streak in the Morgans; was there a streak of madness in the family, also?

He heard a faint sound from Hermina and caught a glimpse of her face above the sheet as she turned her head. The maid moved to one side, opened a small cabinet and took out a bottle so delicately shaped that it might contain an exotic perfume; she removed the stopper and poured a little liquid into a spoon kept in the same place. Next she raised Hermina's head from the pillow and with the precision of long practice parted the lips with the tip of the spoon and poured the contents in. Hermina swallowed without protest—she, too, was used to being dosed this way. The maid put the bottle back in the cabinet.

"She will sleep now. May I prevail on you to take a cup of tea or coffee?"

"Some tea would be most welcome," Richard accepted gratefully. "Then if you will follow me."

She led the way and soon Richard found himself in a small and pleasant room, in one corner a kettle singing over a grease lamp of unusual design. As the woman busied herself he was aware of the suppleness of her movement and the beauty of her busy hands. Beneath her bonnet her hair was set in ringlets which might be natural, and although she was pale it was not the pallor of poor health. She had wide-set blue eyes and a clear, translucent skin.

When she brought the tea and sat opposite him with a cup for herself, he sipped it thankfully, finding the warmth and fragrance welcome and his companion restful after the fury of Hermina's hysteria. She was regarding him with a quizzical expression, as if amused.

"Have you served Hermina long?" he asked.

"I have known her most of her life," the other replied.

Known? Not served? His puzzlement must have shown in his face for she went on, her eyes smiling at him in a most refreshing way:

"I am Susan, the widow of Gabriel Morgan, who was Hermina's cousin."

"*Gabriel!*" he exclaimed.

"Son of Gabriel the First, who was the son of Ebenezer the First for whom your grandfather once worked, Mr. Richard. If you wonder how I came by that information, remind yourself that Mr. Simon collects information as a magpie collects trinkets. There was never a man so interested in family trees! My husband's father, the first Gabriel, was transported to America but was allowed a free life there —bought by old Ebenezer. When his son was born the boy was sent to England and was brought up by his grandfather. Our marriage was brief, for shortly afterward he died of the pox. If I talk too freely it is because I presume on my erstwhile position."

"You need to *work*," Richard exclaimed.

"Did you not know that Gabriel the Second took his inheritance and squandered it at the gambling tables? Then you cannot frequent such hallowed places as Brook's and White's," she teased.

Richard shook his head in mock horror, then got to his feet. The tea and Susan's company had done him good, but now he must go home. Yet if he did, what would he find—Simon alone or Simon still with Lucy? It would be better for him to ride to Chelsea, where a room was always kept ready for him.

"Will Hermina recollect all that took place?" he asked.

"Vividly," answered Susan. "And she will be free of remorse but not without fear."

"Of Simon?"

"Yes. If you should inform him—"

"It would not occur to me to inform him," Richard interrupted.

"May I so reassure her?" Susan asked him in a very quiet voice.

"You have my word."

"You are very gracious," Susan said. "She will be greatly relieved." She studied him closely over the rim of her cup as she went on: "It will be advisable if you and I are able to tell Simon exactly the same things, Richard. Will it suffice to say that she was greatly distressed and that I gave her laudanum to help quiet her?"

"Is that what you gave her?"

Susan nodded.

"Then that is what I shall tell Simon," Richard promised, "and what you should say to him if he comes here before I see him. I am going to Chelsea," he added.

And if she wondered why, she did not ask.

CHAPTER *37*

Another Marshall for Minshall

IN HIS early thirties, Frederick Jackson was one of the Bow Street foot patrol which usually operated near Piccadilly but which had been pressed into service for the search for Timothy McCampbell-Furnival's murderers. It was the greatest man hunt ever known, he was told by the Runner who had briefed him and a dozen others outside the court.

The instructions were simple: search everyone and everywhere if the slightest suspicion attached, from boats and ships to shops and private houses—everywhere. The Bow Street men and those from the various magistrates' offices took constables and volunteers with them so as to go in pairs for their own safety.

Frederick Jackson was alone. He did not greatly mind this for he often worked so, sometimes as a spy sitting among thieves. It was he who some years before had informed Simon Rattray-Furnival of the plan to raid Great Furnival Square and he had been well rewarded, a substantial addition to his meager sixteen shillings a week. He would get a bigger reward if he made a capture on this occasion; bigger still if he made it singlehanded.

The constable who had been with him had stubbed a foot on the sprawling body of a drunken man and had pitched onto his face, injuring his nose so badly that it was thought to be broken. He had recovered well enough to return alone to Bow Street and report the casualty, so Jackson was likely to have a new companion shortly.

Jackson was a tall, very lean young man with a reputation at Bow Street as a pugilist, better with the use of his fists than with any weapons, although he carried a staff and had a pistol, loaded, stuck into his waistband, as well as a wooden rattle. He was now in Westminster, close to one of the places where the sewers debouched into the Thames, and the stink grew worse as he neared the spot. Few people were about, and this made him suspicious of a group of men gathered around two small boats which were drawn up on the sludge at the riverbank. They appeared to be digging.

He saw one of the boats pushed farther into the water and a man vault into it and begin to pole toward midstream. The men still on the mudbank, four or five—Jackson could not be sure because of the shadows—kept on the move. Then another small boat which must have been just inside the sewer's mouth appeared; once again a man leaped into it.

Now Jackson realised what was going on; there were several boats in that hiding place and one by one each was being taken across the river. Suddenly he sensed that he might be close to a big reward.

He could do nothing by himself, but the quicker he sent word to Bow Street, the better. Swinging around, he almost banged into a man creeping up behind him, a huge fellow with arm upraised. One second later and his cudgel would have come crashing down onto Jackson's head.

Swift almost as light, Jackson leaped forward, smashing two blows against his assailant's jaw. Then, as the man fell to the ground, he turned and ran toward the end of Westminster Bridge, not too fast for he did not know how far he would have to run, but with long, easy strides. He did not once look back. When he reached the bridge he saw a party of Bow Street men placing a barricade halfway across and he whirled his rattle until two came hurrying toward him.

Soon they were all gathered about Jackson's unconscious assailant, and while messengers were sent over the bridges, men of the river police went across in skiffs, so that the whole of that section of the river was cordoned off. A Redbreast, as Bow Street officers were popularly known, set off on horseback to inform Simon Rattray-

Furnival, and small boats closed in on the sewer while others waited farther afield.

The man whom Frederick Jackson had knocked down began to moan, but apart from the two men now standing over him, the others paid him scant attention. One of the constables had retrieved the cudgel from the gravel flat where it had fallen and was examining it in the light of a lantern when one of Simon's officials arrived.

"Have you got them? Are they the men?" he demanded.

"I think this cudgel was used earlier tonight," the constable holding the weapon declared. "It has dried blood on it, but not hard dried, and some gray hairs which may be Mr. McCampbell-Furnival's. By good chance it fell on dry land."

The man on the ground moaned more loudly.

Simon's official glared down at him but did not move until, like all of them, he started at a loud cry from the sewer. Another detachment of Bow Street men had sprung from boats which had crept along the bank and were attacking those who were left inside.

In all they found two laden boats and four empty dinghies and three-quarters of the treasure stolen from Furnival Tower House.

Within the hour, nine men were brought before a Bow Street magistrate and each was committed to Newgate to await trial for complicity in the murder and robbery. Before the last of the newspapers had been printed the news reached Fleet Street; presses were stopped and the names of the accused and a list of the goods recovered were put beneath the story of Timothy McCampbell-Furnival's death.

Late on the following day, with much misgiving, Richard went to call on Simon at his house in Great Furnival Square. Outside, flags were at half-mast; inside, blinds were drawn at every window. There was an atmosphere of gloom all over the square, black crepe on carriages at the curbs, and a lowering sky added to the mood. A footman opened the door and stood aside, almost bumping into a smaller man who carried a pile of letters, no doubt all of condolence. Richard was taken straight up to an anteroom on the second floor, outside which at least a dozen men stood or sat in silence. Almost at once the door opened and Hermina appeared.

She was dressed in black, in a dress high at the neck and with long sleeves. She had put on neither powder nor carmine, and the only colour in her face was in her startlingly bright eyes. She came straight toward him, both hands outstretched, white beneath the ruffles of the cuffs.

"Richard, I am so very glad to see you. Simon will be too."

Without embarrassment she put her face up to be kissed and he touched her cheek with his lips, feeling none of the fire she had once stirred in him. She drew him into the room and closed the door. The murmur of voices came from an adjoining room.

"Simon is with a lawyer and I have not told him that you are here," she said quietly. "I will leave the moment I hear the lawyer go." Her eyes seemed to search his face. "Richard, I can never tell you how deeply sorry I am about your—your last visit. I am—"

"Enough," he interrupted. "I shall tell Simon you were sorely distressed, and that is just as I remember you. I hope—Hermina, I hope nothing that you think you remember will ever prevent us from being close friends."

"Friends," she said slowly. "Friends. Nothing can prevent it if we are really still friends, and you do not hate me."

The words he wanted to express were hard to find. How could he tell her that his feelings toward her had changed so utterly? That he would forever carry a picture of her beauty yet never again be filled with desire? And would this even be true? Though now unmoved by her nearness, how could he be sure that his old feeling for her would not return?

"I could no more hate you than I could hate Simon," he said slowly.

Either the words or the way he expressed them or the look on his face satisfied her, for her anxiety faded and she smiled.

"At times I love Simon to absolute distraction and at times I hate him. I really do!"

She gave a subdued but hard laugh, and there was a false brightness in her eyes which stirred Richard to disquiet. In the moment of silence which followed, the voices sounded louder than before, then footsteps. She turned quickly toward the door which led into the adjoining room and stood for a moment in the doorway.

"Simon, Richard is here."

The last time they had seen each other, Simon had been in Richard's apartment; when Richard had returned in the middle of the following day, Simon had gone. Now the fact which struck Richard was that his friend looked older; if he had ever been in any doubt as to the depth of Simon's love for Timothy it was gone. Simon came

457

toward him, arms outstretched, and it was good to see the pleasure on his face.

"You are the one man in the world I would not willingly keep waiting," he said. "How are you?"

"Rested."

"And the one man in the world who knows exactly what to say to me. Richard, I want you to perform a service."

"You have but to name it."

"You do not know me as well as you think, does he, Hermina?" Simon put an arm about Hermina's waist and drew her to him; it would be impossible to imagine a more handsome couple. "I may ask the impossible of you."

"I do not believe you would expect me to compromise with my conscience."

"You see!" Simon said, smiling at Hermina. "He is never without the perfect answer."

But the next instant his smile faded, and turning on his heel he led Richard into the adjoining room, pointed to a high-backed chair in front of a magnificently carved desk, and moved to a massive chair behind it. He appeared to have completely forgotten Hermina, and her words echoed unbidden in Richard's mind: "At times I love Simon to absolute distraction and at times I hate him." Was this a moment when he could inspire hatred—his sudden apparent unawareness of her existence?

Simon, this older, grim-faced Simon, was appraising him as if trying to read his thoughts. His features did not relax and his lips only just parted as he said, "You know the murderers were caught and are waiting trial. They will be hanged. Had I caught the man who struck the blow myself I would have beaten the life out of him. However, one must control primeval instincts in this civilised age. The gang was caught at such speed only because Godley was in charge and the Bow Street Runners organised the search. It was a masterpiece of organisation and Godley and the man Jackson, who actually found the hiding place, will be suitably rewarded. That is not what I wanted to tell you, however. The main point is that Godley created for one single night a cohesive police force in the streets of London. The river force, already primed, cooperated with speed and efficiency. I have no longer the slightest doubt: you are not, and your grandfather was not, a starry-eyed visionary. London needs an organised police force so that any gang contemplating such an outrage will know in

458

advance what odds are against it. From this moment on I pledge you my full support and cooperation."

As soon as the burden of what Simon had to say became apparent, excitement began to burn in Richard, and when at last the other paused, it was raging within him. But this was not a moment to speak, only to feel. He raised his hands in acknowledgment, making it obvious that he was at a loss for words.

"The means of bringing this reform about has preoccupied me greatly," Simon continued. "Will you hear what I have to propose and—no matter what it is—consider it in all its aspects before giving an answer? Consider for a week, say—by which time many of the problems created by Timothy's death will have been resolved."

"I will consider any proposals," Richard promised. He had no inkling of what these might be, but it seemed that Simon suspected that his first reaction might be unfavourable.

"Splendid!" Simon smiled briefly in satisfaction. "First, I am convinced that the City will not support any measure which does not give it control over a police force within its boundaries. So, I shall work, using the greater influence that I now have, for unity among private forces there, and for all constables and peace officers, no matter what title they may give themselves, to be put under one control. Each company, each parish, each authority, should contribute the sum it now spends on keeping the peace but the force itself will be responsible to a central body led, as in the case of the river police, by a single commander, whatever his title. This will take time but I am sure it can be done."

There was nothing as far as Richard could see which he could do to help; his knowledge of the City was extensive, his influence negligible. He wondered what Colquhoun would think as he asked, "So you would like to see two autonomous police forces within the metropolis, under two separate commissions?"

"Yes, with nine-tenths of the metropolis still policed by parish constables and a few men attached to Bow Street, and at least three-quarters of the people with the same kind of protection—if one can call it protection. Not only Westminster and Middlesex but areas of Surrey and Essex are now or will soon be part of London proper; the metropolis stretches nearly as far as Paddington, Brompton and Chelsea in the west, and Camden Town, Islington and Hackney in the north, Poplar and Bow in the east, and Southwark, Lambeth, Rotherhithe and Bermondsey, Camberwell and Battersea south of the river." Simon opened a leather folder as he spoke, turning it around for Richard to see. "In case your memory needs refreshing, here is the map showing the farthest extent of all major building projects."

"I need little reminding," Richard said, as he studied the map. "There is hardly a part of this I do not visit regularly as 'Mr. Londoner.'" He still could not understand what it was that Simon wanted of him.

"Only a man who knows the whole metropolis and is well known and respected by most law-abiding citizens can do what I want you to do. The parliamentary seat of Minshall, your grandfather's seat for so long, will fall vacant shortly. I want you to contest that seat. I will see that you get all the financial help you need, and that it is a fair and free election. And once you are a Member of the House of Commons, as I know you will be, I want you to fight as you have never fought before for a police force in the rest of the metropolis. *Not* the City. *Not* the river. But all the rest. Because once that is achieved, some kind of amalgamation will be inevitable, and until that day comes, the three forces can work together so that in all but name they are one single police force."

Richard gazed at his friend, dumfounded.

"Put 'Mr. Londoner' second in your thoughts," Simon went on. "Do what you have always said you will not do. Become the conscience of the people in the House of Commons. Work with Colquhoun, Bentham and Harriot, with everyone who will help to force the hand of the government. You can do this where I cannot hope to succeed. Jealousy between the City and Westminster is a form of madness but madness cannot be cured by reason. Anything I say will unite the Commons—except the City members and their lobby—against the idea, but an independent voice will weaken them. So there you have it, Richard! That is what I want you to do."

The issue was with Richard, sleeping as well as waking.

Most of his emotional reaction was against the proposal: he did not wish to be tied to the House of Commons, to be forever at the heart of controversy which could lead to such bitter disappointment as his grandfather and Colquhoun had known. Yet all his intellectual reaction was in favour. He agreed with Simon's reasoning, knew that few men were so farsighted, was utterly convinced that he would forever have Simon's support.

He would win Minshall, of course. Even on his own, without Simon's powerful backing, he believed that he would be able to do that. But his life would never again be wholly his own.

He talked to no one about Simon's proposal because he had no one close enough to confide in, and for the first time in his thirty-two years he became acutely aware of the need of companionship, of someone with whom to discuss personal problems.

His parents were now retired, living near the coast in Cornwall, and he saw little of them, exchanging letters occasionally and sending gifts from time to time. The house at Chelsea, despite his room there, had never been the same since James's death, and he had grown out of touch with his brothers and sisters. Yet on the day of Timothy's funeral—which was attended by the Prime Minister, an emissary of the King and a flock of Members of both Houses of Parliament, as well as most of the leading merchants and bankers of the City— Richard went to Chelsea.

It was half-past six when he arrived.

He heard the babble of infants in one room, a quarrel among elder children in another, and from a third the voice of his Aunt Dorothy complaining bitterly about servants to a woman whom he did not know, so he went upstairs without announcing his arrival, and, on a moment's impulse, turned into his grandfather's old bedroom. Some of James Marshall's books were still on their shelves, and Richard paused beside them. There was light enough for him to see the titles, the worn spines, the dog-eared pages. Least read appeared to be Shakespeare, Milton and Goldsmith, but Henry Fielding was well thumbed, with Daniel Defoe a good second. Bentham was well thumbed, too, and Voltaire, although Richard did not quite know why. Hume, of course, and Samuel Johnson, Smollett and . . .

He moved to lower shelves, packed with reports of parliamentary committees. Next to these, in leather binders not unlike the one he had seen on Simon's desk, were issues of *The Daily Clarion*—selected issues, Richard knew, with annotations on matters which had been of special interest to James Marshall.

He pulled them out. At the front of one of the binders was a printed single sheet with the picture of a man's face—a picture which had a familiarity he could not place. It was a striking-looking face, with boldness in both eyes and expression. Above the picture ran words, badly printed and smeared, as if the ink had not been allowed to dry before the paper had been distributed.

Last Speech and Dying Testament of the Notorious
and Beloved Outlaw and Highwayman
Who was Hanged at Tyburn Fields
on the Fifteenth Day of September 1739

Richard had never seen this actual document before but his grandfather had told him of it, had talked of Jackson and his mistress and of the fact that his own father—Richard's great-grandfather—had been murdered by the man pictured here. Where *had* he seen that face before? Richard turned to his pack, unstrapped it, and took out some copies of *The Daily Clarion* which he wanted to read at leisure. On the same page as that giving the story of Timothy's murder was a picture of a man very like the picture of Frederick Jackson, and beneath *The Daily Clarion's* picture was the caption:

> Frederick Jackson, Bow Street Runner, who apprehended Thomas Garson. Garson is believed to be the man who struck the fatal blow which killed Timothy McCampbell-Furnival.

The same cast of face and the same name. This could hardly be coincidence. That first Jackson had been hanged for murder; and now his grandson—or more likely his great-grandson—had apprehended a murderer and was actually a member of the Bow Street force, created out of the one that, so long ago, had hunted down his own forebear.

Aloud, Richard said, "But this was nearly seventy years ago! Nearly seventy years, and they are still fighting for a police force!" That was the moment when he knew that he would have to stand for Minshall when the by-election came.

When he returned to "Mr. Londoner" that night, he found a stranger walking up and down outside the shop. Youthful-looking and cleanly if poorly dressed, he touched his forehead as he approached Richard.

"It is Mr. Richard Marshall, sir, begging your pardon?"

"Yes," said Richard. "How can I help you?"

"Well, sir, my father said if I ever wanted help from an honest man I could rely on Mr. James Marshall, and you being his son"—Richard did not trouble to correct this—"I thought the same would be true of you, sir. My father is a brother of Mr. Daniel Ross, who used to have a coffee house in Wapping, and I am named Daniel after my uncle. My father keeps a public house near the docks at Wapping, sir

—and they won't renew his licence unless he pays them five hundred pounds."

"*Who* won't?"

"Well, sir, it's complicated, because the magistrate takes the word of the constables and the police court men as to whether a license is worthy. And what with the revenue men wanting a share, and the river police—they're always fighting each other, sir, unless they can squeeze some poor innocent person dry—and the Court Runner wanting their share, the magistrate will be advised *not* to renew, sir. And"— the young man gulped—"there is another prepared to pay a thousand pounds, sir, and you can be sure he'll use the place for giving cover to thieves and hiding what they steal."

"When is the application to be heard?" asked Richard.

"Tomorrow morning, sir."

"That doesn't leave much time," Richard said, frowning. "Do you know the men who want to share this blackmail profit?"

"Oh, yes, sir. They'll all be at the house tonight, pressing hard on my father."

"Tell me the name of the house and how to get there and I'll be at the house by eleven o'clock," Richard promised.

"Do you really think you can help, sir?"

"I can try," Richard said.

When the lad had gone Richard went first to sup, then fetched a horse from stables behind the Strand and rode through the City and the East End. The public house, or inn, was on a corner and oil flares showed the name—the Ball and Chain. It was one of the very old oak-roofed and -beamed buildings. He tied his horse to a post and found inside that the place had the brightness and snugness of a well-kept hostelry. Beyond the bar three men were drinking ale in one corner and were talking to a middle-aged man behind the bar.

The youth passed Richard and said out of the corner of his mouth, "There they are, talking to my father."

Richard crossed to the corner, ordered a tankard of ale, raised it and said, "Your health gentlemen. And to you landlord, another good year of trade." He drank deeply. "I have come to find out if you are being pressed to pay money for the recommendation of the constable to the magistrate tomorrow."

The landlord gasped. "Pressed? *Pressed*, sir? Why, no—" His words faded into nothing.

"Good," approved Richard. "That saves me a lot of trouble. There is much blackmail for these licensed houses, and we are determined to stamp it out. Anyone caught demanding money will not only be instantly dismissed but will be arraigned on charges which I won't mention here."

"And—and who may you be, sir?"

"Oh, I am one of the lawyers who began the inquiries. I shall be in court tomorrow morning."

"But they might have attacked you, might have killed you, sir!" said the youth the next day. "It was wonderful, but powerful risky, Mr. Marshall."

"You tell me a way of dealing with such people without risk," Richard said dryly.

He was driving back to the Strand when, near the church of St. Mary-le-Strand, he heard a great commotion, the clatter of rattles, masses of people running, and what he had first thought were coaches swinging around a corner toward Bow Street—three horse-drawn fire engines in a row. It was more than he could do to stay away from the crowd, and he turned his horse. A gentle wind brought the smell of fire and smoke and soon he could see flames stretching high into the sky. A silhouette against the red glow was from the mass of old, decaying buildings close to the theater, but the fire had also reached the façade of the Royal Opera House itself. Firemen and police were pumping water and controlling the crowd; women were screaming. A great roar followed part of the roof's falling in. It was fiercely hot now, and he was doing more harm than good by staying here. As he turned, a middle-aged woman peered up at him.

"Do you know if Handel's organ is safe? Oh, please God, it must be, it must be!"

"All I know," said a man close by, "is that three firemen are dead of suffocation."

"I know it started after Mrs. Siddons left," a young man volunteered.

"But the organ!" the woman gasped.

The first edition of *The Daily Clarion* which Richard saw next day carried a headline and some facts.

HAVOC CAUSED BY FIRE AT ROYAL OPERA HOUSE,
COVENT GARDEN.
TWENTY-THREE FIREMEN PERISHED.

The famed Handel organ was reduced to nothing. Stage scenery, Mrs. Siddons' wardrobe and all such were destroyed. It is estimated that a large number of people have been rendered homeless although the exact number is not yet known.

It was hours before Richard fell asleep that night, and in the morning even word that Ross had been granted his licence did not cheer him. If he were in the House of Commons, he wondered, could he do anything to reduce the crime, the blackmail, the conditions which led to fires which destroyed great landmarks and killed brave men?

"But I have no intention of retiring," declared the Member for Minshall a few days later. "I do not know what put such an idea into your head."

"It was put there by the offer of ten thousand pounds," replied a man who served Simon Rattray-Furnival. "Ten thousand pounds, of which five will be given to you the moment you have resigned your seat because of bad health, and another five when you land in Lisbon, Portugal, for a rest cure in the warm sunshine you can be sure of finding there."

The Member for Minshall pursed his lips, raised his eyebrows, and then said in a wondering voice, "I could not understand why I had been feeling so short of breath. I am a sick man. There is nothing for it but a long rest in a warm climate."

"Pay him his money and get him out of the country," Simon ordered. "I have a candidate who will most certainly be the next Member for Minshall, and I cannot get him into the House of Commons quickly enough. Is there any news from Godley?"

"No, sir," his secretary told him.

Godley of the Bow Street Runners still had not found the proof he needed to charge Mason, who, he said, was behind so much of London's crime. Simon was not positive whether such a man existed or whether continual procrastination was Godley's way of putting up the price for the investigation. Of one thing Simon was sure: he must bide his time, must not rely only on Godley for information. Frederick Jackson, the man who had actually cracked the gang which had murdered Timothy, might do better.

Simon set himself to find out whether Jackson might prove a more valuable contact than Godley, and more reliable.

Almost at once, however, he was forced to consider other pressing matters. The war with France took a turn for the worse and British ships were again in danger on the high seas. In London, trade was slowing down, and Simon found the problems of supplies and shipping all-demanding. The government, with an eccentric, if not mad, King on the throne, was uncertain except in one thing: to continue the war against France.

The seat for Minshall was left vacant for more than a year, and when eventually Richard was elected there was an utter lack of interest in the police among the people as well as among politicians. The nation was fighting for its colonies, its wealth, its survival.

Richard found himself not only blocked wherever he turned but frustrated because there seemed nothing useful he could do. The war dragged on. Months passed. Then, in 1811, when he had already been in the House for nearly four years, two brutal outrages that left six people murdered set London by the ears.

"Oysters," Mr. Marr said, "that's what I'd like for my supper." He finished stacking the bales of linen on the shelves of his shop while his assistant stifled a yawn. It was nearly midnight and he must be back by seven o'clock the next morning to open the shop. "You go and get two dozen best oysters, girl," Marr said to a maid, and she slipped out to another shop not far along Ratcliffe Street.

She left the door ajar.

None of those in the house or shop heard anyone enter, but suddenly a tornado of violence swept in; a man slashed with chisel and maul, smashing the skulls of the two men, battering Mrs. Marr to death, killing her child in its cradle. When the maid summoned a watchman because the door was locked on her, she stood confronted by the hideous scene.

But the murderer was not found.

A few days later, on December 19, terror struck at The King's Arms, in Gravel Lane, not far from the linen shop. The proprietor, an old man, was found savagely murdered, his throat cut, and a maid-servant was killed in the same way.

Panic began in Wapping and quickly spread. Bow Street men and Runners from the Shadwell office searched all haunts of known men of violence, foreigners were blamed, and when proved innocent, there was always the Irish. Then out of the blue the police found a clue which led them to a Dane named Peterson who led to another man named Williams. Committed to Coldbath Prison to await trial, Williams hanged himself.

So great was the panic caused by these murders that the government was inundated with demands for a force to prevent such things happening again. But still it did nothing.

A few months later a sudden wave of rioting and violence began to run through the country, organised by a group of Luddites. Founded among the hosiers of Nottinghamshire and Derbyshire, Luddites were little known until they spread to the woollen cloth and cotton works in Lancashire and Yorkshire. Hand workers in all these industries, fearing for their livelihood if machines replaced men, smashed and burned the machines. Savage punishment was meted out and troops and yeomanry quelled the riots, but as soon as they were smothered in one place they broke out in another.

In some ways, the next few years were to prove one of the blackest periods in London's history. Slums grew filthier and nothing was done to prevent the spread of disease. When, in 1815, a new Corn Bill was introduced to prohibit the free import of corn into England unless home-produced wheat reached a guaranteed price, Parliament was besieged by rioters demanding the defeat of the bill in a way that brought back memories of the Gordon Riots.

On the eighteenth of June, after months of preparation, Richard was to present a bill for a minor reform of Bow Street, adding to the wages paid to officers and the numbers employed. It was a strange day, although he did not realise it. A Member sitting next to him, known as "Old Puff and Blow" because of his constant wheezing and sneezing, was agog with the news.

Napoleon, his army once again almost as powerful as rumour claimed, had met Wellington's forces at Waterloo, after Blücher's Prussians had been defeated. That much was certain. None but those closest to the Cabinet had any idea what was going on; few knew of the tense hours before the victory, the period when Wellington stood alone, his army battered. Few in England learned until weeks afterward how Blücher appeared at the last moment with his ranks reformed, and how what had promised to be a French triumph was turned to bitter defeat.

On that day in June carrier pigeons brought the first tidings to Westminster as Richard James Marshall sat in the House of Commons, heavyhearted not only because his bill was bound to be postponed but because he was sure that after the sweet glory of victory would come the bitterness of disillusion. Tens of thousands of soldiers would soon be home, vast numbers would not be able to find work and there would be yet another wave of crime, with the hapless home-comers pressed into service by the criminal leaders. And London was no better able to cope than ever.

In the following year, Richard's worst fears were confirmed. Riots were breaking out all over the country. News came from Suffolk and Cornwall and Devon, from Norfolk and Essex, from northern counties, of the burning of houses and destruction. "Bread or blood!" screamed the mob, and when the yeomanry were turned on them they threw or catapulted huge stones, used fireballs, raided church-yards and took cover behind tombstones, hurling huge pieces of brick and stone at their attackers.

"But *why?*" Richard begged young Daniel Ross to tell him.

"Hunger, sir—pure and simple hunger. Can't you do *anything?*" Ross pleaded.

It was almost useless to try. Richard made representations but the Ministers dismissed the riots as trivial and local, and declared through the Prince Regent, "The manufacturers, commerce and revenue of the United Kingdom are in a flourishing condition."

Meanwhile, the people begged or fought for food, and were slaugh-tered, transported or sent to jail for crimes committed out of their hunger. Here and there an employer would follow the example set by Robert Owen, who tried to make his mills clean and well run, would not employ child labour, even paid wages when there was no work to be done.

"*Why?*" he was asked in turn by a parliamentary committee on which Richard sat.

"To prevent crime and its misery," Owen replied. "If the poor cannot procure employment they must either commit crimes or starve."

"Yes, Owen is a good man," Daniel Ross admitted freely to Richard. "With a hundred such there might be hope. With one or two there will be constant conflict. You know yourself, sir, that London has more thieves, more prostitutes, more brothels of both sexes—"

"*Both* sexes!" exclaimed Richard.

"Many men prefer young boys to girls, sir. Don't you shut your eyes to facts, no matter how ugly."

"I won't close them once they are open," Richard promised. He could understand the helplessness, the hopelessness of young men like Daniel Ross.

Yet now and again a flash of good came, and in that same year of 1816 prison took the place of the pillories.

"But it should have happened two hundred years ago," protested Daniel. "Mr. Marshall, I always appear to be complaining to you and I wish it were not so—I know you exert yourself to improve conditions—but my friends are impatient and I am afraid of what may happen. We had a meeting last evening at which one of us complained with great bitterness that the rich can *buy* justice, can *buy* the Bow Street Runners, but these are not at the service of the poor because the cost is too high."

"There is a committee sitting on the subject of the Runners and police work, Daniel," Richard told him. "I will raise this matter."

He sat in the crowded committee room the next day, eyes sore from tobacco smoke, Old Puff and Blow wheezing next to him, listening to the chief magistrate at Bow Street, Sir Nathaniel Conant, giving evidence, his voice rather too loud, as if he not only resented being there but resented the questions asked.

Five times Richard raised his hand to be called; five times he was ignored. On his sixth attempt the chairman of the committee, an elderly Member, said in a croaky voice, "Your question, Mr. Marshall. Your question."

"If a poor man is robbed of a few shillings, which might well mean more to him than hundreds of pounds to a rich one, will the Bow Street men help him?"

"Help him?" echoed Conant. "The men will help anyone, and no charge is made for an investigation into a murder or other atrocious event. But the officers have to live. They have to receive payment for services, for they would starve on their official pay. But the charge is small—one guinea a day plus fourteen shillings for living expenses." He glared at Richard before going on. "But if a bank or wealthy merchant is robbed I will send six or even eight Runners out and charge a one-hundred-pound fee for every thousand stolen. We are not a charity, sir."

"So those who are rich can get justice and those who are poor can get none," Richard said tartly.

"Give me a hundred more officers and *all* will get what help they need," rasped Conant.

"I question that," Richard said. "Is it not more likely that the rich would be even better served whilst the poor would still be rejected?"

The witness clenched his hand.

"Not a question, not a question," the chairman croaked.

"Then I will ask another," Richard persisted. "Is it true that officers will act as or appoint go-betweens to arrange terms for the recovery of stolen goods?"

"And why not, sir? Would you rather that valuable gold or silver plate was melted down than a fair price arranged for its return intact?"

"One final question," Richard found himself asking. "Are you and are your men on the side of the people and justice or on the side of the thieves?"

He sat down to some angry comments, and while he received some support, there was none strong enough to help him develop his theme that justice should be free for all. As he left the House that day he felt a mood of despair; his disillusion about some of the attitudes of the Bow Street patrols and the magistrate was tempered only slightly by the fact that they had the government's approval simply because their system of rewards cost the government little money.

There *must* not be much more delay in creating a force which was free to all and free for everyone.

As was usual when he was angry, Richard rode from Westminster in whatsoever direction his fancy took him. Some magnetic attraction nearly always led him to the Thames, and he rode for the first time over the newly finished Regent Bridge, already called Vauxhall Bridge because it led to the famous gardens, then found his way along lanes and narrow streets to the New Strand Bridge, which was not yet finished for heavy traffic but which could be used by those on foot or on horseback. From either side of the river this bridge revealed an elegance which made it more attractive than any other. There were rumours that its name would soon be changed to the Bridge of Waterloo.

Already he was feeling less obsessed with the problems with which he attempted to cope, and was just about to ride across the river when he saw a big, tall man with long jaw and droll expression and recognised him as Talbot, one of the most successful of the Bow Street Runners. Talbot caught his eye and pushed through the crowd toward him.

"Good evening, Mr. Marshall," he said. "I hear you've been after us poor folk!"

"After you—" Richard began, and then understanding dawned. "Oh, you mean in the House. Has the magistrate told you what questions I put to him?'

470

"Yes, sir, *and* his answers," declared Talbot. "I'm on duty here, sir. Since they put in the gas there have been a lot of pickpockets and cutpurses about and I take my turn. For thirty shillings a week!" He gave a wry grin. "But I'll be relieved in ten minutes and I'd be honoured if you'd have some coffee with me. There's a coffee house on the corner."

"I shall go and keep a table," promised Richard.

He tied his horse outside, tipped a man to keep an eye on it, then went in. The interior, bright with advertisements, serving girls and the new gas lamps, struck warm. Richard selected a corner table where he could face Talbot when he arrived, puzzled but glad of an opportunity to rest. When at last Talbot came in, removed his tall hat and sat down, coffee was already on the table.

"Now, rebuke me," Richard invited, half-smiling.

"Rebuke you, sir? God bless my soul, why should I? For telling the truth? There's help and protection for the rich but little for the poor, and that's a fact. No, sir, I've come to inform you, begging your leave. It's a long time since you—and your grandfather before you—spent much time at Bow Street. Things have changed."

"I imagine that is true."

"It is indeed, sir." Talbot drank coffee and then gave his droll smile. What an enormous jaw he has, thought Richard. "But I don't see how you can hold back change, sir. We Runners do a very good job of work, but we can't do miracles. The condition is a mess, to put it plainly. What with constables from the parishes, the watchmen—poor old creatures—the beadles and others, there are too many in one place, too few in another, with hundreds of different authorities controlling them. The truth is, sir, it's not organised because it's not organisable."

"And you think there should be changes?" asked Richard quietly.

"It may be against my own interests, sir, but yes, I do."

In the months that followed, Richard concluded that there were three major obstacles to an organised police force. First, the mass of people, fed by the prejudice created by the merchants and bankers who wanted at all costs to control their own "police." Second, a small number of Bow Street men, mostly Runners, who were making up to £5,000 a year, largely from rewards, and who wanted the present system to continue. Third, a small but powerful group of magistrates who would lose their power and authority if a new police force was established over which they had no jurisdiction.

He studied reports of riots and mass meetings; heard extreme Tories of the Right call for stricter measures in crushing all forms of incipient revolt; heard the Radicals demand new laws, reform of Parliament, better working conditions for the workers. As troops were called in to put down threats of risings, Richard again felt fear that there might be another eruption in London as terrible as the Gordon Riots.

But the real blow fell in the north. The first Richard heard of it was when the Member for Wexford, an elderly man of moderate opinions, came hurrying toward him waving a single newssheet.

"Marshall! Have you seen this terrible thing?" The Member's voice was so hard that others in the hall came toward him. "It's from *The Northern News*. Eleven people were slaughtered and hundreds were wounded by a saber charge at St. Peter's Fields in Manchester. Such dreadful bloodletting!"

"No trained troops would have behaved so," said a red-faced retired colonel. Then, squaring his shoulders, he added, "But the rabble must be put down! Men like Hunt should be thrown into prison."

In a crowded, uneasy House of Lords, the Duke of Wellington congratulated the authorities in Manchester for their firm handling of a grievous situation, but as he spoke, protests came from several Members; cries of "Shame!" and "Murder!" and "Nonsense!" were hurtled across the floor of the House. It became apparent that the government's information, from a special dispatch, had been incomplete. The newspaper account by an eyewitness was much nearer the truth. Within days Wellington was being jeered both in the House and on the streets.

"The hero of Peterloo!" a man bellowed at him.

"That's right—Peterloo. It's a long way from Waterloo to Peterloo!"

Several Members began to laugh.

Nothing in the situation seemed to Richard even remotely a laughing matter. He had come to respect Wellington as a man and was sure he had welcomed the news because he had been misinformed. But could the nation afford a politician among its leaders who was capable of making so serious a gaffe? There was a slight easing in Richard's mind when he learned that the troops had been local yeomanry, only partly trained, but what would happen if a similar situation arose in London before the creation of a strong police force?

He knew the answer: the troops would be ordered to attack, and the people might well rise in bloody revolution.

In his fifteenth year in the House of Commons, 1822, Richard was appointed to yet another committee, with Home Secretary Peel as its chairman.

After sitting through several tense weeks of argument, he finally heard the committee chairman say, to the accompaniment of deep approval from most of the Members present, "It is difficult to reconcile an effective system of police with that of perfect freedom of action and exemption from interference, which are the great privileges and blessings of society in this country; and your committee think that the forfeiture or curtailment of such advantages would be too great a sacrifice for improvements in police or facilities in detection of crime, however desirable in themselves if abstractly considered."

Had this been all, Richard's disappointment would have been acute, but having rejected the concept, the report went on—at Peel's cunning instigation—recommending the formation of a daytime patrol, to be dressed in the same uniform as the Horse Patrols, to control the principal streets of Westminster and around the City of London. It was to cooperate with the night patrols and, since there was no specific district assigned to it, the Bow Street office should become the official criminal investigation headquarters for the whole country.

For once, no doubt due to Peel's urging, the recommendations were accepted.

Richard was stunned by the significance of the move. London for the first time in its history had a *day and night* police patrol sponsored by the government.

CHAPTER *38*

A Bill Is Prepared

THE NEXT night Richard was to dine with Simon. Despite his general mood of satisfaction, he carried with him the uneasiness he always felt in Hermina's presence, whilst his relationship with Susan was, in its way, as unsatisfying as his relationship with Hermina. He had taken to her from the beginning and she apparently to him, but she had always been evasive. She seemed to anticipate any attempt he made to talk seriously about their friendship and would invariably introduce some subject that made it impossible for him to proceed. At first he had believed this coincidental but at last he concluded that either he gave himself away by his expression or that Susan was possessed of a remarkable sixth sense. Not unnaturally, this teased him into greater interest. He did not at any time feel passionately in love with her but there was a quality about her face and movements which caught and held his attention. True, he did not see her often, although in the years immediately following Timothy's death he had visited the house once or twice each month. When at last he managed to break through her evasiveness sufficiently to ask, "Susan, do you think you would enjoy spending more time with me?" she had said, "Oh, there is nothing I would like better. But I cannot get away. Hermina needs me."

It was always the same, and although Richard had no doubt there was some truth in her answer, he was sure that she used Hermina's need partly as an excuse. Had he met another woman who attracted him, he would have paid Susan less attention and thought about her seldom, but he was fond of neither parties nor socialising, and his habit of going to the theater and to concerts by himself was hardly conducive to an *affaire du coeur*.

One day, when he had called and discovered Susan free, Hermina being with Simon, he had asked more boldly, "Do you ever think of marrying again, Susan? And if you do, would you—"

He was about to add "consider me?" when she answered quickly, touching his hand and saying, "Richard, I feel my responsibility to Hermina very deeply, and although you may not realise it, she is in desperate need of a trustworthy friend. I can tell you, but I ask you on your oath not to reveal it to any human soul, least of all Simon, that she has increasing periods of insanity. When she is taken by an attack only I can do anything with her. We stay in the apartment, sometimes for days on end, until she recovers. It is a very grave responsibility."

Richard could only agree, and there seemed no point in saying that Simon appeared to expect too much of her.

From that time on he was convinced that whatever his future, it was not with Susan. But she did smooth the hours he spent at Simon's, making him still more conscious of the lack of a permanent relationship in his own life.

The next few years went by comparatively uneventfully, with Richard remaining unmarried. Then, one morning late in 1827, as he walked into the Palace of Westminster, Peel came forward to meet him. Peel—out of office now that Canning had formed a government —was with Lord John Russell, a Whig Richard knew well enough to admire, and a youngish man he didn't know.

There was a round of introductions and Richard caught the young man's name: Chadwick.

"Richard," said Peel in an unusually affable mood, "do you think you could sit through another committee?"

"And on what subject is our recommendation to be denied this time?" Richard asked, and there was a general laugh.

"To inquire into the causes of crime," said Lord John Russell.

"But we have the answer in at least twelve committee reports and minority reports and abstracts and treatises since 1739," Richard said. *"Can* there be anything new to say?"

"If you sit with us you can at least tell us what has been recounted before," Peel argued.

"If you wish it, then I will sit," answered Richard. "But I warn you, I am no longer a tongue-tied junior Member. When anyone on the committee appears to me to be talking nonsense, I shall say so."

"I suspect you are going to talk a great deal," young Chadwick remarked dryly.

In fact it was a dull committee, held in a smoke-filled room, every speech interspersed by someone sneezing either from a cold or from snuff. It was obvious from the start that they would get nowhere, and Richard did not understand why Peel had joined the committee.

"When are we going to accept the truth, eh?" one of the older Tory Members kept asking. "Crime is caused by too much leniency. Harsher punishments, that's the answer."

"Nonsense," argued Russell. "As far back as the turn of the century Romilly tried to make us see sense. We need fewer crimes liable to capital punishment—"

"Or none at all," interposed Chadwick.

"Are you mad, sir?" the old Tory demanded. "Take away capital punishment and we'll all be murdered in our beds. A strong force to see that the scoundrels are caught, and the certainty of hanging—*that* will cut down crime."

"I want no more police," Russell declared. "We have too many as things are. We need to reduce capital crimes, and—"

"Upon my soul!" interjected Richard. "I have never heard such nonsense in my life—not even from Members of Parliament. Every police reformer from the Fieldings to Colquhoun, Beccaria and Bentham, even back to John Furnival, knew the answer: reduce the severity of punishment but strengthen the police to make sure criminals are caught and no one can make profit from a capture." As they stared at his rare outburst, he went on: "If you are a Tory, you stand for harsher punishment and strong police, if a Whig, you want lighter punishment and weak police. Why don't you forget your parties and think and act like reasonable human beings?"

The Tory Member spluttered with rage, while Russell said dryly, "You have made your point, Mr. Marshall."

"I will tell you what we *won't* make," retorted Richard. "A recommendation which will do the slightest good."

In one way, he was right. The committee's first report was simply a stopgap.

But after one of the meetings, young Chadwick came to him in the lobby and asked, "Would you do me a service, sir?"

"If I can, gladly."

"I have prepared a memorandum on the use of a preventive police force and would be glad indeed if you would read this. And if you are in general agreement, then I think when the committee meets again we may be more effective."

Chadwick's memorandum was brilliant. Praise came from all sides and his future was assured, while the committee's second report left the situation in Peel's hands.

"I am strongly in favour of a vigorous preventive police, Mr. Marshall, even though you may not always have received this impression from me," he told Richard. "I would be afraid to meddle with the City, but if we were to work out a plan for the nucleus of a single police system in the rest of the metropolis this *might* gain the favour of the House. Will you accept the task of preparing such a plan, Mr. Marshall?"

"I will accept it eagerly," Richard promised. He could not know that his heart now thumped as his grandfather's had when, long ago, the accomplishment of the dream seemed nearer. "May I invite help— from Lord John Russell, for instance?"

"You may call on all who you think would be of value," replied Peel. "What I want, Mr. Marshall, are the facts of the situation as it is, and as precise a proposal as possible. Once I am satisfied that this has good prospect of being approved by the House, then I will present it. I do desire such a police force, Mr. Marshall. Indeed—and in strict confidence—I desire a supplementary bill which will lead eventually to a national police force, a sort of Ministry of Police. I have felt the need ever since reading the pleas made to the government by Sir John Furnival and the Fielding brothers. Your grandfather's efforts and your own have not been entirely wasted, you perceive."

"I could not be more deeply gratified," Richard managed to say.

Peel remained silent for a moment, then leaned forward in his chair. "Mr. Marshall," he said at last, "I must offer a word of caution. We have not yet persuaded the House to pass such a bill into law. There is much to do. And if we are blessed with good fortune in timing—I would not like to present the bill on such a day as *you* first presented one to the House, Mr. Marshall; that might indeed be its Waterloo!—we have to create a police force which will overcome all public prejudices. When the time comes, I predict that such prejudices will be much stronger and more hostile than any we shall meet here at Westminster."

"May I ask who else has your confidence?" asked Richard.

"So that you may discuss the matter," Peel remarked shrewdly. "You are at liberty to talk freely with Edwin Chadwick."

"You know the truth as well as I do," Chadwick said, when he and Richard met for coffee two mornings later. "Pitt failed because his bill tried to do too much; Peel hopes to succeed because he asks so little—at the first bite, in all events."

"He will have all the support I can give him," promised Richard.

Chadwick chuckled as he said, "Can you be unaware that your example has been his inspiration?"

"Oh, nonsense!" Richard actually flushed.

"No more nonsense than his warnings that we shall have opposition from all sides," Chadwick rejoined.

But no warnings dampened Richard's enthusiasm, and on that same evening he called on Simon, who, despite obvious preoccupation, appeared delighted.

By now the pressures and responsibilities weighing upon Simon could be made no easier by the problem of Hermina. The stamp of added years marked his face, and he remarkably resembled a portrait of Sir John Furnival of Bow Street. Although Richard seldom went to the Thamesside building and had little to do with others of the family or the company, he knew several Members of Parliament who were sponsored by them, and was acutely aware of the enormous extent of their power and influence. Furnival's had become one of the three most wealthy banking houses in the City, which meant in the world. Its holdings in the Bank of England had doubled; its share in the East India and the West India companies grew; and its holdings and estates in the United States became enormous.

Over this fabulous empire within the Empire, Simon ruled.

After Simon would come his two sons, Marriott and John. Did he fear for them? Richard wondered. Was he haunted by the dread that they might succumb, as Hermina had succumbed, to the awful curse of madness?

Whatever he thought or felt, Simon concealed it well, and after dinner that night, while he sipped and sniffed a cognac, he said with apparent earnestness, "First get your police force, Richard. Then make the public accept it."

He was virtually echoing Robert Peel's words!

Quietly and with great thoroughness the bill was prepared. During the following months Richard himself interviewed more than a hundred constables, magistrates, Bow Street Runners, Bow Street patrolmen, City guards and river police to assess the needs as comprehensively as he could and to make sure there were no weak links. All of his colleagues laboured with equal zeal. Undoubtedly the greatest fears of those in opposition were that a police force would become a kind of civilian armed force used to repress the people; also that its members would act as spies and would encourage informers.

"Above all we must convince the people that neither is true," Richard insisted.

"You mean the police should carry no arms?" Peel asked.

"That is vital, sir. If they are armed beyond a staff or cudgel it could be fatal to our prospects. And they must strictly avoid the use of spies and informers, even among thieves."

"Then show me how it can be done," Peel urged again. "Have you yet to name this bill, Mr. Marshall?"

"It is provisionally entitled Bill for Improving the Police In and Near the Metropolis, sir."

Peel, once again Home Secretary in a new Cabinet, pursed his lips, appeared to talk to himself, then said aloud, "Bill for Improving the Police In and Near the Metropolis. Hmmm. It has a nice respectable ring about it and appears to threaten nothing new. Politicians are most wary of innovations! It shall be considered. When may I expect to see a draft of this—ah—Bill for Improving the Police In and Near the Metropolis? 'Of London' can be taken as read."

"In six to eight weeks, sir."

"Then there should be time for me to study it and for the Attorney General to savage it and for presentation to the House early in the new year of 1829," Peel declared.

The draft was all but ready, and copies were being made by clerks who were also scholars and attorneys, when a message was brought to Richard in the House of Commons saying simply:

Hermina grievously ill. Can you come to see her?

Simon

"She has been subject to increasing rages and periods of violence," Simon told him, "and has been taking larger and larger doses of laudanum to obtain rest. It is years since we were husband and wife in the true sense. Last night, alone in her room, she took a substantial overdose. The doctors despair of her recovery."

"But I thought Susan was always with her to make sure she did nothing harmful."

"Usually she is," answered Simon, and his tired, darkly shadowed eyes were unwavering as he watched Richard. "But a woman must have some respite and a man with an insane wife some comfort. Susan was with me last night. She is a great solace. In fact, I do not know how I would have sustained myself in the past several years but for her."

In that moment Richard understood why Susan had never been in a mood to talk with him seriously about their relationship. Simon, not he, was her chosen. And that was the moment when Richard wondered, in shock touched with horror, whether Hermina had taken the overdose or whether it had been given to her.

Hermina died before night fell, two doctors in attendance, each ready to swear that death had been caused by excessive internal bleeding, and none had any doubt save those who had reason to suspect the truth. Few knew that Simon had taken Susan to his bed, and that from then on he placed her in charge of his household, preparing for the day when they could marry without arousing comment. Richard went less often to see them, the ugly suspicion never wholly driven from his mind. In any event, he was devoting every hour of his days and many of his nights to preparing the bill. At last it was ready, and in the company of Lord John Russell, he handed the precious document to Peel.

Now the task was done, and Richard suffered a reaction quite different from anything he had ever experienced before. It affected him physically; at times his whole body would go tense, at others it would quiver as if he had an attack of ague. Mentally, he was on edge, and did not trust himself for a while to discuss the police issue with anyone—or, for that matter, to discuss any serious issue. He was virtually sure of the cause of his condition, equally sure that he would not recover until he heard from Peel. He tried to prevent himself from looking back not only over the years he had spent on his task but on those decades spent by others. The date of John Furnival's first detailed proposal to Walpole had been in 1725, one hundred and three years earlier, before his grandfather had been born! Was it possible that after the agony of waiting and struggling, the dream was to be realised? Was it conceivable that he, Richard Marshall, was to be the main instrument by which the actual police force was to be forged?

When Richard had such thoughts he suffered a heavy weight of depression which made him feel terribly alone. And because he did not wish others to know how he was feeling, he kept away from the coffee houses which had been his main source of companionship for so many years. He had a strange feeling of being ostracised, although he knew that this was absurd, since the cause lay within himself.

What had he done to deny himself the warmth and pleasures of marriage? Why had be condemned himself to this loneliness, in which he could share his fears and even his hopes with no one? The only man who would have fully understood his present mood was his grandfather, of course: his grandfather and, perhaps, Simon. But Simon had been thrust—or had thrust himself—into a world in which he and Richard had little in common, and seemed far removed from him.

Richard knew he must not lie to himself.

Since Hermina's death, since Simon had told him of his relationship with Susan, it was his own feelings which had cooled. Susan had become a barrier between them at least as great as Simon's wealth and possessions.

One thing Richard could do to occupy and satisfy himself was to look for articles suitable for "Mr. Londoner"; but although during that Christmas season he had a rare chance to concentrate on the business again, it did not hold him as it should. There were now three adjoining shops with living quarters on the top floors of each. The salesrooms were on the ground floor and the one above, and in these there was hardly room to move among the shelves and display stands on which *objets d'art*, bric-a-brac, small paintings, porcelain, coins— all in great variety—were stored.

Christmas was always a busy time. The shops were thronged with customers from eight in the morning until ten and eleven o'clock at night, but the assistants were always courteous and patient. Those trained to watch for light-fingered "customers" carried out even their most distasteful tasks with great tact. Two watchmen were on duty by day and four by night to throw out any "customers" who clearly came to steal, although these were surprisingly few, and to watch the premises for fire. Now and again some precious piece of furniture was stolen from the store's sheds, and doubtless stood in some poor creature's hovel, a prized possession; but that was the worst of the losses at "Mr. Londoner."

As Christmas drew nearer, Richard, in spite of his misgivings, began to look for the yearly invitation from Simon to spend part of the holiday at Great Furnival Square. Usually this came by special messenger, in the form of a handwritten note, but this year there was no messenger and no invitation. Two days before Christmas Richard, convinced that it would not come, was desolate. Simon would not forget such an occasion; it could only be a deliberate omission. Added to his anxiety and tension over the proposals he had handed to Peel, this brought him to a level of depression which made him near distraught.

On Christmas Eve he sent a cart laden with gifts for the family— including an amber-headed pin for Simon, who liked such trifles— and decided that he must make an effort to shake himself out of his mood. A fast ride in the country would do him good. He went to the stables, which were still behind the shop, and the ostler's boy saddled his big bay. As he rode out, a few flakes of snow drifted down, but he wore a close-fitting hat and a long coat and was not troubled. He turned into St. Martin's Lane, still amazed at the changes. Porridge Island was almost gone, only a few miserable wooden shacks being left, and the Royal Stables had vanished completely. John Nash, though said to be failing—hardly surprising since he was in his seventies—had been commanded by George IV to make this whole area a fitting square to celebrate Nelson's victory at Trafalgar. How long such things took! For an even longer period there had been talk about building the Royal Academy to the north of the site; now it was referred to as the National Gallery, and work was started.

The clearing of slums gave a finer view of St. Martin's in the Fields. He was less familiar with the streets leading north, and could hardly believe how the metropolis had grown! Through Bloomsbury, beyond Camden Town and Kentish Town, the houses spread on either side along the banks of the wide Regent's Canal, one of the main arteries for transport of goods from east to west, and out toward the wooded countryside beyond Hampstead. The air was crisp but not too cold and there was little wind but that created by his own movement. He must soon turn back for he had been riding for two hours and the return would be slower because of the snow. Yet he contemplated this with reluctance. Here on horseback one could be alone, and at this moment he needed solitude.

Nestling in a valley between two low hills was an inn, blue wood smoke rising thick and almost straight from two tall chimneys jutting from the thatched roof. Two small carriages were outside, and three saddled horses, but as Richard drew up, a lad led the horses to cover behind the inn. He ducked beneath the low doorway and stepped into a warm room, with a log fire blazing at one end, brasses gleaming, copper pans glistening, and oak beams dark with polish. In one corner a group of men were sitting and drinking, talking about the coming season's crops, about wenches, about their families. In another corner a middle-aged man and woman were eating pies and drinking coffee.

The place had not only brightness but cleanliness. The man behind the bar, short and thickset, had mutton-chop whiskers and a clean-shaven chin; his ruffled shirt was spotless; so was the polished bar and all the things upon it.

Pinned to one of the beams behind the bar was a copy of the *Police Gazette*, giving details of stolen goods and wanted men; some hand-bills, also issued from Bow Street, were pinned beside it.

"Used to be the old *Hue and Cry*," declared the publican know-ingly. "They do say copies go to over a hundred thousand inns and alehouses, the likes of this, and millions of people read them."

Two million, Richard corrected silently, and reflected that not so long ago the old *Hue and Cry* had appeared only once every three weeks.

"Do you ever see any suspects in here?" he asked.

"I have done, sir, to be sure. And I've always sent word to London by the next stage. It's a wonderful system, sir, wonderful. Well now, what will be your pleasure?"

"I shall have a mug of your best light ale and a piece of the pie you most recommend."

"I dassen't recommend owt, sir. If my wife heard me favour one against the other I'd never hear the last on't! But if you'd care to know what I'd eat myself, I'd have the raised pork."

He smiled broadly, and Richard found himself laughing.

"Will you stand or sit, sir? Plenty of room for both today."

"I'll stand," Richard decided.

The pork pie had a flavour he had long dreamed about but seldom tasted, the kind his grandmother had made. He ate with more gusto than for weeks past, had his dented pewter tankard refilled, and went to a window, stooping to see through the leaded panes. The middle-aged couple had already gone; the men in the corner were standing up, even more boisterous in departure. During the half hour he had been here the snow had fallen thickly and now everything was covered, fields, hedges, trees and buildings were alike beautiful. If he did not leave soon he would not reach London in any comfort; the snow could be six or seven inches deep by the time he reached the Strand.

"Your pardon, sir," a girl said at his side.

He turned in surprise because he had not heard her approach. She was young, fifteen or sixteen perhaps, with a round face and eyes the brighter because of the reflection of the snow. A small bonnet rested at the back of a cluster of yellow curls. Her square-necked dress was cut low to reveal her bosom enticingly, and her eyes were china blue. She was holding a dish of tarts, deep lemon in colour, and once again Richard was reminded of his grandmother, who had cooked lemon curd tarts each week because "Jamey likes them so."

"But they are still not so good as those my mother would make," his grandfather would tease, and Mary would snatch them away from him.

"Why thank you," Richard said, taking one. It was butter-soft, rich, delicious.

He took another and another, pressed her to have one, then became aware of something in her manner which he had not at first noticed, an earnestness which he did not understand until she put a hand on his and said in a near-pleading voice, "You will not be able to ride on in this snow, sir, will you?"

"I had not thought of staying," Richard replied.

"Please, sir, do," she urged. " 'Tis cold as charity outside and the snow will grow thicker, you mark the words of a country girl."

Only half-thinking, he said, "But I've no night clothes, nothing with me."

"We'll find all you need, sir," she replied, "and I'll give you a promise to keep you warm in bed. It will be a wonderful way for you to celebrate Christmas Eve; you'll remember it to your dying day."

Had she been older, Richard might have been beguiled into staying, but this was only a child. Seeing the look on his face she backed away, frightened; but his anger was not with her, only with the conditions which made it necessary for young girls to resort to such methods of earning their livelihood. Taking out his purse he gave her a golden sovereign. She stared at the bright yellow on her palm, the colour of her hair, her mouth wide open, her eyes round and huge. Then he strode from her to the bar, paid the host generously, wished him a merry Christmas, and went briskly out.

Mounting his horse, he rode slowly homeward, for the snow could cover ruts and potholes treacherously, and the faster he rode the harder would be a fall. But he had no mishaps. Few coaches and fewer riders appeared on the road, and if the snow continued, a lot of people would be kept from their beds that night.

Dusk had fallen earlier than usual when he reached the Strand because the leaden skies and thick falling flakes created a strange mingling of brightness and gloom. He took the horse straight to the stables, then walked in the tracks of others to "Mr. Londoner." Even here the snow had kept many people away. When the road should be thronged with traffic, sidewalks crowded and the shops bulging, few people were about. Outside the main doorway of "Mr. Londoner" stood a small carriage, covered with snow so that he could not read the crest on the side; the driver was nowhere in sight. Then, as Richard went into the side entrance, stamping snow off his boots, a man came hurrying from the shop's doorway.

"Mr. Marshall, sir! Mr. Marshall!"

Richard turned to find the coachman, who must have been standing inside the doorway, hurrying toward him. He wore the livery of the House of Furnival and in his hand was a letter. As they went inside the narrow entrance Richard tore this open and his fingers were so unsteady that the thick paper shook.

He read:

> *The dolt who should have brought you my greetings a week ago lost the missive and was too frightened to tell me. I beg you, whatever your plans, come and dine with Susan and me this night. We dine at five-thirty but will delay if we receive word from you. I have sent a man to Chelsea, another to Bow Street and others to all your regular haunts to try to make sure of catching you.*
>
> *Simon*

The weight of relief was so great that Richard stood upright for a few moments, staring out of the open doorway. "I beg you, whatever your plans, come and dine with Susan and me this night. We dine at five-thirty . . ."

It now wanted twenty minutes of four.

"What are your orders?" he asked the coachman at last.

"On finding you, to send messages to Chelsea and Bow Street for the release of the coachmen waiting there, sir, and to wait for you no matter how long you may be."

"Come upstairs and warm yourself in the kitchen," Richard said. "The cook will give you some hot soup."

When he entered the main house at Great Furnival Square, where Simon now lived, there was a welcoming warmth and brightness of candles and trees and holly and mistletoe, although no other guests as yet. It was usual for Simon to have a small dinner party this night and as many of the rest of the family as could come would fill the house tomorrow. Footmen took Richard's cloak, drew off his boots and put on the shoes he carried in the cloak's tail pocket, and escorted him upstairs. There could be no less than a thousand candles in the wall brackets and hanging chandelier, casting both light and shadow on the portraits of past Furnivals which adorned the staircase walls. If the quiet was strange, the beauty and elegance were enchanting.

Suddenly a door opened and Simon came toward him, both hands held out in welcome in the old, familiar way. And it was Simon the friend, not Simon Rattray-Furnival, head of the great house, who linked arms with him and said, "I was desolate lest you should not come. At any other time but Christmas I would have thrown the idiot messenger out into the snow! And any man but Richard would have inquired to find out if any letter had been mislaid. Not Richard, though! What a man you are! At a time when you should be bellowing like a town crier at your triumph you hide yourself!"

He gave Richard no time to ask what he meant by triumph but led the way into a small, exquisitely furnished and lighted room, where the table was laid, silver and glass shimmered, and a fire glowed in the beautiful marble fireplace.

"We shall dine here tonight, Richard, since there are but four of us."

Four? wondered Richard.

Out of a doorway at the other side of the room came Susan, so beautifully gowned that he hardly recognised her; and, a step behind her, another, somewhat younger woman, elegant in dark-green velvet, wearing only a single brooch upon her corsage, amber-pale shoulders glowing in the candlelight. She was taller than Susan, moved with grace, and although was not by most standards beautiful, her eyes had the colour and brightness of emeralds and her lips were generous-looking and full.

"Richard, I am eager to present Mrs. Katherine Hooper. Katherine, you have often heard me talk of my blood brother, Richard. I hope you find him more distracting company than me! Susan, my love, if you will ring for service, we will, I trust, sharpen our appetites."

Almost at once a white-haired butler came in bearing a tray, and when they each held a glass of sherry, Simon said, "To new friends and old customs!"

"New friends," Richard echoed, "and old customs."

Katherine was the widow of Cornelius Hooper, Richard learned, grandson of a former Lord Mayor of London and one of three brothers on the board of Hooper, Rill, Bankers, well known among the smaller independent banking houses. At one time the family had been merchants and shipowners as well as bankers, but they had sold these interests to the House of Furnival and now concentrated on banking.

During the next two days, while they remained as guests—the heavy snow, which had gone on until it would have made traveling even short distances difficult, preventing them from leaving—Richard saw a great deal of Katherine, and learned much about her. Her husband had been twenty-four years older than she; she had been married at seventeen, and the only child of the marriage had died in its first year. She was the daughter of a family of goldsmiths whose business had been absorbed by larger companies, had brothers, sisters, and a host of nieces and nephews. She had spent two years at school in Versailles and spoke French fluently. These facts he was told, some by Susan, some by Katherine herself, but other things he discovered in the course of conversation.

She knew a great deal about the work he had done, had studied social and economic history, and could hold her own with Simon on many aspects of trading and of banking. And she could quote Sir John Furnival, the Fieldings and Bentham and Chadwick as freely as he, Richard. He had never known a woman so familiar with what had been taken for granted as a man's world.

She most astonished him by her knowledge of conditions in London. "And in the last few years there has been little improvement," she asserted. "The whole of London is a rabbit warren of thieves' hiding places. There is one near Fleet Ditch, close to Saffron Hill—"

"Number Three West Street?" Richard interrupted.

"So you know of it!"

"It is famous—or infamous—throughout London, full of ways of escape, secret panels, trap doors, concealed staircases—"

"It is said that Jonathan Wild once lived there," said Katherine.

"It is certain that some who have escaped from the Fleet or Newgate have holed up in the house for months, that whenever the Runners search for stolen goods they have no more than one chance in five of finding what they look for, but always discover the proceeds of some crime, or the skeleton of a man promised succour and then sealed in a wall to die of starvation. And there are six or seven places by which one can reach the roof and a dozen directions to escape from there."

"Do you know, Richard, you sound most excited!" Katherine teased.

"And in my way I am," admitted Richard. "Every time I think about the situation I am more convinced that it must be changed."

"So much has to be changed," Katherine responded quietly. "Reform is needed in workshops, in mills, in the streets, in Parliament. You have concentrated on the police, I know, but one day that will no longer be necessary. What will you turn to then?"

"I shall decide if and when the time comes," replied Richard. "True reform of the peace-keeping and police systems in London is not yet achieved despite a hundred years of striving by men far greater than I."

"Not all men define greatness in the same way," she replied lightly, switching the subject to the Bill for Improving the Police In and Near the Metropolis, of which she knew a surprising amount.

They were walking in the garden which, on the night of the Furnival ball, had been the scene of so much bloodshed. Now the children of a dozen families hurled snowballs or climbed trees and dropped into the snow or, with the help of grownups, made giant snowmen.

"I cannot tell you how glad I am to hear that Mr. Peel likes the bill in its present form," Katherine said suddenly.

Richard stopped in his tracks, staring at her.

"I don't understand you. How can you possibly know the Home Secretary's mind? I have not yet heard from him myself."

"You mean that Simon did not tell you?" Katherine's voice rose in astonishment. "There was some matter of taxation on which Mr. Peel and the Lord of the Treasury sought Simon's advice. Mr. Peel told Simon there was only one word, just a single word, that he wished to change in the bill."

They stood in the snow, facing each other.

Richard saw the admiration in her eyes, as well as their beauty.

She saw this man with the eagle's face and the gray eyes that might have been made of finely tempered steel, this man who talked with the voice of reason, this man whom she knew Simon greatly loved, staring at her openmouthed.

She saw the incredulity in his expression.

And she saw the tears, the actual tears, which filled his eyes.

Very slowly and only when they had turned and begun to move back toward the house did Katherine Hooper say, "So it means so much to you?"

Huskily Richard replied, "It is not possible to tell you how much it means. If I have made a fool of myself I am sorry, but—even now, I can scarcely believe it. Peel *approves*? He will present the bill to the House of Commons?"

"There is even a date set aside," Katherine told him. "It will not be as early as he had wished because there is some work to be done behind the scenes to diminish any likely opposition. If you know anything about Robert Peel you know that he does not like to be defeated in the House of Commons! It is to be in April—as early in April as can be arranged. The Leader of the House is already planning it. Why, I have even been promised permission to be present when Peel introduces the bill." After a few moments she went on. "Does it disappoint you that he, not you, will make the introduction to the House?"

Richard frowned in puzzlement.

"No, no, not in any way. On the contrary. Peel will have ten times the authority I could have." Slowly he shook his head and in a wondering voice went on: "How could Simon *forget* to tell me?"

"In truth I thought I had told you on the night when you arrived," Simon defended himself. "I have the clearest recollection of referring to your triumph. What other triumph could you expect? I assumed that you already knew what I meant and were behaving with your customary humility!"

"If ever a word fitted a man, humility fits Richard," Katherine smiled.

"Peel himself will introduce the bill and I believe the House will approve by a handsome majority," Sir Douglas Rackham told a secret meeting of justices and high constables in the high-ceilinged drawing-room of his home at Kensington. It was furnished with extraordinary effectiveness; the pale-gold and soft-green colouring soothed and warmed. "It will be a waste of time and effort to try to prevent its passing. We must therefore devote ourselves to stirring up hostility among the public so that the new police force becomes a total failure. If, once it is tried, it proves unsuccessful, then we can be done with this nonsense for the rest of our lives."

Every one of the thirty men at that meeting voiced his approval, even the one man on duty as a guard, who at the age of twenty was a Bow Street patrol member. He was Arthur Jackson, son of Frederick Jackson, long since retired. No one present dreamed that Arthur was planning to apply for a post with the New Police while remaining a spy within this group. Not even Todhunter Mason, the man responsible for Timothy McCampbell-Furnival's murder, suspected young Jackson. Had his great-grandfather not been hanged at Tyburn Fields?

Mason, who had a foot in the magistrates' as well as the thieves' camps, listened with approval.

On that sixteenth of April, 1829, a bright and sunny day with great banks of clouds vividly white against the deep blue of the sky, every narrow bench in the House of Commons was full and some Members were actually to stand throughout the first reading and the debate which followed the second. Sitting on a cross-bench between the two parties, Richard was directly opposite the Speaker and had full sight of Peel as he spoke with quiet effectiveness, not haranguing the House but set on keeping the temperature cool.

"I do not wish to disguise that the time is come when, from the increase in its population, the enlargement of its resources and the multiplying development of its energies, we may fairly pronounce that the country has outgrown her police institutions, and that the cheapest *and* the safest course will be the introduction of a new mode of protection."

There was a rustle of movement and calls of approval, with as yet no single voice raised in opposition. Richard sat spellbound as Peel went on.

"Such men will be recruited from the ranks of ex-soldiers and ex-sailors as well as trusted officers already employed by courts such as

Bow Street, with whose Runners they will cooperate. The Runners, of course, will remain the chief detective department. None shall be older than thirty-five or less than five feet seven inches in height, and all must be men of exceptional courage for they will be unarmed save for a staff or stick, so that the charge of being a civilian army established to bend the people to the government's will cannot justly be leveled against them. And so that the new force may be able to rely on the cooperation and good will of the public at large, there shall be the following principles embodied in the instructions given to each member of the force, instructions drawn up with great care by your committee."

This time his pause was obviously for effect, and as he held the attention of the House he bowed first to Lord John Russell on the Whig benches and next, with equal deliberation, to Richard; and he paused again so that Members could call out their approval, as most did.

Among the loudest was Sir Douglas Rackham.

"I shall read those instructions to the House," Peel went on at last.

Richard closed his eyes and listened to the persuasive voice, repeating the words to himself almost as if this were a litany.

"It should be understood at the outset that the principal object to be attained is the prevention of crime. . . . He, the constable, will be civil and obliging to all people of every rank and class. . . . Particular care is to be taken that the constables of the police do not form false notions of their powers or duties."

The approval was deep-throated and universal, and when Richard opened his eyes he saw nearly every Member's mouth open, many papers waving, only here and there a scowl or straight face of disapproval. He had no doubt at all that the bill would soon become an Act of Parliament, that the skeleton organisation could be formed and its leaders named, that an arrangement would be made for recruiting —not a handful, as Furnival and the Fieldings had begged for, not a few dozen men, but a force of police more than three thousand strong.

In the House of Lords, the Duke of Wellington, using much the same phraseology, moved the bill and was warmly received.

That night Sir Douglas Rackham saw several of those Members who were opposed to the bill, and also Todhunter Mason, one of the members of the syndicate that had bought *The Daily Clarion*. No one questioned the accuracy of Rackham's prognostication now; they could not hope to prevent the bill from becoming law.

"So we must use our utmost endeavours to make sure that the law fails," Rackham repeated. "As they plan to build, so must we plan to destroy. But for the time being I shall give limited praise to the new force in the columns of *The Daily Clarion*, so that when the time comes to attack, it cannot be charged that the newspaper has acted out of prejudice. As *The Daily Clarion* is again becoming a popular voice of the people, it will help to sway public opinion whichever way we desire."

"Don't make any mistake about it," said Todhunter Mason, "If this police force is a success, we're done, mates. Finished. Pickled in our own blood and that's the truth. We want trading justices and Runners working together, thieves with one hand and thief-takers with the other, that's what we want! If these new police get too strong, they'll put an end to the Runners sure as I stand here."

There was a roar of agreement from the crowded cellar beneath the Black Swan, and he gave the men time to settle before going on:

"We've got to give them no peace, friends. And if they put spies among us then, God help us, we can provide a few, can't we? Never let a little thing like a thief stop us, did we? So why let a spy or two? We'll plant 'em in the force, and we'll let the magistrates find them when the time's ripe, see. And we'll make those bloody men o' Peel's so drunk they don't know whether they're arresting a thief or a Member of Parliament or a bloody bishop, lads. No corruption, Peel says. God help us, they'll be so corrupt before we've finished with them that Parliament will squeal for us to get back to our legitimate work!"

His talk was punctuated by roars of laughter and much banging of tankards on the deal tables, but all of this paled into insignificance as he went on.

"And we'll put the women onto them, that's what we'll do. Old soldiers, are they? And old sailors? Ever known one of the King's men who didn't like half an hour with his doxy? We'll tell the pretties to give them the eye, then we'll catch them in the act. Rape, that's what we'll get 'em for. Do you know what? I give them a *year*. No I don't!" he bellowed, "I give them six months. They'll want to peel themselves off from Peel by then, don't you worry."

The roar made the walls and the ceiling of the cellar shake.

Again among those present was Arthur Jackson, the Bow Street

Runner, unrecognisable in his disguise of black side whiskers and a mustache as the man who had been at Sir Douglas Rackham's meeting not long ago. So far, he warned himself, this was only drunken talk. He must bide his time, and before he could take any effective action he had to join the new force. A guinea a week, food and lodgings would not set a man up for a lifetime, but Simon Rattray-Furnival would pay handsomely for information—and even more handsomely when he knew that Todhunter Mason was the man he had been seeking for so many years.

"Were you proud?" Katherine asked Richard, smiling at him across their table at Rules, a restaurant and oyster bar of renown in Maiden Lane, one of the narrow streets near Covent Garden. Prints of actors and journalists, authors and Members of Parliament, verses signed by their composers, sketches by both Hogarth and Rowlandson, were on the walls. The food was straightforward English style, the roast beef and steak and oyster pies especially good. Sole fresh caught in the English Channel only that morning was always available, and there was a note of elegance and quality everywhere. That night Richard and Katherine had arrived before the rush which would follow the arrival of the patrons from Drury Lane and the Opera House, and they were in a stall in a corner where they could not be overheard.

"Yes," Richard admitted. "I was very proud indeed. I tried to see you in the Strangers' Gallery but failed."

"I was quieter and less conspicuous than a mouse!"

"Impossible," Richard riposted, and although he laughed there was seriousness in his manner. "Katherine, do you know that I love you as deeply as I am capable of love?"

"You are flattering me," she said, and her eyes danced.

"You know better than that," he declared. "But what you may *not* know is why I have not yet declared myself nor told you that I would be truly proud if you were to marry me."

She sat very still, as if oblivious of everything but his expression and the cool touch of his hand on hers.

"I have assumed that it is because you have doubt of your feelings," she said, no longer smiling.

"None whatsoever," he assured her. "Not a single moment. I am absolutely sure of my feeling for you. But I am almost twenty years older than you, Katherine. You have already been married to a man much your senior in years, and you would not be human if you did not sometimes long for a younger man, one of your own age. If you do, I—" He broke off and pressed her hand firmly before going on. "I would ask you to forgive and forget what I have said. I think—I do believe the new bill has gone to my head like wine so that I dare speak when, sober, I would have the good sense to keep silent."

She did not respond at once.

A waiter drew near and would have come to the table but an older one held him back, shaking his head surreptitiously. Both Richard and Katherine were unmindful of everything and everyone about them.

Richard thought, She is trying to find a gentle way of saying No. I cannot blame her but in God's name I wish it were not so.

At last she spoke.

"I am thirty-seven, Richard. Old enough to understand and love you, young enough, if it is your wish, to bear you children, strong enough to help you where you need help, experienced enough to become impatient with younger men."

She stopped, and he hardly seemed to breathe . . . until he took her hands and drew her closer. A spoon fell and they did not notice, a platter fell and broke and they did not notice. Fleetingly Richard thought, I am fifty-five and she thirty-seven, but please God, I can make her happy.

When at last they walked from Rules to the Strand, where there would be a hackney to take first Katherine and then Richard home, Katherine pointed to a newsboy carrying a placard of *The Times* which contained two words:

POLICE!   POLICE!

Richard felt he needed nothing more.

CHAPTER *39*

Number 31 Great Furnival Square

It was a double wedding. But as Katherine walked down the aisle toward Richard and Simon as they waited, first for her and then for Susan, she had eyes only for Richard.

"Wilt thou take this woman . . ."

"I will."

"Wilt thou take this man . . ."

"I will."

She was aware of Richard's lips against hers, of his hand touching her, of the swelling notes of the ancient organ, the massed voices of choristers and congregation. She was not aware of the emerald beauty of her eyes against the paleness of her face and the rich silk of her gown.

Nor did she notice the ranks of nobles and bankers, merchants and sailors, Members of Parliament and justices, and the guard of honour, half in the honey-brown livery of the House of Furnival, half Bow Street Runners, although for a moment the Runners did pierce her euphoria. Richard had for so long been involved with them and the forging of a police force.

She was virtually oblivious of the gilded coach, liveried footmen, coachmen, youths strewing rose petals on the cobbled road; of the crowd lining the streets eager to watch any great occasion; of the fusiliers and dragoons stationed in various places; of the watchmen and constables, the boatmen and the members of the river police; of the urchins, of the poor who gazed, enraptured and without envy.

She did not see Arthur Jackson or his father Frederick. She did not see Todhunter Mason and his favourite cronies. She did not hear the roar of rattles and the ringing of bells, the hooting of ships from the river, the blowing of trumpets and the clear notes of horns, the hurrahs of the people and the cheers of the children.

She was aware only of Richard.

How could a man come to mean so much to her? she wondered, when love, the need for a satisfying sexual relationship, had lain dormant within her for so long. Now they were passionately alive. Had she come to mean as much to him? Was he as eager as she to bring their love to the fiercest consummation? She felt a sudden stir of uncertainty, perhaps even of apprehension, for she did not really know him and he did not know her. He, especially, had lived by himself for so long that once the excitement of the honeymoon faded he might find a shared life intolerable.

She did not in her heart believe that he would, yet the shadow of the possibility hovered.

She had not thought of love during the arid years of her marriage. Affection, yes, and liking, but love—it belonged to those far-off days, to youth, to yesterday. Yet here was Richard, leading her into the main house of Great Furnival Square and to the wedding breakfast— *her* wedding breakfast. Was it all a dream, she wondered, and would she wake, suddenly and with a shock of aching loss, into reality?

And here was Simon with his new bride Susan. He took both her hands, kissed her on either cheek. "I told you how you would feel about Richard, didn't I?" he said, laughing.

Was he a wizard with Merlin's touch? For he had told her.

"I hope you are so very, very happy," said Susan.

"You cannot wish that more for me than I wish it for you," Katherine told her.

Suddenly she was surrounded by men and women who seemed

strangers, all clamouring to talk to her, and at once all apprehension was gone and she was out of the trance and back in the real world, knowing this was no dream, that these well-wishers were of flesh and blood, her relatives and Richard's, her friends and his. Then, as if at a given signal, everyone moved away, drawn to food, drawn by plans which Simon had made, and Katherine and Richard were alone but for Simon and Susan. Simon was handing Richard a large envelope which appeared to be made of parchment and which bore the great gold seal of the House of Furnival.

"My wedding present to you both," he said. Then, taking Katherine's hands, he gripped them tightly. "I charge you to take care of this rare creature, this good man," he told her gravely. The next moment, as if ashamed of his momentary seriousness, his face broke into laughter and he declared, "You now have one precious hour on your own!"

As quickly as the words fell he took Susan's arm and led her off, while a man whom Katherine did not know, silver-haired and courtly, came into the hall from another doorway and said, "My felicitations to you both. Will you be good enough to follow me?"

"I know my way—" Richard began, but the elderly man appeared not to have heard.

He led them first from the great hall into a passage, closing a heavy shiny door behind them, then to another door. He did not attempt to open this, but bowed, smiled, and said with obvious pleasure, "The key to your home is in the envelope, Mr. Marshall."

"The key to my home?" Richard exclaimed in disbelief.

"Indeed yes, sir—your new home. Also in the envelope are the deeds and the deed of gift from Mr. Simon."

The silver-haired man bowed again and moved back along the way he had come.

"I still can't quite believe it," Richard declared, and his tone held a pitch of doubt. "I have long been aware that Simon was the most generous of men, but this—"

He broke off and turned to Katherine, taking her hands for the first time since they had walked through this house, all of its four floors, even the attic, approached by a narrow back staircase, from which they had looked down onto the long, narrow walled garden on one side of which were the stables and outhouses. Nothing but swift, cursory glances had been possible; at furniture and furnishings, carpets and curtains in most of the rooms, although some had been left empty, obviously for their own choice. These rooms had richly polished oak flooring, paneled walls, and ceilings beautifully painted and patterned.

Now they were in a small room—small, that was, compared with most in the house—plainly furnished yet with a substantial bed and huge wardrobe. Leading off on one side was a room with bath and water closet; one of the walls was a huge mirror. And leading from this second room was a dressing room for Richard.

For the first time since the moment she entered the church, Katherine's thoughts had been drawn from Richard.

The house, with such magnificence yet such scope for comfort and homeliness, was indeed an astounding proof of Simon's generosity; she had not dreamed of anything like this. Hand in hand with Richard she had gone from room to room and floor to floor, neither saying more than a word here, a word there. It was as if each had been struck dumb.

Now, standing at the window and looking down once again at the walled garden, with its green lawn so trim and its borders freshly dug and filled with bushy wallflowers, Richard repeated, "I still can't quite believe it."

Almost on the moment that he finished, his expression changed. He turned, took both her hands and drew her close.

"Katherine," he said huskily, "do you like it?"

"Do I like the house?"

"The house, the gift, the beauty in it. Will this be what you want?"

In a choky voice she said, "I think it can be, my love."

"We had planned to seek for ourselves. Would you prefer that?"

"We could not so rebuff Simon," Katherine replied.

"Yes, we could rebuff Simon," Richard said with sudden fierceness. "I want to give you what you desire. I want nothing to stand between us, nothing which is not—not *right* for us."

Her heart was rejoicing.

"Do you like this house, Richard?"

"That is not the issue. The issue is—"

"Richard," she interrupted, then caught her breath, half doubting whether she should go on with what she meant to ask, "Are you a little afraid of Simon?"

"Afraid?" he echoed, and pursed his lips; then he laughed. "Terrified!"

"Be serious, beloved!"

"He is a man who can strike terror," Richard replied, "and at the same time the kindest man alive. He has a heart of gold and a heart of rock. But for him, you and I would not be here. I owe him you, and I owe him much else. Now this house is—"

"Too much?"

"Overwhelming," Richard admitted. For the first time laughter glinted in his eyes. "It is right to be afraid of a man with power enough to come between you and me on *this* day of days." He drew her close, kissing her with surprising gentleness. "He brought us together . . . presented us with a house fit for a prince and a princess . . . he even graciously allowed us one hour on our own and then stood between us as if he were here in the flesh! Yes, I am terrified of him, lest he should now take you away!"

Moving with a suddenness which surprised her, Richard lifted Katherine bodily and with an ease revealing unsuspected strength. He carried her to the bed and placed her on it, then sat beside her and took her in his arms.

"I am now demonstrating that you are mine and I am yours and nothing and no one can come between us. Katherine, will you ever begin to understand how much I love you?"

Soon she said breathlessly, "I hate the need but we must get up."

"I have been pondering the question," Richard said, kissing her more lightly, "and have to conclude that you are right. I have an uneasy feeling that you are likely to be right about many things. Will you answer me one question?"

Katherine nodded.

"Are you at all apprehensive about tonight?"

She was momentarily puzzled, but understanding came swiftly and with warmth of feeling; she longed to turn this moment into "tonight" and sought some way to reassure him. His face was so close to hers that she could feel the pressure of his body at her side and the gentle stir of his breath. So close. Across a room he was striking to look at, with his thick iron-gray hair and hawklike features; across a table this aquiline handsomeness took on a life, a *zest* for life which was much more part of him than she had dreamed. Inches away, every line, every lash, every hair, every speck in his eyes, were as clear as if seen through a magnifying glass; he was more handsome than she had ever realised.

His eyes began to cloud, as if he expected her answer to be "Yes."

"There is nothing in this world I want more than tonight," she told him.

He lowered his face until once again their lips touched; then he sprang up, startling her with his speed of movement, and stood over her, hands outstretched to help her to her feet.

"Kate, my love." He chuckled. "I feel as if I have become young for the first time!"

As she looked up at him a bell rang in the distance, and in a moment it sounded again, telling them that soon their presence would be needed in the great hall of the house so near to this and yet so far away.

CHAPTER *40*

The Reward

ON MAY 26, 1829, the police bill was passed in the House of Commons. Confident that Peel would discuss the formation of the New Police with him, Richard was, as his grandfather before him, both astonished and hurt when, in the weeks that followed, he found he was not consulted. Indeed, it was through the newspapers that he first learned that on July 19 the bill received the Royal Assent and was now the law of the land.

At first he revealed little of his feelings even to Katherine, and when accosted by some member of the press, he simply declared himself delighted that his long-held dream had at last become a reality. Then, when one morning late in August a fair-haired youth introducing himself as Peter Winship of *The Times* stopped him outside the house in Great Furnival Square, Richard answered his questions with increasing impatience. All were to do with the formation of the New Police; all confirmed Richard's suspicions that Peel had no intention of consulting him. Yet the young man himself was likable and apparently well disposed.

"There is a matter with which you should perhaps be acquainted," he said at last, and Richard quailed at the prospect of still more discouraging news. "You may already be aware of it, sir."

"Tell me, Mr. Winship, and I shall know."

"The strongest possible opposition is being organised against the New Police. It is coming from certain justices and politicians and is being most cunningly spread among the people through taverns and alehouses, flash-houses and brothels—even through the guilds, which, as you know, have much influence. The most effective criticism is that despite Mr. Peel's protestations the new force will be an army used to subdue the people, as at Peterloo."

"And do many people believe this?" asked Richard slowly.

"A great many, sir."

Richard did what he could to ease the young man's mind, then turned and strode into the house. He had never wanted to talk to Katherine more, but she was in the City at some meeting to do with the Gold and Silversmiths' Charities and not likely to be back before midday. It was now a little after eleven o'clock and he was too restless to sit at his desk, restless and troubled. Why had Peel not consulted him about the organisation of the New Police? Was it because the government *did* intend to use them as an extension of the military, simply to put down civil disturbances?

When at last Katherine came home Richard told her of his fears. "And that young man's questions made it quite obvious that, as I suspected, Peel *is* ignoring me in his preparations," he admitted.

"If true, it is wickedly unjust," Katherine said, touching his hand. "But are you sure it *is* true, my love? Soon after you left this morning this letter was delivered by one of Mr. Peel's messengers." She took an envelope from the mantelshelf and held it out to him.

Richard took the envelope, opened it, and drew out a missive in the flowing hand of one of Peel's secretaries:

The Minister for Home Affairs the Rt. Hon. Mr. Robert Peel will be pleased if you and Mrs. Marshall will wait on him at six o'clock this evening at Number 10 Downing Street, where he is in temporary residence. He will appreciate an acknowledgment only if it is not possible for you to attend.

He handed it to Katherine. "Well, Kate," he said slowly, "this will at least give me an opportunity to tell Mr. Peel of my fears. I only hope he has nothing to say which will make me lose my temper—I confess I have never been in greater danger of doing so."

"If you must lose your self-control, then pray wait until you have left him and are alone with me," Katherine counseled. "And now, my love, I must make preparations for our visit. I shall wear my peacock silk."

Since the days of the Gordon Riots, nearly fifty years past, guards had always been stationed at the two approaches to Downing Street, now very different from the country lane it had been when Sir George Downing had built the first house there. Richard and Katherine were twice stopped and questioned before reaching the front door of Number 10, but once they were recognised, the guards stepped back with obvious respect, and at two minutes to six the front door opened and a youthful-looking man stood aside, bowing.

"Good evening, ma'am. Mr. Marshall. Mr. Peel is ready for you to attend him. If I may take your cloak, ma'am."

Only on one other occasion had Richard been in this plain brick house which, from its strange beginnings, had become the official London residence of the First Minister of Great Britain, although the present Prime Minister, the Duke of Wellington, spent much time in the splendour of his own residence at Apsley House. There was a sense of dignity here, and of quiet. The young man led them to a room on the second floor, at the head of the stairs, tapped at the dark oak paneling of the door, and at Peel's deep-voiced "Come in" pushed the door aside and stood back for Richard and Katherine to enter. Peel rose to his feet from behind a large square-topped desk and came forward to greet them.

"It is very good of you to come, ma'am. Mr. Marshall. Do please be seated."

He waited for Richard and Katherine to sit down in the big leather chairs arranged in front of the roaring log fire, then picked up a heavy crystal decanter.

"I have often heard it said that one should take a little wine for the stomach's sake—I trust you will share my pleasure. . . . Good, *very* good."

He filled three glasses, then sat down beside them, stretching his long legs toward the blaze, more like a country squire than a Minister of State.

503

"And now, as you are both no doubt curious, I will come to the point." He turned to Katherine. "I wish to speak to your husband on three matters, ma'am. It is the second and third in which I think you will be interested; I shall be glad if you will bear with me over the first. Mr. Marshall"—he swung to face Richard—"I am extremely anxious that in the formation of the New Police there should be fresh minds and a fresh outlook, and it is for that reason only that I have not called upon your assistance."

Richard did not hear Peel's next words, so great was the flood of relief which surged through him. "... *for that reason only* ..." Thank God his fears that the government would use the New Police against the people had been unjustified! How his grandfather would have rejoiced! How Sir John Furnival—But he must concentrate on what was still being said. Making a conscious effort, Richard forced himself to listen.

"I have already selected two men whom I am considering calling 'commissioners,' " Peel was saying. "As you know, Mr. Marshall, one of the main purposes of the Act is to ensure the apprehension of criminals by the police, while the task of considering the accused persons' interests when they have been formally charged will be the duty of judges, with juries when deemed necessary, and of justices if the crimes can be dealt with summarily. So 'justices' will not long remain the name for the chiefs of the Police Office, and I cannot myself think of any better appellation than 'commissioners.' Can you, Mr. Marshall?"

"On the spur of the moment, no, sir. I have always liked the title."

"I am glad. I will now tell you in confidence, although a public announcement will be made in a few days, that I have appointed Mr. Richard Mayne and Colonel Charles Rowan and am extremely hopeful that they will work well together." Peel gave Richard no time to comment but went on: "They will have as their chief administrator, whose task it will be to enlist the members of the new force and to control its finances, a barrister by name Mr. John Wray. There will be the clearest terms of reference for enlistment. The early leaders of the smaller groups will be enlisted from the Army, in every case retired regimental sergeant majors, used to exerting command and discipline over men of the toughness and caliber needed for the police service. It is to be impressed on these leaders, who will be called sergeants and will have nine or ten men under them, that while these men must impose control, they must at no time be aggressive. Their task is to *keep* the peace, not to break it."

Peel paused and Richard seized his opportunity.

"I am heartily glad to hear it, sir. One great fear expressed to me has been that the police will become a civilian army, if I may be permitted such a contradiction in terms. How do you propose to arm the men, sir?" He only just forbore to add: "If they *are* to be armed."

"With one weapon, and one only," answered Peel, "a weapon to be known as a truncheon."

Putting his hand down the side of his chair he brought up a short cudgel such as that used by the Bow Street patrols. Painted a glossy black, it was about two feet long, thicker at one end than the other, the thinner end ridged to insure a good fingerhold. On the thicker end Richard just glimpsed the magnificently enameled Royal coat of arms, the lion and the unicorn rampant, in crimson and gold, as after one brief flourish Peel deftly slipped the cudgel back out of sight. There had been letters, too, skilfully inscribed in gold, but neither Richard nor Katherine had had time to see them, and it was apparent that Peel did not intend that they should.

"And now the uniform," he went on swiftly. Dipping to the side of his chair once again, he drew forth several sheets of thick paper and riffled through them. "Ah, here is a drawing of that which I most favour. It has the distinction of being unmistakably official yet in no way military."

Richard took the picture.

It was of a tall man wearing—and this was the first thing which struck him—a top hat, higher in the crown than an opera hat or a gentleman's dress hat, yet unmistakably civilian in appearance. The jacket and trousers were dark blue, the jacket high-collared and with bright metal buttons, secured at the waist by a black leather belt. The trousers were loose-fitting, reaching just above the instep. The whole gave an impression of a guard rather than of a soldier or a sailor.

Richard, aware of the intentness of Peel's gaze, at last looked up. "It is admirable, sir. Admirable."

"I am flattered that you say so. I had a variety of sketches submitted and this one by Charles Hebbert is in my opinion by far the best."

Peel stretched out his hand for the sketch, then to both Richard's and Katherine's surprise, he went to the desk and picked up a quill pen. When he returned to his chair he handed the sketch back to Richard. Across one corner were the words: "*To Richard Marshall, M.P., whose unceasing efforts have made an important contribution to the formation of the New Police.*"

"You make my poor efforts worthwhile, sir." Richard's voice was unsteady.

"Mr. Marshall," Peel responded with obvious sincerity, "your efforts have been the reverse of poor. I doubt whether they will ever receive full recognition. I am, of course, aware that on some issues in the House of Commons we shall be on opposite sides of the fence, but never, I am sure, with acrimony. So far as the police are concerned I have requested the two—ah—commissioners to give you all facilities for visiting and inspecting, and you may be sure each will make you very welcome. They will be having an office in Scotland Yard."

"*Where*, sir?" ejaculated Richard.

"In Scotland Yard, near Whitehall Place," answered Peel. "I agree that this is not at the moment the most salubrious of areas and it may well soon be regarded as a substitute for Porridge Island, but there are some substantial buildings and much will be cleared. Does it distress you?"

"Distress?" Richard actually laughed before he explained. "Before he was made magistrate of Bow Street, Sir John Furnival worked at Scotland Yard; he had an office there after he left the Army. It is an astonishing coincidence!"

Peel leaned back in his chair. "A coincidence indeed, and a good omen I hope. And now—" he smiled at Katherine. "You have indeed been patient, ma'am, for which I thank you—we come to the last two matters I wished to mention. Firstly, Mr. Marshall, I should like to recommend to His Majesty that he confer a knighthood upon you, and I have no doubt that he would agree with great alacrity. But for my knowledge of you as an individual I would have no doubt that you would accept—I confess I hope that you will. But"—Peel spread his hands, palms downward—"while you will in no way affront me if you decline, I do not think it would be wise to refuse once His Majesty has approved. May I leave the matter with you?"

For a moment Richard was unable to speak. Then, as Katherine jumped from her seat and ran toward him, clasping his hand, he stammered, "Of—of course, sir. And I am—I am overwhelmed."

"You will soon recover from that," Peel said dryly, rising also. "And now to the third and last matter." Once again he slipped his hand down the side of his chair. "Mrs. Marshall"—he bowed to Katherine—"I trust you will be able to persuade your husband to accept not only the knighthood but also this truncheon, the very first in existence, as a symbol of my sincere gratitude—of the country's gratitude—for his help in establishing the New Police."

He held the truncheon toward Richard, who, stretching an unsteady hand to take it, now saw beneath the Royal coat of arms the words:

Presented to Richard Marshall, Esq., Member of Parliament
for the Constituency of Minshall, by the Commissioners
of the Metropolitan Police.
September 1829

Katherine, weeping with pride and happiness, was unable to read through her tears, but knew only that at last Richard had triumphed, that his dreams were realised. And Richard, turning in his hands the shaft of polished wood, glowing in the light of the fire, saw before him in the dance of the flames the beginning of a new tradition, rule without despotism, order without cruelty, justice without arbitrary harshness, a thin blue line of men who would, in their own way, with these simple weapons, defend civilisation as surely as had the more martial thin red line of men at Waterloo, an army whose mission was peace and justice, and whose task was to defend the helpless and to protect the rights of the people—even those who were guilty. He could not know, in that moment, what Scotland Yard was to become, to stand for, but he knew that in this room a revolution was being celebrated, and that his life's work was done. And turning from the Minister, he took Katherine in his arms and kissed her.